TALES OF THE
TIME SCOUTS

II

BAEN BOOKS BY ROBERT ASPRIN

The Time Scout series with Linda Evans
Time Scout
Wagers of Sin
Ripping Time
The House That Jack Built
Tales of the Time Scouts (Omnibus)
Tales of the Time Scouts: II (Omnibus, forthcoming)

For King and Country with Linda Evans

License Invoked with Jody Lynn Nye

E. Godz with Esther Friesner

Myth-Interpretations: The Worlds of Robert Asprin

ALSO BY LINDA EVANS

Far Edge of Darkness
Sleipnir

Road to Damascus with John Ringo

Hell's Gate with David Weber
Hell Hath No Fury with David Weber

To purchase these and all other Baen Book titles in e-book format,
please go to www.baen.com.

TALES OF THE
TIME SCOUTS

II

ROBERT ASPRIN
LINDA EVANS

BAEN

TALES OF THE TIME SCOUTS II

This is a work of fiction. All the characters and events portrayed in this book are fictional, and any resemblance to real people or incidents is purely coincidental.

A Baen Books Original

Baen Publishing Enterprises
P.O. Box 1403
Riverdale, NY 10471
www.baen.com

ISBN: 978-1-4767-8132-7

Cover art by Alan Pollack

Fist Baen printing, April 2016

Distributed by Simon & Schuster
1230 Avenue of the Americas
New York, NY 10020

Printed in the United States of America

10 9 8 7 6 5 4 3 2 1

(((Contents)))

RIPPING TIME

**Robert Asprin and
Linda Evans**

《 Chapter 1 》

She hadn't come to Shangri-La Station for the usual reasons.

A slight and frightened young woman, Jenna had lost the lean and supple dancer's grace which had been hers . . . God, was it only three days ago? It seemed a year, at least, for every one of those days, a whole lifetime since the phone call had come.

"Jenna Nicole," her aunt's voice had startled her, since Aunt Cassie hadn't called in months, not since before Jenna had joined the Temple, "I want to see you, dear. This evening."

The commanding tone and the use of her full name, as much as the unexpected timing, threw her off stride. "*This evening?* Are you serious? Where are you?" Jenna's favorite aunt, her mother's only sister, didn't live anywhere near New York, only appeared in the City for film shoots and publicity appearances.

"I'm in town, of course," Cassie Tyrol's famous voice came through the line, faintly exasperated. "I flew in an hour ago. Whatever you've got on your calendar, cancel it. Dinner, class, Temple services, anything. Be at Luigi's at six. And Jenna, darling, don't bring your roommate. This is business, family business, understand? You're in deep trouble, my girl."

Jenna's stomach clenched into knots. *Oh, my God. She's found out!* Aloud, she managed to say, "Luigi's at six, okay, I'll be there." Only a lifetime's worth of acting experience and the raw talent she'd inherited from the same family that had produced the legendary Jocasta

"Cassie" Tyrol got that simple sentence out without her voice shaking. *She's found* out, *what'll she say, what'll she do, oh my God, what if she's told Daddy? She wouldn't tell him, would she?* Jenna's aunt hated her father, almost as much as Jenna did.

Hand shaking, Jenna hung up the phone and found Carl staring at her, dark eyes perplexed. The holographic video simulation they'd been running, the one they'd been thrown into fits of giggles over, trying to get ready for their grand adventure, time touring in London, flickered silently behind Jenna's roommate, forgotten as thoroughly as last summer's fun and games. Carl blinked, owl-like, through his glasses. "Nikki? What's wrong?" He always called her by her middle name, rather than her more famous given name—an endearing habit that had drawn her to him from the very beginning. He brushed Jenna's hair back from her brow. "Hey, what is it? You look like you just heard from a ghost."

She managed a smile. "Worse. Aunt Cassie's in town."

"Oh, dear God!" Carl's expressive eyes literally radiated sympathy, which was another reason Jenna had moved in with him. Sympathy was in short supply when your father was *the* John Paul Caddrick, the Senator everybody loved to hate.

Jenna nodded. "Yeah. What's worse, she wants me to meet her by six. At Luigi's, for God's sake!"

Carl's eyes widened. "Luigi's? You're kidding? That's *worse* than bad. Press'll be crawling all over you. Remind me to thank the Lady of Heaven for not giving *me* famous relatives."

Jenna glared up at him. "Some help you are, lover! And just what am I supposed to *wear* to Luigi's? Do you see any six-thousand-dollar dresses in my closet?" Jenna hadn't put on much of anything but ratty jeans since hitting college. "The last time I was seen in public with Aunt Cassie, she had on a *blouse* that cost more than the rent on this apartment for a year! And I still haven't lived down the bad press from that horrible afternoon!" She hid her face in her hands, still mortified by the memory of being immortalized on every television set and magazine cover in the country after slipping headlong into a mud puddle. "Cassie Tyrol and her niece, the mudlark . . ."

"Yep, that's you, Jenna Nicole, the prettiest mudlark in Brooklyn."

Jenna put out her tongue, but Carl's infectious grin helped ease a little of the panic tightening down. He tickled her chin. "Look, it's nearly four, now. If you're gonna be in any shape to walk into Luigi's by six, with a crowd of reporters falling all over the two of you—" Jenna just groaned, at which Carl had the impudence to laugh "—then you'd better jump, hon. In case you hadn't noticed, you look like shit." Carl eyed her up and down, wrinkling his nose. "That's what happens when you stay out 'til four A.M., working on a script due at six, then forget to go to bed when you get back from class."

Jenna threw a rolled up sock at him. He ducked with the ease of a born dancer and the forlorn sock sailed straight through a ghostly, three-dimensional simulation of a young woman laced into proper attire for a lady of style, prim and proper and all set to enjoy London's Season. The Season of *1888*. When Jenna's sock "landed" in the holographic teacup, while the holographic young lady continued smiling and sipping her now-contaminated tea, Jenna's roommate fell down on the floor, howling and pointing a waggling finger at her. "Oh, Nikki, three-point shot!"

Jenna scowled down at the idiot, who lay rolling around holding his ribs and sputtering with laughter. "Thanks, Carl. You're all heart. Remind me to lose your invitation to the graduation party. *If* I ever graduate. God, if Simkins rejects *this* script, I'll throw myself in the East River."

Carl chuckled and rolled over, coming to his feet easily to switch off the holoprojector they'd borrowed from the campus library. "Nah. You'll just film it, win an Oscar or two, and take his job. Can you imagine? A member of the Temple on faculty?"

Jenna grinned—and bushwhacked Carl from behind while he wasn't looking, getting in several retaliatory tickles. He twisted around and stole a kiss, which turned into a clutch for solid ground, because she couldn't quite bring herself to tell Carl the worst part of her news, that her aunt *knew*. Just how much Cassie knew remained to be seen. And what she intended to do about it, Jenna didn't even want to think about. So she just held onto Carl for a long moment, queasy and scared in the pit of her stomach.

"Hey," he said gently, "it isn't that bad, is it?"

She shook her head. "No. It's worse."

"Cassie loves you, don't you know that?"

She looked up, blinking hard. "Yes. That's why it's worse."

His lips quirked into a sad, understanding little smile that wrenched at Jenna's heart. "Yeah. I know. Listen, how about I clean up the place while you're out, just in case she wants to visit, then when it's over, I'll give you a backrub, brush your hair, pamper your feet, spoil you silly?"

She gave him a watery smile. "Lover boy, you got yourself a deal."

Then she sighed and stepped into the shower, where she could let the smile pour away down the drain, wishing the fear would drain away with it. Christ, what could she tell Aunt Cassie? She tried to envision the scene, quailed inwardly. Cassie Tyrol, cool and elegant and *very* Parisian, despite her New Hollywood accent and the ranch up in the hills, where Jenna had spent the happiest summers of her life—the only happy ones, in fact, until college and the Temple and Carl. . . . Aunt Cassie was not likely to take the news well. Not at all. Better, of course, than her father.

Two hours later, Jenna was still quailing, despite the outward charm of her smile for the *maitre d'* at Luigi's, the most fashionable of the restaurants owned by increasingly wealthy members of New York's leading Lady of Heaven Temple. It was little wonder her aunt had chosen Luigi's. Given Cassie's prominence in the New Hollywood Temple, she probably had a stakeholder's share in the restaurant's profits. Jenna's only aunt never did anything by halves. That included throwing herself into her latest religion or making money the way Jenna accumulated rejection slips for her screenplays.

The *maitre d'* greeted her effusively, by name. "Good evening, Ms. Caddrick, your aunt's table is right this way."

"Thank you." She resisted the urge to twitch at her dress. Carl had, while she showered and did her hair and makeup with the most exquisite care she'd used in a year, worked a genuine theatrical miracle. He'd rushed over to the theater department and liberated a costume which looked like a million bucks and had only cost a few thousand to construct, having been donated by some New Hollywood diva who'd needed a tax write-off. Jenna, who existed by her own stubborn insistence on a student's budget that did *not* include dinner at Luigi's or the requisite fashions appropriate to be seen there, had squealed with delight at his surprise.

"You wonderful idiot! If they'd caught you sneaking this out, they'd have thrown you out of college!"

"Yeah, but it'd be worth it, just looking at you in it." He ran his gaze appreciatively across her curves.

"Huh. This dress is a lot more glamorous than I am. Now, if I just had Aunt Cassie's nose, or cheekbones, or chin . . ."

"I like your nose and cheekbones and chin just the way they are. And if you don't scoot, you'll be late."

So Jenna had slid gingerly into the exquisite dress, all silken fringe and swaying sheik, and splurged on a taxi, since arriving on a bicycle in a ten-thousand-dollar dress simply would not do. Jenna followed the *maitre d'* nervously into the glitzy restaurant, aware of the stares as she made her way past tables frequented by New York's wealthiest Templars. She did her best to ignore the whispers, staring straight ahead and concentrating on not falling off her high-heeled shoes and damning her father for saddling her with the price of an infamous family face and name.

Then she spotted her aunt at a dim-lit corner table and swallowed hard, palms abruptly wet. *Oh, God, she's got somebody with her and it's not her latest.*

If this was family only . . . The only person it *could* be was a private detective. Cassie'd hired more than her share over the years. Jenna knew her style. Which meant Jenna was in *really* serious hot water. Worse, her aunt appeared to be absorbed in a violent argument with whoever it was. The dark circles under Cassie Tyrol's eyes shocked her. When Jenna reached the table, conversation sliced off so abruptly, Jenna could actually hear the echoes of the silence left behind. Her aunt managed a brittle smile as she stooped to kiss one expertly manicured cheek.

"Hello, Jenna, dear. Sit down, please. This is Noah Armstrong."

Jenna shook hands, trying to decide if the androgynous individual in a fluid silk suit beside her aunt was male or female, then settled for, "A pleasure, Noah." Living in New York for the past four years—not to mention a solid year plunged into Temple life—had been an education in more ways than one.

"Ms. Caddrick." Firm handclasp, no clue from the voice. Noah Armstrong's eyes were about as friendly as a rabid pit bull challenging all comers to a choice cut of steak.

Jenna ignored Armstrong with a determination that matched Armstrong's dark scowl, sat down, and smiled far too brightly as Cassie Tyrol poured wine. Cassie handed over a glass in which tiny motion rings disturbed the wine's deep claret glint. Jenna hastily took it from her aunt before it could slosh onto snowy linen.

"Well, what a surprise, Cassie." She glanced around the elegant restaurant, surreptitiously tugging at her short skirt to be sure nothing untoward was showing, and realized with a start of surprise there were no reporters lurking. "Gawd. How'd you manage to ditch the press?"

Her aunt did not smile. *Uh-oh.*

"This was not an announced visit," she said quietly. "Officially, I'm still in L.A."

Worse, oh, man, she's gonna let me have it, both barrels . . .

"I see. Okay," she sighed, resigned to the worst, "let's have it."

Cassie's lips tightened briefly. The redness in her eyes told Jenna she'd been crying a great deal, lately, which only added guilt to an already-simmering stew of fear and defensiveness. Jenna, wishing she could gulp down the wine, sipped daintily, instead, determined to maintain at least a facade of calm.

"It's . . ." Cassie hesitated, glanced at Noah Armstrong, then sighed and met Jenna's gaze squarely. "It's your father, Jenna. I've discovered something about him. Something you deserve to know, because it's going to wreck all our lives for the next year or so."

Jenna managed not to spray wine all over the snowy linen, but only because she snorted thirty-dollar-a-glass wine into her sinuses, instead. She blinked hard, eyes watering, wineglass frozen at her lips. When she'd regained control, Jenna carefully lowered the glass to the table and stared at her aunt, mind spinning as she tried to reassess the entire purpose for this clandestine meeting. She couldn't even think of a rejoinder that would make sense.

"Drink that wine," her aunt said brusquely. "You're going to need it."

Jenna swallowed hard, just once. Then knocked the wine back, abruptly wishing this meeting *had* been about her highly secret down-time trip with Carl, a trip they'd been planning for more than a year, to Victorian London, where she and her roommate planned to film the East End terror instilled by Jack the Ripper. They'd bought the tickets fourteen months previously under assumed names, using extremely well-made false identifications she and Carl had managed to buy from an underworld dealer in new identities. New York teemed with such dealers, with new identifications available for the price of a few hits of cocaine; but they'd paid top dollar, getting the best in the business, because Jenna Nicole Caddrick's new identity had to be foolproof. *Had* to be, if she hoped to keep the down-time trip secret from her father. And what her father would do if he found out . . .

Jenna had as many reasons to fear her world-famous father as she had to adore her equally famous aunt. Whatever Cassie was about to lay on her, it promised to be far worse than having her father discover she was going time-touring in the face of the elder Caddrick's ultimatums about never setting foot through any time terminal gate, ever. Voice tight despite her relief at the reprieve, Jenna asked, "Dad, huh? What's the son-of-a-bitch done now? Outlaw fun? He's outlawed everything else."

Noah Armstrong glanced sharply into Jenna's eyes. "No. This isn't about his career as a legislator. Not . . . precisely."

Jenna glanced into his—her?—eyes and scowled. "Who the hell are you, Armstrong? Where do you fit into anything?"

Armstrong's lips thinned slightly, but no reply was forthcoming. Not to her, at any rate. The look Armstrong shot Jenna's aunt spoke volumes, a dismissive, superior look that relegated Jenna to the realm of infant toddlers who couldn't think for themselves or be trusted not to piddle on the Persian carpets.

Jenna's aunt said tiredly, "Noah's a detective, hon. I went to the Wardmann Wolfe agency a few months ago, asked for their best. They assigned Noah to the case. And . . . Noah's a member of the Temple. That's important. More important than you can begin to guess."

Jenna narrowed her eyes at the enigmatic detective across the table. Wardmann Wolfe, huh? Aunt Cassie certainly didn't do things by halves. She never had, come to that. Whatever her father had done, it was clearly more serious than the occasional sex scandals which, decades ago, had rocked the careers of other legislators possessing her father's stature. A chill ran through her, wondering just what Daddy Dearest *was* involved in.

Cassie said heavily, "You remember Alston Corliss?"

Jenna glanced up, startled. "The guy in *Sacred Harlot* with you? Blond, looks like a fey elf, loves Manx cats, opera, and jazz dance? Nominated for an Oscar for *Harlot*, wasn't he? And still a senior at Julliard." Jenna had been impressed—deeply so—by her aunt's talented young co-star. And more than a little envious of that Oscar nomination. And with his good looks, Jenna had just about melted all over the theater seats every time he smiled. Guiltily, she remembered a promise to try and get Carl an autograph, via the connection with her aunt. "Wasn't there some talk of you starring in another film with him? Something about *A Templar Goes to Washington*, sort of a new take on that old classic film?

Her aunt nodded. "Alston wanted to spend a semester interning in Congress. Role research. I . . . I set it up, got him a job in your father's office. Asked him to snoop around for us. Find out things Noah couldn't, didn't have access to." Cassie Tyrol bit a well-manicured lip. "Jenna, he's dead."

"*Dead?*"

Cassie was crying, smudging her careful eye makeup into ruins. "Four hours ago. It hasn't hit the press yet, because the FBI's put a press blackout on it. I know because Noah dragged me out of my house, scared spitless because they'll come after *me*."

Jenna couldn't take this in. Alston Corliss dead, Cassie in danger? "But . . ." Nothing intelligent would form coherently enough to say anything else.

Noah Armstrong spoke quietly, with just a hint of anger far back in those piercing grey eyes. "Surely you've heard the scuttlebutt about people close to your father? To know Senator John Paul Caddrick is to inherit a tombstone?"

White-hot anger blazed at the crude insult, jolting her out of shock sufficiently to glare murderously at the detective. There were *plenty* of reasons to hate John Paul Caddrick, Senator from Hell. But murder wasn't by God one of them! Then she saw the sick, anguished pain in her aunt's eyes. Anger slithered to the floor in a puddle at her feet and Jenna was quite suddenly very cold inside.

Cassie Tyrol's lips trembled. "When we leave here, Jenna, we're going to the FBI. What Noah's found, what your father's been doing, who he's involved with and what *they've* been doing . . . it's got to be stopped. Noah didn't want me to tell you, Jenna, I sneaked away to call you, asked you to meet me here . . ."

She was crying harder, voice shaking. Shocked by her collapse into violent tremors, Jenna reached out, grasped her aunt's chilled fingers, held on tight. "Hey. It's okay," she said gently.

Cassie tightened her fingers around Jenna's, shook her head. "No," she choked out, "it isn't. You're his little girl. It's going to hurt you so much when all of this comes out. I thought you deserved to know. If . . ." she hesitated. "If you want to take off for Europe for a while, I'll pay for the tickets. Take Carl with you, if your roommate wants to go."

Jenna had to scrape her lower jaw off the table.

Cassie tried to smile, failed utterly. "You're going to need a friend, someone to protect you, while this is breaking loose, Jenna, and . . . well, your father and I don't see eye to eye on a lot of things. He's never approved of either of us joining the Lady of Heaven Temple or the food I eat or the men I divorced or the way I make my living, any more than he's ever approved of *your* friends or your choice of career. You're growing up, Jenna. Who you're friends with—or sleep with—is your business, not mine or his or anyone else's, and frankly, a blind man could see Carl's good for you, say what your father will. For one thing," she said bitterly, "you're standing up to that bastard for once in your life, insisting on a film career, and I *know* how much Carl's had to do with that. And I know what's in that bank box of yours. Frankly, I approve. It's why I'm sending him with you. I *know* he'll take care of you for me."

"*What?*" Jenna gasped. *Cripes* . . . Where *did* Aunt Cassie get her information from? But her concern was so genuine, Jenna couldn't even take offense at the invasion of privacy which her really serious snooping represented.

Cassie tried to smile, failed. "Don't be angry with me for prying, sweety, please. I'm just trying to look out for you. So." She slid an envelope across the table. "If you want to go, you can probably get out before the press gets wind of this. And don't go all stubborn and proud on me and tell me you've got to do things on your own. You think the press has been savage before? You have no idea how bad it's going to get, hon. They're going to crucify us. *All* of us. So take it, grab your passports, both of you, and get out of town. Okay, Jenna?"

She just didn't know what to say. Maybe that crazy scheme to get down time to film the Ripper terror wasn't so crazy, after all—and here was her aunt, handing Jenna enough cash to keep her hidden safely down time from the press corps for months, if necessary. Carl, too. Maybe they'd win that Kit Carson Prize in Historical Video, after all, with months to complete the filming, rather than a couple of weeks. The envelope she slid into her handbag was heavy. Thick, heavy, and terrifying. She poured another glass of wine and drank it down without pausing.

"Okay, Cassie. I'll go. Mind if I call Carl?"

Her aunt's attempt at a smile was the most courageous thing Jenna ever seen, braver and more real than anything her aunt had ever done in her presence. "Go on, Jenna. I'll order us dinner while you're gone."

She scooted back her chair and kissed her aunt's cheek. "Love you, Cassie. Be right back." She found the phones in the back beside the bathrooms and dug into her purse for change, then dialed.

"Hello?"

"Carl, it's Jenna. You're never going to believe—"

Gunfire erupted in stereo.

From the telephone receiver *and* the restaurant. Carl's choked-off scream, guttural, agonized, cut straight through Jenna. Rising screams out in Luigi's main dining room hardly registered. "Carl! *Carl!*" Then, as shock sank in, and the realization that she was still hearing gunfire from the direction of her aunt's table: "*Cassie!*" She dropped the receiver with a bang, ignoring its violent swing at the end of its cord.

Jenna ran straight toward the staccato chatter of gunfire, tried to shove past terrified patrons fleeing the dining room.

Someone shouted her name. Jenna barely had time to recognize Noah Armstrong, elegant clothing covered in blood. Then the detective body-slammed her to the floor. Gunfire erupted again, chewing into the man behind Jenna. The wall erupted into splinters behind *him*. The man screamed, jerked like a murdered marionette, plowed into the floor, still screaming. Jenna choked on a ghastly sound, realized the hot, wet splatters on her face were blood. A booming report just above her ear deafened her; then someone snatched her to her feet.

"Run!"

She found herself dragged through Luigi's kitchen. Screams echoed behind them. The gun in Armstrong's hand cleared a magical path. Waiters and cooks dove frantically out of their way. At the exit to the alleyway behind the restaurant, Armstrong flung her against the wall, reloaded the gun with a practiced, fluid movement, then kicked the door open. Gunfire from outside slammed into the door. Jenna cringed, tried to blot from memory the sound of Carl's scream, tried desperately not to wonder where Aunt Cassie was and just *whose* blood was all over Armstrong's fluid silk suit.

More deafening gunfire erupted from right beside her. Then Armstrong snatched her off balance and snarled, "*Run, goddamn you!*" The next instant, they were pelting down an alleyway littered with at least three grotesquely dead men. All three were dressed like middle-easterners, wearing a type of headdress made popular during the late twentieth century by a famous terrorist turned politician, Jenna couldn't recall the name through numb shock. The detective swore savagely, stooped and snatched up guns from dead hands. "It figures! They showed up as *Ansar Majlis!*" Armstrong thrust one salvaged gun into a pocket, shoved the other two into Jenna's shocked hands with a steel-eyed glance. "Don't drop them! If I tell you to shoot, *do it!*"

Jenna stared stupidly at the guns. She'd used guns before, Carl's black-powder pistols, which he carried in action-shooting re-enactments, the ones stored in her bank box along with their time-touring tickets and the diamond ring she didn't dare wear publicly yet, and she'd fired a few stage-prop guns loaded with blanks. The guns Noah Armstrong shoved into her hands were modern, sleek, terrifying. Their last owners had tried to kill her. Jenna's hands shook violently. From the direction of Forty-Second Street, sirens began to scream.

"Come *on,* kid! Go into shock later!"

Armstrong jerked her into motion once more. She literally fell off her high-heeled shoes, managed to kick them off as she stumbled after Armstrong. They pelted down the alleyway and emerged into heavy traffic. Armstrong ran right in front of a yellow taxicab. The car screeched to a halt, driver cursing in a blistering tongue that was not English. Armstrong yanked open the driver's door and bodily tossed the cabby onto the street.

"*Get in!*"

Jenna dove for the passenger's door. She barely had her feet off the pavement before the car squealed into motion. Armstrong, whatever his/her gender, was a maniac behind the wheel of a car. If anyone tried to follow, they ended up at the bottom of a very serious multi-car pileup that strung out several blocks in their wake. Jenna gulped back nausea, found herself checking the guns with trembling fingers to see how much ammunition might be left in them, terrified she'd accidentally set one of them off. She'd never used *any* guns like these. She asked hoarsely, "Aunt Cassie?"

"Sorry, kid."

She squeezed shut her eyes. *Oh, God . . . Cassie . . . Carl . . .* Jenna needed to be sick, needed to cry, was too numb and shocked to do either.

"It's my fault," Armstrong said savagely. "I should *never* have let her meet you. I told her not to wait at Luigi's for you, told her they'd trace her through that goddamned call to your apartment! I *knew* they'd try something, dammit! But Christ, an all-out war in the middle of Luigi's . . . with his own daughter and sister-in-law!"

Wetness stung Jenna's eyes. She couldn't speak, couldn't think. Her hands shook where she gripped the guns Armstrong had shoved at her.

"Forget Europe, kid," the detective muttered. "They're not gonna let you get out of New York alive. They hit your apartment, didn't they? Killed your fiancé? Carl, wasn't it?"

She nodded, unable to force any sound past the constriction in her throat.

Whoever Armstrong was, he or she could out-curse a rodeo rider. "Which means," the detective ended harshly, "they were going to hit you anyway, even if Cassie hadn't met you. Just on the chance she might have *mailed* it to you. And they had to kill Carl, in case you'd said something to *him*. God*damn* them!"

"Who's 'them'?" she managed to choke out, not quite daring to ask what Cassie might have mailed, but hadn't.

Armstrong glanced sidelong at her for just an instant, long enough for Jenna to read the pity in those cold grey eyes. "Your father's business associates. One royal bastard in particular, who's been paying off your father for years. And the goddamned terrorists they're bringing into the country. Right past customs and immigration, diplomatic fucking immunity."

Jenna didn't want to hear anything more. She'd heard all the slurs, the innuendo, the nasty accusations in the press. She hadn't believed any of it. Who would've believed such filth about her own father, for Chrissake, even a father as lousy as hers had been over the years? Jenna had learned early that politics was a dirty, nasty game, where rivals did their damnedest to smear enemies' reputations with whichever reporters they'd paid off that week. It was one reason she'd chosen to pursue a career in film, following her aunt's lead, despite her father's furious opposition. *Oh, God, Aunt Cassie . . . Carl . . .* Her eyes burned, wet and swollen, and she couldn't get enough air down.

"Ever been time-touring, kid?" Armstrong asked abruptly.

"Wh-what?"

"Time-touring? Have you ever been?"

She blinked, tried to force her brain to function again. "No. But . . ." she had to swallow hard, "Carl and I, we were going to go . . . through TT-86, to London. Got the tickets and everything, used false ID to buy them, to keep it a secret . . ."

The taxi slewed around another corner, merged with traffic on

Broadway, slowed to a decorous pace. "Kid," Armstrong said softly, "those tickets might just save your life. Because the only by-God way out of this city now is through TT-86. Where did you hide them? Do you still have the fake ID's you bought?"

She'd begun to shake against the cracked plastic of the taxi's front seat, was ashamed of the reaction, couldn't hide it. "Yeah, we've still— I've still—" she was trembling violently now, unable to block the memory of Carl's agonized screams. "Locked them up in . . . in my lock box . . ." The other secret hidden in that lock box brought the tears flooding despite her best efforts not to cry. Carl's ring, the one she couldn't wear openly, yet, not until she'd turned twenty-one, making her legally and financially independent of her hated father, lay nestled in the lock box beside the tickets.

Noah glanced sharply into her eyes. "Lock box? A bank box? Which bank?"

Jenna told him.

Twenty minutes later, after a brief stop at a back-alley stolen-clothes huckster for new clothes—something without blood on it—Jenna clutched the entire contents of her bank account—which wasn't much—and the false identification papers and tickets she and her secret fiancé had bought to go time-touring, a grand adventure planned in innocence, with dreams of making a film that would launch both their careers . . . and so much more. Jenna rescued the ring from the safe, too, still closed up its little velvet box that had once been Carl's mother's, wanting at least that much of Carl's memory with her.

She also carried a thick case which held Carl's two black-powder 1858 Remington Beale's pistols she'd kept in the vault, the heavy .44-caliber pistols Carl had carried during re-enactments of Gettysburg and First Manassas and the Wilderness campaigns, the ones he'd taught her to use, after he'd won that action-shooting match in up-state New York last month. The ones her father would've exploded over, had he known Jenna was keeping them in her bank box. Armstrong eyed the heavy pistols silently, that glance neither approving nor disapproving, merely calculating. "Do you have ammo for those?"

Jenna nodded. "In the bottom of the gun case."

"Good. We'll have to ditch this modern stuff before we enter TT-86. I'd just as soon be armed with *something*. How do you load them?"

Wordlessly, Jenna began loading the reproduction antique guns, but Noah's steel-cold voice stopped her. "Not yet."

"Why not?" Jenna demanded shrilly. "Just because it's illegal? My own father wrote those laws, dammit! It didn't stop . . ." Her voice shattered.

Noah Armstrong's voice went incredibly gentle. "No, that isn't it. We just won't be able to take loaded guns through TT-86's security scans. We can take them through as costume accessories, but not loaded and ready to fire. Tell me *how* to load them, and we'll do that the second we're on station."

Jenna had to steady down her thoughts enough to explain how to pour black powder into each cylinder and pull down the loading lever to seat bullets, rather than more traditional round balls, in each chamber of the cylinder, how to wipe grease across the openings to prevent flame from setting off the powder in adjoining chambers, how to place percussion caps . . . The necessity to think coherently helped draw her back from raw, shaking terror.

"They're probably going to figure out where we went," Armstrong said quietly when she'd finished. "In fact, they'll be hitting TT-86, too, as soon as possible." The detective swore softly. "*Ansar Majlis* . . . That's the key, after all, isn't it? After today, it's even money they'll hit *her* the next time Primary cycles. Part of their goddamned terrorist plan."

Jenna glanced up, asking the question silently.

"Those bastards at Luigi's were *Ansar Majlis*. Never heard of 'em? I wish to Christ I hadn't. Your aunt is—was—a prominent public supporter of the Lady of Heaven Temples. So are the owners of Luigi's. And half the patrons. The bastard behind that attack back there sent a death-squad of *Ansar Majlis* to do his dirty work for him. You've heard of Cyril Barris? The multi-billionaire? Believe me, kid, you *don't* want to know how he made all that money. And he can't afford to have your aunt's murder tied to *him*. Or to your father. Getting the

Ansar Majlis involved makes goddamned sure of that. And *those* bastards have lined up another 'terrorist' hit, aimed right at the very soul of the Lady of Heaven Temples . . ."

Jenna gasped, seeing exactly where Armstrong was going with this.

The detective's glance was grudgingly respectful. "You see it, too, don't you, kid?"

Jenna truly, genuinely didn't want to know anything else about this nightmare.

Armstrong told her, anyway. Showed her the proof, sickening proof, in full color and stereo sound, proof which the elfin actor on the miniature computer screen in Jenna's hands had managed to give Armstrong before his death.

It killed what little respect for her father she'd still possessed.

In the year 1853, a stately man with a high forehead and thick, dark hair that fell down across his brow from a high widow's peak was inaugurated as the fourteenth U.S. President under the name of Franklin Pierce. Armed conflict between Russia and Turkey heralded the beginning of the disastrous Crimean War. Further south, Britain annexed the Mahratta State of Nagpur, while in the British home islands, Charlotte Bronte published "Villette" and another writer on the opposite side of the Atlantic, American Nathaniel Hawthorne of *Scarlet Letter* fame, brought out the "Tanglewood Tales." Noted historian Mommsen wrote "A History of Rome" and the legendary impressionist painter Vincent Van Gogh was born. European architecture enjoyed a renaissance of restoration as P.C. Albert began the rebuilding of Balmoral Castle, Aberdeenshire, Scotland, and— across the English Channel—Georges Haussmann began the reconstruction of Paris with the Boulevards, Bois de Boulogne.

In New York, Mr. Henry Steinway began manufacturing fine pianos. On the Continent, Italian composer Verdi wrote his great operas *Trovatore* and *La Traviata* and German composer Wagner completed the text of the masterwork *Der Ring des Nibelungen*. Alexander Wood shot his first patient with a subcutaneous injection from a hypodermic syringe and Samuel Colt, that American legend of firearms design, revolutionized British small-arms manufacture with his London factory for machine-made revolvers.

In London, Queen Victoria ensured the increasing popularity of the previously little-trusted chloroform as a surgical anesthetic by allowing herself to be chloroformed for the birth of her seventh child. Britain established the telegraph system in India and made smallpox vaccinations mandatory by law. In America, the world's largest tree, the *Wellingtonia gigantea,* was discovered growing in a California forest. And in Middlesex Street, Whitechapel—otherwise known as Petticoat Lane, after the famous market which lined that cobbled thoroughfare—a child was born to Lithuanian immigrant Varina Boleslaus and English dock laborer John Lachley.

The child was not a welcome addition to a family of six subsisting on John Lachley's ten shillings a week, plus the shilling or two Varina added weekly from selling hand-crafted items made on her crocheting hook. In fact, in many parts of the world during that year of 1853, this particular child would have been exposed to the elements and allowed to die. Not only could its parents ill afford to feed the baby, clothe it, or provide an education, the child was born with physical . . . peculiarities. And in 1853, the East End of London was neither an auspicious time nor a hospitable place to be born with marked oddities of physique. The midwife who attended the birth gasped in horrified dismay, unable to answer every exhausted mother's first, instinctive question: *boy or girl?*

Statistically, the human gene pool will produce children with ambiguous genitalia once in every thousand live births, perhaps as often as once in every five hundred. And while true hermaphrodites—children with the genital tissues of both sexes—account for only a tiny fraction of these ambiguously genitaled infants, they still can occur once in every one million or so live human births. Even in modern, more culturally enlightened societies, surgical "correction" of such children during infancy or early childhood can give rise to severe personality disorders, increased rates of suicide, a socially inculcated sense of guilt and secrecy surrounding their true sexual nature.

In the year 1853, London's East End was an ethnically diverse, poverty-stricken, industrial cesspool. The world's poor clustered in overcrowded hovels ten and twelve to a room, fought and drank and fornicated with rough sailors from every port city on the globe, and traded every disease known to humanity.

Women carrying unborn children swallowed quack medical remedies laced with arsenic and strychnine and heavy metals like sugar of lead. Men who would become fathers worked in metal-smelting foundries and shipyards, which in turn poured heavy metals into the drinking water and the soil. Sanitation consisted of open ditches where raw sewage was dumped, human waste was poured, and drinking water was secured. In such areas, a certain percentage of embryos whose dividing cells, programmed with delicate genetic codes, inevitably underwent massive genetic and teratogenic alterations.

And so it was that in Middlesex Street, Whitechapel, in that year of 1853, after a protracted debate, many condemnations of a God who would permit such a child to be born, and a number of drunken rages culminating in beatings of the woman who had produced this particular unfortunate offspring, the child was named John Boleslaus Lachley and reared as a son in a family which had already produced four dowerless sisters. Because he survived, and grew to manhood in London's East End, where he was tormented into acquiring a blazing ambition and the means to escape, the infant born without a verifiable gender grew in ways no innocent should ever have to grow. And once grown, John Lachley made very certain that the world would never, ever forget what it had done to him.

On a quiet, rainy Saturday morning in the waning days of August, 1888, Dr. John Lachley, who had long since dropped the foreign "Boleslaus" from his name, sat in a tastefully decorated parlour in an exceedingly comfortable house on Cleveland Street, London, opposite his latest patient, and brooded over his complete dissatisfaction with the entire morning while daydreaming about his last encounter with the one client who would finally bring into his life everything his soul yearned to possess.

The room was cold and damp, despite the coal fire blazing in the hearth. August in London was generally a fine month, with flowers in bloom and warm breezes carrying away the fog and coal smoke and damp chill of early autumn with glorious blue skies and sunshine. But rain squalls and thunderstorms and an unseasonable chill had gripped the whole South of England for months, leaving arthritic bones aching and gloomy spirits longing for a summer that had seemed indefinitely postponed and then abruptly at an end before it had properly begun. John Lachley was tired of hearing the week's complaints, never mind those which had been lodged in all the previous weeks since winter had supposedly ceased to plague them.

He had little tolerance for fools and whiners, did John Lachley, but they paid his bills—most handsomely—so he sat in his parlour with the curtains drawn to dim the room and smiled and smiled at the endless parade of complainers and smiled some more as he collected his money and let his mind drift to remembered delights in another darkened room, with Albert Victor's hands and mouth on his body and the rewards of Albert Victor's social status firmly within his grasp.

He had been smiling steadily for the past hour or more, concealing his loathing for his current patient with an air of concerned understanding, while the bloody idiot of a Liverpudlian who'd appeared on his doorstep rambled on and endlessly on about his health, his illnesses, his medicines, his incessant chills and shaking hands, his itching skin and aching head . . .

It was enough to drive a sane man round the twist and gone. Which was where, in John Lachley's private opinion, this pathetic cotton merchant had long since departed. Hypochondria was the least of Mr. James Maybrick's woes. The fool daily swallowed an appalling amount of "medicinal" strychnine and arsenic in the form of powders prescribed by his physician, some doddering imbecile named Hopper, who should have known better than to prescribe arsenic in such enormous quantities—five and six doses a day, for God's sake. And as if that weren't enough, Maybrick was *supplementing* the powdered arsenic with arsenic *pills*, obtained from a chemist. And on top of that, he was downing whole *bottles* of Fellow's Syrup, a quack medicine available over any chemist's counter, liberally laced with arsenic and strychnine.

And Maybrick was so dull of mind, he honestly could not

comprehend why he now suffered acute symptoms of slow arsenic poisoning! *Grant me patience,* Lachley thought savagely, *the patience to deal with paying customers who want any answer but the obvious one.* If he simply told this imbecile, "Stop taking the bloody arsenic!" Maybrick would vanish with all his lovely money and never darken' Lachley's doorstep again. He would also, of course, die somewhat swiftly of the very symptoms which would kill him, anyway, whether or not he discontinued the poisonous drug.

Since the idiot would die of arsenic poisoning either way, he might as well pay Lachley for the privilege of deluding him otherwise.

Lachley interrupted to give Maybrick the one medication he *knew* would help—the same drug he gave *all* his patients before placing them into a mesmeric trance. Most people, he had discovered, could easily be hypnotized without the aid of drugs, but some could not and every one of his patients expected some spectacular physical sensation or other. His own, unique blend of pharmaceuticals certainly guaranteed that. Success as a mesmeric physician largely depended upon simple slight-of-hand tricks and the plain common sense of giving his patients precisely what they wanted.

So he mixed up his potent chemical *aperitif,* served in a glass of heavy port wine to help disguise the unpleasant flavor, and said, "Now, sir, drink this medicine down, then give me the rest of your medical history while it takes effect."

The drug-laced wine went down in two gulps, then Maybrick kept talking.

"I contracted malaria, you see, in America, trading for cotton shares in Norfolk, Virginia. Quinine water gave me no relief, so an American physician prescribed arsenic powder. Eleven years, I've taken it and the malaria rarely troubles me, although I've found I require more arsenic than I used to. . . . Poor Bunny, that's my wife, I met her on a return trip from Norfolk, Bunny worries so about me, dear child. She hasn't a brain in her pretty American head, but she does fret. God knows I have tried to gain relief. I even contacted an occultist once, for help with my medical disorders. A Londoner, the lady was. Claimed she could diagnose rare diseases by casting horoscopes. Told me to stop taking my medicines! Can you imagine anything more absurd? That was two years ago, sir, and my health has grown so alarmingly worse and Dr. Hopper is such a bumbling fool. So when I decided to visit my brother Michael, yes, that's right, Michael Maybrick, the composer, he publishes under the name Stephen Adams, I said to myself, James, you must consult a London specialist, your life is most assuredly worth the time and money spent, what with the wife and children. So when I saw your advert in *The Times*, Dr. Lachley, that you were a practicing physician and an occultist with access to the guidance of the spirit world for diagnosis of difficult, rare illnesses, and that you use the latest techniques in mesmeric therapies, well, I simply knew I must see you . . ."

And on, and on, *ad infinitum, ad nauseum*, about his *nux vomica* medications, his New York prescriptions that Dr. Hopper had so insultingly torn up . . .

John Lachley sat and smiled and thought, *If I were to jab my fingers into his larynx, I could put him on the floor without a sound, cut off his testicles, and feed them to him one bollock at a time. If he even has any. Must have, he said he'd fathered children. Poor little bastards. Might be doing them a favor, if I simply slit their father's throat and dumped his body in the Thames. Wonder what Albert Victor is doing now? Christ, I'd a thousand times rather be swiving Victoria's brain-damaged grandson than listening to this idiot. Dumb as a fence post, Albert Victor, but what he can do with that great, lovely Hampton wick of his . . . And God knows, he will be King of England one day.*

A small, satisfied smile stole across John Lachley's narrow face. It wasn't every Englishman who could claim to have balled the future monarch of the British Empire. Nor was it just any Englishman who could tell a future king where to go, what to say, and how to behave— and expect to be slavishly obeyed. Stupider than a stick, God bless him, and John Lachley had him wrapped right around his finger.

Or rather, a point considerably lower than his finger.

Albert Victor, secretly bi-sexual outside certain very private circles, had been ecstatic to discover John's physical . . . peculiarities. It was, as they said, a match created in—

"Doctor?"

He blinked at James Maybrick, having to restrain the

instantaneous impulse to draw the revolver concealed in his coat and shoot him squarely between the eyes.

"Yes, Mr. Maybrick?" He managed to sound politely concerned rather than homicidal.

"I was wondering when you might be able to perform the mesmeric operation?"

Lachley blinked for a moment, then recalled Maybrick's request to be placed in a mesmeric trance in order to diagnose his disease and effect a "mesmeric surgical cure." Maybrick was blinking slowly at him, clearly growing muzzy from the medication Lachley had given him.

"Why, whenever you are ready, sir," Lachley answered with a faint smile.

"Then you do think there is hope?"

Lachley's smile strengthened. "My dear sir, there is always hope." *One can certainly hope you will pass into an apoplectic fit while in trance and rid the world of your unfortunate presence.* "Lie back on the daybed, here, and allow yourself to drift with the medication and the sound of my voice." Maybrick shifted from the overstuffed chair where he'd spent the past hour giving his "medical history," moving so unsteadily, Lachley was required to help him across to the daybed.

"Now, then, Mr. Maybrick, imagine that you are standing at the top of a very long staircase which descends into darkness. With each downward step you take, your body grows heavier and more relaxed, your mind drifts freely. Step down, Mr. Maybrick, one step at a time, into the safe and comfortable darkness, warm and cozy as a mother's embrace . . ."

By the end of twenty-five steps, Mr. James Maybrick, Esquire, was in deep trance, having been neatly drugged into a state of not-quite oblivion.

"Can you hear my voice, Mr. Maybrick?"

"Yes."

"Very good. You've been ill, Mr. Maybrick?"

"Yes. Very ill. So many different symptoms, I can't tell what is wrong."

Nothing new, there. "Well, then, Mr. Maybrick, what is it that is troubling you the most, just now?"

It was an innocent question, completely in keeping with a patient suffering from numerous physical complaints. All he was really interested in was narrowing down which symptom troubled the fool the most, so he could place post-hypnotic suggestions in the man's drugged mind to reduce the apparent levels of that symptom, something he had done successfully with a score of other patients suffering more from hysteria and nervousness than real illnesses. He had been following the work of that fellow in Vienna, Dr. Freud, with considerable interest, and had begun a few experiments of his own—

"*It's the bitch!*"

John Lachley nearly fell backward out of his chair.

Maybrick, his drugged face twisting into a mask of rage, snarled it out. "*She* troubles me! The goddamned *bitch*, she troubles me more than anything in the world! Faithless whore! Her and her whoremaster! I'll kill them both, I swear to God, the way I killed that filthy little prostitute in Manchester! Squeezed the life out of her with my own hands, thinking of that bitch the whole time! Wasn't pleasurable, though, damn her eyes, I wanted it to be pleasurable! I'll squeeze the life out of that bitch, I swear I will, I'll cut her wide open with a knife, god*damn* Brierly, fucking my own wife . . ."

Stunned, open-mouthed silence gripped John Lachley for long moments as he stared at the raving cotton merchant, for once completely at a loss as to how he ought to proceed. He'd never stumbled across anything even remotely like this homicidal fury. What had he said? . . . *killed that filthy little prostitute in Manchester . . . squeezed the life out of her with my own hands . . .* Lachley gripped the upholstered arms of his chair. *Dear God! Should I contact the constabulary? This madman's murdered someone!* He started to speak, not even sure what he was going to say, when a frantic knocking rattled the front door, which was situated just outside the closed parlour. John Lachley started violently and slewed around in his chair. In the hallway just outside, his manservant answered the urgent summons.

"Your Highness! Come in, please! Whatever is wrong, sir?"

"I must see the doctor at once, Charles!"

Prince Albert Victor . . . In a high state of panic, too, from the sound of it.

John Lachley glared furiously at the ranting cotton merchant on the daybed, who lay there muttering about ripping his wife open with a knife for sleeping with some arsehole named Brierly, about keeping a diary some servant had almost discovered, nearly ending in a second murder, and something about a room he'd rented in Middlesex Street, Whitechapel, so he could kill more filthy whores, and hated James Maybrick with such an intense loathing, he had to clench his fists to keep from shooting him on the spot. The crisis of his career was brewing outside and this homicidal maniac had to be dealt with first!

Outside, Charles was saying, "Dr. Lachley is with a patient, Your Highness, but I will certainly let him know you're here, immediately, sir."

Lachley bent over Maybrick, gripped the man's shoulders hard enough to bruise, hissed urgently, "Mr. Maybrick! I want you to be quiet now! *Stop talking at once!*"

The drugged merchant fell silent, instantly obedient.

Thank God . . .

Lachley schooled his features and stilled his hands, which were slightly unsteady, then crossed the parlour in two hurried strides, just as Charles knocked at the door.

"Yes, Charles? I heard His Highness arrive. Ah, Your Highness," he strode forward, offering his hand to the visibly distraught grandson of Queen Victoria, "welcome back to Tibor. You know my house is always open to you, whatever the time of day. Please, won't you come back to the study?"

Charles bowed and faded into the back of the house, his duty having been discharged. Prince Albert Victor Christian Edward was a tall, good-looking young man with an impressive dark moustache, a neck so long and thin he had to wear exaggeratedly high collars to disguise the deformity, and the dullest eyes John Lachley had ever seen in a human face. He was twisting expensive grey kidskin gloves into shreds. He followed Lachley down the corridor into the study with jerky, nervous strides. John closed the door carefully, guided his star client to a chair, and poured him a stiff shot of brandy straight away. Albert Victor, known as Eddy to his most intimate friends—and John Lachley was by far the most intimate of Eddy's current friends—gulped it down in one desperate swallow, then blurted out his reason for arriving in such a state.

"I'm ruined, John! Ruined . . . dear God . . . you must help me, tell me what to do . . ." Eddy gripped Lachley's hands in desperation and panic. "I am undone! He can't be allowed to do this, you know what will become of me! Someone must stop him! If my grandmother should find out—dear Lord, she can't ever find out, it would destroy her good name, bring such shame on the whole family . . . my God, the whole government might go, you know what the situation is, John, you've told me yourself about it, the Fenians, the labor riots, what am I to *do?* Threats—*threats!*—demands for money or else ruination! Oh, God, I am destroyed, should word leak of it . . . Disgrace, *prison* . . . he's gone beyond his station in life! Beyond the bounds of civilized law, beyond the protection of God, may the Devil take him!"

"Your Highness, calm yourself, please." He pulled his hands free of Eddy's grip and poured a second, far more generous brandy, getting it down the distraught prince's throat. He stroked Eddy's absurdly long neck, massaging the tension away, calmed him to the point where he could speak coherently. "Now, then, Eddy. Tell me very slowly just exactly what has happened."

Eddy began in a shaken whisper, "You remember Morgan?"

Lachley frowned. He certainly did. Morgan was a little Welsh nancy boy from Cardiff, the star attraction of a certain high-class West End brothel right here on Cleveland Street, a boulevard as infamous for its homosexual establishments as it was famous for its talented artists, painters, and art galleries. Hard on the heels of learning that his ticket to fame and fortune and considerable political power was banging a fifteen-year-old male whore on Cleveland Street, he had drugged Eddy into a state of extreme suggestibility and sternly suggested that he break off the relationship immediately.

"What about Morgan?" Lachley asked quietly.

"I . . . I was indiscreet, John, I'm sorry, it's only that he was so . . . so damned beautiful, I was besotted with him . . ."

"Eddy," Lachley interrupted gently, "how, exactly, were you indiscreet? Did you see him again?"

"Oh, no, John, no, I wouldn't do that, I haven't been with him since you told me to stop seeing him. Only women, John, and you . . ."

"Then what did you do, Eddy, that was indiscreet?"

"The letters," he whispered.

A cold chill slithered down John Lachley's back. "*Letters?* What letters?"

"I . . . I used to write him letters. Just silly little love letters, he was so pretty and he always pouted so when I had to leave him . . ."

Lachley closed his eyes. *Eddy, you stupid little bastard!*

"*How many letters, Eddy?*" The whiplash of his voice struck Eddy visibly.

"Don't hate me, John!" The prince's face twisted into a mask of terror and grief.

It took several minutes and a fair number of intimate caresses to convince the terrified prince that Lachley did not, in fact, hate him. When he had calmed Albert Victor down again, he repeated his question, more patiently this time. "How many letters, Eddy?"

"Eight, I think."

"You think? You must be certain, Eddy. It's very important."

Eddy's brow creased. "Eight, it must be eight, John, I saw him eight weeks in a row, you see, and I sent him a letter each week, then I met you and didn't need to see him any longer. Yes, it's eight letters."

"Very good, Eddy. Now, tell me what's happened to upset you so deeply about these eight letters."

"He wants money for them! A great deal of money! Thousands of pounds, John, or he'll send the letters to the newspapers, to the Scotland Yard inspectors who arrest men for crimes of sodomy! John, I am ruined!" Eddy covered his eyes with his hands, hiding from him. "If I don't pay him everything he wants . . ."

"Yes, yes, Eddy, he'll make the letters public and you will go to prison. I understand that part of the situation, Eddy, very thoroughly, indeed. Now then, how has he demanded payment? Where is the money to be delivered and who is to take it there?"

"You know I enjoy little jaunts in to the East End, occasionally, dressed as a commoner? So no one suspects my identity?"

Lachley refrained from making a tart rejoinder that Eddy was the only person in London fooled by those pitiful disguises. "Yes, what about your little trips?"

"I'm to take the money to him there, tomorrow night, alone. We're to meet at Petticoat Lane and Whitechapel Road, at midnight. And I must be there! I must! If I don't go, with a thousand pounds, he'll send the first letter to the newspapers! Do you realize what those newspapermen—*what my Grandmother*—will do to me?" He hid his face in his hands again. "And if I don't pay him another thousand pounds a week later, the second letter will go to the police! His note said I must reply with a note to him today, I'm to send it to some wretched public house where he'll call for it, to reassure him I mean to pay or he will post the first letter tomorrow."

"And when you pay him, Eddy, will he give you back the letters?"

The ashen prince nodded, his thin, too-long neck bobbing like a bird's behind the high collars he wore as disguise for the slight deformity, which had earned Eddy the nickname Collars and Cuffs. "Yes," he whispered, moustache quivering with his distress, "he said he would bring the first letter tomorrow night if he receives my note today, will exchange it for the money. Please, John, you must advise me what to do, how to stop him! *Someone must make him pay for this!*"

It took several additional minutes to bring Eddy back to some semblance of rationality again. "Calm yourself, Eddy, really, there is no need for such hysteria. Consider the matter taken care of. Send the note to him as instructed. Morgan will be satisfied that you'll meet him tomorrow with your initial payment. Lull him into thinking he's won. Before he can collect so much as a shilling of his blood money, the problem will no longer exist."

Prince Albert Victor leaned forward and gripped John's hands tightly, fear lending his shaking fingers strength. Reddened eyes had gone wide. "What do you mean to do?" he whispered.

"You know the energies I am capable of wielding, the powers I command."

The distraught prince was nodding. John Lachley was more than

Eddy's lover, he was the young man's advisor on many a spiritual matter. Eddy relied heavily upon Dr. John Lachley, Physician and Occultist, touted as the most famous scholar of antiquities and occult mysteries ever to come up out of SoHo. And while most of his public performances—whether as Johnny Anubis, Whitechapel parlour medium or, subsequent to earning his medical degree, as Dr. John Lachley—were as fake as the infamous seances given by his greatest rival, Madame Blavatsky, not everything Dr. John Lachley did was trickery.

Oh, no, not by any means everything.

"Mesmerism, you must understand," he told Prince Albert Victor gently, patting Eddy's hands, "has been used quite successfully by reputable surgeons to amputate a man's leg, without any need for anesthesia. And the French are working the most wondrous marvels of persuasion one could imagine, making grown men crow like chickens and persuading ladies they have said and done things they have never said or done in their lives."

And in the parlour down the hall from this study, a homicidal Liverpudlian cotton merchant had just been spilling his darkest secrets under Lachley's considerable influence.

"Oh, yes, Eddy," he smiled, "the powers of mesmerism are quite remarkable. And I am, without modesty, quite an accomplished mesmerist. Don't trouble yourself further about that miserable little sod, Morgan. Contact him, by all means, promise to pay the little bastard whatever he wants. Promise him the world, promise him the keys to your grandmother's palace, for God's sake, just so long as we keep him happy until I can act. We'll find your letters, Eddy, and we'll get back your letters, and I promise you faithfully, before tomorrow night ends, there will be no more threat."

His oh-so-gullible, most important client gulped, dull eyes slightly brighter, daring to hope. "You'll save me, then? John, promise me, you will save me from prison?"

"Of course I will, Eddy," he smiled, bending down to plant a kiss on the prince's trembling lips. "Trouble yourself no more, Eddy. Just leave it in my capable hands."

Albert Victor was nodding, childlike, trusting. "Yes, yes of course

I shall. Forgive me, I should have realized all was not lost. You have advised me so admirably in the past . . ."

Lachley patted Eddy's hands again. "And I shall continue to do so in future. Now then . . ." He walked to his desk, from which he retrieved a vial of the same medication he had given James Maybrick. Many of his patients preferred to consult with him in a more masculine and private setting such as his study, rather than the more public and softly decorated parlour, so he kept a supply of his potent little mixture in both locations. "I want you to take a draught of medicine before you leave, Eddy. You're in a shocking state, people will gossip." He splashed wine into a deep tumbler from a cut-crystal, antique Waterford decanter, stirred in a substantial amount of the powder, and handed the glassful of oblivion to Eddy. "Sip this. It will help calm your frayed nerves."

And leave you wonderfully suggestible, my sweet and foolish prince, for you must never recall this conversation or Morgan or those thrice-damned letters ever again. Eddy was just sufficiently stupid, he could well blurt out the entire thing some night after a drinking spree in the East End. He smiled as Eddy swallowed the drugged wine. Lachley's one-time public persona, Johnny Anubis, might have been little more than a parlour trickster who'd earned ready cash with the mumbo-jumbo his clients had expected—indeed, demanded. Just as his new clients did, of course.

But Dr. John Lachley . . .

Dr. Lachley was a most accomplished mesmerist. Oh, indeed he was.

He would have to do something about that drugged cotton merchant down the hall, of course. It wouldn't do to leave a homicidal maniac running about who could be associated with him, however innocently; but the man had mentioned an incriminating diary, so Lachley might well be able to rid himself of that problem fairly easily. A man could be hanged even for murdering a whore, if he were foolish enough to leave proof of the crime lying about. And James Maybrick was certainly a fool. John Lachley had no intention of being even half so careless when he rid the world of Eddy's blackmailing little Morgan.

His smile deepened as Prince Albert Victor Christian Edward leaned back in his chair, eyes closing as the drug that would leave him clay in Lachley's hands took hold, allowing him to erase all memory of that frightened, desperate plea:

Make him pay . . . !

Oh, yes. He would most assuredly make young Morgan pay.

No one threatened John Lachley's future and lived to tell the tale.

Senator John Paul Caddrick was a man accustomed to power. When he gave an order, whether to a senatorial aide or to one of the many faceless, nameless denizens of the world he'd once inhabited, he expected that order to be executed with flawless efficiency. Incompetence, he simply did not tolerate. So, when word that the hit he'd helped engineer at New York's exclusive Luigi's restaurant had failed to accomplish its primary objective, John Paul Caddrick backhanded the messenger hard enough to break cartilage in his nose.

"*Imbecile!* What the hell do you mean, letting that little bastard Armstrong get away? And worse, with my *daughter!* Do you have any idea what Armstrong and that vindictive little bitch will do if they manage to get that evidence to the FBI? My God, it was bad enough, watching Cassie turn my own daughter into a crusading, stage-struck fool! And now you've let her escape with enough evidence to electrocute the lot of us?"

The unfortunate lackey chosen to carry the bad news clutched at his nose. It bubbled unpleasantly as he whimpered, "I'm sorry, Senator, we sent six men to your daughter's apartment, *ten* into that restaurant! Who'd have figured Armstrong was such a slippery snake? Or that your kid would leave the table just before the hit went down?"

John Caddrick vented his rage with another backhand blow, then paced the dingy little hotel room, muttering curses under his breath and trying to figure out what that little bastard Armstrong would do next. High-tail it to the FBI? Maybe. But with Jenna Nicole in tow? Armstrong was good at disguises—as John Caddrick had discovered, much to his chagrin—but Jenna was instantly recognizable. If they tried to go anywhere near the New York FBI offices, the men he and Gideon Guthrie had hired would nail them. The trouble was,

Armstrong was bound to realize that. No, that meddlesome bastard would attempt getting them both out of the city. But how? And where would the detective go? Armstrong was more than smart enough to know they'd be watching the bus stations, the airports, the car rental agencies, the ferry launches, anything and everything that offered a way out of the city.

Caddrick swore explosively again. Dammit! After everything he'd worked to achieve, with the timetable counting down to the final few days, along comes that goddamned, nosy bastard *Armstrong*. . . . He paused in his pacing. Armstrong knew that timetable, knew enough of it, anyway, to calculate their next major move. And the rat-assed little detective was a Templar, too, same as the Senator's worthless daughter and now-deceased sister-in-law. If Armstrong and Jenna Nicole didn't try to rescue the next target slated to die, John Caddrick didn't know Templars.

"They'll go to TT-86," Caddrick muttered under his breath. "Get your butt onto that station with a hand-picked team. I want Armstrong dead."

"And your daughter?" the lackey quavered.

John Paul Caddrick shut his eyes, hating Cassie Tyrol for turning his daughter against him, for bringing her into this mess, for showing her the evidence. . . . And John Caddrick's employers would demand blood. At this stage, security leaks had to be plugged. Fast. Regardless of whose family got in the way. So he snarled out, "I won't by God let *anybody* screw this up. Not as close as we've come!"

Speaking through a handful of blood, the messenger asked, "Same M.O. as Luigi's?"

"Hell, yes!" He ran a distracted hand through his hair. "We've already got *Ansar Majlis* on station, thank God. Infiltrated 'em into that construction crew weeks ago. The second your team sets foot on that station, I want them activated. Major blowup. Whatever it takes to make it look good."

"Yes, sir."

"Well, don't just stand there, goddammit! Move!"

The lackey scrambled for the door.

John Caddrick yanked open the hotel room's wet bar and upended an entire, miniature bottle of scotch, then hurled the empty against the wall. The thing didn't even have the decency to shatter. It just bounced off. His ragged temper left a considerable hole in the drywall above the television set, along with a broken lamp and three overturned chairs. *Damn* that meddling detective! And Goddamn that brainless bitch, Cassie Tyrol! His only child . . . who'd never quite forgiven him for all the missed birthday parties and recitals and graduation ceremonies, stranded on the campaign trail or conducting Congressional business . . .

But there wasn't a stinking, solitary thing he could do to save his little girl. And once Jenna knew the truth, Caddrick's ungrateful wretch of a daughter would do whatever it took to see her own father behind bars. If he wanted to keep his butt out of the electric chair, he'd better make damned sure she died. And before this business was done, Noah Armstrong would bitterly regret having ever interfered in Caddrick's business. The Senator ripped out another savage oath, then stalked out of the hotel.

Cassie had finally been paid in full for the trouble she'd caused.

All that remained now was to finish the job.

(((Chapter 2)))

Of all the souls wandering the Commons of Time Terminal Eighty-Six, none felt as out of place Skeeter Jackson. He wasn't lost, which was more than he could say of three-quarters of the people around him. But his status was so changed, he couldn't help but reflect wryly on how odd it was to be trundling a heavy cart stencilled "Station Maintenance" through Edo Castletown, past crowds of kimono-clad tourists jostling elbows with Victorian gents and bustled ladies and a few forlorn, middle-aged men with paunches, bald knees, and Roman tunics.

Confidence man to bathroom-cleaning man wasn't quite the transition Skeeter had hoped for, when he'd decided to give up his life of petty crime. There wasn't much glamor in a cart full of mops, detergent bottles, and vending-machine supplies. On the other hand, he did *not* miss having to dodge station security every ten minutes, or sweating bullets every time some chance acquaintance glanced his way. And while he didn't eat high on anybody's hog, at least he didn't regularly miss meals, anymore, thanks to the uncertainty of a pickpocket's income.

Skeeter was very glad he'd switched careers. But he wasn't quite used to it yet.

A wry smile tugged at the corners of his mouth. As confused as *he* sometimes felt, the other up-time residents were goggle-eyed with shock to find La-La Land's most notorious confidence artist walking the straight and narrow, working the first honest job of his life. It had only taken an act of God and Ianira Cassondra to get him that job. But he couldn't have continued in his old career, not after the pain his greed and stupidity had caused the only friends he possessed in the world. He frequently marveled that he still possessed any friends at all. Never mind ones close enough to help him start his life over again. After what Skeeter had done, he wouldn't have blamed Marcus and Ianira if they'd never spoken to him again. Whatever their reasons, he wouldn't let them down.

As Skeeter maneuvered his cart through the bustling hoards of eminently lost humanity trying to find their way back to hotels, to restaurants that were impossible to find in the station's sprawling maze, or simply standing still and screaming for junior at the top of panic-stricken lungs, the public address system came to life from speakers five stories overhead. "Your attention, please. Gate One is due to open in three minutes. All departures, be advised that if you have not cleared Station Medical, you will not be permitted to pass Primary. Please have your baggage ready for customs inspection by agents of the Bureau of Access Time Functions, who will assess your taxes due on down-time acquisitions . . ."

A familiar voice, the sound of friendship in the middle of all the chaos, sounded at his ear. "Double-gate day, yes?"

Startled, Skeeter turned to find Ianira Cassondra smiling up at him.

"Ianira! What are you doing up here in Edo Castletown?" The lovely *cassondra* of ancient Ephesus could usually be found at her kiosk down in Little Agora, surrounded by her adoring up-time acolytes. Ianira's self-proclaimed worshipers flocked to TT-86 by the thousands each year, on pilgrimage to honor the woman they considered the Goddess incarnate on earth.

Ianira, blithely ignoring the adoring worshippers who trailed her like pilot fish in the wake of an ancient schooner, swept long strands of glossy, raven's-wing hair back from her forehead. "I have been to visit Kit Carson, at the Neo Edo. The Council of Seven asked him to participate in the Festival of Mars next week."

Kit Carson, the planet's most famous and successful individual ever to enter the business of scouting the gates through time, had retired to TT-86. Having pushed most of the famous tour gates now operating through the terminal, Kit Carson was one of the station's major tourist draws, in his own right, despite his status as essentially a recluse who had vowed never to return to that up-time world again. Skeeter, however, steered clear of Kit whenever possible, on general principle. He tended to avoid the older male relatives of any girl he'd tried to finagle into bed with him. Kit, he avoided even more cautiously than others. Kit Carson could seriously cripple a man, just looking crosswise at him. The day Kit had hunted him down and read him the riot act about staying away from Kit's granddaughter, Skeeter would've welcomed a double-gate day. He'd have crawled through an unstable gate, if one had been available, by the time Kit had finished with him.

Skeeter smiled ruefully. "Double-gate day, is right. And I've got this funny feeling we'll be neck deep in lunatics before the day's over. First Primary, then Britannia, and tomorrow, *another* double-gate day."

"Yes," Ianira nodded. "The Wild West Gate opens tomorrow."

"And that new tour gate they're ripping half the station apart over, adding to the Commons."

"At least, there won't be any tourists coming through for it, yet," Ianira smiled.

"No. For now, it's the Britannia tours, packing in the loons. In record numbers." He shook his head. "Between your acolytes and all those crazies coming in for the Ripper Season, this place is turning into the biggest nuthouse ever built under one roof. And those Scheherazade Gate construction workers . . . eergh!" He gave a mock shudder. "What slimy boulder did they turn over, hiring that bunch of thugs?"

As Ianira fell into step alongside Skeeter's push cart, she glanced up with a reproachful glint in her eyes. "You must not be so irritated by the construction workers, Skeeter. Most of them are very good men. And surely you, of all up-timers on station, must understand their beliefs and customs are different? As a down-timer, I understand this very well."

"Oh, I understand, all right. But some of the guys on the Scheherazade Gate crew are throwbacks to the Dark Ages. Or maybe the Stone Ages. Honestly, Ianira, everybody on station's had trouble with some of them."

She sighed. "Yes, I know. We do have a problem, Skeeter. The Council of Seven has met about them, already. But you, Skeeter," she changed the subject as they navigated a goldfish pond with its ornate bridge and carefully manicured shrubbery, "you are ready for the Britannia? There are only seven hours left. Your case is packed? And you will not be late?"

Skeeter let go the heavy handle of his push cart with one hand and rubbed the back of his neck in embarrassment. "Yes, I'm packed and ready. I still can't believe you pulled off something like that." About seven hours from now, the first official Ripper Watch tour of the season was scheduled to arrive in London, on the very evening of the first murder officially attributed to Jack the Ripper. And thanks to Ianira, Skeeter would spend the next eight days in London, courtesy of Time Tours, working the gate as a baggage porter. Hauling suitcases wasn't the world's greatest job either; but carrying rich tourists' luggage beat hell out of scrubbing La-La Land's bathrooms for a living. He'd been doing that for weeks, now. And Ripper Watch tour tickets were selling for five-digit figures on the black market, when they could be found at all. Every one of the Ripper tours had been sold out for over a year.

Skeeter rubbed his nose and smiled wryly. "Time Tours baggage porter. Who'd've believed that, huh? They never would've trusted me, if you hadn't offered to replace anything that went missing on my watch."

"They will learn," she said firmly, giving him a much-needed boost of confidence. Ianira rested a hand on his arm. "You will do well, Skeeter. But will you try to go with the scholars? To see who is this terrible man, the Ripper?"

Skeeter shook his head. "No way. The videotapes will be bad enough."

"Yes," Ianira said quietly. "I do not wish to see any of them."

"Huh. Better avoid Victoria Station, then," Skeeter muttered as he bumped his cart across the division between Edo Castletown and Victoria Station, the portion of Commons which served the Britannia Gate. Bottles of cleaning solution rattled and boxes of toilet paper rolls, feminine supplies, and condoms (latex, spray-on, and natural for those going to appropriate down-time destinations) bounced and jiggled as he shoved the cart across the cobblestones. Mop handles sticking out the top like pungee stakes threatened tourists too slow to dodge—and on every side, pure-bred lunatics threatened everything in sight, including Skeeter and his awkward cart.

"God help us," Skeeter muttered, "Ripper Watch Season is really in full swing."

Ripperoons had come crawling out of the woodwork like swarming termites. So had the crazies preying on them. Saviors of the Gates, convinced the Savior would appear through one of the temporal gates . . . the Shifters, who drifted from station to station seeking Eternal Truth from the manifestations of unstable gates . . . Hell's Minions, whose up-time leader had convinced his disciples to carry out Satan's work with as many unsuspecting tourists and down-timers as possible . . . and, of course, the Ripper Cults.

Those were visible everywhere, holding hand-scrawled signs, peddling cheap literature and ratty flowers, hawking cheap trinkets in the shape of bloody knives. Most of them carried as sacred talismans the authentic surgical knives Goldie Morran was selling out of her shop, and all of them were talking incessantly in a roar of excited conversation about the one topic on *everyone's* mind.

"Do you suppose they'll catch him?"

"—listen, my brothers, I tell you, Jack is Lord, traveling to this world from another dimension to show us the error of our sins! Repent and join with Jack to condemn evil, for He cannot die and He knows the lust in your hearts—"

"No, how can they catch him, no one in 1888 ever discovered who he was."

"—I don't care if you *do* have a ticket for the Britannia, you can't take that surgical knife with you, it's against BATF rules—"

"—let the Sons of Jack show you the way to salvation! Condemn all whores and loose women! A whore is the downfall of righteousness, the destruction of civilization. Follow the example of Jack and rid our great society of the stain of all sexual activity—"

"Yes, but they're putting video cameras at all the murder sites, so maybe *we'll* find out who he was, at least!"

"—somebody ought to confiscate all those goddamned knives Goldie's selling, before these loons start cutting one another up like Christmas turkeys—"

"—a donation, please, for Brother Jack! He will come to Shangri-La to lead us into the paths of truth. Support his good works with your spare change—"

"A hundred bucks says it's that crazy cotton merchant from Liverpool, what's-his-name, Maybrick."

"Go back up time, you sick lunatics! What kind of idiots are you? Jack the Ripper, an alien from another planet—?"

"Hah! Shows what you know! A hundred-fifty says it was the Queen's personal physician, Sir William Gull, hushing up the scandal over Victoria's grandson and his secret marriage, you know, the Catholic wife and daughter!"

"—you want me to *what?* I'm not following Brother Jack or anybody else in a crusade against evil. My God, mister, I'm an *actress!* Are you trying to put me out of work?"

"—help us, please, Save Our Sisters! S.O.S. is determined to rescue the Ripper's victims before he can strike, they're so unimportant, surely we can change history just this once—"

"Oh, don't tell me you bought that Royal Conspiracy garbage? There's absolutely no evidence to support that cockamamie story! I tell you, it's James Maybrick, the arsenic addict who hated his unfaithful American wife!"

"—all right, dump that garbage into the trash bin, nobody wants to read your pamphlets, anyway, and station maintenance is tired of sweeping them up. We've got parents complaining about the language in your brochures, left lying around where any school kid can find them—"

"No, you're both wrong, it's the gay lover of the Duke of Clarence, the queen's grandson, the tutor with the head injury who went crazy!"

Skeeter shook his head. La-La Land, gone *totally* insane. Everyone was trying to out-guess and out-bet one another as to who the real Ripper would turn out to be. Speculation was flying wild, from genuine Scotland Yard detectives to school kids to TT-86's shop owners, restauranteurs, and resident call girls. Scholars had been pouring into the station for weeks, heading down time to cover the biggest murder mystery of the last couple of centuries. The final members of the official Ripper Watch Team had assembled three days ago, when Primary had last cycled, bringing in a couple of dandified reporters who'd refused to go down time any sooner than absolutely necessary and a criminal sociologist who'd just come back from another down-time research trip. They'd arrived barely in time to make the first Ripper murder in London. And today, of course, the first hoard of tourists permitted tickets for the Ripper Season tours would be arriving, cheeks flushed, bankrolls clutched in avaricious hands, panting to be in at the kill and ready to descend on the station's outfitters to buy everything they'd need for eight days in London of 1888.

"Who do you think it is?" Ianira asked, having to shout over the roar.

Skeeter snorted. "It's probably some schmuck nobody's ever heard of before. A sick puppy who just snapped one day and decided to kill a bunch of penniless prostitutes. Jack the Ripper wasn't the only madman who ripped up women with a knife, after all. The way those Ripperologists have been talking, there were hundreds of so-called 'rippers' during the 1880s and 1890s. Jack was just better with his PR, sending those horrible letters to the press."

Ianira shuddered, echoing Skeeter's own feelings on the subject.

If Skeeter had still been a betting man, he might have laid a few wagers, himself. But Skeeter Jackson had learned a very harsh lesson about making wagers. He'd very nearly lost his home, his life, and his only friends, thanks to that last ill-considered, ruinous wager he'd made with Goldie Morran. He'd finally realized, very nearly too late, that his life of petty crime hurt a lot more people than just the rich, obnoxious tourists he'd made a living ripping off. For Skeeter, at any rate, ripping time was over. For good.

Unfortunately, for the rest of La-La Land, it was just getting started.

As though on cue, the station's PA system crackled to life as Primary cycled open. The station announcer blared out instructions for the newly arriving tourists—and at Skeeter's side, Ianira Cassondra faltered. Her eyes glazed in sudden pain and a violent tremble struck her, so hard she stumbled against him and nearly fell.

"Ianira!" He caught and held her up, horrified by the tremors ripping through her. All color had drained from her face. Ianira squeezed shut her eyes for a long, terrifying moment. Then whatever was wrong passed. She sagged against him.

"Forgive me . . ." Her voice came out whispery, weak.

He held her up as carefully as he would've held a priceless Ming vase. "What's wrong, Ianira, what happened?"

"A vision," she choked out. "A warning. Such power . . . I have never Seen with such power, never have I felt such fear . . . something terrible is to happen . . . is happening now, I think . . ."

Skeeter's blood ran cold. He didn't pretend to understand everything this seemingly fragile woman he braced so carefully was capable of. Trained in the ancient arts of the Temple of Ephesus as a child, some twenty-five hundred years before Skeeter's birth, Ianira occasionally said and did things that raised the hair on the back of Skeeter's neck. Ianira's acolytes, who followed her everywhere, pressed closer, exclaiming in worry. Those farther back, unable to see clearly, demanded to know what was wrong.

"Dammit, get back!" Skeeter turned on the whole lot of them. "Can't you see she needs air?"

Shocked faces gawped at him like so many fish, but they backed away a few paces. Ianira sagged against him, trembling violently. He guided her toward a bench, but she shook her head. "No, Skeeter. I am fine, now." To prove it, she straightened and took a step under her own power, wobbly, but determined.

Worried acolytes formed a corridor for her. Skeeter glared silently at them, guiding her by the elbow, determined not to allow her to fall. Speaking as quietly as possible, in the probably vain hope their vidcams and tape recorders wouldn't pick up the question, he murmured, "What kind of vision was it, Ianira?"

She shivered again. "A warning," she whispered. "A warning of dark anger. The darkest I have ever touched. Violence, terrible fear . . ."

"Sounds like everyday life, up time." He tried to make light of it, hoping to make her smile.

Ianira, the gifted Cassondra of Ephesus, did not smile. She shuddered. Then choked out, "It is from up time the danger comes."

He stared down at her. Then a prickle ran up his back. It occurred to him that Primary had just cycled. Skeeter narrowed his eyes, gazing off toward the end of Commons where Primary precinct would be filled with tourists shoving their way into the station. *Screw the bathroom floors. I'm not letting her out of my sight.*

They reached the junction between five of the terminal's major zones, a no-man's land where the corners of Urbs Romae and Victoria Station ran into El Dorado, Little Agora, and Valhalla, not too far from the new construction site where the Arabian Nights sector was going up. It was there in that no-man's land, with Ianira's acolytes making it impossible to see for any distance, that Skeeter heard the first rumbles. An angry swell of voices heralded the approach of trouble. Skeeter glanced swiftly around, trying to pin down the source. It sounded like it was coming from two directions at once—and was apparently triangulating straight toward them.

"Ianira . . ."

Four things occurred simultaneously.

Tourists screamed and broke into a dead run. A full-blown riot engulfed them, led by enraged construction workers shouting in Arabic. A wild-eyed young kid burst through the crowd and yelled something that sounded like, "*No! Aahh!*"—then pointed an enormous black-powder pistol right at Skeeter and Ianira. Gunfire erupted just as someone else lunged out of the crowd and swept Ianira sideways in a flying tackle. The blow slammed her against Skeeter, knocked them both sideways. They crashed to the floor. The maintenance cart toppled, spilling ammonia bottles, mop handles, and toilet paper rolls underfoot. Screams and alarm klaxons deafened him. Skeeter rolled awkwardly under running feet and came to his hands and knees, searching wildly for Ianira. He couldn't see her anywhere. Couldn't see anything but fleeing tourists and spilled cleaning supplies and embattled construction workers. *They* were locked in hand-to-hand combat with Ianira's howling acolytes.

"Ianira!"

He gained his feet, was rocked sideways by a body blow as a cursing construction worker smashed into him. They both went down. Skeeter's skull connected with El Dorado's gold-tinted paving stones. He saw stars, cursed furiously. Before he could roll to his hands and knees again, security killed the station lights. The entire Commons plunged into utter blackness. Shrieking riot faded to an uncertain roar. Somebody stumbled over Skeeter in the darkness, tripped and went down, even as Skeeter clawed his way back to his feet.

"*Ianira!*"

He strained for any sound of her voice, heard nothing but the sobs and cries of frantic tourists, maddened acolytes, and screaming, erstwhile combatants. Somebody ran past him, with such purpose and certainty it could only be security. They must be using that night-vision equipment Mike Benson had ordered before the start of Ripper Season. The riot helmets had their own infrared light-sources built in, for just this kind of station emergency. Then the lights came up and Skeeter discovered himself hemmed in by a solid wall of security officers, armed with night sticks and handcuffs. They waded in, cuffing more rioters, breaking up combatants with scant regard for who was attempting to throttle whom. "Break it up! Move it—"

Skeeter peered wildly through the crowd, recognized the nearest officer. "Wally! Have you seen Ianira Cassondra?"

Wally Klontz stared at him, visibly startled. "What?"

"Ianira! Some crazy kid shot at us! Then somebody else knocked us both down and now she's missing!"

"Oh, Jeezus H., that's *all* we need! Somebody taking pot-shots at the most important religious figure of the twenty-first century!" A brief query over Wally's squawky produced a flat negative. Nobody from security had seen her, anywhere.

Skeeter let loose a torrent of fluent Mongolian curses that would've impressed even Yesukai the Valiant. Wally Klontz frowned and spoke into the squawky again. "Station alert, Signal Eight-Delta, repeat, Signal Eight Delta, missing person, Ianira Cassondra. Expedite, condition red."

The squawky crackled. "Oh, shit! Ten-four, that's a Signal Eight-Delta, Ianira Cassondra. Condition red. Expediting."

More sirens hooted insanely overhead, a shrieking rhythm that drove Skeeter's pulse rate into the stratosphere and left his head aching. But the pain in his head was nothing to the agony in his heart. Wally let him pass the security cordon around the riot zone, then he fought his way clear of the riot's fringe, searching frantically for a flash of white Ephesian gown, the familiar gloss of her dark hair. But he couldn't find her, not even a trace. Skeeter bit his lip, shaking and sick. He had allowed the unthinkable to happen. *Someone* wanted Ianira Cassondra dead. And whoever that someone was, they had snatched her right out of his grasp, in the middle of a *riot*. If they killed Ianira . . .

They wouldn't get out of Shangri-La Station alive.

No one attacked the family of a Yakka Mongol and lived to boast of it.

Skeeter Jackson, adopted by the Khan of all the Yakka Mongols, a displaced up-time kid who had been declared their living *bogda,* spirit of the upper air in human form, the child named honorary uncle to an infant who one day would terrorize the world as Genghis Khan, had just declared blood feud.

Margo Smith glanced at her wristwatch for the tenth time in three minutes, fizzing like a can of soda shaken violently and popped open. Less than seven hours! Just seven more hours and she would step through the Britannia Gate into history. And, coincidentally, into her fiancé's arms. She could hardly wait to see Malcolm Moore's face when she showed up at the Time Tours gatehouse in London, guiding the final contingent of the Ripper Watch Team. Malcolm had been in London for a month, already, acclimating the other Ripper Watch Team members. Margo hadn't lived through four longer, lonelier weeks since that gawdawful misadventure of hers in southern Africa, going after Goldie Morran's ill-fated diamonds.

But she'd learned her lessons—dozens of them, in fact—and after months of the hardest work she'd ever tackled, her gruelling efforts had finally paid off. Her grandfather was letting her go back down time again. And not through just any old gate, either. The Britannia! To study the most famous murder mystery since the disappearance of the Dauphin during the French Revolution. All that stood between her and the chance to earn herself a place in scholarly history—not to mention Malcolm Moore's embrace—was seven hours and one shooting lesson.

One she dreaded.

The elite crowd gathered in the time terminal's weapons range talked nonstop in a fashion unique to an assemblage of late-arriving wealthy tourists, world-class scholars, and self-important reporters—each hotly defending his or her own pet theories as to "whodunnit." They ignored her utterly, even when she stuffed earmuffs and lexan-lensed safety glasses into their gesticulating, waving hands. Most of the students stationed along the firing line were tourists holding ordinary tickets, many of them for the Wild West tour set to leave tomorrow.

The Denver-bound tourists, headed for some sort of action cowboy shoot down time, cast envious glances at the lucky ones who'd managed to beg, borrow, buy, or steal Ripper Watch tickets. *Those* were Margo's new charges, although they didn't know it yet. The mere tourists heading for London, Margo ignored. Her attention was focused on the three individuals with whom she would be spending the next three solid months, as their time guide.

Dominica Nosette, whose name, face, and body seemed quintessentially *French,* yet who was as staidly British as kippers and jellied eels, was chattering away with her partner Guy Pendergast. And Shahdi Feroz . . . Margo gulped, just approaching Dr. Feroz where she stood locked in conversation with a Ripper Watch tourist at the next lane over. Dr. Feroz had spent the past four months studying the rise of cults and cult violence in Imperial Rome, through the Porta Romae. At previous training classes like this one, Margo had met all the other team members now in London, before they'd left the station with Malcolm. But none of the others possessed the credentials or the fieldwork record Shahdi Feroz did. Not even the team's nominal leader, Conroy Melvyn, a seedy-looking Englishman who bore the impressive title of Scotland Yard Chief Inspector.

Looking as Persian as her name and voice sounded, Dr. Feroz *awed* Margo. Not only was she exotic and beautiful in a way that made Margo feel her own youth and inexperience as keenly as a Minnesota winter wind, Shahdi Feroz was absolutely brilliant. Reading Dr. Feroz' work, virtually all of it based on first-hand study of down-time populations, reminded Margo of what she'd seen in New York during her agonizing, mercifully short stay there, and of things she'd seen during her few, catastrophic trips through TT-86's time gates. Not to mention—and she winced from the memory—her own childhood.

Margo's lack of education—a high-school GED and one semester of college which Kit had arranged for up time, augmented with months of intensive study on the station—caused her to stammer like a stupid schoolgirl with stagefright. "Dr. Feroz. Your, uh, safety goggles and muffs, earmuffs, I mean, for your ears, to protect them . . ." *Oh, for God's sake, stop shaking, Margo!*

"Thank you, my dear." The inflection of dismissal in her voice reduced Margo to the status of red-faced child. She fled back down the line of shooting benches, toward Ann Vinh Mulhaney, resident projectile weapons instructor, and the reassuring familiarity of a routine she knew well: preparing for a shooting lesson. Ann, at least, greeted her with a warm smile.

"So, are you all set for London?"

"Oh, boy, am I just! I've been packed for two whole days! I still can't believe Kit managed to swing it with Bax to let me go!" She had no idea what it had taken to convince Granville Baxter, CEO of Time Tours, Inc. on station, to give Margo that gate pass. And not just a one-cycle pass, either, but a gate pass that would let her stay the entire three months of East End Ripper murders.

Ann chuckled. "Grandpa wants you to get some field experience, kid."

Margo flushed. "I know." She glanced at the journalists, at the woman whose scholarly work was breaking new ground in the understanding of the criminal mind in historical cultures. "I know I haven't really got enough experience to guide the Ripper Watch Team through the East End. Not yet, even though I've been to the East End once." *That* trip, and her own greenhorn mistakes, she preferred not to remember too closely. "But I'll get the experience, Ann, and I'll do a good job. I know I can do this."

Ann ruffled Margo's short hair affectionately. "Of course you can, Margo. Any girl who could talk Kit Carson into training her to become the world's first woman time scout can handle mere journalists and eggheads. Bet Malcolm will be happy to see you, too," Ann added with a wink.

Margo grinned. "He sure will! He'll finally have somebody else to send on all the lousy errands!"

Ann laughed. "Let's get this class started, shall we?"

"Right!"

Margo needed to prove to Ann, to Kit, and to Malcolm that she was capable of time scouting. And—perhaps most importantly— Margo needed to prove it to herself. So she dredged up a bright smile to hide her nervousness, hoped she didn't *look* as young as she felt in such illustrious, enormously educated company, and wondered if the team members could possibly take seriously a hot-headed, Irish alley- cat of a time guide who'd just turned seventeen-and-a-half last week . . .

Her smile, which had been known to cause cardiac arrest, was one of the few weapons currently available in her self-defense arsenal, so she dredged up a heart-stopping one and got to work. "Hi! Is everybody ready to get in some weapons practice?"

Heads swivelled and Margo was the abrupt focus of multiple, astonished stares.

Oh, Lordy, here we go. . . . "I'm Margo Smith, I'll be one of your time guides to London—"

"You?" The sound was incredulous, just short of scathing. Another voice from further down the line of shooting benches said, "What high school is that kid playing hooky from?"

Margo's face flamed. So did her temper. She bit down on it, though, and forced a brittle smile. Ann Mulhaney, the rat, just stood off to one side, waiting to see how she handled herself. *Oh, God, another test. . . .* One she'd better pass, too, drat it. So Margo ignored the incredulous looks and scathing remarks and simply got on with the job. "Most of the other guides are already in London," she said firmly. "I've been assigned the job of shepherding you through weapons training, so let's get organized, shall we? We've got a lot to do. Everyone's signed in, been assigned a lane and a shooting partner? Yes? Good. We'll get started, then."

Dominica Nosette interrupted, in a voice acid enough to burn holes through solid steel. "Why d'you insist we learn to shoot? It isn't proper, isn't decent, handling such things. I'm a photojournalist, not some macho copper swaggering about and giving orders with a billycock, nor yet some IRA terrorist. I'm not about to pick up one of those nasty things."

Hoo boy, here we go . . .

Margo said as patiently as possible—which wasn't very—"You don't have to carry one with you. But you will have to pass the mandatory safety class if you want to be a part of the Ripper Watch Team. Not my rules, sorry, but I will enforce them. London's East End is a very dangerous neighborhood under the best of conditions. We're going into areas that will be explosive as a powderkeg. Tempers will be running hot. In the East End, gangs of thieves and cutthroat muggers routinely knife prostitutes to death, just to steal the few pence in their pockets. Any stranger will be singled out by suspicious minds—"

"Oh, sod off, I've never needed a gun, not on a single one of my photo shoots, and I've trailed mob hit men!"

Oh, man, it's gonna be a long three months . . .

Margo steeled herself to keep smiling if it killed her, and vowed to cope. "Ms. Nosette, I am fully aware of your credentials. No one is questioning your status as a competent journalist. But you may not appreciate just how dangerous it's going to be for us, even for the team members born in England, trying to blend in with Victorian East End Londoners. It's your right to choose not to carry a personal weapon. But the rules of the Ripper Watch Team are clear. You must be familiar with their use, because many of us *will* be carrying them. And the more you know about the kind of gun some Nichol-based gang member pulls on you, the more likely you'll be to survive the encounter—"

"Miss Smith," Dr. Shahdi Feroz interrupted gently, "I am sorry to disagree with you, but I have been to London's East End, several years ago. Most of the Nichol gangs did not carry guns. Straight razors were the weapon of choice. So popular, laws against carrying them were suggested by London constables, even by Parliament."

Margo was left with her mouth hanging open and blood scalding her checks until her whole face hurt. She wanted desperately to dig a hole through the concrete floor with the toe of her shoe and crawl down through it, pulling the top in after herself. Before she could recover her shattered composure, never mind think of anything to say that wouldn't sound completely witless, the station's alarm klaxons screamed out a warning that shook through the weapons range like thunder. Margo gasped, jerking her gaze around.

"What's going on?" Dominica Nosette demanded.

"Station emergency!" Margo shouted above the strident *skronkk!* Ann had already bolted toward her office. Margo was right behind, literally saved by the bell. *Oh, God, how'm I ever gonna face that bunch again?* Ann flung open her office door, snatched up the telephone, dialed a code that plugged her into the station's security system. Margo crowded in, then barricaded the doorway so tourists and the Ripper Watch Team couldn't barge in, as well. A moment later, Ann hung up, white-faced and shaken. "There's been a shooting! Skeeter and Ianira! Security's just put out a station-wide alarm. Ianira's *missing!* And there's a station riot underway!"

Her voice carried out through the doorway to the milling throng of tourists and Ripperologists. For one agonizing second, indecision crucified Margo. Ianira was a friend, a good friend, but Margo had a job to do here. And no matter how desperately she wanted to run from her own embarrassing mistake, she had to finish that job.

Dominica Nosette and Guy Pendergast, however, showed no such hesitation.

They grabbed equipment bags and ran.

"Margo! Go after those idiots!" Ann was already striding toward the exit, blocking the way with her body. "Nobody else leaves this range, is that clear? *Nobody!*" Diminutive as she was, none of the others challenged her. They'd all seen her shoot. And nobody wanted to face down the Royal Irish Constabulary revolvers she abruptly clutched in either hand, rather than wearing benignly in twin holsters.

Margo, however, broke and ran, pounding up the stairs after the fleeing British reporters. "Hey! Wait!" *Yeah, like they're really gonna stop just because I said so . . .*

They didn't even slow down.

Seconds later, Margo—hard on their heels and gaining ground—emerged straight into chaos. A seething mass of frightened, confused tourists tried to rush in fifty-eleven directions at once, kids crying, women shouting for husbands, fathers grimly dragging youngsters toward anything that promised shelter. The awesome noise smote Margo like a physical blow, a fist made up of alarm klaxons, medi-van sirens, and screaming, shouting voices. Security squads raced past. Officers were jamming riot helmets on, even as they ran.

Margo's AWOL reporters surged right into the thick of utter chaos, dragging out cameras and recorders on the fly and pounding along in the wake of security. Margo swore under her breath and darted after them. She was small enough to dodge and weave with all the skill of a trained acrobat. An instant later, however, total darkness crashed down, engulfing the whole Commons. Margo skidded to a halt—or tried to, anyway. She caromed into at least half-a-dozen shrieking people before she managed to stop her headlong rush. Sobs of terror rose on every side. The insane wail of the klaxons shook through the darkness.

Margo stood panting in a film of sweat. The hair on her arms stood starkly erect. Unreasoning fear surged. Booted feet pounded past through the total blackness, startling Margo until she realized those odd helmets she'd seen security putting on were Mike Benson's new night-vision helmets. What seemed hours, but couldn't have been longer than a few minutes later, the lights started coming back up, moving gradually inward from the far edges of Commons. Margo blinked as the overhead lights flickered back to life in banks, illuminating Edo Castletown at one far end of the station and the Anachronism's Camelot sector and Outer Mongolia at the other end, around several twists and turns where the Commons snaked through the massive cave system into which TT-86 had been built.

Tourists clung to one another, badly shaken. Margo searched the crowd for her charges and finally caught a glimpse of purposeful movement. The Ripper Watch reporters were on the move again. She swore in gutter Latin that would've shocked Cicero and pounded after them. "Are you crazy?" she demanded, catching up at last. "You can't go in there!"

Dominica Nosette flashed her a pitying smile. "Love, never tell a reporter what she can't do—*can't* is one word we don't understand."

Then they reached the zone of destruction. They'd beat SLUR-TV, the in-station televison news crew, to the punch. Dominica and Guy started filming steadily on every side as more reporters arrived, trailing cameras and lights and microphones. Then Margo caught her first glimpse of the blood and the broken bones.

Oh, my God . . .

While the newsies interviewed shaken eyewitnesses, station security zipped up a body bag with an extremely deceased individual inside. It wasn't the first time Margo had seen a dead person. Not even the second. And her mother's murder had been far more brutal a shock. But blood had stained the golden "bricks" of El Dorado's floor, leaking down between the paving stones in rivulets and runnels, where Margo had never expected to see it. And if that glimpse into the body bag had been accurate, the dead man had been shot in the face, point-blank.

With a very large caliber firearm.

What in God's name happened up here?

Margo began to tremble violently as the remembered smell of burnt toast and spreading, stinking puddles of blood smashed into her from her own childhood, from that long-ago morning when it had been her mother's body zipped up and carted out, and her father led away in handcuffs. . . . She wrapped both arms around herself, biting her lips to keep them from shaking. Violence like this happened in places like New York or London or even Minnesota, where drunkards beat their wives to death. But murder wasn't supposed to happen in a place like La-La Land, not where happy tourists gathered for vacations of a lifetime, where residents pursued dreams that came true every single day, where delightful amounts of money changed hands and everybody had fun in the process. Margo discovered she'd pressed the back of her hand against her mouth, unable to drag her gaze away from the macabre load as security carried away the grey zippered bag with the remains of a stranger inside.

Who is he? she wondered grimly. Or, rather, who had he been? He hadn't been dressed in a tourist costume, or as one of those construction workers building the new section of the station. More than a dozen of the Arabian Nights crewmen, bruised and bleeding, were being dragged off in handcuffs. Then station medical arrived, having to fight their way past newsies filming white-faced, bleeding, dazed survivors. Among the worst injured were the Lady of Heaven Templars, members of the cult which had singled out Ianira as their prophetess. And Ianira was missing, might be dead. . . . Ugly cuts, swollen bruises, and visibly broken bones had so badly injured more than a dozen Templars, medi-vans were required to rush them out of the riot zone.

"Margo!"

She stumbled around, dazed, and found her grandfather cutting through the crowd like an ice-breaking ship plowing through arctic seas. Margo ran to him, threw her arms around him. "Kit!"

Her grandfather hugged her close for a long moment, then murmured, "Hey, it's over, Imp, what's wrong?" He peered worriedly into her eyes.

"I know." She gulped, feeling stupid from lingering shock. "It's just . . . stuff like that isn't supposed to happen. Not *here.*"

Lines of grief etched deeper into Kit's lean cheeks. "I know," he said quietly. "It isn't. I hate it, too. Which is why we're going to do something about it."

"Do *what?* I mean, what can we possibly do? And what happened, exactly? I got here a little late."

Kit thinned his lips. "*Ansar Majlis* is what happened."

"Answer who?"

The grim look in his eyes frightened Margo, worse than she was already. "*Ansar Majlis,*" he said it again. "The *Ansar Majlis* Brotherhood is one of the most dangerous cults to form up time in the past fifty years. Where's Ann?"

"On the weapons range. She stayed with Dr. Feroz and the tourists, to keep anybody else from leaving. I tried to catch up with the reporters. They went charging straight up here, but they out-ran me." She ducked her head. "I'm sorry. I did try to stop them."

Kit muttered under his breath. "I'm sure you did. Listen, Imp, we've got *big* trouble on this station, with Ianira Cassondra missing. I don't have to tell you the repercussions of that, both on station and up time. And with the *Ansar Majlis* involved, this riot may be the first of a whole *lot* of station riots. When word of this gets out . . ." He thinned his lips. "Next time Primary cycles, we are going to be neck deep in more trouble than you can shake an entire tree at. I want you to find Marcus. Try the Down Time Bar & Grill. Tell him we need search parties organized, Found Ones as well as up-time residents. And see if you can find out how Skeeter is."

"Skeeter's hurt? Ann said there'd been a shooting . . ." She swallowed hard, abruptly queasy to her toes. Margo and Skeeter Jackson might have a mutually uncivil history, but the idea of someone having shot the admittedly charming, one-time con artist left Margo sicker and colder than before. She'd gradually been changing her opinion of Skeeter Jackson, particularly since he'd become Marcus and Ianira's latest rescue project. An apparently successful one.

But Kit was shaking his head. "No, not shot, just banged up. Security said he had a lump on his temple the size of a goose egg. Should've had medical look at it, but he bolted into this mess, trying to find Ianira. Get Marcus busy organizing the Found Ones, okay? And find out if Marcus needs help looking after the girls."

Margo drew a shaky breath. "Kit . . ."

If we can't find Ianira, ever . . .

"Yes, I know. When you've got all that set up, meet me at the aerie."

"Bull's office? Won't Bull be busy conducting the official investigation?"

"Yes. Which is why you and I are going to be there." When Margo gave him her best look of blank befuddlement, Kit explained. "In a major station emergency, every single time scout in residence becomes a *de facto* member of station security. Same with the independent guides, the ones not on a company payroll, or with specific tour commitments to meet. And I'd say a riot, a murder, and a kidnapping qualify as a major station emergency in anybody's book. We're going to be busy, Margo, busier than you've been since you arrived on station."

He must have noticed the sudden panic Margo couldn't choke down, try as she might, because he said more gently, "Don't worry about the Ripper Watch tour, kid. You'll get to London, all right. But the Britannia doesn't open for almost six and a half hours and right now, we've got a murderer loose somewhere in this station. A killer who's very likely got Ianira Cassondra in his hands."

Margo shuddered. It was one thing, studying a serial murderer like Jack the Ripper, whose victims were quite well known. Hunting for a madman loose in TT-86 was another prospect altogether—one that terrified her. "Okay, Kit." She managed to keep her voice fairly steady. "I'll find Marcus, get the down-timers organized, try to find out about Skeeter, then meet you at Bull's office."

"Good girl. And for God's sake, Imp, *don't* let those damned newsies follow you!"

She tried to imagine the kind of story *any* reporter would take up time about this disaster, tried to imagine the impact that story would have, particularly the disappearance of the inspiration for the fastest-growing cult religion in the world, and nodded, jaw clenched.

"Right."

"Get moving, then. I'll see you later."

Margo turned her back on the chaos of the riot zone and headed for the popular residents' bar where Marcus worked, wondering how badly Skeeter had been injured and just who had grabbed Ianira—and what they were doing to her, now they had her. Margo bit her lip. What would Marcus do if they couldn't find her? Or if—she swallowed hard at the thought—if they didn't find her *alive?* And their little girls? They weren't even old enough to understand what had happened . . .

Margo's fear edged over into terror, mingled with helpless anger. If those little girls had been left motherless . . . Today's riot would be small potatoes compared to the explosion yet to come. And violence of that magnitude could get a station closed down, permanently. Even one as famous and profitable as TT-86. After the bombing destruction of TT-66 by whichever group of middle eastern religious fanatics had blown the station sky-high, all it would take was another major station rocked by violence to shut down the whole time-tourism industry. There was already a powerful up-time Senator trying to close down the stations. If TT-86 went under because of riots and on-station murders, Kit wouldn't need to kick her out of time-scout training to wreck her dreams.

Up-time politics would wreck them for her.

(((Chapter 3)))

Marcus had not known such fear since his one-time master had tricked him through the station's Roman gate and sold him back into a slavery from which Skeeter Jackson had rescued him. Abandoning the Down Time's bar without a backward glance, he bolted into the chaos loose on Commons, hard on the heels of Robert Li, the antiquarian who'd burst into the bar with the white-faced news: "Marcus! Someone's shot at Skeeter and Ianira!"

Ianira! Fear for her robbed breath he needed for running. Everything that was good and beautiful in his life had come through her, through the miracle of a highly born woman who had been treated cruelly by her first husband, who had still managed, somehow, to love Marcus enough to want his touch, to want the love he had offered as very nearly the only thing in his power to give her. He had been a slave and although Marcus was free now in a way he had never dreamed possible, he would never be a wealthy man, could never give Ianira the kind of life she deserved.

If anything had happened to her, *anything* . . . He could not conceive of a life without her. And their children, how could he tell their beautiful little girls they would never see their mother again? *Please,* he prayed to the gods of his Gallic childhood, to the Roman gods of his one-time masters, but especially to the many-breasted Artemis of Ephesus, the Great Mother of all living creatures, whose temple Ianira had served as a child in that ancient goddess' holy city, *please let her be unharmed and safe . . .*

Marcus was struggling to thrust himself through a packed crowd at the edge of Urbs Romae when a hand closed around his arm. A voice he didn't recognize said, "As you value your children's lives, come with me."

Shocked, he turned—and found himself staring into haunted grey eyes.

He could not have said if the person watching him so narrowly was male or female. But there was pain in those grey eyes, desperate pain and fear and something else, something dark and deadly that made his pulse shudder.

"Who—?"

"Your wife is safe. For the moment. But I can't keep her safe forever, not from the people who want her dead. And your children are in terrible danger. Please. I can't tell you why, not here. But I swear to you, if you'll just come with me and bring your little girls, I'll do everything in my power to keep all of you alive."

It was insane, this impulse to trust. Too many people had betrayed Marcus over the years, and too much that was precious to him, more precious than his own life, depended on his making the right choice. *This is Shangri-La Station,* he found himself thinking desperately, *not Rome. If I am betrayed here, there are people who will move heaven and stars to come to our aid . . .*

In the end, it came down to one simple fact: this person knew where Ianira was. If Marcus wanted to see her, he *had* to go. And the girls?

"I will not risk my children until I know Ianira is safe."

Impatience flared in those grey eyes. "There's no time for this! My God, we've already killed one of them, before he could shoot her. They'll murder your little girls, Marcus, in cold blood. I've seen how they kill! Cassie Tyrol died right in front of me and there was nothing I could do to save her—"

Marcus started. "The woman from the movies? Who played the priestess of Artemis, the Temple harlot? She is dead?"

Pain shone in those grey eyes. "Yes. And the same people who killed her are trying to kill Ianira, her whole family. Please, I'm begging you . . . get your little girls out of danger while there's still time. I'll tell you everything, I swear it. But we have to move *now.*"

Marcus pressed clenched fists to his temples, tried to think clearly, wishing he possessed even a hundredth the skill Ianira did in reading people's hearts and intentions. Standing irresolute in the middle of a panic-stricken crowd jammed into Commons, voices echoing off the girders of the ceiling five stories overhead, Marcus had never felt more alone and afraid in his life. Not even as a child, thrust into chains and caged like an animal for sale. Then, the only person at risk had been himself. Now . . .

"They are at the school and daycare center," he decided, voice brusque. "This way."

He still didn't know if the grey-eyed person at his side was a man or a woman.

But when they reached the daycare center and interrupted an ugly, heart-stopping tableau, Marcus discovered that his shaky trust in his new companion was well-founded. They skidded through the daycare center's doors at an all-out run—and found an armed Arabian Nights construction worker holding Harriet Banks at gunpoint. Another armed man was dragging Artemisia and Gelasia away from the other children. Rage and terror scalded Marcus, blinded him, sent him forward with fists clenched, even as the grey-eyed person with him erupted with a violence that would have struck terror, had that violence been aimed at his family.

Marcus barely had time to see the gun before it discharged. The roar deafened in the confines of little daycare center. His ears rang even as smoke bellied out from the antique gun's barrel. Children screamed and scattered like frightened ants. The construction worker closest to them, the one holding a gun on Harriet Banks, jerked just once, then fell like a man whose legs have been abruptly jerked out from beneath him. The hole through the back of his skull was far smaller than the one through his face, where the bullet had plowed through on its way out. Shock caught Marcus like a fist against the side of his head—then the black-powder pistol discharged again and the man holding Artemisia's wrist plowed into the floor, obscenely dead.

Marcus snapped out of shock with the grotesque thud as the second body landed on the daycare center's floor. He flung himself toward his screaming children. "Hush . . . it's all right, Daddy's here . . ."

He gathered the girls close, hugged them, wept against their hair.

"Marcus! Come *on,* man! More of the bastards are headed this way!"

Marcus had no time to say anything to Harriet Banks, who was trying to get the other children out through the back door, away from the carnage in the playroom. He simply scooped up his daughters and ran with them, following his unknown benefactor into the chaos on Commons. There were, indeed, more construction workers racing toward them, with weapons clutched in their hands as tourists screamed and scattered.

His benefactor's voice cut through shock and terror. "Do you know any better way to reach the Neo Edo Hotel? They're between us and any safety we've got on this station."

Marcus took one look at the burly construction workers running toward them and swore savagely in the language only he, alone of all residents on TT-86, could understand. His Gaulish tribe was as extinct as the language they'd spoken. But his children were still alive. He intended to keep them that way. "This way," he snarled, spinning around and plunging toward Residential. "Down-timers know *all* the secret ways through this station!"

Skeeter had taught Marcus routes he'd never suspected could be used to get from one side of the station to the other. Those escape routes had proven useful when he and Ianira had needed to slip away from the pressing attentions of her adoring acolytes, trying to gain a little privacy for themselves. Marcus had never dreamed he would need them to save his little family from cold-blooded murder. Why anyone would want to kill them, he could not imagine. But he intended to find out.

Marcus might be nothing more than an ex-slave, a down-timer without legal rights. But he was a husband and a father and an " 'eighty-sixer," a member of the insane, fiercely independent, intensely loyal community of residents who called Time Terminal Eighty-Six home. Whoever sought to kill them, they had failed to take that particular fact into account. 'Eighty-sixers took care of their own.

Even if it meant breaking up-time laws to do so.

By the time Skeeter arrived at the aerie, Bull Morgan's glass-walled office was packed, standing room only. And that was *without* the howling mob of reporters trying to get past security to the elevator and stairs that led up to the station manager's ceiling-level office. The elevator had been crowded, too, with 'eighty-sixers responding to the emergency call for search teams. Connie Logan, owl-eyed behind her thick glasses and dressed as outlandishly as ever in bits and pieces of various costumes she'd been testing when the call had gone out, stood crammed into one corner, trying not to jab anybody with the pins sticking out of her clothes. Arley Eisenstein, restauranteur of one of the ten most famous restaurants on the planet and married to the station's head of medicine, stared at the elevator doors with his jaw muscles clenched so tight, Skeeter wondered why his teeth hadn't broken yet. Brian Hendrickson, station librarian and a man who hadn't forgotten the circumstances of Skeeter's disastrous wager with Goldie, any more than he'd forgotten anything else he'd ever seen, heard, or read, was swearing colorfully in a language Skeeter had never heard in his life. Ann Vinh Mulhaney had come upstairs from the weapons range in company with a woman Skeeter recognized as one of the Ripper Watch Team members. Both women were as silent as ghosts and very nearly as pale.

Dr. Shahdi Feroz, Skeeter knew, was not just a world-renowned Ripperologist, she was also the team's cult-phenomena expert. She had made a life's study of criminal cults and intended to research first-hand Victorian London's teeming subculture of spiritualists, occult worshipers, Celtic-revivalists, magic practitioners, and the city's numerous flourishing, quasi-religious cult groups. It had led her to support some rather unusual ideas about the Ripper murders. What she knew about down-time occult groups made for a terrifying parallel to what Skeeter knew of *up*-time cults. He'd seen his share of them in New York. And over the past few years, the new ones popping up like malignant mushrooms made those older ones look positively apple-pie ordinary. Which was doubtless why Bull Morgan had personally requested her presence at this meeting. Shahdi Feroz, as elegant and composed as a Persian queen, dark hair upswept in a mass of thick, raven's-wing waves, glanced at Skeeter, evidently aware of his intent scrutiny, and started to speak—

And the elevator doors slid open onto pandemonium.

Shahdi Feroz turned aside at once, stepping out of the elevator to make room for the others. She glanced over at Ann through dark, worried eyes as they all crowded off the elevator and tried, somewhat vainly, to find space in Bull's packed office.

"I didn't expect quite so many people to be here." Her speech was rich and fluid. Skeeter, fascinated by the rising and falling inflections of her exotic voice, managed to locate a space that hid him from most people's view.

Ann answered in a strained undertone. "I did. In fact, I'm betting we won't be the last to arrive."

When the weapons instructor glanced around, her gaze paused on Skeeter. The look in Ann's eyes caused him to stiffen. Skeeter clenched his jaw and looked away first, unsure which was worse: the pity or the deep, lingering suspicion that Skeeter had only been using Ianira, the way most 'eighty-sixers thought he used everyone he came into contact with. There was nothing he could say, no explanation he could—or cared to—offer that anyone in this room would believe. With the down-timers on station, it was different. But in a room crammed shoulder-to-jowl with *up*-time 'eighty-sixers, Skeeter felt as alone and isolated as he'd felt in Yesukai's felt tent, a lost little boy of eight without the ability to understand a word spoken around him or to go home again to a family that didn't want him, anyway.

He set his jaw and wished to hell Bull would get this meeting underway. He needed to be down on Commons, searching. He'd only come to this meeting because he was not, by God, going to let them leave him out of whatever decisions were made on where and how to search for her. A door near the back of Bull's office opened and Ronisha Azzan, the deputy station manager, appeared, looking worried. She said something to Bull, too low for Skeeter to overhear. Bull ground his teeth over the stubby end of an unlit cigar, then spat debris into an ornate brass spittoon strategically positioned on one corner of his desk. Margo arrived a moment later via the elevator, breathless, her green eyes clouded with fear. She spotted Ann Vinh Mulhaney and Shahdi Feroz and bit her lower lip, then pushed past to Bull's desk. "I can't find Marcus," she said flatly. "He ran out of the Down Time with Robert Li and nobody's seen him since. Robert said Marcus was behind him one minute and he'd vanished into the crowd the next." Ronisha Azzan stepped into the office behind Bull's, swearing under her breath.

Skeeter knew a moment of fear almost as deep as when Ianira had vanished right in front of *him*. Then reason reasserted itself, helped by the white-knuckled hands he used to push back heavy locks of hair sticking to his damp brow. Marcus would be with other Found Ones, searching, of course, there was no reason to panic, no up-timer on station knew the back routes the way the down-timers did, somebody had obviously got to him and maybe even told him they'd seen her somewhere . . .

Station alarms screamed to life again.

Fear tightened down once more, driving daggers through Skeeter's nerves. He very nearly pulled out two fistfuls of his own hair. Skeeter clenched his jaw and made himself wait, while sweat prickled out over his entire torso. Bull Morgan snatched the security phone off his desk and shouted, "What the hell is it *now*?"

Whatever was said on the other end, Bull's florid face actually lost color. The unlit cigar he chewed went deathly still. Then he spat out the cigar with a furious curse and snarled, "Turn this station upside down, dammit, but *find* them! And I want every construction worker in this goddamned station locked up on suspicion of attempted murder, do you hear me, Benson? *Do it!* Ronisha!" The phone didn't quite bend when he slammed the receiver back down, but a crack appeared in the plastic casing.

The deputy station manager, African-patterned silks swirling around her tall figure, reappeared from the back office, talking urgently to someone via squawky. She was snarling, "I don't care who you have to slap in the brig! Control that mess or find yourself another job! Yes?" she asked, turning her attention to Bull.

"Get down to the war room! Coordinate the search from down

there. Have Benson's security teams report directly to you there. We've got another helluva mess breaking loose."

Ronisha fled down the back stairs, squawky in hand. La-La Land's station manager faced the expectant hush from the crowd in his office. The silence in the glass-walled office was as unbearable as the sound of fingernails on a blackboard.

Bull said heavily, "There's been a shooting at the daycare center. Two construction workers messily dead, dozens of children in hysterics. Marcus and his little girls vanished in the middle of the shooting." Nausea bit Skeeter's throat. He forced himself not to bolt for the elevator, forced himself to wait, to hear the rest of it. "A couple of Scheherazade construction workers were trying to take his daughters out at gunpoint when Marcus showed up with someone Harriet didn't recognize. Whoever it was, they shot both construction workers dead and took Marcus and the girls out of there." Bull craned to peer through the crowd of white-faced, furious residents. "Is Dr. Feroz here yet?"

Shahdi Feroz pushed through the throng to the front of Bull's office. "Yes, Mr. Morgan, I am here. How may I help?"

"I want to know what we're up against. Kit Carson told security the bastards who've attacked Ianira and her family are members of the *Ansar Majlis* Brotherhood. He's not here yet, or I'd ask him to brief us."

Shahdi Feroz moved sharply at the mention of the Brotherhood, as though wanting to deny what he'd just said. Then she sighed, tiredly. "*Ansar Majlis*... This is very bad, very dangerous. The *Ansar Majlis* Brotherhood began when Islamic fundamentalist soldiers began recruiting down-time Islamic warriors for *jihad* through the gates where TT-66 used to be. The station is destroyed, but the gates still function, of course."

She spoke with a bitterness Skeeter understood only too well. He hadn't known anyone personally on the station, but hundreds of innocents had died when the station had been blown sky-high. The elevator's soft *ping!* sent Skeeter two inches straight up the wall. But it was only Kit Carson, face haggard, eyes bleak. He moved quietly into the office as Dr. Feroz continued her explanation.

"Since the station was destroyed, thousands of down-time recruits have been brought through to fight *jihad*. Some of these soldiers have banded together to form a brotherhood. They have styled themselves after the nineteeth-century *Ansar*, fanatical religious soldiers of the Mahdi, an Islamic messiah who drove the British out of the Sudan and killed General Gordon at Khartoum. It operates very much like the social structure of a nomadic tribe. Those in the brotherhood are fully human; those outside are not. And the lowest, least human of all are the women of the Lady of Heaven Temples. Such women are considered evil and heretical by these soldiers. A female priesthood, a female deity . . ." She shook her head. "They have sworn the destruction of the Artemis Temple and all Templars. There has been trouble with them in the Middle East, but they were for many years contained there. It seems they are contained no longer. If they have managed to establish cells in major cities like New York, there will be terrible violence against the Temple and its members. The whole purpose of this cult is to destroy the Lady of Heaven Temples as completely as if they had never existed. It is *jihad*, Mr. Morgan, a particularly virulent, fundamentalist form of hatred."

Skeeter wanted to close his hands around someone's throat, wanted to center the bastards responsible for these attacks on Ianira and her family in the sights of any weapon he could lay hands on. Instead, he forced himself to wait. He had learned patience from Yesukai, had learned that to destroy an enemy, one must first know and understand him.

Bull Morgan clenched his teeth over the stub of his cigar, which he'd retrieved from his desk top and was now shredding between molars once again. "All of which explains the attack on Ianira. And her kids, goddamn it. But those construction workers have been on station for weeks. Why wait until now to attack? Why today?"

Margo spoke up hesitantly. "Maybe someone came through Primary today with orders? I mean, the whole thing blew up within minutes of Primary cycling."

Bull pinned her with a sharp stare. Kit nodded silently, clearly agreeing with that assessment. It made sense to Skeeter, as well. Too much sense. And there was that terrifying vision of Ianira's, right before the violence had erupted. Right *after* Primary had cycled.

Bull picked up his security phone again. "Ronisha, I want a dossier on every man, woman, and child who came through Primary today. Complete history. Anybody who might have ties to the Middle East or the *Ansar Majlis* Brotherhood, I want questioned."

Skeeter wanted to question two other individuals, too: the wild-eyed young kid who'd shot whoever it was behind Ianira and Skeeter in that riot, and the person who'd knocked both Ianira and Skeeter to the floor in time for that kid to do the shooting. Skeeter wondered which one of that pair had done the killing in the daycare center. Whoever they were, they clearly knew about the threat to Ianira and her family. But why were they trying to protect her? Were they Templars? Someone else? Skeeter intended to find out, if he had to take them apart joint by joint to learn the truth.

Only to do that, he had to find them first.

He edged toward the elevator, impatient to do something besides stand here and listen. Bull hung up the phone again and started spitting orders. "All right, I want the biggest manhunt in the history of this station and I want it yesterday. Hotels, restaurants, shops, residential, library, gym, weapons ranges, physical plant and maintenance areas, waste management, storage, *everything*. Organize search teams according to the station's emergency management plan. Presume these bastards are armed and dangerous. Personal weapons are not only permitted, but encouraged. Questions?"

Nobody had any.

Least of all Skeeter.

"Let's move it, then, people. I want Ianira and her family found."

Skeeter got to the elevator before anybody else and found himself sharing a downward ride with Kit Carson, of all people. The retired time scout glanced at him as others crowded into the elevator. "You'll organize the Found Ones?"

The question surprised Skeeter. He and Kit Carson were hardly on civil terms, not after his ill-conceived attempt to get Margo into bed with that ruse about being a time scout, himself. Of course, he hadn't known Margo was Kit's granddaughter at the time. In point of fact, not even Kit had known, then. But when the scout *had* discovered the truth, his visit to Skeeter had been anything but grandfatherly—and nothing even remotely resembling cordial. Kit's concern now surprised Skeeter, until he realized that it had nothing to do with Skeeter and everything to do with how Kit felt about Janira Cassondra.

So he nodded with a short jerk of his head. "They'll be organized already, but I'll join them."

"Let me know if you need anything."

Again, Skeeter stared. He said slowly, grudgingly, "Thanks. We're pretty organized, but I'll let you know if something comes up we can't handle." Not that he could think of anything. The Found Ones' Council of Seven had made certain the resident down-timers on station were as prepared as possible for any station crisis that threatened them. The down-timers were, in fact, as prepared as Sue Fritchey's Pest Control officers were for an invasion of anything from hordes of locusts to prehistoric flying reptiles—which, in point of fact, TT-86 had been forced to deal with, just a few months previously.

Kit's next question startled the hell out of Skeeter.

"Would you mind if Margo and I joined you and the Found Ones to search?"

Skeeter's brows dove down as suspicion flared. "Why?"

Kit held his gaze steadily. "Because if anyone on this station has a chance of finding them, it's the down-timers. I'm aware of those meetings held in the subbasements. And I know how underground organizations operate. I also want rather badly to be there if and when we *do* find whoever is responsible for this."

Skeeter had known for a long time that Kenneth "Kit" Carson was a thoroughly dangerous old man, the sort you didn't want as an enemy, ever. It came as a slight shock, however, to realize that the retired time scout would relish taking apart whoever had done this as thoroughly as Skeeter, himself, would. He hadn't expected to share anything in common with the world's most famous recluse.

"All right," he found himself saying tightly. "You're on. But when we do find them . . ."

"Yes?"

He looked the man he was mortally afraid of straight in the eye. "They're *mine*."

Kit Carson's sudden grin was as lethal as the look in his eyes. "Deal."

Skeeter was left with the terrifying feeling that he'd just made a deal with a very formidable devil, indeed. A deal that was likely to lead him places he truly didn't want to go. Before he could worry too intensely about it, however, the elevator bumped to a halt and the doors opened with a swoosh. Five minutes later, he was leading the way through Commons, an unlikely team leader for a search team consisting of himself, Kit Carson, the fiery tempered Margo, and—surprisingly—Dr. Shahdi Feroz.

"The Britannia opens in less than six hours," Margo said pointedly when she insisted on joining them.

"Yes, it does. And I am as ready as I will ever be. I may not know how to shoot a gun yet, but I am certain you can remedy that for me once we reach London, Miss Smith."

The look Margo shot the breathtakingly beautiful older woman wavered somewhere between pleased surprise and wary assessment. Skeeter wondered why, but he didn't have the time to pursue it. Then he spotted Bergitta, a young down-timer who'd fallen through an unstable gate from medieval Sweden. She'd been crying, to judge from her reddened, swollen eyes. She'd hooked up with young Hashim ibn Fahd, a down-time teenager who'd fallen through the Arabian Nights gate, and with Kynan Rhys Gower, whose face was a lethal mask of fury.

Bergitta gave a glad cry when she spotted him. "Oh, Skeeter! We have looked and looked . . ."

Kit was already speaking rapidly in Welsh with the bowman, who had sworn an oath of fealty to Kit down that unstable gate into sixteenth-century Portuguese southern Africa. Skeeter gave Bergitta's hands a swift and reassuring squeeze. "The search teams are organized and out?"

"Yes, Skeeter, and I am told to say to you, please search the escape routes from Little Agora to Frontier Town. You will need a team . . ."

"They're with me," Skeeter said roughly, nodding at the others. "Not my choice, but they're good."

It was a monumental understatement, one of his all-time best, in fact.

Bergitta, who knew their reputations perfectly well, for all that she'd been on station only three months, widened pretty blue eyes; then nodded. "Kynan and Hashim and I go to search also, then." She hugged him, very briefly, but it didn't take more than a fleeting contact to feel the tremors shaking through her.

"We'll find them, Bergitta." Skeeter forced the conviction in his voice. *We have to find them. Dear God, please let us find them soon . . . and safe.*

She nodded and tried to smile, then departed with Kynan Rhys Gower and Hashim, whose glance looked ready to kill anyone who hurt Ianira, despite his youth. Skeeter found Margo's speculative gaze on Bergitta as she moved away into the crowd. What he read in her eyes defied translation for several moments. At first, he thought it was simply distaste for sharing company with a girl who'd been forced by circumstances to sell the only commodity she possessed to make a living on the station: herself. Then he looked again, struck forcibly by the memories lurking in Margo's shadowed green eyes, which had filled with pain, shame, remorse. But for what? He knew how other kids Margo's age had been forced to make a living in New York. He rather doubted Margo had been there long enough to get into serious trouble, given her determination to get onto TT-86 and begin her career as a trainee time scout. But with the kind of pain and the depth of shame he could see in Margo's eyes, Skeeter found himself wondering how she'd raised the money for a ticket through Shangri-La Station's expensive Primary gate.

If Kit's granddaughter *had* resorted to . . . that . . . Skeeter wasn't sure how Grandpa would take the news. Or—Christ, talk about complications—Malcolm, who planned to marry her. *Noneya*, Skeeter told himself severely. Whatever the reason for that look in Margo's eyes, it was very much none of Skeeter's business.

"We'll start in Little Agora," he said gruffly. "It's closer. Let's go, I've waited too long as it is."

Wordlessly, his little search party followed.

Jenna Nicole Caddrick didn't take Ianira to the hotel room she'd reserved nearly a year previously in Carl's married sister's name. She hadn't dared try to check into the luxury hotel, not with Ianira Cassondra draped, unconscious, across her back and shoulders in a fireman's carry where Noah Armstrong had put her. "Get her to the hotel!" the detective had ordered. "Take the stairways to the basement—I've got to find her husband and kids!"

So, staggering with every step, because Jenna was not that much larger than Ianira, herself, she carried the sacred prophetess through the station's Commons during security's riot-control blackout, bumping into people and stumbling into walls until she finally found a staircase, its emergency "Exit" sign glowing in the stygian darkness. The lights down here, at least, hadn't been shut off. Shangri-La Station's basement was a twisting montage of pipes and conduits and crowded storage rooms where, with any luck—and the Lady alone knew they deserved a little of that—the *Ansar Majlis* wouldn't think to look. Or anyone else, for that matter, not right away, at least. Jenna, legs and arms trembling with the effort, joints all but cracking, finally spotted a thick pile of hotel towels, in a big packing crate that someone had pried open to remove part of its contents. Moving gingerly, she lowered Ianira onto the piled towels. The prophetess was still as death, with a nasty bruise along her brow where Noah had slammed her to the floor, saving her life.

Jenna didn't know much about medicine or first aid, but she knew how to test a pulse, anyway, and remembered that a shock victim had to be kept warm. So she covered Ianira with a whole pile of the crated towels and tested her pulse and wondered if slow and regular might be good or bad news. She bit one lip, then wondered how to let Noah Armstrong know where to find them. *We'll meet at the Neo Edo, kid, that's where you've got reservations and they'll expect you to show up.*

Yeah, she thought glumly. But not with an unconscious prophetess across her shoulder. Showing up with Ianira, Cassondra of Ephesus, in a state of coma was a great way to get the attention of all the wrong people, *fast*. When Jenna heard the footfalls and the distant murmur of voices, she spun on her heel, gripping Carl's reproduction pistol in both hands, terrifying herself with that blurred, instinctive reaction. *I don't want to get used to people trying to kill me . . . or having to kill them.* The thundering shock of shooting down a living human being up on Commons would have left Jenna on hands and knees, vomiting, if Ianira Cassondra's life hadn't been in mortal jeopardy with every passing second. She wanted to go into shock now, *needed* to be sick, was shaking violently with the need, but there was someone coming and she couldn't let them kill Ianira.

The voices drew closer, voices she didn't recognize. Jenna scowled, fist tight on the reproduction antique weapon in her hand, trying to make sense of what they were saying. She realized abruptly that the words weren't *going* to fall into any recognizable patterns because they weren't in English. Whatever it was, it sounded like . . . Classical Latin, maybe? Would the *Ansar Majlis* speak Latin? She couldn't imagine it, not a pack of medieval terrorists imported from the war-wracked Middle East for the express purpose of destroying the Temple which formed the bedrock of Jenna's faith.

Then the speakers rounded an abrupt corner and Jenna gasped, giddy with relief. "*Noah!*"

Armstrong swung around sharply, recognized her, relaxed a death grip on the trigger. "Kid," Noah muttered, "you are gonna get yourself shot one of these days, doing that. Where is she?"

Jenna pointed, eyeing the people who accompanied Noah. The ashen-faced young man in jeans and an ordinary short-sleeved work shirt, she recognized as the Cassondra's husband—the Roman slave—and the two little girls with him looked so much like their mother it closed Jenna's throat. Another young man with them was a kid, really, younger than Jenna. A lot younger. At the moment, Jenna Nicole Caddrick felt about a thousand years old and aging rapidly.

"Ianira!" Marcus cried, running toward his wife.

"She's unconscious," Jenna said, voice low and unsteady. "She hit her head on the floor . . ."

Marcus and the teenager broke into a voluble spate of Latin, Marcus nodding his head vehemently up and down, the kid looking stubborn. A fragment of historical research for a film class came back to her, that Romans bobbed their heads up and down to indicate disagreement, not wagging them from side to side the way moderns did. At length, the younger kid muttered something that sounded foul and trotted away into the dim-lit basement.

"Where's he going?" Jenna asked. What if they brought the station authorities in? If that happened, Ianira and Marcus and those beautiful little girls would die. *Nobody* could protect them, not as long as they remained on this station.

Marcus didn't even glance up. He was stroking his wife's hair back from her bruised forehead, holding her cold hand. Their little girls whimpered and clung to his leg, too young to know or comprehend what was happening around them, but old enough to know terror. "He goes to bring medicine. Food, water, blankets. We will hide her in the Sanctuary."

Jenna didn't know exactly what or where Ianira's Sanctuary might be, although she suspected it was hidden deep under the station. But she knew enough to blurt out, "You can't! It won't be safe there. These bastards will hunt through every inch of this station, looking for her. For you, too, and the children."

Frightened brown eyes lifted, met hers. "What can we do, then? We have friends here, powerful friends. Kit Carson and Bull Morgan—"

Armstrong cut him off. "Not even Kit Carson can stop the *Ansar Majlis*," Noah bit out, bitterness darkening the detective's voice, leaving it harsh and raw. "You have to get completely off this station. The faster, the better. We sure as hell are," Noah nodded toward Jenna. "The only place that's gonna be safe is someplace down time. There's a whole lot of history to hide in, through this station's gates. We hide long enough, stay alive long enough, I can slip back through the station in disguise—and I'm damned good at disguises—and get the proof of what we know to the up-time authorities. If we're going to stop the bastards responsible for this," Noah jerked a glance toward Ianira, curled up on her side, fragile as rare porcelain, "the *only* way is to destroy them, make sure they're jailed for life or executed. And we can't do that if *we're* dead."

"*Who is it?*" Marcus grated out. "I will kill them, whoever they are!"

Jenna believed him. Profoundly. Imagination failed her, trying to comprehend what this ordinary-seeming young man in blue jeans and a checkered shirt had already lived through. Noah told Marcus what they were up against. All of it. In thorough and revolting detail. The suspicion that flared in Marcus' eyes when he looked at Jenna wounded her.

"I'm not my father!" she snapped, fists aching at her sides. "If that son-of-a-bitch were in front of me right now, I'd blow his head off. He always was a lousy, rotten, stinking bastard of a father. I just never knew how *much*. 'Til now."

The suspicion in the other man's brown eyes melted away while something else coalesced in its place. It took a moment to recognize it. When he did, it shook Jenna badly. *Pity*. This ex-slave, this man whose family was targeted for slaughter, pitied *her*. Jenna turned roughly aside, shoved her pistol through her belt and her hands into her pockets, and clenched her teeth over a flood of nausea and anger and fright that left her shaking. A moment later, Noah settled a hand on her shoulder.

"You never killed a man before." It wasn't a question, didn't have to be a question, because it was perfectly obvious. Jenna shook her head anyway. "No." Noah sighed, tightened fingers against her shoulder for a moment. "They say it's never easy, kid. I hadn't either, you know, until that hit in New York." Jenna glanced up, found deep pain in Noah's enigmatic eyes. "But I always knew I might have to, doing the job I chose. It's worse for you, probably. When a kid comes to the Temple young as you are, she's hurting inside already. You got more reason than most. And Cassie told me you cried when you accidentally ran over a mongrel dog on the road out to the ranch."

She clenched her teeth tighter and tried to hold back tears she did not want the detective to witness. Noah didn't say anything else. Just dropped the hand from Jenna's shoulder and turned away, moving briskly around the confined space Jenna had chosen to defend, making up a better bed for Ianira. That it was necessary only upset Jenna more, because she hadn't done a good enough job of it, herself. The Latin-speaking teenager returned a few silent minutes later, bringing a first aid kit, a heavy satchel that wafted the scent of food when he lifted the flap, blankets piled over one shoulder, and a couple of stuffed toys, which he gave to Ianira's daughters. The children grabbed hold of the shaggy, obviously home-made bears, and hugged them with all their little-girl strength. Jenna's eyes stung, watching it. No child only three years old should ever look at the world through eyes that looked like *that.* And Artemisia's sister was even younger, barely a year old. Barely walking, yet.

"We can't stay here long," Noah was saying, voice low. "They'll be searching for her. We'll have to smuggle her up into the hotel room Jenna's reserved. We can hide there until the Britannia Gate opens." The detective checked a wristwatch. "We won't need to hide long. But we've got to outfit for the gate between now and then. And find a way to smuggle Ianira through."

"Us," Marcus said sharply. "We all go through."

But Noah was shaking a head that ought to've gone grey by now, if the detective's private life was anything like what they'd already lived through. "No. They're going to send a death squad after us, Marcus. They'll send somebody through every gate that opens during the next week, trying to get her. I won't risk all of you anywhere in one group. Just in case the worst happens and the bastards who follow her through the gate *do* catch up."

"Not the Britannia," Marcus insisted stubbornly. "They cannot get through the Britannia. It is Ripper Season. There have been no tickets for today's gate for over a year. I could get through working as a porter hauling baggage, because I am a station resident, but no one else."

"Don't underestimate these people, Marcus. If necessary, they'll kill one of the baggage handlers, take his place, and get through that way, using their victim's ID and timecard."

Marcus' already pale cheeks ran dead white. "Yes," he whispered. "It would be easy. Too easy."

"So." Noah's voice, so difficult to pin down as either a man's light voice or a woman's deep one, was cold and precise. "We put Ianira in a steamer trunk. Same thing for the girls. You," the detective nodded at Marcus, "go through one of the other gates with your children. And we'll disguise you as a baggage handler, since they're almost invisible. The problem is, which gate?"

The teenager spoke up at once. "The Wild West Gate opens tomorrow."

Jenna and Noah exchanged glances. It was perfect. Too perfect.

The *Ansar Majlis* would track Marcus and the girls straight through that gate, figuring it would be the one gate Jenna was likeliest to choose. The tour gate into Denver of 1885 was the only gate besides the sold-out Britannia where the natives spoke English. And Carl had been such a nut about that period of American history, the killers tracking them would doubtless figure Jenna had cut and run through the gate she and Carl would've known the most about, the only one she could get tickets for, not knowing, thank the Lady, that Jenna had secretly bought tickets through the Britannia in another name more than a year ago.

Noah, however, was frowning in concentration, studying Marcus closely. "It could work. Put you and the girls down Denver's Wild West Gate, with me as guard, send Jenna and Ianira through to London."

"But—" Jenna opened her mouth to protest, terrified at the prospect of Noah abandoning her.

A dark glance from steel-cold grey eyes shut her up. "There are two of us. And two groups of them." The detective nodded at Marcus and Ianira, who still lay unmoving except to breathe. Fright tightened down another notch, leaving Jenna to wonder if she'd ever be hungry again, her gut hurt so much. Noah said more gently, "We have to split up, kid. If we send Marcus and the girls through without a guard . . . hell, kid, we might as well shoot them through the head ourselves. No, we *know* they're going to follow whoever goes through the Wild West Gate. So I'll go with them, pose as somebody they're likely to think is you, use a name they'll think is something you'd come up with, something you'd think is clever—"

The teenager interrupted. "You don't look like her. Not anything like her. Nobody would believe you *were* her. You are too tall."

For the first time, Jenna Nicole Caddrick saw Noah Armstrong completely flummoxed. The detective's mouth opened onto shocked silence. But the kid who spoke Latin—which probably meant he was a down-timer, too, same as Marcus—wasn't finished. "I look more like her than any of us. I'll go in her place. If I dress up like a rich tourist, wear a wig the color of her hair, pretend to be rude and obnoxious, wear a bonnet low over my eyes and swear a lot, the people hunting *her,*" the kid nodded toward Jenna, "will think she's *me.* Or I'm her. It *will* work," he insisted. "There is a tour leaving tomorrow that plans to shoot in a special competition, men and women both. I *have* watched every John Wayne movie ever made, twice, and I have seen thousands of tourists. I can pretend to be a woman cowboy shooter with no trouble at all."

The very fact that he'd come up with the idea in the first place told Jenna a great deal about how much the residents of this time station loathed tourists. Obnoxious and rude . . . It probably would work beautifully, given half a chance. "You realize you're risking your life?" she asked quietly.

The teenager stared her down. "Yes. They have tried to murder Ianira."

It was all that needed to be said.

"Julius—" Marcus started to protest.

"No," Julius swung that determined gaze toward his older friend. "If I die, then I will die with honor, protecting people I love. What more can any man ask?"

How did a kid that young end up that wise? Jenna thought about ancient Rome and what men did to other men there and shuddered inside. The fact that she, herself, had done exactly what this boy was volunteering to do didn't even occur to her. Jenna, too, was risking her own life to save Ianira's.

"That's settled, then," Noah said briskly. "Julius, I don't have words to thank you. Right now, I'd better go up to Commons, check into the hotel under the name on my station pass, find an outfitter. You, too, Jenna. I'll need help getting those steamer trunks back to the hotel, and all the gear we've got to buy along with it." The detective glanced at Marcus and Julius. "We'll bring the steamer trunks back right away, get Ianira and the rest of you into a hotel room until the gate goes. We're going to hide you right in the open, in a perfectly ordinary hotel room, and let them tear the basement and the rest of the station apart, looking for you. Then I'm going to establish my Denver persona with a vengeance, draw the attention of the bastards after us, so they'll concentrate on Denver, rather than London. There's going to be one more rude and obnoxious cowboy added to the station's population, today, I believe, the sooner the better. With a name that ought to grab somebody's attention."

The purloined letter . . . Jenna grimaced. She sure as hell didn't have any better ideas. Noah had gotten her out of New York alive. She was pretty sure Noah could get them all out of the station alive, too. Whether or not she and Ianira stayed that way in London was up to Jenna. She prayed she was up to the job. Because there just wasn't anybody else around to do it. Thoughts of her father brought her teeth together, hard and brutal. *You're gonna pay for this, you son-of-a-bitch. You'll pay, if it's the last thing I ever do on this earth!*

Then she headed up to Commons on Noah Armstrong's heels to fetch a steamer trunk.

(((Chapter 4)))

Shangri-La Station was an Escheresque blend of major airport terminal, world-class shopping mall, and miniature city, all tucked away safely inside a massive cavern in the heart of the uplifted limestone massifs of the Himalayan mountains, a cavern which had been gradually enlarged and remolded into one of the busiest terminals in the entire time-touring industry. Portions of the station emerged into the open sunshine on the mountain's flank, or would have, if Shangri-La's engineers hadn't artificially extended that rocky flank to cover the station's outer walls in natural-looking concrete "rock" faces. Because the terminal's main structure followed the maze of the cave system's inner caverns, TT-86 was a haphazard affair that sprawled in unexpected directions, with tunnels occasionally boring their way through solid rock to connect one section of the station with another.

The major time-touring gates all lay in the Commons, of course, a vast area of twisting balconies, insane staircases and ramps, and all the glitter of high-class shops and restaurants that even the most discriminating of billionaires could wish to find themselves surrounded with. But because Commons followed the twists and turns of the immense cavern, there was no straight shot or even line-of-sight view from one end to the other. And station Residential snaked back into even more remote corners and crannies, with apartments tucked in like cells in a beehive designed by LSD-doped honeybees.

The underpinnings of the station descended multiple stories into the mountain's rocky heart, where the nitty-gritty, daily business of keeping a small city operational was carried out. Machinery driven by a miniature atomic pile hummed in the rocky silence. The trickle and rush of running water from natural underground streams and waterfalls could be heard in the sepulchral darkness beyond the station's heating, cooling, and waste-disposal plants. Down here, anybody could hide anything for a period of many months, if not years.

Margo had realized long ago that Shangri-La Station was immense. She just hadn't realized how big it really was. Not until Skeeter Jackson led them down circuitous, narrow tunnels into a maze he clearly knew as well as Margo knew the route from Kit's palatial apartment to her library cubicle. Equally clearly, Skeeter had taken full advantage of this rat's maze to pull swift disappearing acts from station security and irate tourists he'd fleeced, conned, or just plain robbed.

Probably what saved his life when that enraged gladiator was trying to skewer him with a sword, she thought silently. Under Skeeter's direction, their search party broke apart at intervals, combing the corridors and tunnels individually, only to rejoin one another further on. She could hear the footsteps and voices of other search parties off in the distance. The echoes, eerie and distorted, left Margo shivering in the slight underground chill that no amount of central heating could dispel. Occasional screams and girder-bending shrieks drifted down from the enormous *pteranodon sternbergi* which had entered the station through an unstable gate into the era of dinosaurs.

The size of a small aircraft, the enormous flying reptile lived in an immense hydraulic cage that could be hoisted up from the sub-basements right through the floor to the Commons level for "feeding demonstrations." The pterodactyl ate several mountains of fish a day, far more than they could keep stocked through the gates. So the head of pest control, Sue Fritchey, had hatched an ambitious project to keep the big *sternbergi* fed: breeding her own subterranean food supply from an up-time hatchery and any down-time fingerlings they could bring in. The sub-basement corridors were lined with rows and high-stacked tiers of empty aquariums, waiting to be filled with the next batch of live fingerlings. Piles and dusty stacks of the empty glass boxes left the tunnels under Little Agora and Frontier Town looking like the ghost of a pet shop long since bankrupt, its fish sold below cost or dumped down the nearest toilet.

It was a lonely, eerie place to have to search for a missing friend.

Margo glanced at her watch. How long had they been searching, now? Four hours, twenty minutes. Time was running out, at least for her and anyone else heading down the Britannia Gate. She bit one lip as she glanced at Shahdi Feroz, who represented in one package very nearly everything Margo wanted to be: poised, beautiful, a respected professional, experienced with temporal gates, clocking in nearly as much down time as some Time Tours guides. Time Tours had actually approached Dr. Feroz several times with offers to guide "seance and spiritualist tours" down the Britiannia. She'd turned them down flat, each and every time they'd offered. Margo admired her for sticking by her principles, when she could've been making pots and kettles full of money. Enough to fund her down-time research for the next century or two.

And speaking of down-time research . . .

"Kit," Margo said quietly, "we're running short of time."

Her grandfather glanced around, checked his own watch, frowned. "Yes. Skeeter, I'm sorry, but Margo and Dr. Feroz have a gate to make."

Skeeter turned his head slightly, lips compressed. "I'm supposed to work that gate, too, you know. We're almost directly under Frontier Town now. We finish this section of tunnels, then they can run along and play detective down the Britannia as much as they want."

Margo held her breath as Kit bristled silently; but her grandfather held his temper. Maybe because he, too, could see the agony in Skeeter's eyes. Kit said only, "All right, why don't you take that tunnel?" and nodded toward a corridor that branched off to the left. "Dr. Feroz, perhaps you'd go with Margo? You can discuss last-minute plans for the tour while you search."

Margo squirmed inwardly, but she couldn't very well protest. She was going to spend the next three months of her life in this woman's company. She'd have to face her sooner or later and it might as well be sooner.

Kit pointed down one of the sinuous, winding tunnels. "Take that fork off to the right. I'll go straight ahead. We'll meet you—how much farther?" he asked Skeeter.

"Fifty yards. Then we'll take the stairs up to Frontier Town."

They split up. Margo glanced at Shahdi Feroz and felt her face redden. Margo barely had a high school diploma and one semester of college. She had learned more in Shangri-La's library than she had in that stuffy, impossible up-time school. And she had learned, enormously. But after that mortifying mistake, with Shahdi Feroz correcting her misapprehension about Nichol gangs' weapons of choice, it wouldn't matter that Margo had logged nearly two hundred hours through the Britannia or that she spoke fluent Cockney. Kit had drilled her until she could not only make sense of the gibberish that passed for Cockney dialect, but could produce original conversations in it, too. Without giving herself too savage a headache, remembering all the half-rhymes and word-replacement games the dialect required. None of that would matter, not when she'd goofed on the very first day, not when Margo's lack of a diploma left her vulnerable and scared.

Shahdi Feroz, however, surprised Margo with an attempted first gesture at friendliness. The scholar smiled hesitantly, one corner of her lips twisting in chagrin. "I did not mean to embarrass you, Miss Smith. If you are to guide the Ripper Watch Tour, then you clearly have the experience to do so."

Margo almost let it go. She wanted badly to have this woman think she really did know what she was doing. But that wasn't honest and might actually be dangerous, if they got into a tight spot and the scholar thought she knew more than she did. She cleared her throat, aware that her face had turned scarlet. "Thanks, but I'm not, really." The startled glance Dr. Feroz gave her prompted Margo to finish before she lost her nerve. "It's just that I'm in training to be a time scout, you see, and Kit wants me to get some experience doing fieldwork."

"Kit?" the other woman echoed. "You know Kit Carson that well, then, to use his first name? I wish I did."

Some of Margo's nervousness drained away. If Dr. Shahdi Feroz could look and sound that wistful and uncertain, then maybe there was hope for Margo, after all. She grinned, relief momentarily transcending worry and fear for Ianira's family. "Well, yeah, I guess you could say so. He's my grandfather."

"Oh!" Then, startling Margo considerably, "That must be very difficult for you, Miss Smith. You have my sympathy. And respect. It is never easy, to live up to greatness in one's ancestors."

Strangely, Margo received the impression that Shahdi Feroz wasn't speaking entirely of Margo. "No," she said quietly, "it isn't." Shahdi Feroz remained silent, respecting Margo's privacy, for which she was grateful. She and the older woman began testing doors they came to and jotting down the numbers painted on them, so maintenance could check the rooms later, since neither of them had keys. Margo did rattle the knobs and knock, calling out, "Hello? Ianira? Marcus? It's Margo Smith . . ." Nobody answered, however, and the echoes that skittered away down the tunnel mocked her efforts. She bit her lower lip. How many rooms to check, just like these, and how many miles of tunnels? God, they could be *anywhere.*

No, she told herself, not just anywhere. If they had been killed, the killer would either have needed keys to unlock these doors or would've had to use tools to jimmy the locks. And so far, neither Margo nor Shahdi Feroz had found any suspicious scratches or toolmarks indicating a forced door. So they might still be alive.

Somewhere.

Please, God, let them still be alive, somewhere . . .

Their tunnel twisted around, following the curve of the cavern wall, and re-joined the main tunnel fifty yards from the point they'd left it. Kit was already there, waiting. Skeeter, grim and silent, arrived a moment later.

"All right," Skeeter's voice was weary with disappointment, "that's the whole section we were assigned." The pain in his voice jerked Margo out of her own worry with a stab of guilt. She hadn't lost anything, really, in that goof with Shahdi Feroz, except a little pride. Skeeter had just lost his only friends in the whole world.

"I'm sorry, Skeeter," she found herself saying, surprising them both with the sincerity in her voice.

Skeeter met her gaze steadily for a long moment, then nodded slowly. "Thanks. I appreciate that, Margo. We'd better get back up to Commons, get ready to go through the Britannia." He grimaced. "I'll carry the luggage through, because I agreed to take the job. But I won't be staying."

No, Margo realized with a pang. He wouldn't. Skeeter would come straight back through that open gate and probably kill himself searching, with lack of sleep and forgetting to eat. . . . They trooped wordlessly up the stairs to the boisterous noise of Frontier Town. With the Wild West gate into Denver set to open tomorrow, wannabe cowboys in leather chaps and jingling spurs sauntered from saloon to saloon, ogling the bar girls and pouring down cheap whiskey and beer. Rinky-tink piano music drifted out through saloon doors to mingle with the voices of tourists speculating on the search underway, the fate of the construction workers who'd attacked Ianira, her family, and her acolytes, on the identity of the Ripper, and what sights they planned to see in Denver of 1885 and the surrounding gold-mining towns.

In front of Happy Jack's saloon, a guy with drooping handlebar moustache, who wore an outlandish getup that consisted of low-slung Mexican sombrero, red silk scarf, black leather chaps, black cotton shirt, black work pants tucked into black, tooled-leather boots, and absurdly roweled silver spurs, was staggering into the crowd, bawling at the top of his lungs. "Gonna win me that medal, y'hear? Joey Tyrolin's the name, gonna win that shootin' match, l'il lady!"

He accosted a tourist who wore a buckskin skirt and blouse. She staggered back, apparently from the smell of his breath. Joey Tyrolin, drunker than any skunk Margo had yet seen in Frontier Town, drew a fancy pair of Colt Single-Action Army pistols and executed an equally fancy roadhouse spin, marred significantly by the amount of alcohol he'd recently consumed. One of the .45-caliber revolvers came adrift mid-air and splashed into a nearby horse trough. Laughter exploded in every direction. A scowl as dark as his clothes appeared in a face that matched his red silk bandanna.

"Gonna win me that shootin' match, y'hear! Joey Tyrolin c'n shoot th' eye outta an eagle at three hunnerd yards . . ." He bent, gingerly fishing his gun out of the horse trough.

Margo muttered, "Maybe he'll fall in and drown? God, am I ever glad we're going to London, not Denver."

Kit, too, eyed the pistolero askance. "Let's hope he confines his shooting to that black-powder competition he's bragging about. I've seen far too many idiots like that one go down time to Denver and challenge some local to a gunfight. Occasionally, they choose the wrong local, someone who can't be killed because he's too important to history. Now and again, they come back to the station in canvas bags."

Shahdi Feroz glanced up at him. "I should imagine their families must protest rather loudly?"

"All too often, yes. It's why station management requires the hold harmless waivers all time tourists must sign. Fools have a way of discovering," Kit added with a disgusted glance toward the drunken Joey Tyrolin, who now dripped water all over the Frontier Town floor and any tourist within reach, "that the laws of time travel, like the laws of physics, have no pity and no remorse."

Skeeter said nothing at all. He merely glared at the drunken tourist and clamped his lips, eyes ravaged by a pain Margo could literally feel, it was so strong. Margo reached out hesitantly, touched his shoulder. "I'm sorry, Skeeter. I hope you find them. Tell them . . . tell them we helped look, okay?"

Skeeter had stiffened under her hand. But he nodded. "Thanks, Margo. I'll see you later."

He strode away through the crowd, disappearing past Joey Tyrolin, who teetered and abruptly found himself seated in the horse trough he'd just fished his pistol out of. Laughter floated in Skeeter's wake. Margo didn't join in. Skeeter was hurting, worse than she'd ever believed it possible for him to hurt. When she looked up, she found Kit's gaze on her. Her grandfather nodded, having read what was in her eyes and correctly interpreted it, all without a word spoken. It was one of the reasons she was still a little in awe of him—and why, at this moment, she loved him more fiercely than ever.

"I'll keep looking, too, Imp," he promised. "You'd better scoot if you want to get into costume and get your luggage to the gate on time."

Margo sighed. "Thanks. You'll come see us off?"

He ruffled her hair affectionately. "Just try and keep me away."

She gave him a swift, rib-cracking hug, having to blink salty water out of her eyes. "Love you, Kit," she whispered.

Then she fled, hoping he hadn't noticed the tears.

Time scouting was a tough business.

Just now, Margo didn't feel quite tough enough.

The night dripped.

Not honest rain, no; but a poisonous mist of coal smoke and river fog and steam that carried nameless scents in the coalescing yellow droplets. Above a gleam of damp roofing slates, long curls of black, acrid smoke belched from squat chimney pots that huddled down like misshapen gargoyles against an airborne, sulphurous tide. Far above, an almost forgotten moon hung poised above the city, a sickle-shaped crescent, the tautly drawn bow of the Divine Huntress of the Night, pure as unsullied silver above the foul murk, taking silent aim into the heart of a city long accustomed to asphyxiating beneath its own lethal mantle.

Gas jets from scattered street lamps stung the darkness like impotent bees. The fog dispersed their glow into forlorn, hopeless little pustules of light along wet cobblestones and soot-blackened walls of wood and stone and ancient, crumbling brick. Diffuse smells lurked in eddies like old, fading bruises. The scent of harbor water thick with weeds and dead things afloat in the night drifted in from the river. Wet and half-rotted timbers lent a whiff of salt and moldering fungus. Putrefied refuse from the chamber pots and privies of five million people stung the throat and eyes, fighting for ascendency over the sickly stench of dead fish and drowned dogs.

The distant, sweet freshness of wet hay and muddied straw eddying down from the enormous hay markets of Whitechapel and Haymarket itself lent a stark note of contrast, reminding the night that somewhere beyond these dismal brick walls, fresh air and clean winds swept across the land. Closer at hand came the stink of marsh and tidal mud littered with the myriad flotsam cast up by the River Thames to lap against the docks of Wapping and Stepney and the Isle of Dogs, a miasma that permeated the chilly night with a cloying stink like corpses too long immersed in a watery grave.

In the houses of respectable folk, rambling in orderly fashion to the west along the river banks and far inland to the north, candleshades and gas lamps had long since been extinguished. But here in the raucous streets of Wapping, of Whitechapel and of Stepney, drunken voices bellowed out the words of favorite drinking tunes. In rented rooms the size of storage bins, huddled in ramshackle brick tenements which littered these darkened streets like cancerous growths, enterprising pimps played the blackmail-profitable game of "arse and twang" with hired whores, unsuspecting sailors, and switchblade knives. Working men and women stood or sat in doorways and windows, listening to the music drifting along the streets from public houses and poor-men's clubs like the Jewish Working Men's Association of Whitechapel, until the weariness of hard work for long, squalid hours dragged them indoors to beds and cots and stairwells for the night. In the darkened, shrouded streets, business of another kind rose sharply with the approach of the wee hours. Men moved in gangs or pairs or slipped singly from shadow to shadow, and plied the cudgels and prybars of their trade against the skulls and window casements of their favorite victims.

Along one particular fog-cloaked street, where music and light spilled heedlessly from a popular gathering place for local denizens, bootheels clicked faintly on the wet cobbles as a lone young man, more a fair-haired boy than a man fully grown, staggered out into the wet night. A working lad, but not in the usual sense of the word, he had spent the better part of his night getting himself pissed as a newt on what had begun as "a quick one down to boozer" and had steadily progressed—through a series of pints of whatever the next-closest local had been selling cheapest—into a rat-arsed drunken binge.

A kerb crawler of indeterminate years appeared from out of the yellow murk and flashed a saucy smile. "You look to be a bloke what likes jolly comp'ny, mate." She took his arm solicitously when he reeled against a sooty brick wall, leaving a dark streak of damp down his once-fine shirt, which had seen far better days in the fashionable West End. She smiled into his eyes. "What about a four-penny knee trembler t' share wiv a comfy lady?" A practiced hand stole along the front of his shapeless trousers.

He grabbed a handful of the wares for sale, since it was expected and he had at least the shreds of a reputation to maintain, then he sighed dolefully, as though a sluggish, drunken thought had come to him. He carefully slurred his voice into the slang he'd heard on these streets for weeks, now. "Ain't got a fourpence, luv. No ackers a'tall. Totally coals an' coke, 'at's what I am, I've spent the last of what I brung 'ome t'night on thirty-eleven pints."

The woman eyed him more closely in the dim light. "I know 'at voice . . ."

When she got a better look, she let out a disgusted screech and knocked his hand away. " 'Oo are you tryin' t'fool, Morgan? Grabbin' like it's me thripenny bits you'd want, when it's cobbler's awl's you'd rather be gropin' after? Word's out, 'bout you, Morgan. 'At Polly Nichols shot 'er mouth good, when she were drunk, 'at she did." The woman shoved him away with a harsh, "Get 'ome t' yer lovin' Mr. Eddy—if th' toff'll 'ave you back, whoever he might be, unnatural sod!" She gave a short, ugly bark of laughter and stalked away into the night, muttering about wasting her time on beardless irons and finding a bloke with some honest sausage and mash to pay her doss money for the night.

The cash-poor—and recently infamous—young drunk reeled at her sharp shove and plowed straight into the damp wall, landing with a low grunt of dismayed surprise. He caught himself ineffectually there and crumpled gradually to the wet pavement. Morgan sat there for a moment, blinking back tears of misery and absently rubbing his upper arm and shoulder. For several moments, he considered seriously what he ought to do next. Sitting in muck on a wet pavement for the remainder of the night didn't seem a particularly attractive notion. He hadn't any place to go and no doss money of his own and he was very far, indeed, from Cleveland Street and the fancy West Side house where he'd once been popular with a certain class of rich toffs— and until tomorrow night, at least, when Eddy would finally bring him the promised money, he would have nothing to buy food, either.

His eyes stung. Damn that bitch, Polly Nichols! She was no better than he was, for all the righteous airs she put on. Just a common slattern, who'd lift her skirts for a stinking fourpence—or a well-filled glass of gin, for that matter. Word on the streets hereabout was, she'd been a common trollop for so many years her own husband had tossed her out as an unfit mother and convinced the courts to rescind the order for paying her maintenance money. Morgan, at least, had plied his trade with respectably wealthy clients; but thinking about that only made the hurt run deeper. The fine West End house had tossed him out, when he'd lost their richest client. *Wasn't my fault Eddy threw me over for that bloody mystic of his, with his fancy ways and fine house and his bloody deformed . . .*

And Polly Nichols, curse the drunken bitch, had found out about that particular house on Cleveland Street and Morgan's place in it, had shoved him against a wall and hissed out, "I know all about it, Morgan. All about what you let a bloke do t'you for money. I've 'eard you got a little rainy day fund put aside, savin's, like, from that 'ouse what tossed you onto the street. You 'and it over, Morgan, maybe I won't grass on you, eh? Those constables in H Division, now, they might just want to know about an 'andsome lad like you, bendin' over for it."

Morgan had caught his breath in horror. The very last thing Morgan needed was entanglements with the police. Prostitution was bad enough for a woman. A lad caught prostituting himself with another *man* . . . Well, the death penalty was off the books, but it'd be prison for sure, a nice long stretch at hard labor, and the thought of what would happen to a lad like himself in prison . . . But Morgan had come away from the house on Cleveland Street with nothing save his clothes, a half-crown his last client had given him as a bonus, which he'd managed to hide from the house's proprietor, and a black eye.

And Eddy's letters.

"Here . . ." He produced the half-crown, handed it over. "It's everything I've got in the world. Please, Polly, I'm starving as it is, don't tell the constables."

"An *'alf a crown?*" she screeched. "A mis'rable *'alf-crown?* Bleedin' little sod! You come from a fine 'ouse, you did, wiv rich men givin' it to you, what do you mean by givin' me nuffink but a miserly 'alf-crown!"

"It's all I've got!" he cried, desperate. "They took everything else away! Even most of my clothes!" A harsh, half-strangled laugh broke loose. "Look at my face, Polly! That's what they gave me as a going away present!"

"Copper's'll give you worse'n bruises an' a blacked eye, luv!" She jerked around and started to stalk away. "Constable!"

Morgan clutched at her arm. "Wait!"

She paused. "Well?"

He licked his lips. They were all he had . . . but if this drunken whore sent him to prison, what good would Eddy's letters do him? And he didn't have to give them all to her. "I've got one thing. One valuable thing."

"What's 'at?" She narrowed her eyes.

"Letters . . ."

"Letters? What sort of fool d'you tyke me for?"

"They're valuable letters! Worth a lot of money!"

The narrow-eyed stare sharpened. "What sort o' letters 'ave you got, Morgan, that'd be worth any money?"

He licked his lips once more. "Love letters," he whispered. "From someone important. They're in his handwriting, on his personal stationery, and he's signed them with his own name. Talks about everything he did to me when he visited me in that house, everything he planned to do on his next visit. They're worth a fortune, Polly. I'll share them with you. He's going to give me a lot of money to get them back, a *lot* of money, Polly. Tomorrow night, he's going to buy back the first one, I'll give you some of the money—"

"You'll give me the letters!" she snapped. "Hah! Share wiv *you?* I'll 'ave them letters, if you please, y'little sod, you just 'and 'em over." She held out one grasping hand, eyes narrowed and dangerous.

Morgan clenched his fists, hating her. At least he hadn't told the bitch how many letters there were. He'd divided them into two packets, one in his trouser pocket, the other beneath his shirt. The ones in his shirt were the letters Eddy had penned to him in English. The ones in his trouser pocket were the *other* letters, the "special surprise" Eddy had sent to him during that last month of visits. The filthy tart wouldn't be able to read a word of them. He pulled the packet from his trouser pocket and handed them over. "Here, curse you! And may you have joy reading them!" he added with a spiteful laugh, striding away before she could realize that Prince Albert Victor had penned those particular letters in *Welsh*.

Now, hours later, having managed to find himself a sailor on the docks who wanted a more masculine sort of sport, Morgan was drunk and bitter, a mightily scared and very lonely lad far away from his native Cardiff. He rubbed his wet cheek with the back of his hand. Morgan had been a fool, a jolly, bloody fool, ever to leave Cardiff, but it was too late, now, to cry about it. And he couldn't sit here on his bum all night, some constable would pass and then he *would* be spending the night courtesy of the Metropolitan Police Department's H Division.

Morgan peered about, trying to discern shapes through the fog, and thought he saw the dark form of a man nearby, but the fog closed round the shadow again and no one approached nearer, so he decided there was no one about to help him regain his feet, after all. Scraping himself slowly together, he elbowed his way back up the wall until he was more or less upright again, then coughed and shivered and wandered several yards further along the fog-shrouded street. At times, his ears played tricks with the echoing sounds that spilled out onto the dark streets from distant public houses. Snatches of laughter and song came interspersed faintly with the nearer click of footfalls on pavement, but each time he peered round, he found nothing but swirling, malevolent yellow drifts. So he continued his meandering way down the wet street, allowing his shoulder to bump against the sooty bricks to guide and steady him on his way, making for the hidey hole he used when there was no money for a doss-house bed.

The entrance to a narrow alley robbed him of his sustaining wall. He scudded sideways, a half-swamped sailboat lashed by a sudden and brutal cross-wise gale, and stumbled into the dark alley. He tangled his wobbling feet, met another wet brick wall face on, and barely caught himself from a second ignominious slide into the muck. He was cursing softly under his breath when he heard that same, tantalizing whisper of faint footfalls from behind. Only this time, they were no trick of his hearing. Someone was coming toward him through the fog, hurrying now as he clung to the dirty brick wall in the darkness of the alley.

Another tart, perhaps, or a footpad out to pinch what he didn't any longer possess. Alarm flared slowly through his drunken haze. He started to turn—but it was far too late. A blow from something heavy smashed across his skull from behind. Light exploded behind his eyes in a detonation of pain and terror. Unable even to cry out, he crumpled straight down into darkness.

As Morgan toppled toward the filthy alley, a wiry man in his early thirties, dark-skinned with the look of Eastern Europe in his narrow face and eyes and dark moustache, caught him under the arms. This second man grunted softly, curling his lip at the reek of alcohol and sweat which rose from the boy's grimy, once fancy clothes. This was no time, however, for fastidiousness. He twisted the boy around with a practiced jerk and heaved the dead weight over one shoulder. A swift glance told him the thick fog and darkness of the narrow alleyway had concealed the attack from any chance observation.

Well, Johnny my boy, he smiled to himself, *you've made a good start. Now to finish this pathetic little cockerel.* Dr. John Lachley was as pleased with the enshrouding yellow murk as he was with his swift handiwork and the drunken little fool he'd trailed all evening, who'd finally wandered so conveniently close to a place he could strike. He'd feared he might have to trail the boy all the way back to the filthy hole he'd been living in, on the first floor of a ramshackle, abandoned warehouse along the docks, so dilapidated and dangerous it was in the process of being torn down.

Quite a come-down, eh, pretty Morgan?

Dark-haired, dark-eyed, darker-souled, John Lachley moved deeper into the darkness of the alleyway, staggering slightly under his burden until he found his new center of balance. The alley was narrow, clotted with rubbish and stench. A rat's eyes gleamed briefly in the foggy gloom. A street—little wider than the alley he followed—appeared through the murk. He turned to his right, moving toward the invisible docks a mere three blocks away, which were concealed from sight by grim warehouses and tumble-down shacks. Their bricks leaned drunkenly in the night, whole chunks of their walls missing in random patterns of darkness and swirling, jaundiced eddies.

John Lachley's clothes, little cleaner than those of his victim, revealed very little about their current owner; neither did the dark cloth cap he wore pulled low over his eyes. During daylight, his was a face that might well be recognized, even here, where many years ago Johnny Anubis had once been a household name, sought out by the poorest fishwives in search of hope; but in the darkness, in such rough clothing, even a man of his . . . notoriety . . . might go unremarked.

He smiled and paused at the entrance to one of the soot-streaked blocks of ramshackle flats. An iron key from his pocket unlocked a shabby wooden door. He cast a glance overhead and spotted the waning horns of the sickle-shaped moon. He smiled again. "Lovely night for scything, Lady," he said softly to the sharp-edged crescent. "Grant me success in mine, eh?"

Sulphurous fog drifted across the faintly glowing horns of that wicked sickle, seeming almost to catch and tear on the sharp points. He smiled again; then ducked inside, swung his victim's legs and head clear, and locked the door behind him. He needed no light to navigate the room, for it contained nothing but coal dust and scattered bits of refuse. A savage barking erupted from the darkness of the next room, sounding like every hound in hell had been loosed. Lachley spoke sharply. "Garm!"

The barking subsided into low growls. Heaving his burden into a slightly more comfortable position on his shoulder, John Lachley entered the next room and swung shut another heavy door which he located by feel alone. Here he paused to grope along the wall for the gas light. The gas lit with a faint hiss and pop; dim light sprang up. The windowless brick walls were barren, the floor covered with a cheap rug. A wooden bed frame with a thin cotton tick stood along one wall. A battered dry sink held a jug and basin, a lantern, and a grimy towel. An equally battered clothes press leaned drunkenly in one corner. The chained dog crouched at the center of the room stopped growling and thumped its tail in greeting.

"Have a pleasant evening, Garm?" he addressed the dog, retrieving a meat pie from one pocket, which he unwrapped from its greasy newspaper wrapping. He tossed it carelessly to the huge black hound. The dog bounded to its feet and snatched the food mid-air, wolfing it down in one bite. Had anyone besides himself entered this room, the dog would have shredded them to gobbets. Garm had earned his meat pies on more than one occasion.

Lachley dumped his victim onto the bed, then pulled back the rug and prised up a wooden trap door cut into the floorboards. He heaved this to one side, lit the lantern and set it beside the gaping hole in the floor, then retrieved the unconscious boy from the bed and shouldered his inert burden once again. He paused when he approached the edge and felt downward with one foot, finding the top step of a steep, narrow staircase. Lachley descended cautiously into darkness, retrieving his lantern as he moved downward. A wet, fetid smell of mold and damp brick rose to meet him.

Light splashed across a clammy wall where a rusty iron hook protruded from the discolored bricks. He hung the lantern on this, then reached up and dragged the trapdoor back into place. It settled with a scrape and hollow bang. Dust sifted down into his hair and collar, peppering his clothes as well as his victim's. He dusted off his palms, brushed splinters from a sleeve, then rescued his lantern from its hook and continued the descent. His feet splashed at the bottom. Wavering yellow light revealed an arched, circular brick tunnel through the bowels of Wapping, stretching away into blackness in either direction. The filthy brick was chipped and mottled with algae and nameless fungi. He whistled softly as he walked, listening to the echoes spill away like foam from a mug of dark ale.

As Lachley paralleled the invisible Thames, other tunnels intersected the one he'd entered. The sound of rushing water carried through the sepulchral darkness from underground streams and buried rivers—the Fleet River, which had blown up in 1846 from the trapped rancid and fetid gasses beneath the pavements, so toxic was the red muck leaking from the tanneries above; the once-noble Walbrook, which ran through the heart of the City of London; and River Tyburn, which had lent its name to the triple-tree where convicts were hanged at the crossroads—each of them was now confined beneath London's crowded, filthy streets, churning and spilling along their former courses as major sewers dumping into the mighty Thames.

John Lachley ignored the distant roar of water as he ignored the sewer stench permeating the tunnels. He listened briefly to the echoes of his footfalls mingle with the squeals of rats fighting over a dead dog's corpse and the distant sound of mating cats. At length, he lifted his lantern to mark the exact spot where the low entrance loomed. He ducked beneath a dripping brick arch, turned sharp left, and emerged in a narrow, coffin-sized space set with a thick iron door. An brass plaque set into it bore the legend *"Tibor."*

Since the word was not English, the owner of this door had little fear of its meaning being deciphered should anyone chance to stumble across the hidden chamber. Lachley was not Hungarian by birth, but he knew the Slavic tongues and more importantly, their legends and myths, had studied them almost since boyhood. It amused him to put a name that meant "holy place" on the door of his private retreat from workaday London and its prosaic, steam-engine mentality.

Another key retrieved from a coat pocket grated in the lock; then the stout door swung noiselessly open, its hinges well oiled against the damp. His underground Tibor welcomed him home with a rush of dark, wet air and the baleful glow of perpetual fire from the gas jet he, himself, had installed, siphoning off the requisite fuel from an unsuspecting fuel company's gas mains. Familiar sights loomed in the dim chamber: vaulted ceiling bricks stained with moss and patchy brown mold; the misshapen form of gnarled oak limbs from the great, dead trunk he'd sawn into sections, hauled down in pieces, and laboriously fitted back together with steel and iron; the eternal gas fire blazing at its feet from an altar-mounted nozzle; huddled cloaks and robes and painted symbols which crawled across the walls, speaking answers to riddles few in this city would have thought even to ask; a sturdy work table along one wall, and wooden cabinets filled with drawers and shelves which held the paraphernalia of his self-anointed mission.

The reek of harsh chemicals and the reverberations of long-faded incantations, words of power and dominion over the creatures he sought to control, spoken in all-but-forgotten ancient tongues, bade him welcome as he stepped once more across the threshold and re-entered his own very private Tibor. He dumped his burden carelessly onto the work table, heedless of the crack of his victim's head against the wooden surface, and busied himself. There was much to do. He lit candles, placed them strategically about the room, stripped off his rough working clothes and donned the ceremonial robes he was always careful to leave behind in this sanctuary.

White and voluminous, a mockery of priestly vestments, and hooded with a deep and death-pale hood which covered half his face when he lowered it down, the semi-Druidic robes had been sewn to his specifications years previously by a sweatshop seamstress who had possessed no other way to pay for the divinations she'd come to him to cast for her. He slipped into the robes, shook back the deep hood for now, and busied himself with the same efficient industry which had brought him out of the misery of the streets overhead and into the life he now sought to protect at all cost.

John Lachley searched the boy's appallingly filthy, empty pockets, then felt the crackle of paper beneath Morgan's shirt. When he stripped off his victim, a sense of triumph and giddy relief swept through him: Morgan's letters were tucked into the waistband of his trousers, the foolscap sheets slightly grimy and rumpled. Each had been folded into a neat packet. He read them, curious as to their contents, and damned Albert Victor for a complete and bumbling fool. Had these letters come into the hands of the proper authorities . . .

Then he reached the end and stared at the neatly penned sheets of foolscap.

There were only four letters.

John Lachley tightened his fist down, crushing the letters in his hand, and blistered the air. *Four!* And Eddy had said there were *eight!* Where had the little bastard put the other half of the set? All but shaking with rage, he forced himself to close his fists around empty air, rather than the unconscious boy's throat. He needed to throttle the life out of this little bastard, needed to inflict terror and ripping, agonizing hurt for daring to threaten *him,* Dr. John Lachley, advisor to the Queen's own grandson, who should one day sit the throne in Victoria's stead . . .

With a snarl of rage, he tossed Morgan's clothing into a rubbish bin beneath the work table for later burning, then considered how best to obtain the information he required. A slight smile came to his lips. He bound the lad's hands and feet, then heaved him up and hauled him across the chamber to the massive oak tree which dominated the room, its gnarled branches supported now by brackets in ceiling and walls.

He looped Morgan's wrist ropes over a heavy iron hook embedded in the wood and left him dangling with his toes several inches clear of the floor. This done, he opened cabinet doors and rattled drawers out along their slides, laying out the ritual instruments. Wand and cauldron, dagger, pentacle, and sword . . . each with meanings and ritual uses not even those semi-serious fools Waite and Mathers could imagine in their fumbling, so-called studies. Their "Order of the Golden Dawn" had invited him to join, shortly after its establishment last year. He had accepted, naturally, simply to further his contacts in the fairly substantial social circles through which the order's various members moved; but thought of their so-called researches left him smiling. Such simplicity of belief was laughable.

Next he retrieved the ancient Hermetic deck with its arcane trumps, a symbolic alphabetical key to the terrible power of creation and transformation locked away aeons previously in the pharoahonic *Book of Thoth*. After that came the mistletoe to smear the blade, whose sticky sap would ensure free, unstaunchable bleeding . . . and the great, thick-bladed steel knife with which to take the trophy skull . . . He had never actually performed such a ritual, despite a wealth of knowledge. His hands trembled from sheer excitement as he laid out the cards, mumbling incantations over them, and studied the pattern unfolding. Behind him, his victim woke with a slow, wretched groan.

It was time.

He purified the blade with fire, painted mistletoe sap across its flat sides and sharp edge, then lifted his sacred, deep white hood over his hair and turned to face his waiting victim. Morgan peered at him through bloodshot, terrified eyes. Morgan's throat worked, but no sound issued from the boy's bloodless lips. He stepped closer to the sweating, naked lad who hung from Odin's sacred oak, its gnarled branches twisting overhead to touch the vaulted brick ceiling. A ghastly sound broke from his prisoner's throat. Morgan twisted against the ropes on his wrists, to no avail.

Then Lachley shook back his hood and smiled into the lad's eyes. Blue eyes widened in shock. *"You!"* Then, terror visibly lashing him, Morgan choked out, "What—what'd I ever do to you, Johnny? Please . . . you got Eddy for yourself, why d'you want to hurt me now? I already lost my place in the house—"

He backhanded the little fool. Tears and blood streamed. *"Sodding little ponce! Blackmail him, will you?"*

Morgan whimpered, the terror in his eyes so deep they glazed over, a stunned rabbit's eyes. John Lachley let out a short, hard laugh. "What a jolly little fool you are, Morgan. And look at you now, done up like a kipper!" He caressed Morgan's bruised, wet face. "Did you think Eddy wouldn't tell me? Poor Eddy . . . Hasn't the brains God gave a common mollusk, but Eddy trusts me, bless him, does whatever I tell him to." He chuckled. "Spiritualist advisor to the future King of England. I'm at the front of a very long line of men, little Morgan, standing behind the rich and powerful, whispering into their ears what the stars and the gods and the spirits from beyond the grave want them to say and do and believe. So naturally, when our distraught Eddy received your message, he came straight to my doorstep, begging me to help him hush it all up."

The lad trembled violently where he dangled from the ropes, not even bothering to deny it. Not that denial would have saved him. Or even spared him the pain he would suffer before he paid the price for his schemes. Terror gleamed in Morgan's eyes, dripped down his face with the sweat pouring from his brow. Dry lips worked. His voice came as a cracked whisper. "W-what do you want? I swear, I'll leave England, go back to Cardiff, never whisper a word . . . I'll even sign on as deck hand for a ship out to Hong Kong . . ."

"Oh, no, my sweet little Morgan," Lachley smiled, bending closer. "Hardly that. Do you honestly think the man who controls the future King of England is so great a fool as that?" He patted Morgan's cheek. "The first thing I want, Morgan, is the other four letters."

He swallowed sharply. "H-haven't got them—"

"Yes, I know you haven't got them." He brushed a fingertip down Morgan's naked breastbone. "Who *has* got them, Morgan? Tell me and I may yet make it easier for you."

When Morgan hesitated, Lachley slapped him, gently.

The boy began shaking, crying. "She—she was going to tell the constables—I hadn't any money left, all I had was the letters—gave her half of them to keep her quiet—"

"*Who?*" The second blow was harder, bruising his fair skin.

"Polly!" The name was wrenched from him. He sobbed it out again, "Polly Nichols . . . filthy, drunken tart . . ."

"And what will Polly Nichols do with them, eh?" he asked, twisting cruelly a sensitive bit of Morgan's anatomy until the boy cried out in sharp protest. "Show them to all her friends? How much will *they* want, eh?"

"Wouldn't—wouldn't do any good, all she has is my word they're worth anything—"

He slapped Morgan again, hard enough to split his lips. "Stupid sod! Do you honestly think she won't read your pitiful letters? You *are* a fool, little boy. But don't ever make the mistake of thinking I am!"

Morgan was shaking his head frantically. "No, Johnny, no, you don't understand, she *can't* read them! They're not in English!"

Surprise left John Lachley momentarily speechless. "Not in English?" It came out flat as a squashed tomato. "What do you mean, not in English? Eddy doesn't have the intelligence to learn another language. I'm surprised the dear boy can speak his *own*, let alone a foreign one. Come, now, Morgan, you'll have to do better than that."

Morgan was crying again. "You'll see, I'll get them for you, Johnny, I'll show you, they're not in English, they're in Welsh, his tutor helped him—"

He backhanded the sniveling liar. Morgan's head snapped violently sideways.

"*Don't play me for a fool!*"

"Please," Morgan whimpered, bleeding from cut lips and a streaming nose, "it's true, why would I lie to you *now,* Johnny, when you promised you wouldn't hurt me again if I told you the truth? You have to believe me, *please . . .*"

John Lachley was going to enjoy coercing the truth from this pathetic little liar.

But Morgan wasn't done blubbering yet. His eyes, a watery blue from the tears streaming down his face, were huge and desperate as he babbled out, "Eddy *told* me about it, right after he sent the first one in Welsh, asked me if I liked his surprise. He thought it was a grand joke, because the ever-brilliant Mr. James K. Stephen—" it came out bitter, jealous, sounding very much, in fact, like Eddy "—was always so smart and learned things so easily and made sure Eddy was laughed at all through Cambridge, because everybody but a few of the dons knew it was *Mr. James K. Stephen* writing Eddy's translations in Latin and Greek for him, so Eddy could copy them out correctly in his own hand! He *told* me about it, how much he paid dear Jamesy for each translation his tutor did for him while they were still at Cambridge! So when Eddy wanted to write letters nobody else could read, he got the doting Mr. James K. Stephen to help him translate *those* for him, too, paid him ten sovereigns for each letter, so he wouldn't whisper about them afterwards . . ."

It was, Lachley decided, just possible that Morgan was telling him the truth. Paying his tutor to translate his Latin and Greek at University was very Eddy-like. So was paying the man to translate his love letters, God help them all. He caught Morgan's chin in one hand, tightened down enough to bruise his delicate skin. "And how much did Eddy pay his tutor to keep the secret that he was writing love letters in Welsh to a male whore?"

"He didn't! Tell him, I mean. That I'm a boy. He told Mr. Stephen that 'Morgan' was a pretty *girl* he'd met, from Cardiff, said he wanted to impress her with letters in her own native Welsh, so Mr. Stephen wouldn't guess Eddy was writing to *me.* He's not so very bright, Eddy, but he doesn't want to go to prison! So he convinced Mr. Stephen I was a girl and the gullible idiot helped Eddy write them, I swear it, Eddy said he stood over his shoulder and told him all the right Welsh words to use, even for the dirty parts, only when Eddy wrote out the second copies to me in private, he changed all the words you'd use for a girl's body to the right ones for a boy, because he looked that up, himself, so he'd know—"

"*Second copies?*"

Morgan flinched violently. "*Please, Johnny, please don't hit me again!* Eddy thought it would be funny, so he sent me the first copies attached to the ones he wrote out especially for me . . ."

His voice faded away as Lachley's white-faced fury sank in, mistaking Lachley's rage honestly enough. *My God, the royal bastard is stupider than I thought! If it would do any good, I'd cut off Eddy's bollocks and feed them to him! Any magistrate in England would take one look at a set of letters like that and throw away the bloody key!*

He no longer doubted Morgan's sordid little tale about Welsh translations. Eddy was just that much of a fool, thinking himself clever with such a trick, just to impress a money grubbing, blackmailing little *whore* not fit to sell his wares for a crust of bread, much less royal largesse.

Morgan was gasping out, "It's true, Johnny, I'll prove it, I'll get the letters back and *show* you . . ."

"Oh, yes, Morgan. We will, indeed get those letters back. Tell me, just where might I find this Polly Nichols?"

"She's been staying at that lodging house at 56 Flower and Dean Street, the White House they call it, rooming with a man, some nights, other nights sharing with Long Liz Stride or Catharine Eddowes, whoever's got the doss money for the night and needs a roommate to share the cost . . ."

"What did you tell Polly Nichols when you gave her the letters?"

"That they were love letters," he whispered. "I didn't tell her who they were from and I lied, said they were on his personal stationery, when they're on ordinary foolscap, so all she'll know is they've been signed by someone named Eddy. Someone rich, but just Eddy, no last name, even."

"Very good, Morgan. Very, very good."

Hope flared in the little fool's wet eyes.

He patted Morgan's cheek almost gently.

Then Lachley brought out the knife.

(((Chapter 5)))

The reporters were waiting outside his office building, of course.

Senator Caddrick stepped out of his chauffeured limo and faced the explosion of camera flashes and television lights with an expression of grief and shock and carefully reddened eyes.

"Senator! Would you comment on this terrorist attack—"

"—tell us how it feels to lose your sister-in-law to terrorists—"

"—any word on your daughter—"

Caddrick held up his hands, pled with the reporters. "Please, I don't know anything more than you do. Cassie's dead . . ." He paused, allowing the catch in his voice to circle the globe live via satellite. "My little girl is still missing, her college roommate has been brutally murdered, that's all I know, really . . ." He was pushing his way through the mob, his aide at his side.

"Is it true the terrorists were members of the *Ansar Majlis*, the down-time organization that's declared *jihad* against the Lady of Heaven Temples?"

"Will this attack cause you to re-open your campaign to shut down the time terminals?"

"Senator, are you aware that Senator Simon Mukhtar al Harb, a known *Ansar Majlis* sympathizer, is spearheading an investigation into the Temples—"

"Senator, what do you plan to do about this attack—"

He turned halfway up the steps leading to his office and faced the cameras, allowing his reddened eyes to water. "I intend to find my daughter," he said raggedly. "And I intend to find the bastards responsible for her disappearance, and for murdering poor Cassie . . . If it turns out these down-timer terrorists *were* responsible for Cassie's murder, if they've kidnapped my only child, then I will do whatever it takes to get every time terminal on this planet shut down! I've warned Congress for years, the down-timers flooding into the stations are a grave threat to the stability of our up-time world. And now this . . . I'm sorry, that's all I can say, I'm too upset to say anything else."

He fled up the steps and into his office.

And deep in his heart, smiled.

Phase Two, successfully launched . . .

Ianira Cassondra regained consciousness while Jenna and Noah were still packing. The faint sound from the hotel bed where she rested brought Jenna around, hands filled with the Victorian notion of ladies' underwear, which she'd purchased specifically for Ianira with Aunt Cassie's money. Jenna would be going through to London in disguise as a young man, something that left her shaking with stage fright worse than any she'd ever experienced. Seeing Ianira stir, Jenna dumped corsets and woolen drawers into an open steamer trunk and hurried over to join Marcus. Noah glanced up from the telephone, where the detective was busy scheduling an appointment with the station's cosmetologist. Armstrong wanted Jenna to go in for some quick facial alterations before the gate opened, to add Victorian-style whiskers to Jenna's too-famous, feminine face. Noah frowned, more reflectively than in irritation, then finished making the appointment and joined them.

Ianira stirred against the pillow. Dark lashes fluttered. Jenna discovered she was clenching her hands around her new costume's trousers belt. The leather felt slippery under the sweat. She realized with a sinking sensation in her gut that it was one thing to carry the prophetess on earth unconscious through the station's basement. It was quite another to gaze eye-to-eye with the embodiment of all that Jenna had come to believe about life and how it ought to be lived.

bones. She got the rest out in a rush, trying to hold onto her nerve. "As long as the *Ansar Majlis* were kept bottled up in the Middle East, where they started coming through the down-time gates, they were pretty much harmless. But a lot of people would like to see the Temples destroyed, or at least hurt badly enough they're not a political threat, anymore. Some of the lunatics who live up time have been helping that murdering pack of terrorists . . ."

"Your father," she said quietly. "He is among them."

Jenna didn't have to answer; Ianira *knew*. Jenna bit one lip, ashamed of the blood in her own veins and furious that she couldn't do anything besides smash Ianira's world to pieces. "He gave the orders, yes. To a death squad. They murdered my mother's sister. And my . . . my best friend from college . . ." Jenna's voice went ragged.

Ianira reached across, touched Jenna's hand. "They have taken him from you," she whispered, the sympathy in her voice almost too much to bear, "but you have his final gift to you. Surely this must bring some consolation, some hope for the future?"

Jenna blinked, almost too afraid of this woman to meet those dark, too-wise eyes. "What . . . what do you mean?"

Ianira brushed fingergips across Jenna's abdomen, across the queasiness which had plagued her for nearly a full week, now. "You carry his child," Ianira said softly.

When the room greyed out and Jenna clutched at the edge of the bed in stupid shock, the prophetess spoke again, very gently. "Didn't you know?"

Someone had Jenna by the shoulders, kept her her from falling straight to the floor. *Dear God . . . it's not fear sickness, it's morning sickness . . . and I am late, oh, God, I'm going to Victorian London with Daddy's killers trying to find me and I'm carrying Carl's baby. . . .* How long would they have to hide in London? Weeks? Months? Years? *I can't go disguised as a man, if I'm pregnant!* But she had no real choice and she knew it. Her father's hired killers would be searching for a frightened girl in the company of a detective, not a lone young man travelling with several large steamer trunks. When she looked up, she found Ianira's dark gaze fastened on her and, more surprisingly, Noah Armstrong's grey-eyed gaze, filled with worry and compassion.

"You're . . . sure . . . ?" Jenna choked out.

Ianira brushed hair back from Jenna's brow. "I am not infallible, child. But about this, yes, I am certain."

Jenna wanted to break down and cry, wanted to curl up someplace and hide for the next several decades, wanted to be held and rocked and reassured that everything would be all right. But she couldn't. She met Ianira's gaze again. "They'll kill us all, if they can." She wrapped protective arms around her middle, around the miracle of Carl's baby, growing somewhere inside her. A fierce determination to protect that tiny life kindled deep within. "I'd be in a morgue someplace, already, undergoing an autopsy, if Noah hadn't dragged me out of that trap where Aunt Cassie died. I'm not going to let them win. Not if I have to spend the next forty years on the run, until we can find a way to stop them."

"And they have come here," Ianira whispered, fingers tightening around Jenna's arm, "to destroy the world we have built for ourselves."

Jenna wanted to look away from those too-knowing eyes, wanted to crawl away and hide, rather than confirm it. But she couldn't lie to the prophetess, even to spare her pain. "Yes. I'm sorry . . ." She had to stop for a moment, regain her composure. "We can get you off station, make a run for it down time. I don't give a damn about the laws forbidding down-timers to emigrate through a gate."

Ianira's gaze went to her children. Mute grief touched those dark eyes. "They cannot come with me?"

Noah answered, voice firm. "No. We don't dare risk it. They'll find a way to follow us through every gate that opens this week. If we put your children in the same trunk we smuggle you out of the station in, and their assassins get to Jenna . . ."

Ianira Cassondra shuddered. "Yes. It is too dangerous. Marcus . . ."

He gripped her hands hard. "I will guard them. With my life, Ianira. And Julius has pledged to help us escape. No one else must know. Not even our friends, not even the Council of Seven. Julius only knows because he was using the tunnels to run a message from one end of Commons to the other. He found us."

At the look that came into her eyes, a shudder touched its cold finger to Jenna's spine. Ianira's eyelids came clenching down. "The death that stalks us is worse than we know . . . two faces . . . two faces beyond the gates . . . and bricks enclose the tree where the flame burns and blood runs black . . . be wary of the one with grey eyes, death lives behind the smile . . . the letters are the key, the letters bring terror and destruction . . . the one who lives behind the silent gun will strike in the night . . . seeks to destroy the soul unborn . . . will strike where the newborn bells burn bright with the sound of screams . . ." She sagged against her husband, limp and trembling.

Jenna, too, was trembling, so violently she could scarcely keep her feet where she crouched beside the bed.

Marcus glanced up, eyes dark and frightened. "I have never seen the visions come to her so powerfully. Please, I beg of you, be careful with her."

Jenna found herself lifting Ianira's cold hands to warm them. They shook in Jenna's grasp. "Lady," she whispered, "I'm not much good at killing. But they've already destroyed the two people I cared about more than anything in the world. I swear, I will kill anything or anyone who tries to hurt *you*."

Ianira's gaze lifted slowly. Tears had reddened her eyes. "I know," she choked out. "It is why I grieve."

To that, Jenna had no answer whatever.

Dr. John Lachley had a problem.

A very serious problem.

Polly Nichols possessed half of Eddy's eight letters, written to the now-deceased orphan from Cardiff. Unlike Morgan, however, whom nobody would miss, Polly Nichols had lived in the East End all her life. When she turned up rather seriously dead, those who knew her were going to talk. And what they knew, or recalled having seen, they would tell the constables of the Metropolitan Police Department's H Division. While the police were neither well liked nor respected in Whitechapel, Polly Nichols *was*, despite her infamous profession. Those who liked and respected her would help the police catch whoever did to her what John Lachley intended to do to *anyone* who came into possession of Eddy's miserable little letters.

God, but he had enjoyed carving up that little bastard, Morgan . . .

The very memory made his private and unique anatomy ache.

So . . . he must find Polly Nichols, obtain her letters, then cut her up the same delightful way he had cut Morgan, as a message to all blackmailing whores walking these filthy streets, and he must do it without being remarked upon or caught. He would disguise himself, of course, but John Lachley's was a difficult face to disguise. He looked too foreign, always had, from earliest childhood in these mean streets, a gift from his immigrant mother. Lachley knew enough theatrical people, through his illustrious clientele, to know which shops to visit to obtain false beards and so on, but even that was risky. Acquiring such things meant people would recall him as the foreigner who had bought an actor's bag of makeup and accouterments. That was nearly as bad as being recalled as the last man seen with a murdered woman. Might well prove worse, since being remembered for buying disguises indicated someone with a guilty secret to hide. How the devil did one approach the woman close enough to obtain the letters and murder her, afterwards, without being *seen?*

He might throw suspicion on other foreigners, perhaps, if he disguised himself as one of the East End's thousands of Jews. A long false beard, perhaps, or a prayer shawl knotted under his overcoat . . . Ever since that Jew, what was his name, Lipski, had murdered that little girl in the East End last year, angry Cockneys had been hurtling insults at foreigners in the eastern reaches of London. In the docklands, so many refugees were pouring in from the Jewish communities of Eastern Europe, the very word "foreigner" had come to mean "Jew." Lachley would have to give that serious consideration, throwing blame somehow onto the community of foreigners. If some foreign Jew hanged for Lachley's deeds, so much the better.

But his problem was more complicated than simply tracing Polly Nichols, recovering her letters, and silencing her. There was His Highness' tutor to consider, as well. The man knew too much, far too much for safety. Mr. James K. Stephen would have to die. Which was the reason John Lachley had left London for the nearby village of Greenwich, this morning: to murder Mr. James K. Stephen.

He had made a point of striking up an acquaintance with the man on the riding paths surrounding Greenwich just the morning previously. Lachley, studying the layout of the land Stephen preferred for his morning rides, had casually trailed Stephen while looking for a place to stage a fatal accident. The path Eddy's tutor habitually took carried the riders out into fields where farm workers labored to bring in the harvest despite the appalling rain squalls, then wandered within a few feet of a large windmill near the railway line. Lachley gazed at that windmill with a faint smile. If he could engineer it so that Stephen rode past the windmill at the same time as a passing train . . .

So he followed Stephen further along the trail and cantered his horse up alongside, smiling in greeting, and introduced himself. "Good morning, sir. John Lachley, physician."

"Good morning, Dr. Lachley," Eddy's unsuspecting tutor smiled in return. "James Stephen."

He feigned surprise. "Surely not James *K.* Stephen?"

The prince's former tutor stared in astonishment. "Yes, in fact, I am."

"Why, I am delighted, sir! Delighted! Eddy has spoken so fondly of you! Oh, I ought to explain," he added at the man's look of total astonishment. "His Highness Prince Albert Victor is one of my patients, nothing serious, of course, I assure you. We've become rather good friends over the last few months. He has spoken often of you, sir. Constantly assigns to you the lion's share of the credit for his success at Cambridge."

Stephen flushed with pleasure. "How kind of His Highness! It was my priviledge to have tutored him at university. You say Eddy is quite well, then?"

"Oh, yes. Quite so. I use certain mesmeric techniques in my practice, you see, and Eddy had heard that the use of mesmeric therapy can improve one's memory."

Stephen smiled in genuine delight. "So naturally Eddy was interested! Of course. I hope you have been able to assist him?"

"Indeed," John Lachley laughed easily. "His memory will never be the same."

Stephen shared his chuckle without understanding Lachley's private reasons for amusement. As they rode on in companionable conversation, Lachley let fall a seemingly casual remark. "You know,

I've enjoyed this ride more than any I can recall in an age. So much more refreshing than Hyde Park or Rotten Row, where one only appears to be in the countryside, whereas this is the genuine article. Do you ride this way often?"

"Indeed, sir, I do. Every morning."

"Oh, splendid! I say, do you suppose we might ride out together again tomorrow? I should enjoy the company and we might chat about Eddy, share a few amusing anecdotes, perhaps?"

"I should enjoy it tremendously. At eight o'clock, if that isn't too early?"

"Not at all." He made a mental note to check the train schedules to time their ride past that so-convenient windmill. "Eight o'clock it shall be." And so they rode on, chatting pleasantly while John Lachley laid his plans to murder the amiable young man who had helped Eddy with one too many translations.

Early morning light, watery and weak, tried vainly to break through rainclouds as Lachley stepped off Greenwich pier from the waterman's taxi he'd taken down from London. The clock of the world-famous Greenwich observatory struck eight chimes as Lachley rented a nag from a dockside livery stable and met James Stephen, as agreed. The unsuspecting Stephen greeted him warmly. "Dr. Lachley! Well met, old chap! I say, it's rather a dismal morning, but we'll put a good face on it, eh? Company makes the gloomiest day brighter, what?"

"Indeed," Lachley nodded, giving the doomed tutor a cheery smile.

The scent of the River Thames drifted on the damp breeze, mingling with the green smell of swampy ground from Greenwich Marshes and the acrid, harsh smell of coal smoke, but Dr. John Lachley drew a deep, double-lungful and smiled again at the man who rode beside him, who had but a quarter of an hour to live.

Riding down the waterfront, past berths where old-fashioned, sail-powered clipper ships and small, iron-hulled steamers creaked quietly at anchor, Lachley and Mr. Stephen turned their nags up King William Walk to reach Greenwich Park, then headed parallel to the river past the Queen's House, built for Queen Anne of Denmark by

James the First in 1615. Greenwich boasted none of London's stink, smelling instead of fresh marshes and late-autumn hay and old money. Tudor monarchs had summered here and several had been born in Greenwich palaces. The Royal Naval College, once a Royal Hospital for Seamen, shared the little village on the outskirts of London with the Royal Observatory and the world-famous Greenwich Meridian, the zero line of oceanic navigation.

As they left behind the village with its royal associations, riding out along the bridle path which snaked its way between Trafalgar Road and the railway line, Lachley began sharing an amusing story about Eddy's latest forays into the East End, a low and vulgar habit Eddy had indulged even during his years at Cambridge, in order to drink and make the rounds of the brothels, pubs, and even, occasionally, the street walkers and fourpence whores who could be had for the price of a loaf of bread.

". . . told the girl he'd give her quid if she'd give him a four-penny knee-trembler and the child turned out to be an honest working girl. Slapped his face so hard it left a hand-print, little dreaming she'd just struck the grandson of the queen. And poor Eddy went chasing after her to apologize, ended up buying every flower in her tray . . ."

They were approaching the fateful windmill Lachley had spied the previous morning. The screaming whistle of a distant train announced the arrival of the diversion Lachley required for his scheme. He smiled to himself and slowed his horse deliberately, to be sure of the timing, leaning down as though concerned his horse might be drawing up lame. Stephen also reined in slightly to match pace with him and to hear the end of the story he was relating.

The train whistle shrieked again. Both horses tossed their heads in a fretting movement. *Good* . . . Lachley nodded approvingly. A nervous horse under Mr. James K. Stephen was all the better. The sorrel Stephen rode danced sideways as the train made its roaring, smoking approach. A moment later they were engulfed in a choking cloud of black smoke and raining cinders.

Lachley whipped his hand into his coat pocket and dragged out the lead-filled sap he'd brought along. His pulse thundered. His nostrils dilated. His whole body tingled with electric awareness. His vision narrowed, tunnelling down to show him the precise spot he would strike. They passed the whirling blades of the windmill, engulfed in the deafening roar of the passing train. *Now!* Lachley reined his horse around in a lightning move that brought him alongside Stephen's sweating mount. Excitement shot through him, ragged, euphoric. He caught a glimpse of James Stephen's trusting, unsuspecting face—

A single, savage blow was all it took.

The thud of the lead sap against his victim's skull jarred Lachley's whole arm, from wrist to shoulder. Pain and shock exploded across Stephen's face. The man's horse screamed and lunged sideways as its rider crumpled in the saddle. The nag bolted straight under the windmill, crowded in that direction by Lachley's own horse and the deafening thunder of the passing train. Stephen pitched sideways out of the saddle, reeling toward unconsciousness. And precisely as Lachley had known it would, one of the windmill vanes caught Stephen brutally across the back of the skull. He was thrown violently to one side by the turning blade. The one-time tutor to Prince Albert Victor Christian Edward landed in a crumpled heap several feet away. Lachley sat watching for a long, shaking moment. The sensations sweeping through him, almost sexual in their intensity, left him trembling.

Then, moving with creditable calm for a man who had just committed his second murder with his own hands—and the first in open view of the public eye—John Lachley wiped the lead sap on his handkerchief and secreted his weapon in his pocket once more. He reined his horse around and tied it to the nearest tree. Dismounting from the saddle, he walked over to the man he'd come here to kill. James K. Stephen lay in a broken heap. Lachley bent down . . . and felt the pulse fluttering at the man's throat.

The bastard was still alive! Fury blasted through him, brought his vision shrieking down to a narrow hunter's focus once more. He stole his hand into his pocket, where the lead sap lay hidden—

"Dear God!" a voice broke into his awareness above the shriek and rattle of the train. Lachley whirled around, violently shaken. Another man on horseback had approached from the trail. The stranger was jumping to the ground, running towards them. Worse, a striking young woman with heavy blond hair sat another horse on the trail, watching them with an expression of shock and horror.

"What's happened?" the intruder asked, reasonably enough.

Lachley forced himself to calmness, drew on a lifetime's worth of deceit and the need to hide who and what he was in order to survive, and said in a voice filled with concern, "This gentleman and I were riding along the trail, here, when the train passed. Something from the train struck him as it went by, I don't know what, a large cinder perhaps, or maybe someone threw something from a window. But his horse bolted quite abruptly. Poor devil was thrown from the saddle, straight under the windmill blades. I'd just reached him when you rode up."

As he spoke, he knelt at Stephen's side, lifted his wrist to sound his pulse, used his handkerchief to bind the deep wound in his head, neatly explaining away the blood on the snowy linen. The stranger crouched beside him, expression deeply concerned.

"We must get him to safety at once! Here . . . cradle the poor man's head and I'll lift his feet. We'll put him in my saddle and I'll ride behind, keep him from falling. Alice, love, don't look too closely, his head's a dreadful sight, covered in blood."

Lachley ground his teeth in a raging frustration and gave the man a seemingly relieved smile. "Capital idea! Splendid. Careful, now . . ."

Ten minutes later the man he'd come all this way to murder lay in a bed in a Greenwich Village doctor's cottage, in a deep coma and not—as the doctor said with a sad shake of his head—expected to survive. Lachley agreed that it was a terrible tragedy and explained to the village constable what had occurred, then gave the man his name and address in case he were needed again.

The constable said with genuine concern, "Not that there's likely to be any inquest, even if the poor chap dies, it's clearly an accident, terrible freak of an accident, and I appreciate your help, sir, that I do."

The bastard who'd come along at just the wrong instant gave the constable his own name, as well, a merchant down from Manchester, visiting London with his younger sister. Lachley wanted to snatch the lead sap out of his pocket and smash in the merchant's skull with it.

Instead, he took his leave of the miserable little physician's cottage while the constable arranged to contact James Stephen's family. It was some consolation, at least, that Stephen was not likely to survive much longer. And, of course, even if Stephen did live, the man would not realize that the blow which had struck him down had been an intentional one. The story of the accident would be relayed to the victim by the constable, the village doctor, even his own family. And if Stephen did survive . . .

There were ways, even then, of erasing the problem he still represented.

The matter being as resolved as he could make it at this juncture, John Lachley set his horse toward Greenwich Village pier for the return trip to London and set his seething mind toward Polly Nichols and the problems *she* represented.

He was still wrestling with the problem when he returned home to find a letter which had arrived, postmarked, of all places, Whitechapel, London, Liverpool Street Station. "My dearest Dr. Lachley," the missive began, "such a tremendous difference you have made! Many of my symptoms have abated immeasurably since my visit to your office, Friday last. I feel stronger, more well, than I have in many months. But I am still troubled greatly by itching hands and dreadful headaches. I wondered if you would be so good as to arrange another appointment for me in your surgery? I am certain you can do me more good than any other physician in the world. As I have returned to London on business, it would be most kind of you to fit me into your admittedly busy schedule. I eagerly await your response. Please contact me by return post, general delivery, Whitechapel."

It was signed James Maybrick, Esquire.

John Lachley stared at the signature. Then a slow smile began to form. James Maybrick, the murderous cotton merchant from Liverpool . . . With his delightful *written* diary and its equally delightful confession of murder. And not just any murder, either, but the murder of a *whore,* by damn, committed by a man with all the motive in the world to hate prostitutes! Maybrick wasn't a Jew, didn't look even remotely foreign. But if Lachley recruited Maybrick into this hunt for Polly Nichols, worked with him, there would be *two* descriptions for eyewitnesses to hand police, confounding the issue further, throwing the constables even more violently off Lachley's trail. Yes, by damn, Maybrick was just the thing he required.

It was so simple, he very nearly laughed aloud. He would meet the man in Whitechapel this very night, by God, induce a state of drugged mesmeric trance, then turn that lethal rage of his into the perfect killing machine, a weapon he could direct at will against whatever target he chose. And the diary would ensure the man's death at the end of a rope. Lachley chuckled, allowing the seething frustration over his failure to silence the prince's tutor to drop away. He would encourage Maybrick to dutifully record every sordid detail of Polly Nichols' murder, would even place mesmeric blocks in Maybrick's mind to prevent the imbecile from mentioning *him* in the diary.

James Maybrick was a godsend, by damn, a genuine godsend!

But as he turned his thoughts toward the use he would make of Maybrick, the enormity of the threat Polly Nichols represented drained away his jubilant mood. God, that Nichols bitch had been in possession of the letters long enough, she might have found someone to translate the bloody letters into English! He had to move quickly, that much was certain. Tonight. He would risk waiting no longer than that.

Lachley opened his desk and removed pen, paper, and penny-post stamps, then composed a brief reply to his arsenic-addicted little cotton merchant. "My dear sir, I would be delighted to continue your treatment. It is an honor to be entrusted with your health. I am certain I can make a changed man of you. Please call upon me in my Cleveland Street surgery this evening by eight P.M. If you are unable to keep this appointment, please advise me by telegram and we will arrange a mutually agreeable time."

He left the house to post the letter, himself, wanting to be certain it would go out in plenty of time for the late afternoon mail delivery bound for Liverpool Street Station, Whitechapel—no more than a handful of miles from his house in Cleveland Street. London was the envy of Europe for its mail service, with multiple pickups a day and delivery times of only a few hours, particularly for general delivery mail service. Lachley smiled to himself and whistled easily as he strolled past the fashionable artists' studios which lined Cleveland Street, giving it the air of respectability and fashion its other, less reputable inhabitants could never hope to achieve. Men of wealth and high station patronized the studios on Cleveland Street, commissioning paintings for their homes, portraits of their wives and progeny, immortalizing themselves on the canvasses of talented artists like Walter Sickert and the incomparable Vallon, who'd recently painted a canvas which the Prime Minister, Lord Salisbury, had just purchased for the astonishing sum of five hundred pounds, merely because members of his family were included in the work.

John Lachley had chosen Cleveland Street for his residence because of its association with the highly fashionable artistic community. Here, a mesmeric physician and occultist appeared to his wealthy clientele as a model of staid respectability compared with the somewhat more Bohemian artists of the district. Lachley knew perfectly well he would have been considered outlandish in more sedate surroundings such as Belgravia. So to Cleveland Street he had come, despite the reputations of one or two of its pubs and houses, which catered to men of Eddy's persuasion. And it was in Cleveland Street where he had first met the darling prince Albert Victor Christian Edward and turned that chance meeting to his considerable advantage. His scheme was certainly paying handsome dividends.

All he had to do now was protect his investment.

Polly Nichols didn't yet know it, but she had less than a day to live. Lachley hoped she spent it enjoying herself. He certainly intended to enjoy her demise. He hastened his footsteps, eager to post his letter and set into motion the events necessary to bring him to that moment. James Maybrick would make the perfect weapon. Why, he might even let Maybrick have the knife, once Lachley, himself, had vented his rage.

He chuckled aloud and could have kissed the fateful letter in his gloved hand.

Tonight, he promised Polly Nichols. *We meet tonight.*

When Margo arrived at the Britannia Gate's departures lounge, Victoria Station had taken on the chaotic air of a tenting circus in the process of takedown for transit to the next town. Not a cafe table in sight, either on the Commons floor or up on one of the balconies, could be had for less than a minor king's ransom and it was standing room only on every catwalk and balcony overlooking Victoria Station. If many more spectators tried to crowd onto the concrete and steel walkways up there, they'd have balconies falling three and four stories under the weight.

Besides the ordinary onlookers, the loons were out in force, as well, carrying placards and holding up homemade signs. Delighted news crews filmed the chaos while Ripperoons and assorted lunatics gave interviews to straight-faced camera operators about how Lord Jack was going to appear through an unstable gate created by a passing meteor and step off into the open Britannia amidst a host of unheavenly demons charged with guarding his most unsacred person from all earthly harm . . .

It might almost have been funny if not for the handful of real crazies demanding to be allowed through, tickets or no tickets, to serve their lord and master in whatever fashion Jack saw fit. Margo, jockeying for position in the crowd, trying to get her luggage cart through, stumbled away from one wild-eyed madman who snatched at her arm, screaming, "Unchaste whore! Jack will see your sins! He will punish you in this ripping time . . ." Margo slipped out of his grasp and left him windmilling for balance, unprepared for someone who knew Aikido.

Security arrived a moment later and Margo waved at Wally Klontz as the nutcase came after her again. "Wally! Hey! Over here!"

"What's the prob—oh, shit!" Wally snatched out handcuffs and grabbed the guy as he lunged again at Margo and screamed obscenities. More security waded in as a couple of other frenzied nutcases protested the man's removal. Violence broke out in a brief, brutish scuffle that ended with Margo gulping down acid nervousness while security agents hauled away a dozen seriously deranged individuals—a couple of them in straightjackets. Standing in the midst of a wide-eyed crowd of onlookers and glassy camera lenses, Margo brought her shudders under control and shoved her way past news crews who thrust microphones and cameras into her face.

"Aren't you Margo Smith, the Time Tours special guide for the Ripper Watch—"

"—true you're training to become a time scout?"

"—give us your feelings about being accosted by a member of a 'Jack is Lord' cult—"

"No comment," she muttered again and again, using the luggage cart as a battering ram to force the newsies aside. If things were this bad on station . . . What was it really going to be like in London's East End, when the Ripper terror struck?

And what if it'd been one of those madmen who'd grabbed Ianira? As a sacrifice to Jack the Ripper? It didn't bear thinking about. Margo thrust the thought firmly aside and turned her luggage over to Time Tours baggage handlers, securing her claim stubs in her reticule, then lunged for the refuge of the departures lounge, where the news crews could follow her only with zoom lenses and directional microphones. It wasn't privacy, but it was the best she could do under the circumstances and Margo had no intention of giving anybody an interview about anything.

Once in the Time Tours departures lounge, she searched the crowd, looking for her new charges, Shahdi Feroz and the two journalists joining the Ripper Watch Team. She'd made one complete circuit of the departures area and was beginning to quarter it through the center when the SLUR-TV theme music swelled out over the crowds jamming Commons and a big screen television came to life. Shangri-La's new television anchor, Booth Hackett, voiced the question of the hour in booming tones that cut across the chaos echoing through Commons.

"It's official, Shangri-La Station! Ripper Season is underway and the entire world is asking, who really was Jack the Ripper? The list of suspects is impressive, the theories about conspiracies in high-government offices as convoluted as any modern conspiracy theorist could want. In an interview taped several hours ago with Dr. Shahdi Feroz, psycho-social historical criminologist and occult specialist for the team . . ."

Margo tuned it out and kept hunting for the Ripper scholar and wayward journalists, who should've been here by now. She wasn't interested in what that ghoul, Hackett, had to say and she already knew all the theories by heart. Kit had made sure of that before consenting to send her down the Britannia. First came the theories involving cults and black magic—hence Shahdi Feroz's inclusion on the team. Robert Donston Stephenson, who had claimed to know the Ripper and his motives personally and was at the top of several suspect lists, had been a known Satanist and practitioner of black magic. Aleister Crowley was on the cult-member suspect list, as well, although the evidence was slim to non-existent. Neither man, despite individual notoriety, fit the profile of a deranged psychopathic killer such as the Ripper. Margo wasn't betting on either of them.

She didn't buy any of the Mary Kelly theories, either—and some of them were among the weirdest of all Ripper theories. Honestly, Queen Victoria ordering the Prime Minister to kill anyone who knew that her grandson had secretly married a Catholic prostitute and fathered a daughter by her, guaranteeing a Catholic heir to the throne? Not to mention the Prime Minister drafting his pals in the Masonic Temple to re-enact some idiot's idea of Masonic rituals on the victims? It was just too nutty, not to mention the total lack of factual support. And she didn't think Mary Kelly's lover, the unemployed fish porter Joseph Barnett, had cut her up with one of his fish-gutting knives, either, despite their having quarrelled, or that he'd killed the other women to "scare" her off the streets. No, the Mary Kelly theories were just too witless . . .

"You are looking very irritated, Miss Smith."

Margo jumped nearly out of her skin, then blinked and focused on Shahdi Feroz' exquisite features. "Oh! Dr. Feroz . . . I, uh, was just looking . . ." She shut up, realizing it would come out sounding like she was irritated with the scholar if she said "I was looking for you," then turned red and stammered out, "I was thinking about all those stupid theories." She nodded toward the big-screen television where Dr. Feroz' taped interview was still playing, then added, "I mean, the ones about Mary Kelly."

Shahdi Feroz smiled. "Yes, there are some absurd ones about her, poor creature."

"You can say that again! You're all checked in and your luggage is ready?"

The scholar nodded. "Yes. And—oh *bother!*"

Newsies. Lots of them. Leaning right across the departures lounge barricades, with microphones and cameras trained on Shadhi Feroz and Margo. "This way!" Margo dragged the scholar by the wrist to the most remote corner of the departures lounge, putting a mass of tourists between themselves and the frustrated news crews. As Margo forced their way through, speculation flew wild amongst the tourists milling around them in every direction, eager to depart.

"—I think it was the queen's grandson, himself, not just some alleged lover."

"The queen's grandson? Duke of Clarence? Or rather, Prince Albert Victor? He wasn't named Duke of Clarence until after the Ripper murders. Poor guy. He's named in at least three outlandish theories, despite unshakable alibis. Like being several hundred miles north of London, in *Scotland,* for God's sake, during at least one of the murders . . ."

A nearby Time Tours guide in down-time servant's livery, was saying, "Ducks, don't you know, just *everybody* wants it to've been a nice, juicy royal scandal. Anytime a British royal's involved in something like the Ripper murders or the drunk-driving death of the Princess of Wales, back near the end of the twentieth century, conspiracy theories pop up faster than muckraking reporters are able to spread 'em round."

They finally gained the farthest corner, out of sight of reporters, if not out of earshot of the appalling noise loose in Victoria Station. "Thank you, my dear," Shadhi breathed a sigh. "I should not be so churlish, I suppose, but I am tired and reporters . . ." She gave an elegant shrug of her Persian shoulders, currently clad in Victorian watered silk, and added with a twinkle in her dark eyes, "So you believe none of the theories about Mary Kelly?"

"Nope."

"Not even the mad midwife theory?"

Margo blinked. *Mad midwife?* Uh-oh . . .

Shahdi Feroz laughed gently. "Don't be so distressed, Miss Smith. It is not a commonly known theory."

"Yes, but Kit made me study this case inside out, backwards and forwards—"

"And you have been given, what? A few days, at most, to study it? I have spent a lifetime puzzling over this case. Don't feel so bad."

"There really is a mad midwife theory?"

Shahdi nodded. "Oh, yes. Mary Kelly was three months pregnant when she died. With a child she couldn't afford to feed. Abortions were illegal, but easily obtained, particularly in the East End, and usually performed by midwives, under appalling conditions. And midwives could come and go at all hours, without having to explain blood on their clothing. Even Inspector Abberline believed they might well be looking for a woman killer. This was based on testimony of a very reliable eyewitness to the murder of Mary Kelly. Abberline couldn't reconcile the testimony any other way, you see. A woman was seen wearing Mary Kelly's clothes and leaving her rented room the morning she was killed, several hours *after* coroners determined that Mary Kelly had died."

Margo frowned. "That's odd."

"Yes. She was seen twice, once between eight o'clock and eight-thirty, looking quite ill, and again about an hour later outside the Britannia public house, speaking with a man. This woman was seen both times by the same witness, a very sober and reliable housewife who lived near Mary Kelly, Mrs. Caroline Maxwell. Her testimony led Inspector Abberline to wonder if the killer might perhaps be a deranged midwife who dressed in the clothing of her victim as a disguise. And there certainly were clothes burned in Mary Kelly's hearth, shortly after the poor girl was murdered."

"But she died at four A.M.," Margo protested. "What would've kept her busy in there for a whole four hours? And what about the mutilations?"

"Those," Shahdi Feroz smiled a trifle grimly, "are two of the questions we hope to solve. What the killer did between Mary Kelly's death and his or her escape from Miller's Court, and why."

Margo shivered and smoothed her dress sleeves down her arms, trying to smooth the goose chills, as well. She didn't like thinking about Mary Kelly, the youngest and prettiest of the Ripper's victims, with her glorious strawberry blond hair. Margo's memories of her mother were sharp and terrible. Long, thick strawberry blond hair, strewn across the kitchen floor in sticky puddles of blood . . .

The less Margo recalled about what her mother had been and how she'd died, the better. "A mad midwife sounds nutty to me," she muttered. "As nutty as the other theories about Mary Kelly. Besides, there probably was no such person, just a police inspector groping for a solution to fit the testimony."

Shahdi Feroz chuckled. "You would be wrong, my dear, for a mad midwife did, in fact, exist. Midwife Mary Pearcey was arrested and hanged for slashing to death the wife and child of her married lover in 1890. Even Sir Arthur Conan Doyle suggested the police might have been searching for a killer of the wrong gender. He wrote a story based on this idea."

"That Sherlock Holmes should've been searching for *Jill* the Ripper, not *Jack* the Ripper?"

Shahdi Feroz laughed. "I agree with you, it isn't very likely."

"Not very! I mean, women killers don't do that sort of thing. Chop up their victims and eat the parts? Do they?"

The Ripper scholar's expression sobered. "Actually, a woman killer is quite capable of inflicting such mutilations. Criminologists have long interpreted such female-inflicted mutilations in a psychologically significant light. While lesbianism is a perfectly normal biological state for a fair percentage of the population and lesbians are no more or less likely than heterosexuals or gays to fit psychologically disturbed profiles, nonetheless there is a pattern which some lesbian killers do fit."

"*Lesbian* killers?"

"Yes, criminologists have known for decades that one particular profile of disturbed woman killer, some of whom happen to be lesbians, kill their lovers in a fit of jealousy or anger. They often mutilate the face and breasts and sexual organs. Which the Ripper most certainly did. A few such murders have been solved only after police investigators stopped looking for a male psychotically deranged sexual killer and began searching, instead, for a female version of the psychotic sexual killer."

Margo shuddered. "This is spooky. What causes it? I mean, what happens to turn an innocent little baby into something like Jack the Ripper? Or Jill the Ripper?"

Shahdi Feroz said very gently, "Psychotic serial killers are sometimes formed by deep pyschological damage, committed by the adults who have charge of them as young children. It's such a shocking tragedy, the waste of human potential, the pain inflicted. . . . The adults in such a person's life often combine sexual abuse with physical abuse, severe emotional abuse, and utter repression of the child's developing personality, robbery of the child's power and control over his or her life, a whole host of factors. Other times . . ." She shook her head. "Occasionally, we run across a serial killer who has no such abuse in his background. He simply enjoys the killing, the power. At times, I can only explain such choices as the work of evil."

"Evil?" Margo echoed.

Shahdi Feroz nodded. "I have studied cults in many different time periods, have looked at what draws disturbed people to pursue occult power, to descend into the kind of killing frenzy one sees with the psychotic killer. Some have been badly warped by abusers, yet others simply crave the power and the thrill of control over others' lives. I cannot find any other words to describe such people, besides a love of evil."

"Like Aleister Crowley," Margo murmured.

"Yes. Although he is not very likely Jack the Ripper."

Margo discovered she was shuddering inside, down in the core of herself, where her worst memories lurked. Her own father had been a monster, her mother a prostitute, trying to earn enough money to pay the bills when her father drank everything in their joint bank account. Margo's childhood environment had been pretty dehumanized. So why hadn't *she* turned out a psychopath? She still didn't get it, not completely. Maybe her parents, bad as they'd been, hadn't been quite monstrous enough? The very thought left her queasy.

"Are you all right?" Shahdi asked in a low voice.

Margo gave the scholar a bright smile. "Sure. Just a little weirded out, I guess. Serial killers are creepy."

"They are," Shahdi Feroz said softly, "the most terrifying creation the human race has ever produced. It is why I study them. In the probably vain hope we can avoid creating more of them."

"That," Margo said with a shiver, "is probably the most impossible quest I've ever heard of. Good luck. I mean that, too."

"What d'you mean, Miss Smith?" a British voice said in her ear. "Good luck with what?"

Margo yelped and came straight up off the floor, at least two inches airborne; then stood glaring at Guy Pendergast and berating herself for not paying better attention. *Some time scout trainee you are! Stay this unfocused and some East End blagger's going to shove a knife through your ribcage. . . .* "Mr. Pendergast. I didn't see you arrive. And Miss Nosette. You've checked in? Good. All right, everybody's here. We've got—" she craned her head to look at the overhead chronometers "—eleven minutes to departure if you want to make any last-minute purchases, exchange money, buy a cup of coffee. You've all got your timecards? Great. Any questions?" *Please don't have any questions . . .*

Guy Pendergast gave her a friendly grin. "Is it true, then?"

She blinked warily at him. "Is what true?"

"Are you really bent on suicide, trying to become a time scout?"

Margo lifted her chin a notch, a defiant cricket trying to impress a maestro musician with its musicality. "There's nothing suicidal about it! Scouting may be a dangerous profession, but so are a lot of other jobs. Police work or down-time journalism, for instance."

Pendergast chuckled easily. "Can't argue that, not with the scar I've got across me arse—oh, I beg pardon, Miss Smith."

Margo almost relaxed. Almost. "Apology accepted. Whenever I'm in a lady's attire," she brushed a hand across the watered silk of her costume, "please watch your speech in my presence. But," and she managed a smile, "when I put on my ragged boy's togs or the tattered skirts of an East End working woman, don't be shocked at the language I start using. I've been studying Cockney rhyming slang until I speak it in my dreams at night. One thing I'm learning as a trainee scout is to fit language and behavior to the role I play down time."

"I don't know about the rest of the team," Dominica Nosette flashed an abruptly dazzling smile at Margo and held out a friendly hand, completely at odds with her belligerence over the shooting lesson, "but I would be honored to be assigned to you for guide services. And of course, the *London New Times* will be happy to pay you for any additional services you might be willing to render."

Margo shook Dominica's hand, wondering what, exactly, the woman wanted from her. Besides the scoop of the century, of course. "Thank you," she managed, "that's very gracious, Ms. Nosette."

"Dominica, please. And you'll have to excuse my scapegrace partner. Guy's manners are atrocious."

Pendergast broke into a grin. "Delighted, m'dear, can't tell you how delighted I am to be touring with the famous Margo Smith."

"Oh, but I'm not famous."

He winked, rolling a sidewise glance at his partner. "Not yet, m'dear, but if I know Minnie, your name will be a household word by tea time."

Margo hadn't expected reporters to notice her, not yet, anyway, not until she'd really proved herself as an independent scout. All of which left her floundering slightly as Dominica Nosette and Guy Pendergast and, God help her, Shahdi Feroz, waited for her response. *What would Kit want me to do? To say? He hates reporters, I know that, but he's never said anything about what I should do if they talk to me . . .*

Fortunately, Doug Tanglewood, another of the guides for the Ripper Watch tour, arrived on the scene looking nine feet tall in an elegant frock coat and top hat. "Ah, Miss Smith, I'm so glad you're here. You've brought the check-in list? And the baggage manifests well in hand, I see. Ladies, gentlemen, Miss Smith is, indeed, a time scout in training. And since we will be joining her fiancé in London, I'm certain she would appreciate your utmost courtesy to her as a lady of means and substance."

Guy Pendergast said in dismay, "Fiancé? Oh, bloody *hell!*" and gave a theatrical groan that drew chuckles from several nearby male tourists. Doug Tanglewood smiled. "And if you would excuse us, we have rather a great deal to accomplish before departure."

Doug nodded politely and drew Margo over toward the baggage, then said in a low voice, "Be on your guard against those two, Miss Smith. Dominica Nosette and Guy Pendergast are notorious, with a reputation that I do not approve of in the slightest. But they had enough influence in the right circles to be added to the team, so we're stranded with them."

"They were very polite," she pointed out.

Tanglewood frowned. "I'm certain they were. They are very good at what they do. Just bear this firmly in mind. What they do is pry into other people's lives in order to report the sordid details to the world. Remember that, and there's no harm done. Now, have you seen Kit? He's waiting to see you off."

Margo's irritation fled. "Oh, where?"

"Across that way, at the barricade. Go along, then, and say goodbye. I'll take over from here."

She fled toward her grandfather, who'd managed to secure a vantage point next to the velvet barricade ropes. "Can you believe it? Eight minutes! Just eight more minutes and then, wow! Three and a half *months* in London! Three and a half very *hard* months," she added hastily at the beginnings of a stern glower in her world-famous grandfather's eyes.

Kit kept scowling, but she'd learned to understand those ferocious scowls during the past several months. They concealed genuine fear for her, trying to tackle this career when there was so much to be learned and so very much that could go wrong, even on a short and relatively safe tour. Kit ruffled her hair, disarranging her stylish hat in the process. "Keep that in mind, Imp. Do you by any chance remember the first rule of surviving a dangerous encounter on the streets?"

Her face went hot, given her recent lapses in attention, but she shot back the answer promptly enough. "Sure do! Don't get into it in the first place. Keep your eyes and ears open and avoid anything that even remotely smells like trouble. And if trouble does break, run like hel—eck." She really was trying to watch her language. Ladies in

Victorian London did not swear. *Women* did, all the time; *ladies,* never.

Kit chucked her gently under the chin. "That's my girl. Promise me, Margo, that you'll watch your back in Whitechapel. What you ran into before, in the Seven Dials, is going to look like a picnic, compared with the Ripper terror. *That* will blow the East End apart."

She bit her lower lip. "I know. I won't lie," she said in a sudden rush, realizing it was true and not wanting to leave her grandfather with the impression that she was reckless or foolhardy—at least, not any longer. "I'm scared. What we're walking into . . . The Ripper's victims weren't the only women murdered in London's East End during the next three months. And I can only guess what it's going to be like when the vigilance committees start patrolling the streets and London's women start arming themselves out of sheer terror."

"Those who could afford it," Kit nodded solemnly. "Going armed in that kind of explosive atmosphere is a damned fine idea, actually, so long as you keep your wits and remember your training."

Margo's own gun, a little top-break revolver, was fully loaded and tucked neatly into her dress pocket, in a specially designed holster Connie Logan had made for her. After her first, disastrous visit to London's East End with this pistol, Margo had drilled with it until she could load and shoot it blindfolded in her sleep. She just hoped she didn't need to use it, ever.

Far overhead, the station's public address system crackled to life. "Your attention please. Gate Two is due to cycle in two minutes. All departures . . ."

"Well," Margo said awkwardly, "I guess this is it. I've got to go help Doug Tanglewood herd that bunch through the gate."

Kit smiled. "You'll do fine, Imp. If you don't, I'll kick your bustled backside up time so fast, it'll make your head swim!"

"Hah! You and what army?"

Kit's world-famous jack-o-lantern grin blazed down at her. "Margo, honey, I *am* an army. Or have you forgotten your last Aikido lesson?"

Margo just groaned. She still had the bruises. "You're mean and horrible and nasty. How come I love you?"

Kit laughed, then leaned over the barricade to give her a hug. "Because you're as crazy as I am, that's why." He added in a sudden, fierce whisper, "Take care of yourself!"

Margo hugged him tight and gave him a swift kiss on one lean, weathered cheek. "Promise."

Kit's eyes were just a hint too bright, despite the now-familiar scowl. "Off with you, then. I'll be waiting to test you on everything you've learned when you get back."

"Oh, God . . ." But she was laughing as she took her leave and found Douglas Tanglewood and their charges. When the Britannia Gate finally rumbled open and Margo started up the long flight of metal stairs, her computerized scout's log and ATLS slung over her shoulder in a carpet bag, Margo's heart was pounding as fast as the butterflies swooping and circling through her stomach. Three and a half months of Ripper Watch Tour wasn't exactly scouting . . . but solving the most famous serial murder of all time was just about the next best thing. She was going to make Kit proud of her, if it was the last thing she ever did. Frankly, she could hardly wait to get started!

《 Chapter 6 》

Polly Nichols needed a drink.

It'd been nearly seven hours since her last glass of gin and she was beginning to shake, she needed another so badly. There was no money in her pockets, either, to buy more. Worse, trade had been miserably slow all day, everywhere from the Tower north to Spitalfields Market and east to the Isle of Dogs. Not one lousy whoreson during the whole long day had been willing to pay for the price of a single glass of gin to calm her shaking nerves. She hadn't much left to sell, either, or pawn, for that matter.

Polly wore cheap, spring-sided men's boots with steel-tipped heels, which might've been worth something to a pawn broker, had she not cut back the uppers to fit her small legs and feet. Worse, without boots, she could not continue to ply her trade. With rain falling nearly every day and an unnatural chill turning the season cold and miserable, she'd catch her death in no time without proper boots to keep her feet warm and dry.

But, God, how she needed a drink . . .

Maybe she could sell her little broken mirror. Any mirror was a valuable commodity in a doss house—which made Polly reluctant to give it up. For a woman in her business, a mirror was an important professional tool. She frowned. What else might she be able to sell? Her pockets were all but empty as she felt through them. The mirror . . . her comb . . . and a crackle of paper. *The letters!* Her fingers trembled slightly as she withdrew the carefully folded sheets of foolscap. That miserable little puff, Morgan, had lied to her about these letters. There was no name on the paper, other than a signature. She suspected she could figure out who the letter-writer was if she could only get the letters translated from Welsh into English. A translation would make Polly a rich woman. But that wouldn't get her a drink right now.

Well, she could always sell some of the letters, couldn't she? With the agreement that as soon as they found out the identity of the author, they would share the spoils between them. Or, if Polly found out quickly enough, she might simply buy them back by saying she'd had them translated and Morgan had lied to her and the letters were worthless. Yes, that was what she would do. Sell three of the four now, to get her gin money, then get them back with a lie and figure out who to blackmail with the whole set of four. But who to convince to buy them in the first place?

It must be someone as desperate for money as herself, to buy into the scheme. But it couldn't be anyone like an ordinary pawn broker. No, it had to be someone she could trust, someone who would trust her. That left one of a few friends she had made on the streets. Which meant she wouldn't be able to get much up front. But then, Polly didn't need much right now, just enough to buy herself a few glasses of gin and a bed for a night or two. She could always get the letters back the moment she had money from her next paying customer, if it came to that.

The decision as to which of her friends to approach was made for her when Polly saw Annie Chapman walking down Whitechapel Road. Polly broke into a broad smile. Annie Chapman was a prostitute, same as herself, and certainly needed money. Dark Annie ought to buy into a blackmail scheme, all right. Annie was seriously ill, although to look at her, a body wouldn't guess it. But she was dying slowly of a lung and brain ailment which had put her into workhouse infirmaries occasionally and siphoned much of what she earned on the streets for medicines.

Yes, Annie ought to be quite interested in making a great deal of money quickly.

"Well, if it isn't Annie Chapman!" she said with a bright smile.

The other woman was very small, barely five feet tall, but stoutly built, with pallid skin and wide blue eyes and beautiful teeth that Polly, herself, would have given much to be able to flash at a customer when she smiled. Annie's dark brown hair was wavy and had probably been lustrous before her illness had struck. Her nose was too thick for beauty and at forty-five she was past her best years, but she was a steady little individual, meeting life quietly and trying to hold on in the face of overwhelming poverty, too little to eat, and an illness that sapped her strength and left her moving slowly when she was able to walk at all.

Annie Chapman smiled, genuinely pleased by the greeting. "Polly, how are you?"

"Oh, I'm good, Annie, I'm good. I'd be better if I 'ad a gin or two, eh?"

The two women chuckled for a moment. Annie was not the drinker Polly was, but the other woman enjoyed her rum, when there was enough money to be spared for it, same as most other women walking these dismal streets.

"Say, Annie, 'ow's your 'ealth been these past few weeks?"

The other woman's eyes darkened. "Not good," she said quietly, with a hoarse rasp in her voice. "It's this rain and cold. Makes my lungs ache, so it's hard to breathe." She *sounded* like it hurt her to breathe.

"I'd imagine a good bit more money would 'elp, eh? Maybe even enough to take you someplace warm and dry, right out o' London?"

"Daft, are you, love?" Annie laughed, not unkindly. "Now, just tell me Polly, how would I get that sort of money?"

Polly winked and leaned close. "Well, as it 'appens I just might be set to come into a small fortune, y'see. And I might be willin' to share it." She showed Annie the letters in her pocket and explained her scheme—and let on like she knew who the author was and was only willing to share the money because she was totally broke, herself, and needed a bed for the night. When she finished her proposition, Annie glared at her. "But Polly! That's blackmail!" The anger in the other woman's eyes and rasping voice astonished Polly.

She drew herself up defensively. "An' if it is? Bloke should 'ave thought of that before 'e went about dippin' 'is Hampton into a bloke's arse'ole! Besides, Annie, this 'ere bastard's rich as sin. And what've you got, eh? A dead 'usband and a sickness eatin' away at you, 'til you can't 'ardly stand up. If we went to a magistrate, this 'ere bloke would go t'prison. I'm not talkin' about 'urting a decent sort of chap, I'm talkin' about makin' a right depraved bastard pay for 'is crimes against God an' nature. An' 'ow better *should* 'e pay, than to 'elp a sick woman? I ask you that, Annie Chapman, 'ow better to pay for 'is sins than to 'elp a woman 'oo needs it most? Think of it, Annie. Enough money t'go someplace where it don't rain 'alf the year an' the fogs don't make it near impossible to breathe of a night. Someplace warm, even in winter. A decent 'ouse wiv a roof over and enough to eat, so's you aren't weak all the time, wot lets the sickness gets a better grip than ever. Annie, think of it, enough money to pay a real doctor an' get the sort of medicines rich folk 'ave . . ."

Annie's expression had crumpled. Tears filled her eyes. "You're right," she whispered. "Isn't my fault I'm sick. Not my fault this nasty chap went out and seduced a half-grown boy, either. God, to have enough money for real medicine. A warm place to live . . ." She coughed, swaying weakly. Misery and longing ploughed deep gullies into her face.

Polly patted her shoulder. "That's right, Annie. I'll share wiv you. There's four letters. You take three of 'em. All I need's enough money to pay me doss 'ouse for a few nights. Can you spare that much, Annie? A few pence for now . . . and a lifetime of medicine and rest in warm beds, after?"

Annie was searching through her pockets. "I've got to have enough for my own doss house tonight," she muttered, digging out a few coins. "I've had some luck today, though. Made enough money to pay for almost a week's lodging. Here." She gave Polly a shilling. "That's fourpence a letter. Is it enough?" she asked anxiously.

Polly Nichols had to work hard not to snatch the shilling out of Annie's hand. She was looking at enough money to buy four brimming *glassfuls* of gin. "Oh, Annie, that's a gracious plenty." She accepted the shilling and handed over three of her precious letters. "An' 'ere you are, luv, three tickets to the life you deserve."

Annie actually hugged her.

Polly flushed and muttered, "I'll not forget this, Annie. An' we'll send the letter to this nasty Mr. Eddy together, eh? Tomorrow, Annie. Meet me at the Britannia pub tomorrow an' we'll compose a lovely letter to Mr. Eddy an' send it off. You got a better education than I 'ave, you can write it out all posh, like, eh?"

By tomorrow she would have found someone to translate her remaining letter for her and be able to keep that promise. And she just might let Annie keep one of the letters, after all, rather than buying them all back.

Annie smiled at her, eyes swimming with gratitude. "You're a grand friend, Polly Nichols. God bless you."

They said their goodbyes, Annie tucking three of the letters into her pockets while Polly pocketed the remaining letter and her precious shilling. As they went their separate ways, Polly smiled widely. Then she headed for the nearest public house as fast as her steel-capped boots would carry her there. She needed a drink, all right.

To celebrate!

Skeeter wasn't certain what, exactly, he was looking for as he worked the Britannia Gate's baggage line. But the Britannia was the first gate to cycle since Ianira's disappearance. If Skeeter had kidnapped someone as world-famous as Ianira Cassondra, intending something more subtle than simply killing her and dumping the body somewhere, he'd have tried to smuggle her out through the first open gate available.

For one thing, it would be far easier to torture a victim down a gate. Fewer people to hear—or at least care about—the screams. And if her abductor really was the person who'd shoved her out of the way of an assassin's bullet, if he actually was interested in keeping her alive, then getting her off the station would be imperative. Too many people had far too many opportunities to strike at Ianira on station, even if her rescuer tried to keep her hidden. In a gossip-riddled place like La-La Land, *nothing* stayed secret for long. Certainly not an abduction of someone as beloved and strikingly recognizable as Ianira.

So Skeeter had abandoned his search of the station, donned a shapeless working man's shirt and the creaseless trousers of the Victorian era—the costume worn by all Time Tours baggage handlers working the Britannia—and reported for work, as planned. As Ianira had planned . . . He couldn't think about that now, couldn't dwell on the fear and the dull, aching anger, not if he hoped to catch what might be a very fleeting, subtle clue betraying a smuggler.

How someone might successfully sneak someone through a gate occupied Skeeter's thoughts as hotel bellhops arrived in steady streams from hotels up and down Commons, bringing cartloads of luggage tagged for London. Tourists generally carried no more on their person than an average passenger was permitted to carry aboard a jetliner, which meant—and Skeeter stared in dismay at the flood of baggage carts on direct approach to the Britannia's lounge—that bellhops and baggage handlers had to transport every last trunk, carpet bag, portmanteau, and ladies' toiletry case from hotel room door to down-time destination, through a gate which opened only so wide and stayed open only so long.

Sloppy handling, broken contents, and lost luggage had resulted in the firing of many a baggage handler, not to mention four baggage *managers* in just the past few months. And Celosia Enyo, the latest in that dismal line of unhappy managers, was not the kind of woman to tolerate mistakes by anyone, not on this gate's cycle, anyway. After all, this wasn't just *any* gate opening. This was a Shangri-La Event: Ripper Season's official kickoff. And true to 'eighty-sixer predictions, the social gala on the other side of the departures-lounge barricades had roared to boisterous, ghoulish life.

"I don't care what those experts say," a severely dressed woman was saying as she passed through the check-in procedures, "I think it was that barber-surgeon, the bigamist. George Chapman."

Her companion, an equally severe woman with upswept, greying hair, said, "Chapman? His real name was Severin Klosowski, wasn't it? I don't think he was a very likely suspect."

"Well, Inspector Abberline named him as a leading candidate! Klosowski killed lots of women. Wives, mistresses, girlfriends—"

"Yes, but he didn't use a knife, my dear, he poisoned them. The

Ripper wasn't that devious. Klosowski killed his women when they got too inconvenient. Or too expensive to keep. Jack the Ripper killed for the pleasure of it."

And behind those two, a professonrial-looking little man in a seedy suit was holding forth at length to a drab little woman with a dumpy build and a rabbitty, frightened look in her eyes: "A serial killer needs to punish the woman or women he hated in his own life. He acts out the violence he wished he'd had the nerve to commit against the women who injured him. Jack the Ripper simply transferred that violence to the prostitutes of London's East End. That's why it can't be Klosowski," he added, nodding at the two severely dressed women in line ahead of him. "Personally, I favor the Mysterious Lodger, that Canadian chap, G. Wentworth Bell Smith. He went about in rubberized boots, changing clothes at all hours, railing against loose women. I'd stake my reputation on it, Bell Smith's the man . . ."

The nearest of the ladies championing Chapman rounded on the Bell-Smith supporter. "A killer proven is a killer proven!" she insisted, refusing to be swayed in her convictions by any amount of evidence or reason. "Mark my words, Claudia," she turned back to her friend, "Chapman or Klosowski, whichever name you prefer, he'll turn out to be the Ripper! I'm sure of it . . ."

While overhead, on the immense SLUR television screen, the scholarly debate raged on. "—a very common pattern," Scotland Yard Inspector Conroy Melvyn was saying in a taped interview with fellow Ripper Watch Team member Pavel Kostenka, "for a male serial killer to attack and kill prostitutes. Bloke sees 'em as a substitute for the powerful woman in 'is life, the one 'e feels powerless to strike at, instead."

"Indeed," Dr. Koskenka was nodding. "Not only this, but a prostitute represents a morally fallen woman. And prostitutes," Dr. Kostenka added heavily, "were and still are the most easily available women to such killers. Add to that the historical tendency of police to dismiss a prostitute's murder as less important than the murder of a 'respectable' woman and streetwalkers surge into prominence as victims of mass murderers—"

Skeeter tuned out the debate as best he could and grunted under the weight of massive steamer trunks, portmanteaus, carpet bags, leather cases, smaller trunks and satchels until his back ached. The arriving luggage was transferred case by case to a growing pile at the base of a newly installed, massive conveyor system which Time Tours' new baggage manager had finally had the good sense to install. Skeeter glanced up to the gate platform, five stories overhead. Thank God for the conveyer. Some of those steamer trunks weighed more than Skeeter did. Considerably more. He eyed the gridwork stairs he'd be climbing soon and blessed that conveyer system fervently.

Geographically speaking, the Britannia was the highest of Shangri-La's active tour gates. When it opened, tourists climbed up to an immense metal gridwork platform which hovered near the steel beams and girders of the ceiling. Until the advent of that conveyer, sweating baggage handlers and porters had climbed that same ramp, gasping and hurrying to make it through before the gate disappeared into thin air once more.

"Sheesh," Skeeter muttered, grabbing another trunk by its leather handles and hauling it over to the conveyer, "what's in some of these monsters? Uranium bricks?" One of the other baggage handlers, a down-timer who worked most gate openings as a porter, grunted sympathetically as Skeeter groused, "They're only staying in London eight days, for Chrissake. And they'll be bringing back more than they left with!"

They would, too. Right down to the last yammering, whining kid in line. Parents had to pay a hefty amount of extra cash demanded by Time Tours, Inc., for children's tickets, a policy put into place after a couple of kids had managed to get themselves fatally separated from tours out of other stations. Children on a time tour were like gasoline on an open campfire. But parents still brought their brats with them in droves, and a surprising number paid the extra fees for kids' tickets. Others simply dropped the kids off at the station school to "have fun" in the zany world of the station while Mommy and Daddy went time hopping.

Skeeter dragged over another portmanteau. Why anybody would take a child into something like the Ripper terror . . . He could see it now. *My summer vacation: how a serial killer cut up women who make their living sleeping with strangers for money.* And kids had grown up fast in *his* day.

"C'mon, Jackson," an angry voice snapped practically in his ear, "enough goofing off! Put your back into it! Those baggage carts are piling up fast. And more are coming in from the hotels every minute!"

Skeeter found the baggage manager right behind him, glaring at him through narrowed, suspicious eyes. He resisted the urge to flip her a bird and said, "Yes, ma'am!" Just exactly how he was supposed to work faster than top speed, Skeeter wasn't quite sure, but he made a valiant effort. He cleared the cart in front of him and shoved it out of the way so another could take its place. Celosia Enyo watched him sharply for the next couple of minutes, then stalked further down the line, browbeating some other unfortunate. At least she was impartially horrible to everyone. Of course, after the miserable track record her four immediate predecessors had compiled between them, Enyo doubtless sweat bullets every time a gate opened, hoping she'd still have a job when it closed again. Skeeter could sympathize. Not much, maybe—anybody that universally rude deserved a dose of unpleasantness right back, again. But he could sympathize some.

Of course, Skeeter grunted sharply and dropped another case onto the stack, by that same logic, he'd still be working off his own karma when he was four-hundred ninety. *Yeah, well, at least I was never obnoxious to anybody I ripped off. . . .* A polite thief, that's what he'd been, by God. But no longer a thief, thanks to Marcus and Ianira.

Skeeter blinked sweat out of his eyes, fighting a sudden tightness in his chest as he emptied yet another baggage cart. Surely Marcus realized he could trust Skeeter? After what Skeeter'd gone through in Rome, damn near dying in that gladiatorial combat in the Circus Maximus before wrenching Marcus out of slavery again, surely Marcus could've trusted him enough to let him know they were alive, at least? Whoever was trying to kill them, he had to realize that Skeeter, of all people, wouldn't betray him and his daughters?

He ground his teeth in silent misery. If somebody had tried to shoot *his* wife, if he'd walked into *his* daughters' daycare center to find two armed thugs trying to drag off *his* kids, would *he* have risked contacting anybody? Just on the remote chance they might be followed, trying to bring help? Skeeter knew he wouldn't have. Wouldn't have dared risk his loved ones, no matter what risks he, himself, might have been willing to run. The realization hurt, even as he was forced to admit he understood the silence. But the girls were just babies, Artemisia not yet four, Gelasia barely turned one. Marcus couldn't stay in hiding with them, not for long. Which was doubtless what the faceless bastards trying to kill them were counting on. If Skeeter were Marcus, he'd seriously consider trying to jump station. Through *any* gate that opened.

Skeeter closed his hands around the stout handles of yet another steamer trunk and heaved it into place, wishing bitterly he could get his hands on whoever had dragged Ianira away through that riot. It must have been staged. Create a perfect diversion, shoot her down in the midst of the chaos . . . Only somebody had interrupted the attempt. Had the shooter dragged her off? To finish the job at his leisure? Or someone else? Skeeter couldn't bear to keep thinking in ragged circles like this, but he couldn't *not* think about her, either, not considering what he owed her.

Skeeter wiped sweat from his forehead. Just another few minutes, he told himself fiercely. Another few minutes and the gate would have cycled, all this ridiculous luggage would be on the other side of the Britannia, and he could get back to combing the station with the finest-toothed comb ever invented by humanity.

Meanwhile . . .

Watching the freakshow beyond the barricades helped keep his mind off it and watching the tourists inside the barricades occupied the rest of his mind, searching faces for clues, for any similarity to the face in his memory, that wild-eyed kid with the black-powder pistol. Gawkers formed an impenetrable barrier around the edges of the departures lounge, so thick, security had formed cordons to permit ticketed tourists, uniformed Time Tours employees, freelance guides, baggage handlers, and supply couriers to reach the roped-off lounge. The noise was appalling. Troops of howler monkeys had nothing on the mob of humanity packed into the confined spaces of Victoria Station. And every man-jack one of 'em wanted to be able to tell his grandchildren some day, "I was there, kids, I was there when the first Ripper tour went through, let me tell you, it was *something . . .*"

It was something, all right.

There weren't words disgusting enough to describe it, that electric air of anticipation, of excitement that left the air supercharged with the feeling that a major event is happening right before your eyes, an excitement sensed in the nerve endings of skin and hair, completely independent of sight and sound and smell. Skeeter was the kind of soul who loved excitement, thrived on it, in fact. But this . . . this kind of excitement was a perversion, even Skeeter could sense that, and Skeeter Jackson's moral code, formed during his years with the Yakka Mongols, didn't exactly mesh with most of up-time humanity's. What was it going to be like when *next* week's gate opened? When all these people and probably a couple hundred more, besides, newly arrived through Primary, jammed in to learn who the ghoul *really* was?

Maybe after he dragged all this luggage through the Britannia and came back to look for Ianira some more, he'd volunteer to haul baggage to Denver for a couple of weeks, just to miss out on the whole sordid thing? The Wild West Gate opened tomorrow, after all, and Time Tours was perennially short of baggage handlers. If only they'd found Ianira by then, and Marcus, and little Artemisia and bright-eyed, laughing Gelasia.

If, *if, IF!*

It was the not knowing that was intolerable, the not knowing or being able to find out. He wanted this job over with, so he could get back to searching. Skeeter stared intently through the crowd, trying to spot anybody he might recognize from The Found Ones. Any news was better than none. But he couldn't see a single down-timer in that crowd who wasn't already busy to distraction hauling luggage. Which meant they wouldn't know spit about the search underway, either.

God, how much longer until this blasted gate cycled?

He peered up at the huge chronometer boards suspended from the distant ceiling, picking out the countdown for Gate Two: five minutes. At the rate time was creeping past, it might as well be five years.

"Jackson! Do you really like scrubbing toilets that much?"

He started so violently he nearly dropped the carpet bag dangling from his hands. Celosia Enyo was glaring at him, lips thinned to a murderous white line.

"Sorry, ma'am," he muttered. "I was hoping I might see someone who'd heard about Ianira—"

"We're all worried! But that gate doesn't give a damn who's missing or found. We get that—" she jabbed a finger toward the small mountain of luggage "—through the gate on time or some millionaire will have your head on his dinner platter for having to buy a new wardrobe in London. Worry about your friends on your own time. Or by God, your own time is all you'll have!"

She was absolutely right, in a cold-blooded, mercenary sense. The moment she turned away to snarl at someone else, Skeeter gave her a flying eagle salute and dragged another portmanteau off a groaning luggage cart. He scowled at the enormous stack of luggage on the conveyer already, mentally damning Time Tours for insane greed. No wonder the last four baggage managers had failed disastrously with gate logistics. Time Tours was sending through too many blistering tourists at once.

Never mind *way* too many trunks per tourist.

If he'd kept accurate count, the last five steamer trunks and three portmanteaus alone had belonged to the same guy. Benny Catlin, whoever the hell he was. Rich as sin, if he could cart that much luggage through in just one direction. The big conveyer rumbled to life with one jolting squeal and a grating of metal gears. Then the rubberized surface began moving upward, ready to carry all that luggage to the platform overhead. Skeeter glanced around to look for the boss. Enyo wasn't in sight, but the shift supervisor was busy sending handlers aloft. He caught Skeeter's eye and said, "Get up top, Jackson. Start hauling that stuff off the conveyer as it arrives."

"Yessir!"

The climb up to the Britannia platform was a long one, particularly after all the hauling he'd done in the past few minutes, but the view was spectacular. Commons spread out beneath his feet, a full five stories deep, riotous with color and sound. Costumed tourists scurried like rainbow-hued bugs whipped around in the currents and eddies of a slow-motion river. Great banners—bright holiday-colored ribbons curling and floating through a hundred-foot depth of open air from balconies and catwalks— proclaimed to the world that Ripper Season had begun, and advertised other not-to be-missed down-time events. A cat's-cradle tangle of meshwork bridges stretched right across Commons from one side to the other, supported from below by steel struts or suspended from above by steel cables disappearing into the ceiling. The noise from hundreds of human throats lapped at the edges of the high platform like crashing surf against jagged rocks, leaping and splashing back again, indistinct and unintelligible from sheer distance.

And booming above it all came the voice of the public address system, echoing down the vast length of Commons: "Your attention, please. Gate Two is due to open in two minutes . . ."

The first luggage on the conveyor belt arrived with a jolt and scrape against the gridwork platform. Skeeter joined a human-chain effort, hauling luggage clear of the moving conveyor and piling it on the platform. Railings ran all the way around, with a wide metal gate set into one side. Until the Britannia actually opened, that wide metal gate led to a sheer, hundred-foot drop to the cobblestones of Victoria Station. Despite the railing, Skeeter stayed well away from the edge as he hauled, piled, and stacked a steadily increasing jumble of trunks, cases, and soft-sided carpet bags across the broad stretch of platform.

At the far corner, a second conveyor system rumbled to life, moving downward rather than up. Celosia Enyo was testing the system, making sure everything was ready for the returning tour and all of *its* luggage. So engrossed was Skeeter in the monumental task of shifting the arriving baggage, the gate's opening took him by surprise. A skull-shaking backlash of subharmonics rattled his very bones. Skeeter jumped, wanting instinctively to cover his ears, although that wouldn't have done any good. The gate's frequency was too low for actual human hearing. He glanced around—and gasped.

A kaleidoscope of shimmering color, dopplering through the entire rainbow spectrum, had appeared in the middle of empty air right at the edge of the platform. The colors scintillated like a sheen of oil on water, sunlight on a raven's glossy feathers. The hair on Skeeter's arms stood starkly erect. He'd seen gates open hundreds of times, had stepped through a number of them, when he'd had the money for a tour or had conned someone else into paying for it. But he'd never been this close to the massive Britannia as it began its awe-striking cycle a hundred feet above the Commons floor.

From below, a wall of noise came surging up to the platform, gasps and cries of astonishment from hundreds of spectators. A point of absolute darkness appeared dead center in the wild flashes of color. The blackness expanded rapidly, a hole through time, through the very fabric of reality . . . Something hard banged into Skeeter's elbow. He yelped, jumped guiltily, then grabbed the steamer trunk thrust at him. It went awkwardly onto the top of the stack, canted at an angle, too unstable for anything else to go on top. The next portmanteau to arrive thudded against the steel gridwork, starting a new pile.

Skeeter rearranged wetness on his brow with a limp, soaked sleeve, then straightened his aching back and started piling up the next stack, all while keeping one eye on the massive gate rumbling open behind him. The blackness widened steadily until it stretched the full width of the platform. A Time Tours guide climbed up from the Commons floor and opened the broad metal gate at the edge of the platform to *its* full extent, as well.

A blur of motion caught his eye and the first returnee arrived, rushing at them with the speed of a runaway bullet train. Skeeter resisted the urge to jump out of the way. Then the apparent motion slowed and a gentleman in fancy evening clothes, protected by a wet India-rubber rain slicker, stepped calmly onto the platform and turned to assist the returning tourists through. Men and women in silks and expensively cut garb, most of them holding 1880's style umbrellas and brushing water off their heavy cloaks, jostled their way through, many chattering excitedly. Quite a few others had gone slightly greenish and stumbled every few steps. Guides in servants' uniforms and working men's rougher clothes helped those who seemed worst off to stagger through the open gate. Porters rushed through on their heels, tracking mud onto the platform, then a mad scramble ensued to get all the arriving luggage—every bit of it slick

with what must be
gate—onto the dow
up the five flights o
Skeeter worked fien
down time onto the
clear the jam at the g
outbound tourists ru
they stepped off the e
insisted was a hundre

"Get that outboun

Skeeter lunged to t
staggered through the
garden. It was nearly da
foot traffic across it, mu ~~~~ with slick leaves. There
was a flagstone path, but that was crowded with tourists and guides
and gatehouse staff holding umbrellas. The porters didn't have time
to wait for them to clear out of the way. Following the lead of more
experienced baggage handlers in front of him, Skeeter plunged into
the muddy grass and slogged his way toward the gatehouse. The rain
was icy, slashing against his clothing and soaking him to the skin. He
dumped his first load at the back door of the three-story gatehouse
and pelted back through the open gate to grab another load. The
sensation was dizzying, disorienting.

Then he was through and staggering a little, himself, across the
platform. His muddy shoes slipped on wet metal. Skeeter windmilled
and lurched against a stack of luggage waiting to be ferried through.
The topmost steamer trunk, a massive thing, slid sideways and started
to topple toward the edge of the platform. The corner of the trunk
was well out beyond the periphery of the open Britannia gate,
teetering out where it would plunge the full hundred feet to the
Commons floor. As Skeeter went to one bruised knee, furious shouts
and blistering curses erupted. Then somebody lunged past him to
grab the steamer trunk by the handle before it could fall.

"Don't just sit there, goddamn you!" A short, skinny tourist stood
glaring murderously down at him, arms straining to keep the trunk
from falling. The young man's whiskered face had gone ashen under

nk! I can't hold the weight!" The
, furious.

where he'd landed on it, but Skeeter
nd leaned over the piles of trunks and cases
ed grip on the corner that had already gone over
latform. Hauling together, Skeeter and the tourist
eavy trunk back onto the platform. The tourist was
aking, whether with fright or rage, Skeeter wasn't certain.
t he wasn't so shaken he didn't blow up in Skeeter's face. "*What
e hell did you think you were doing?* Were you *trying* to shove that
trunk over the edge? Goddammit, do you have any idea what
would've happened if that trunk had gone over? If you've been
drinking, I'll make sure you never work on this station again!" The
young man's face was deathly pale, eyes blazing against the unnatural
pallor of his skin and the dark, heavy whiskers of his mutton-chop
sideburns and moustache, which he must've acquired from Paula
Booker's cosmetology salon, because up-time men didn't grow facial
hair in that quantity or shape any more. The furious tourist, fists
balled up and white-knuckled, shrilled out, "My God, *do you realize
what you almost caused?*"

"Well, it didn't fall, did it?" Skeeter snapped, halting the tirade
mid-stream. "And if you stand there cursing much longer, you're
gonna miss your stinking gate!" Skeeter shouldered the trunk himself,
having to carry it across his back, the thing was so heavy. The short
and brutish little tourist, white-lipped and silent now, stalked through
the open gate on Skeeter's heels, evidently intent on following to make
sure Skeeter didn't drop it again. *So much for my new job. After this guy
gets done complaining, I'll be lucky if I still have the job scrubbing toilets.*

It was, of course, still raining furiously in the Spaldergate House
garden. Skeeter did slip again, the muddy ground was so churned up
beside the crowded flagstone walkway. The furious man on his heels
grabbed at the trunk again as Skeeter lurched and slid sideways.
"Listen, you drunken idiot!" he shouted above steady pouring of the
rain. "Lay off the booze or the pills before you show up for work!"

"Stuff it," Skeeter said crudely. He regained his feet and finally
gained the house, where he gratefully lowered his burden to the floor.

"Where are you going?" the irate young man demanded when Skeeter headed back into the downpour.

He flung the answer over one aching shoulder. "Back to the station!"

"But who's going to cart this out to the carriage? Take it to the hotel?"

"Carry it yourself!"

The skinny, whiskered little tourist was still sputtering at the back door when Skeeter re-entered the now-visibly shrunken Britannia Gate. He passed several other porters bent double under heavy loads, trying to get the last of the pile through, then was back on the metal gridwork platform. All that remained of the departing tour was a harried Time Tours guide who plunged through as Skeeter reappeared. Then he was alone with the mud and a single uniformed Time Tours employee who swung shut the big metal safety gate as the Britannia shrank rapidly back in on itself and vanished for another eight days.

Skeeter—wet, shivering, exhausted—slowly descended the stairs once again and slid his timecard through the reader at the bottom, "clocking out" so his brief stay in the London timestream would be recorded properly. The baggage manager was waiting, predictably irate. Skeeter listened in total, sodden silence, taking the upbraiding he'd expected. This evidently puzzled the furious Enyo, because she finally snapped, "Well? Aren't you going to protest your innocence?"

"Why bother?" Skeeter said tiredly. "You've already decided I'm guilty. So just fire me and get it over with so I can put on some dry clothes and start looking for my friends again."

Thirty seconds later, he was on his way, metaphoric pink slip in hand. *Well, that was probably the shortest job on record. Sixty-nine minutes from hired to fired.* He never had liked the idea of hauling luggage for a bunch of jackass tourists, anyway. Scrubbing toilets was dirtier, but at least more dignified than bowing and scraping and apologizing for being alive. And when the job was over, *something*, at least, was clean.

Which was more than he could say of himself at the moment. Mud covered his trousers, squelched from his wet shoes, and dripped with the trickling rainwater down one whole sleeve where he'd caught himself from a nasty fall, that last time through. *Wonder what was in that lousy trunk, anyway? The way he acted, you'd've thought it was his heirloom china. God, tourists!*

Maybe that idiot would do them all a favor and get himself nice and permanently lost in London? But that thought only brought the pain surging back. Skeeter blinked away wetness that had nothing to do with the rainwater dripping out of his hair, then speeded up. He had to get out of these wet, filthy clothes and hook up with the search teams again. Very few people knew this station the way Skeeter did. If he couldn't find her . . .

He clenched his jaw muscles.

He had to find her.

Nothing else mattered at all.

(((Chapter 7)))

Rain had stopped falling over the slate rooftops and crockery chimney pots of London by the time the arriving tour sorted itself out at the Time Tours Gatehouse and departed via carriages to hotels, boarding houses, and rented flats—a British word for apartment that one of the guides had needed to explain to her. Jenna Nicole Caddrick sat hunched now in a rattling carriage, listening to the sharp clop as the horses, a teamed pair of them in harness, struck the cobblestoned street with iron-shod hooves in a steady rhythm.

She shivered and hugged her gentleman's frock coat more tightly around her, grateful for the first time that she was less well endowed than she'd have liked through the chest, and grateful, too, for the simple bulkiness of Victorian men's clothing, which helped disguise bulges that shouldn't have been there. Jenna huddled into her coat, miserable and scared and wishing like anything that Noah had come through with her. She hadn't expected London to be so cold or so wet. It was only the end of August here, after all; but the guides back at the gatehouse had told them London's entire summer had been cold and wet, so there wasn't any use complaining to *them* about the miserable weather.

Miserable was right. The ride jounced her sufficiently to shake her teeth loose, if she hadn't been clenching them so tightly. The air stank, not like New York, which smelt of car exhaust fumes and smog, but rather a dank, bleak sort of stench compounded of whatever was rotting in the River Thames and coal smoke from hundreds of thousands of chimneys and horse dung scattered like shapeless anthills across the streets and a miasma of other stinks she couldn't identify and wasn't sure she wanted to, either. Everything was strange, even the lights. Gaslight didn't look like electric light, which was a phenomenon all those period-piece movies hadn't been able to capture on film. It was softer and yellower, adding a warm and yet alien color to everything where it spilled out across window sills or past half-closed shutters.

What the jouncing, jarring ride was doing to Ianira Cassondra, folded up like last week's laundry and nestled inside an enormous steamer trunk, Jenna didn't even want to consider. They'd cushioned her with blankets and fitted her with a mask for the oxygen canisters supplied in every hotel room in Shangri-La, in case of a station fire. Every hotel room stocked them, since TT-86 stood high in the Himalayas' rarified air. Ianira had clung briefly to Marcus, both their faces white with terror, had kissed her little girls and whispered to them in Greek, then she'd climbed into the trunk, folded herself down into the makeshift nest, and slipped on the oxygen mask.

Noah had been the one to close and latch the lid.

Jenna couldn't bring herself to do it, to lock her in, like that.

She'd wanted to call in a doctor, to look at the nasty bruise and swelling along Ianira's brow where the Prophetess had struck her head on the concrete floor. But risking even a doctor's visit, where questions *would* be asked, meant risking Ianira's life, as well as risking her whole family. And Noah and Jenna's lives, too . . . She clenched down her eyelids. *Please, Goddess, there's been enough killing, let it stop. . . .*

Jenna refused to let herself recall too acutely those ghastly seconds on the platform high above the Commons floor, when Ianira's trunk had teetered and nearly fallen straight off the edge. Jenna's insides still shook, just remembering. She'd have blamed the baggage handler for being a member of the death squad on their trail if the man hadn't obviously been a long-time station resident. And the guy had gone back to the station, too, in a state of churlish rage, which he wouldn't have done, if he'd been sent to murder Jenna and Ianira. No, it'd just been one of those nightmarish, freakish near-accidents that probably happened every time a gate opened and too many people with too much luggage tried to cram themselves through a hole of finite dimensions and duration.

Don't think about it, Jenna, she didn't fall, so don't think about it. There's about a million other things to worry about, instead. Like, where to find refuge in this sprawling, sooty, foul-smelling city on the Thames. She was supposed to stay at the Piccadilly Hotel tonight, in her persona as Mr. Benny Catlin, up-time student doing post-doctoral work in sociology. "Benny" was supposed to be filming his graduate work, as part of the plan she and Carl had come up with, a lifetime ago, when the worst terror she'd had to face was having her infamous father find out she planned to go time touring.

Carl should've been the one playing "Benny Catlin," not Jenna. If Noah'd been able to go with her, the detective would've played the role of the non-existent Mr. Catlin. But they *had* to split up, so Jenna had exchanged identification with Noah. That way, the female "tourist" using the persona she and Carl had bought from that underworld identity seller in New York would cash in her Britannia Gate ticket, then buy one for Denver, instead, leading the *Ansar Majlis* on a merry chase down the wrong gate from the one Jenna and Ianira had really gone through. With any luck, Jenna and the Prophetess would reach the Piccadilly Hotel without incident.

But they wouldn't be staying in the Piccadilly Hotel for long, not with the probability that they'd been followed through the Britannia Gate by *someone* topping out somewhere around a hundred ten percent. Jenna knew she'd have to come up with some other place to stay, to keep them both safe. Maybe she should check into the Piccadilly Hotel as scheduled, then simply leave in the middle of the night? Haul their luggage down the back stairs to the hotel livery stable and take off with a wagon. Maybe vanish into the East End somewhere for a while. It was the least likely place any searchers would think to look for them, not with Jack the Ripper stalking those dismal streets.

Jenna finally came up out of her dark and miserable thoughts to realize that the carriage driver—a long-term Time Tours employee— was talking steadily to someone who hadn't been listening. The man was pattering on about the city having taken out a whole triangular-shaped city block three years previously. "Demolished the entire length of Glasshouse Street, to cut Shaftesbury Avenue from Bloomsbury to Piccadilly Circus. Piccadilly hasn't been a true circus since, y'see, left it mighty ugly, most folks are saying, but that new Shaftesbury Avenue, now, it's right convenient, so it is . . ."

Not that Jenna cared a damn what streets were brand new, but she tried to pay more attention, because she was going to have to get used to living here, maybe for a long time. Longer than she wanted to think about, anyway. The carriage with its heavy load of luggage passed through the apparently blighted Piccadilly Circus, which looked perfectly fine to Jenna, then jolted at last to a halt in front of the Piccadilly Hotel, with its ornate wrought-iron dome rising like the bare ribs of Cinderella's pumpkin coach. The whole open-work affair was topped by a rampant team of horses drawing a chariot. Wet streets stood puddled with the recent rain. As Jenna climbed cautiously down, not wanting to fall and break a bone, for God's sake, thunder rumbled overhead, an ominous warning of more rain squalls to come.

The driver started hauling trunks and cases off the luggage shelf at the back of the carriage while Jenna trudged into the hotel's typically fussy Victorian lobby. The room was dark with heavy, ornately carved wood and busy, dark-hued wallpaper, crowded with breakables and ornate ornamentation in wrought iron. Jenna went through the motions of signing the guest register, acquiring her key, and climbing the stairs to her room, all in a daze of exhaustion. She'd been running ever since Luigi's in New York, didn't even want to think about how many people had died between then and now. The driver arrived on Jenna's heels and waited with a heavy load of luggage while Jenna unlocked her stuffy, overly warm room. A coal fire blazed in a hearth along one wall. The driver, puffing from his exertions, was followed in by a bellman who'd assisted the driver in lugging up the immense trunk where Ianira Cassondra lay safely hidden. At least, Jenna hoped she was safe inside that horrible cocoon of leather and brass fittings. When the bellman nearly dropped one end, Jenna's ragged temper exploded again.

"Careful with that!" It came out far more sharply than she'd meant it to, sharp and raggedly frightened. So she gulped and tried to explain her entirely-too-forceful concern. "It has valuable equipment inside. Photographic equipment."

"Beggin' your pardon, sir," the uniformed bellman huffed, gingerly setting down his end, "no wonder it's so heavy, cameras are big things, and all those glass plates and suchlike."

"Yes, well, I don't want anything in that trunk damaged."

The Time Tours driver gave Jenna a sour look. Clearly he'd been on the receiving end of too many tourists' cutting tongues. Driver and bellman vanished downstairs to fetch up the rest of the baggage, making short work of it. Jenna tipped the hotel employee, who left with a polite bow, closing the door after himself. The driver showed her how the gas lights worked, lighting them, then turning one of them out again, the proper way. "If you just blow it out, gas'll still come flooding out of the open valve. They haven't started putting in the smelly stuff yet, so you'd never even notice it. Just asphyxiate yourself in your sleep, if you didn't accidentally strike a spark and blow yourself out of this room."

Jenna was too tired for lectures on how the whole Victorian world operated, but she made a valiant effort to pay attention. The Time Tours driver was explaining how to summon a servant and how to find "Benny Catlin's" rented flat in Cheapside, across the Holborn Viaduct—whatever that was. Jenna didn't know enough about London and hadn't been given a chance to finish her library research for the trip she and Carl had planned to make. "We'll send an express wagon round in the morning, Mr. Catlin, help you shift to your permanent lodgings. Couldn't have you arriving at the flat this late in the evening, of course, the landlady would have a cultured fit of apoplexy, having us clatter about and disturb her seances or whatever she'll have there tonight, it's always something new . . ."

A polite tap at the door interrupted. "Mr. Catlin?" a man's voice inquired.

"Yes, come in, it isn't locked." *Yet* . . . The moment the driver was gone, Jenna intended locking the door and putting a small army of little up-time burglar alarms she'd brought with her on every windowsill and even under the doorknob. The door swung open and Jenna caught one glimpse of the two men in the hallway. Jenna registered the guns they held faster than with the driver. Jenna dove sideways with a startled scream as the pop and clack of modern, silenced semi-autos brought the driver down with a terrible, choked sound. Jenna sprawled to the floor behind the bed, dragging frantically at the Remington Beale's revolver concealed in her coat pocket. The driver was screaming in pain on the far side of the bed. Then Jenna was firing back, bracing her wrists on the feather-ticking of the mattress to steady her hands. Recoil kicked her palms, jarred the bones of her wrists. The shattering noise of the report left Jenna's ears ringing. But one of the bastards went down with a surprised grunt and cry of pain.

Jenna kept shooting, trying to hit the other one. The second shooter had danced into the corridor again, cursing hideously. Smoke from her pistol hung like fog, obscuring her view of the doorway. The wounded driver, gasping with the effort, managed to grab the leg of a nearby washstand. He brought the whole thing crashing down across the wounded gunman's head. The crockery basin shattered, leaving a spreading pool of blood in its wake. Then bullets slammed into the wallpaper beside Jenna's head. She ducked, doing some swearing of her own, wet and shaky with raw terror. Jenna fired and the pistol merely clicked. Hands trembling, she fumbled for her other pre-loaded revolver.

The driver, grey-faced and grunting with the effort, was dragging himself across the floor. He left a sickening trail of blood, as though a mortally wounded garden snail had crawled across the carpets. Jenna fired above the man's head, driving the gunman in the doorway back into the corridor again, away from the open door. Then the driver was close enough. He kicked the door shut with his feet, hooked an ankle around a chair and gave a grunting heave, dragged it in front of the door. Then collapsed with a desperate groan.

Jenna lunged over the top of the bed, scrambled across the floor on hands and knees to avoid the bullets punching through the wooden door at head height, and managed to snap shut the lock. Then she grunted and heaved and shoved an entire bureau across the door, toppling it to form a makeshift barricade. The door secured, Jenna dragged the driver's coat aside. What she found left her shaking and swearing under her breath. She didn't have time, dammit . . . but she couldn't just let the man lie there and bleed to death, could she? It was all Jenna's fault the man had been shot at all. She stripped a coverlet off the bed, managed to tear it into enough strips and pieces to form a tight compress. She had to yank off her gentleman's gloves to tie knots in the makeshift bandages.

"What in hell's going on, Catlin?" the driver gasped out, breathing shallowly against the pain.

"Long story," Jenna gasped. "And I'm really sorry you got dragged into it." She ran a distracted hand through her cropped and Macassar-oiled hair, felt the blood on her hands, wiped them on the remnants of the coverlet. A pause in the shooting outside indicated the gunman's need to change magazines or maybe even guns, temporarily stopping him from turning the solid wooden door into a block of swiss cheese. Jenna bit one lip, then scrambled across the floor on hands and knees. "Look, I can't do much for you. I've got to get the hell out of here. I'm really sorry." She handed the driver a pistol scavenged from the dead gunman. Then Jenna retrieved the Remington she'd emptied at their attackers and wished there was time to reload it, but the gun was so slow and difficult to load, she just shoved it into the waistband of her trousers beside the partially loaded one.

Then she wrenched up the nearest window sash and let in a flood of relatively fresh, wet air. It stank, but coal smoke smelled better than the coppery stench of blood and burnt gunpowder in the room's close confines. Jenna glanced down, judged the drop. Even with Ianira, she ought to be able to manage it without injury. Maybe ten feet. She opened the trunk, barely able to control her fingers. Holding the trunk lid open with one hand, she dragged Ianira up out of the protected cocoon in which she'd traveled. The Prophetess was fumbling with the oxygen mask and bottle, clumsy and slow from the cramped confines of the trunk. Jenna tore them loose and dropped them back in. "Trouble," she said tersely. "They hit us faster than I expected."

Ianira was taking in the blood, the corpse on the carpet, the wounded driver. Her eyes had gone wide, dark and terrified. She had to lean against Jenna just to remain on her feet, which terrified *Jenna*.

"What the hell—?" The driver was staring. "Who's *that?*"

Jenna gave him a sharp stare. "You don't know?"

"Should I? Been living in London for the past eight years. Haven't been back on the station in at least seven . . ."

If this guy didn't know who Ianira Cassondra was, Jenna wasn't about to tell him.

"I'm going to lower you out the window," Jenna whispered tersely, so her voice wouldn't carry beyond the door. "Hold onto my wrists *tight*." Ianira climbed over the sill and held onto Jenna's wrists with enough force to leave bruises. Jenna grunted and shifted her weight, swinging Ianira out, lowering her as far down along the wall as she could reach. "Now! Jump!"

Ianira plunged downward, staggered, landed. "Hurry!" the prophetess called up.

Jenna climbed cautiously across the windowsill, carefully balancing herself, and inched around until she was facing the hotel room. Bullets had started punching through the stout wooden door again. The gunman was shoving at it, too, trying to break it down or splinter the lock out of the doorframe. Thank God for solid Victorian construction, plaster and lathe walls and genuine wooden doors, not that hollow-core modern crap.

"Sorry, really," Jenna gasped, meeting the driver's bewildered, grey-faced gaze. "If he gets through that door, shoot him, will you? If you don't, he'll kill you." Then she scraped her way down until she was just hanging by her fingertips and let go her hold on the window. Jenna shoved outward slightly to keep her face from bashing against the wall on the way down. The drop was longer than she expected, but she landed well. Only went to one knee, jarring the soles of her feet up through her ankles. When she straightened with a pained gasp, her legs even condescended to work. Ianira grabbed her hand and they stumbled toward the carriage.

And the gunman charged out of the hotel's entryway. Gun in hand, he was heading for the window they'd just jumped from. But he hadn't seen them yet . . . Jenna dragged her loaded gun out of her waistband again, cursing herself for not holding onto it, and shoved Ianira behind her. The gunman saw them just as Jenna fired. She managed to loose off a couple of shots that drove their pursuer back into the hotel while smoke bellied up from her pistol and hung in the air like wet fog.

Jenna didn't wait for a second opportunity. She turned and ran, dragging Ianira with her, unable to reach the carriage without exposing them both to fatal fire. Ianira couldn't run very fast at first, but found her stride as they whipped through an alleyway, dodged into the street beyond, and gained speed. "Is he still back there?" Jenna gasped, not wanting to risk a wrenched ankle despite a driving terror that she would feel a bullet through her back at any second.

"Yes . . . I cannot see him . . . but he still comes, not far behind . . ."

Jenna decided she didn't want to know how Ianira knew that. She cut down side streets, running flat out, then heard a bullet ricochet off the wall beside her. Jenna shoved Ianira ahead, whirled and snapped off a couple of wild shots, then ducked down another street with one hand around Ianira's wrist. They wove in and out between horse-drawn phaetons and heavier carriages, running flat out. Drivers and passengers shouted after them, stared open-mouthed and hurled curses as horses reared in surprised protest. Then they were running down yet another street, dodging past the biggest greenhouse Jenna had ever seen.

They were nearly to a columned portico beyond, which offered better cover, when something slammed against her hips. Jenna screamed in pain and fright. She crashed to the ground, trying to roll onto her back. Jenna jerked the gun around, fired point-blank into the gunman's belly—

And the pistol clicked over an empty chamber.

She'd shot it dry.

"*Run!*" Jenna kicked and punched whatever she could reach, scrambled to hands and knees, saw Ianira racing for the shelter of the portico. Shadowy movement behind the columns suggested someone watching. *Please God, let it be someone who can help.* Jenna gained her feet, staggered forward a single stride. A hand around her ankle brought her down again. The glint of a knife caught her peripheral vision. Jenna kicked hard, felt bone crunch under the toe of her boot. The gunman screamed. Jenna rolled frantically, tried to free herself as the bastard swung the knife in a smashing blow toward her unprotected belly—

A gunshot exploded right above Jenna. She screamed, convinced she'd just been shot. Then she realized she wasn't hit. A stranger had appeared from the darkness. The newcomer had fired that shot, not the man trying to murder her. The bullet had plowed straight through the back of the paid assassin's head. The hit-man who'd hunted them through the Britannia was dead. *Messily* dead. The explosive aftermath left Jenna shuddering, eyes clenched shut. Blood and bits of human brain had spattered across her face and neck and coat. She lay on her side, panting and shaking and fighting back nausea. Then she looked up, so slowly it might've taken a week just to lift her gaze from the wet street to the stranger's face. She expected to find a constable, recalled a snatch of memory that suggested London constables had not carried firearms in 1888, and found herself looking up into the face of a man in a dark evening coat and silk top hat.

"Are you unharmed, sir? And the lady?"

Ianira had fallen to her knees beside Jenna, weeping and touching her shoulder, her arm, her blood-smeared face. "I . . ." Jenna had to gulp back nausea. "I think I'm okay."

The stranger offered a hand, calmly putting away his pistol in a capacious coat pocket. Jenna levered herself up with help. Once on her feet, she gently lifted Ianira and checked her pulse. Jenna didn't like the look of shock in the Cassondra's eyes or the desperate pallor of her skin, which was clammy and cold under her touch.

The stranger's brows rose. "Are you a doctor, sir?"

Jenna shook her head. "No. But I know enough to test a pulse point."

"Ah . . . As it happens, I *am* a medical doctor. Allow me."

The down-timer physician took Ianira's wrist to test her pulse, himself. And the Prophetess snapped rigid, eyes wide with shock. The Cassondra of Ephesus uttered a single choked sound that defied interpretation. She lifted both hands—gasped out something in

Greek. The doctor stared sharply at Ianira and spoke even more sharply—also in Greek. While Jenna was struggling to recall a snatch of history lesson, that wealthy men of society had learned Greek and Latin as part of a gentleman's education, the physician snarled out something that sounded ugly. Naked shock had detonated through his eyes and twisted his face.

The next moment, Jenna found herself staring down the wrong end of his gun barrel. "Sorry, old chap. Nothing personal, you know."

He's going to kill me!

Jenna flung herself sideways just as the gun discharged. Pain caught her head brutally and slammed her to the street. As the world went dark, she heard shouts and running footsteps, saw Ianira's knees buckle in a dead faint, saw the stranger simply scoop her up and walk off with her, disappearing into the yellow drizzle.

Then darkness crashed down with a fist of brutal, black terror.

(((Chapter 8)))

Malcolm Moore had done a great deal of hard work during his career as freelance time guide. But nothing had come even remotely close to the bruising hours he'd put in setting up a base camp in a rented hovel in Whitechapel Road, guiding scholars and criminologists through the East End from well before sunup until the early morning hours, sleeping in two- and three-hour snatches, assisting them in the task of learning everything the scholars and Scotland Yard Inspectors wanted to know before the terror broke wide open on the final day of August.

The last thing Malcolm expected when the Britannia cycled near dusk, just nine hours before the first Ripper murder was what he found in the Spaldergate parlour. Having rushed upstairs from his work with the scholars ensconced in the cellar, he stood blinking in stupid shock at the sight of her. "*Margo?*"

"Malcolm!" His fiancée flung herself toward him, arms outstretched, eyes sparkling. "Oh, Malcolm! I *missed* you!"

The kiss left his head spinning. Giddy as a schoolboy and grinning like a fool, Malcolm drew back at last, reluctant to break away from the vibrant warmth of her, and stared, amazed, into her eyes. "But Margo, whatever are you *doing* here?"

"Reporting for duty, sir!" she laughed, giving him a mock salute. "Kit worked it out with Bax," she said in a rush, eyes sparkling. "I'll be guiding for the rest of the Ripper Watch tour, whatever you think I can handle, and Doug Tanglewood came through to help out, too, your message asking for assistance came through loud and clear!"

Malcolm grinned. "Bloody *marvelous!* It's about time those dratted johnnies at Time Tours listened to me. How many additions to the Team did you bring through?"

Margo grimaced expressively.

"Oh, dear God," he muttered, "that many?"

"Well, it's not too bad," Margo said guardedly. "Dr. Shahdi Feroz finally made it in. Mostly, it's those reporters. Guy Pendergast and Dominica Nosette. I don't know which is worse, honestly, the scholars or the newsies. Or the tourists," she added, rolling her eyes at the flood of Ripperoons crowding into Spaldergate's parlour.

"That, I can believe," Malcolm muttered. "We haven't much time to get them settled. Polly Nichols is scheduled to die at about five o'clock tomorrow morning, which means we'll have to put our surveillance gear up sometime after two A.M. or so, when the pubs close and the streets grow a little more quiet. Daren't put up the equipment sooner, someone might notice it. It's not likely, since the wireless transmitters and miniaturized cameras and microphones we'll be setting up are so small. Still and all . . . Let's get them settled quickly, shall we, and take them downstairs to the vault. We've a base camp out in Whitechapel, but the main equipment is here, beneath Spaldergate, where we've the power for computers and recording equipment."

Margo nodded. "Okay. Let's get them moving. And the sooner we get those reporters under wraps, the better I'll feel. They don't listen at all and don't follow rules very well, either."

Malcolm grunted. "No surprise, there. The tourists the past few weeks have been bad enough, trying to duck out on their tour guides so they can cheat and stay long enough to see one of the murders. I expect the reporters will be even more delightful. Now, let's find Mrs. Gilbert, shall we, and assign everyone sleeping quarters . . ."

An hour later, Malcolm and his fiancée escorted the newly arrived team members down into the vault beneath the house, where a perfectly ordinary wooden door halfway across a perfectly standard Victorian cellar opened to reveal a massive steel door that slid open on pneumatics. Beyond this lay a brightly lit computer center and modern infirmary. The scholars greeted one another excitedly, then immediately fell to squabbling over theories as well as practical approaches to research, while the newly arrived reporters busied themselves testing their equipment. Technicians nodded satisfactorily at the quality of the images and sound transmitted by cable from the carefully disguised receiving equipment on the roof of the house above this bubble of ultra-modern technology.

While the scholars and journalists worked, Margo quietly brought Malcolm up to date about events on the station. The news left Malcolm fretting, not just because the station was in danger if the riots continued, but because there was literally nothing he could do to help search for Ianira or her family while trapped on this side of the Britannia Gate. "I've heard about the *Ansar Majlis*," Malcolm said tiredly, rubbing his eyes and the bridge of his nose. "Too much, in fact."

"You had friends on TT-66, didn't you?" Margo asked quietly, laying one gentle hand on his sleeve.

Malcolm sighed. "Yes. I'm afraid I did."

"Anyone . . ." she hesitated, looking quite abruptly very young and unsure of herself.

Malcolm stroked her cheek. "No, Margo. No one like that." He drew her close for a moment, blessing Kit for sending her here. He'd have to turn around and send her into danger out on the streets, he knew that, it was part of the dream which burned inside her and made her the young woman he loved so much; but for the moment, he was content merely to have her close. "Just very good friends, guides I'd known for years."

She nodded, cheek rubbing against the fine lawn of the expensive gentleman's shirt he'd put on to greet the new team members. "I'm sorry, Malcolm."

"So," he sighed, "am I. How much of the station had they managed to search before you had to leave?"

Margo's description of search efforts on station was interrupted by the shrill of the telephone on the computer console behind them. Hooked into a much more antique-looking telephone in the house above, it was a direct link between the outside world and the vault. Malcolm pulled reluctantly away and snagged the receiver. "Yes?"

It was Hetty Gilbert, co-gatekeeper of the Time Tours Gatehouse. The news she had was even worse than Margo's. All color drained from Malcolm's cheeks as he listened. "Oh, dear God. Yes, of course. We'll come up straight away."

"What is it?" Margo asked breathlessly as he hung up again.

"Trouble. Very serious trouble." He glanced at the monitor where, a few hours from now, they hoped to record the identity of Jack the Ripper. Weeks, he'd put in, preparing for that moment. And now it would have to wait. Reluctantly, Malcolm met Margo's gaze again.

"What *is* it?" Margo demanded, as if half-afraid to hear the answer.

"We have a tourist missing," he said quietly. "A male tourist."

"Oh, my God."

"Yes. His name is Benny Catlin. The Gilberts are asking for our help with the search teams. Evidently, he has already killed someone in a brutal shooting at the Piccadilly Hotel. A Time Tours driver is in critical condition, should be arriving within minutes for surgery. He managed to telephone from the hotel before he collapsed."

The animated excitement of the anticipated search for the Ripper's identity drained from Margo's face. Malcolm hated seeing the dread and fear which replaced it. Missing tourist . . . any time guide's worst nightmare. And not just any tourist, either, but one who'd already committed murder in a quiet Victorian hotel. A missing and homicidal tourist, search teams combing London at the beginning of the Ripper's reign of terror . . . and back on the station, riots and murders and kidnappings . . . Malcolm met Margo's frightened gaze, read the same bleak assessment in her eyes which coursed through his entire being. Margo's budding career as a time scout, her dreams, were as much on the line as his own. Malcolm hadn't seen Margo look so frightened since that horrible little prison cell in Portuguese Africa.

Wordlessly, he took her hand, squeezed her fingers. "We'd better get up there."

They headed upstairs at a dead run.

※ ※ ※

John Lachley hadn't planned to walk down past the Royal Opera, tonight.

But he'd emerged from his lecture at the Egyptian Hall to find the street blocked by an overturned carriage, which had collided with a team of drays, spilling the contents of a freight wagon and several screaming, hysterical ladies into the street, more frightned than injured. Glancing impatiently at his pocket watch, he'd determined that there was time, after all, before meeting Maybrick at his surgery in Cleveland Street, and rendered medical assistance, then pushed his way through the crowd and snarled traffic in search of a hansom he might hire.

It was sheer, blind chance which sent him down toward the Opera, where a rank of cabs could normally be found waiting for patrons. Sheer, bloody chance that had sent him straight into the path of a young woman who appeared from the murk of the wet night, gabbling out a plea for help. John Lachley had been at the wrong end of many an attack from vicious footpads, growing up in the East End, a target for nearly everyone's scorn and hatred. Rage had detonated through him, watching an innocent young man struggle with a knife-wielding assailant, fighting for his life.

So Lachley drew the pistol he'd concealed for the night's work with Maybrick and strode forward, ridding the street of this particular vermin with a single shot to the back of the skull. He expected the young man's shock, of course, no one reacted well to having blood and bits of brain spattered across his face, and he even expected the young woman's distraught reaction, nearly fainting under the strain of their close call.

But he did not expect what happened when he sounded the beautiful young woman's pulse. The words came pouring out of her, in flawless Greek, *ancient* Greek, even as she snapped rigid, straining away from him: *Death hangs on the tree beneath the vault . . . down beneath the bricks where the boy's sightless skull rests . . . and six shall die for his letters and his pride . . .*

This girl could not *possibly* know about the letters, about Tibor, about Morgan's skull, sitting as a trophy atop the flame-ringed altar, or the massive oak on which the little bastard had died. But she did.

And more, she had prophesied that five *others* should die for the sake of Eddy's accursed letters . . .

Who?

He couldn't even hazard an educated guess. But he intended to find out. Oh, yes, he most certainly intended to find out. He reacted with the swiftness a childhood in the East End had taught him, brought up the pistol to eliminate the young man whose life he'd just saved. "Sorry, old chap. Nothing personal . . ."

He discharged the gun at the same instant the shaken young man realized Lachley's intent. The blood-spattered man flung himself violently sideways, trying to save himself. The bullet grazed the side of his skull, sending him reeling, wounded, to the ground. Lachley snarled out an oath and brought the pistol up to fire again, while the girl screamed and fainted—

"Jenna!"

The shout was from almost directly in front of him. Lachley jerked his gaze up and found a wild-eyed woman in a shabby dress racing toward him, twenty yards away and closing fast. She had an enormous revolver in one hand and was pointing it right at Lachley. With only a split-second to decide, Lachley loosed off a wild shot at the approaching woman to delay her and snatched up the unconcious girl at his feet. A gunshot ripped through the damp night and a bullet whipped past his ear, knocking his top hat to the street. Lachley swore and bolted with his prize, flung her across one shoulder and ran down toward Drury Lane and SoHo's maze of mean, narrow streets.

He fully expected to hear the hue and cry sounded as constables were summoned; but no cry came, nor did any footsteps chase after him. Lachley slowed to a more decorous pace, discovering he was halfway down Drury Lane, and allowed his pulse to drop from its thunderous roar in his ears. With the panic of flight receding, rational thought returned. He paused for a moment in a narrow alley, shaking violently, then mastered himself and drew deep, gulping lungfuls of wet air to calm the tremors still ripping through him. *Dear God* . . . What was he to make of this?

He shifted the unconscious girl, cradled her in both arms, now, as though he were merely assisting a young lady in distress, and stared down at her pallid features. She was a tiny little thing, delicate of stature. Her face was exquisite and her rich black hair and olive cast of skin bespoke Mediterranean heritage. She'd gabbled out her plea for help in English, but the words spoken in shock—almost, he frowned, in a trance—had been the purest Greek he'd ever heard. But not modern Greek. *Ancient* Greek, the language of Aristotle and Aristophanes . . . yet with a distinctive dialectic difference he couldn't quite pin down.

He'd studied a great deal, since his charity school days, educated as a scholarship pupil at a school where the other boys had tormented him endlessly. He'd learned everything he could lay hands on, had drunk in languages and history the way East End whores downed gin and rum, had discovered a carton of books in the back of the school's dingy, mouldering library, books donated by a wealthy and eccentric patroness who had dabbled in the occult. John Lachley's knowledge of ancient languages and occult practices had grown steadily over the years, earning him a hard-earned reputation as a renowned SoHo scholar of antiquities and magical practices. Lachley could read three major ancient dialects of Greek, alone, and knew several other ancient languages, including Aramaic.

But he couldn't quite place the source of this girl's phrasing and inflections.

Her half-choked words spilled through his memory again and again, brilliant as an iron welder's torch. Who *was* this insignificant slip of a girl? As he peered at her face, stepping back out into Drury Lane to find a gaslight by which to study her, he realized she couldn't be more than twenty years of age, if that. Where had she learned to speak ancient Greek? Ladies were not routinely taught such things, particularly in the Mediterranean countries. And where in the names of the unholy ancient gods which Lachley worshiped had she acquired the clairvoyant talent he'd witnessed outside the Opera House? A talent of that magnitude would cause shockwaves through the circles in which Lachley travelled.

He frowned at the thought. Revealing her might prove dangerous at this juncture. Surely someone would miss the girl? Would search for her? No matter. He could keep her quite well hidden from any search and he intended to exploit her raw talent in every possible way he could contrive. His frown deepened as he considered the problem. It would be best to drug her for a bit, keep her quietly hidden at the top of the house, locked into a bedroom, until he could determine more precisely who she was, where she'd come from, and what efforts would be made to locate her by the young man and the poorly dressed woman with the revolver.

Beyond that, however . . .

Lachley smiled slowly to himself. Beyond that, the future beckoned, with this girl as the instrument by which he viewed it and Prince Albert Victor as the key to controlling it. John Lachley had searched for years, seeking a true mystic with such a gift. He'd read accounts in the ancient texts, written in as many languages as he had been able to master. His fondest dream had been to find such a gifted person somewhere in the sprawling metropolis that was capitol city to the greatest empire on earth, to bring them under his mesmeric control, to use their powers for his own purposes. In all his years of searching, he had found only charlatans, like himself, tricksters and knaves and a few pathetic old women mumbling over tea leaves and cut crystal spheres in the backs of Romany wagons. He had all but lost hope of finding a real talent, such as the ancient texts had described. Yet here she was, not only vibrantly alive, she'd quite literally run straight into his arms, begging his help.

His smile deepened. Not such a bad beginning to the evening, after all. And by morning, Eddy's letters would be safely in his hands.

Really, the evening was turning out to be most delightful, an adventure truly worthy of his skills and intellect. But before he quite dared celebrate, he had to make certain his prize did not succumb to shock and die before he could make use of her.

Lachley's hands were all but trembling as he carried her through increasingly poorer streets, down wretched alleyways, until he emerged, finally, with many an uneasy glance over his shoulder, onto the broad thoroughfare of the Strand, where wealth once again flaunted its presence in the houses of the rich and the fine shops they patronized. He had no trouble, there, flagging down a hansom cab at last.

"Cleveland Street," he ordered curtly. "The young lady's quite ill. I must get her to my surgery at once."

"Right, guv," the cabbie nodded.

The cab lurched forward at an acceptably rapid pace and Lachley settled himself to sound his prize's pulse and listen to the quality of her breathing. She was in deep shock, pulse fast and thready, skin clammy and chill. He cradled her head almost tenderly, wondering who the young man with her had been and who had attacked them. A Nichol footpad, most likely. They prowled the area near the Opera, targeting the wealthy gentlemen who frequented the neighborhood, so close to the slums of SoHo. That particular footpad's fatal loss, however, was his immense gain.

The cab made excellent time, bringing him to his doorstep before she'd even regained consciousness from her dead faint. Charles answered the bell, since fumbling for his key was too awkward while carrying her. His manservant's calm facade cracked slightly at the sight of his unconscious prize. "Whatever has happened, sir?"

"The young lady was attacked by footpads on the street. I must get her to the surgery at once."

"Of course, sir. Your scheduled patient has arrived a little early. Mr. Maybrick is waiting in the study."

"Very good, Charles," Lachley nodded, leaving the butler to close and lock the door. James Maybrick could jolly well wait a bit longer. He had to secure this girl, quickly. He carried her back through the house and set her gently onto the examining table, where he retrieved his stethoscope and sounded her heartbeat. Yes, shock, right enough. He found blankets, elevated her feet, covered her warmly, then managed to rouse the girl from her stupor by chafing her wrists and placing warm compresses along her neck. She stirred, moaned softly. Lachley smiled quietly, then poured out a draught of his potent aperitif. He was lifting the girl's head, trying to bring her round sufficiently to swallow it, when Charles appeared at the door to the surgery.

"Dr. Lachley, I beg pardon, sir, but Mr. Maybrick is growing quite agitated. He insists on seeing you immediately, sir."

Lachley tightened his hands around the vial of medicine and forcibly fought back an unreasoning wave of rage. *Ill-timed bastard!*

I'll bloody well shoot him through the balls when this night's business is done! "Very well!" he snapped. "Tell him I'll be there directly."

The girl was only half-conscious, but more than awake enough to swallow the drug. He forced it past her teeth, then held her mouth closed when she struggled, weak and trembling in his grasp. A faint sound of terror escaped from between ashen lips before she swallowed involuntarily. He got more of the drug down her throat, then gave curt instructions to the waiting manservant. "Watch her, Charles. She's quite ill. The medicine should help her sleep."

"Of course, sir."

"Move her to the guest room as soon as the medicine takes hold. I'll check on her again after I've seen Mr. Maybrick."

Charles nodded and stepped aside to let him pass. Lachley stormed past, vowing to take a suitable vengeance for the interruption. Then he drew multiple calming breaths, fixed in place a freezing smile, and steeled himself to suffer the slings and arrows of a fortune so outrageous, even the bloody Bard would've been driven to murder, taking up arms against it. *One day,* he promised himself, *I shall laugh about this.*

Preferably, on the day James Maybrick dropped off a gallows.

Meanwhile . . .

He opened the door briskly and greeted the madman waiting beyond. "My dear Mr. Maybrick! So delighted to see you, sir! Now, then, what seems to be the trouble this evening . . ."

Beyond James Maybrick's pasty features, beyond the windows and their heavy drapes and thick panes of wavy glass, lightning flickered, promising another storm to match the one in Lachley's infuriated soul.

Kit Carson knew he was a hopelessly doting grandfather when, twenty-four hours after Margo's departure for London, he was seriously considering going through the Britannia the next time it opened, just to be near her. He missed the exasperating little minx more than he'd have believed possible. The apartment they shared was echoingly empty. Dinner was a depressingly silent affair. And not even the endless paperwork waiting for him at the Neo Edo's office could distract him from his gloom. Worse, they'd found no trace of Ianira

Cassondra, her husband Marcus, or the *cassondra's* beautiful children, despite the largest manhunt in station history. Station security hadn't been any more successful finding the two people who'd shot three men on station, either, despite their being described in detail by a full two dozen eyewitnesses.

By the next day, when the Wild West Gate cycled into Denver's summer of 1885, tempers amongst the security squads were running ragged. Ianira's up-time acolytes—many of them injured during the rioting—were staging protests that threatened to bring commerce in Little Agora to a screeching halt. And Kit Carson—who'd spent a fair percentage of his night working with search teams, combing the rocky bowels of the station for some trace of the missing down-timers— needed a drink as badly as a dehydrated cactus needed a desert rainstorm in the spring.

Unshaven and tired, with a lonely ache in his chest, Kit found himself wandering into Frontier Town during the pre-gate ruckus, looking for company and something wet to drown his sorrows. He couldn't even rely on Malcolm to jolly him out of his mood—Malcolm was down the Britannia with Margo, lucky stiff. A sardonic smile twisted Kit's mouth. Why he'd ever thought retirement would be any fun was beyond him. Nothing but massive doses of boredom mingled with thieving tourists who stripped the Neo Edo's rooms of everything from towels to plumbing fixtures, and endless gossip about who was doing what, with or to whom, and why. *Maybe I ought to start guiding, just for something to do?* Something that didn't involve filling out the endless government paperwork required for running a time-terminal hotel . . .

"Hey, Kit!" a familiar voice jolted him out of his gloomy maunderings. "You look sorrier than a wet cat that's just lost a dogfight."

Robert Li, station antiquarian and good friend, was seated at a cafe table outside Bronco Billy's, next to the Arabian Nights contruction crew foreman. Li's dark eyes glinted with sympathetic good humor as he waved Kit over.

"Nah," Kit shook his head, angling over to grab one of the empty chairs at Robert's table, "didn't lose a dogfight. Just missing an Imp."

"Ah," Robert nodded sagely, trying to look his inscrutable best. A maternal Scandinavian heritage had given the antiquarian his fair-skinned coloring, but a paternal Hong Kong Chinese grandfather had bequeathed Li his name, the slight almond shape of his eyes, and the self-ascribed duty to go inscrutable on command. "The nest empties and the father bird chirps woefully."

Kit smiled, despite himself. "Robert?"

"Yeah?"

"Save it for the tourists, huh?"

The antiquarian grinned, unrepentant, and introduced him to the foreman.

"Kit, meet Ammar Kalil Ben Mahir Riyad, foreman of the Arabian Nights construction team. We've just been discussing pre-Islamic Arabian artwork. He's worried about the Arabian Nights tourists, because they're going to try smuggling antiquities out through the gate and he wanted to know if I could help spot the thefts."

"Of course," Kit nodded, shaking hands across the table and greeting him in Arabic, of which he knew only a few words. The foreman smiled and returned the greeting, then his eyes turned serious. "I will stay only a moment longer, Mr. Carson, our work shift begins again soon." He hesitated, then said, "I wish to apologize for the problems some of my workers have caused. I was not given any choice in the men I brought into TT-86. Others did the hiring. Most of us are Suni, we have no quarrel with anyone, and even most up-time Shi'ia do not agree with this terrible Brotherhood. I did not know some of the men were members, or I would have refused to take them. If I could afford to send away those who started the fighting, I would. But it is not in my power to fire them and we are already behind schedule. I have docked their wages and written letters of protest to my superiors, which I will send through Primary when it opens. I have asked for them to be replaced with reliable workers who will not start riots. Perhaps," he hesitated again, looking very worried, "you could speak with your station manager? If the station deports them, I cannot be held responsible and my superiors will have to send reliable men to replace them, men who are not in the *Ansar Majlis*."

"I'll talk to Bull Morgan," Kit promised.

Relief touched his dark eyes. "Thank you, Mr. Carson. Your word means a great deal." He glanced at Robert and a hint of his smile returned. "I enjoyed very much discussing my country's ancient art with you, Mr. Li."

"The pleasure was mine," Robert smiled. "Let's meet again, when you have more time."

They shook hands, then the foreman took his leave and disappeared into the crowds thronging Frontier Town. Robert said, "Riyad's a good man. This trouble's really got him upset."

"Believe me, I'll take it up with Bull. If we don't stop this trouble, there won't be a station left for Riyad to finish working on."

Robert nodded, expression grim, then waved over a barmaid. "Name your poison, Kit. You look like you could use a dose. I know I could."

"Firewater," Kit told the barmaid. "A double, would you?"

"Sure, Kit." She winked. "One double firewater, coming right up. And another scotch?" she added, glancing at Robert's half-empty glass.

"No, make mine a firewater, too."

Distilled on station from God alone knew what, firewater was a favorite with residents. Tourists who'd made the mistake of indulging had occasionally been known to need resuscitation in the station infirmary. As they waited for their drinks to arrive, a slender young man in black, sporting a badly stained, red silk bandana, reeled toward them in what appeared to be the terminal stages of inebriation. His deeply roweled silver spurs jangled unevenly as he staggered along and his Mexican sombrero lay canted crookedly down over his face, adding to his air of disconsolate drunkenness.

"I'd say that kid's been tippling a little too much firewater, himself," Li chuckled.

The kid in question promptly staggered against their table. Robert's drink toppled and sloshed across the table. A lit candle dumped melted wax into Robert's plate and silverware scattered all over the concrete floor. The *caballero* rebounded in a reeling jig-step that barely kept him on his feet, and kept going, trailing a stench of whiskey and garlic that set both Kit and Robert Li coughing. A baggage porter, bent nearly double under a load of luggage, trailed gamely after him, trying to keep his own course reasonably straight despite his employer's drunken meanderings through the crowd.

"Good God," Kit muttered, picking up scattered silverware as Robert mopped up the spill on the table, "is that idiot *still* drunk?"

"Still?" Robert Li asked as the waitress brought their drinks and whisked away the mess on the table.

"Yeah," Kit said, sipping gingerly at his firewater, "we saw him yesterday. Kid was bragging about winning some shooting competition down the Wild West Gate."

"Oh, that." Robert nodded as the drunken tourist attempted to navigate thick crowds around the Denver Gate's departures lounge. He stumbled into more people than he avoided, leaving a trail of profanity in his wake and more than a few ladies who made gagging noises when he passed too close. "Yes, there's a group of black-powder enthusiasts from up time going through this trip, mostly college kids, some veteran shooters. Plan to spend several weeks at one of the old mined-out ghost towns. They're running a horseback, black-powder competition, one that's not bound by Single Action Shooting Society rules and regulations. Paula Booker, of all people, came in the other day, told me all about it. She's taking a vacation, believe it or not, plans to compete for the trophy. Bax told the tour organizers they had to take a surgeon with 'em, in case of accidents, so Paula made a deal to trade her skills in exchange for the entry fee and a free gate ticket."

Kit chuckled. "Paula always was a smart lady. Good for her. She hasn't taken a vacation in years."

"She was all excited about the competiton. They can't use anything but single-action pistols in up-time sanctioned competitions any more, which kind of takes the variety out of a shooting match that's supposed to be based on actual historical fact."

Kit snorted. "I'd say it would. Well, if that idiot," he nodded toward the wake of destruction the drunken tourist was leaving behind him, "would sober up, maybe he'd have a chance of hitting something. Like, say, the side of a building. But he's going to waste a ton of money if he keeps pouring down the whiskey."

Li chuckled. "If he wants to waste his money, I guess it's his business. I feel sorry for his porter, though. Poor guy. His boss already needs a bath and they haven't even left yet."

"Maybe," Kit said drily, "they'll dump him in the ghost town's gold-mining flume and scrub him off?"

Robert Li lifted his glass in a salute. "Here's to a good dunking, which I'd say he deserves if any tourist ever did."

Kit clinked his glass against his friend's and sipped, realizing as he did that he felt less lonely and out of sorts already. "Amen to that."

Bronco Billy's cafe was popular during a cycling of the Wild West Gate because its "outdoor" tables stood close enough to the departures lounge, they commanded a grand view of any and all shenanigans at the gate. Which was why Robert Li had commandeered this particular table, the best of the lot available. They spotted Paula in the departures lounge and waved, then Kit noticed Skeeter Jackson working the crowd. "Now, there's a kid I feel for."

Robert followed his gaze curiously. "*Skeeter?* For God's sake, why? Looks like he's up to his old tricks is all."

Kit shook his head. "Look again. He's hunting, all right. For Ianira and Marcus and their kids."

Robert glanced sidelong at Kit for a moment. "You may just be right about that."

Skeeter was studying arrivals intently, peering from face to face, even the baggage handlers. The expression of intense concentration, of waning hope, of fear and determination, were visible even from this distance. Kit understood how Skeeter felt. He'd had friends go missing without a trace, before. Scouts, mostly, with whom the odds had finally caught up, who'd stepped through a gate and failed to return, or had failed to reach the other side, Shadowing themselves by inadvertently entering a time where they already existed. It must be worse for Skeeter, since no one expected resident down-timers to go missing in the middle of a crowded station.

Kit sat back, wondering how long Skeeter would push himself, like this, before giving up. Station security already had. The wannabe gunslinger approached the ticket counter to present his ticket and identification. He had to fish through several pockets to find it.

"Joey Tyrolin!" he bellowed at a volume loud enough to carry clear across the babble of voices to their table. "Sharpshooter! Gonna win me tha' shootin' match. Git me that gold medal!"

The unfortunate ticket agent flinched back, doubtless at the blast of garlic and whiskey fired point-blank into her face. Kit, who'd been able to read lips for several decades, made out the pained reply, spoken rapidly and to all appearances on one held breath: "Good-evening-Mr.-Tyrolin-let-me-check-you-in-sir-yes-this-seems-to-be-in-perfect-order-go-right-on-through-sir . . ."

Kit had never seen any Time Tours employee check any tourist through any gate with such speed and efficiency, not in the history of Shangri-La Station. Across the table, Robert Li was sputtering with laughter. The infamous Mr. Tyrolin, weaving on his cowboy-booted feet, turned unsteadily and peered out from under his cockeyed sombrero. He hollered full blast at the unfortunate porter right behind him. "Hey! Henry or Sam or whoever y'are! Get m'luggage over here! Li'l gal here's gotta tag it or somethin' . . ."

The poor baggage handler, dressed in a working man's dungarees and faded check shirt, staggered back under the blast, then ducked his head, coughing. His own hat had already slid down his brow, from walking bent double. The brim banged his nose, completely hiding his face as the unlucky porter staggered up to the counter and fumbled through pockets for his own identification. He presented it to the ticket agent along with Mr. Tyrolin's baggage tags and managed, in the process, to drop half his heavy load. Cases and leather bags scattered in a rain of destruction. Tourists in line behind him leaped out of the way, swearing loudly. The woman directly behind the hapless porter howled in outrage and hopped awkwardly on one foot.

"You *idiot!* You nearly broke my foot!" She hiked up a calico skirt and peered at her shoe, a high-topped, multi-buttoned affair with a scuff visible across the top where a case had crashed down on top of it. Tears were visible on her face beneath the brim of her calico sunbonnet. "Watch what you're doing, you fumble-fingered moron!"

The porter, mouthing abject apologies, was scrambling for the luggage while the ticket clerk, visibly appalled, was rushing around the counter to assist the injured tourist.

"Ma'am, I'm so dreadfully sorry—"

"You ought to be! For God's sake, can't you get him out of the way?" The unfortunate porter had lost his balance again and nearly crashed into her a second time. "I paid six thousand dollars for this ticket! And that clumsy jackass just dropped a trunk on my foot!"

The harried ticket agent was thrusting the porter's validated ticket into the nearest pocket she could reach on his dungarees, while waving frantically for baggage assistance and apologizing profusely. "I'm terribly sorry, we'll get this taken care of immediately, ma'am, would you like for me to call a doctor to the gate to see your foot?"

"And have them put me in a cast and miss the gate? My God, what a lot of idiots you are! I ought to hire a lawyer! I'm sorry I ever signed that stupid hold harmless waiver. Well don't just stand there, here's my ticket! I want to sit down and get off my poor foot! It's swelling up and hurts like hell!"

Time Tours baggage handlers scrambled to the porter's assistance, hauling scattered luggage out of the way so the irate, foot-sore tourist could complete her check-in procedure and hobble over to the nearest chair. She sent endless black and glowering glares at the drunken Joey Tyrolin and his porter, who was now holding his employer's head while that worthy was thoroughly sick into a decorative planter. Another Time Tours employee, visibly horrified, was fetching a wet cloth and basin. Paula Booker and the other Denver-bound tourists crowded as far as possible from Joey Tyrolin's corner of the departures lounge. Even Skeeter Jackson was steering clear of the mess and its accompanying stench.

"Oh, Kit," Robert Li was wiping tears, he was laughing so hard. "I feel sorry for Joey Tyrolin when he sobers up! That lady is gonna make his life one miserable, living nightmare for the next two weeks!"

Kit chuckled. "Serves him right. But I feel sorrier for the porter, poor sap. *He's* going to catch it from both of 'em."

"Too true. I hope he's being well paid, whoever he is. Say, Kit, I haven't had a chance to ask, who do *you* think the Ripper's going to turn out to be?"

"Oh, God, Robert, not you, too?" Kit rolled his eyes and downed another gulp of firewater.

"C'mon, Kit, 'fess up. Bets are running hot and heavy it turns out to be some *up*-timer. But I know you. *I'm* betting you won't fall for that. Who is it? A deranged American actor appearing in *Dr. Jekyll and Mr. Hyde*? Mary Kelly's lesbian lover? Francis Tumblety, that American doctor who kept women's wombs pickled in jars? Aaron Kosminski or Michael Ostrog, the petty thief and con artist? Maybe Frederick Bailey Deeming, or Thomas Neil Cream, the doctor whose last words on the gallows were 'I am Jack—'? Or maybe a member of a Satanic cult, sacrificing victims to his Dark Lord? Like Robert Donston Stephenson or Aleister Crowley?"

Kit held up a hand, begging for mercy. "Please, enough! I've heard all the theories! I'd as soon believe it was Lewis Carroll or the queen's personal physician. The evidence is no better for them than for anybody else you've just named. Personally? If it wasn't James Maybrick, and the case against him is a pretty good one, if you don't discount the diary as a forgery—and the forensic and psychological evidence in favor of the diary are pretty strong—then I think it was a complete stranger, someone none of our Ripperologists has identified or even suspected."

"Or the Ripperoons who *think* they're Ripperologists," Li added with a mischievous glint in his eye. Every resident on station had already had a bellyful of the self-annointed "experts" who arrived on station to endlessly argue the merits of their own pet theories. "Well," Robert drawled, a smile hovering around the corners of his mouth, "you may just be right, Kit. Guess we'll find out next week, won't we?"

"Maybe," Kit chuckled. "I'd like to see the faces of the Ripper Watch Team if it *does* turn out to be somebody they've never heard of."

Robert laughed. "Lucky Margo. Maybe she'll take pictures?"

Kit gave his friend a scowl. "She'd better do more than take a few snapshots!"

"Relax, Grandpa, Margo's a bright girl. She'll do you proud."

"That," Kit sighed, "is exactly what I'm afraid of."

Robert Li's chuckle was as unsympathetic as the wicked twinkle in his eyes.

When, Kit wondered forlornly, did he get to start *enjoying* the role of grandpa? *The day she gives up the notion of scouting,* his inner voice said sourly. Trouble was, the day Margo gave up the dream of scouting, both their hearts would break. Sometimes—and Kit Carson was more aware of the fact than most people—life was no fair at all. And, deep down, he knew he wouldn't have wanted it any other way. Neither would Margo. And that, Kit sighed, was one reason he loved her so much.

She was too much like him.

God help them both.

Ianira Cassondra did not know where she was.

Her mind was strangely lethargic, her thoughts slow and disjointed. She lay still, head aching, and knew only cold fear and a sickening sense of dislocation behind her eyelids. The smells and distant sounds coming through the fog in her mind were strange, unfamiliar. A harsh, acrid stink, like black dust in the back of her throat . . . a rhythmic ticking that might have been an old-fashioned clock like the ones in Connie Logan's shop or perhaps the patter of rain against a roof . . . That wasn't possible, of course, they couldn't hear rain in the station.

Memory stirred, sharp and terrible despite the lassitude holding her captive, whispered that she might not be in the station. She'd been smuggled out of TT-86 in Jenna Caddrick's steamer trunk. And something had gone terribly wrong at the hotel, men had come after them with silenced, up-time guns, forcing them to flee through the window and down the streets. She was in London, then. But where in London? Who had brought her to this place? One of the men trying to kill them? And why did she feel so very strange, unable to move or think clearly? Other memories came sluggishly through the murk. The attack in the street. Running toward the stranger in a top hat and coat, begging his help. The belch of flame and shattering roar of his pistol, shooting the assassin. The touch of his hand against her wrist—

Ianira stiffened as shock poured through her, weak and disoriented as she was. *Goddess!* The images slammed again through her mind, stark and terrible, filled with blood and destruction. And with that memory came another, far more terrible: their benefactor's pistol raised straight at Jenna's face, the nightmare of the gun's discharge, Jenna's long and terrible fall to the pavement, blood gushing from her skull . . .

Ianira was alone in London with a madman.

She began to tremble and struggled to open her eyes, at least.

Light confused her for a moment, soft and dim and strange. She cleared her vision slowly. He had brought her to an unknown house. A fire burned brightly in a polished grate across from the bed where she lay. The room spoke of wealth, at least, with tasteful furniture and expensive paper on the walls, ornate decorations carved into the woodwork in the corners of the open, arched doorway leading to another room, she had no idea what, beyond the foot of her bed. Gaslight burned low in a frosted glass globe set into a wall bracket of polished, gleaming brass. The covers pulled up across her were thick and warm, quilted and expensive with embroidery.

The man who had brought her to this place, Ianira recalled slowly, had been dressed exceedingly well. A gentleman, then, of some means, even if a total madman. She shuddered beneath the expensive covers and struggled to sit up, discovering with the effort that she could not move her head without the room spinning dizzily. *Drugged . . .* she realized dimly. *I've been drugged. . . .* Fear tightened down another degree.

Voices came to her, distantly, male voices, speaking somewhere below her prettily decorated prison. *What does he want of me?* She struggled to recall those last, horrifying moments on the street with Jenna, recalled him snarling out something in her own native language, the ancient Greek of her childhood, realized it had been a curse of shock and rage. *How did a British gentleman come to know the language of ancient Athens and Ephesus?* Her mind was too slow and confused to remember what she had learned on station of Londoners beyond the Britannia Gate.

The voices were closer, she realized with a start of terror. Climbing toward her. And heavy footfalls thudded hollowly against the sound of stairs. Then a low, grating, metallic sound came to her ears and the door swung slowly open. "—see to Mr. Maybrick, Charles. The medication I gave him will keep him quiet for the next several hours. I'll come down and tend to him again in a bit, after I've finished here."

"Very good, sir."

Their voices sounded like the Time Tours Britannia guides, like the movies she and Marcus had watched about London. About—and her mind whirled, recalling the name this man had spoken, the name of Maybrick, a name she recognized with a chill of terror—about Jack the Ripper . . .

Then the door finished opening and he was there in the doorway, the man who had shot Jenna Caddrick and brought Ianira to this place. He stood unsmiling in the doorway for a long moment, just looking down into her open eyes, then entered her bedroom quietly and closed the door with a soft click. He turned an iron key in the lock and pocketed it. She watched him come with a welling sense of slow horror, could see the terrible blackness which hovered about him like a bottomless hunger . . .

"Well, then, my dear," he spoke softly, and pulled a chair close to sit down at her side. "I really didn't expect you to awaken so soon."

She would have cowered from the hand he rested against her temple, had she been able to move. The rage surrounding this man slammed into her senses. She cried aloud, as though from a physical blow.

"No need to be afraid, my dear. I certainly won't be harming you." He laughed softly, at some joke she could not fathom. "Tell me your name."

Her tongue moved with a will of its own. "Ianira . . ." The drugs in her veins roared through her mind, implacable and terrifying.

"Ianira? Where are you from? What last name have you?"

They called her Cassondra, after her title as priestess of Artemis. She whispered it out, felt as well as saw the surprise that rippled through him. "Cassondra? Deuced odd surname. Where the devil did you come from?"

Confusion tore through her. "The station—" she began.

"No, not the bloody train station, woman! Where were you born?"

"Ephesus . . ."

"*Ephesus?*" Shock tore through his eyes again. "You mean from the region of Turkey where that ancient place used to be? But why, then, do you speak Greek, when Turkestani is the language of that part of the world? And how is it you speak the Greek of Pericles and Homer?"

Too many questions, blurring together too quickly . . . He leaned across, seizing her wrist in a brutal grip. "Answer me!"

She cried out in mortal terror, struggled to pull away from the swamping horror of what she sensed in his soul. "Artemis, help me . . ." The plea was instinctive, choked out through the blackness flooding across her mind. His face swam into focus, very close to hers.

"Artemis?" he whispered, shock blazing through his eyes once more. "What do you know of Artemis, the Many-Breasted Goddess of Ephesus?"

The pain of his nearness was unendurable. She lapsed into the language of her childhood, pled with him not to hurt her, so . . .

He left her side, allowing relief to flood into her senses, but was gone only for a moment. He returned with a leather case, which he opened, removing a heavy, metal tube with a needle protruding from one end. "If you are unable to speak with what I've given you already," he muttered, "no power of hell itself will keep you silent with this in your veins."

He injected something into her arm, tore the sleeve of her dress to expose the crook of her elbow and slid the needle in. New dizziness flared as the drug went in, hurting with a burning pain. The room swooped and swung in agonizing circles.

"Now then, Miss Cassondra," the voice of her jailor came through a blur, "you will please tell me who you are and where you come from and who the man was with you . . ."

Ianira plunged into a spinning well of horror from which there was no possible escape. She heard her voice answer questions as though in a dream, repeated answers even she could not make sense of, found herself slipping deep into prophetic trance as the images streamed into her mind, a boy hanging naked from a tree, dying slowly under this man's knife, and a pitiful young man with royal blood in his veins, whose need for love was the most tragic thing about him, a need which had propelled him into the clutches of the man crouched above her now. Time reeled and spun inside her mind and she saw the terrified face of a woman, held struggling against a wooden fence, and other women, hacked to pieces under a madman's knife . . .

She discovered she was screaming only when he slapped her hard enough to jolt her from the trance. She lay trembling, dizzy and ill, and focused slowly on his eyes. He sat staring down at her, eyes wide and shocked and blazing with an unholy sort of triumph. "By God," he whispered, "what else can you do?"

When she was unable to speak, he leaned close. "Concentrate! Tell me where Eddy is now!"

The tragic, lonely young man flashed into her mind, surrounded by splendour such as Ianira had never dreamed might exist. He was seated at a long table, covered with gleaming silver and crystal and china edged in gold. An elderly woman in black Ianira recognized from photographs presided over the head of the table, her severe gaze directed toward the frightened young man.

"You are not to go wandering about in the East End again, Eddy, is that understood? It is a disgrace, shameful, such conduct. I'm sending you to Sandringham soon, I won't stand for such behavior . . ."

"Yes, Grandmama," he whispered, confused and miserable and frightened to be the object of her displeasure.

Ianira did not realize she had spoken aloud, describing what she saw until her jailor's voice shocked her back into the little room with the expensive coverlets and the gas lights and the drugs in her veins. "*Sandringham?*" he gasped. "The queen is sending him to Scotland? Bloody *hell* . . ." Then the look in his eyes changed. "Might be just as well. Get the boy out of the road for a bit, until this miserable business is finished. God knows, I won't risk having him connected with it."

Ianira lay trembling, too exhausted and overwhelmed by horror to guess at her fate, trapped in this madman's hands. He actually smiled down at her, brushing the hair back from her brow. "Your friends," he whispered intimately. "Will they search for you?"

Terror exploded. She flinched back, gabbled out the fear of pursuit, the gunmen in the hotel, the threat to her life from faceless men she had never met . . . Fear drained away at the sound breaking from him. *Laughter.* He was staring down into her eyes and laughing with sheer, unadulterated delight. "Dear God," he wheezed, leaning back in his chair, "they *daren't* search for you! Such a bloody piece of luck! No doubt," he smiled, "someone influential was disquieted by what you can do, my dear lady. Never fear, I shall protect you from all harm. You are much too precious, too valuable a creature to allow anyone to find you and bring you to grief." He leaned close and stroked the back of her hand. "Mayhap," he chuckled, "I'll even take you to wife, as an added precaution."

She closed her eyes against horror at such a fate.

He leaned down and brushed his lips to hers, then murmured, "I've work to do, this evening, my lovely pet, very serious work, which must take me from your side. And you must rest, recover from the shocks to your system. Tomorrow, however . . ." He chuckled then stroked her brow, the chill of her wet cheek. "Tomorrow should prove most entertaining, indeed."

He left her, drugged and helpless, in the center of the bed and carefully locked the door behind him. Ianira lay weeping silently until the medication he had given her dragged her down into darkness.

They didn't intend to stay long.

In fact, they hadn't intended to take the train to Colorado Springs with the rest of the tour group, or ride all the way out to the derelict mining camp in the mountains far to the west of the train station, not at all. Not with Artemisia and Gelasia asleep in a big, awkward trunk, sedated and breathing bottled oxygen from the same type of canisters they'd sent with Ianira into London. Marcus, terrified for his children's safety, had packed away a spare oxygen bottle for each of the girls, just in case something went wrong. And it had. Badly wrong.

They'd been followed through the Wild West Gate.

Just as Noah had predicted.

"His name's Sarnoff," Noah Armstrong muttered, pointing him out with a slight nod of the head. "Chief of security for a real bad sort named Gideon Guthrie. And Guthrie's specialty is making people disappear when they're too much of a threat. Real sweet company, Jenna's Daddy keeps. We can't do a damned thing yet. If we bolt now, he's just going to follow us. Then *he'll* choose the time and place, when there aren't a truckful of witnesses nearby. But if we head for that mining camp with the rest of the shooting competition tour, he'll *have* to follow us, with all those up-time witnesses lurking everywhere. Then *we* can choose the time and place, jump *him* when he's not expecting it."

"I can stick a knife through his ribs," Julius offered, glaring out from under the calico bonnet he'd donned in his role doubling for Jenna.

The detective said sharply, "No, not here!" When Julius looked like arguing, Noah shot a quelling look at the down-time teenager. "Too many witnesses. If we have to explain why murder is really self-defense, it'll just give the next death squad they send after us the chance they need to hit us while we're cooling our heels in the station's jail. So we wait until we're up in the mountains. Marcus, you'll be riding with the baggage mules when we leave the train station. Keep the trunk with the girls at the very back of the mule train. It's a long ride out there, so we'll have to switch out the oxygen canisters partway. Tell the other porters the mule's thrown a shoe or something, just get that trunk open and switch out the bottles. They'll both sleep until sometime tonight, but they'll need air in a few hours."

So that was what they did, Marcus trembling at the thought of the danger to his little girls. And he had no assurance that Ianira was safe, either, that no one had followed her to London. He bit one lip, wishing desperately they had all been able to go through one gate together as a family. But Jenna Caddrick and Noah Armstrong had argued the point forcefully.

Unfortunately, they hadn't brought anything like enough supplies to take his precious children all the way out to the rugged mining camp where the shooting competition was to be held. They'd planned for Marcus and the girls to bolt out of Denver, to ditch the tour and take a train east into the Great Plains which he had seen in so many cowboy movies. They would hide in one of the big cities like Chicago or St. Louis for three or four cycles of the Wild West Gate, just long enough for Noah to eliminate any threat which might come through from up time on the next cycle of the gate.

Then they could slip back onto the station, after Noah had gone back up time, taking to the legal authorities the proof which the detective had brought onto the station. Only when the men responsible for the murderous attacks had been jailed, would Marcus and his little family be safe again. And Julius, too. The teenage leader of Shangri-La's Lost and Found Gang had come through the Porta Romae, same as Marcus had. Julius was playing his part as Jenna's double with superb skill, laying a false trail for their pursuers to follow. His act at the departures lounge, dressed as an aggrieved lady tourist bawling about her injured foot had convinced onlookers, while Noah, acting the role of the drunken Joey Tyrolin, had drawn all attention away from Marcus, who'd needed to remain anonymous until safely on the other side of the gate.

Marcus had taken Julius' own station identification, so he could act as "Joey Tyrolin's" baggage porter to disguise his own identity. Julius had used a fake ID produced by the ever-resourceful Noah Armstrong. Jenna Caddrick had furnished it, as well as the money for the Denver Gate tickets. Marcus' throat closed, just thinking of the risk Noah and Jenna and young Julius were running to keep his family safe. Ianira and his children had never seemed so fragile to Marcus, never more precious to him. They had agreed to the charade, because they'd had no other choice.

But Marcus had never ridden a horse in his life. And while he had once been accustomed to the burning brilliance of a Mediterranean sun, he'd lived for several years in the sunless world of TT-86. Despite the broad-brimmed hat which shaded his face, by the time they were an hour out on the trail, Marcus was sunburnt, sore in more places than he'd realized his body possessed, and miserably homesick for the station and his wife and his many 'eighty-sixer friends.

"We'll go through with the itinerary we set up," Noah Armstrong told them on the trail. "That way, the bastard following us will think we haven't twigged to who he is. Any edge we can find, we need." Dressed in a cowboy's gear, Noah Armstrong was more difficult than ever to pigeonhole as a man or a woman. Each time Marcus thought he'd gathered enough clues to decide, the up-time detective did or said something which threw all his theories into chaos again.

Marcus had seen individuals like Noah Armstrong before, in the slave markets of Rome. Ambiguous in the way their bodies grew into adulthood, developing into neither man nor woman, such people were exceedingly rare in nature. But they were pitifully common on auction blocks. Boys in Roman slave markets were routinely castrated as children to preserve a child's sexless features and mannerisms, so they would grow into eunuchs. Neither male nor female, such artificially created eunuchs were valuable slaves. But those *born* that way fetched astronomical prices in Roman slave pens. Marcus had seen one such slave fetch half a million sesterces at auction—ten times the going rate for a highly educated scribe or Greek tutor. Romans, Marcus had learned over the years, were avaricious collectors. And the more unusual the item, or the individual, the greater the status in claiming its ownership. Whoever Noah was, the detective was luckier than he or she knew, to've been born up time, not down the Porta Romae.

As they rode out of Colorado Springs with dust from the horses' hooves hanging on the hot air, Julius frowned slightly under his calico bonnet brim. "Do you want me to go ahead and enter the shooting contest, then? I've watched a lot of movies, but I don't really know how to shoot a black-powder pistol."

"Don't worry about that," Armstrong reassured Marcus' young friend. "I'll show you how to load and operate the pistols tonight at camp, and I'll teach you to fire them. You don't have to shoot well enough to win or even qualify. Just make it look good, that's all we need. Long before the competition's over, we'll have nailed this bastard Sarnoff, so we can go back to Denver. When we've eliminated him, I'll want you to go with Marcus and the girls to the nearest train station. As soon as the men responsible for this have been arrested, I'll send word and we can bring everyone home again."

It sounded so simple . . .

But Marcus had learned the hardest way possible that nothing in life was ever simple, least of all a high-stakes game in which religion, political power, and human life were the stakes. During the long hours it took them to reach the mining camp, refurbish the ghost town to a livable state, and set up the shooting course, with Marcus periodically checking on his precious little girls to be sure they still slept and breathed comfortably in their snug cocoon, Marcus couldn't help glancing over his shoulder every few minutes, expecting disaster to strike them down at any moment.

He searched the faces of the others on the tour, the eager college-age kids who had gathered for a try at the medal, the older shooters who'd clearly been at this sport longer than the kids had been alive; he studied the guides supplied by Time Tours, the baggage handlers and mule drovers who tended the line of stubborn, slack-eared mules which had toted the equipment and personal baggage of the entire competition; and wondered what it must be like to be free to come and go as one pleased through the up-time world, through any gate, so long as the money was there to pay for a ticket. And each time the silent, hired killer who'd come through the gate with them glanced sidelong at Julius and himself, Marcus sweat into his dungarees and swallowed back sour fright.

Some of the tourists were talkative, laughing and bragging or sharing stories about other competitions they'd participated in. Some of them talked about re-enactments of historical battles involving thousands of people and weapons ranging from pistols to full-sized cannons. Marcus had seen cannons only in photographs and movies. Other tour members were loners, keeping to themselves, cleaning and oiling their guns regularly, working hard at tasks assigned to get the competition's complex course of fire laid out and the buildings refurbished, speaking little and wolfing down their supper in silence at mealtime. Impromptu sing-alongs and amateur musicians provided entertainment for those with the desire to socialize.

There was even—and their happiness left Marcus feeling more lonely and isolated than ever—a young couple who planned to marry during the competition. They had brought along a wedding dress, a bridesmaid, a best man, an officiant, and photographer for the happy occasion. The photographer snapped pictures of everything and everyone in sight with a digital camera, much to the irritation of Noah Armstrong. The one person in the tour Marcus avoided like plague was Paula Booker, the station's cosmetic surgeon. She was preoccupied, at least, by the fun of her vacation, and paid little attention to the baggage handlers where they sat in the shadows, eating their meal in silence.

But when Artemisia and Gelasia woke up from their long, drugged sleep, all hell broke loose—and Paula Booker recognized him. Her eyes widened in shock and she opened her mouth to speak . . . then closed it again, looking abruptly frightened. *She understands,* he realized with a jolt of hope, *she understands we are in danger, even if she is not sure of the cause.*

Meanwhile, the whole camp had erupted and the baggage manager, who was not an 'eighty-sixer, but an up-timer hired by the tour organizers, demanded to know what insanity had prompted him to bring two toddlers off the station. The uproar echoed off the black-shadowed mountains hemming them in.

Nearly stammering under the close scrutiny of Sarnoff, aware that Noah Armstrong's hand was poised on the grip of a pistol at the detective's side, Marcus offered the only explanation he could: "I am a down-timer and we are never allowed off the station, sir. My little girls have never seen the sun . . ."

It was true enough and more than a plausible reason. In fact, several women burst into tears and offered the sleepy girls candy and ribbons for their hair while other tourists, irate at such a notion, vented their wrath on the head baggage handler, protesting the cruelty of enforcing a law that didn't even permit down-timers' *children* to leave the station.

"It's not healthy!" one woman glared at the hapless Time Tours guides, men who lived full time down the Denver Gate, rarely returning to the station. They did not recognize him, thank all the gods. One woman in particular, the wedding photographer, was thoroughly incensed. "I've never heard of such an awful thing in all my life! Not letting little children go through a gate for some real sunshine! When I get home, you can believe I'm writing my congresswoman a nasty letter about this!"

Julius, playing the part of Cassie Coventina, added, "You certainly can't expect two little girls to sleep in that disgusting, filthy livery stable!" The disguised down-timer boy glanced at him, giving him and the children a winning smile, "They can stay in my cabin tonight. Every night, in fact. I've got plenty of room."

"Thank you," Marcus said with an exhausted, grateful smile.

So the girls moved into Julius' protective custody and Marcus and Noah watched the killer sent to stalk them, tracking him during their every waking moment, and Paula Booker followed them silently with her gaze, biting her lip now and again, clearly wanting to approach him and fearing to jeopardize his life, or perhaps her own, by doing so, while all of them, killer included, waited for the chance to strike. The man stalking them was too clever to wander off alone, where one or more of them could have sent him back to whatever gods had created him. They couldn't strike in front of witnesses any more than he could, but the chance everyone was waiting for came all too soon, during the endurance phase of the shooting games.

Marcus, burned to lobster red by the sun, was assigned the job of riding shadow on Julius' heels for this portion of the competition. The "endurance round" involved riding a looping, multiple-mile trail through the sun-baked mountains around the dusty gold-mining camp. The competitors were to pause at predetermined intervals to fire at pop-up targets placed along the trail like ambushes. Noah, deeply wary of Julius riding alone through the wild countryside, told Marcus quietly, "I want you to trail him, just far enough behind to stay in earshot. I'll trail you, same way."

Marcus, heart in his throat, just nodded. He couldn't keep his hands from trembling as he mounted his stolid plug of a horse and urged the animal into a shambling trot. He set a course that took him away from camp on a tangent, allowing him to loop back around and pick up Julius' trail just beyond the first ridge outside camp.

The sun blazed down despite the earliness of the hour. At least Julius' persona, Cassie Coventina, had drawn one of the early slots for riding the endurance course, so it wasn't too unbearably hot, yet. Dust rose in puffs where Marcus' horse plodded along the narrow, twisting trail. He urged the nag to a slightly faster shamble until he caught sight of "Miss Coventina" ahead, riding awkwardly in a high-pommeled side saddle. Marcus eased back, cocking his head to listen, reassured when Julius began to whistle, leaving him an audible trail to follow. Marcus glanced back several times and thought he caught a glimpse of "Joey Tyrolin" once or twice through the heat haze behind him.

Saddle leather squeaked and groaned under his thighs. Marcus began to sweat into his cotton shirt. He worried about the girls, back at camp, even though they were surrounded by fifteen adoring women who weren't riding the endurance trail until later in the afternoon, or who were part of the wedding and weren't competing at all. The mingled scent of dust and sweating horse rose like a cloud, enveloping his senses and drawing his mind inexorably back to the years he'd spent as a slave working for the master of the chariot races and gladiatorial games and bestiaries at the great Circus Maximus. The scent of excited, sweating race horses and dust clogged his memory as thoroughly as the scream of dying animals and men—

The sharp animal scream that ripped through the hot morning was no memory.

Marcus jerked in his saddle. Blood drained from his face as the scream came again, a horse in mortal agony. Then a high, ragged shriek of pain, a *human* shriek, tore the air . . . and the booming report of a gun firing shook the dusty air . . .

Marcus kicked his horse into a startled canter. He wrenched at the gun on his hip. From behind him, a clatter of hooves rattled in a sudden burst of speed. Noah Armstrong swept past as though Marcus' horse were plodding along at a sedate walk. Another gunshot split the morning air. Then Marcus was around the bend in the trail and the disaster spread out in front of him.

Julius was down.

His horse was down, mortally wounded.

Dust rose in a cloud along the trail, where Noah pursued whoever had shot down Marcus' friend. He hauled his own horse to a slithering halt and slid out of the saddle, then flung himself to the young Roman's side. Julius was still alive, ashen and grey-lipped, but thank the gods, still alive . . .

"Don't move!" Marcus was tearing at the boy's clothing, ripping open the dress he wore as disguise. The calico cotton was drenched with dark stains that weren't sweat. The bullet had gone in low, missing the heart, plowing instead through the gut. The boy moaned, gritted his teeth, whimpered. Marcus was already stripping off his own shirt, tearing it into strips, placing compresses to staunch the bleeding. In the distance, a sharp report floated back over the rocky hills, followed by three more cracking gunshots. Then hoofbeats crashed back toward them. Marcus snatched up his pistol again. Noah Armstrong appeared, riding hell for leather toward them. Marcus dropped the gun from shaking hands and tied the compresses tighter.

The detective slithered out of a sweaty saddle and crouched beside the fallen teenager. "Hold on, Julius, do you hear me? We'll get you back to camp. To that surgeon, Paula Booker."

"No . . ." The boy was clawing at Noah's arm. "They'll just kill you . . . and Marcus . . . the girls . . . he'll kill you . . ."

"Not that one," Noah said roughly. "He's dead. Shot the bastard out of his saddle. Left him for the buzzards."

"*Then they'll send someone else!*"

If they hadn't already . . .

The unspoken words hung in the air, as hot and terrifying as the coppery smell of Julius' blood. "Please . . ." Julius was choking out the words, "you can't afford to take me back. I'll only slow you down. Just get the girls and run, please. . . ." Marcus tried to hush the frantic boy. Guilt ripped through him. He'd allowed Julius to help—this was his fault. "Please, Julius, do not speak! You have not the strength. Here, can you swallow a little water?" He held his canteen to the boy's lips.

"Just a sip," Noah cautioned. "There, that's enough. Here, help me get him up. No, Julius, we have to go back to camp anyway, to rescue the kids. You're coming with us, so don't argue. Marcus, we'll put him on your horse." The detective glanced up, met Marcus' gaze. "He's right, you know. They will send someone else. And someone after that."

"What can we do?" Marcus felt helpless, bitterly afraid, furious with himself for bringing his young friend into this.

"We leave Julius with the camp surgeon, that's what. As soon as we get back to camp, you get the girls and take them back to the livery stable with you. During the confusion, you and I will leave camp with the kids. Take our horses and our gear and ride out. By the time they figure out we're gone, we'll be far enough away to catch a train out of the territory."

Marcus swallowed exactly once. "And go where?" he whispered.

"East. *Way* East. To New York." Noah held Marcus's gaze carefully, reluctance and regret brilliant in those enigmatic eyes. "And eventually," the detective added softly, "to London. Jenna and your wife will be there. We'll meet them."

Three *years* from now . . .

Marcus looked down into his young friend's ashen face, his pain-racked eyes, and knew they didn't have any choice. Three years in hiding . . . or this. When next Ianira saw their children, just hours after dropping them off at daycare, from her perspective, Artemisia would be nearly seven, Gelasia almost four. Gelasia might not even *remember* her mother. Ianira might well never forgive him. But he had no choice. They couldn't risk going back to the station, not even long enough to crash through the Britannia Gate. And crashing it was the only way they could get through the Britannia, because there wasn't a single ticket available for months, not until after the Ripper Season closed. Marcus bowed his head, squeezed shut his eyes. Then nodded, scarcely recognizing his own voice. "Yes. We will go to London. And wait." Three entire *years* . . .

Wordlessly, he helped the detective lift Julius to Marcus' saddle. Wordlessly, he climbed on behind his dying friend, steadied him and kept the boy from falling. Then turned his horse on the dusty, blood-spattered trail and left Julius' groaning, gut-shot mount sprawled obscenely across the path. A sharp report behind him, from Noah's gun, sent his pulse shuddering; but the agonized sounds tearing from the wounded horse cut off with that brief act of mercy. He tightened his hands around the sweaty wet leather of his reins.

And swore vengeance.

Jenna woke to the sensation of movement and the deep shock that she was still alive to waken at all. For a moment, the only thing in her mind was euphoria that she was still among the breathing. Then the pain hit, sharp and throbbing all along the side of her skull, and the nausea struck an instant later. She moaned and clenched her teeth against the pain—which only tightened the muscles of her scalp and sent the pain mushrooming off the scale. Jenna choked down bile, felt herself swoop and fall . . .

Then she lay propped across something hard, while she was thoroughly sick onto the street. Someone was holding her up, kept her from falling while she vomited. Memory struck hard, of the gun aimed at her face, of the roar and gout of flame, the agony of the gunshot striking her. She struggled, convinced she was in the hands of that madman, that he'd carried her off to finish her or interrogate her . . .

"Easy, there."

Whoever held her was far stronger than Jenna; hard hands kept her from moving away. Jenna shuddered and got the heaves under control, then gulped down terror and slowly raised her gaze from the filthy cobblestones. She lay propped across someone's thigh, resting against rough woolen cloth and a slim torso. Then she met the eyes of a woman whose face was shadowed by a broad-brimmed bonnet which nearly obscured her face in the darkness. Through the nausea and pain and terror, Jenna realized the woman was exceedingly poor. Her dress and coat were raggedy, patched things, the bonnet bedraggled by the night's rain. Gaslight from a nearby street lamp caught a glint of the woman's eyes, then she spoke, in a voice that sounded as poor and ragged as she was.

"Cor, luv," the woman said softly, "if you ain't just a sight, now. I've 'ad me quite a jolly time, so I 'ave, tryin' t' foller you all the way 'ere, an' you bent on getting yourself that lost and killed."

Jenna stared, wondering whether or not the woman had lost her mind, or if perhaps Jenna might be losing hers. Mad, merry eyes twinkled in the gaslight as a sharp wind picked up and pelted them with debris from the street. The shabby woman glanced at the clouds, where lightning flared, threatening more rain, then frowned. "Goin' t'catch yer death, wivout no coat on, and I gots t'find a bloody surgeon what can see to that head of yours. It's bled a fright, but in't as bad as it seems or likely feels. Just a scrape along above the ear. Bloody lucky, you are, *bloody* lucky." When Jenna stared at her, torn by nausea and pain and the conviction that she was in the hands of yet another down-time lunatic, the madwoman leaned closer still and said in a totally different voice, "Good God, kid, you really don't know me, do you?"

Jenna's mouth fell open. "*Noah?*"

The detective's low chuckle shocked her. Jenna had never heard Noah Armstrong laugh. They hadn't found much to laugh about, since their brutal introduction three days previously. Then she blinked slowly through the fog in her mind. *Three days?* But Noah and Marcus had gone down Denver's Wild West Gate. Or rather, *would* be going down the Wild West Gate. Tomorrow morning, on the station's timeline. Noah Armstrong shouldn't be *here* at all, on the night of Jenna's arrival. The night *before* Noah and Marcus were due to leave the station for Denver . . .

Mind whirling, Jenna asked blankly, "Where did you come from? How did you get here?"

The detective was pulling off a shabby black coat, which served to protect Jenna's head from the cold, damp wind. When Jenna touched gingerly, she found rough, torn cloth tied as makeshift bandages. They were wet and sticky. Noah said, "Let me carry you again, kid. You're just about done in from exhaustion and shock. I'll get you someplace safe and warm as soon as I can."

Jenna lay in a daze as Noah gently lifted her and started walking steadily eastward. "But—how—?"

"We came across from New York, of course. Hopped a train in Colorado and lost ourselves nice and thoroughly in Chicago and points east." The detective's voice darkened. "That down-timer kid from the station, Julius? He was disguised as you, Jenna, dressed in a calico skirt, wearing a wig." Noah paused, eyes stricken in the light streaming from a nearby house window. "They shot him. My fault, dammit, I shouldn't have let that kid out of my sight! I knew Sarnoff would follow us, I just didn't figure he'd slip ahead and ambush the kid so fast. We got him back to the camp surgeon, but . . ."

"No . . ." Jenna whimpered, not wanting to hear.

"I'm sorry, Jenna. He didn't make it. Poor bastard died before we could slip out of camp. I had a helluva time getting us out in the middle of the uproar, with Time Tours guides and the surgeon demanding to know exactly what had happened."

Jenna's vision wavered. "Oh, God . . ." She didn't want to accept the truth. Not that nice kid, the down-timer she'd met in the basement under the Neo Edo hotel. Julius was younger than she was. . . . Her eyes burned and she nearly brought up more acid from her stomach as she fought not to sob aloud. How many people were going to die, trying to keep her alive?

Then she remembered Ianira. "Oh, God! *Ianira!*"

Noah's stride faltered for just a moment. "I know." The detective's voice was rough. "I tried to follow him, the instant I knew you weren't critically wounded. But he disappeared into that rat's maze of streets down in SoHo. Which, coincidentally, is exactly the same thing we did. I had to get us out of there fast, after all the shooting left that hit-man dead in front of the Opera House. The door man and some people in a passing carriage went shouting for a constable."

"But—but Noah, he's got her—"

"Do you have any idea who he was?"

She gulped down terror, tried to think past the memory of that gun levelled at her face, that mad, calm voice telling her it was nothing personal. "He said he was a doctor. Ianira found him, while I was struggling with that killer. I think he was down by those columns."

Noah nodded. "That'd be the Opera House, it's just down the way from where you were attacked."

"He took Ianira's pulse and she . . . she went into shock. Tried to get away from him, starting ranting something that sounded awful. In ancient Greek. Whatever she said, he understood it and his face . . . he *snarled* at her. I've never seen such hatred, such murderous fury . . ."

Noah's quiet voice intruded. "That's damned odd, don't you think?"

Jenna just shivered and huddled closer to the detective's warmth. "He looked at me. Just looked at me and said, 'Sorry, old chap, nothing personal,' and shot me."

"*Damned* odd," Noah muttered. "Doesn't sound like an up-time hit at all."

"No." Then, voice breaking, "*We have to find her!* I let him . . . let him take her away . . ."

"No, you didn't. Don't argue! For Christ sake, Jenna, you've been on the run for three solid days, in shock from the murders in New York, and the shock of being pregnant and shooting a man to death in TT-86, and you damned near got shot at the Piccadilly Hotel, then almost knifed to death in front of the Opera, then some lunatic down-timer shot you in the head, and you blame yourself? After all that? Kid, you did one helluva job. And you're not even a pro. I *am*. And I screwed up royally. I didn't manage to grab you aside at Spaldergate House, damn near got caught stealing a horse to follow the carriage you took, and still arrived at the Piccadilly Hotel too damned late to do you any good. And by the time the shooting started outside the hotel, I'd tied that damned horse up a block down the street and had to chase after you on foot, in these heavy, damned wet skirts. Kid, I fucked up, plain and simple, and ended up letting that guy shoot you and kidnap Ianira. Don't you *dare* blame yourself, Jenna Caddrick. You did one helluva job getting her out of that hotel in one piece."

Very quietly and very messily, Jenna began to cry down the front of Noah's rough woolen dress.

"Aw, shit . . ." Noah muttered, then speeded up. "I gotta get you out of this raw air." Noah braced her head against a solid shoulder, easing the coat to protect her face from the cold, and hurried through the darkened city. Occasional carriages rattled past, a greyed-out blur to Jenna's overtaxed senses. Pain, dull and endless, throbbed through her head. Nausea bit the back of her throat, without letup. *God, if I really am pregnant, please let the baby be all right . . .*

At least half an hour later, Noah Armstrong carried Jenna into a snug little house near Christ Church, Spitalfields. Marcus, who seemed to have aged terribly since the last time she'd seen him, greeted them with a cry of fear. "*What has happened? Where is Ianira?*"

Noah spoke curtly. "Jenna ran into bad trouble, getting away from the gatehouse. I've got to carry her upstairs to bed. Heat a water bottle and bring up some extra blankets, then go out and ask Dr. Mindel to come. Jenna's been shot, not seriously, but she needs medical attention and she's in shock."

"Ianira?" Marcus whispered again.

The detective paused. "She's alive. Somewhere. It's complicated. A man helped them, shot one of the hit-men. But when he touched her, she went into prophetic trance and whatever she said, it really upset him. He shot Jenna without warning and was about to finish her off when I finally caught up. He took a potshot at me and I fired back, but missed, dammit, and he grabbed Ianira and took off down Drury Lane. I'm sorry, Marcus. We'll find her. I swear it, we *will* find her."

The ex-slave had gone ashen, stood trembling in the shabby house they'd rented, eyes wet and lips unsteady. At a slight sound behind him, he turned his shaken gaze downward.

"Daddy?" A beautiful little girl of about seven had appeared in the doorway from the back of the house. "Daddy, did Noah bring Mama?"

Jenna had to grasp Noah's shoulders as the whole room spun. Ianira's little girl, Artemisia . . . only she was too old, much too old, and Marcus had aged, as well, there was grey in his hair and she didn't understand . . .

"No, Misia," Marcus choked out, going to his knees to hug the little girl close. "Noah and Jenna tried, honey, but something went wrong and a bad man took Mama away. We'll find her, sweetheart, we'll look all through London and find her. But Jenna's been hurt, trying to protect your mother, and we have to help her, now. I need to go for a doctor, Misia, and Noah has to watch Jenna until the doctor comes, so we all need you to help us out, tonight, okay? Can you watch Gelasia for us, make sure she's had her milk and biscuits?"

The little girl nodded, wide eyes wet and scared as she stared up at Jenna.

"This is Jenna," Noah said gently. "She helped me save your mommy's life tonight. The bad men we ran away from a long time ago chased her, honey, then another man hurt her and took your mother. I'm sorry, honey. We'll get her back."

No child of seven should possess eyes like Artemisia's, dark as mahogany and too wise and haunted for her age, eyes which had, like her mother's, seen far too much at far too early a point in life. She disappeared into the back of the house. Marcus said raggedly, "I will bring the hot water bottle, then go for Dr. Mindel."

"Good. And take my Colt Thunderer with you. Put it up, when you get back, someplace where the girls can't reach it."

Marcus took Noah's revolver and disappeared into the kitchen.

Noah carried Jenna up a narrow, dark staircase that smelled of dampness and recent, harsh soap. "Noah?" she whispered, still badly shaken.

"Yeah?" The detective carried her into a neat, heartlessly plain bedroom and settled her gently into a deep feather bed.

"Why . . . why is Artemisia so much older? I don't understand . . ."

Noah dragged off the wet, bedraggled bonnet which hid the detective's face, pulled blankets up across her, then gently removed Jenna's makeshift bandages and peered anxiously at the side of her head before pouring out a basin of water and wetting a cloth to sponge away dried blood, all without answering. Jenna found herself staring into Noah's eyes, which had gone dark with an even deeper sorrow Jenna didn't want to know the reasons for. Noah met her frightened stare, paused, then told her.

"You're too foggy to work it out, aren't you? The Denver Gate opens into 1885. The Britannia opens into 1888. It's been three years for us, kid. There wasn't any other way."

The whole bed came adrift under Jenna's back. She found herself a foggy stretch of time later floating in a grey haze while Noah very gently removed her clothing and eased her into a nightshirt, then replaced the blankets. Jenna slowly focused on the detective's haunted eyes. "Three *years?*" she finally whispered, her foggy mind catching up at last. "My God . . . Even if we find her . . . Ianira's little girls won't even know their own mother. And poor Ianira . . . God, three *years* of their lives, gone . . ."

"I know." Quiet, that voice, filled with regret and hushed pain. "Believe me, we wanted there to be some other way. There wasn't." The detective kept talking, voice low, giving Jenna a lifeline to cling to while her world swung in unpredictable circles all over again. "We've been in London for nearly two-and-a-half years, now. Waiting for you. I showed up at Spaldergate tonight, hoping to catch your attention, but . . . You know how that ended."

The shock, the misery of what Jenna had caused, was too much. She squeezed shut her eyes over hot tears. *What else could I have done? Could any of us have done?* They could've brought the girls through with Ianira, at least. But Noah'd been right to guess hit men would be sent through both gates after them. If they *had* brought the little girls through with Ianira, none of them would have escaped the Piccadilly Hotel alive. There really hadn't been any other choice. Knowing that didn't help much, though, with Ianira missing somewhere in this immense city, in the hands of God alone knew what kind of madman, and those beautiful little girls downstairs, unable to remember the mother they'd waited three years to meet again and deprived of her once more by violence and death. *None* of them had expected Marcus and the children to have to stay down time in Denver long enough to catch up to the Britannia Gate.

The knowledge that none of them were safe, yet, after everything they'd already been through, was a pain too deep to express. So Jenna just lay there, staring blankly at the stained ceiling, waiting for the doctor to arrive while Noah slipped a hot water bottle under the blankets to warm her and brought a basin full of hot, steaming water that smelled strongly of disinfectant to wash the gash in her head. She was grateful that Noah Armstrong had managed, at least, to set up a hiding place in London, ready and waiting for her. Outside, lightning flared and thunder rumbled through the dismal streets of Spitalfields as rain poured from leaden skies.

Their safe haven was at least well hidden by grinding poverty. It was probably the last place on earth her father's hired killers would think to look for them. London's violent and poverty-stricken East End during the middle of the Ripper horror . . .

When Dr. Mindel finally arrived, he praised Noah's "nursing" and sutured up Jenna's scalp, then fed her some foul-tasting medicine that left her drifting in darkness. The final awareness to impinge on her exhausted mind was the sound of Marcus in the hallway, talking quietly with Noah, with the cold and granite sound of murder in his voice as they made plans to find his missing wife.

Then she drifted into pain-free oblivion and knew no more.

Malcolm tilted his pocketwatch toward the light of a gas lamp on the street corner, putting the time at half-past eight when he alighted from his hansom cab at the corner of Bow and Hart Streets. Clouds, shot through with lightning, swirled in thick drifts and eddies above the rooftops, muting the sounds of a boisterous Thursday evening with the imminent threat of more rain. Although they were past the official end of the annual London social season, cut short yearly when Parliament adjourned each August twelfth, not everyone was fortunate enough to escape London immediately for their country homes or the rural estates of friends. Business matters had to be wound up and some gentlemen remained trapped in London year-round, particularly those of the aspiring middle classes, who had acquired the tastes and pursuits of the wealthy without the means of fleeing London at the end of the social season.

As a result, cultured male voices the length of Bow Street could be heard discussing theater and dinner plans, birds they planned to shoot on favorite grouse moors up in Scotland now that grouse season had opened, or the ladies who inhabited the country houses they would visit during the fall's leisurely hunting seasons, beginning with grouse, graduating to partridge and pheasant, and ending lastly—but perhaps most importantly—with the noble fox.

Also drifting through the damp night came the light laughter of women Malcolm could not actually see, whose carriages rattled invisibly past in the murk that was not quite rain but not quite fog, either. The jingle of harness and the sharp clopping of horse's hooves struck the lime-rock gravel bed of the street with a thick, thumping sound, carrying the hidden ladies off to bright dinner parties. Carefully orchestrated affairs, such dinners were designed to bring together eligible young ladies and equally eligible gentlemen for the deadly serious purpose of finding suitable spouses for the unmarried daughters of the house.

It being a Thursday evening, many such dinner parties throughout the ultra-fashionable west end would be followed by musical and other soirees, theater or the opera, and after that, the final, few elegant balls of the year, at which silk-clad young ladies still unmarried and desperate would swirl across dance floors and sip wine with smartly dressed young gentlemen until three in the morning, with a fair number of those young gentlemen equally desperate to find an heiress, even from a fortune made in *trade,* God help them all for having to stoop to such measures, just to bolster the finances of blue-blooded but cash-poor noble houses.

Above the jingle of harness as carriages rattled past, filtering through the sounds of gay laughter and merrymaking, came other, more plaintive cries, the calls of flower girls and eel-pie vendors hawking their wares to the genteel folk who frequented this fashionable district on such evenings. Malcolm could just make out one such girl, stationed beneath the nearest street lamp where she would be most visible in the drizzle and murk. She held a heavy tray of carnations and pinks suspended from cords around her neck. Her dress, damp in patches from the raw night, was made of cheap, dark cotton, much mended and several years out of fashion. The toes of the shoes peeping out from beneath her skirts had been cut open to accommodate the growth of her feet.

As Malcolm watched, three gentlemen emerged from the darkness and paused briefly to purchase boutonnieres for their lapels. They strolled on toward Malcolm, nodding and smiling as they passed, locked deep in conversation about the best methods of cubbing the young foxes and adolescent fox hounds once cub season opened. Malcolm nodded in return, wishing them a pleasant, "Good evening" as they crossed Bow Street and moved past the looming edifice of the Royal Opera House down Hart Street in the direction of Covent Garden Theater.

Then he was alone again on the pavement, turning over in his mind everything the Spaldergate staff had learned about Mr. Benny Catlin's disappearance. Foul play was now the major fear consuming everyone at Spaldergate. Catlin's abandoned luggage, the corpse in Catlin's hotel room, and the wounded Time Tours carriage driver had led police constables straight to Spaldergate House, asking about the body at the Piccadilly Hotel and a second grisly corpse found outside the Royal Opera. The police, comparing witness descriptions, had concluded that the Piccadilly Hotel shooting and the Opera House shooting had been committed by the same desperate individual.

The Time Tours driver injured at the Piccadilly Hotel had, thank God, arrived at the gatehouse unconscious but still alive, driven by one of the gatehouse's footmen dispatched to fetch him back. Catlin's luggage had been impounded, but the footman had managed to secure Catlin's bloodstained gloves from the room before police could arrive, giving the Spaldergate staff at least some chance of tracing Catlin with bloodhounds. Weak from shock and blood loss, the wounded driver had barely been alive by the time he'd been rushed downstairs to surgery.

A massive police manhunt was now on for the missing Mr. Catlin and for anyone who might have been involved in the fatal shootings. Marshall Gilbert, gatehousekeeper, was faced with the worst crisis of his career, trying to assist the police while keeping the secrets of Spaldergate House very much under wraps.

Malcolm dreaded the coming night's work and the lack of sleep this search would mean. At least—and he consoled himself with the prospect—he wouldn't be searching alone. For good or ill, Margo would be assisting him. He needed her close, tired and soul-sore as he was from weeks spent plunged into the misery of the East End, preparing for the coming horror.

When two hansom cabs traveling close behind one another pulled up and halted at the corner of Bow and Hart, Malcolm pocketed his watch and moved rapidly forward to greet the occupants alighting on the pavement. "Ah, Stoddard, very good, I've been awaiting your arrival. Miss Smith, I'm so dreadfully sorry about this trouble, I do wish you had reconsidered coming along this evening. Madame Feroz, frightfully decent of you to accompany her, I know the demands upon your time are keen. And this must be Mr. Shannon?"

The man who had jumped to the pavement behind Spaldergate's stable master, hanging slightly back as Malcolm greeted Margo and Shahdi Feroz in turn, was a temporal native, a stringy, tough old Irishman in an ill-cut suit. He was assisting another passenger to alight, a striking young woman in very plain garments. The girl's skirt was worn but had been made of good quality cloth when new, and her coat, also faded, was neat and clean. Her hair was a glorious copper in the gaslight, her face sprinkled with far too many freckles for her to be considered a beauty by Victorian standards. But she had a memorable face and a quiet air of utter and unshakable self-confidence. She'd wrapped one hand around the leash of a magnificent Alsatian or—had Malcolm been in America—a beautiful black-and-tan German Shepherd dog with bright, intelligent eyes.

The grizzled Irishman, who was doubtless far stronger than his slight frame suggested, shook Malcolm's hand. "That's me, sir, Auley Shannon. This is me granddaughter, Maeve Shannon, Alfie's 'er dog, trained 'im she did, 'er own self, won't find a better tracker in London."

"Malcolm Moore," he smiled in return, offering his hand. "My pleasure, Mr. Shannon, Miss Shannon."

The inquiry agents whom Stoddard had been sent to fetch shook Malcolm's hand firmly. Miss Shannon kept her dog on a short leash, even though the animal was immaculately behaved, sitting on his haunches and watching the humans with keen eyes, tongue lolling slightly in the damp air.

Malcolm turned to Spaldergate's stable master. "Stoddard, you have the gloves that were found when poor Mr. Catlin disappeared from his hotel?"

"I do, sir." He produced a small cloth bag, inside which nestled a gentleman's pair of kid gloves. Relatively fresh blood stains indicated that they had, in fact, been on Catlin's person when the shootout at the Piccadilly Hotel had occurred and Catlin had rendered life-saving first aid, just as the wounded driver had described via telephone before losing consciousness.

Malcolm nodded briskly. "Very good. Shall we give the dog the scent, then? I'm anxious to begin. Poor Miss Smith," and he bowed to Margo before returning his attention to the Shannons, "is understandably distraught over her fiancé's absence and who can blame the dear child?"

Margo was doing a very creditable job, in fact, of imitating someone in deep distress, shredding her own gloves with jerking, nervous movements and summoning tears through God-alone knew what agency. "Please, can't you find him?" Margo gasped out, voice shaking, one hand clutching at Mr. Shannon's ill-fitting jacket sleeve.

His granddaughter spoke, not unkindly. "Now, then, get 'old of yourself, miss, wailin' and suchlike won't do 'im a bit o' good an' you're like t'give yourself a fit of brain fever."

"Maeve," her grandfather said sharply, "the lady 'as a right to be upset, so you just give Alfie the scent an' mind your tongue! Or I'll give yer me German across yer Hampsteads, so I will."

"You an' what army, I'm wonderin'?" she shot right back, not cowed in the slightest by her grandfather's uplifted hand. "Give Alfie a sniff o' them gloves, now," she instructed Stoddard briskly.

"Where were the chap last spotted?" the elder Shannon wanted to know as the dog thrust an eager nose into the gloves held out to him.

Malcolm nodded toward the opera house across the road. "There, between the Opera and the Floral Hall. The doorman caught a glimpse of him engaged in what he described as a desperate fight with another man and ran to fetch the constables he'd just seen pass by. This other man was evidently shot dead and abandoned by Mr. Catlin in his terror to escape. Probably one of those desperate, criminal youths in one of those wretched, notorious Nichol gangs. Their depredations have all London in an uproar. God help us, what are we coming to when young boys no older than fourteen or fifteen roam the streets as armed thugs and break into homes, stealing property and dishonoring women—" he lifted his hat apologetically to the ladies "—and attacking a man in front of the Floral Hall, for God's sake? The last time anyone saw Mr. Catlin, he was down Bow Street that way, just past the Floral Hall, fighting for his life."

"Let's cross, then," Maeve Shannon said briskly, "an' we'll give Alfie the scent off them gloves again when we've got right up to where 'e were at the time."

They dodged carriages and ghostly, looming shapes of horses across the road, carriage lamps and horses' eyes gleaming in the raw night. Clouds of white vapour streamed from the horses' distended nostrils, then they were across and the copper-haired girl held the gloves to her dog's nose again while her grandfather tapped one impatient foot. The shepherd sniffed intently, then at a command from his trainer began casting along the pavement. A sharp whine reached them, then Alfie strained out into the road, following the scent. The dog paused at a dark stain on the cobbles, which, when the elder Shannon crouched down and tested it, proved to be blood.

Margo let out an astonishing sound and clutched at Malcolm's arm. "Oh, God, poor Benjamin . . ."

"There, there," Mr. Shannon soothed, wiping his sticky hand on a kerchief, "it's most like the blagger wot attacked 'im, 'oo bled on these 'ere cobbles. Police took 'is body away to the morgue, so it's not like as to be Mr. Catlin's blood. Not to fret, Miss, we'll find 'im."

Miss Shannon said, "Alfie, seek!" and the dog bounded across the road and headed down a drizzle-shrouded walk which passed beneath the graceful colonnaded facade of the Royal Opera House. The dog led the way at a brisk walk. Malcolm and Philip Stoddard, escorting Margo and Shahdi Feroz solicitously, hastened after them. The darkened glass panes of the Floral Hall loomed up from the damp night. The high, domed roof of the magnificent glasshouse glinted distantly in the gaslights from the street, its high, curved panes visible in snatches between drifting eddies of low-blown cloud.

The eager Alsatian, nose casting along the pavement as the dog traced a scent mingled with thousands of other traces where gentlemen, ladies, horses, dogs, carters, and Lord knew what all else had passed this way today, drew them eagerly to Russell Street, where Alfie cast sharp left and headed rapidly away from Covent Garden. They moved down toward the massive Drury Theater, which took up the better part of the entire city block between Catherine Street and Drury Lane. The drizzling fog swirled and drifted across the heavy stone portico along the front, with its statue at the top dimly lit by gaslight from hanging lamps that blazed along the entrance. Malcolm worried about the scent in weather like this. If the drizzle turned to serious rain, which rumbled and threatened again overhead, no dog born could follow the scent. The deluge would wash it straight into the nearest storm sewer. Which, upon reflection, might be why the dog was able to follow Catlin's trail so easily—most of the competing scents *had* been washed away, by the night's earlier rainstorm.

God alone knew, they needed a piece of luck, just now.

More carriages rattled past in the darkness, carrying merry parties of well-to-do middle-class theater goers to the Drury's bright-lit entrance. Voices and laughter reached across the busy thoroughfare as London prepared for yet another evening of sparkling gaiety. The straining shepherd, however, ignored Catherine Street altogether and guided the way down Russell Street along the huge theater's left-hand side, where a portico of Ionic columns loomed like a forest of stone trees in the darkness. Malcolm felt his hopes rise at the dog's sharp eagerness and ability to discern Catlin's trail. *Good idea, Margo*, he approved silently, grateful to her for thinking of a bloodhound when the rest of them had been struck stupid with shock.

Their footsteps echoed eerily off tall buildings when the dog led them straight down Drury Lane. The fact that Benny Catlin had come this way suggested to Malcolm he *had* been forced away by someone with a weapon. The Royal Opera House, Drury Lane Theater, and the Covent Garden district stood squarely in a well-to-do, middle-class neighborhood, eclipsed in finery only by the wealthiest of the upper-class districts to the west. But once into Drury Lane itself, wealth and even comfort dropped away entirely. As the eager shepherd drew them down the length of that famous street, poverty's raw bones began to show. These were the houses and shops of London's hard-working poor, where some managed to eke out moderate comfort while others descended steeply into want and hunger.

Piles of wooden crates stood on the pavements outside lower-class shops, where wagons had made daytime deliveries. The deeper they pressed into the recesses of Drury Lane, which dwindled gradually in width as well as respectability, the meaner and shabbier grew the houses and the residents walking the pavements. Pubs spilled piano music and alcoholic fumes into the streets, where roughly clad working men and women gathered in knots to talk and laugh harshly and stare with bristling suspicion at the well-dressed ladies and frock-coated gentleman passing in the company of a liveried servant, with an older man and younger woman of their own class controlling a leashed dog.

Malcolm made mental note of where the pubs lay, to locate potential witnesses for later questioning, and pressed his arm surreptitiously against the lump of his concealed pistol, making certain of it. Margo, he knew, also carried a pistol in her pocket, as did Philip Stoddard. He wished he'd thought to ask Shahdi Feroz whether or not she was armed, but this was neither the time nor the place to remedy that lack. Preternaturally aware of the shabby men and women watching them from shadows and from the lighted doorways of mean houses and rough pubs, Malcolm followed the eager dog and his mistress, listening to the click of their footfalls on the pavement and the scrape and scratch of the dog's claws.

Whatever Benny Catlin's motive, whether flight from trouble or the threat of deadly force taking him deeper into danger, it had carried him the length of Drury Lane. The dog paused briefly and sniffed again at a dark spot on the pavement. This time, Mr. Shannon was not able to explain away the spots of blood so glibly. Margo clutched at Malcolm, weeping and gulping back evident terror. Malcolm watched Shannon wipe blood from his hand again, knowing, this time, it must be Benny Catlin's blood, and was able to console himself only with the fact that not enough had been spilled here to prove immediately fatal. But untended, with wounds of unknown severity . . . and perhaps in the grip of footpads who would kill him when they had obtained what they'd forced him here for . . .

Grimly, Malcolm signalled to continue the hunt. Even Shahdi Feroz's eyes had taken on a strained, hopeless look. The Ripper scholar clearly knew Catlin's odds as well as Malcom did.

They reached the final, narrow stretches of Drury Lane where Wych Street snaked off to the left, along a route that would eventually be demolished to create Aldwych. That upscale urban renewal was destined to gobble up an entire twenty-eight acres of this mean district. They kept to the right, avoiding the narrow trap of Wych Street, but even this route was a dangerous one. The buildings closed in, ill-lit along this echoing, drizzle-shrouded stretch, and still the Alsatian shepherd strained eagerly forward, nose to the pavement. When they emerged at last into the famous Strand, another juxtaposition of wealth in the midst of slums, their first sight was St. Mary le Strand church, which stood as an island in the middle of the broad street.

Philip Stoddard muttered, "What the devil was after him, to send him walking down this way in the middle of the night?"

Malcolm glanced sharply at the stable master and nodded warningly toward the Shannons, then said, "I fear Miss Smith is greatly distressed."

Margo was emitting little sounds of horror as she took in their surroundings. She had transferred her act to the Ripper scholar and clung to Shahdi Feroz' arm as though to a lifeline, tottering at the end of her strength and wits. "Where can he be?" Margo was murmuring over and over. "Oh, God, what's happened to him? This is a terrible place, dreadful . . ."

Auley Shannon glanced over his shoulder. "Could be another answer, guv, if 'e never got clean away from th' blokes wot attacked 'im outside the opera. Alfie's 'eadin' straight for 'olywell Street. Might've been brought down 'ere for reasons I'd as soon not say in front o' the ladies."

A chill touched Malcolm's spine. Dear God, not *that*. . . . The dog was dragging them past Newcastle Street directly toward the cramped, dark little lane known as Holywell, which ran to the left of the narrow St. Mary le Strand church on a course parallel to the Strand. On the Strand itself, Malcolm could just see the glass awning of the Opera Comique, a theater sandwiched between Wych and Holywell Streets, reachable only through a tunnel that opened out beneath that glass canopy on the Strand. The neighborhood was cramped and seemingly picturesque, with exceedingly aged houses dating to the Tudor and Stuart periods crowding the appallingly narrow way.

But darkened shop windows advertising book sellers' establishments the length of Holywell were infamous throughout London. In the shops of "Booksellers' Row" as Holywell was sometimes known, a man could obtain lewd prints, obscene books, and a pornographic education for a mere handful of shillings. And for a few shillings more, a man could obtain a young girl—or a young boy, come to that, despite harsh laws against it. The girls and young men who worked in the back rooms and attics of these nasty, crumbling old shops had often as not been drugged into captivity and put to work as whores, photographed nude and raped by customers and jailors alike. If some wealthy gentleman, with or without a title, had requested a proprietor on Holywell Street to procure a young man of a specific build and coloring, Benny Catlin might well have been plunged into a Victorian hell somewhere nearby.

Although the shops were closed for the night and certainly would have been closed when Benny Catlin had passed this way earlier in the evening, women in dark skirts were busy carrying out hasty negotiations with men in rough workingmen's garments. Several of the women cast appraising glances at Malcolm, who looked—to them—like a potential wealthy customer passing by in the close darkness, despite the presence of ladies with him.

"What does Mr. Shannon mean?" Margo whispered *sotto voce.* "What is it about Holywell Street that's so awful he won't say?"

Malcolm cleared his throat. "Ah . . . perhaps some other time might be better for explanations, Miss Smith? I rather doubt that what Mr. Shannon referred to is what has actually happened." Malcolm wished he could be as certain as he sounded, but he had no intention of requiring Margo to play out her role by displaying complete hysterics over the notion of her fiancé having been sold to someone to be photographed and raped by a dealer in pornographic literature.

The rough-clad women watching them so narrowly were clearly trying to judge whether or not to risk openly approaching him with *their* business propositions. Had Malcolm been quite alone, he suspected he would have been propositioned no fewer than a dozen times within fifty paces. And had he been quite alone, Malcolm's hand would never have left the pocket concealing his pistol. A man dressed as Malcolm was, venturing unaccompanied into the deep, semi-criminal poverty of Holywell, would be considered fair game by any footpad who saw him. There was more safety in numbers, but even so, Malcolm's hand never strayed far from the entrance to his pocket.

When Malcolm spotted a woman lounging by herself against a bookshop wall, standing directly beneath a large, projecting clock that stuck out perpendicularly from the building, he paused, carefully gesturing the ladies on ahead with Mr. Stoddard. A gas street lamp nearby shed enough light to see her worn dress, work-roughened hands, and tired face beneath a bedraggled bonnet.

"Good evening, ma'am."

She stood up straighter, calculation jumping into her eyes. "Evenin', luv. Whatcher' wantin', then?"

"I was wondering if you might have seen someone pass this way earlier this evening? A gentleman dressed much the same way I am? My cousin's gone missing, you see," he added at the sharp look of distrust in her face. "I'm quite concerned over my cousin's safety and his fiancée, there, is in deep distress over it." He gestured toward Margo, who was clinging to Shahdi Feroz and biting her lip, eyes red and swollen. He must remember to ask her how she managed to conjure tears on command.

"Yer cousin, eh? Well, that's diff'rent, innit?" She shrugged. "Right about when might 'e 'ave gone by, luv?"

"Half-eight or shortly thereafter."

"I weren't 'ere at 'alf-eight, tonight nor any other. I got a job at the Black Eagle Brewery, I 'ave, what I gets up at six o'clock of a morning for, t' earn shilling an' sixpence a week, an' I don't leave brewery 'ouse til nigh on 'alf-nine of a night. Weren't 'ere at 'alf-eight, luv."

A shilling and sixpence. Eighteen cents a week, for a job that started at six A.M. and ran fifteen hours or more a shift. It was little wonder she was out here on the street after dark, trying to earn a few extra pence however she could. He sighed, then met her narrow-eyed gaze. "I see, madame. Well, thank you, anyway." He held up a shining silver florin. "If you could think of anyone who might have been hereabouts at that hour?"

She snatched the coin—nearly two weeks' wages—from his fingers. "G'wan down to Davy's, ask round there. Pub's open til all hours, anybody could've seen 'im. Ain't like we see gents every night o' th' week, these parts."

"Indeed? Thank you, ma'am, and good evening."

He was aware of her stare as he rejoined the ladies and followed the straining Alfie at the end of his leash. By dawn, the story of the missing gent and his grieving fiancée would be news from one end of the district to the other. With any luck, word of Benny Catlin might yet shake loose—particularly in the hopes of a cash "donation" for information given. Meanwhile, Alfie was whining and straining in the direction of Davy's Pub at the end of Holywell Street where it rejoined the Strand once more. Music and laughter reached up the narrow lane as they approached the busy public house, brightly lit by a multitude of gas lamps. Its windows and placard-plastered walls advertised Scotch and Irish Whiskeys . . . Wainey, Comb, and Reid fine ales . . . favorite brands of stout . . . and, of course, Walker's.

Malcolm wasn't dressed for mingling in such a crowd, but Auley Shannon was. He nodded slightly at Malcolm, then disappeared into the packed pub. Malcolm waited patiently with Margo and Shahdi Feroz and the others, noting the location of another pub, The Rising Sun, across the road where Wych Street emerged just the other side of Davy's. Beyond, in the wide avenue that lay beyond the conjunction of the two narrow, old streets, lay the ancient facade of St. Clement Danes Church, another island church built in the center of the Strand. Its high steeple was topped with what appeared to be a miniature, columned Greek temple, barely visible now between drizzle-laden clouds and streaks of jagged lightning.

And in another of London's abrupt transitions, where glittering wealth shared a line of fenceposts with criminal poverty, where the narrow Wych and Holywell Streets intersected the Strand, a sharp line of demarcation divided the dark poverty-stricken regions behind them, separating it from the expensive, well-to-do houses and shops right in front of Malcolm, shops and houses that stood in a stately double row to either side of the street, lining the Strand, itself. Such abrupt changes from deepest poverty to startling wealth, within half-a-block of one another, placed destitute men and women with no hope at all side-by-side with socially ambitious businessmen and their ladies, ensconced in fine houses, with servants and carriages and luxuries their neighbors could never aspire to owning through any means except thievery.

And thievery was exactly how many a denizen of SoHo obtained such items.

Studying the intersection and judging the lay of the land and the inhabitants of the various buildings within view, Malcolm realized they'd need to field a good-sized search party through this area just to question all the potential witnesses. Five minutes later, Shannon emerged from Davy's, looking hopeful. "Blokes are suspicious o' strangers," he said quietly, "an' rightly so, what wiv coppers lookin' t'nick 'alf the blokes in there, I'd reckon, but I pointed out Miss Smith, 'ere, give 'em the bare bones of what's 'appened. Got a few of 'em t'thaw a bit, seein' the lady cryin' and all. Must be 'alf a dozen blokes said they saw a bloke wot might've been 'im." He paused, with a glance toward Margo, then cleared his throat. "Wot they saw was a woman walk past, Mr. Moore, carryin' a wounded gentleman. Walkin' quick-like, as if to find a surgeon. Blokes remembered, on account of that poor streetwalker, Martha Tabram, 'oo got 'erself stabbed to death August Bank 'oliday, an' on account of it were so queer, seein' a woman in a patched dress and ragged bonnet, carryin' a gentleman in a fine suit wiv a shabby old coat wrapped round 'is head."

Malcolm paled, even as Margo blanched and clutched at Shahdi Feroz. "Odd," Malcolm muttered, "How deuced *odd*."

"You've the right o' that, sir."

"It's unlikely a woman would have attacked Mr. Catlin. Perhaps she found him lying on the street, injured, and was, indeed, carrying him to safety with a surgeon. Mr. Catlin was a slightly built young man, after all, and wouldn't have proved difficult to lift and carry, for a stout woman." Margo nodded, wiping tears from her face with the back of one gloved hand. "Mr. Shannon, Miss Shannon, lead on, please. Let's see how much farther this trail will take us."

As it happened, that was not much farther at all. Alfie crossed the Strand right along the front of the old Danish church, where the street curved around to the south. Tailors' establishments and boot sellers' shops advertised their wares to wealthy families able to afford their trade. But where Millford Lane cut off to the south near the rear corner of St. Clement Danes, the skies cut loose with a stinging downpour of rain and Alfie lost the trail. The dog hesitated, cast about the wet pavement in confusion and ever-widening circles, and finally sat back on its haunches, whining unhappily while runoff poured, ankle deep, past their feet in the gutters. Maeve pulled her coat collar up around her neck, then bent and patted the dog's shoulder and ruffled its wet, clamped back ears, speaking gently to it.

Malcolm noted the presence of a few hansom cabs along the Strand, waiting hopefully for customers from amongst the wealthier gentlemen Malcolm could see here and there along the street, some of them escorting well-dressed ladies out to carriages under cover of taut umbrellas, and said, "Well, perhaps Mr. Catlin's benefactress hired a cab?"

It was, at least, worth the asking, although he doubted a woman as shabbily clad as the one the men in Davey's pub had described would've been able to afford the cost of a hansom cab fare.

Miss Shannon patted her dog's wet side and glanced around. "Pr'aps, sir. I'm that sorry, I am, 'bout the rain. 'E's a good tracker, Alfie is, but no dog born wot'll trace a man through a downpour like this."

"I fear not. Very well," Malcolm said briskly, "we shall simply have to proceed along different lines. Mr. Shannon, I believe the terms of our agreement include pressing inquiries amongst potential witnesses at whatever point your fine Alsatian lost the trail? If you and your granddaughter would be so good as to assist us, I feel we might yet make good progress this evening. Try the cabbies, there, if you please. Stoddard, if you'll broach the denizens of the Rising Sun Pub, I'll endeavor to strike up a conversation with some of the gentlemen out for the evening's merriment and dinner parties. Ladies, if you would be so good as to secure a hansom cab? I hope we may need one shortly."

"Yes, sir."

"Of course, Mr. Moore."

"Right, sir. Let's give 'er a go, then, Maeve."

Over the course of the next half-hour, Malcolm spoke with dozens of gentlemen and their stout, respectable wives, the latter dressed in satins and bonnets with drooping feathers under widespread umbrellas, inquiring politely about an ill-dressed woman assisting a wounded gentleman of their class. The answers he received were civil, concerned, and entirely negative, which left Malcolm increasingly frustrated as well as thoroughly soaked. Lightning flared overhead, sizzled down to strike chimney pots and church steeples with crashes of thunder that sent the well-dressed citizenry scrambling for doorways and covered carriages.

They couldn't stay out in this kind of weather any longer, searching.

London was a vast maze of streets and lanes. The number of places an unwary time tourist could go fatally astray would have sobered the most optimistic of searchers. Malcolm hurried back down the Strand, calling for Stoddard and the Shannons. They rejoined Margo and

Shahdi Feroz, who had secured the services of the nearest hansom cab and were huddled inside it, out of the downpour. None of the others had found so much as a trace, either.

"There's nothing more to be done, here, in this weather," Malcolm shouted above the crash of thunder.

Margo's performance inside the hansom cab, weeping distraughtly and leaning against Shahdi Feroz, left Mr. Shannon clearing his throat in sympathy. Maeve Shannon stepped up onto the running board and leaned in to put a comforting hand on Margo's shoulder, said something too low for Malcolm to hear, at which Margo nodded and replied, "Thank you, Miss Shannon. Thank you . . ."

"I'm that sorry, I am, miss, but I'm sure it'll come right." Maeve smiled at Margo, then stepped back down to the pavement and called her dog to heel. Malcolm handed over Mr. Shannon's fee for the night's work and a bonus for Maeve's unexpected sympathy to Margo, which he felt deserved recognition of some kind. The Shannons might be accustomed to the harshness of life in Whitechapel, where they kept their inquiry agency, but they were good and decent people, nonetheless. The inquiry agent and his granddaughter wished him luck and hurried off into the downpour with Alfie trotting between them, seeking shelter from the rising storm. Malcolm sighed heavily, then secured a cab of his own to follow Margo and Shahdi Feroz back to Spaldergate, and settled down for a clattering ride through night-shrouded streets. Stoddard, riding silently beside him, was grim in the actinic glare of lightning bolts streaking through London's night sky.

Somewhere out there, Benny Catlin *was* known, to someone.

Malcolm intended finding that someone. All it required was a bit of luck added to the hard work ahead. In the swaying darkness of the hansom, Malcolm grimaced. This was not a good time for reminding himself that before Margo had come into his life, Malcolm's luck had run to the notoriously bad. Malcolm Moore was not a superstitious man by nature, but he couldn't quite shake the feeling that on this particular hunt, luck just might not be with him.

He could only pray that it *had* been with Benny Catlin.

If not, they might yet locate him in a morgue.

((Chapter 9))

Gideon Guthrie poured a drink from an expensive cut-crystal decanter and moved quietly to the window. Night had fallen across the city, turning the filthy sprawl of New York into a fairy-land jewel at his feet. Behind him, the television flickered silently, sound muted. Gideon frowned slowly, then sipped at his scotch. John Caddrick had given quite a performance for the press today. How the sociopathic bastard was able to summon tears for the cameras, Gideon didn't know. But the press had eaten it up, delighted with the ratings points Caddrick's grief gave them. Which played quite nicely into Gideon's plans. What worried Gideon, however, and it worried *his* boss, as well, was Caddrick's tendency to explosive fits of temper. They played a very delicate game, Gideon and Cyril Barris and the Senator, a damned delicate game. Caddrick's notorious temperament was just as likely to prove a liability as an asset.

It was too bad about the girl, in a sense, although Caddrick didn't seem to give a damn that Gideon had ordered a fatal hit on the Senator's own daughter. Of course, Caddrick wasn't stupid and there'd never been any love lost between those two. If Gideon and his political ally played it right, Cassie Tyrol's impulsive decision to tell her niece would play into Cyril Barris' long-range plans brilliantly. All Gideon had to do was keep Caddrick's temper from screwing things up. A man like John Caddrick was priceless in Congress, where that temper and his ruthless ability to play the filthy game of politics made him a devastating enemy and a cunning advocate. But Caddrick's flair for playing the press could easily backfire, if they weren't incredibly careful. The Senator's call for investigating the *Ansar Majlis*, claiming they'd kidnapped his daughter, worked wonders for television ratings. And it would doubtless fire up a world-wide demand for the destruction of the very terrorists Gideon had chosen to further his employer's plans. Which was, ultimately, the precise outcome both Cyril Barris and Gideon, himself, wanted.

But too close an investigation into the *Ansar Majlis* could prove risky.

Very risky.

He'd have to keep a close watch on John Caddrick, all right. Their timetable was moving along right on schedule, with only one minor hitch, which ought to've been effectively eliminated, by now. He'd sent a good team onto TT-86 to destroy Ianira and her whole family, not to mention finishing up the job with Jenna Caddrick and that miserable, meddlesome detective, Noah Armstrong. Gideon scowled and poured himself another scotch. *That* was one complication he hadn't anticipated. Cassie Tyrol, actress, six-time divorcee, and scatter-brained Templar, was the last person Gideon had expected to hire a detective, for God's sake, to investigate her own brother-in-law's business practices. And who'd have guessed she would come so damned unglued over the seemingly accidental death of that little bastard, Alston Corliss, who'd taped all the evidence on Caddrick? How, in fact, had she even known about it, so soon? She'd bolted *hours* before the FBI had leaked word to the press. Armstrong again, no doubt.

Alston Corliss was yet another reason to worry about the Senator. If a goddamned *actor* could ferret out that kind of evidence on the Senator's activities. . . .When this was over and done with, maybe it would be a good idea to bring about Caddrick's political downfall. Do it subtly, so Caddrick would never suspect Gideon had orchestrated it. Yes, he'd have to look into that. Suggest it to Cyril Barris as a potential course of action for the future, after they'd culled everything useful they could from Caddrick's position in government. Meanwhile, Noah Armstrong had somehow absconded with a copy of that goddamned incriminating tape, the original of which they'd found and destroyed. Maybe Corliss had used the stinking Internet to send it, with streaming video technology. However he'd gotten the tape to Armstrong, out in California, it spelled certain disaster for their plans if they didn't get it back before Armstrong found a way to contact the authorities.

Gideon knocked back the scotch and swore under his breath. Complications like this, he did not need. But he had the situation under control again, thank God, so all he had to do now was keep an eye on John Caddrick and make sure nothing else went wrong. If anything else did . . . Heads would by God roll. Gideon scowled. The Senator had believed for years *he* was calling the shots. Fine. Let him. If Caddrick screwed up one more time, he'd find out the bitter truth, fast. It would almost be worth the trouble, to see the shock on his face.

Gideon switched off the television and settled himself to set in motion the events necessary to bring about the end of a powerful politician's career.

❰❰ Chapter 10 ❱❱

It was a vastly subdued Margo who returned to Spaldergate House in a driving downpour, with lightning sizzling in the night skies and Benny Catlin missing and wounded somewhere beyond their reach. After the preoccupation of their abortive search, it was actually a shock to return to the warmth and brightness of Spaldergate and the lively discussion amongst the Ripper scholars, who cared absolutely nothing about a missing time tourist. All except Shahdi Feroz. Margo still wondered why she'd volunteered to accompany them.

An argument broke out the moment they returned, as to which scholars would go into the East End to help place the final surveillance equipment at the first murder scene. Not to be outdone, Dominica Nosette and Guy Pendergast joined the fray.

"We're coming along, as well."

Pavel Kostenka said, "You are not qualified—"

"I've been on more undercover photoshoots than you have credentials strung out behind your name!"

"And you are a two-bit, muckraking—"

"*Two-bit my arse!* I'll have you know—"

"Enough!" Malcolm's stern voice cut through the babble and silenced the entire lot of them. "*I'll* make the decision as to who goes and who stays! Is that clear?"

Even Margo gulped, staring wide-eyed at her infuriated fiancé.

"Now. Miss Nosette, Mr. Pendergast, the terms of the Ripper Watch contract include you as the only journalists. It would be remiss of us if you did not accompany the team members placing the equipment, tonight, to record the attempt for posterity. I presume you've brought low-light, miniaturized cameras?"

"I know my trade," the blond reporter said with an icy chill in her voice, glaring at Kostenka. "And my equipment."

Kostenka just shrugged and pretended to find the carpet utterly absorbing.

"Very well. I would suggest you go and get that equipment ready. We'll leave the house at two A.M. If you're not dressed for the East End and waiting in the carriage drive, we'll leave without you. Now then, Margo, please be good enough to help them select costumes. They haven't been into the East End. Assist Dr. Feroz with that as well. I'll want you along, Inspector," he glanced at Conroy Melvyn, the Scotland Yard chief inspector who'd been named head of the Ripper Watch Team, "and the others can prepare the relay and recording equipment on the roof and down in the vault."

There were grumbles, but clearly, the Ripper Watch Team had grown accustomed to taking Malcolm's orders when it came to his decisions as head guide.

"Very good. I expect you all have someplace better to be than standing about in the parlour, with your mouths hanging open."

The assembled scholars and journalists dispersed quickly. Only Conroy Melvyn seemed to find the situation humorous. The police inspector winked at Malcolm as he strolled out in the wake of the disgruntled scholars. Then Margo was alone with Malcolm, at last.

"Margo, I'm afraid you're not going to like what I have to say next."

"Oh, no, Malcolm, please let me come with you!"

He grimaced. "That isn't it. Quite the opposite, in fact." He rubbed the back of his neck distractedly. "It's this blasted business with Catlin. Thank God you've come. I've got to work with the Gilberts, organize some plan of attack to search for him. We'll try the hospitals, the workhouse infirmaries, anywhere Catlin might have gone seeking medical attention."

Margo gulped, seeing abruptly where this was leading. "Malcolm . . . I—I'm not ready to guide that bunch by myself—"

Malcolm grinned. "Good. I'm glad you've the sense to admit it. I didn't intend sending you alone. Tanglewood's a good man, an experienced guide, and he's been in the East End a fair bit."

Margo frowned. "Isn't that kind of an odd place for tourists to go?"

Malcolm merely cleared his throat. "Zipper jockey tours."

Oh. "That's disgusting!"

"It isn't his fault, Margo. He's a Time Tours employee. If he wants to keep his job, he goes where the paying customers want to visit. Even if it's some back-alley brothel in Wapping."

"Huh. I hope they catch a good dose of something nasty!"

"Occasionally," Malcolm said drily, "they do. Spaldergate's resident surgeon keeps rather a generous supply of penicillin on hand. There is a reason London's courtesans wore death's-head rings, even as early as the eighteenth century."

Margo shivered. Poor women, reduced to such poverty they'd no choice but to risk syphillis and its slow, certain deterioration toward madness and death in an era predating antibiotics.

"Very well," Malcolm said tiredly, "that's settled, then. I would suggest you go in costume as a girl, rather than a street ruffian. You'll be less apt to run into serious trouble, particularly in company with the members of the Ripper Watch Team. But go armed, love. It's no busman's holiday I'm sending you into, out there."

She nodded. "Believe me, I will be. I'll watch over them, get them back here safe again, as soon as their equipment is in place."

Malcolm held out his arms and she walked into his embrace, just holding onto him tightly for a long moment. He kissed her with such hunger, it left her head swimming. Then he broke the contact and leaned his brow against hers and sighed. "I would give anything . . . But I must get on with the search for Benny Catlin."

"I know."

He kissed her one last time, then went in search of the Spaldergate House gatekeepers. Margo found her way upstairs and helped the new arrivals pick out costumes ragged enough for the East End, then showed Dominica Nosette how to get into the costume. Shahdi Feroz had, at least, been down the Britannia before.

"In the West End, mostly," she said with a slight smile, glancing at the garments Margo had authorized. "But I do know how the underthings, at least, go on."

Dominica Nosette expected Margo to assist her as lady's maid, a task she did not relish. *Three months of this?* Margo groused silently, yanking at the strings on Miss Nosette's stays. *I'll lop off her pretty blond hair and put her in a boy's togs, first!*

By the time the mantle clocks throughout Spaldergate chimed two A.M. and they were ready to leave in one of the Time Tours carriages, which would take them as far as the Tower of London, Malcolm had been gone for hours, out combing the hospitals and workhouse infirmaries for some trace of their missing tourist. Douglas Tanglewood ushered them all into a stylish Calash Coach, which possessed a hard, covered roof and curtains to screen them from outside scrutiny, since they were dressed as roughly as any dockhand out of Stepney. They rode in a silence electric with anticipation. Even Margo, who fretted over Malcolm's safety, searching for a man who had already been involved in two fatal shootings, found herself caught up in the air of excitement.

In three hours, they would *know.*

After more than a century and a half of mystery, they would finally *know.*

If nothing went wrong. If she did her job right. If the equipment didn't fail . . .

When they finally alighted at the Tower, which stood at the very gateway to the East End, dividing it from more prosperous areas to the west, Dominica Nosette gasped in astonishment and pointed through the darkness toward a misshapen silhouette outlined now and again by flashes of lightning.

"The Bridge!" she gasped. "What's wrong with the Bridge? Who's destroyed it?"

Douglas Tanglewood chuckled softly. "Miss Nosette, Tower Bridge hasn't suffered any damage. They simply haven't finished building it, yet." Flickers of lightning revealed naked iron girders which only partly spanned the River Thames in the darkness. The famous stone covering had not yet been put into place. "There's been quite a controversy raging about the Bridge, you know. Stone over iron, unheard of, risky."

"Controversy?" the blonde sniffed, clearly thinking Tanglewood was feeding her a line. "Absurd. Tower Bridge is a national monument!"

"Will be," Margo put in. "Right now, it's just another bridge. Convenient for trans-shipping cargo from the docks on this bank to the docks on the South Side, since it'll cut five miles out of the draymen's one-way journey, but just a bridge, for all its convenience."

"Nonsense!"

Margo shrugged. "Suit yourself. This isn't the London you left a couple of days ago, Miss Nosette. I'd advise you to keep that in mind. Let's get moving, all right? We don't have any time to waste, standing around arguing about a stupid bridge that isn't even finished, yet."

They set out, Doug Tanglewood in the lead, Margo and Shahdi Feroz bringing up the rear, while Dominica Nosette and Guy Pendergast, voices low, deadlocked in a debate with Conroy Melvyn of Scotland Yard as they walked through the dark, rainy streets. Pubs had just closed down and houses were mostly dark, gas lights turned out while the working poor found what sleep they could before dawn sent them reeling out once more to earn a living however they could manage.

"There's a lot of evidence against Frederick Bailey Deeming, isn't there?" Pendergast asked softly.

"A small-time swindler with brain fever," Conroy Melvyn said with a dismissive air. "Killed his wife and children, slashed their throats. They hanged him in '92."

"Didn't the press dub him the official Ripper, though?" Dominica Nosette pressed the argument. "And Scotland Yard, as well? For years, the Yard exhibited his death mask as the Ripper's."

Conroy Melvyn shrugged. "Well, he was a right popular chap at the time, so he was, violent and known t'be in Whitechapel during the murders. Carried knives, so witnesses told police. Not," the uptime Scotland Yard inspector added drily, "that anybody had any real evidence against him. Prob'ly just an epileptic, drunken lout of a sailor with a violent temper and a nasty habit of killing off family when they got inconveniently expensive to support."

"Nice guy," Margo muttered, earning a sardonic glance from Shahdi Feroz.

Dominica Nosette, who had secreted a miniature video camera system under her clothing and bonnet, turned to glance at the Scotland Yard inspector—thus adroitly filming the "interview" as well.

"Who do *you* think did it, then?"

"I dunno, ma'am, and that's what we're doin' tonight, innit? Taking a bit of a look-see for ourselves, eh?"

Dominica Nosette, clearly not one to be dismissed so easily, dropped back to where Margo and Shahdi Feroz walked behind the chief inspector and Guy Pendergast. "Who do you think did it, Dr. Feroz? You never did name your top suspect, back on the station, despite all those marvelous theories about Satanists and mad lesbian midwives. Come, now, Dr. Feroz, who's your favorite suspect?"

Neither Shahdi Feroz nor Dominica Nosette noticed the sharp stare from a roughly dressed man nearly invisible in the shadows of a dark alleyway. A man who abruptly changed course to follow them. But Margo did. And she noticed the heavy sap in his hand and the covetous look he cast at Shahdi Feroz and her carpet bag. He'd clearly heard Dominica Nosette call Shahdi Feroz "doctor" and doubtless figured there was something valuable in her satchel. Medicines, maybe, which could be sold for cash. Margo rounded on him in scalding language that brought the ill-dressed villain—and the entire Ripper Watch Team—to a screeching halt in the middle of Whitechapel Road.

"Cor, 'ave a nice butcher's, will you?" Margo shrilled, fists clenched as she advanced menacingly on him. "Ain't you never clapped yer bleedin' minces on no missionary doctor before, you gob-smacked lager lout? Takin' 'er to London Horse Piddle, so I am, an' you lay a German on 'er, I'll clout you upside yer pink an' shell-like, so I will! I ain't no gormless git, I ain't, I know wot a blagger like you is up to, when 'e follows a lady, so g'wan, then, 'ave it away on yer buttons!

Before I smack you in the 'ampsteads wiv a bleedin' sap! C'mon, get yer finger out!"

Margo was, in fact, gripping a lead-filled leather sap of her own, so hard her knuckles stood out white. The shabbily dressed man following them had halted, mouth dropping open as he stared. Then he let out a bark of laughter past blackened teeth.

"Grotty-mouthed bit, ain't yer? Don't want no bovver, not 'at bad, I don't. Sooner go back to me cat an' face me ruddy knife, so I would, after she's copped an elephant."

The man faded back into the darkness, his harsh laughter still floating back to them. Margo relaxed her grip on the lead-filled sap one finger joint at a time, then glanced up to discover Douglas Tanglewood hovering at her side, pistol concealed behind one hip. "Well done," he said quietly, "if a bit theatrical. Ladies, gentlemen, we have a schedule to keep. Move along, please."

It was only then, as Margo herded the Ripper Watch Team members down the street, casting uneasy glances over her shoulder, that she noticed the open-mouthed stares from Guy Pendergast, Dominica Nosette, and—of all people—Shahdi Feroz, who broke the stunned silence first. "I am amazed! Whatever did you say to that man? It wasn't even in English! Was it?" she added uncertainly.

Margo cleared her throat self-consciously. "Well, no, it wasn't. That was Cockney dialect. Which isn't exactly English, no."

"But what did you *say?*" the Ripper scholar insisted. "And what did *he* say?"

"Well . . ." Margo tried to recall, exactly, what it was she'd actually said. "I asked him if he'd had a good look, hadn't he ever laid eyes on a missionary doctor, and I was taking you to London Hospital. So if he laid a hand on you, I'd hit him across the ear with a sap. Told him to go away, or I'd smack him in the teeth, and told him to hurry it up. Then he said I had a dirty mouth and told me he didn't want any trouble. Said he'd rather go home and face his wife after she'd been drinking than mix it up with me." Margo smiled a little lamely. "Actually, he was right about the dirty mouth. Some of what I said was really awful. Bad enough, a proper lady would've fainted from the shock, if she'd understood half of it."

Dominica Nosette laughed in open delight. "My dear, you are a treasure! Really, you've a splendid career ahead. What made you want to scout? Following in your grandfather's footsteps, no doubt?"

Margo didn't really want to talk about her family. Too much of it was painful. So she said, "We really shouldn't discuss anything from up time while we're here, Miss Nosette. That jerk started following us because he overheard what we were saying. You called Madame Feroz, there, by her professional title, which left him dangerously curious about us and the contents of her bag. There are very few women doctors in 1888 and it caught his attention. If you want to talk about scouting later, at the gatehouse, we can talk about it then, but not now. And please don't ask so many questions about the suspects while we're out on the streets. You-know-who hasn't even struck yet, despite the deaths on Easter Monday and August Bank Holiday, both of which will be attributed to him by morning. And since the nickname isn't made public in the newspapers until after September thirtieth, with the Dear Boss letter that's published after the double murders, conversation on that subject should be confined strictly to the gatehouse."

Dominica gave her one rebellious glance, then smiled sweetly. "Oh, all right. I'm sure you're only trying to watch out for our safety, after all. But I will get that interview, Miss Smith!"

Margo didn't know whether to feel flattered or alarmed.

Then they reached the turn-off for Buck's Row and all conversation came to a halt as the Ripper Watch Team went to work. They set up their surveillance equipment efficiently, putting in place miniature cameras, low-light systems, tiny but powerful microphones, miniaturized transmitters that would relay video and audio signals up to the rooftops and across London. They worked in silent haste, as the factory cottages terraced along the road were occupied by families who slept in the shadow of the factories where they worked such long and gruelling shifts. Conroy Melvyn had just finished putting the last connection in place when the constable assigned to this beat appeared at the narrow street's end, sauntering their way with a suspicious glance.

"Wot's this, then?" the policeman demanded.

"Don't want no barney, guv," Doug Tanglewood said quickly, "just 'aving a bit of a bobble, ain't we? C'mon, mates, let's 'ave a pint down to boozer, eh?"

"Oh, aye," Margo grumbled, "an' you'll end pissed as a newt again, like as not!"

"Shut yer gob, eh? Bottle's goin' t'think you ain't got no manners!"

The constable watched narrowly as Douglas Tanglewood and Margo herded the others out of Buck's Row and back toward Whitechapel Road. But he didn't follow, just continued along his assigned beat. Margo breathed a sigh of relief. "Whew . . ."

And did her dead-level best to keep the scholars and journalists out of trouble the whole way back to Spaldergate House, where Margo grew massively absorbed in the unfolding drama in the East End. They did a test recording, which captured a disturbance underway in one of the terraced cottages. The screaming fight which erupted on the heels of a drunken man's return home was not in English. Or Cockney, either. Bulgarian, maybe . . . Lots of immigrants lived in the East End, so many it was hard to distinguish languages, sometimes. The fight flared to violence and breaking crockery, then subsided with a woman sobbing in despair.

The street and the houses lining it grew quiet again. The constable walked his beat past the cameras several times during the next three hours, virtually alone on the dark stretch of road where no public gas lights burned anywhere within reach of the camera pickups. The silence in the street was mirrored by a thick silence in the vault, as they waited, downing cupfuls of coffee, fidgeting with the equipment, occasionally muttering and adjusting connections. As the clock ticked steadily toward Zero-Hour, the excitement, the electric tension in the vault beneath Spaldergate House was thick enough to cut with the Ripper's knife. Ten minutes before the earliest estimated time of death, they switched on the recording equipment, videotaping the empty stretch of cobbled street.

"Check those backup recordings," Conroy Melvyn muttered. "Be bloody sure we're getting multiple copies of this."

"Number two recording."

"Number three's a go."

"Four's copying just fine."

"Got a sound-feed problem on number five. I'm on it."

Margo, who had nothing to do but watch the others huddle tensely over consoles, fiddling with computer controls and adjusting sound mixers, wondered with a lonely pang what Malcolm was doing and why he hadn't returned, yet. Hours, it'd been, since he'd left on the search of London's hospitals. How many were there in London? She didn't know. After all the work he'd put in during the past weeks, setting up the base camp and helping the scholars learn their way around the East End, he was missing the historical moment when they would finally discover who Jack the Ripper really was. Lousy idiot of a tourist! Why Benny Catlin had chosen tonight, of all nights, to get himself into a gunfight at the Piccadilly Hotel . . .

"Oh, my God!" Pavel Koskenka's voice sliced through the tense silence. "There they are!"

Margo's breath caught involuntarily.

Then Jack the Ripper walked calmly into view, escorting Polly Nichols, all unknowing, to her death.

The night resembled the entire, waning summer: wet and cold. Rain slashed down frequently in sharp gusting showers which would end abruptly, leaving the streets puddled and chilly, only to pour again without warning. Thunder rumbled through the narrow cobbled streets like heavy wagon wheels laboring under a vast tonnage of transport goods. Savage flares of lightning pulsed through low-lying clouds above the wet slate rooftops of London. For the second time that night, a hellish red glow bathed the underbellies of those clouds as another dock fire raged through the East End. It was nearly two-thirty in the morning of a wet, soggy Friday, the last day of August.

James Maybrick paused in the puddled shadows along Whitechapel Road, where he watched the exceedingly erratic progress of the woman he had been following all evening, now. His hands, thrust deep into the pockets of his dark overcoat against the chill of the wet night, ached for the coming pleasure. His right hand curled gently around the hard wooden handle of the knife concealed in his coat's deep pocket. He smiled and tugged down his dark felt cap, one of many caps and hats he had purchased recently in differing parts of the city, preparing for this work.

The woman he followed at a discreet distance staggered frequently against the wall as she made her way east down Whitechapel Road ahead of him. She was a small woman, barely five feet two inches in height, with small and delicate features gone blowzy and red from the alcohol she had consumed tonight. High cheekbones, dark skin, and grey eyes, framed by brown hair beginning to show the signs of age . . . She might have been anywhere from thirty to thirty-five, to look at her, but Maybrick knew her history, knew everything it was possible to discover about this small, alcoholic woman he stalked so patiently. John Lachley had told Maybrick all about Polly Nichols. About her years of living as a common whore on the streets of White-chapel.

She was forty-four years old, this "Hooker" as the Americans in Norfolk would have called her, after the general who had supplied such women in the camps during the Civil War. Not a handsome woman, either. She must have a dreadful time luring customers to pay for the goods she offered up for sale. Polly's teeth were slightly discolored when she smiled and just above her eyes, Polly's dark complexion was marred by a scar on her brow. She was married, was "Polly" Nichols, married and a mother of five miserable children, God help them, to have such a mother. Mary Ann Walker, as Lachley had told him was her maiden name, had married William Nichols, subsequently left him five or six times (by William Nichols' own disgusted admission), and had finally left him for good, abandoning her children to take up a life of itinerant work "in service" between stints in workhouses and prostitution. William, poor sod, had convinced the courts to discontinue her maintenance money by proving that she was, in fact, living as a common whore.

Not even her father, Edward Walker, a respectable blacksmith in Camberwell, had been able to live with her during her slide into the miserable creature James Maybrick stalked through this rainy and unseasonably chilly August night. Her own father had quarreled violently with her over her drunkenness, precipitating her departure from his doorstep. Her most recent home—and Maybrick curled his lip at the thought of calling such lodgings home—had been the cold, unheated rooms she'd paid for in various "doss" houses along the infamous Flower and Dean Street and the equally notorious Thrawl Street, establishments which catered primarily to destitute whores. Hundreds of such lodging houses existed in Whitechapel, some of them even permitting men and women to share a bed for the night, as scandalous a notion as that was. The "evil quarter mile" as the stretch of Commercial Road from Thrawl Street to Flower and Dean was known, had for years been vilified as the most dangerous, foul street in London.

James Maybrick knew this only too well, for he had lived, briefly, in Whitechapel during the earliest years of his career as a cotton merchant's clerk, had met and married a pretty working girl named Sarah here, where she had still lived, unknown to the wealthy and faithless bitch he'd married many years later and settled in a fine mansion in Liverpool. Florie, the whore, had discovered Sarah's existence not so many weeks ago, had dared demand a divorce, after what she, herself, had done with Brierly! James had laughed at her, told her to consider her own future carefully before taking such a step, to consider the massive debts she'd run up at dressmakers' shops, debts she could not pay. If she hoped to avoid disgrace, to avoid bringing shame upon herself and her innocent children, she would jolly well indulge his appetites, leave poor Sarah in peace, and keep her mouth shut.

James had visited Sarah tonight, before arriving at Dr. Lachley's. He had enjoyed the conjugal visit with his precious first wife, who bore his need for Florie's money and social position stoically and lived frugally on the money Maybrick provided for her. Sarah was a good, God-fearing girl who had refused to leave Whitechapel and her only living relatives and ruin his social chances. Sarah, at least, would never have to walk these streets. Even the local Spitalfields clergy despaired of the region and its violent, criminal-minded denizens.

James Maybrick smiled into the wet night. They would not despair over one particular denizen much longer. Three and a half hours previously, he had quietly followed Polly Nichols down Whitechapel Road as she set out searching for her evening's doss money, the fourpence needed to secure a place to sleep, and had watched from the shadows as his guide, his mentor, Dr. John Lachley, had accosted her. The disguise his marvelous teacher wore had changed his appearance remarkably, delighting James to no end, as much as the secret retreat beneath the streets had delighted him. The false theatrical beard Maybrick had obtained for him from a cheap shop in SoHo and the dye used to color it left Lachley as anonymous as the thousands of other shabbily dressed working men wandering Whitechapel, wending their way from one gin palace to the next on a drunken pub crawl.

Lachley, stepping out into Polly Nichols' path, had smiled into her eyes. "Hello, my dear. It's a raw evening, isn't it?"

The doctor, whose medical treatments had left Maybrick feeling more powerful, more vigorous and invincible than he'd felt in years, glanced briefly past the whore's shoulder to where Maybrick stood in concealment, nodding slightly to indicate that this was Polly Nichols, herself, the woman he had brought James here to help murder. Dressed in a brown linsey frock, Polly Nichols had smiled up at John Lachley with a whore's calculating smile of greeting.

"Evening. Is a bit wet, innit?"

"A bit," Lachley allowed. "A lady such as yourself shouldn't be out with a bare head in such weather."

"Ooh, now aren't you the polite one!" She walked her fingers coyly up his arm. "Now, if I were to 'ave the coin, I might buy me a noice, fancy bonnet and keep the rain off."

"It just so happens," Lachley smiled down into her brown eyes, "that I have a few coins to spare."

She laughed lightly. "An' what might a lady need t'do to share that wealth, eh?"

"Consider it a gift." The physician pressed a silver florin into her palm.

She glanced down at the coin, then stared, open-mouthed, down at her grubby hand. "A *florin*?" This pitiful alcoholic little trollop now held in her hand a coin worth twenty-four pence: the equivalent of *six times* the going rate for what she was selling tonight. Or, marketed differently, six glasses of gin. Polly stared up at Lachley in sudden suspicion. "What you want t'give me an whole, entire florin for?" Greed warred with alarm in her once delicate little face.

John Lachley gave her a warm smile. "It's a small token of appreciation. From a mutual friend. Eddy sends his regards, madam." He doffed his rough cloth cap. "It has come to his attention that another mutual friend, a young man by the name of Morgan, loaned you a few of his personal letters. Eddy is desirous of re-reading them, you see, and asked me if I might not do him the favor of speaking with you about obtaining them this evening."

"*Eddy?*" she gasped. "Oh, *my!* Oh, blimey, the *letters!*"

Deep in his pocket, Maybrick gripped the handle of his knife and smiled.

John Lachley gave the filthy little trollop a mocking little bow. "Consider the florin a promise of greater rewards to come, in appreciation of your discretion in a certain, ah, delicate matter."

"Oh, I'm most delicate, I am, and it's most generous of Mr. Eddy to send a token of 'is good faith. But you see, I don't exactly 'ave those letters on me person, y'see. I'd 'ave to go an' fetch them. From the safe place I've been keepin' 'em 'idden, y'see, for Morgan," she added hastily.

"Of course, madam. Shall we meet again when you have obtained them? Name the time and place and I will bring a far better reward than that paltry florin, there."

"Oh, yes, certainly! Give me the night, say? Maybe we could meet in the morning?"

Maybrick tightened his hand on the knife handle again, in anger this time. *No!* He would *not* wait a whole day! The bitch must be punished now! Tonight! Visions of his wife, naked in her lover's arms, tormented James Maybrick, drove him to a frenzy of hatred, instilled in him the burning desire to kill this filthy prostitute posturing in front of them as though she were someone worthy of breathing the same air they did. Polly Nichols was nothing but a blackmailing, dirty little whore . . .

"You must understand," John Lachley was saying to her, "Eddy is most anxious to re-read his letters. I will meet you again here, later tonight, no later than, say, three-thirty in the morning. That should give you more than adequate time to fetch the letters, buy yourself something to drink at a public house and get a little something to eat, perhaps even buy yourself a nice new bonnet to keep this miserable rain off your lovely hair."

She bobbed her head in excitement, now. "Oh, yes, that'd be fine, three-thirty in the morning, no later. I'll be 'ere, I will, with them letters."

"Very good, madam." Lachley gave her another mocking bow. "Be sure, now, to find yourself a nice bonnet, to keep out the wet. We don't want you catching your death on a raw night like this." Lachley's lips twitched at the silent joke.

The doomed whore laughed brightly. "Oh, no, that would never do, would it? Did you want to go someplace dry and comfy, then?" She was caressing Lachley's groin vulgarly.

The thought tickled Maybrick's sense of humor, that this dirty little trollop would sell herself to the very man who was bringing about her murder. The thought excited him, almost as much as the thought of killing her did. He hoped Lachley dragged her to the nearest private spot and commenced banging her as hard as possible, toothless blackmailing bitch that she was.

John Lachley gave her a wry little smile. "Indeed, madam," he lifted his cap again, "little would give me greater pleasure, but duty recalls me to Eddy's side, I fear."

"Oh! Well, then, tell Mr. Eddy I'm that grateful for the money and I'll buy a proper bonnet before we meet again."

Maybrick reined in his seething frustration and disappointment with barely restrained violence. He gripped the wicked new knife inside his pocket until his whole hand ached. He wanted to strike *now,* curse it! But he had to wait until the tart found Lachley's letters, had hours to wait, yet. *I will rip her apart,* he thought savagely, *rip her wide open and let the rain wash the filth from the bleeding womb she sells so freely . . .*

Lachley gave her a courteous bow she did not merit and left her walking down Whitechapel Road. Maybrick's clever mentor had carefully instructed him in the exact method he must use to murder this bitch, to keep the blood from splashing across his clothes when he struck. The brilliant physician and occultist had guided him to the worst of the slatterns walking these streets—deserving targets of the monumental rage he carried against the bitch who lay with her lover, tonight, in Liverpool. Maybrick almost loved his mentor, in that moment, as he thought of what delights lay ahead. As Polly wobbled drunkenly off into the night, Lachley circled around silently, sent a secretive little smile in Maybrick's direction, and followed Polly Nichols once again.

Maybrick trailed at a leisurely distance, smiling to himself, now, and caressed the handle of his concealed knife with loving fingertips. Polly Nichols, stumbling ahead of them, first visited an establishment that sold clothing of dubious origins. There she acquired a reddish brown ulster to keep off the rain, which fastened up with seven large brass buttons, and a fetching little black straw bonnet with black velvet trim and lining. She giggled as she put it on, then paraded down the wet streets to pub after pub, steadily drinking the remaining change from the silver florin.

Twice, both he and Lachley paused in dense, wet shadows while she disappeared into a secluded spot with a customer to earn three or fourpence "for my doss money" she explained each time. And twice, after she had earned a few more pence, they followed along behind again as she found yet another pub in which to spend the money on gin. Well past midnight, she staggered out of the locally famous Frying Pan Public House, just one more in a long series of pubs, and found herself another customer with whom to earn another fourpence. She spent this money just as quickly as she had the rest, pouring it down her alcoholic gullet.

And so the night waned into the small hours. At nearly one-thirty in the morning, she returned to a lodging house at 18 Thrawl Street and remained inside its kitchen for several minutes, until the lodging house deputy escorted her to the door and said, "Get your doss money, ducks, an' don't come back 'til you 'ave it."

"Won't you save a bed for me?" she asked the man. "Never mind! I'll soon get my doss money. See what a jolly bonnet I've got now?" And she touched the black, velvet-lined straw hat with caressing fingers. "I've 'ad money tonight and I'll get more just as easy, I will, an' I'll be back wiv my doss money soon enough."

And so out onto the streets she wandered again, clearly searching for another customer to procure more gin to while away the time before their three-thirty appointment—presumably having retrieved the letters Lachley sought from the room she was not yet able to pay for and would not be needing, ever again. Maybrick followed her silently, as did the all-but-invisible John Lachley, a mere shadow of a shape in the darkness ahead, the paler blur of Lachley's skin lit now and again by the lightning flaring across the sky. The rumble of thunder threatened more rain. It would need rain, to wash away the blood James would spill into these streets . . .

Polly Nichols stumbled and staggered her way through the better part of an hour, approaching and being turned down by one prospect after another, leading James and his mentor eventually toward the corner of Whitechapel Road and Osborn Street. There, she put out a hand to brace herself and greeted a woman coming up Osborn. "Well, if it in't Emily 'olland," she slurred, "where you been?"

Emily Holland was a woman considerably older than Polly Nichols, closer to Maybrick's own age, he suspected, although she looked considerably older than Maybrick's fifty years. Emily greeted the drunken prostitute with considerable surprise. "Polly? I didn't expect to find you at this hour! Whatever are you doing wandering around so late? Me, I've been down to Shadwell Dry Dock. To see the fire." Emily gestured toward the distant docks, where the sky glowed a sullen red from the dockside disaster. It was the second fire that night which had reddened the clouds scudding so low above Whitechapel's broken and dilapidated rooftops. "What are you doing out at this hour, Polly? I thought you were coming back down to Flower and Dean Street, with Annie and Elizabeth and me. You were at the White House with us last night."

" 'At's right," Polly nodded, slurring the words. "But I've got to get me doss money, yet. Bastard wouldn't let me stay 'til I've got it."

"Polly, it's two-thirty in the morning!" Almost as an echo, a nearby church clock struck the time. "Hear that? Why don't you have your doss money by now?"

"Oh, I 'ad it. Three times today, I've 'ad it." She touched her pretty new bonnet in an absent little gesture. But she didn't explain about the florin and the letters, which was just as well, since that would have required Maybrick to murder this new trollop, Holland, also. Lachley had made it clear that none of these filthy whores must be allowed to know about such important letters. Truly, Maybrick was doing all England a great service, ridding the streets of the kind of filth Polly Nichols represented.

Polly was saying in a deeply slurred voice, "Three times, Emily, I've 'ad me doss money, but I've drunk it all. Every las' penny of it. Three times. Never you fret, though. I'll 'ave my doss money before long, I will, and I'll be back wiv you and the girls." She patted her pocket and let out a drunken giggle. "Won't be long at all, now."

Whereupon Polly took her leave of Emily Holland and staggered away on a new course, down Osborn Street in the direction of the Shadwell dock fire, where she might presumably find paying customers in abundance. The other woman called a low-voiced, "Good night!" after her and watched Polly for a moment longer, shaking her head sadly, then shrugged and pulled her shawl more tightly about her shoulders and continued on her way, down Osborn Street in the opposite direction. James Maybrick waited impatiently until Emily Holland had disappeared into the wet night before moving down Whitechapel Road in pursuit, once more. John Lachley also broke from hiding.

Polly's voice, badly slurred, drifted back to Maybrick. "Be nice, 'aving an 'ot fire to warm me cold fingers by." She laughed drunkenly and reached the edge of the crowd which had gathered at Shadwell to watch the docks burn. Utter chaos reigned. Firemen swept continuous streams of water back and forth across the blazing dry dock and several doomed warehouses. Fire boats in the river added their drenching spray, trying to contain the inferno before it spread to any other warehouses with valuable contents.

More than two centuries might have passed since the Great Fire, but London had never forgotten the devastation which had destroyed all but one tiny corner of Britain's capital city. The only good to come of *that* fire, which had forced thousands to flee, only to watch their homes and livelihoods burn to ashes, had been the complete eradication of the Black Death. Afterwards, plague had never broken out in London again.

Not a plague of *that* sort, in any case. A plague of whores and prostitutes and bitches, however, had swelled to number in the thousands. Tonight, Maybrick would begin his campaign to eradicate this latest deadly plague to strike the greatest city in the greatest Empire on the earth. He smiled, marshaled his patience, and kept watch on Polly Nichols as she trolled for customers.

Despite the late hour, thousands of spectators jammed the narrow streets to watch this latest London fire. The electric thrill of danger was a tangible presence in the wet night. Maybrick hung well back, as did Lachley, losing sight of the drunken Polly Nichols in the crowd. The atmosphere in Shadwell was a carnival madness. Alcohol flowed in prodigious quantities. Maybrick, seething like the jagged lightning overhead, downed pint after pint of dark ale, himself, feeding his rage, nursing the hunger in his soul. John Lachley, too, had vanished through the crowd, leaving Maybrick to wait. He wanted to shout obscenities, he was so weary of walking and endlessly *waiting*. He gripped the handle of his knife so tightly he was sure there would be bruises across his palm by morning.

Nearly an hour later, with the fire still blazing furiously, Maybrick finally caught another glimpse of Polly Nichols' black, velvet-trimmed bonnet. She was just emerging through the door of a jam-packed public house which had thrown open its doors in all defiance of the closing-hour laws. She staggered mightily under the influence of God-only-knew how much more alcohol. She passed Maybrick without even seeing him, stumbled straight past a doorway from which John Lachley subsequently emerged, and headed down Osborn Street toward Whitechapel Road.

It was time for her to keep her rendezvous with murder.

The game was in Maybrick's blood, now, the stop and start of shadowing his prey down wet streets with the growl of thunder snarling overhead like a savage beast loose in the night. They waited, strolling quietly along, until they were well away from the crowd at the fire. Polly reached the now-deserted Whitechapel Road and turned east, moving unsteadily toward the spot they'd agreed to meet. John Lachley started out into the open, making his move to retrieve the letters. Then halted abruptly. So did Maybrick, cursing their foul luck.

A rough man dressed like a dockhand, also coming from the direction of the Shadwell Dry Dock fire, had appeared at the end of the block and accosted her first.

Maybrick and his mentor melted back into the shadows of dark overhanging doorways, on opposite sides of the narrow street. The dockhand and the drunken whore bent their heads together and spoke quietly. A low laugh broke from the man and Maybrick heard Polly say, "Yes." A moment later, the two of them sought deeper shadows, so close to James Maybrick's hiding place, he could literally *smell* them from where he stood.

Maybrick's pulse flared like the lightning overhead as he stood there in the darkness, listening to the rustle of skirts and clothing hastily switched about, the sharp sounds of the dockhand shifting his hobnailed boots on the pavement as he pressed the cheap trollop back into a convenient corner, the heavy breaths and meaty sounds of flesh coming together, slow and rhythmic and hard. Maybrick's nostrils flared. He gripped the wooden handle of his knife, listened eagerly to the gasp of breath as the whore ground her hips against her customer's. He could all but see the clutch of the dock worker's hands against a straining breast, a naked thigh, skirts and petticoats lifted high to either side to accommodate him. He imagined his wife's face where the strumpet's was, saw his wife's glorious, strawberry blond hair falling down across her naked breasts as the unwashed dockhand shoved into her, took her right here on the street like the slut she was, heard his wife's voice gasping in the close darkness . . .

Low, breathy obscenities drifted on the night air, his voice, then hers, encouraging him. *Hurry,* she must be thinking, *hurry up and finish, I'm drunk and need a bed for the night and they'll be along with the money for the letters soon, so get on with it and spend your spunk, you great ugly lout of a dockhand . . .*

Maybrick clutched his knife, hand thrust deep in his pocket, and breathed hard as she whispered to the man using her. " 'At's right, lovey, 'at's good, Friar me right good, you do, 'at's grand . . ."

Friar Tuck . . . the rhyming slang of the streets . . .

A low, masculine grunt finally drifted past Maybrick's hiding place.

He waited for their breaths to slow from the frantic rush.

Waited for the sounds of clothing going back down, the jingle of coins in a pocket, the whisper of, " 'Ere's threepence, pet, and a shiny penny besides." The sound of a wet kiss came, followed by the muffled smack of a hand against a cloth-covered backside. "An' a right nice trembler it was, too."

Maybrick waited, pulse pounding like the thunder overhead, as the dockhand's hobnailed boots clattered away down the pavement in the direction of the docks and the still-burning fire. As his footfalls died away, Polly's low, slurred voice drifted to Maybrick. "Eh, then, got my doss money, just like I told Emily I would. I've 'ad a lovely new bonnet tonight and a warm new ulster and thirty-eleven pints and still got my doss money. And there's still the money for the letters to collect, too!" A low laugh reached Maybrick's hiding place.

He waited in a fever of impatience while she staggered out into the open again, heading down Whitechapel Road with the money she'd just earned in her pocket. Across the street, Lachley, silent on the rubberized overshoes they'd both bought, the same shoes worn by several million ordinary domestic servants to silence their footfalls, stole after her down Whitechapel Road. They crept up behind . . .

"Hello, love," Lachley whispered.

She gave a tiny, indrawn shriek and whirled, with semi-disastrous results.

Lachley steadied the small woman easily. "There, now, I didn't mean to terrify you. Steady."

She peered up at him, face pinched from the shock. "Oh, it's you," she breathed out, "you give me such a fright!" She smiled happily, then, and touched her bonnet. "See? I got me that bonnet, just like you said. Innit a fine one?"

"Very fine. Very becoming. Velvet trim, isn't it? A lovely bonnet. I trust you have the letters we discussed earlier?"

A crafty smile stole across the woman's face. "I've got one of 'em, so I 'ave."

Only Maybrick saw the flicker of murderous wrath cross Lachley's face. Then he was smiling down at her again. "*One* of them? But, my dear, there were four! Mr. Eddy really is most anxious to obtain the full set."

"Course 'e is, an' I don't blame 'im none, I don't, but y'see, I only 'ad the one letter. An' I've looked for my friend, looked an' looked everywhere, what 'as the other three—"

"Friend?" Lachley's voice came to Maybrick as a flat, blank sound of astonishment. "*Friend?*"

The stupid whore didn't even notice the cold rage in her murderer's voice.

"I 'adn't so much as a single 'apenny to me name and it were ever so cold an' raining ever so 'ard. An' I 'adn't drunk no gin in an whole day, y'see, so I give three of the letters to Annie an' she give me a shilling, so I could pay for a doss 'ouse an' not be caught by some constable sleepin' rough and get sent back to Lambeth Work'ouse. She's only 'olding 'em for me, like, 'til I get the shilling back to repay 'er the loan . . ."

Lachley touched her gently, tipping up her chin. "Who is this friend, Polly? What is her name?"

"Annie. I said that, Annie Chapman, what lives in the doss 'ouses over to Flower and Dean Street, same as me. She's 'oldin' the other three letters for me, but I'll 'ave 'em back by tomorrow morning, swear I will."

"Of course you will." Lachley was smiling again.

Maybrick's hand was sweaty where he gripped his knife.

Polly blinked anxiously up into Lachley's face. "Say, you finish up your business with Mr. Eddy for the night?" She leaned against Lachley, still reeking of the dockworker's sweat. "Maybe we could go someplace b'fore I go back to me doss 'ouse an' find Annie?"

"No, my business tonight is not quite finished," Lachley said with fine irony. Maybrick admired the man more and more. He gestured Maybrick forward with a motion of his head. "But I've a friend here with me who has a little time in hand."

Polly turned, so drunk on the gin she'd guzzled that Lachley had to keep her from falling. "Well, then, 'ello, luv."

"Good evening, ma'am." Maybrick tipped his hat.

"Polly," John Lachley said with a faint smile, "this is James. He is a dear friend of mine. James will take care of you this evening. Now. Here is the money for the letter you have with you." Lachley held out a palmful of glittering sovereigns.

Polly gasped. Then fumbled through her pocket and produced a crumpled letter.

Lachley took it gently from her, swept his gaze across what had been written on the grubby sheets of foolscap, and put the money in her hand, then glanced up at Maybrick with a quirk of his lips. Polly wouldn't be keeping her money long.

"There, now. First payment, in good faith. Payment in full very soon. Shall Mr. James, here, escort you someplace quiet?"

Polly smiled up at Maybrick in turn and moved her hand downward along the shapeless workmen's trousers he wore. "Grand."

Maybrick's breaths came faster. He smiled down into her eyes, pulse beating a savage rhythm at his temples. He said to his whore, "This way, my dear."

They had timed the rounds of the constables of the H Division all through this area, he and Lachley. Maybrick knew very well that the next few minutes would provide him with exactly the opportunity he needed. Lachley doffed his cap and bid Polly goodnight and disappeared down Whitechapel Road at a brisk walk, whistling merrily to himself. James knew, of course, that his mentor would circle around to Buck's Row by way of quiet little Baker's Row and meet him again soon . . . very soon.

Maybrick took Polly's arm and gave her a brilliant smile, then guided her off the main road, down Thomas Street, a narrow bridge road which led across the rail line of the London and Northern Railway, twenty feet below. Beyond the railway line lay the exceedingly narrow street known as Buck's Row, lined by high brick warehouses, a board school, and several terrace houses, which served as cottages for the tradesmen who worked in Schneiders Cap Factory and several high, dark warehouses: the Eagle Wool Warehouse, which supplied fabric for the cap factory, and the massive warehouse called Essex Wharf.

James knew Schneider of old, a dirty little foreigner, which in this dismal region meant only one thing: Jew. James had chosen his killing ground carefully, most carefully, indeed. It was the filthy foreigners flooding into London who were destroying the moral fibre of the English Empire, bringing in their foreign ways and unholy religious practices and speaking every tongue heard at the Tower of Babel except the Queen's good English. Yes, James had chosen this spot with great care, to leave a message on the very doorstep of the bastards destroying all that was English.

The place he wanted was an old stableyard which stood between the school and the workers' cottages. The only street lamp was at the far end of Buck's Row, where it met Baker's Row to the west. As they entered the cramped, cobbled street, which was no more than twenty feet wide from housewalls on the one hand to warehouse walls opposite, Maybrick slipped his right hand into his coat pocket again. He closed his hand around the handle of the beautiful, shining knife and gripped it tightly. His pulse raced. His breath came in short, unsteady gasps. The smell of cheap gin and sex and greed was a poison in his brain. Her whispered obscenities to the dockworker rang in his ears. His hand sweat against the wood. *Here,* his mind shrieked. *Quick, before the bloody constables come back!* He drew another breath, seeing in his mind his beautiful, faithless wife, naked and writhing under the lover who impaled her in that hotel he'd seen them coming out of together, the one in Liverpool's fashionable Whitechapel Street.

Maybrick glanced toward Baker's Row. Saw Lachley appear from the blackness at the end of Buck's Row. Saw him nod, giving the signal that all was clear. Maybrick's breath whipsawed, harsh and urgent. He tightened his left hand on the whore's arm. Moving her almost gently, Maybrick pressed her back against the stableyard gate. It was solid as iron. She smiled up at him, fumbling with her skirts. He slid his hand up her arm, toyed with a breast, slipped his fingers upwards, toward her neck—

Then smashed a fist into her face.

Bone crunched. Several of her teeth broke loose. She sagged back against the fence, stunned motionless. Maybrick tightened a savage grip around her throat. Her eyes bulged. Her abruptly toothless mouth worked. Shock and terror twisted across her once-delicate face.

High cheekbones flushed dark as he cut off her air. His wife's face swam before his eyes, gaping and toothless and terror stricken. He dug his thumb into dear, faithless Florie's jaw, bruising the right side of her face. The bitch struggled feebly as he tightened down. He dented and bruised the flesh of her throat, the left side of her face with his fingers, ruthless and drunk with the terror he inflicted. *She* was so drunk, she wasn't able to do more than claw weakly at his coat sleeve with one hand.

James Maybrick smiled down into his whore's dying eyes . . .

. . . and brought out his shining knife.

Skeeter Jackson pushed his heavy maintenance cart toward the men's room in Little Agora, bottles rattling and mops threatening to crash against the protestors who screamed and carried signs and picketed fifteen feet deep around Ianira's vacant booth, threatening to shut down commerce with their disruptive presence and threatening to shut down the station with the violence that broke out between them and the Arabian Nights construction workers at least once every couple of hours.

Nuts, he groused, maneuvering with difficulty through the packed crowd, *we are neck deep in nutcases.* He finally gained the bathroom, which he was already fifteen minutes overdue to scrub, slowed down on his schedule by the crowds of protestors and uneasy tourists, and turned on the hot water to fill his mop bucket. He'd just added soap when the trouble broke loose.

A sudden scuffle and a meaty smack and thump shook the whole bank of stalls behind him. Skeeter came around fast, mop gripped in both hands like a quarterstaff. A pained cry, high-pitched and frightened, accompanied another thud and violent slap. Then a stall door burst open and a burly guy with Middle Eastern features, who wore jeans and a work shirt and a burnoose-style headdress, strode out. He looked smug and self-satisfied. He was still zipping his fly. A muffled, startlingly feminine sob came from the now-open stall.

Skeeter narrowed his eyes at the construction worker, who wore a wicked linoleum knife in a sheathe on his belt. These creeps had been involved in the attacks on Ianira and her family. He was convinced they might yet know where she was, despite their protests of innocence to station security. They were trouble, wherever they went on station and it looked very much like more trouble was breaking loose right in front of him.

"You want to tell me what that was all about?" Skeeter asked quietly, placing himself carefully between the heavily muscled worker and the exit.

The dark-eyed man smirked down at Skeeter, measuring his shorter height and lighter frame contemptuously. "Little girls should not demand more money than they are worth."

"Is that a fact?" Skeeter balanced lightly on the balls of his feet, aware that he played a potentially lethal game. These guys carried tools that doubled as deadly weapons. But he wasn't going to let this creep just walk out of here, not with somebody back there crying in that stall like a hurt child. "Hey, you okay in there?" he called out to the pair of grubby tennis shoes visible under the partially open door. "I'll call the station infirmary if you need help."

"S-Skeeter?" The voice was familiar, quavering, terrified.

When the voice clicked in Skeeter's memory, the anger that burst through him was as cold and deadly as the winter winds howling down off the mountains onto the plains of the Gobi. *"Bergitta?"* The girl huddled in the back of the stall was younger than Skeeter. She'd helped search for Ianira, that first terrible day, had searched along with the other down-timers long after station security had given up the job. The Found Ones had been teaching her modern technical skills so she could make a living doing something besides selling herself.

"Skeeter, please . . . he . . . he will hurt you . . ."

Skeeter had no intention of abandoning a member of his adopted down-timer family to the likes of this smirking lout. "How much did he agree to give you, Bergitta?" he asked, carefully keeping his gaze on the construction worker who now eyed him narrowly.

"T-twenty—but it is okay, please . . ."

Skeeter gave the angry construction worker a disgusted glare. *"Twenty?* Geez, last of the big spenders, aren't we? You can't hardly buy a *burger* around here for that. Listen, asshole, you pay my friend, there, what you promised and get the hell out of here, maybe I won't get nasty."

Incredulous black eyes widened. "*Pay* her?" His laugh was ugly, contemptuous. "Out of my way, you stupid little cockerel!"

Skeeter stood his ground. The other man's eyes slitted angrily. Then the construction worker started forward, moving fast, one fist cocked, the other reaching for his belt. Skeeter caught a glint of light off that wicked linoleum knife—

He whirled the mop handle in a blurred, sweeping arc.

It connected solidly with a solar plexus that came to an abrupt halt.

A sharp, ugly grunt tore loose. The knife clattered to the tiled floor. The would-be knife-fighter folded up around the end of Skeeter's mop, eyes bugged out. Skeeter kicked the knife away with one foot. It clattered across the floor and skidded into a puddle under a distant urinal, then Skeeter assisted the gagging construction worker face-first into the steaming mop bucket at his feet. He landed with a *skloosh!* While he was upended, Skeeter lifted his wallet with light-fingered skill and extracted its contents. Curses gurgling underwater blew the most interesting soap bubbles Skeeter had ever seen.

As soon as he'd secured Bergitta's money, Skeeter hauled the former customer up by the shirt collar. "Now," he said gently, "you want to tell me about Ianira Cassondra?"

The reply was in Arabic and doubtless obscene.

Skeeter fed him more soap bubbles.

By the fourth dunking, the man was swearing he'd never laid eyes on Ianira Cassondra and would've strewn petals at her feet, if it would've helped keep his head above water. Reluctantly, Skeeter decided the bastard must be telling the truth. He shoved the guy's wallet between soapy teeth and said, "Twenty for services rendered and the rest for damages wrought. Now get the hell out of here before I break ribs. Or call security."

One twist of the mop handle and the dripping construction worker found it necessary to launch himself across the tiled floor, out the doorway, and past the "Slippery When Wet" sign just beyond. From the startled shrieks and angry shouts outside, he cannoned straight into a group of protestors. A moment later, security whistles sounded and a woman's voice drifted in, shrill with indignation. "He knocked me down! Yes, he ran that way . . ."

Skeeter crossed the bathroom, flexing a slightly strained shoulder, and peered into the open stall. Bergitta had clutched one side of her face, which was already swollen and turning purple. The simple dress she wore was torn. Anger started a slow burn as he gazed down at his terrified friend. "Are you okay?" he asked gently.

She nodded. Then burst into tears and slid to the tiled floor, trembling so violently he could hear the scrape of her identification bracelet—a gift from the Found Ones—against the wall. Skeeter bit his lip. Then sighed and waded in to try and pick up the shattered pieces. He crouched beside her, gently brushed back Bergitta's hair, a glorious, platinum blond, thick and shining where the lights overhead touched it.

"Shh," he whispered, "he's gone now. You're safe, shh . . ." When she'd stopped crying, he said gently, "Bergitta, let's take you down to the infirmary."

She shook her head. "No, Skeeter, there is no money . . ."

Skeeter held out the cash he'd liberated. "Yes, there is. And I've got some money put aside, too, so don't you worry about that, okay?" He'd been saving that cash for his rent, but what the hell, he could always sleep in the Found Ones' council chamber down in the station's sub-basement until he could afford to rent another apartment.

Bergitta was crying again, very quietly and very messily down her bruised face. Skeeter retrieved a towel from his push cart and dried her cheeks, then helped her to her feet. When she wobbled, shaking violently, Skeeter simply picked her up and carried her. She clung to his shoulders and hid her face from the curious onlookers they passed. When he carried her into the infirmary, Rachel Eisenstein was just stepping out of her office.

"Skeeter! What's happened? Not another riot?" she asked worriedly.

"No. Some asshole construction worker blacked Bergitta's face and God knows what else before I interrupted. Tried to disembowel me with a linoleum knife when I protested."

Rachel's lips thinned. "Bring her into the back, Skeeter, let's see how badly hurt she is. And we'd better file an official complaint with security. The more complaints we log, the more likely Bull is to push the issue and toss the men responsible for all this trouble through Primary, schedule or no schedule. Kit's already been after Bull to do just that."

So Rachel took charge of Bergitta, and Skeeter found himself giving a statement to security. He identified the man from a file of employment photos. "That's him. Yeah, the creep came at me with a linoleum knife."

"You realize we can't press charges for what he did to Bergitta?" the security officer said as he jotted down notes. "She's a down-timer. No legal rights."

"Yeah," Skeeter muttered darkly, "I know." They'd search for Ianira Cassondra, move heaven and earth to find her, because of the Templars and the phenomenal popularity and power of the Lady of Heaven Temples, but Bergitta was just another down-timer without rights, trapped on the station with no way off and no protection from the people who ran her new world. Worse, she was a known prostitute. Security didn't give a damn when a girl like Bergitta got hurt.

The guard said, "If *you* want this creep charged with assault and battery with a deadly weapon, plus anything else I can think up, you got it, but that's all we can nail him for, Skeeter."

"Yes, I want him charged," Skeeter growled. "And tossed off station, if you can swing it. Along with his pals."

"Don't hold your breath. That crew's already running behind schedule and the first tour's slated for next month. We might be able to work out a trial up time after the new section of Commons is finished, but getting him tossed off station before that job's done is flogging a dead horse. Not my idea, but that's how it is. Just figured you'd want to know up front."

Skeeter muttered under his breath. "Thanks. I know you're doing your best."

Rachel put in appearance just then, returning from the exam room where Bergitta rested. "She's badly shaken up and her face is going to be sore for a while, along with some other nasty bruises he left, but she's basically all right. No internal hemorrhaging, no broken bones."

Skeeter relaxed marginally. "Thank God."

Rachel eyed him curiously. "You fought a man with a knife, protecting her?"

Skeeter shrugged. "Wasn't much of a contest, really. I had a mop, he never got close to me with it."

"Well, whatever you think, it was still a risky thing to do, Skeeter."

He realized she was trying to thank him. Skeeter felt his cheeks burn. "Listen, about the bill, I've got some money—"

"We'll talk about that later, all right? Oh-oh . . ."

Skeeter glanced around and blanched.

His boss was inbound and the head of station maintenance did not look happy.

"Is it true?" Charlie Ryan demanded.

"Is what true?" Skeeter asked, wary and on his guard.

"That you beat up a construction worker over a goddamned down-timer whore? Then brought her up here while you're still clocked in officially on my dime?"

Skeeter clenched his fists. "Yes, it's true! He was beating the shit out of her—"

"I don't pay you to rescue your down-timer pals, Jackson! I looked the other way when it was Ianira Cassondra, but this by God tears it! And I sure as hell don't pay you to put hard-working construction professionals in the brig!"

Rachel tried to intervene. "Charlie, everyone on station's had trouble with those guys and you know it."

"Stay out of this, Rachel! Jackson, I pay you to mop bathrooms. Right now, there's a bathroom in Little Agora that's not getting mopped."

"I'll clean the stinking bathroom!" Skeeter growled.

Charlie Ryan look him up and down. "No, you won't. You're fired, Jackson."

"Charlie—" Rachel protested.

"Let it go, Rachel," Skeeter bit out. "If I'd known I was working for a stinking bigot, I'd've quit weeks ago."

He stalked out of the infirmary and let the crowds on Commons swallow him up.

What he was going to do now, he honestly did not know.

He walked aimlessly for ages, hands thrust deep into his pockets, watching the tourists practice walking in their rented costumes and laughing at one another's antics and buying each other expensive lunches and souvenirs, and wondered if any of them had the slightest notion what it was like for the down-time populations stranded on these stations?

He was sitting on the marble edging of a fountain in Victoria Station, head literally in hands, when Kynan Rhys Gower appeared from out of the crowd, expression grim. "Skeeter, we have trouble."

He glanced up, startled to hear the Welshman's voice. "Trouble? Oh, man, *now* what?"

"It is Julius," Kynan said quietly. "He is missing."

Skeeter just shut his eyes for a long moment. "Oh, no . . ." Not another friend, missing. The teenager from Rome had organized the down-timer kids into a sort of club known affectionately as the Lost and Found Gang. Under Ianira's guidance, the "gang" had turned its attention to earning money guiding lost tourists back to their hotel rooms, serving as the Found Ones' eyes and ears in places where adults would have roused suspicion, running errands and proving their value time and again. The children's work had allowed the Found Ones to learn rather a good bit more about the cults active on station than Mike Benson or anyone in security had managed to discover.

"How long has he been missing?" Skeeter asked tiredly.

"We are not sure," Kynan sighed. "No one has seen him since . . ." The Welshman hesitated. "He was supposed to be running an errand for the Found Ones, just before the riot broke out, the one Ianira disappeared in. No one has seen him, since."

"Oh, God. What's going on around this station?"

Kynan clenched his fists in visible frustration. "I do not know! But if I find out, Skeeter, I will take apart whoever is responsible!"

Of that, Skeeter had no doubt whatsoever. Skeeter intended to help. "Okay, we've got to get another search organized. For Julius, this time."

"The Lost and Found Gang are already searching."

"I want them to get as close to those creeps on the Arabian Nights construction crew as they can. And those crazy Jack the Ripper cults, too. *Any* group of nuts on this station who might have a reason to want Ianira to disappear, to stir up trouble, is on the suspect list."

Kynan nodded. "I will get word to the children. They are angry, Skeeter, and afraid."

"Huh. So am I, Kynan Rhys Gower. So am I."

The Welshman nodded slowly. "Yes. A brave man is one who admits his fear. Only a fool believes himself invincible. The Council of Seven has called an emergency meeting. *Another* one."

"That's no surprise. What time?"

"An hour from now."

Skeeter nodded. At least he wouldn't have to worry about losing his job, sneaking off to attend it. Kynan Rhys Gower hesitated. "I have heard what happened, Skeeter. Bergitta is all right?"

"Yeah. Bruised, scared. But Rachel said she's okay."

"Good." The one-time longbowman's jaw muscles bunched. "Charlie Ryan is a pig. He hires us because he does not have to pay, what is the up-time word? Union wages."

"Yeah. Tell me about it."

"Skeeter . . ."

He glanced up at the ominous growl in the other man's voice.

"Accidents happen."

"No." Skeeter shoved himself to his feet, looked the Welshman straight in the eyes. "No, it's his right to fire me. And I *was* doing a lousy job, spending all my time looking for Ianira and Marcus instead of working. I happen to think he's got his priorities screwed up, but I won't hear of anything like that. I appreciate it, but it'd just be a waste of effort. Guys like Charlie Ryan are like mushrooms. Squash one, five more pop up. Besides, if anybody's going to loosen his teeth, it's gonna be me, okay?"

Kynan Rhys Gower clearly considered arguing, then let it go. "That is your right," he said quietly. "But you have earned more this day than you have lost."

Skeeter didn't know what to say.

"I will see you at the Council meeting," the Welshman told him quietly, then left him standing in the glare and noise of Commons, wondering why his eyes stung so harshly. "I'll be there," Skeeter swore to empty air.

How many more of his friends would simply vanish into thin air before this ugly business was done? What had Julius seen or overheard, to cause someone to snatch him, too? When Skeeter got his hands on whoever was responsible for this . . . That someone would learn what it meant to suffer the summary justice of a Yakka Mongol clansman. Meanwhile, he had another friend missing.

Skeeter had far too few friends to risk losing any more of them.

Margo craned forward, so excited and repelled at the same time, she felt queasy. Then she saw the face and gasped as she recognized him. "*James Maybrick!*" she cried. "It's James Maybrick! The cotton merchant from Liverpool!"

"Shh!" The scholars motioned frantically for silence, trying to hear anything the murderer and his victim might say, even though everything was being recorded, including Polly Nichols' final footfalls. Margo gulped back nausea, watched in rising horror as Maybrick escorted his victim down to the gate where he would strangle and butcher her. When he struck with his fist, Margo hid her face in her hands, unable to watch. The sounds were bad enough . . .

Then Conroy Melvyn burst out, "Who the bloody hell is *that*?"

Margo jerked her gaze up to the television screen . . . and found herself staring, right along with the rest of the shocked Ripper Watch Team. A man had crept up behind Jack the Ripper, who was still hacking away at his dead victim.

"James . . . enough." Just the barest thread of a whisper. Then, when Maybrick continued to hack at the dead woman's neck, as though trying to cut loose her entire head, "*She's dead, James. Enough!*"

Whoever this man was, he clearly knew James Maybrick. More importantly, Maybrick clearly knew *him*. The maniacal rage in Maybrick's eyes faded as he glanced around. Maybrick's lips worked wetly. "But I wanted the head . . ." Plaintive, utterly mad.

"There's no time. Fetch me the money from her pockets. Be quick about it, the constable will be arriving momentarily."

The Buck's Row cameras, fitted with low-light equipment, picked up the lean, saturnine face, the drooping moustache of a total stranger who stepped up to peer at Polly Nichols. As Maybrick stooped to crouch over the dead woman, the newcomer closed a hand around Jack the Ripper's shoulder, a casual gesture which revealed a depth of meaning to anyone who knew the stiff etiquette of Victorian Britain. These men knew each other well enough for casual familiarities. Maybrick was wiping his knife on Polly's underskirts.

"Very good, James. You've done well. Strangled her first, as instructed. Not more than a wineglass of blood. Very good." Voice pitched to a low whisper, the tones and words were clearly those of an educated man, but with hints of the East End in the vowels, hints even Margo's untrained ear could pick out. Then, more sharply, "The money, James!"

"Yes, Doctor!" Maybrick's voice, thick with sexual ecstasy, trembled in the audio pickup. The arsenic-addicted cotton merchant from Liverpool bent over the prone remains of his victim and searched her pockets, retrieving several large coins that glinted gold like sovereigns. "No other letters, Doctor," he whispered.

"Letters?" Pavel Kostenka muttered, leaning closer to the television monitor to stare at the stranger's face. "What letters? And Dr. *Who?*"

Across the room, the British police inspector Conroy Melvyn choked with sudden, silent laughter for some completely unfathomable reason. Margo resolved to ask him what he could possibly find funny, once this macabre little meeting in Buck's Row had ended.

On the video monitor, the stranger muttered impatiently, "No, of course there won't be any other letters. She said she'd sold them, drunken bitch, and I believed her when she said it. Come, James, the H Division Constables will be along momentarily. Wipe your shoes clean, they're bloody. Then come with me. You've done well, James, but we have to hurry."

Maybrick straightened up. "I want my medicine," he said urgently.

"Yes, I'll be sure and give you more of the medicine you need, before you catch your train for home. *After* we've reached Tibor."

Maybrick's eyes glittered in the low-light pickup. He gripped the other man's arm. "*Thank you,* doctor! Ripping the bitch like that . . . she opened like a ripe peach . . . so bloody wonderful . . ."

"Yes, yes," the narrow-faced man said impatiently, "You can write it all down in your precious diary. *Later.* Now, you must come with me, we haven't much time. This way . . ."

The two men moved away from the camera's lens, walking quickly but not so fast as to arouse suspicion should anyone happen to glance out a window. The crumpled body of Polly Nichols lay beside the gate where she'd died, her disarranged skirts hiding the ghastly mutilations Maybrick's knife had inflicted. Margo stared after the two men who—clearly—were conspirators in some hideous game that involved unknown letters, payments made to prostitutes, and murder. The game made no rational sense to Margo, any more than it did to the openly stunned Ripper scholars. Who was this mysterious doctor and why was Maybrick involved with him? And why hadn't Maybrick's diary even once hinted at such a turn of events? That diary, explicit as to detail, with its open, candid mention of the many people in Maybrick's life—his unfaithful American wife, their young children and the little American girl staying with the Maybrick family, his brothers, employees, murder victims, friends— that diary had never even once hinted at a co-conspirator in the murder of the five Whitechapel prostitutes Maybrick had taken credit for killing.

Who, then, was this dark-skinned, foreign-looking man? A man who, Margo realized abruptly, fit perfectly some of the Ripper eyewitness descriptions. And Maybrick, with his fair skin and light hair and thick gold watch chain, fit other eyewitness descriptions to the last detail. The many witnesses questioned by London police had described two very different-appearing men—for the perfectly simple reason that there'd been *two* killers. "The eyewitness accounts," Margo gasped, "no wonder they differed, yet were so consistent. There *were* two of them! A dark-haired, foreign-looking man *and* a fair-haired one. And Israel Schwartz, the Jewish merchant who'll see Elizabeth Stride attacked, he saw *both* of them! Working together!"

She grew aware of startled stares from the Ripper Watch scholars.

Shahdi Feroz, in particular, was frowning; but not, Margo sensed, in disapproval. She looked merely thoughtful. "Yes," Dr. Feroz nodded, "that would certainly account for much of the confusion. It is not so unheard of, after all."

Margo gulped. "What's not so unheard of?"

Shahdi Feroz glanced up again. "Hmm? Oh. It is not unheard of, this collusion between psychopaths. A weaker psychopathic serial killer will sometimes attach himself to a mentor, a personal god, if you will. He worships the more powerful killer, does his bidding, learns from him." She was frowning, dark eyes agitated. "This is very unexpected, very serious. It is, indeed, possible that more of the murders during this time period *should* be attributed to the Ripper, if the Ripper was, in fact, *two* men. Two very disturbed men, working as a team, master and worshiper. They might well have struck in different *modus operandi,* which would explain the confusion over which women were killed by the Ripper."

"Yes," Inspector Melvyn broke in, "but what about these letters? What letters? And just who *is* this bloke? Doesn't fit any of the known profiles. Not a bloody, damned one of 'em!"

Dr. Kostenka shook his head, however. "Not one of the named profiles, no; but a profile, yes. He is a doctor. A man with medical knowledge. It is this doctor, clearly, who warned James Maybrick to strangle his victims first, to avoid drenching his clothing with blood from arterial spurts. If Maybrick's victim had been alive when he slashed her neck and throat, he would have ended covered in the 'red stuff' of which he writes in his diary."

The passages to which Kostenka referred had been labeled as damning Americanisms, which had caused some experts to call the diary a hoax. Of course, Maybrick had lived for years in Norfolk, Virginia, and married an American girl, so he would've been intimately familiar with American slang from the late Victorian period. Sometimes, so-called experts could be as blind as an eyeless cave shrimp.

Kostenka was frowning thoughtfully at the TV monitor. "Whoever he is, the man is foreign-looking and of genteel appearance, just as the witnesses described. A man of education."

Margo heard herself say, "And he's spent time in the East End. You can hear it in his voice."

Once again, she was the abrupt focus of startled stares from the Ripper Watch experts. Then Guy Pendergast grinned. "She's right, y'know, Melvyn. Rerun the tape. Heard it, meself. Just didn't twig to it quite so fast. Used to hearing that sound, hear it every day, just about, on a job."

Shahdi Feroz was nodding. "Yes, whereas Miss Smith has needed to listen very carefully to East End accents, to pick up the vowel sounds and the rhythms of the speech. Very well done, Margo."

A warm glow ignited in her middle and spread deliciously through her entire being. She smiled at the famous scholar, so proud of herself, she felt like she must be floating a couple of inches above the floor.

Dominica Nosette said abruptly, "Well, I intend to find out who our mystery doctor is! Anybody else game to give it a go?"

Guy Pendergast lunged for cameras and recorders.

"Oh, no you don't!" Margo darted squarely in front of the exit to Spaldergate House's main cellar. "I'm sorry," she said firmly, "but there will be an official police investigation getting underway in Buck's Row a few minutes from now. And no one, *not one member of this tour,* is going to be anywhere near that spot when the police arrive. We have remote cameras and microphones in place and every second of this is being recorded."

"Listen," Guy Pendergast began, "you can't just keep us locked up in this cellar!"

"I have no intention of locking anybody in this cellar!" Margo shot back, trying to sound reasonable as well as authoritative, when she felt neither. "But there's no point in leaving Spaldergate for the East End right now. Maybrick has been positively identified. His companion has remained a mystery for nearly a hundred fifty years. We'll certainly begin working to identify him. Carefully. Discreetly. Word of this murder is going to send shockwaves through Whitechapel. Especially the mutilations, when the workhouse paupers who clean the body tomorrow finally remove Mrs. Nichols' clothing and discover them. It's been less than a month, after all, since Martha Tabram was savagely slashed to death in the East End."

"August seventh," Shahdi Feroz put in, "August Bank Holiday. And don't forget Emma Smith, stabbed to death Easter Monday. To the residents of the East End, April fourth wasn't all that long ago. Not when women are being cut to pieces and nobody feels safe walking the streets."

"Yes," Margo said forcefully. "So everyone out there will assume this is the *third* murder, not the first. We are *not* going to go charging into the East End asking, 'Say, have you seen a foreign-looking doctor hereabouts, friend of James Maybrick's?' The investigators of the day had no inkling that James Maybrick was involved, let alone this other guy, whoever he turns out to be. So we'll use extreme caution in proceeding with this investigation. Do I make myself perfectly clear on that point?"

Dominica Nosette looked petulant, but nodded. Slowly, her partner agreed, as well, grumbling and visibly irritated, but compliant. At least for the moment.

"Good. I'd suggest we analyze the tapes we've got for further clues. Inspector Melvyn, if you would rewind one of the backup copies while the master tape and other backups continue running?"

As they viewed the footage again, Shahdi Feroz pursed her lips thoughtfully. "He is familiar to me. The face is not quite right, but the voice . . . I have heard it somewhere. I would swear that I have." She shook her head, visibly impatient with her own memory. "It will come to me, I am certain. There are so many I have studied in so many different places and time, over the past few years. I spent several weeks in London, alone, looking into occult groups such as the Theosophical Society and various Druidic orders. And if he is a friend to James Maybrick, he, too, may be a Liverpudlian, not a Londoner. But I know that I have seen or heard him before. Of that, I am completely certain."

What Shahdi Feroz might or might not have remembered at that moment would never be known, however, because the telephone rang with the news that Malcolm and the search teams had returned for the night. There was no news of Benny Catlin, although from the sound of Malcolm's voice, there was something worse which he wasn't telling her. Margo narrowed her eyes and frowned at the monitors where the Ripperologists were studying their tapes. At least Benny Catlin didn't look anything like their unknown Ripper, thank God. And an American graduate student wouldn't sound like an East End Londoner, particularly not one who'd taken pains to train poverty from his voice. The notion that they were facing two wrenching murder mysteries, an up-time shootout *and* the Ripper slayings, left Margo deeply disturbed as she quietly left the vault to meet her fiancé in the house upstairs.

"What's wrong, Malcolm?" Margo whispered after he'd hugged her close and buried his face in her hair.

"Oh, God, Margo . . . we are in a great deal of trouble with Catlin."

She peered up into his eyes, alarmed by the exhaustion she found there. "What now?"

"The men who were killed? At the hotel and the opera? They're not down-timers, as we'd all assumed. Not Nichol gang members or any other native footpads."

Margo swallowed hard. "They're not?"

He shook his head. "No. The constables of the Metropolitan police asked Mr. Gilbert and me to come to the police morgue, to see if we might be able to identify either man, since Mr. Catlin had been a guest in Spaldergate for a brief time." He paused fractionally. "Margo, they're up-timers. Baggage handlers from TT-86. Gilbert recognized them, said they came through with your group, he saw them earlier in the evening hauling steamer trunks out to carriages for the newly arrived tour group. Then they vanished, abandoned a wagonload of luggage and half a dozen tourists at Paddington Station and went haring off on their own. The Spaldergate footman in charge of the wagon thought perhaps they were reporters who'd slipped through as baggage handlers and tried to follow, but lost them within minutes and returned to help the stranded tourists."

Margo rubbed her eyes with the heels of her hands. "I don't get it, Malcolm," she moaned softly, "why would a couple of baggage handlers ditch their jobs to chase halfway across London and try to murder a graduate student at the Piccadilly Hotel?"

"And failing that, chase him all the way to the Royal Opera?" Malcolm added. "I don't know, Margo. I haven't the faintest bloody idea. It simply makes no rational sense."

"Maybe Catlin's involved somehow with organized crime?" Margo wondered with a shiver.

"God knows, it could be anything. I don't want to think about it for a while. What's the news from the Ripper Watch?" he added quietly, drawing her closer to him and burying his lips in her hair once again.

"You're not gonna believe it," Margo muttered against his coat.

Malcolm's face, wet from the rain that had been falling again, drew down into a whole ladder of exhausted lines and gullies. "That bad?"

"Bad enough." She told him what they'd just discovered, down in the vault.

Malcolm let out a low whistle. "My God. A ruddy pair of them? And you're sure the other chap isn't Catlin?"

"Not unless he brought a plastic surgeon with him. And knows how to walk on stilts. This guy's a lot taller than Benny Catlin."

"Well, that's one breath of good news, anyway. Whatever's up with Catlin, he's not a psychopathic serial murderer."

"No," Margo said quietly. "Given what's happened on station, though, and what you just found out about the guys he killed tonight, quite frankly, I'd feel better if Catlin *had* turned out to be the Ripper."

"My dear," Malcolm sighed, "I wish it weren't so distressing when you're right."

To that, Margo said nothing at all. She simply guided her weary fiancé up to bed and did what she could to help them both forget the night's horrors.

(((Chapter 11)))

Kit Carson was in the back room of the Down Time Bar & Grill, doing his best to beat Goldie Morran at pool—and losing his shirt, as usual—when Robert Li appeared, dark eyes dancing with an unholy glee.

"What's up?" Kit asked warily as Goldie sank another ball in the corner pocket with a rattle like doom.

The antiquarian grinned. "Oh, goodie! You haven't heard yet!"

"Heard what?" Goldie glanced up before pocketing another fifty bucks of Kit's money. "We didn't get a riot when Primary opened, did we?"

"No," Robert allowed, eyes twinkling. "But you're not gonna believe the news from up time!"

Kit scowled. "Oh? Don't tell me. Some up-time group of nuts sent an official protest delegation to the station?"

Li's eyes glinted briefly. "As a matter of fact, they did, but not about Jack the Ripper or his victims."

Kit grunted. A vocal group calling themselves S.O.S.—Save Our Sisters—had been lobbying for the right to intervene and save the London prostitutes the Ripper would kill, despite the fact that it wasn't possible to alter important historical events. Their argument went that since these women were nobodies, the effort ought to at least be made, but Kit didn't see how, since Jack the Ripper was one of the most important murder cases in the past couple of centuries.

"Well," Kit said as Goldie lined up another shot, "if it's not the S.O.S. or some group like Jack is Lord, what is it?"

Robert grinned. "Those *Ansar Majlis* Brothers involved in the riot, the ones Mike Benson threw in the brig? Their up-time brothers have been raising holy hell. Attacks on the Lady of Heaven Temples and important Templars, riots in the streets, you name it. And a whole bunch of somebodies figured out trouble was likely to break out here, because of Ianira Cassondra. The first group through is already demanding the release of the creeps Mike Benson jailed. Seems it's a violation of their human rights to throw in jail a pack of down-time terrorists who left their home station illegally and came to another station to commit murder."

Kit just grimaced. "Why am I not surprised?" Behind him, another fifty bucks of his hard-earned cash dropped into a little round hole. He winced. "But," he added hopefully, "that's not what you came to tell us, is it?"

Li's glance was sympathetic as Goldie dropped yet another ball with a fateful clunk, into a side pocket this time. "Well, no, actually. That news is even better."

Goldie glanced up from lining up her next shot. "Oh, my. Something even better than a bunch of nuts who want to protect the non-existent rights of down-time terrorists?"

Li nodded. "Yep. Better, even, than the arrival of an Angels of Grace Militia Squadron. First thing *they* did was pick a fight with the idiots agitating for the release of the Brothers in jail. A *big* fight. Wrecked three kiosks, a lunch stand, and the costume Connie Logan was modeling. She's suing for damages. The costume was a custom order, worth eight grand."

Kit just groaned.

Goldie muttered, "Lovely, this is all we need. What could possibly be worse than a pack of militant feminists whose sole aim in life is to ram their religion down other people's throats at the point of a bayonet?"

Li let the bombshell drop just as Goldie lined up another shot. "You remember Senator John Caddrick, don't you? That nut who outlaws everything he doesn't agree with? The one who's been agitating about the dangers to modern society from time tourism? Well, it seems the *Ansar Majlis* have kidnapped his only kid. *After* killing his sister-in-law and about sixty other people in a New York restaurant. He's threatening to shut down every time terminal in the business unless his little girl's returned to him alive and well."

Goldie's shot went wild. So wild, in fact, the five ball jumped *off* the table and smacked into the floor with a thud. Goldie's curse peeled paint off the ceiling.

"Ooh, Goldie," Robert looked about as contrite as a well-fed cat, "sorry about that, Duchess."

The hated nickname which Skeeter Jackson had given La-La Land's most infamous money changer, combined with the ruin of her game, sent Goldie into a rage so profound, she couldn't even squeeze sound past the purple-hued knot of distended veins in her throat. She just stood there glaring at the antiquities dealer, cue in hand, sputtering like a dying sparkler.

Kit threw back his head and crowed. "Robert, you are a prince among men!" He snatched up his pool cue, replaced the five ball on the felt, and calmly ran the table while Goldie stood flexing the narrow end of her pool cue until Kit feared the wood would crack. When the final ball rattled into the far corner pocket, Kit bowed, sweeping his arm around in a courtly flourish. "Goldie, thank you for a *lovely* game."

He stuck out a hand to collect his winnings.

She paid up with a seething glare and stalked stiff-legged out of the pool room, a wounded battle destroyer running under the gun for home port. Her deflated reputation trailed after her like the tail of a broken kite. Kit pocketed Goldie's money with a broad grin, then danced a jig around the pool table, whooping for sheer joy. "I did it! Damn, I finally did it! I beat Goldie at pool!"

Robert chuckled. "Congratulations. How many decades have you been waiting to do that?"

Kit refused to be baited. "Noneya, pal. Buy you a drink?"

"Sure!"

They ambled out into the main room of the bar, where an astonishing amount of money was changing hands in the aftermath of Kit's unexpected victory. Excited laughter echoed through the Down Time Bar & Grill as 'eighty-sixers celebrated, relishing the victory almost as much as Kit. La-La legend held that Goldie Morran had never lost a game of pool in the entire millennium or so she'd been on station.

As they fought their way through the crowd toward the bar, Kit had to raise his voice to be heard. "Listen, were you serious about Caddrick threatening to shut down the time terminals?"

Robert Li's smile vanished. "As a heart attack, unfortunately."

"Damn. That man is the most dangerous politician of this century. If he's declared war on us, we're all in trouble. Big trouble."

Li nodded. "Yeah, that's how I've got it figured. And the riots on station won't play in our favor, either. We're going to look like a war zone, with the whole station out of control. Every news crew on station sent video footage up time with couriers."

Kit scowled. "Once the newsies get done with us, Caddrick won't need to shut us down. The tourists will just stay home and do it for him."

Robert Li's worried gaze matched Kit's own. They both had too much to lose, to risk letting anyone shut down Shangri-La Station. Shangri-La was Robert's life as much as it was Kit's. For one thing, they both owned priceless objects which neither could take up time, not legally, anyway. And what *was* legal to take with them, would break them financially with the taxes BATF would impose. Never mind that Shangri-La was *home,* where they had built dreams and brought something good and beautiful to life, where Kit's only grandchild was building her own dreams and trying to build something good for *herself.*

"Molly," Kit muttered, sinking into a seat at the bar, "we need a drink. Make it a double. *Two* doubles. Apiece."

The down-timer barmaid, who had come into Shangri-La Station through the Britannia Gate, gave them a sympathetic smile and poured. Despite the impromptu party roaring all around them, somehow Molly knew *they* were no longer celebrating Kit's victory over Goldie Morran. Kit watched her pour the drinks with a sinking sensation inside his middle. If the station were closed, where Molly would go? Molly and the other down-timer residents? Kit didn't know. "Those idiots demanding human rights for the *Ansar Majlis* are defending the wrong down-timers. Doesn't anybody up time give a damn about folks like Molly and Kynan Rhys Gower?"

Robert Li muttered into his glass, "Not unless it makes for good press, no."

That was so depressingly true, Kit ordered another double.

And wondered when somebody would figure out that the down-timer problem facing every time terminal in the business would have to be solved one of these days. He just hoped Shangri-La Station was still open for business when it happened.

When Skeeter heard that Charlie Ryan had hired Bergitta to take his place on the station maintenance crew, his first thought was that maybe Ryan had a soul, after all. Then he wondered if maybe Kynan Rhys Gower hadn't paid him a little visit anyway? Whatever the case, Bergitta finally had a job that would give her enough income to pay for her closet-sized apartment and food and station taxes.

But when she learned that she'd been hired only because he'd been fired, she showed up on his doorstep in tears, vowing to quit.

"No," he insisted, "don't even think such a thing. It is not your fault I lost my job."

"But Skeeter . . ."

"Shh." He placed a fingertip across her lips. Her face was still bruised where that creep had hit her, but the swelling along her eye had gone down, at least. "No, I won't hear it. You need the job, Bergitta. I can get work doing anything. I only took the maintenance job because it was the first one they offered me."

Her stricken expression told Skeeter she knew full well it had been the only job anyone had offered him. What he was going to do to earn enough money to pay rent, buy food, keep the power turned on, and pay his own station taxes, Skeeter had no idea. But that wasn't important. Taking care of the few friends he had left was. So he locked up his dreary little apartment and placed Bergitta's hand through his arm. "Let's go someplace and celebrate your new job!"

Commons was still Skeeter's favorite place in the world, despite the loneliness of knowing that Marcus and Ianira weren't anywhere to be found on station. The bustle of excited tourists, the vibrant colors of costumes and bright lights and glittering merchandise from around the world and from Shangri-La's many down-time gates, the myriad, mouth-watering scents wafting out of restaurants and cafes and lunch stands, all washed across them like a tidal wave from heaven as soon as Bergitta and Skeeter emerged from Residential.

"How about sushi?" Skeeter asked teasingly, since Bergitta adored fish but could not comprehend the desire to eat it raw.

"Skeeter!"

"Okay," he laughed, "how about yakitori, instead?"

The little bamboo skewers of marinated chicken had become one of the Swedish girl's all-time favorite up-timer foods. "Yes! That would be a real celebration!"

So they headed up toward Edo Castletown, where the Japanese lunch stands were concentrated. Skeeter paused as they shouldered their way through Victoria Station and bought a single rose from a flower girl, another down-timer who had sewn her own street-vendor costume and grew her flowers in the station's lower levels. The Found Ones had set up hydroponics tanks to supplement their diets with fresh vegetables, and to grow flowers as a cash crop. They kept the crops healthy with special grow lights Ianira had purchased with money made at her kiosk.

Skeeter's throat tightened at the thought of Ianira and everything she'd done for these people, but he made himself smile and handed the rose to Bergitta. She dimpled brightly, then hugged him on impulse. Skeeter swallowed hard, then managed, "Hey, I'm starved. Let's go find that yakitori."

They were halfway through Victoria Station, with Bergitta sniffing at her flower's heady perfume every few moments—the down-time varieties of roses the Found Ones grew had been carefully chosen for scent, as well as beauty—when they came upon Molly, the London down-time barmaid, surrounded by an improbable hoard of reporters.

"I dunno 'oo 'e is," Molly was protesting, "an' I don't want ter know! G'wan, now, I got a job to get back to, don't want t'be late or they'll dock me wages . . ."

"But you're a down-timer from the East End!" a reporter shouted, shoving a microphone into Molly's face.

"And didn't you earn your living as a streetwalker?" another newsie demanded. "What's your opinion on prostitution in the East End?"

"How would you feel if you were back in London now?"

"Did any of your customers ever rough you up? Were you ever attacked?"

At Skeeter's side, Bergitta began to tremble. She clutched at Skeeter's arm, holding on so tight, blood stopped flowing down to his hand. "Do something, Skeeter! How can they ask her such things? Have they no heart?"

Molly, sack lunch in hand and clearly on break from her job at the Down Time Bar & Grill, glared at the reporters hemming her in. "Blimey, 'ark at the lot of you! Arse about face, y'are, if you Adam I'll give it some chat! Don't give me none of your verbals, I'll clout you round the ear'ole, I will, you pack o' bloody wind-up merchants! Clear off, the rabbitin' lot of you!"

When Molly plowed straight through the pack of gaping newsies, not one of whom had understood a single word in five, given their round eyes and stunned silence, Skeeter burst into laughter. "I think Molly can fend for herself," he chuckled, patting Bergitta's hand. "I'll wager she's the stroppiest bit they've seen in a while. Come on, let's go find that lunch stand."

Bergitta waved at Molly as the other woman sailed past, trailing uncertain reporters after her, then she turned a smile up at Skeeter. "Yes, I feel sorry now for the newsies!"

Skeeter bought yakitori skewers for both of them and brimming cups of hot green tea, which they carried with them, sipping and munching as they strolled Commons, just taking in the sights. Frontier Town was quiet, but Camelot was gearing up for an impending invasion by re-enactors of the Society for Creative Anachronism, since the Anachronism Gate was scheduled to cycle in a few days. Floods of tournament-bound pseudo-medievalists would pour through the station, complete with horses, hooded hunting falcons, and all the attendant chaos of two separate month-long tournaments trying to flood through one gate, moving in opposite directions.

"I heard BATF plans to start watching the Mongolian Gate more closely," Skeeter said as they passed a shop where a Camelot vendor was putting up advertisements for falconry equipment. "Word is, that pair who went through last time are bird smugglers. Mongolian falcons are worth a fortune up time, especially to Arab princes. Some of the species have gone extinct, up time. Monty Wilkes wants to make sure those two don't try to smuggle out a suitcase load of rare falcons or viable eggs."

"Skeeter," Bergitta frowned, dabbing at her mouth with a paper napkin to wipe sauce off her lips, "why do they worry so about it? If there are no such birds on the other side of Primary, would it not be good to bring them through?"

Skeeter snorted. "You'd think so. Actually, if you get the special permits, you *can* bring extinct birds and animals back through a gate. What's illegal is *smuggling* them through to sell them to rich collectors, without paying taxes on them. First law of time travel: Though Shalt Not Profit from the Gates."

Bergitta shook her head, clearly baffled by the up-time world. "My brother is a trader," she said, eyes dark with sorrow. Bergitta would never again be able to see her family. "He would say such a law is not sane. If no one is to profit, how can the world do business?"

"My dear Bergitta," Skeeter chuckled, "you just asked the sixty-four-million-dollar question. Me, I think it's crazy. But I'm just an ex-thief, so who's going to listen to me?"

"I would," Bergitta said softly.

A sudden lump blocked Skeeter's throat. He gulped tea just to hide the burning in his eyes, and nearly strangled, because his throat was still too constricted to swallow. He ended up coughing while Bergitta thumped his shoulder blades. "Sorry about that," he finally wheezed. "Thanks."

Their wandering had brought them down into Little Agora, where Skeeter and Bergitta ran into total chaos. The news-hungry reporters up in Victoria Station were small potatoes compared with Little Agora's cult lunatics and militant groups like—God help them all—

the Angels of Grace Militia, which had so recently arrived amid a flurry of violence. The Angels were determined to protect the station's down-timers and Lady of Heaven Templars, whether they wanted protection or not.

Everywhere Skeeter glanced, Templars were picketing and shouting, many of them reading from scriptural compilations of Ianira's recorded "words of wisdom." Angels of Grace strutted in black uniforms, their red emblems resembling a running Mirror of Venus which had mated with a swastika, prowling like rabid wolves, moving in packs. Some of them resembled female linebackers or maybe animated refrigerators in jackboots; others were lithe and deadly as ferrets. The psychological effect of all those black uniforms was undeniable. Even Skeeter shivered in their presence. Monty Wilkes had ordered his BATF agents to break out their "dress uniforms"— the red ones with black chevrons on the sleeves—to keep BATF agents from being mistaken for Angel Squads.

Nutcases in sympathy with the *Ansar Majlis* Brotherhood picketed the picketing Templars, chanting for the release of their oppressed Brothers. Other up-time protesters who didn't agree with terrorism in any form, but wanted the Temples shut down for reasons of their own, stalked through Little Agora with hand-lettered signs that read, "MY GOD'S A FATHER—YOURS IS A WHORE!" and "DRIVE OUT THE MONEYCHANGERS IN THE TEMPLE! THE LADY OF HEAVEN IS A FRAUD AND A FRONT FOR ORGANIZED CRIME!"

And seated on the floor by the dozens, locked in human protest chains around the shops and kiosks of Little Agora, blocking exits to residential and public bathrooms, were shocking *droves* of keening, disconsolate acolytes. Everywhere Skeeter turned his glance, security was running ragged, trying to keep fights from exploding out of control every half hour or so.

"I wonder," Skeeter muttered, "how soon the violence on this station is going to close Shangri-La down for good?"

Bergitta's rosy cheeks lost color. "Would they really do this, Skeeter? Everyone says it could happen, but there are so many people here, so much business and money . . . and where could we go? They will not let us walk through Primary and it is not legal for us to go to live down another gate, either. And my gate will never open again. It was unstable."

"I know," Skeeter said quietly, trying to hide his own worry. The thought of living somewhere else—anywhere else—stirred panic deep in his soul. And the thought of what might become of his friends, his adopted family, left him scared spitless. He'd heard rumors that Senator Caddrick was talking internment camps, run like prisons . . .

Bergitta peered toward the ceiling, where immense chronometers hanging from the ceiling tracked date and time on station, down each of the station's multiple active gates, and up time through Primary. "Oh," she exclaimed in disappointment, "it is time for me to go to work!" She hugged Skeeter again, warm and vibrant against him for a brief moment. "Thank you, Skeeter, for the yakitori and the beautiful rose. I . . . I am still sorry about the job."

"Don't be." He smiled, hoping she couldn't sense his worry, wondering where he was going to line up another job, when his search for *that* job had broken world records for the shortest job interview category. "You'd better scoot. Don't want *you* to be late."

When she reached up and kissed his cheek, Skeeter reddened to his toes. But the warmth of the gesture left him blinking too rapidly as she hurried away through the crowds, still clutching her single rose. He shoved hands into pockets, so abruptly lonely, he could've stood there and cried from the sheer misery of it. He was turning over possibilities for job applications when a seething whirlwind of shrieking up-timer kids engulfed him. Clearly dumped by touring parents, the ankle-biters, as Molly called them, were once again playing hooky from the station school. Screaming eight- through eleven-year-olds swirled and foamed around Skeeter like pounding surf, yelling and zooming around, maddened hornets swarming out of a dropped hive. Skeeter found himself tangled up in the coils of a lasso made from thin nylon twine. He nearly fell, the coils wound so tightly around his body and upper legs. Skeeter muttered under his breath and yanked himself free.

"Hey! Gimme that back!" A snot-mouthed nine-year-old boy glared up at him as Skeeter wound the lasso into a tight coil and stuffed it into his pocket. Skeeter just grabbed the kid by the collar and dragged him toward the nearest Security officer in sight, Wally Klontz, whose claim to fame was a schnoz the size of Cyrano de Bergerac's. "Hey! Lemme go!" The kid wriggled and twisted, but Skeeter had hung onto far slipperier quarries than this brat.

"Got a delinquent here," Skeeter said through clenched teeth, hauling the kid over to Wally, whose eyes widened at the sight of a screeching nine-year-old dangling from Skeeter's grasp. "Something tells me this one is supposed to be in school."

Wally's lips twitched just once, then he schooled his expression into a stern scowl. "What did you catch him doing, Skeeter?"

"Lassoing tourists."

Wally's eyes glinted. "Assault with a deadly weapon, huh? Okay, short stuff. Let's go. Maybe you'd prefer a night in jail, if you don't want to sit through your classes."

"Jail? You can't put me in jail! Do you have any idea who my daddy is? When he finds out—"

"Oh, shut up, kid," Wally said shortly. "I've hauled crown princes off to the brig, so you might as well give it up. Thanks, Skeeter."

Skeeter handed the wailing brat over with satisfaction and watched as Wally dragged the kid away, trailing protests at the top of his young lungs. Then Skeeter shoved hands into pockets once again, feeling more isolated and lonely than ever. For just a moment, he'd felt a connection, as though Wally Klontz had recognized him as an equal. Now, he was just Skeeter the unemployed mop man again, Skeeter the ex-thief, the man no one trusted. Unhappiness and bitter loneliness returned, in a surge of bilious dissatisfaction with his life, his circumstances, and his complete lack of power to do the one thing he needed to do most: find Ianira Cassondra and her little family.

So he started walking again, heading up through Urbs Romae into Valhalla, past the big dragon-prowed longship that housed the Langskip Cafe. Skeeter tightened his fingers through the coils of the plastic lasso in his pocket and blinked rapidly against a burning behind his eyelids. *Where is she? God, what could have happened, to snatch them all away without so much as a trace? And if they slipped out through a gate opening, how'd they do it?* Skeeter had worked or attended every single opening of every single gate on station since

Ianira and Marcus' disappearance, yet he'd seen and heard nothing. If they'd gone out in disguise, then that disguise had been good enough to fool even him.

He cut crosswise down the edge of Valhalla and shouldered past the crowd thronging around Sue Fritchey's prize *Pteranodon sternbergi*. Its enormous cage could be hoisted up from the basement level—where it spent most of its noisy life—to the Commons "feeding station" which had been built to Sue's specifications. The flying reptile's wing span equaled that of a small aircraft, which meant the cage was a big one. Expensive, too. And that enormous *pteranodon* had literally been eating Pest Control's entire operations budget. So the creative head of Pest Control had devised a method whereby the *tourists* paid to feed the enormous animal. Every few hours, tourists lined up to plunk down their money and climb a high ramp to dump bucketloads of fish into the giant flying reptile's beak. The sound of the *sternbergi's* beak clacking shut over a bucketload of fish echoed like a monstrous gunshot above the muted roar on Commons, two-by-fours cracking together under force.

Ianira had brought the girls to watch the first time the ingenious platform cage had been hoisted up hydraulically through the new hole in the Commons floor. Skeeter had personally paid for a couple of bucketloads of fish and had hoisted the girls by turns, helping them dump the smelly contents into the huge pteranodon's maw. They'd giggled and clapped gleefully, pointing at the baleful scarlet eye that rolled to glare at them as the gigantic reptile tried to extend its wings and shrieked at them in tones capable of bending steel girders. Skeeter, juggling Artemisia and a bucketful of fish, had sloshed fish slime down his shirt, much to his chagrin. Ianira had laughed like a little girl at his dismayed outburst . . .

Throat tight, Skeeter clenched his fists inside his jeans pockets, the plastic lasso digging into his palm, and stared emptily at the crowd thronging into Valhalla from El Dorado's nearby gold-tinted paving stones. And that was when he saw it happen. A well-timed stumble against a modestly dressed, middle-aged woman . . . a deft move of nimble fingers into her handbag . . . apologies given and accepted . . .

You rat-faced little—

Something inside Skeeter Jackson snapped. He found himself striding furiously forward, approached close enough to hear, "— apologize again, ma'am."

"It is nothing," she was saying as Skeeter closed in. *Spanish,* Skeeter pegged the woman, who was doubtless here for the next Conquistadores Gate tour. *Doesn't look rich enough to afford losing whatever's in that wallet, either. Probably spent the last five or six years saving enough money for this tour and that fumble-fingered little amateur thinks he's going to get away with every centavo she's scraped up!* Skeeter closed his fingers around the loops of plastic lasso in his pocket and came to an abrupt decision.

"Hello there," Skeeter said with a friendly smile dredged up from his days as a deceitful confidence artist. This screaming little neophyte didn't know the first thing about the business—and Skeeter intended to impart a harsh lesson. He offered his hand to the pickpocket. Startled eyes met his own as the guy shook Skeeter's hand automatically.

"Do I know you?"

"Nah," Skeeter said, still smiling, looping the plastic lasso deftly through the pickpocket's nearest belt loop with his other hand, "but you will in a minute. Care to explain what you're doing with the lady's wallet in your back pocket?"

He bolted, of course.

Then jerked to a halt with a startled, *"Oof!"* as the lasso snapped taut at his waist. Skeeter grabbed him and trussed him up, wrists behind his back, in less time than it took the man to regain his balance. The pickpocket stood there sputtering in shock, completely inarticulate for long seconds; then a flood of invective broke loose, crude and predictable.

Skeeter cut him off with a ruthless jerk on his bound wrists. "That's about enough, buddy. We're going to go find the nearest security officer and explain to him why you've got this lady's property in your pocket. Your technique stinks, by the way. *Am-a-teur.* Oh, and by the way? You're gonna love the isolation cells in this place. Give you plenty of time to consider a career change." Skeeter turned toward the astonished tourist. "Ma'am, if you'd be good enough to come with us? Your testimony will see this rat behind bars and, of course, you'll have your property returned. I'm real sorry this happened, ma'am."

Her mouth worked for a moment, then tears sprang to her eyes and a torrent of Spanish flooded loose, the gist being that Skeeter was the kindest soul in the world and how could she ever repay him and it had taken her ten years to save the money for this trip, *gracias, muchas, muchas gracias, señor* . . .

The stunned disbelief in Mike Benson's eyes when Skeeter handed over his prisoner and eyewitness at the security office was worth almost as much as the woman's flood of gratitude. Skeeter swore out his deposition and made certain the lady's property was safely returned, then turned down the reward she tried to give him. Broke he might be, but he hadn't done it for the money and did not want to start accepting cash rewards for one of the few decent things he'd ever done in his life. Mike Benson's eyes nearly popped out of his skull when Skeeter simply smiled, kissed the lady's hand gallantly, leaving the proffered money in her fingers, and strode out of Security HQ feeling nine feet tall. For the first time since Ianira's disappearance, he didn't feel helpless. He might never be able to find Ianira Cassondra or Marcus and their children; but there was something he *could* do, something he knew she'd have been proud of him for doing.

His throat tightened again. It was probably the least likely occupation he could have stumbled across. And the station wasn't likely to give him a salary for it. But Skeeter Jackson had just discovered a new purpose and a whole new calling. Who better to spot and trip up pickpockets, thieves, and con artists than a guy who knew the business inside out? *Okay, Ianira,* he promised silently, *I won't give up hope. And if there's the slightest chance I can find you, I'll jump down an unstable gate to do it. Meanwhile, maybe I can do some good around here for a change. Make this a better place for the Found Ones to raise their kids* . . .

Skeeter Jackson found himself smiling. La-La Land's population of petty crooks had no idea what was about to hit them. For the first time in days, he felt good, really and truly good. Old skills twitching at his senses, Skeeter headed off to start the unlikeliest hunt of his life.

✕ ✕ ✕

Margo Smith had spent her share of rough weeks down temporal gates. Lost in Rome with a concussion, that had been a bad one. Lost in sixteenth-century Portuguese Africa had been far worse, stranded on the flood-swollen Limpopo with a man dying of fever hundreds of miles from the gate, followed by capture and rape at the hands of Portuguese traders . . . At seventeen, Margo had certainly lived through her fair share of rough weeks down a gate.

But the first week after their arrival in London was right up there with the best of them. The Ripper Watch Team's second foray into the East End, the morning after Polly Nichols' brutal murder, put Margo in charge of security and guide services for the up-time reporters Guy Pendergast and Dominica Nosette, as well as Ripper scholars Shahdi Feroz and Pavel Kostenka. Doug Tanglewood was going along, as well, but Malcolm, swamped with the search for Benny Catlin, not to mention demands from the rest of the Ripper Watch Team, couldn't come with them.

So Malcolm, eyes glinting, told Margo, "They're all yours, Imp. Handle them, you can handle anything."

Margo rolled her eyes. "Oh, thanks. I'll remember to send you invitations to the funeral."

"Huh. Theirs or yours?"

Margo laughed. "With your shield or on it, isn't that what the Roman matron told her son? You know, as he went off to die gloriously in battle? The way I figure it, any run-in with that crew is gonna be one heck of a battle."

"My dear girl, you just said a bloody mouthful. Give 'em hell for me, too, would you? Just get them back in one piece. Even," he added with a telling grimace, "those reporters. Those two are a potential nightmare, snooping around for the story of the century, with the East End set up blow like a powder keg on a burning ship of the line. Doug's good in a routine tour and he's taken a lot of zipper jockeys into the East End, but frankly, he hasn't the martial arts training you do. Remember that, if it comes to a scrap."

"Right." It was both flattering and a little unsettling to realize she possessed skills that outranked a professional guide's. Doug

Tanglewood, one of those nondescript sort of brown fellows nobody looks at twice, or even once, and who occasionally shock their neighbors by dismembering small dogs and children, was delighted that he wouldn't have to shepherd the Ripper Watch Team through the East End by himself.

"You handle the reporters," Margo told him as they left the gatehouse to climb into the carriage that would take them to the East End. "I'll tackle the eggheads."

Hitching up her long, tattered skirts, Margo clambered awkwardly up into the carriage in pre-dawn darkness, just an hour after Polly Nichols' murder, then assisted Shahdi Feroz up into the seat. Pavel Kostenka and Conroy Melvyn climbed up and found seats, as well. As soon as everyone was aboard, the driver shook out his whip and they pulled away from the dark kerb and headed east.

Margo still couldn't quite believe that she was herding world-class scholars into the East End on such an important guiding job. She'd ordered the whole crew dressed in Petticoat Lane castoffs, once again. They looked as bedraggled as last year's mudhens. Margo, as disreputable as the rest in a streetwalker's multiple layers and fifth-hand rags, complete with strategic mud smears, carried a moth-eaten haversack which concealed her time scout's computerized log. A tiny camera disguised as one of several mismatched coat buttons transmitted data which her log converted to digitized and compressed video, allowing her to record every moment of their excursion. By popping out and replacing the google-byte disks, Margo could extend her recording capacity almost infinitely, limited only by the number of google disks she could carry.

And, of course, limited by the simple opportunity to switch them out without being caught at it. The Ripper scholars and newsies also carried scout's logs and a large supply of spare googles, as did Doug Tanglewood, who remained typically reserved and quiet during the ride. Dominica chatted endlessly as the carriage rattled eastward through London, navigating in the near darkness of predawn, asking questions that Doug answered in monosyllables whenever possible. Clearly, the Time Tours guide didn't think much of up-time newsies, either. Margo sighed inwardly. *It's going to be a long day.*

By the time they reached the dismal environs of Whitechapel and Wapping, the sun was just climbing above the slate and broken tar-paper rooftops, all but invisible through a haze compounded of fog, drizzle, and acrid, throat-biting coal smoke. As the carriage rattled to a halt in the stinking docklands, the black smoke they were all breathing had already dulled Margo's shapeless white bodice to a smudged and dirty grey. She apologized to her lungs, wriggled her toes inside her grubby boots to warm them, and said, "All right, first stop, Houndsditch and Aldgate. Everybody out, please."

Watching the Spaldergate carriage vanish back through the murk toward the west, leaving them bereft as orphans, Margo's pulse lurched slightly. Her long, entangling skirts hampered her as they started walking, but not as much as they might've had she chosen a more current fashion. She'd opted, instead, for a dress ten years out of style, one that gave her leg room. And if need be, running and fighting room.

The reporters were eager, eyes shining, manner alert. The scholars were no less eager, they were simply more restrained, or maybe just more conscious of their stature as dignitaries. Margo had long since lost any idea that dignity was anything important while down a gate. What mattered was getting the job done with the least amount of damage to her person, not what her person looked like. Dignity, like vanity, did not rank as a survival trait for a wannabe time scout.

As they set out through the early dawn murk, the clatter and groaning of heavy wagons rumbled down Commercial Road, only a couple of blocks farther east. Margo couldn't even guess at the raw tonnage of finished goods, coal, grain, brick, lumber, and God knew what else, transported from the docks through these streets on any given day. Shops were already throwing back their shutters and smoke belched from factory chimneys.

The roar of smelting furnaces could be heard and the scent of molten metal, rotting vegetables, and dung from thousands of horses hung thick on the air. Human voices drifted through the murk as well. Dim shapes resolved occasionally into workmen and flower girls and idle ruffians lurking in dark alleyways. The East End was getting itself busily up and at its business, right along with the chickens cackling and clucking and crowing mournfully on their way to the big poultry markets further west or scratching for whatever scraps might've been left from breakfast in many a lightless, barren kitchen yard.

Dogs slunk past, intent on canine business as muddy daylight slowly gathered strength. Cats' eyes gleamed from alleyways, their shivery whiskers atwitch in the cold air, paws flicking in distaste as they navigated foul puddles of filthy rainwater from the previous night's storm. Along those same alleyways, ragged children sat huddled in open doorways. Most of the children clustered together for warmth, faces dirty and pinched with hunger, eyes dull and suspicious. Their mothers could be heard inside the dilapidated cribhouses they called home, often as not shouting in ear-bending tones at someone too drunk to respond. "Get a finger out, y' lager lout, or there'll be no supper in this cat an' mouse, not tonight nor any other . . ."

Margo glanced at her charges and found a study in contrasts. The reporters were taking it all in stride, studying the streets and the people in them with a detached sort of eagerness. Conroy Melvyn looked like the police inspector he was: alert, intelligent, dangerous, eyes taking in minute details of the world unfolding around him. Pavel Kostenka was not so much oblivious as simply unmoved by the shocking poverty spreading out in every direction. He was clearly intent on objective observation without the filter of human emotion coloring his judgements.

Dr. Feroz, on the other hand, was as quietly alert as the chief inspector from Scotland Yard, her dark eyes drinking in the details as rapidly as her miniature, concealed camera, but there was a distinctive shadow of grief far back in her eyes as she recorded the same details: children toting coal in wheelbarrows, tinkers with their donkey carts crying their trade, knife grinders carrying their sharpening wheels on harnesses strapped to their shoulders, little boys with leashed terriers and caged ferrets heading west to the neatly kept squares and tree-lined streets of the wealthy to offer their services as rat catchers.

Margo said quietly, "We'll want to be outside the police mortuary when the news breaks. When the workhouse paupers clean her body, they'll tell half of London's reporters what they found. We'll have to walk fast to make it in time—"

"In time?" Dominica Nosette interrupted, eyes smouldering as she rounded on Margo like a prizefighter coming in for the kill. "If we're likely to be late, why didn't the carriage take us directly there? What if we miss this important event because you want us to *walk?*"

Margo had no intention of standing on a Whitechapel street corner locked in argument with Dominica Nosette, so she kept walking at a brisk clip, ushering the others ahead of her. Doug Tanglewood took Miss Nosette's arm to prevent her being separated from the group. The photographer took several startled, mincing steps, then jerked her arm loose with a snarled, "Take your hand off me!" She favored Margo with a cool stare. "Answer my question!"

"We did not take the carriage," Margo kept her voice low, "because the last thing we want to do is attract attention to ourselves. Nobody in this part of London arrives in a chauffeured carriage. So unless you enjoy being mugged the instant you set foot on the pavement, I'd suggest you resign yourself to hoofing it for the next three months."

As the poisonous glare died away to mere hellfire, Margo reminded herself that Dominica Nosette's work in clandestine photography had been done in the comfortable up-time world of air-conditioned automobiles and houses with central heating. Margo told herself to be charitable. Dominica Nosette's first daylight glimpse of London's East End was probably going to leave her in deep culture shock—she just didn't know it, yet.

When they reached the corner of Whitechapel and Commercial Roads, one of the busiest intersections in all London, they ran afoul of one of the East End's most famous hallmarks: the street meeting. Idle men thrown out of work by the previous night's dock fire had joined loafing gangs of the unemployed who roamed the streets in loose-knit packs, forming and breaking and reforming in random patterns to hash through whatever the day's hot topic might be, at a volume designed to deafen even the hardest of hearing at five hundred paces. From the sound of it, not one man—or woman—in the crowd had ever heard of Roberts' Rules of Order. Or of taking turns, for that matter.

"—why should I vote for 'im, I wants t'know? Wot's 'e goin' t'do for me an' mine—"

"—bloody radicals! Go an' do good to somebody wot might appreciate it, over to Africa or India, where them savages need civilizing, an' leave us decent folk alone—"

"—let the bloke 'ave 'is say, might be good for a laugh, eh, mate—"

"—give me a job wot'll put food in me Limehouse Cut, I'd vote for 'im if 'e were wearin' a devil's 'orns—"

"—say, wot you radical Johnnies in this 'ere London County Council goin' to do about them murders, eh? Way I 'eard it, another lady got her throat cut last night, second one inside a month, third one since Easter Monday, an' me sister's that scared to walk out of a night—"

Near the edge of the crowd, which wasn't quite a mob, a thin girl of about fifteen, hair lank under her broken straw bonnet, leaned close against a man in his fifties. He'd wrapped his hand firmly around her left breast. As Margo brushed past, she heard the man whisper, "Right, luv, fourpence it is. Know of anyplace quiet?"

The girl whispered something in his ear and giggled, then gave the older man a sloppy kiss and another giggle. Margo glanced back and watched them head for a narrow gate that led, presumably, to one of the thousands of sunless yards huddled under brick walls and overlooked by windows with broken glass in their panes and bedsheets hung to keep the drafts out. As the girl and her customer vanished through the gate, a sudden, unexpected memory surged, broke, and spilled into her awareness. Her mother's voice . . . and ragged screams . . . a flash of bruised cheek and bleeding lips . . . the stink of burnt toast on the kitchen counter and the thump of her father's fists . . .

Margo forcibly thrust away the memory, concentrating on the raucous street corner with its shouting voices and rumbling wagons and the sharp clop of horses' hooves on the limerock and cobbled roads—and her charges in the Ripper Watch Team. Furious with herself, Margo gulped down air that reeked of fresh dung and last week's refuse and the tidal mud of the river and realized that no more than a split second had passed. Dominica Nosette was stalking down Whitechapel Road, oblivious to everything and Doug Tanglewood was hot on her trail so she wouldn't step straight in front of an express wagon loaded with casks from St. Katharine's Docks. Guy Pendergast was still talking to people at the edge of the crowd, asking questions he probably shouldn't have have been asking. Dr. Kostenka was intent on recording the political rally, a historic one, Margo knew. The speaker at the center of the crowd was supporting the first London County Council elections, a race hotly contested by the radicals for control of London's East End. Conroy Melvyn was staring, fascinated, at the man speaking.

Only Shahdi Feroz had noticed Margo's brief distress. Her dark-eyed gaze rested squarely on Margo. Her brows had drawn down in visible concern. "Are you all right?" she asked softly, moving closer to touch Margo's arm.

"Yes," Margo lied, "I'm fine. Just cold. Come on, we'd better get moving."

She genuinely didn't have time to deal with *that;* certainly not here and now. She had a job to do. Remembering her mother—anything at all about her mother—was worse than useless. It was old news, ancient history. She didn't have time to shed any more tears or even to hate her parents for being what they'd been or doing what they'd done. If she hoped to work as an independent time scout one day, she had to keep herself focused on *tomorrow.* Not to mention *today . . .*

"Come on," she said roughly, all but dragging Guy Pendergast and Conroy Melvyn down the street. "We got a schedule, mates, let's 'ave it away on our buttons, eh? Got a job waitin', so we 'ave, time an' tide don't wait for nobody."

They were amenable to being dragged off, at least, clearly eager to get the story they'd come here for, rather than intriguing side stories. They reached the police mortuary in time, thank God, and contrived to position themselves outside where a whole bevy of London's native down-time reporters had gathered. Several of them added foul black cigar smoke to the stench wafting out of the mortuary. Margo took up a watchful stance where she could record the events across the street, yet keep a cautious eye on her charges, not to mention everyone else who'd joined the macabre vigil, waiting for word about the third woman hideously hacked to death in these streets since spring.

The native reporters, every one of them male, of course, were speculating about the dead woman, her origins, potential witnesses they'd already tracked down and plied with gin—"talked to fifty women, I tell you, fifty, and they all described the same man, big foreign-looking bastard in a leather apron." Everyone wondered whether or not the killer might be caught soon, based on those so-called witness accounts. The man known as "Leather Apron," Margo knew, had been one of the early top suspects. The unfortunate John Pizer, a Polish boot finisher who also happened to be Jewish, and a genuinely innocent target of East End hatred and prejudice, would find himself in jail shortly.

Of course, he would soon afterward collect damages from the newspapers who had libeled him, since he'd been seen by several witnesses including a police constable, at the Shadwell dock fire during the time Polly Nichols had been so brutally killed. But this morning, nobody knew that yet—

A male scream of horror erupted from the mortuary across the road. "Dear God, oh, dear God, constable, come quick!"

Reporters broke and ran for the door, which slammed abruptly back against the sooty bricks. A shaken man in a shabby workhouse uniform appeared, stumbling as he reached the street. His face had washed a sickly grey. He gulped down air, wiped his mouth with the back of his hand in a visible effort not to lose the meager contents of his stomach. Questions erupted from every side. The workhouse inmate shuddered, trying to find the words to describe what he'd just witnessed.

"Was 'orrible," he said in a hoarse voice, "ripped 'er open like a . . . a butchered side of beef . . . from 'ere to 'ere . . . dunno 'ow many cuts, was 'orrible, I tell you, couldn't stay an' look at 'er poor belly all cut open . . ."

Word of the mutilations spread in a racing shockwave down the street. Women clutched at their throats, exclaiming in horror. Men stomped angrily across the pavement, cursing the news and demanding that something be done. A roar of angry voices surged from down the street. Then Margo and Doug Tanglewood and their mutual charges were buried alive by the mob which had, just minutes previously, been heckling the radical politicians running for council office. Angry teenage boys flung mud and rocks at the police mortuary. Older men shouted threats at the police officials inside. Margo was shoved and jostled by men taller and heavier than she was, all of them fighting for the best vantage points along the street. The sheer force of numbers thrust Margo and her charges apart.

"Hold onto one another!" Margo shouted at Shahdi Feroz. "Grab Dominica's arm—and I don't care what she says when you do it! Where's Doug?"

"Over there!" The wide-eyed scholar pointed.

Margo found the Time Tours guide trying to keep Guy Pendergast and Conroy Melvyn from being separated. Margo snagged the police inspector's coat sleeve, getting his shocked attention. "Hold onto Guy! Grab Doug Tanglewood's arm! We can't get separated in this mob! Follow me back!" She was already fighting her way back to the women and searching for Dr. Kostenka, who remained missing in the explosive crowd. She'd just reached Shahdi Feroz when new shouts erupted not four feet distant.

"Dirty little foreigner! It's one o' your kind done 'er! That's wot they're sayin', a dirty little Jew wiv a leather apron!"

Margo thrust Shahdi Feroz at the Time Tours guide. "Get them out of here, Tanglewood! I've got a bad feeling that's Dr. Kostenka!"

She then shoved her way through the angry mob and found her final charge, just as she'd feared she would. Pavel Kostenka clutched at a bleeding lip and streaming nose, scholarly eyes wide and shocked. Angry men were shouting obscenities at him, most of them in Cockney the scholar clearly couldn't even comprehend.

Oh, God, here we go. . . . "Wot's this, then?" Margo shouted, facing down a thickset, ugly lout with blood on his knuckles. "You givin' me old man wot for, eh? I'll give you me Germans, I will, you touch 'im again!" She lifted her own fist, threatening him as brazenly as she dared.

Laughter erupted, defusing the worst of the fury around them at the sight of a girl who barely topped five feet in her stockings squaring off with a man four times her size. Voices washed across her awareness, while she kept her wary attention on the man who'd punched Kostenka once already.

"Cheeky little begger, in't she?"

"Don't sound like no foreigner, neither."

"Let 'er be, Ned, you might break 'er back, just pokin' at 'er!" This last to the giant who'd smashed his fist into Pavel Kostenka's face.

Ned, however, had his blood up, or maybe his gin, because he swung at Margo anyway. The blow didn't connect, of course, which infuriated the burly Ned. He let out a roar like an enraged Kodiak grizzly and tried to close with her. Margo slid to one side in a swift Aikido move and assisted him on his way. Whereupon Ned was obliged to momentarily mimic the lowly fruit bat, flying airborne into the nearest belfry, that being the brick wall of the church across the street. Ned howled in outraged pain when he connected with a brutal thud. A roar of angry voices surged. So did the mob. A filthy lout in a ragged coat and battered cap took a swing at her. Margo ducked and sent him on his way. Then somebody else took offense at having his neighbor come careening head first into the crowd. Margo dodged and wove as fists swung like crazed axes in the hands of drunken lumberjacks. Then she grabbed Kostenka by the wrist and yelled, "Run, you bloody idiot!"

She had to drag him for two yards. Then he was running beside her, while Margo put to use every Aikido move Kit and Sven had ever drilled into her. Her wrists and arms ached, but she did clear a path out. The riot erupting behind them engulfed the entire street. Margo steered a course toward the spot where she'd last seen the other members of her little team. She found them, wide-eyed in naked shock, near the edge of the crowd. Doug Tanglewood had wisely dragged them clear as soon as she'd yelled at him to do so.

"Dr. Kostenka!" Shahdi Feroz cried. "You're injured!"

He was snuffling blood back into his sinuses. Margo hauled a handkerchief out of one pocket and thrust it into his hand. "Come on, let's clear out of here. We got what we came for. Pack this into your nostrils, hold it tight. Come *on!*" That, to Guy Pendergast, who was still intent on filming the riot with his hidden camera. "If we get to the

Whitechapel Working Lads' Institute now, we can scramble for the best seats at the inquest."

That got the reporter's attention. He turned, belatedly, to help steer Dr. Pavel Kostenka down the street and away from the mortuary riot. Margo escorted her shaken charges several blocks away before pausing at a coffee stall to buy hot coffee for everyone. "Here, drink this," she said, handing Dr. Kostenka a chipped earthenware mug. "You're fighting shock. It'll warm you up."

Dominica Nosette too, was battling shock, although hers was emotional rather than from physical injuries sustained. Margo got a mugful of coffee down her, as well, and Doug bought crumpets for everyone. "Here you go. Carbs and hot coffee will set you to rights, mates." Pavel Kostenka had seated himself on the chilly stone kerb, elbows propped on knees, shabby boots in the gutter. He was trembling so violently, he had trouble holding Margo's now-stained handkerchief against his battered nose. Margo crouched beside him.

"You okay?" she asked quietly.

He shuddered once, then nodded, slowly. When he lowered the handkerchief to his lap, he left a smear of blood down his chin. "I do believe you saved my life, back there."

She shrugged, trying to make light of her own role in the near-disaster. "It's possible. That flared up a lot faster than I expected it to. Which means you got hurt and you shouldn't have. I knew people would be in a mean mood. And I knew about the anti-Semitism. But I didn't figure on a full-blown riot that fast."

He stared for a long moment into the cup Margo handed him, where dark and bitter coffee steamed in the cold morning air. "I have seen much anger in the world," he said quietly. "But nothing like this. Such murderous hatred, simply because I am different . . ."

"This isn't the twenty-first century," she said in a low voice. "Not that people are perfect in our time, they're not. But down a gate, you *can't* expect people to behave the way up-timers do. Socials norms do change over a century and a half, you know, more than you realize, just reading about it. Me? I'm just glad I was able to pull you out of there in one piece. Next time we come out here, we're gonna be a whole lot more careful about getting boxed into potential riots."

He finally met her gaze. "Yes. Thank you."

She managed a wan smile. "You're welcome. Ready to tackle that inquest?"

His effort to return the smile was genuine, even if the twist of his lips was a dismal failure in the smile department. "Yes. But this time, I think I shall not say anything at all, even if my foot is trod on hard enough to break the bones."

"Smart choice. Through with that coffee yet?"

The shaken scholar drained the bitter stuff—what did the British *do* to coffee, to produce such a ghastly flavor?—then climbed to his feet. "Thank you. From now on, whatever you suggest, I will do it without question."

"Okay. Let's find the Working Lads' Institute, shall we? I want us to keep a low profile." She glanced at the reporters. "No interviewing potential mobs, okay? You want this story, you get it by keeping your mouth shut and your cameras rolling."

This time, none of her charges argued with her. Even Guy Pendergast and Dominica Nosette, whose dress was torn, were momentarily subdued by the flash-point riot. For once, Margo actually felt in *charge*.

She wondered how long it would last.

(((Chapter 12)))

The smell of tension was thick in Kit's nostrils as he threaded his way through Edo Castletown, answering a call from Robert Li to meet him for the antics at Primary and to ask his expert opinion on a recent aquisition he'd made. So Kit abandoned several stacks of bills and government forms in his office at the Neo Edo Hotel and set out, curious about what the antiquities dealer might have stumbled across this time and wondering what new horror Primary's cycle might bring onto the station.

Kit had never seen a bigger crowd for a gate opening and that was saying a lot, after being caught in the jam-packed mass of humanity which had come to see the last cycling of the Britannia. Kiosks that hadn't existed just a week previously cluttered the once-wide thoroughfares of Commons, overflowing into Edo Castletown from its border with Victoria Station. Their owners hawked crimson-spattered t-shirts and tote bags, Ripper-suspect profiles, biographies and recent photos of the victims, anything and everything enterprising vendors thought might sell.

Humanity, he thought darkly—watching a giggling woman in her fifties plunking down a wad of twenties for a set of commemorative china plates with hand-painted portraits of victims, suspects, police investigators, and crime scenes—*humanity is a sick species.*

"Is she honestly going to display those hideous things in her house?"

Kit glanced around at the sound of a familiar voice at his elbow. Ann Vinh Mulhaney was gazing in disgust at the woman buying the plates.

"Hello, Ann. And I think the answer's yes. I'm betting she'll not only display them, she'll put them right out in the middle of her china hutch."

Ann gave a mock shudder. "God, *Ripperoons* . . . You wouldn't believe the last class of them I had to cope with." She glanced up at Kit, who gave her a sardonic smile. Kit had seen it all—and then some. "On second thought, you probably would believe it. Have you seen Sven yet? He came up before I did."

"No, I just got here. Robert said something about finding a spot to watch Primary go and said he wanted my opinion on something."

"Really?" Ann's eyes glinted with sudden interest. "That something wouldn't have anything to do with Peg Ames, would it?"

Kit blinked. "Good God. Have I missed something?"

Ann laughed, pulling loose the elastic band holding her long dark hair, and shrugged the gleaming tresses over one shoulder. She'd clearly just come from class, since she still wore a twin-holster rig with a beautiful pair of Royal Irish Constabulary Webley revolvers. Unlike the big military Webleys, which came open on a top-break hinge for reloading and were massive in size, the little RIC Webley was a solid-frame double-action that loaded like the American single-action Army revolver through a gate in the side, and came in a short-barrelled, concealable version popular with many time tourists heading to London. At .442 caliber, they packed a decent punch and were easier to hide than the much larger standard Webleys. Kit had shot them several times during his down-time escapades—and had cut his finger more than once on the second trigger, a needle-type spur projecting down behind the main trigger.

As she pocketed her hair band, Ann glanced side-long at Kit. "You really have been moping with Margo gone, haven't you? Honestly, Kit, they've been thick as mosquitoes in a swamp for *days*. Rumor has it," and she winked, "that Peg had a line on a Greek bronze that was going up for auction in London and Robert was just about nuts, trying to find somebody to snitch it quietly for him the night the auction warehouse goes up in smoke. Or rather, went up in smoke. It burned the night of Polly Nichols' murder, in a Shadwell dry-dock fire."

Kit grinned as he escorted Ann through the crowds. Robert Li was engaged in an ongoing, passionate love affair with any and all Greek bronzes. "I hope he gets it. Peg Ames will make him the happiest man in La-La Land if he can lay hands on another one for his collection."

The IFARTS agent and resident antiquarian had personally rescued from destruction a collection of ancient bronzes that most up-time museum directors would've gnashed their teeth over, had they known about them. Rescuing artwork from destruction was perfectly legal, of course, and constituted one of the major exceptions to the first law of time travel. Collectors who salvaged such art could even sell it on the open market, if they were willing to pay the astronomical taxes levied by the Bureau of Access Time Functions. Many an antiquarian and art dealer made a good living doing just that.

But Robert Li would sooner have sold his own teeth than part with an original Greek bronze, even one acquired through perfectly legitimate means. Of course, snitching one from a down-time auction warehouse before it burned did *not* qualify as a "legitimate" method of acquisition. To rescue a doomed piece of art, one had to rescue it during the very disaster destined to destroy it. Li was a very honest and honorable man. But when it came to any man's abiding passion, honesty occasionally went straight out the nearest available window. Certainly, many another antiquarian had tried smuggling out artwork that was not destined for down-time destruction. Hence the existence of the International Federation for Art Temporally Stolen, which tried to rescue such purloined work and return it to its proper time and place of origin. Robert Li was the station's designated IFARTS agent, a very good one. But if he had a line on a Greek bronze that was scheduled to be destroyed by some method it couldn't easily be rescued from, or one that had just disappeared mysteriously, he wouldn't be above trying to acquire it for his personal collection, whatever the means.

"Wonder which bronze?" Kit mused as they threaded their way toward Primary.

"Proserpina, actually," Robert Li's voice said from behind him.

Kit turned, startled, then grinned. "Proserpina, huh?"

"Yeah, beautiful little thing, about three feet high. Holding a pomegranate."

"Is that what you wanted to ask me about?"

The antiquities dealer chuckled and fell into step beside them. "Actually, no." He held up a cloth sack. "I wondered if you might know more about these than I do. A customer came into the shop, asked me to verify whether or not they were genuine or reproduction. He'd bought 'em from a Templar who came through with a suitcase full of 'em and is selling them down in Little Agora to anyone who'll pony up the bucks."

Curious, Kit opened the sack and found a pair of late twentieth-century, Desert Storm-era Israeli gas masks, capable of filtering out a variety of chemical and nerve agents.

"Somebody," Kit muttered, "has a sick sense of humor."

"Or maybe just a psychic premonition," Ann put in, eyeing the masks curiously. "It's illegal to discharge chemical agents inside a time terminal, but nothing would surprise me around here, these days."

As Kit studied the gas masks, looking for telltale signs of recent manufacture, he could hear, in the distance, the sound of live music and chanting. Startled, Kit glanced up at the chronometers. "What's going on, over toward Urbs Romae?"

"Oh, that's the Festival of Mars," Ann answered, just as Kit located the section of the overhead chronometers reserved for displaying the religious festivals scheduled in the station's timeline.

Kit smacked his forehead, belatedly recalling his promise to Ianira that he'd participate in the festival. "Damn! I was supposed to be there!"

"All the down-timers on station are participating," Robert said with a curious glance at Kit.

Ann's voice wobbled a little as she added, "Ianira was supposed to officiate, you know. They're holding the festival anyway. The way I hear it, they plan on asking the gods of war to strike down whoever's responsible for kidnapping Ianira and her family."

A chill touched Kit's spine. "With all the crazies we've got on station, that could get ugly, fast." Before he'd even finished voicing the thought, shouts and the unmistakable sounds of a scuffle broke out close by. Startled tourists in front of them scrambled in every direction. A corridor of uninhabited space opened up. Two angry groups abruptly faced one another down. Kit recognized trouble when he saw it—and this was *Trouble*.

Capital "T" that rhymed with "C" and that stood for Crazies.

Ann gasped. A group of women in black uniforms and honest-to-God jackboots formed an impenetrable wall along one flank, blocking any escape in that direction. *Angels of Grace Militia* . . . And opposing the Angels ranged a line of burly construction workers, the very same construction workers who'd been involved in the *last* station riot.

"*Unchaste whores!*"

"*Medieval monsters!*"

"*Feminazis!*"

"*Get out of our station, bitches!*"

"You're not *my* goddamned brothers!"

"Go back to the desert and beat up your own women, you rag-headed bastards! Leave ours alone!"

Kit had just enough time to say, "*Oh, my God . . .*"

Then the riot exploded around them.

To Margo's relief, they found the Working Lads' Institute without further incident. When the doors were finally opened for the inquest into Polly Nichols' brutal demise, the Ripper scholars and up-time reporters in her charge surged inside with the rest of the crowd. The room was so jam-packed with human bodies, not even a church mouse could have forced its way into the meeting hall. The coroner was a dandified and stylish man named Wynne Edwin Baxter, who arrived with typical flair, straight from a tour of Scandinavia, dressed to the nines in black-and-white-checked trousers, a fancy white waistcoat, and a blood-red scarf. Baxter presided over the inquest with a theatrical mien, asking the police surgeon, Dr. Llewellyn, to report on his findings. The Welsh doctor, who had been dragged from his Whitechapel surgery to examine the remains at the police mortuary, cleared his throat with a nervous glance at the crowded hall, where reporters hung expectantly on every word spoken.

"Yes. Well. Five teeth were missing from the victim's jaw and I found a slight, ah, laceration on the tongue. A bruise ran along the lower part of the lady's jaw, down the right side of her face. This might have been caused by a fist striking her face or, ah, perhaps a thumb digging into the face. I found another bruise, circular in nature, on the left side of her face, perhaps caused by fingers pressing into her skin. On the left side of her neck, about an inch below the jaw, there was an, ah, incision." The surgeon paused and cleared his throat, a trifle pale. "An, ah, an incision, yes, below the jaw, about four inches in length, which ran from a point immediately below the ear. Another incision on this same side was, ah, circular in design, severing tissues right down to the vertebrae."

A concerted gasp rose from the eager spectators. Reporters scribbled furiously with pencils, those being far more practical for field work than the cumbersome dip pens which required an inkwell to resupply them every few lines.

Dr. Llewellyn cleared his throat. "The large vessels of the neck, both sides, were all severed by this incision, at a length of eight inches. These cuts most certainly were inflicted by a large knife, a long-bladed weapon, moderately sharp. It was used with considerable violence . . ." The doctor shuddered slightly. "Yes. Well. Ah, there was no blood on the breast, either her own or the clothes, and I found no further injuries until I reached the lower portion of the poor lady's abdomen." A shocked buzz ran through the room. Victorian gentlemen did not speak about ladies' abdomens, not in public places, not anywhere else, for that matter. Dr. Llewellyn shifted uncomfortably. "Some two to three inches from the left side of the belly, I discovered a jagged wound, very deep, the tissues of the abdomen completely cut through. Several other, ah, incisions ran across the abdomen as well, and three or four more which ran vertically down the right side. These were inflicted, as I said, by a knife used violently and thrust downward. The injuries were from left to right and may possibly have been done by an, ah, left-handed person, yes, and all were without doubt committed with the same instrument."

A reporter near the front of the packed room shouted, "Dr. Llewellyn! Then you believe the killer must have stood in front of his victim, held her by the jaw with his right hand, struck with the knife in his left?"

"Ah, yes, that would seem to be indicated."

Having watched the brutal attack in Buck's Row via video camera, Margo knew that was wrong. James Maybrick had strangled his victim, then shoved her to the ground and ripped her open with the knife gripped in his right hand. Criminologists had long suspected that would be the case, just from the coroners' descriptions of wound placement and surviving crime scene and mortuary photos. But in London of 1888, the entire science of forensics was in its infancy and criminal psychology hadn't even been invented yet, never mind profiling of serial killers.

"Dr. Llewellyn . . ."

The inquest erupted into a fury of shouted questions and demands for further information, witness names, descriptions, anything. It came out that a coffee-stall keeper named John Morgan had actually seen Polly Nichols shortly before her death, a mere three minutes' walk from Buck's Row where she'd died. Morgan said, "She were in the company of a man she called Jim, sir."

Whether or not this "Jim" had been James Maybrick, Margo didn't know and neither did anybody else, since they hadn't rigged a camera at Morgan's coffee stall. But the description Morgan gave didn't match Maybrick's features, so it might well have been another "Jim" who'd bought what poor Polly had been selling, as well as her final cup of bitter, early-morning coffee. If, in fact, Morgan wasn't making up the whole story, just to gain the momentary glory of police and reporters fawning over him for details.

Margo sighed. *People don't change much, do they?*

Once the inquest meeting broke up, Margo and Doug Tanglewood parted company. Tanglewood and the reporters, accompanied by Pavel Kostenka and Conroy Melvyn, set out in pursuit of the mysterious doctor they'd captured on video working with James Maybrick. Margo and her remaining charge, Shahdi Feroz, plunged into the shadowy world inhabited by London's twelve hundred prostitutes.

"I want to walk the entire murder area," Shahdi said quietly as they set out alone. Most of this lay in the heart of Whitechapel, straying only once into the district of London known as The City. Margo glanced at the older woman, curious.

"Why the whole area now? We'll be rigging surveillance on each site."

Shahdi Feroz gave Margo a wan smile. "It will be important to my work to get a feel for the spatial relationships, the geography of the killing zone. What stands where, how the pattern of traffic flows through or past the murder sites. Where Maybrick and his unknown accomplice might meet their victims. Where the prostitutes troll for their customers."

When Margo gave her a puzzled stare, she said, "I want to learn as much as I can about the world the prostitutes live in. To me, that is the important question, the conditions and geography of their social setting, how they lived and worked as well as where and why they died. This is more important than the forensics of the evidence. The basic forensics were known *then;* what is not known is how these women were treated by the police sent undercover to protect them, or how these women coped with the terror and the stress of having to continue working with such a monstrous killer loose among them. We have studied such things in the modern world, of course; but never in Victorian England. The social rules were so very different, here, where even the chair legs are covered with draperies and referred to as limbs, even by women who sell their bodies for money. It is this world I need to understand. I have worked in middle class London and in areas of wealth, but never in the East End."

Margo nodded. That made sense. "All right. Buck's Row, we've seen already. You want to do the murder sites in numerical order, by the pattern of the actual attacks? Or take them as we come to them, geographically? And what about the murder sites on the question list? The ones we're not sure whether they were Jack's or not? Like the Whitehall torso," she added with a shudder. The armless, legless, headless woman's body, hacked to pieces and left in the cellar of the partially constructed New Scotland Yard building on Whitehall, would be discovered in October, during the month-long lull between confirmed Ripper strikes.

"Yes," Shahdi Feroz said slowly, narrowing her eyes slightly as she considered the question. "With two men working in tandem, it would be good, I think, to check all the murder sites, not just the five traditionally ascribed to the Ripper. And I believe we should take the sites in order of the murders, as well. We will follow the killer's movements through the territory he staked out for himself. Perhaps we might come to understand more of his mind, doing this, as well as how he might have met his victims. Or rather, how they met their victims, since there are two of them working together." Her smile was rueful. "I did not expect to have the chance to study such a dynamic in this particular case. It complicates matters immensely."

Even Margo, with no training in psychology or criminal social dynamics, could understand that. "Okay, next stop, Hanbury Street." Margo intended to get a good look at the yard behind number twenty-nine Hanbury. Seven days from now, she'd be slipping into that yard under cover of darkness, to set up the Ripper Watch Team's surveillance equipment.

Number twenty-nine Hanbury proved to be a broken-down tenement in sooty brick. It housed seventeen souls, several of whom were employed in a nearby cigar factory. It was a working-man's tenement, not a doss house where the homeless flopped for the night. Two doors led in from the street. One took residents into the house proper and another led directly to the yard behind the squat brick structure. Margo and Shahdi Feroz chose this second door, opening it with a creaking groan of rusting hinges. The noise startled Margo.

And brought instant attention from an older woman who leaned out a second-story window. "Where d'you think you're going, eh?" the irate resident shouted down. "I know your kind, missies! How many times I got to tell your kind o' girls, keep out me yard! Don't want nuffink to do wiv the likes o' you round me very own 'ouse! Go on wiv you, now, get on!"

Caught red-handed trying to sneak into the yard, Margo did the only thing she could do, the one thing any East End hussy would've been expected to do. She let the door close with a bang and shouted back up, "It's me gormless father I'm after, nuffink else! Lager lout's said 'e 'ad a job, workin' down to Lime'ouse docks, an' where do I see 'im, but coming out the Blue Boy public 'ouse, 'at's where! Followed 'im I did, wiv me ma, 'ere. Sore 'im climb over the fence into this 'ere yard. You seen 'im, lady? You do, an' you shout for a bottle an' stopper, y'hear?"

"Don't you go tellin' an old woman any of your bloody Jackanories! Off wiv you, or I'll call for that copper me own self!"

"Ah, come on, ma," Margo said loudly to Shahdi Feroz, taking her arm, "senile owd git ain't no use. We'll catch 'im, 'e gots to come 'ome sometime, ain't 'e?"

As soon as they had gained enough distance, Shahdi Feroz cast a curious glance over her shoulder. "How in the world will Annie Chapman slip through that door with seventeen people asleep in the house and *nobody hear a thing?*"

Margo shot the scholar an intent glance. "Good question. Maybe one of the working girls got tired of having that busybody interfere with using a perfectly suitable business location? One of them could've poured lamp oil on the hinges?"

"It's entirely possible," Dr. Feroz said thoughtfully. "Pity we haven't the resources to put twenty-four-hour surveillance on that door for the next week. That was quick thinking, by the way," she added with a brief smile. "When she shouted like that, I very nearly lost my footing. I had no idea what to say. All I could imagine was being placed in jail." She shivered, leaving Margo to wonder if she'd ever seen the inside of a down-time gaol, or if she just had a vivid imagination. Margo, for one, had no intention of discovering what a Victorian jail cell looked like, certainly not from the inside. She had far too vivid a memory of sixteenth-century Portuguese ones.

"Huh," she muttered. "When you're caught stealing the cookies, the only defense is a counterattack with a healthy dose of misdirection."

Shahdi Feroz smiled. "And were you caught stealing the cookies often, my dear Miss Smith?"

Margo thrust away memory of too many beatings and didn't answer.

"Miss Smith?"

Margo knew that tone. That was the *Something's wrong, can I help?* tone people used when they'd inadvertently bumped too close to something Margo didn't want bumped. So she said briskly, "Let's see, next stop is Dorset Street, where Elizabeth Stride was killed in Dutfield's Yard. We shouldn't have any trouble getting in there, at least. Mr. Dutfield has moved his construction yard, so the whole place has been deserted for months." She very carefully did not look at Shahdi Feroz.

The older woman studied her for a long, dangerous moment more, then sighed.

Margo relaxed. She'd let it go, thank God. Margo didn't want to share those particular memories with anyone, not even Malcolm or Kit. Especially Malcolm or Kit. She realized that Shahdi Feroz, like so many others since it had happened, meant well; but raking it all up again wouldn't help anyone or solve anything. So she kept up a steady stream of chatter about nothing whatsoever as her most useful barrier to well-intentioned prying. She talked all the way down Brick Lane and Osborn Street, across Whitechapel Road, down Plumber Street, past jammed wagon traffic on Commercial Road, clear down to Berner Street, which left her badly out of breath, since Berner Street was all the way across the depth of Whitechapel parish from number twenty-nine Hanbury.

Dutfield's Yard was a deserted, open square which could be reached only by an eighteen-foot alleyway leading in from Berner Street. A double gate between wooden posts boasted a wooden gate to the right and a wicker gate to the left, to be used when the main gate was closed. White lettering on the wooden gate proclaimed the yard as the property of W. Hindley, Sack Manufacturer and A. Dutfield, Van and Cart Builder. The wicker gate creaked when Margo pushed it open and stepped through. She held it for Shahdi Feroz, who lifted her skirts clear of the rubbish blown against the base by wind from the previous night's storm.

The alleyway, a dreary, dim passage even in daylight, was bordered on the north by the International Workers' Educational Club and to the south by three artisans' houses, remodeled from older, existing structures. Once into the yard proper, Margo found herself surrounded by decaying old buildings. To the west lay the sack factory, where men and teenaged boys could be seen at work through dull, soot-grimed windows. Beside the abandoned cart factory stood a dusty, dilapidated stable which clearly hadn't been used since Arthur Dutfield had moved his business to Pinchin Street. Terraced cottages to the south closed in the yard completely. The odor of tobacco wafted into the yard from these cottages, where cigarettes were being assembled by hand, using sweatshop labor. The whir of sewing machines, operated by foot treadles, floated through a couple of open windows in one of the cottages; a small sign announced that this establishment was home to two separate tailors. The rear windows of the two-story, barnlike International Workers' Educational Club overlooked the yard, looming above it as the major feature closing in this tiny, isolated bit of real estate. The club, a hotbed of radical political activity and renowned for its Jewish ownership, also served as a major community center for educational and cultural events.

Standing in the center of the empty construction yard, Margo gazed thoughtfully at the rear windows of the popular hall. "Bold as brass, wasn't he?" she muttered.

Shahdi Feroz was studying the yard's only access, the eighteen-foot blind alley. She glanced up, first at Margo, then at the windows Margo was gazing at. "Yes," the scholar agreed. "The hall was—will be—filled with people that night."

It would be the Association's secretary, in fact, jeweler Louis Diemshutz, who would discover Elizabeth Stride's body some four weeks hence. Margo frowned slowly as she gazed, narrow-eyed, at the ranks of windows in the popular meeting hall. "Doesn't it strike you as odd that he chose this particular spot to kill Long Liz Stride?"

Shahdi frowned. "Odd? But it is a perfectly natural spot for him to choose. It is completely isolated from the street. And it will be utterly dark, that night. What more natural place for a prostitute to take her customer than a deserted stable in an abandoned yard?"

"Yes . . ." Margo was trying to put a more concrete reason to the niggling feeling that this was still an odd place for Jack to have killed his victim. "But she didn't want to come back here. She was struggling to escape when Israel Schwartz saw her. Given the descriptions he gave of the two men, I'm betting it's our mystery doctor who knocked her to the ground and Maybrick who ran Schwartz off."

Shahdi turned her full attention to Margo. "You know, that has always puzzled me about Elizabeth Stride," the Ripper scholar mused. "Why she struggled. As a working prostitute, this is not in character. And she had turned down a customer earlier that evening."

Margo stared. "She had?"

Shahdi nodded. "One of the witnesses who remembered seeing her said this. That a man had approached her and she said, 'No, not tonight.' And yet we know she needed money. She had quarreled with the man she lived with, had been seen in a doss house, admitted to a friend that she needed money. Why would she have refused one customer, then struggled when a second propositioned her? What did they discuss, that he attacked her?"

"Maybe," Margo said slowly, narrowing her eyes slightly, "she didn't need the money as much as we thought she did."

Shahdi's eyes widened. "The letters," she whispered, abruptly excited. Her eyes gleamed with quick speculation. "Perhaps these mysterious letters are worth a great deal of money, yes? Clearly, our friend the doctor is most anxious to retrieve them. And he recovered several gold sovereigns from Polly Nichols' pockets, which she must have been given by him earlier in the evening, as payment for these letters."

"Blackmail?" Margo breathed. "But blackmail against who? Whom, I mean. And if all these penniless women are being systematically hunted down because they've got somebody's valuable letters, why didn't they cash in on them? Every one of Jack's victims was drunk and soliciting just to get enough money for a four-penny bed for the night."

Shahdi Feroz shook her, visibly frustrated. "I do not know. But I intend to find out!"

Margo grinned. "Me, too. Come on, let's go. My feet are freezing and it's a long walk to Mitre Square and Goulston Street."

To reach Mitre Square, they traced one of the possible routes the Ripper might have taken from Berner Street where his bloody work with Elizabeth Stride had been—would be—interrupted by Louis Diemshutz. "One thing I find interesting," Margo said as they followed Back Church Lane up to Commercial Road and from there hiked down to Aldgate High Street and Aldgate proper, further west. "He knew the area. Knew it well enough to pull a stunt like switching police jurisdictions after getting away from Dutfield's Yard. He knew he was going to kill again. So he deliberately left Whitechapel and Metropolitan Police jurisdiction and hunted his second victim over in The City proper, where The City police didn't get on with Scotland Yard at all."

The "City of London" was a tiny district of government buildings in the very heart of London. Fiercely independent, The City maintained its own Lord Mayor and its own police force, its own laws and jurisdictions, separate from the rest of London proper, and was exceedingly jealous about maintaining its autonomy. It was confusing from the get-go, particularly to up-time visitors. In the case of Jack the Ripper's murder spree on the night of September thirtieth, it would confuse the devil out of London's two rival constabularies, as well. And it would lead to destruction of vital evidence by bickering police officials trying to keep the East End from exploding into anti-Semitic riots.

"That," Shahdi mused, "or he simply didn't meet Catharine Eddowes until he'd reached The City's jurisdiction. She had just been released from jail and was heading east, while Jack was presumably heading west."

"Well, even if he did just happen to meet her in The City, he doubled back into Whitechapel again, so it'd be the Metropolitan Police who found the apron he left for them under his chalked message, not constables from The City police. Somehow, Maybrick doesn't strike me as quite that clever."

"Perhaps, perhaps not," Shahdi said thoughtfully. "But one thing is quite clear. Our doctor is *very* clever. How has he managed, I wonder, to work so closely with Mr. Maybrick, yet keep all mention of himself out of Maybrick's incriminating diary?"

"Yeah. And why did Maybrick write a diary like that at all? I mean, that's tempting fate just a little too much, isn't it? His wife knew he was married to another woman, that he was a bigamist *and* having other affairs, probably with his own maidservants. At Florie's trial, everybody commented on how gorgeous all the Maybrick maids were. Florie might have gone looking for clues to who the other women were and found the diary. Or one of those nosy maids might have. They certainly helped themselves to Mrs. Maybrick's clothes and jewelry."

Shahdi Feroz was shaking her head in disagreement. "Yes, they did, but you may not realize that Maybrick kept his study locked at all times with a padlock. He kept the only key and straightened the room himself. Very peculiar for a businessman of the time. And he threatened to kill a clerk who nearly discovered something incriminating. Presumably the diary, itself. As to why he wrote the diary, many serial killers have a profound need to confess their crimes. A compulsion to be caught. It is why they play taunting games with the police, with letters and clues. A serial killer is under terrible pressure to murder his victims. By writing down his deeds, he can relieve some of this pressure, as well as relive the terrible thrill and excitement of the crime. Maybrick is not alone, in this. The risk of being caught, either through the diary or at the crime scene, is as addictive to the serial killer as the murder itself, is."

"God, that's really sick!" Margo gulped back nausea.

Shahdi nodded, eyes grim. "Maybrick's diary has always rung with authenticity on many levels. To forge such a thing, a person would have needed to comprehend a vast array of information, technical and scientific skills ranging from psychopathic serial killer psychology to the forensics of ink and handwriting and linguistic styles. No, I never believed the diary to be a forgery, even before we taped Mr. Maybrick killing Polly Nichols, although many of my colleagues have believed it to be, ever since it was discovered in the twentieth century. The thing I find most intriguing, however, is his silence in the diary about this doctor who works with him. Through the whole diary, he names people quite freely, including doctors he has consulted, both in Liverpool and London. Why, then, no mention of *this* doctor?"

"He mentions a doctor in London?" Margo said eagerly. "That's the guy, then!"

"No," Shahdi shook her head. "There are records of this doctor. He does not fit the age or physical description profile of the man on our video. I had already thought of this, of course, but we brought with us downloaded copies of everything known on this case. It is not the same man."

"Oh." Margo couldn't hide the disappointment in her voice.

Shahdi smiled. "It was a good thought, my dear. Ah, this is where we turn for Mitre Square."

They had to dodge heavy freight wagon traffic across Aldgate to reach Mitre Street, from which they could take one of the two access routes into the Square. This was a rectangle of buildings almost entirely closed in on four sides by tall warehouses, private residences, and a Jewish synagogue. The only ways in and out lay along a narrow inlet off Mitre Street and through a covered alleyway called Church Passage, which ran from Duke Street directly beneath a building, as so many odd little streets and narrow lanes in London did. Empty working men's cottages rose several stories along one side of the square. School children's voices could be heard in one corner, reciting lessons through the open windows of a small boarding school for working families with enough income to give their children a chance at a better future.

As they studied the layout of the narrow square, a door to one of the private houses opened. A policeman in uniform paused to kiss a woman in a plain morning dress. "Good day, m'dearie, an' keep the doors locked up, what with that maniac running about loose, cutting ladies' throats. I'll be back in time for supper."

"Do take care, won't you?"

"Ah, Mrs. Pearse, I always take care on a beat, you know that."

"Mr. Pearse," his wife touched his face, "I worry about you out there, say what you will. I'll have supper waiting."

Margo stared, not so much because Mr. and Mrs. Pearse had addressed one another so formally. That was standard Victorian practice, using the formal address rather than first names in public. The reason Margo stared was because Mr. Pearse was a police constable. "My God," Margo whispered. "Right across the street from a *constable's* house!"

Shahdi Feroz was also studying the policeman's house with great interest. "Yes. Most interesting, isn't it? Playing cat and mouse with the constables on the very night he was nearly caught at Dutfield's Yard. Giving the police a calculated insult. I am willing to bet on this. Maybrick hated Inspector Abberline already, by the night of the double murder."

"And one of them had already started sending those taunting letters to the press, too," Margo muttered. "No wonder the handwriting on the Dear Boss letters and note didn't match Maybrick's. This mysterious doctor of ours must have written them."

Shahdi Feroz gave Margo a startled stare. "Yes, of course! Which raises very intriguing questions, Miss Smith, most intriguing questions. Such letters are almost always sent by the killer to taunt police with his power. Yet the letters do *not* match Maybrick's handwriting, even though they use the American phrases Maybrick certainly would have known."

"Like the word 'boss,'" Margo nodded. "Or the term 'red stuff' which isn't any kind of Britishism. But Maybrick didn't need to disguise his handwriting, because Maybrick didn't send them, the *doctor* did. But why?" Margo wondered. "I mean, why would he write letters taunting the police using language deliberately couched to sound like an American had written them? Or somebody who'd been to America?"

Shahdi's eyes widened. "Because," she said in an excited whisper, "*he meant to betray James Maybrick!*"

Margo's mouth came open. "My God! He sent them to *frame his partner*? To make sure Maybrick was hanged? But ... surely Maybrick would've turned him in, if he'd been arrested? Which he wasn't, of course. Maybrick dies of arsenic poisoning next spring." Margo blinked, thoughts racing. "Does this mean something happens to the partner? To stop him from turning Maybrick over to the police?"

Shahdi Feroz was staring at Margo. "A very good question, my dear. We *must* find out who this mysterious doctor is!"

"You're telling me! The sooner the better. We've only got a week before he kills Annie Chapman." Margo was staring absently at the building across the square, while something niggled the back of her mind, some little detail she was missing. "If he knew the East End as well as I'm guessing—" She broke off as it hit her, what she was seeing. "*Oh, my God!* Look at that! The *Great Synagogue!* Another *Jewish connection!* First the Jewish Workingmen's Educational Club, then he kills Catharine Eddowes practically on the doorstep of a *synagogue.* And then he chalks anti-Semitic graffiti on a tenement wall on Goulston Street!"

Shahdi stared at the synagogue across Mitre Square. "Do you realize, this has never been noticed before? That a synagogue stood in Mitre Square? I am impressed, Miss Smith. Very much impressed. A double message, with one killing, leaving her between a policeman's home and a Jewish holy place of worship. A triple message, if one considers the taunt to police represented in his crossing police jurisdictions to chalk his message of hatred."

Margo shivered. "Yeah. All this gives me the screaming willies. He's *smart.* And that's scary as hell."

"My dear," Shahdi said very softly, "all psychopathic serial murderers are terrifying. If only we could only eliminate the abuse and poverty and social sickness that create such creatures . . ." She shook her head. "But that would leave the ones we cannot explain, except through biology or a willful choice to pursue evil pleasure at the expense of others' lives."

"No matter how you look at it," Margo muttered, "when you get down to it, human beings aren't really much better than killer plains apes, are they? Just a thin sugar-coating of civilization to make 'em look prettier." Margo couldn't disguise the bitterness in her voice. She'd had enough experience with human savagery to last a lifetime. And she wasn't even eighteen years old yet.

Shahdi's eyes had gone round. "Whatever has happened to you, my dear, to make you say such things at so young an age?"

Margo opened her mouth to bite out a sharp reply; then managed to bite her tongue at the last instant. "I've been to New York," she said, instead, voice rough. "It stinks. Almost worse than this." She waved a hand at the poorly dressed, hard-working people bustling past, at the women loitering in Church Passage, women eyeing the men who passed, at the ragged children playing in the gutter outside the Sir

John Cass School, children whose parents couldn't afford to send them for an education, children who couldn't even manage to be accepted as charity pupils, as Catharine Eddowes had been many years previously, whose parents kept them out of compulsory public-sector schools in defiance of the new laws, to earn a little extra cash. How many of those dirty-faced little girls tossing a ball to one another would be walking the streets in just a few years, selling themselves for enough money to buy a loaf of bread and a cupful of gin?

They left Mitre Square and headed east once more, crossing back into Metropolitan Police jurisdiction, and made their way up Middlesex Street, jammed with the clothing stalls which had given the street its nickname of Petticoat Lane. Margo and Shahdi pushed their way through the crowd, recording the whole scene on their scout logs. Women bargained prices lower on used petticoats, mended bodices and skirts, on dresses and shawls and woolen undergarments called combinations, while men poked through piles of trousers, work shirts, and sturdy boots. Children shouted and begged for cheap tin toys their mothers usually couldn't afford. And men loitered in clusters, muttering in angry tones that "somefink ought to be done, is wot I says. We got no gas lamps in the streets, it's dark as pitch, so's anybody might be murdered by a cutthroat. And them constables, now, over to H Division, wot they care about us, eh? Me own shop was robbed three times last week in broad daylight by them little bastards from the Nichol, and where was a constable, I ask you? Don't care a fig for us, they don't. Ain't *nobody* gives a fig for us, down 'ere in the East End . . ."

And further along, "Goin' to be riots in the streets again, that's wot, mate, goin' to be riots in the streets again, an' they don't give us a decent livin' wage down to docks. I got a brother in a factory, puts in twelve hours a day, six days a week, an' don't bring 'ome but hog an' sixpence a week, t' feed a wife an' five children. God 'elp if 'e comes down ill, God 'elp, I say. Me own sister-in-law might 'ave to walk the streets like that poor Polly Nichols, corse I can't feed 'er, neither, nor 'er starvin' dustpan lids, I got seven o' me own an' the shipyard don't pay me much over a groat more'n me brother brings 'ome . . ."

Margo cut across to Bell Lane, just to get away from the press of unwashed bodies and the miasma of sweat and dirt and despair rising from them, then led the way north along Crispin to Dorset Street, one of London's most infamous thoroughfares, lined with shabby, unheated doss houses. It was even money that every second or third woman they saw on the street was up for sale at the right price. "Dosset Street," as it was nicknamed by the locals, was still half-asleep despite the fact that the sun had been high over London's rooftops for hours. Many of the women who used these doss houses worked their trade until the early hours of the morning, five and six A.M., then collapsed into the first available bed and slept as late as the caretakers would let them.

Miller's Court, site of the fifth known Ripper murder, lay just off Dorset Street, through an archway just shy of Commercial Road. Directly across the street from the entrance to Miller's Court lay Crossingham's Lodging House, where Annie Chapman stayed by preference when she possessed the means. The killer had chosen his victims from a very small neighborhood, indeed.

Margo and Shahdi Feroz ducked beneath the archway, passing the chandler shop at number twenty-seven Dorset Street. This shop was owned by Mary Kelly's landlord, John McCarthy. Six little houses, each whitewashed in a vain attempt to make them look respectable, stood in the enclosed court where the final Ripper murder would take place, some three months from now. McCarthy's shop on the corner did a brisk business, it being a Friday. The younger McCarthys' voices were audible through the open windows, squabbling in a boisterous fashion.

At one of the cottage windows, a strikingly beautiful young woman with glorious strawberry blond hair leaned out the window to number thirteen. "Joseph! Come in for breakfast, love!"

Margo started violently. Then stared as a thickset man hurried across the narrow court to open the door to number thirteen. He gave the beautiful blonde girl a hearty kiss. *My God! It's Mary Kelly! And her unemployed lover, the fish-porter, Joseph Barnett!* Mary Kelly's laughter floated out through the open window, followed by her light, sweet voice singing a popular tune. "Only a Violet I Plucked From My Mother's Grave . . ." Margo shuddered. It was the same song she'd be heard singing the night of her brutal murder.

"Let's get out of here!" Margo choked out roughly. She headed for the narrow doorway that led back to Dorset Street. She had barely reached the chandler's shop when Shahdi Feroz caught up to her.

"Margo, what is it?"

Margo found dark eyes peering intently into her own. Shadows of worry darkened their depths even further. "Nothing," Margo said brusquely. "Just a little shook up, that's all. Thinking about what's going to happen to that poor girl . . ."

Mary Kelly had been the most savagely mutilated of all, pieces of her strewn all over the room. And nothing Margo could do, no warning Margo could give, would save her from that. She understood, in a terrible flash of understanding, how that ancient prophetess of myth, Cassandra of Troy, for whom Ianira Cassondra was named, must have felt, looking into the future and glimpsing nothing but death—with no way to change any of it. The feeling was far worse than during Margo's other down-time trips, worse, even, than she'd expected, knowing it was bound to strike at some point, during her Ripper Watch duties.

Margo met Shahdi Feroz's gaze again and forced a shrug. "It just hit me a lot harder than I expected, seeing her like that. She's so pretty and everything . . ."

The look Shahdi Feroz gave her left Margo's face flaming. *You're young,* that look said. *Young and inexperienced, for all the down-time work you've done . . .*

Well, it was true enough. She might be young, but she wasn't a shrinking violet and she wasn't a quitter, either. Memory of her parents had not and *would not* screw up the rest of her life! She shoved herself away from the sooty bricks of McCarthy's chandler shop. "Where did you want to go, now? Whitehall? That's where the torso will be found in October." The decapitated woman's torso, discovered between the double-event murders of Elizabeth Stride and Catharine Eddowes and the final murder of Mary Kelly, generally wasn't thought to be a Ripper victim. The *modus operandi* simply wasn't the same. But with two killers working together, who knew? And of course, the rest of London would firmly believe it to be Jack's work, which would complicate their task enormously as hysteria and terror deepened throughout the city.

Shahdi Feroz, however, was shaking her head. "No, not just yet. To reach Whitehall, we must leave the East End. I have other work to do, first. I believe we should go to the doss houses along Dorset Street, listen to what the women are saying."

Margo winced at the idea of sitting in a room full of street walkers who would remind her of what she'd fought so hard to escape. "Sure," she said gamely, having to force it out through clenched teeth. "There's only about a million of 'em to choose from."

They set out in mutual silence, walking quickly to keep warm. Margo would've faced the prospect of viewing piles of people left dead by the Black Death with less distaste than the coming interview with doss-house prostitutes. But there literally wasn't a thing she could do to get out of it. *Chalk it up to the price of your training,* she told herself grimly. After all, it wasn't nearly as awful as being raped by those filthy Portuguese traders and soldiers had been. She'd survived Africa. She'd survive this. Her life—and Shahdi Feroz'—might well depend on it. So she clenched her jaw and did her best to stay prepared for whatever might come next.

(((Chapter 13)))

Cold and rainy weather inflicts enormous suffering on those with lung ailments. The dampness and the chill seep down into the chest, worsening congestion until each breath drawn is a struggle to lift the weight of a boulder which has settled atop the ribcage, crushing the lungs down against the spine. Worse than the aching heaviness, however, are the prolonged coughing spells which leave devastating weakness in their wake, transforming a simple stroll across six feet of floor space into a marathon-distance struggle.

Cold, wet weather is bad enough when the air is clean. Add to it the smoke of multiple millions of coal-burning fireplaces and stoves, the industrial spewage of factory smokestacks, smelting plants, and iron works, and the rot and mold of anything organic left lying on the ground or in the streets or stacked along water-logged, dockside marshes, and the resulting putrid filth will irritate already-burdened lungs into a state of chronic misery. Toss in the systemic, wasting effects of tuberculosis and the slow deterioration of organs, brain tissues, and mental clarity brought on by advanced syphillis and the result is a slow, pain-riddled slide toward death.

Eliza Anne Chapman had been sliding down that fatal slope for a long time.

The summer and early autumn of 1888 had broken records for chilly temperatures and heavy rainfall. By the first week of September, Annie was so ill, she was unable to pay for her room at Crossingham's lodging house on Dorset Street with anything approaching regularity. Most of what she earned or was given by Edward Stanley—a bricklayer's mate with whom she had established a long-term relationship after the death of her husband—went to pay for medicines. A serious fight with Eliza Cooper, whom Annie had caught trying to palm a florin belonging to a mutual acquaintance, substituting a penny for the more valuable coin, had left Annie bruised and aching, with a swollen temple, blackened eye, and bruised breast where the other woman had punched her.

She had confidently expected to receive money soon for the letters she'd bought from Polly Nichols, to pay for the medicines she desperately needed. But no money was forthcoming from Polly or from the anonymous writer of the letters she carried in her pocket. Then, to Annie's intense shock, Polly was brutally murdered, more hideously stabbed and mutilated than poor Martha Tabram had been, back on August Bank Holiday. Even if Annie had wanted to ask Polly who the letter writer had been, it was now impossible. So Annie had dug out the letters to look at them more closely—and realized immediately there would *be* no money coming, either, not anytime soon. Had Annie been able to read Welsh, she might have been able to turn the letters into a substantial amount of cash very quickly. But Annie couldn't read Welsh. Nor did she know anyone who could.

Which left her with a commodity worth a great deal of money and no way to realize the fortune it represented. So she did the only thing she could. She sold the letters, just as Polly had sold them to her. One went to a long-time acquaintance from the lodging houses along Dorset Street. Long Liz Stride was a kind-hearted soul born in Sweden, who bought the first letter for sixpence, which was enough for Annie to go to Spitalfields workhouse infirmary and buy one of the medications she needed.

The second letter went to Catharine Eddowes for a groat, and the third Annie sold to Mr. Joseph Barnett, a fish porter who'd lost his job and was living in Miller's Court with the beautiful young Mary Kelly. Mr. Barnett paid Annie a shilling for the last letter, giving her a wink and a kiss. "My Mary lived in Cardiff, y'know, speaks Welsh like a native, for all she was born in Ireland. Mary'll read it out for me, so

she will. And if it's as good as you say, I'll come back and give you a
bonus from the payout!"

The groat, worth fourpence, and the shilling, worth twelve,
bought Annie the rest of the medicine she needed from Whitechapel
workhouse infirmary, plus a steady supply of beer and rum for the
next couple of days. Alcohol was the only form of pain medication
Annie could afford to buy and she was in pain constantly. She felt too
ill most of the time to walk the streets, particularly all the way down
to Stratford, where she normally plied her trade; but the medicine
helped. If only the weather would clear, she might be able to breathe
more easily again.

Annie regretted the sale of the letters. But a woman had to live,
hadn't she? And blackmail was such a distasteful trade, no matter how
a body looked at it. Polly had dazzled her with fanciful dreams of real
comfort and proper medicines, but in Annie's world, such dreams
were only for the foolish, people who didn't realize they couldn't
afford to indulge their fancies when there was food to be gotten into
the stomach and medicine to be obtained and a roof and bed to be
paid for, somehow . . .

Being a practical woman, Annie put those brief, glittering dreams
firmly behind her and got back to the business of staying alive as long
as humanly possible in a world which did not care about the fate of one
aging and consumptive widow driven to prostitution by sheer poverty.
It wasn't much of a life, perhaps. But it was all she had. So, like countless
thousands before her, "Dark Annie" Chapman made the best of it she
could and kept on living—without the faintest premonition that utter
disaster hung over her head like the executioner's sword.

Skeeter Jackson had an uncanny nose for trouble.

And this time, he landed right in the middle of it. One moment,
he was intent on reaching Urbs Romae to join the Festival of Mars
procession, having been delayed by a man moving suspiciously
behind a woman gowned in expensive Japanese silk. The next, Skeeter
found himself stranded between a solid wall of Angels of Grace
Militia on his left and a whole pack of *Ansar Majlis* sympathizers and
construction workers to his right.

He tried to backpedal, but it was far too late. Somebody's fist connected with an *Ansar Majlis* sympathizer's nose. Blood spurted. A roar went up from both sides, *Ansar Majlis* Brotherhood *and* Angels of Grace Militia. The crowd surged, fists swinging. A kiosk full of t-shirts and Ripper photo books toppled. Someone yelled obscenities as merchandise was trampled underfoot. A reek of sweat abused Skeeter's nostrils. Combatants plunged, dripping, into Edo Castletown's goldfish ponds, sending prehistoric birds flapping and screeching in protest from the trampled shrubbery. Then a ham-handed fist clouted his shoulder and the riot engulfed him.

Skeeter spun away from the blow. He tripped and teetered over the edge of the overturned kiosk, trying to keep his balance. Somebody hit him from the side. Skeeter yelled and slammed face first into a total stranger. He found himself tangled up with a viciously swearing woman, who sported a bleeding nose and a black uniform. Her eyes narrowed savagely. Angels of Grace hated *all* men, unless they worshipped the Lady of Heaven, and even then, they were suspicious of treason. Skeeter swore—and ducked a thick-knuckled fist aimed at *his* nose. He twisted, using moves he'd learned scrapping in the camp of the Yakka Mongols, trying to stay alive when the camp's other boys had decided to test the fighting skills and agility of their newly arrived *bogdo*.

Skeeter's lightning move sent the screeching woman into the waiting arms of a roaring *Ansar Majlis* construction worker. The collision was spectacular. Skeeter winced. Then yelped and ducked behind the toppled kiosk, dodging another pair of locked, grappling combatants. He stared wildly around for a way out and didn't find anything remotely resembling an escape route. Not four feet away, Kit Carson stood calmly at the center of the riot, casually tossing bodies this way and that, regardless of size, mass, onrushing speed, or religious and political affiliations. The retired scout's expression wavered between disgust and boredom. A whole pile of bodies had accumulated at his feet, growing steadily even as Skeeter watched, awestruck.

Then a crash of drums and a screaming wail from a piper jerked Skeeter's attention around. The Festival of Mars processional had arrived. Just in time to be engulfed in battle. Skeeter caught a confused glimpse of misshapen, shaggy shapes like hirsute kodiak bears. Women in ring-mail armor who resembled a cartoonist's vision of ancient *valkyries* staggered into view, complete with shields, spears, and swords. Mixed in were several keen-eyed old women in ragged skins, whose screeches in Old Norse lifted the hair on Skeeter's nape.

Kynan Rhys Gower appeared from out of the melee, dressed in the uniform he'd been wearing when the Welsh bowman had stumbled through that unstable gate into the Battle of Orleans, fighting the French army under the command of Joan of Arc. Several other down-timers sported Roman-style armor, hand-made for this very festival out of metal cans and other scraps salvaged from the station's refuse bins. There was even a Spaniard clutching a blunderbuss, wild-eyed and shouting in medieval Spanish as the procession slammed headlong into the riot.

The shock of collision drove tourists scattering for their very lives.

Shangri-La's down-timers fought a pitched battle—and they fought *dirty*.

A wild-eyed construction worker reeled back from a sword blow, blood streaming down his face from the gash in his scalp. A black-unformed ferret staggered past, locked in mortal combat with a six-foot bearskin draped over the head and down the back of a six-foot-eight Viking berserker. Skeeter dimly recognized the man under the bearskin as Eigil Bjarneson, a down-timer who'd stumbled through Valhalla's Thor's Gate several months previously. A sushi lunch stand swayed and crashed to the floor, spilling water and live fish underfoot. Several combatants slipped on the wriggling, slippery contents of the broken aquarium and fell. Skeeter caught a glimpse of onrushing motion from the corner of one eye and jumped back instinctively. A spear missed his midriff by inches, whistling past to embed itself in the wooden slats of a bench behind him

The spear's intended victim, a roaring *Ansar Majlis* sympathizer, pulled a mortar trowel from his tool belt and launched himself at the ring-mail clad woman who'd thrown the spear. Then a giant Angel in black, screaming obscenities in tones to bend metal, lunged right at Skeeter. Obligingly, Skeeter grasped the woman's outstretched arms and assisted her on her way, planting one foot and turning his hip in an effortless Aikido move he'd been practicing for months, now. For just an instant, the startled Militia Angel was airborne. Then the park bench behind Skeeter, complete with protruding spear, splintered under the Angel's landing. If Skeeter hadn't been practicing—and teaching his down-time friends—martial arts moves like that one, he'd have been *under* that mountain of curse-spitting Angel.

Then a man in a red shirt and burnoose, eyes wild and distorted, came in from Skeeter's off-side, and caught him while he still teetered off balance. Skeeter went down hard. He knew, at least, how to fall without doing himself injury, another legacy of scrapping fights with Yakka Mongol youngsters heavier and stronger than he was. Unfortunately, the man in red was heavy, too. A great deal heavier than Skeeter. And he landed right on top of Skeeter's chest, fists pounding everything within reach. Which mainly constituted Skeeter. A blow caught his ribs. Skeeter grunted, half-stunned. His own jab at the man's eyes narrowly missed the mark, but he raked the bastard's nose with a fist and popped his Adam's apple with the side of his arm. Blood welled from both nostrils. The man roared, even as Skeeter twisted under him, trying to wriggle free. Another smashing blow landed against Skeeter's ribs. He gasped, trying to breathe against blossoming pain—

And somebody snatched the bastard up by his red shirt and dragged him off. Skeeter heard a meaty blow and a howl of pain, a curse in Arabic . . . Skeeter rolled to his hands and knees, gasping and cursing a little, himself. His ribs ached, but nothing felt broken. He staggered to his feet, aware of his exposed vulnerability on the floor. Then he blinked. The roar of battle had died away, almost to a whimper. Security had arrived in force. Several dozen uniformed officers were tossing weighted nets and swinging honest-to-God lassos, bringing down combatants five and six at a time. And the Arabian Nights construction foreman was directing more of his crew to help Security, throwing nets across enraged construction workers and dragging them out none too gently, holding them for security to handcuff. In seconds, the fight was effectively over.

Skeeter caught his breath as uniformed bodies waded in, yanking combatants off balance and cuffing them with rough efficiency. Weapons clattered to the cobblestones and lay where they'd fallen, abandoned by owners who found themselves abruptly under arrest. As Skeeter stood swaying, his shirt in shreds where he'd tried to wriggle away from the guy in the red shirt, he realized who'd helped him out. None other than Kit Carson was standing over the fallen *Ansar Majlis* sympathizer, breathing easily, gripping a cotton rag mop in both hands like a quarterstaff. An overturned mop bucket spread a puddle of dirty water behind the retired time scout, where someone on the maintenance crew had been caught up in the riot, as well. At least it wasn't Bergitta—she wasn't anywhere in sight. Judging from the trail of bruised, groaning figures behind Kit, leading from the jumbled pile of combatants Kit had already put down, the retired time scout knew how to use a quarterstaff effectively, too. The jerk in red on the floor was moaning and not moving much.

Then Kit glanced up, caught Skeeter's gaze, and relaxed fractionally. "You okay, Skeeter?"

He nodded, then winced at the bruising along his ribs. "Yeah. Thanks."

"My pleasure." He said it like he meant it. Literally. A feral grin had begun to stretch his lips. "Whoops, here comes Mike Benson. *Him,* you don't need breathing down your neck. Scoot, Skeeter. I'll catch you later."

Skeeter blinked, then made tracks. Kit was right about one thing. The last person Skeeter wanted to tangle with was Mike Benson cleaning up a riot. Skeeter disappeared into the stunned crowd as Rachel Eisenstein's medical team arrived, setting broken bones and sewing up gashes. Fortunately, from the look of things, they wouldn't be dealing with anything fatal. *How,* he wasn't sure. Spears, swords, knives, construction tools of half a dozen shapes and lethal potentialities . . . He shook his head in amazement. One member of the Angels of Grace Militia sported gashes down her face from a fistful of bear claws, where she'd made the mistake of taking a swing at Eigil Bjarneson.

And right at the edge of the riot zone, down at the border between Edo Castletown and Victoria Station, Skeeter found Ann Vinh

Mulhaney, totally unscathed despite her tiny size. The petite firearms instructor was sitting calmly atop a wrought iron lamp post, with a small, lethal-looking revolver clutched in each hand. It was clear from the path of wreckage that no one had cared to challenge either her position or her person. Skeeter grinned and waved. Ann smiled and nodded, then holstered her pistols and slithered down the lamp post, lithe and agile as a sleek hunting cat. She landed lightly on the cobbles and headed Skeeter's way.

"Good God, Ann," he said, eying the guns she'd used to defend her perch, "you could've held off an army from up there. Those pistols of yours are cute little things. What are they?"

The petite instructor chuckled. "Webleys, of course. The Royal Irish Constabulary Webley, a different animal altogether from your later military Webley. Pack quite a punch for their size, too, in a delightfully concealable package. Lots of Britannia tourists have been renting them for the Ripper tours."

"No wonder nobody challenged you up there."

She laughed easily. "Occasionally, we get a tourist or two with brains. I don't know about anybody else, but after all that excitement, I could use a drink to cool my throat. Come with us, why don't you, Skeeter?"

He flushed crimson, aware that what little money he had left wouldn't even cover the cost of a beer. "Uh, thanks, but I've got work to do. I'll, uh, take a raincheck, okay?" She probably knew he'd been fired, the whole station knew that, by now, but a guy had his pride, after all.

"Well, all right," she said slowly, studying him with her head tilted to one side. "See you around, then, Skeeter. Hey, Kit! Over here! I saw Robert headed toward Urbs Romae. What say we stop at the Down Time for a quick drink before Primary cycles? We'll probably catch up to Robert there and I heard they had a cask of Falernian . . ."

Skeeter edged his way deeper into the crowd as Kit exclaimed, "Falernian? When did they bring in a cask of heaven?"

Even Skeeter knew that Falernian was the Dom Perignon of ancient Roman wines. And Kit Carson was a connoisseur of fine wines and other potent potables. Skeeter sighed, wondering how marvellous it really tasted, aware that he wouldn't have been able to afford a glass of Falernian even if he had still been employed. But since he wasn't . . .

He cut around the damaged riot zone the long way, heading for Primary again. Skeeter dodged around one corner of the Shinto Shrine which had been built in the heart of Edo Castletown, and wheeled full-tilt into a short, stout woman. The collision rocked her back on her heels. Skeeter shot out a steadying hand to keep her from falling. Familiar blue eyes flashed indignantly up at him. "Cor, blimey, put a butcher's out, won't you, luv? Right near squashed me thrip'nny bits, you 'ave!"

That patter identified her faster than Skeeter could focus on her features. Molly, the down-timer Cockney barmaid who worked at the Down Time Bar & Grill, favorite haunt of station residents, was rubbing her substantial chest with one arm and grimacing. "Molly! What are you doing halfway to Primary Precinct?" Skeeter had to shout above the roar of voices as she tugged her dress to rights and glared sourly up at him. "I thought you were working late today? Did you get caught up in the Festival of Mars procession after all?"

Molly's expressive grimace encapsulated a wealth of disdain, loathing, and irritated anger into one twist of her mobile face. "Nah. Bleedin' newsies invaded, bad as any whirlin' dervishes, they are, wot broke a British square. Devil tyke 'em! I'd like t'see 'em done up like kippers, so I would. Got the manners of a gutter snipe, won't let a lady put 'er past be'ind 'er, not for all the quid in the Owd Lady of Threadneedle Street." When Skeeter drew a blank on that reference, as he often did with Molly's colorful Cockney, she chuckled and patted his arm. "Bank of England, me owd china, that's wot we called 'er, Owd Lady of Threadneedle Street."

"Oh." Skeeter grinned. "Me owd china, is it? I'm honored, Molly." She didn't admit friendship to many, not even among the down-timers. He wondered what he'd done to earn her good opinion. Her next words gave him the answer.

"I come up 'ere t'find Bergitta. Needs a place t'stay, is afraid o' that blagger wot blacked 'er face, livin' alone an' all, an' I got room in me flat, so I 'ave. It'd be cheaper, too, wiv two of us sharin' the bills."

Skeeter didn't know what to say. He found himself swallowing hard.

"You ain't seen 'er, then?"

He shook his head. "No. I was heading for Primary, when that riot broke out."

"Might come along, me own self," Molly mused. "Got nuffink better to do, 'til I finds Bergitta, anyway."

Skeeter grinned. "I'd be honored to escort you, Molly."

She fell into step beside him.

"I've *never* seen this many people at an opening of Primary." Skeeter had to shout above the roar of voices. Using elbows and a few underhanded moves, Skeeter shoved his way through the mob until he found a good vantage point where he and Molly could settle themselves to wait.

Gaudy splashes of color marked long lines of departing tourists and the hundreds of spectators arriving just to watch the show. Montgomery Wilkes, ruling head of BATF on station, wasn't in sight yet. Security officers were scarce, too, in the wake of the riot.

BATF carels, manned by tax-collection agents of the Bureau of Access Time Functions, carefully clad in dress-uniform red, lined the route into and out of Primary Precinct. Once past the BATF carels, inbound tourists and visitors arriving at TT-86 had to run a gauntlet of medical stations, a whole double row of them, which formed the entryway into the time terminal.

Tourists inbound had to scan their medical records into the station's database files before entering Shangri-La. This gave station medical baseline data to compare the tourists' health with, once they returned from their time tours. All departing tourists were required to undergo an intensive physical before leaving the station, as a quarantine procedure against exporting anything nasty up time. The system had stopped an outbreak of black death a couple of years back on TT-13, keeping the deadly plague from reaching the up-time world. The medical screening system wasn't foolproof, of course— nothing in life was—but it kept time tourism operational, which was the lifeblood of a station like Shangri-La.

Skeeter just hoped, with a superstitious shiver, that the irate up-time Senator whose daughter had been kidnapped failed to swing enough votes to shut down the time terminals. If station violence on TT-86 continued much longer, he just might get those votes. If BATF was worried about it, however, that worry didn't show in the attitudes of its agents. They were as rude as ever, from what Skeeter could see of the check-out procedures underway. BATF agents ignored the increasing crush of onlookers, busy valuing souvenirs brought back from down-time gates. The agents' main job on station was to establish taxes due on whatever was brought up time from the gates and to levy fines for anyone caught smuggling out contraband. They searched luggage—and occasionally, the tourists and the couriers who ran supplies and mail back and forth through Primary—for anything undeclared that might be considered taxable. At one tax kiosk, a middle-aged lady with diamonds on every finger was protesting loudly that she hadn't any idea how those granulated Etruscan gold earrings and necklaces had come to be sewn into her Victorian corset. *She* hadn't put them in her suitcase, why, they must have been planted in her luggage by some ruffian . . .

"Tell it to the judge," the red-clad BATF agent said in a bored tone, "or pay the taxes."

"But I tell you—"

"Lady, you can either pay the five-thousand-dollar tax fine due on this jewelry, or you can turn it over to a representative of the International Federation of Art Temporally Stolen, to see that it's returned to its proper place of origin, or you can go to prison for violating the Prime Rule of time travel. You can't profit illegally from a time gate. Robert Li is the designated IFARTS agent for Shangri-La Station. His studio is in Little Agora. You have exactly a quarter of an hour to dispose of it there or pay the taxes due here."

The woman sputtered indignantly for a long moment, then snapped, "Oh, all right! Will you take a check?"

"Yes, ma'am, if you have three forms of identification with a permanent address that matches the information you gave in your records when you entered Shangri-La Station. Make it payable to the Bureau of Access Time Functions."

"Fine!" She was digging into a large, exquisitely wrought handbag.

That bag had walked out of some designer's studio in Paris, or Skeeter didn't know high fashion. And since Skeeter had made it a lifelong practice to keep tabs on *haute couture* as well as cheap knock-offs, as a way of distinguishing rich, potential marks from wannabe pretenders, he was pretty sure it was the real McCoy. She dragged out a checkbook cover made from genuine ostrich leather with a diamond insignia in one corner and scribbled out a check. Five thousand was probably what she dropped on restaurant tables as tips in the course of an average month. Skeeter shook his head. The richer they were, the more they tried to pull, sneaking out contraband past customs.

The BATF agent verified her identification and accepted the check.

The lady stuffed her Etruscan gold back into her corset with wounded dignity and snapped shut the case, moving deeper into the departures area with an autocratic sniff.

"Next!"

Gate announcements sounded every ten minutes until the five-minute mark, after which the loudspeaker warnings began coming every minute, reminding stragglers they were running out of time. At the three-minute warning, a familiar voice from somewhere behind him startled Skeeter into glancing around.

"Skeeter!"

He caught a glimpse of Rachel Eisenstein pushing through the crowd. She was panting hard, clearly having run most of the way from the infirmary.

"Rachel? What's wrong?" He entertained momentary, panic-stricken visions of Bergitta having thrown a blood clot from that beating or something else equally life threatening. As Shangri-La' Station's chief of medicine pushed her way through to Skeeter and Molly, he grasped her hand. "What is it? What's *wrong?*"

Rachel blinked in startled surprise. "Wrong? Oh, Skeeter, I'm sorry, of course you'd think something's happened to Bergitta. Nothing's wrong at all, other than I just finished triage from that riot and decided I'd better work Primary, too, just in case." She patted a heavy hip pack. "Brought all the essentials. I was just trying to get here before the gate opened, hoping I might find someone I recognized who already had a good spot. Hi, Molly!"

Skeeter drew a long, deep breath and slowly relaxed. "Well, we've got a decent spot. You're welcome to share."

"Thanks, this *is* a great spot." Rachel pushed back damp hair from her brow. "God, I hope we don't have another riot on the heels of that mess."

"Me, either," Skeeter muttered. "Because now I've got *two* ladies to look out for, if the fists start flying."

The slim surgeon smiled, dark eyes sparkling. "Skeeter, I'm touched, really. I didn't know you cared. What brings *you* out here in all this madness?"

"Me?" Skeeter shrugged, wondering if she'd believe the truth. "I, uh, was wondering how many pickpockets and con artists I might spot on their way in."

Rachel Eisenstein shot him a surprisingly intent stare. "I have been paying attention, you know, Skeeter. I'm not sure, exactly, what triggered it, although I suspect it had something to do with Ianira."

He flushed. "You could say that." Skeeter shrugged. "I'm just trying to make things better around here. For the down-timers." He glanced at Molly, whose eyes reflected a quiet pride that closed his throat. "Folks like Molly, here, they've got a rough enough time as it is, trying to survive, without some jerk stealing them blind." Skeeter shrugged again and changed the subject. "I've been keeping count of outgoing departures. I was up to nearly a hundred before you got here. Want to bet we get more inbound than we send back outbound?"

Rachel chuckled. "No bets!"

Skeeter grinned. "Wise woman."

The klaxon sounded again, blasting away at Skeeter's eardrums. *"Your attention please.* Gate One is due to open in one minute. All departures, be advised that if you have not cleared Station Medical, you will not be permitted to pass Primary. Please have your baggage ready for customs . . ."

The departures in line hastily gathered up their luggage. Those still at the customs tables scrambled to pay the astromical taxes demanded as a condition of departure. Then the savage lash of subharmonics which heralded the opening of a major temporal gate struck Skeeter square in the skull bones. A fierce headache comprised of equal parts low blood sugar, stress, and gate subharmonics blossomed, causing him to wince. Skeeter resisted the urge to cover his ears, knowing it wouldn't shut out the painful noise that wasn't a noise, and simply waited.

The sight was always impressive as Primary opened up out of thin air. A point of darkness appeared five feet above the Commons floor. It grew rapidly, amoebalike, its black, widening center an oil stain spreading across the air. The outer edges of the dark hole in reality dopplered through the whole visible spectrum, with the spreading fringes shimmering like a runaway rainbow. A stir ran through the spectators. Every person in the station had seen temporal gates open before, of course, but the phenomenon never failed to raise chill bumps or the fine hairs along the back of the neck as the fabric of reality shifted and split itself wide open . . .

A flurry of startled grunts and a rising flood of profanities sounded behind them. Skeeter turned to crane his head above the crowd. "Aw, nuts . . ."

Literally.

The Angels of Grace Militia, at least the portion that had escaped arrest during the riot, was on a crash-course drive for Primary, shoving their way through by brute force.

"What is it?" Rachel asked, trying to see.

"Angel Squad, inbound."

Molly's comment was in obscure Cockney, defying translation.

Rachel rolled her eyes. "Oh, God. Please don't tell me *they're* expecting reinforcements from up time, too?"

"Well," Skeeter scratched his ear, "scuttlebutt has it their captain was seen buying a ticket for some general of theirs who's coming in for a Philosopher's Gate tour. Wants to see the city where Ianira lived in subjugation to an evil male of the species."

"Oh, God, Skeeter, I *told* you not to tell me they were bringing in reinforcements!"

"Sorry," he grinned sheepishly.

Rachel scowled up at him and stood on tiptoe, trying to spot the onrushing Angels. Molly just thinned her lips and moved into a slightly aggressive stance, waiting for whatever might come next. Moving in a close-packed wedge, the Angel Squad drove through the waiting crowd on an unstoppable course, shoving and bullying their way through. One brief altercation ended with a tourist clutching at a bloodied nose while Angels burst past him on a course that would bring them out right about where Skeeter stood with Molly and Rachel. He braced for bad trouble for the second time in a quarter hour, wondering whether it might not be wiser to simply cut and run, taking himself, Molly, and Rachel out of their path, or whether he ought to stand his ground on general principles.

At that instant, an ear-splitting klaxon shattered the air.

Skeeter jerked his gaze around just in time to see it. Primary had opened wide enough to begin the transfer of out-bound tourists. Only they hadn't gotten very far. A writhing, entangled mass of humanity crashed straight through Primary, *inbound.*

Rachel gasped. "What in the world—? *Nobody* crashes Primary!"

But a howling swarm of people had done just that, shoving through into Shangri-La Station before the outgoing departures could get off to a good start. Klaxons blared insanely. The mad, hooting rhythm all but deafened. Nearly a hundred shouting people stormed into Shangri-La Station in a seething mass, rushing past medical stations, past screaming tourists and howling BATF agents, past everything in their path, as though they owned the entire universe.

"Has every nut in the universe decided to converge on Primary today?"

"I don't know!" Rachel shook her head. "But this could get ugly, whoever they are."

Skeeter agreed. Whoever the new arrivals were, they were headed right this way. And where were those damned Angels? He tried to peer back through the crowd where the Angels of Grace still plowed toward them, a juggernaut at full steam. At that moment, Montgomery Wilkes shot from his office at a dead run, driving forward like a hurtled war spear straight into the boiling knot of close-packed humanity crashing through Primary. The head of BATF wielded his authority like a machete. "HALT! Every one of you! Stop *right now!* And I mean—"

Monty never finished.

Someone in that on-rushing maelstrom shoved him. *Hard.*

The seething head of BATF slammed sideways, completely out of the swarm inbound through Primary. Wilkes careened headlong into the chaos of the departure line. Windmilling wildly, he inadvertently knocked down a woman, three kids, and a crate of sixteenth-century Japanese porcelain which had just been valued and taxed by Monty's agents. Its owner, a departing businessman, teetered for an instant, as well. Monty, staggering and stumbling in a half-circle, caromed off the businessman and continued on through the line into the concrete wall beyond. They connected—Monty's face and the wall—with a sickening SPLAT!

Wilkes slid, visibly dazed, to the floor just as the Japanese businessman went down. He landed as badly as his irreplacable porcelain. *That* didn't fare nearly as well when it hit the concrete. Japanese curses—which followed the confirmation of utter ruin— poured out above the noise of yelling voices and screaming klaxons. Monty Wilkes simply sat on the floor blinking wet eyes. His agents gaped, open-mouthed, for a long instant, motionless with shock. Then they scattered, antlike. Some broke toward the gate crashers and others raced to their employer's rescue. Sirens and klaxons wailed like storm winds on the Gobi—

Skeeter abruptly found himself tangled up in the outer edges of a churning cyclone of vid-cam crews, remote-lighting technicians, and shouting newsies. Skeeter staggered. A long boom microphone attached to a human being slammed violently sideways. It very nearly knocked him off his feet. Pain blossomed down the side of his head and through his shoulder. Skeeter spat curses and tried to protect Rachel's head when a heavy camera swung straight toward her skull. Molly went spinning under a body slam from someone twice her height.

Then another jostling, shouting mob slammed into them from *behind.*

The Angels of Grace had arrived.

The seething chaos crashing Primary staggered as the juggernaut of black-clad Angels crashed into it, full speed. Skeeter heard shouts and threats and screeches of protest. A fist connected with someone's nose. An ugly exchange of profanity exploded into the supercharged air . . .

"Armstrong!"

Hard, grasping hands forcibly jerked Skeeter around. A tall, powerful stranger yanked him forward. *"Armstrong, you son-of-a-bitch! Where's my daughter?"*

Over the shoulder of the gorilla breaking his arm, Skeeter glimpsed a living wall of newsies and camera operators. They stared right at him, eyes and mouths rounded. Skeeter blinked stupidly into a dimly familiar face . . .

One that darkened as sudden shock and anger registered. "You're not Noah Armstrong! Who the hell are *you?*"

"Who am I?" Skeeter's brain finally caught up. He dislodged the man's grip with a violent jerk of his arm. "Who the hell are *you?*"

Before anybody could utter a single syllable, the embattled Angels exploded.

"Death to tyrants!"

"Get him!"

For just an instant, Skeeter saw a look of stupefied surprise cross the stranger's face. The man's mouth sagged open. Then his whole face drained absolutely white. Not in fear. In *fury*. The explosion went off straight into Skeeter's face. *"What in hell is going on in this God-cursed station?"*

Skeeter's mouth worked, but no sound emerged.

"What are those *lunatics*"—he jabbed a finger at the Angels— "doing brawling with my staff? Answer me! Where's your station security? You!" The man who'd mistaken him for somebody named Noah Armstrong grabbed Skeeter's arm again, yanked him off balance. "Take me to your station manager's office! Now!"

"Hey! Take your hands off me!" Skeeter wrenched free. "Didn't anybody teach you assault's illegal?"

The stranger's eyes widened fractionally, then narrowed into angry grey slits. "Just who do you think you're talking to? I'd better get some cooperation out of this station, starting with *you*, whoever you are, or this station's jail is going to be full of petty officials charged with obstruction of justice!"

Skeeter opened his mouth again, not really sure what might come out of it, but at that moment, Bull Morgan, himself, strode through the chaos at Primary. The station manager moved with jerky strides as he maneuvered his fireplug-shaped self on a collision course with Skeeter and the irate stranger.

"Out of the way," Bull growled, shouldering aside newsie crews and BATF agents with equal disregard for their status. He puffed his way up like a tugboat and stuck out one ham-sized hand. "Bull Morgan, Station Manager, Time Terminal Eighty-Six. I understand you wanted to see me?"

Skeeter glanced from Bull's closed and wary expression to the stranger's flushed jowls and seething grey eyes and decided other climes were doubtless healthier places to take himself . . .

"Marshal!" the stranger snapped.

A red-faced bull moose in a federal marshal's uniform detached itself from the chaos boiling around them. Said moose produced a set of handcuffs, which he promptly snapped around Bull Morgan's wrists.

Skeeter's jaw dropped.

So did Bull's. His unlit cigar hit the floor with an inaudible thud.

"Mr. Clarence Morgan, you are hereby placed under arrest on charges of kidnapping, misuse of public office, willful disregard of public safety, violation of the prime directive of temporal travel—"

"*What?*"

"—and tax evasion. You are hereby remanded to federal custody. You have the right to remain silent. Anything you say can and will be used against you in a court of law—"

From somewhere directly behind Skeeter, a woman in a black uniform let out a strangled bellow. "*You slimy little dictator!* Take your trumped up charges and your Stalinist terror tactics off our station!"

Somebody threw a punch . . .

The riot erupted in every direction. A camera smashed to the concrete floor. Somebody sprawled into Skeeter's line of vision, clutching at a bloody nose and loosened teeth. Another black-clad Angel loomed out of the crowd, fists cocked. Molly's gutter Cockney scalded someone's ears. A newsie went flying and somebody screamed—

The tear gas hit them all at the same instant.

Riot turned abruptly to rout.

Skeeter coughed violently, eyes burning. Rachel Eisenstein staggered into him, bent almost double. A ring of uniformed federal officers materialized out of the spreading cloud, masked against the gas, spewing chemical spray from cannisters in a three-sixty-degree swath. They surrounded Bull Morgan and the infuriated, cursing stranger, making sure the latter didn't collapse onto the floor. Moving with neat, deadly calm, more than a dozen federal agents took charge. Snub-nosed riot guns flashed into a bristling circle, muzzles pointed outward.

Newsies fell over one another as they tried to evade armed feds, livid BATF officers, residents trying to get away through the chaos, Shangri-La Security arriving too late to prevent disaster, screaming Angels, and panic-stricken tourists. As the tear gas spread, the inbound traffic arriving through Primary disintegrated into a shambles.

Skeeter grabbed Rachel's wrist and hauled her bodily toward Edo Castletown. They had to get clear of this insanity. Weird, distorted shouts and cries rose on all sides. He couldn't see Molly anywhere. He could barely see, at all. They slithered feet-first into a goldfish pond and nearly fell, then splashed through knee-deep water and ran into screaming, wailing tourists and floating timbers where one of the Edo Castletown bridge railings had collapsed. Skeeter scrambled up the other side of the pond, pulling Rachel up behind him, and half-fell through a screen of shrubbery, then they stumbled into a miraculous pocket of clear air. Skeeter dragged down a double lungful of it, coughing violently. He tried to keep Rachel on her feet, but was hardly able to keep his own.

"Let me help!"

The familiar voice rang practically in his ear. Someone got an arm around Rachel and drew her forward, then somebody grasped

Skeeter's elbow and hauled him out of the chaos on tottering feet. Blinded by the tear gas, Skeeter allowed himself to be propelled along. Noise and confusion faded. Then someone else got an arm around him and a few moments later, he found his face buried in blessedly cool, running water. He coughed again and again, blinked streaming, burning eyes. He managed to choke out, "Rachel?"

"She's all right, Skeeter. Damned good job you did, getting her out of that mess."

He heard her coughing somewhere beside him and wondered with an anxious jolt what had become of Molly. Skeeter rinsed his eyes again, swearing under his breath, furious with himself for failing yet again to protect a friend in the middle of a station riot. He was finally able to blink his eyes and keep them open without burning pain sending new tears streaming down his face.

Skeeter was standing, improbably, in what looked like the bathrooms off the Neo Edo Hotel lobby. The mirror showed him a sodden mess that had once been his face. He shook his head, spraying water, and started to scrub his face with both hands. Someone grabbed his wrists and said hastily, "Wash them off, first. They're covered with CS." Slippery liquid soap cascaded across his fingers.

That voice sounded so familiar, Skeeter glanced up, startled. And found himself staring eyeball to reddened eyeball with Kit Carson.

Skeeter's mouth fell open. The lean and grizzled former time scout smiled, a trifle grimly. "Wash your hands, Skeeter. Before you rub tear gas into your eyes again." Behind Kit's shoulder, Robert Li, the station's resident antiquarian, bent over another sink, helping Rachel rinse tear gas out of her eyes. Belatedly, Skeeter noticed the floppy rubber gas mask dangling from Kit's neck. Where the devil had Kit Carson found a gas mask? Surely he hadn't bought one from that Templar selling them down in Little Agora? Wherever he'd stashed it—probably that fabled safe of his, up in the Neo Edo Hotel's office—there'd been two of 'em, because Robert Li wore one, too. Well, maybe Kit had bought them from that Templar, after all. He was smart enough to prepare for any kind of trouble. Wordlessly, Skeeter washed his hands.

When he'd completed the ritual, which helped him regain his composure and some measure of his equilibrium, he straightened up and met Kit's gaze again. He was startled by the respect he found there. "Thanks," Skeeter mumbled, embarrassed.

Kit merely nodded. "Better strip off those clothes. The Neo Edo's laundry staff can clean the tear gas out of them."

Well, why not? Skeeter had done stranger things in his life than strip naked in front of Kit Carson and the station's leading antiquities expert in the middle of the most expensive bathroom in Shangri-La Station while a riot raged outside. He was down to his skivvies when Hashim Ibn Fahd, a down-time teenager who'd stumbled, shocked, through the new Arabian Nights gate, arrived. Dressed in Neo Edo Hotel bellhop livery, which startled Skeeter, since Hashim hadn't been employed two days previously, the boy carried a bundle of clothing under one arm and a large plastic sack.

"Here," Hashim said, holding out the sack. "Put everything inside, Skeeter."

"Have you seen Molly?"

"No, Skeeter. But I will search, if Mr. Carson allows?"

Kit nodded. "I didn't realize she was caught in that mess, too, or I'd have pulled her out along with Skeeter and Rachel."

The down-timer boy handed over his plastic sack and ran for the door. Skeeter dumped in his dress slacks and his shirt, the one the irate construction worker had ripped not thirty minutes previously. The jingle of important things rattled in his pockets. "Uh, my stuff's in there."

"We'll salvage everything, Skeeter," Kit assured him. "There's an emergency shower in that last stall, back there. Sluice off and get dressed. This is going to get mighty ugly, mighty fast. I don't want you anyplace where that asshole out there," he nodded toward the riot still underway outside the Neo Edo, "can lay hands on you. Not without witnesses."

That sounded even more ominous than the riot.

"Uh, Kit?" he asked uncertainly.

The retired time scout glanced around. "Yes?"

Skeeter swallowed nervously. "Just who was that guy, anyway? He looked sorta familiar . . ."

Kit's eyes widened. "You didn't recognize him? Good God. And here I thought you had a set the size of Everest. That was Senator John Caddrick."

Skeeter's knees jellied.

Kit gripped his shoulder. "Buck up, man. I don't think you'll be going to jail anytime in next ten minutes, anyway, so shower that stuff off. We'll convene a council of war, after, shall we?"

There being nothing of intelligence Skeeter could say in response to that, he simply padded off barefooted across the marble floor of the Neo Edo's luxurious bathroom, wondering how in hell Kit Carson proposed to get Skeeter out of *this* one. He groaned. Oh, God, this was *all* they needed, with Ianira Cassondra's suspicious disappearance, fatal shootings on station during two major station riots, *not* counting today's multiple disasters . . .

Why *Senator Caddrick,* of all people? And why *now?* If Caddrick was here, did that mean his missing, kidnapped kid had been brought here, too? By the *Ansar Majlis?* Skeeter held back a groan. He had an awful feeling Shangri-La Station was in fatal trouble.

Where that left Skeeter's adopted, down-timer family . . .

Skeeter ground his molars and turned on the emergency shower. Shangri-La Station wasn't going down without a fight! If Senator Caddrick meant to shut them down, he was in for the biggest battle of his life. Skeeter Jackson was fighting for the very survival of his adopted clan, for everything he held sacred and decent in the world.

Yakka Mongols, even adopted ones, were notoriously dirty fighters.

And they did not like to lose.

Chief Inspector Conroy Melvyn, as head of the Ripper Watch Team, had the right to tell Malcolm what he wanted to try when it came to searching for the Ripper's identity, and what Conroy Melvyn wanted was to know who this mysterious doctor was, assisting James Maybrick. Malcolm, exhausted by days of searching for Benny Catlin, didn't think Melvyn's latest scheme was going to work. But he was, as they said in the States, the boss, and what the boss wanted . . .

Nor could Margo tackle this particular guiding job. Not even Douglas Tanglewood was properly qualified. But Malcolm was. So

Malcolm Moore dressed to the nines and ordered the best carriage Time Tours' Gatehouse maintained, and set his teeth against weariness as they jolted through the evening toward Pall Mall and the gentlemen's clubs for some trace of a doctor answering their mystery Ripper's description.

Conroy Melvyn, Guy Pendergast, and Pavel Kostenka rode with him, the latter agreeing to remain silent throughout the evening, since men of foreign birth were *not* welcomed in such clubs unless they were widely known as prominent international celebrities, which Pavel Kostenka was not—at least, not in 1888. And he was still very much shaken by the riot which had endangered his life in Whitechapel earlier in the week. Conroy Melvyn would also have to remain close-mouthed in these elite environs, given his working-class accent; if pressed, Malcolm would explain that he was with the police, investigating a case, but hoped to avoid any such scene, which would irretrievably damage his own reputation. No gentleman would be forgiven for bringing a low and vulgar creature like a policeman into an establishment such as the Carlton Club, their first destination for the evening.

Of the three men Malcolm would be guiding this evening, Guy Pendergast would be the least restrained by circumstances. And he remained the most ebulliently convinced of his own immortality, as well, constantly suggesting mad "research" schemes which Malcolm and Douglas and Margo had to veto, sometimes forcefully. Undaunted, Pendergast chatted amiably the whole ride, trying to draw out the Ripper scholars on the subject of the evening's search and chuckling at their close-mouthed irritation.

They finally reached Robert Smirke's famous clubhouse of 1836, which was fated for destruction by Nazi bombs in 1940, and Malcolm told the carriage driver to wait for an hour, then entered the ornately popular Carlton Club, which lay situated beautifully between ultra-fashionable St. James' Square—with its statue of William III and the minaret-steepled church of St. James' Piccadilly visible above the tall, stately buildings—and Carlton House Terrace on the opposite side. The lovely Carlton Gardens ran along Carlton Club's open, easterly facing side, completing the stately club's picturesque, fashionable setting.

Malcolm was known here, as he was in all of the gentlemen's clubs of Pall Mall and Waterloo Place, having procured memberships in each for business purposes as a temporal guide. He greeted the doorman with a nod and introduced his guests, anglicizing Dr. Kostenka's name, then ushered them into the familiar, tobacco-scented halls of the gentleman's private domain. Massive mahogany furniture and dark, rich colors dominated. There was no trace of feminine frills, of the crowding of bric-a-brac, or the typical housewifely clutter which dominated most gentlemen's private homes. Malcolm and his guests checked their tall evening hats, canes, and gloves, but Malcolm declined to check his valise, which held his log and ATLS, pleading business matters.

"I would suggest, gentlemen," he told his charges, "that we begin in one of the gaming rooms where card tables have been set up."

Conversation flowed thick as the brandy and the heavy port wines in evidence at every elbow. Voices raised in laughter swirled around others engaged in conversation which was not deemed socially proper for mixed company, accompanied by blue-grey clouds of tobacco smoke. Copies of infamous publications such as *The Pearl*, a short-lived but popular pornographic magazine, could be seen in a few hands where gentlemen lounged beneath gas lights, reading and trading jokes.

"—meeting of the Theosophists, this evening?" a passing gentleman asked his companion.

"Where, here? No, I hadn't realized. What an intriguing set of gentlemen, although I daresay they would do well to be rid of that horrid Madame Blavatsky!"

Both gentlemen laughed and climbed an ornate staircase for the second floor of the club. Malcolm paused, wondering if he ought not follow his instincts.

"What is it?" Pendergast asked.

"Those gentlemen just spoke of a Theosophical meeting here this evening."

Pendergast frowned. "A what meeting?"

"Theosophical Society. One of London's foremost occult research organizations."

Pendergast chuckled. "Bunch of lunatics, no doubt. Too bad Dr. Feroz couldn't accompany us, eh?"

Conroy Melvyn, keeping his voice carefully low, said, "You thinkin' what I am, Moore? Our man might be a member, eh? Respected doctor, what? Any number of medical men were attracted to such groups."

"Precisely. I believe it might be worth our while to attend this evening's meeting."

They fell in behind a group of gentlemen heading for the same staircase, following a snatch of conversation which marked them as probable Theosophists.

"—spoke to an American fellow once, from some cotton-mill town in South Carolina. Claimed he'd spoken to an elderly gentlemen who raised the dead."

"Oh, come now, what guff! It's one thing to debate the existence of an ability to *converse* with the departed. I've seen what a spiritualist medium can do, in seances and with automatic writing and what have you, but *raise* the dead? Stuff and falderol! I suppose next you'll be claiming this Yank thought himself Christ Jesus?"

Malcolm moved his hand unobtrusively, very carefully switching on the scout's log concealed in the valise he carried, with its tiny digital camera disguised as the stickpin in his cravat. He followed the gentlemen, listening curiously as they crossed a grand lounge and neared the staircase.

"No, no," the first gentleman was protesting, "not literally raise the dead, raise the *spirit* of the dead, to converse with it, you know. Without a medium or a mysteriously thumping table tapping out inscrutable messages. To accomplish the feat, one had to procure the rope used to hang a man, stake it out around the grave of the chap you wished to raise and repeat some gibberish in Latin, I don't recall what, now, then the poor sod's spirit would appear inside the rope and *voila!* You're able to converse at your leisure until cock crow. Of course, the spirit couldn't leave the confines of the roped-off ground . . ."

"And you didn't tumble to the fact that this Yank was having you on?"

A low rumbling chuckle reached through the pall of smoke. "No,

I assure you, he was not. Senile as they come, I daresay, the chap was ninety if he was a day, but perfectly sincere in his beliefs."

Malcolm was about to take his first step toward the second floor when a voice hailed him by name. "I say, it's Moore, isn't it!"

The unexpected voice startled him into swinging around. Malcolm found himself looking into the bemused and vivid blue eyes of a gentleman he vaguely thought he was supposed to know. He was a young man, barely past his early twenties, handsome in a Beau Brummel sort of fashion, with wavy dark hair, the brilliant blue eyes and fair skin of an Irishman, and the same elegant, almost effete fastidiousness of the trend setter whose name had been synonymous with fashion during the Regency period some sixty-eight years previously.

"It *is* Malcolm Moore, isn't it?" the young man added with a wry smile. A trace of Dubliner Irish in the man's voice echoed in familiar ways, telling Malcolm he was, indeed, supposed to know this friendly faced young man.

"Yes, I am, but I fear you've the advantage of me, sir."

"O'Downett's the name, Bevin O'Downett. We met, let me see, it would have been nearly a year ago, I believe, at last summer's Ascot Races." Eyes twinkling merrily, Mr. O'Downett chuckled, a good-natured sound. "I recall it quite distinctly, you see. We bet on the same rotten nag, came in dead last."

The face and name clicked in Malcolm's memory. "Of course! Mr. O'Downett, how good to see you again!" They shook hands cordially as Malcolm grimaced in rueful remembrance. He, too, had excellent cause to recall that race. He'd placed that losing bet on behalf of a client who'd hired him as guide, a millionaire who considered himself an expert on sport, particularly on the subject of horse racing. Malcolm had warned the fool not to bet on that particular horse, aware as he was of its record in past races, but the client is, as they say, always right . . . Both Malcolm and this young Irishman, Mr. O'Downett, here, had lost spectacularly.

Malcolm introduced his unexpected acquaintance to his guests. "Mr. O'Downett, may I present Mr. Conroy Melvyn and Mr. Guy Pendergast, of London, and Dr. Kosten, of America."

"Pleasure to meet you," O'Downett smiled, shaking hands all around. "I say," he added, "where've you been keeping yourself, Moore? Oh, wait, I recall now, you're from the West Indies, knock about the world a good bit. Envy you that, you know."

Malcolm was trying for the life of him to recall anything about Mr. O'Downett, other than one ill-placed bet. "And you?" he asked a bit lamely.

"Ah, well, fortune smiles and then she frowns, as they say. But I did manage to publish a volume of poetry. A slim one, true, but published, nonetheless." His eyes twinkled again, laughing at himself, this time. "Druidic rubbish, nothing like the serious verse I prefer, but it sells, God knows, it does sell. This Celtic renaissance will make gentlemen of us Dubliners, yet." He winked solemnly.

Malcolm smiled. "It does seem to be rather popular. Have you been to the Eisteddfod, then, since Druidic verse appeals to the book-buying masses?"

"Hmm, that Welsh bardic thing they put together over in Llangollen? No, I haven't, although I suppose if I'm to represent the Celtic pen, I had probably ought to go, eh? Have you attended one?"

"As a matter of fact, no, although I intend to do so when they hold another." Malcolm laughed easily. "Moore's a French name, you know, originally, anyway. It's whispered that the back of our family closet might have contained a Gaulish Celt or two rattling round as skeletons."

O'Downett clapped him heartily on the shoulder. "Well said, Moore! Well said! It is, indeed, the day of the Celtic Fringe, is it not? I've spoken to gentlemen whose grandsires were Prussian generals who were 'Celts' and pure London Saxons who were 'Celts' and, God forbid, a half-caste Indian fellow in service as a footman who was a 'Celt' at least on his father's side!"

Malcolm shared the chuckle, finding it doubly humorous, since there was a wealth of evidence—linguistic, literary, musical, legal, and archaeological—to suggest that the Celtic laws, languages, customs and arts of Ireland, Wales, Cornwall, Scotland, and Gaulish France bore direct and striking ties to Vedic India.

"And speaking of grand and glorious Celts," Mr. O'Downett said, eyes twinkling wickedly, "here comes the grandest of all us Celtic poets. I say, Willie, have you come for our little meeting this evening? I'd thought you would be haunting Madame Blavatsky's parlour tonight."

Malcolm Moore turned . . . and had to catch his breath to keep from exclaiming out loud. His chance acquaintance had just greeted the most profoundly gifted poet ever born in Ireland, the soon-to-be world-famous William Butler Yeats.

"Willie" Yeats smiled at O'Downett, his own eyes glowing with a fire-eaten look that spoke of a massively restless intellect. "No, not tonight, Bevin. The good lady had other plans. Occasionally, even our peripatetic madame pursues other interests." Yeats was clearly laughing at himself. The Dubliner Irish was far more pronounced in the newcomer's voice. Yeats was still in his twenties, having arrived with his parents from Dublin only the previous year, 1887.

Bevin O'Downett smiled and made introductions. "Willie, I say, have you met Mr. Malcolm Moore? West Indian gentleman, travels about a good bit, met him at Ascot last year. Mr. Moore, my dear friend, Mr. William Butler Yeats."

Malcolm found himself shaking the hand of one of the greatest poets ever to set pen to paper in the English language. "I'm honored, sir."

"Pleasure to meet you, Mr. Moore," Yeats smiled easily.

Malcolm felt almost like the air was fizzing. Yeats was already considered an occult authority, despite his relative youth. Malcolm thanked that unknown American ghost-summoner for inducing him to turn on the scout's log in his valise. He managed to retain enough presence of mind to introduce his own companions, who shook Yeats' hand in turn. Guy Pendergast didn't appear to have the faintest notion who Yeats was—or would be—but Conroy Melvyn's face had taken on a thunderstruck look and even Pavel Kostenka was staring, round-eyed, at the young poet who would legitimize Irish folk lore as a serious art form and subject of scholarly interest, as no other Irishman had managed in the stormy history of Irish-Anglo relations, and would be branded the most gifted mystic writer since William Blake.

Bevin O'Downett winked at his fellow Irishman. "Mr. Moore, here, was just sharing a piece of his family history," he chuckled. "A Gaulic Celt or two, he says, rattled about in earlier branches of the family's gnarled old tree."

Yeats broke out into an enthusiastic smile. "Are you a Celtic scholar, then, Mr. Moore?" he asked, eyes alight with interest.

"No, not really." Malcolm smiled, although he probably knew more about Celtic and Druidic history than any expert alive in Great Britain tonight. "My real interest is antiquity of another sort. Roman, mostly."

O'Downett grinned, bending a fond look on his friend. "Willie is quite the antiquarian, himself."

Yeats flushed, acutely embarrassed. "Hardly, old bean, hardly. I dabble in Celtic studies, really, is all."

"Stuff and nonsense, Willie here is a most serious scholar. Helped co-found the Dublin Hermetic Society, didn't you? And Madame Blavatsky finds your scholarship most serious, indeed."

Malcolm, anxious to put the young poet at ease, gave Yeats a warm, encouraging smile. "You're interested in Theosophy, then, Mr. Yeats?" He knew, of course, that Yeats pursued a profound interest in Theosophy and any other studies which touched on the occult. The new and wildly popular organization established by Madame Blavatsky devoted itself to psychical and occult studies along the lines of the "Esoteric Buddhism" which she and so many other practitioners were popularizing.

Clearly uncertain where Malcolm stood on the issue, the young Irish poet cleared his throat nervously. "Well, sir, yes, I am, sir. Most interested in Theosophy and, ah, many such studies."

Malcolm nodded, endeavoring to keep his expression friendly, rather than awestruck. "You've read Wise's new *History of Paganism in Caledonia*? Intriguing ideas on the development of religion and philosophy."

The young poet brightened. "Yes, sir, I have, indeed, read it! Borrowed a copy as soon as I arrived in London last year, as it had just been published. And I've read Edward Davies, of course, and D.W. Nash on Taliesin."

"Ah, the British druid who was said to have met Pythagoras. Yes, I've read that, as well."

Malcolm did not share his opinion on Nash's theories about the so-called British druid, whose existence had been fabricated whole cloth. Probably not by Nash, for the myth was widespread and persistent, but it was myth, nonetheless. "And have you read Charles Graves' latest work?"

"The Royal Commission's study of ancient Irish Brehon laws? Absolutely, sir!"

And the young poet's smile was brilliant, filled with understandable pride in the accomplishments of his forebears, who had been recognized throughout the western world in past centuries as the finest physicians, poets, musicians, and religious scholars of medieval Europe. The Brehon legal system of medieval Ireland had included such "modern" concepts as universal health care and even workman's compensation laws.

"Excellent!" Malcolm enthused. "Marvellous scholarship in that work. Graves is expanding the knowledge of ancient Britain tremendously. And do you, Mr. Yeats, hold that the Druids built Stonehenge?"

Yeats flushed again, although his eyes glowed with delighted interest. "Well, sir, I'm not an archaeologist, but it strikes me that the standing stones must be of considerable antiquity. At least centuries old, I should think?"

Malcolm smiled again. "Indeed. Millennia, to be more precise. Definitely pre-Roman, most definitely. Even the greatest Egyptologist of our day, Mr. W.M. Flinders Petrie, agrees on that point. Keep up the scholarship, Mr. Yeats. We need good, strong research into our own islands' histories, eh? By God, ancient Britain has a history to be proud of! This Celtic revival is a fine thing, a very fine thing, indeed!"

Bevin O'Downett nodded vehement agreement. "Quite so, sir! I say, have you heard that fellow speak down at the Egyptian Hall? That Lithuanian-looking chap, although he's as British as a gold sovereign, what's he calling himself? I heard some reporter say he used to go by some Egyptian-sounding moniker, back in his younger days over in

SoHo, before he studied medicine and the occult and became a respectable mesmeric physician."

Malcolm hadn't the faintest idea who O'Downett might mean, although he did notice Guy Pendergast lean forward, sudden interest sharp in his eyes. Once a reporter, always a reporter, although Malcolm couldn't imagine why Guy Pendergast would be so acutely interested in a SoHo occultist.

Yeats, however, nodded at once, clearly familiar with the fellow Bevin O'Downett had mentioned. "Yes, I have seen him speak. Intriguing fellow, although he hasn't actually gone by the name of Johnny Anubis in several years. Oh, I know it's an absurd name," Yeats said, noticing the amused tilt of Bevin O'Downett's brows, "but a man must have some way to attract the attention of the public when he's come up from that sort of background. And despite the theatrics of his early career, his scholarship really is sound, astonishing for a self-made man from Middlesex Street, Whitechapel."

Malcolm paused, caught as much by the edge of bitterness in the young poet's voice as by the niggling suspicion that he was missing something important, here. He glanced into Yeats' brilliant, fire-eaten eyes—and was struck motionless by the pain, the anger and pride that burned in this young Irishman's soul. Forthright fury blazed in those eyes for every slight ever made by an Englishman against the Irish race, fury and pain that the achievements of the Celtic peoples were only now, in the latter half of the nineteenth century, being hailed as genius by overbearing English scholars—and then, only by *some* scholars, in a decade when Welshmen, descendants of the original Celtic settlers of Britain, were still belittled as savage subhumans and advised to give up their barbarous tongue if they would ever redeem themselves into the human race, while the Irishman was kicked and maltreated as the mangiest dog of Europe. Yet despite the kicks and slurs, there blazed in Yeats' brilliant, volcanic eyes a fierce, soul-igniting pride, lightning through stormclouds, a shining pride for the history of a nation which for centuries had carried the torch of civilization in Europe.

Malcolm stood transfixed, caught up in the power of the young poet's presence, aware with a chill of awe that he was witnessing the birth of an extraordinary religious and literary blaze, one which would sweep into its path the ancient lore, the mysterious rite and religious philosophy of the entire world, a blaze which would burn that extraordinary learning in the crucible of the poet's fiery and far-reaching intellect, until what burst forth was not so much resounding music as rolling, thunderous prophecy:

> *Mere anarchy is loosed upon the world,*
> *The blood-dimmed tide is loosed, and everywhere*
> *The ceremony of innocence is drowned;*
> *The best lack all conviction, while the worst*
> *Are full of passionate intensity . . .*
> *Now I know*
> *That twenty centuries of stony sleep*
> *Were vexed to nightmare by a rocking cradle,*
> *And what rough beast, its hour come round at last,*
> *Slouches toward Bethlehem to be born?*

Malcolm's favorite Yeats poem, "The Second Coming," could easily have been written in prophecy of Malcolm's own time, when mad cults multiplied like malignant mushrooms and insanity seemed to be the rule of the day. To be standing here, speaking with Yeats, before the poem had even been written . . .

"I say, Mr. Moore," Bevin O'Downett chuckled, shattering with a shock like icewater the spell of Yeats' as-yet-embryonic power, "you might want to close your mouth before a bird seizes the chance to perch on your teeth!"

Malcolm blinked guiltily. Then gathered his wits and composure with profound difficulty. "Sorry. I've just been trying to recall whether I'd read anything by this fellow you were just mentioning. Er, what's his name, did you say? Anubis?"

Yeats nodded. "Yes, but he doesn't use that name any longer. The man's a physician, actually, an accomplished mesmerist, Dr. John Lachley. Holds public lectures and spiritualist seances at places like the Egyptian Hall, but he keeps a perfectly ordinary medical surgery in his rooms in Cleveland Street, calls his house Tibor, I believe, after some ancient holy place out of East European myth. He's quite a serious scholar, you know. An acquaintance of mine, Mr. Waite, invited him to join an organization he's recently founded, and was absolutely delighted when Dr. Lachley agreed. He's been awarded Druidic orders, at the Gorsedd, carries the Druidic wand, the *slat an draoichta*. Lachley's been called the most learned scholar of antiquities ever to come out of SoHo."

Malcolm's gaze sharpened. *Waite?* The famous co-founder of the Hermetic Order of the Golden Dawn? Waite had helped develop the most famous Tarot deck in existence. This mesmeric scholar moved in most intriguing circles. "John Lachley, you say? No, I'm afraid I haven't heard of him. Of course," Malcolm gave the intense young Irishman a rueful smile, "I travel so widely, I often find myself having to catch up on months of scholarly as well as social activities which have transpired in my absence. I shall certainly keep his name in mind. Thank you for bringing his work to my attention."

"Well, that's grand," Bevin O'Downett smiled, visibly delighted at having introduced Malcolm to his scholarly young friend. "I say, Moore, you were just on your way up when I detained you. Have I interrupted any plans?"

Malcolm smiled. "Actually, we'd heard there was to be a meeting here this evening, of Theosophists, and wanted to learn a bit more."

Yeats brightened. "Splendid! We'll be meeting upstairs, sir, in a quarter of an hour."

Malcolm glanced at Conroy Melvyn, who nodded slightly. "Excellent! I believe I'll tell my carriage driver to return rather later than I'd anticipated. We'll join you shortly, I hope?"

The two Irish poets took their leave, heading upstairs, and Malcolm turned towards the entrance, intent on letting the driver know they'd be longer than an hour—and paused, startled. Their party was one short. "Where the devil is Mr. Pendergast?"

Conroy Melvyn, who had been peering up the staircase after the poets, started slightly. The police inspector looked around with a sheepish expression. "Eh?"

"Pendergast," Malcolm repeated, "where the deuce has he gone?"

Pavel Kostenka swallowed nervously and said in a whisper that wouldn't carry very far, "I cannot imagine. He was here just a moment ago."

"Yes," Malcolm said irritably, "he was. And now he isn't. Bloody reporters! We'd better search for him at once."

Within ten minutes, it was clear that Guy Pendergast was no longer anywhere inside the Carlton Club, because he had been seen retrieving his hat, cane, and gloves. The doorman said, "Why, yes, Mr. Moore, he left in a tearing hurry, caught a hansom cab."

"Did you hear him give the driver directions?"

"No, sir, I'm afraid I didn't."

Malcolm swore under his breath. "Damn that idiot journalist! Gentlemen, I'm afraid our mission on your behalf will simply have to wait for another evening. Dr. Kostenka, Mr. Melvyn, we must return to Spaldergate immediately. This is very serious. *Bloody* damned serious. A reporter on his own without a guide, poking about London and asking questions at a time like this . . . He'll have to be found immediately and brought back, before he gets himself into fatal trouble."

The Ripper scholars were visibly furious at having their evening's mission cut short, particularly with the meeting getting underway upstairs, but even they realized the crisis another missing up-timer represented. The Scotland Yard inspector at least had the good grace to be embarassed that he'd allowed the reporter to give them the slip so easily. The driver of the Time Tours carriage which had brought them to the Carlton Club hadn't noticed Pendergast leave, either, and berated himself all the way back to Spaldergate House for his careless inattention. "Might've followed the bloody fool," the driver muttered under his breath every few moments. "Dammit, why'd the idiot go and hire a hansom cab? I'd have taken him anywhere he wanted to go!"

Malcolm had his own ideas about that, which were confirmed less than half an hour later, when they re-entered Time Tours' London gatehouse. Guy Pendergast had returned to Spaldergate, very briefly. Then he and Dominica Nosette had left again, taking with them all their luggage and one of Spaldergate's carriages—without obtaining the Gilberts' permission first.

Fresh disaster was literally staring them square in the face.

Not only had they lost the tourist Benny Catlin, they had now lost two members of the Ripper Watch Team, who clearly had defected to pursue the case on their own. Malcolm, operating on less than three hours' sleep a night for several weeks straight, tried to think what Guy Pendergast might possibly have seen or heard tonight to send him haring off on his own, defying all rules set for members of the Ripper Watch tour. Malcolm had been so focused on Yeats, he hadn't been doing his job. And that was inexcusable. Only once before had Malcolm lost a tourist: Margo, that ghastly day in Rome, in the middle of the Hilaria celebrations. It did not improve his temper to recall that both times, he'd been focused on his own desires, rather than the job at hand.

Without the faintest idea where to begin searching for the renegade reporters, Malcolm did the only thing he *could* do and still remain calm. He stalked into the parlour, poured himself a stiff scotch, and started reviewing potential alternative career options.

Crossingham's doss house smelled of mildew and unwashed clothes, of sweat and stale food and despair. When Margo and Shahdi Feroz stepped into the kitchen, it was well after dark and bitterly cold. They found a sullen, smoking coal fire burning low in the hearth and nearly twenty people crowded nearby, most of them women. There were no chairs available. Most of the room's chairs had been dragged over to the hearth by those lucky enough to have arrived early. The rest of the exhausted, grubby occupants of Crossingham's kitchen sat on the floor as close to the fire as they could manage. The floor was at least neat and well-swept despite its worn, plain boards and deep scuffs from thousands of booted feet which had passed across it.

Margo paid the lodging house's caretaker, Timothy Donovan, for a cuppa and handed it over to Shahdi, then paid for another for herself. " 'ere, luv," Margo said quietly to the Ripper scholar, using her best Cockney voice, "got a cuppa tea for you, this'll warm you up nice."

The tea was weak and bitter, with neither sugar nor milk to alter the nasty flavor. Margo pulled a face and sipped again. Recycled tea leaves, no doubt—if there was even any real tea in this stuff. The demand for tea was so high and the price of new leaves so steep, an enormous market existed for recycled tea. Used leaves, carefully collected by housewives and servants, were sold to the tea men who came door-to-door, buying them up in bulk. The tea men, in turn, redried them, dyed them dark again, pressed them into "new" bricks, and resold them to cheaper chandlers' shops scattered throughout the East End. There was even a black market in counterfeit tea, with leaves of God-alone knew what and even bits of paper dyed to look like tea, sold in carefully pressed little bricks to those unable to afford real tea often enough to know the difference in taste.

Margo tucked up her skirts and found a spot as close to the fire as she could manage, then balanced Shahdi's teacup for her so the scholar could sit down. Both of them carefully adjusted their frayed carpet bags with the irreplaceable scout logs inside, so they lay across their laps and out of reach of anybody with lighter-than-average fingers. Margo noticed curious—and covetous—glances from several nearby women and most of the men. Very few of the people in Crossingham's owned enough goods in this world to put *into* a carpet bag.

"Wotcher got in the bag, eh, lovie?" The woman beside Margo was a thin, elderly woman, somewhere in her mid-sixties, Margo guessed. She stank of gin and spilt ale and clothes too many months—or years—unlaundered.

Margo made herself smile, despite the stench. "Me owd clothes, wot I'm aimin' to pawn, soon's I got a place to sleep. That an' me lovin' father's shirts, may God send 'im to burn, drunken bastard as 'e is. Was, I mean. They 'anged 'im last week, for 'is tea leafin' ways."

"Never easy, is it," another woman muttered, "when the owd bastard thieves 'is way through life 'til 'e's caught an' 'anged, leavin' a body to make 'er own way or starve. Better a live blagger, I says, than a dead 'usband or father wot ain't no use to anybody. Nobody save the grave digger an' the bleedin' worms."

"Least 'e won't black me face never again," Margo muttered, "nor drink me wages down to boozer. Good riddance, I says, good riddance to the owd bastard. Could've 'anged 'im years ago, they could, an' I'd 'ave been that 'appy, I would, that I would 'ave."

"You got a job, then?" a girl no older than Margo asked, eyes curious despite the fear lurking in their depths. She reminded Margo of a rabbit hit once too often by a butcher's practice blows.

"Me?" Margo shrugged. "Got nuffink but me own self, that an' me mother, 'ere." She nodded to Shahdi Feroz. "But we'll find something, we will, trust in that. Ain't afraid t' work 'ard, I ain't. I'll do wot a body 'as t' do, to keep a roof over an' bread in me Limehouse an' a bite or two in me ma's, so I will."

A timid looking girl of fourteen swallowed hard. "You mean, you'd walk the streets?"

Margo glanced at her, then at Shahdi Feroz, who—as her "mother"—cast a distressed look at her "daughter." Margo shrugged. "Done it before, so I 'ave. Won't be surprised if it comes to the day I 'as to do it again. Me ma ain't well, after all, gets all tired out, quick like, an' feels the winter's cowd more every year. Me, I'd sleep rough, but me ma's got to 'ave a bed, don't she?"

Over in the corner, a woman in her forties who wore a dress and bonnet shabby as last summer's grubby canvas shoes, started to rock back and forth, arms clenched around her knees. "Going to die out there," she moaned, eyes clenched shut, "going to die out there and who'd care if we did, eh? Not them constables, they don't give a fig, for all they say as how they're here to protect us. We'll end like poor Polly Nichols, we will." Several women, presumably Irish Catholics, crossed themselves and muttered fearfully. Another produced a bottle from her pocket and upended it, swallowing rapidly. "Poor Polly . . ." the woman in the corner was still rocking, eyes shut over wetness. Her voice was rough, although she'd clearly had more education than the other women in the room. Margo wondered what had driven her to such desperate circumstances. "Oh, God, poor Polly . . . Bloody constable saw me on the street this morning, told me to move on or he'd black my eye for me. Or I could pay him to stay on my territory. And if I hadn't any money, I'd just have to give him a four-penny knee-trembler, for free. Stinking bastards! They don't care, not so long as they get theirs. As for us, it's walk or starve, with that murdering maniac out there . . ." She'd begun to cry messily, silently, rocking like a madwoman in her corner beside the hearth.

Margo couldn't say anything, could scarcely swallow. She clenched her teeth over the memories welling up from her own past. No, they didn't care, damn them . . . The cops never cared when it was a prostitute lying dead on the street. Or the kitchen floor. They didn't give a damn what they did or said or how young the children listening might be . . .

"I knew Polly," a new voice said quietly, grief etched in every word. "Kinder, nicer woman I never knew."

The speaker was a woman in her fifties, faded and probably never pretty, but she had a solemn, honest face and her eyes were stricken puddles, leaking wetness down her cheeks.

"Saw her that morning, that very morning. She'd been drinking again, poor thing, the bells of St. Mary Matfellon had just struck the hour, two-thirty it was, and she hadn't her doss money yet. She'd drunk it, every last penny of it. How many's the time I've told her, 'Polly, it's drink will be the ruin of you'?" A single sob broke loose and the woman covered her face with both hands. "I had fourpence! I could've loaned it to her! Why didn't I just give her the money, and her so drunk and needing a bed?"

A nearby woman put an arm around her shoulders. "Hush, Emily, she'd just have drunk it, too, you know how she was when she'd been on the gin."

"But she'd be alive!" Emily cried, refusing to be comforted. "She'd be alive, not hacked to pieces . . ."

This was Emily Holland, then, Margo realized with a slow chill of shock. One of the last people to see Polly Nichols alive. The two women had been friends, often sharing a room in one of the area's hundreds of doss houses. How many of these women knew the five Ripper victims well enough to cry for them? Twelve hundred prostitutes walking the East End had sounded like a lot of people, but there'd been more students than twelve hundred in Margo's high school and she'd known all of them at least by sight. Certainly well enough to've been deeply upset if some maniac had carved them into little bits of acquaintance.

Margo gulped down acrid tea, wishing it were still hot enough to drive away the chill inside. At least they were gathering valuable data.

She hadn't read anywhere, for instance, about London's constables shaking down the very women they were supposed to be protecting. So much for the image of British police as gentlemen. Margo snorted silently. From what she'd seen, most men walking the streets of Great Britain tonight viewed any woman of lower status not decently married as sexually available. And in the East End and in many a so-called "respectable" house, where young girls from streets like these went into service as scullery maids, the gentlemen weren't overly fussy about taking to bed girls far too young to be married. It hadn't been that long since laws had been passed raising the age of consent from *twelve*.

No, the fact that corrupt police constables were forcing London's prostitutes to sleep with them didn't surprise Margo at all. Maybe that explained why Jack had been able to strike without the women raising a cry for help? Not even Elizabeth Stride had screamed out loudly enough to attract the attention of a meeting hall-full of people. A woman in trouble couldn't count on the police to be anything but worse trouble than the customer.

Shahdi Feroz, with her keen eye for detail, asked quietly, "Are you cold, my dear?"

Margo shook her head, not quite willing to trust her voice.

"Nonsense, you are shaking. Here, can you scoot closer to the fire?"

Margo gave up and scooted. It was easier than admitting the real reason she was trembling. Sitting here surrounded by women who reminded her, with every word spoken, exactly how her entire world had shattered was more difficult than she'd expected it would be, back on station studying these murders. And she'd known, even then, it wouldn't be easy. *Get used to it,* she told herself angrily. Because later tonight, Annie Chapman was going to walk into this kitchen and then she was going to walk out of it again and end up butchered all over the yard at number twenty-nine Hanbury Street. And Margo would just have to cope, because it was going to be a long, *long* night. Somehow, between now and five-thirty tomorrow morning, she would have to slip into that pitch-dark yard and set up the team's low-light surveillance equipment.

Maybe she'd climb the fence? She certainly didn't want to risk that creaking door again. Yes, that was what she'd better do, go over the wall like a common thief, which meant she'd need to ditch the skirts and dress as a boy. Climbing fences in this getup was out of the question. She wondered bleakly what Malcolm was doing, on his search for their unknown co-killer, and sighed, resting her chin on her knees. She'd a thousand times rather have gone with Malcolm, whatever he was doing, than end up stuck on the kitchen floor in Crossingham's, trying vainly to ignore how her own mother had died.

As she blinked back unshed tears, Margo realized she had one more excellent reason she couldn't risk falling apart, out here. Kit might—just might—forgive her for screwing up on a job, might chalk it up to field experience she had to get some time. But if she came completely unglued out here, Malcolm would know the reason why or have her skin, one or the other. And if she was forced to tell Malcolm that she'd messed up because she couldn't stop thinking about how her mother had died, he was going to discover the truth about that, too.

Try as she might, Margo simply could not imagine that Malcolm Moore would be willing to marry a girl whose drunken father had died in prison while serving a life sentence for murder, after beating to death his wife in front of his little girl because he'd discovered she was a whore. Far worse than losing Malcolm, though—and Margo loved Malcolm so much, the thought of losing him left her cold and bleak and empty—would be the look in her grandfather's eyes if Kit Carson ever found out how and why his only daughter had really died.

For the first time in her young life, Margo Smith discovered that hurting the people you loved was even worse than being hurt, yourself. Which was why, perhaps, in the final analysis, her mother and so many of the women in this room and out on these streets had sunk to the level of common prostitute. They were trying to support families any way they could. Margo's mouth trembled violently. Then she simply squeezed shut her eyes and cried, no longer caring who saw the tears. She'd think up a good reason to give Shahdi Feroz later.

Just now, she needed to cry.

She wasn't even sure who she was crying for.

When Shahdi Feroz slipped an arm around her shoulder and pulled her close, just holding her, Margo realized it wasn't important at all, knowing who her tears were for. In the end, it didn't matter. The only thing that really mattered was protecting the people you cared about. In that moment, Margo forgave her mother everything. And cried harder than she had since those terrible moments in a blood-spattered Minnesota kitchen, with the toast burnt on the counter and the stink of death in her nostrils and her father's rage pursuing her out the door into the snow.

I'm sorry, Mom, I'm sorry . . .

I'm sorry I couldn't stop him.

I'm sorry I hated you . . .

Did Annie Georgina Chapman, Dark Annie Chapman's daughter, who'd run away from her poverty-stricken, prostituted mother to join a French touring circus, hate her mother, too? Margo hoped not. She blinked burning salt from her eyes and offered up one last apology. *And I'm sorry I can't stop him from killing you, Annie Chapman . . .*

Margo understood at last.

Kit had warned her that time scouting was the toughest job in the world.

Now she knew why.

(((Chapter 14)))

Skeeter Jackson was just climbing into the clothes Kit had loaned him, in the Neo Edo bathrooms, when a slim, wraithlike little girl named Cocheta, a mixed-blood Amer-Indian who'd stumbled through the Conquistadores Gate and joined the Lost and Found Gang of downtimer children, skidded into the Neo Edo men's room, out of breath and ashen. Her dark eyes had gone wide, glinting with terror. "Skeeter! Hashim sent me for you! There is bad trouble! Please hurry!"

"What's wrong?"

"It is Bergitta! They have taken her away—the men from the construction site!"

The roar of insanity outside the Neo Edo, where the riot was still spreading, faded to a whisper. Skeeter narrowed his eyes over a surge of murderous rage. *"Show me!"*

Cocheta snatched his hand, led him through the craziness running amok in Edo Castletown. "The Lost and Found Gang is following them! Hurry, Skeeter! They took her from the bathroom they just finished building in the new part of the station, when she went to clean the floor."

"How many?" Dammit, he didn't have any weapons with him, not even a pocket knife, and those construction workers would all be carrying heavy tools. Any one of which could cut a man's throat or spill his intestines with a single swiping blow.

"Twenty! They knocked unconscious the foreman and several of the other men who did not agree with them, locked them into a supply room. We sent word to the Council for help. I was told to find you, Skeeter, and Hashim said where you were."

As soon as they cleared the mob in Edo Castletown, Skeeter and the girl tugging at his hand broke into a dead run. Cocheta led him through Victoria Station and Urbs Romae, through Valhalla, down toward the construction site, which was ominously silent. There should've been an ear-splitting roar of saws, drills, and pneumatic hammers echoing off the distant ceiling, but they found only silence and a deserted construction zone, tasks left abandoned on every side. The timing of the attack on Bergitta left Skeeter scowling. With the antics at Primary to preoccupy station security and most of the tourists, nobody was likely to notice the work stoppage. Or the disappearance of one down-timer from her job scrubbing bathroom floor tiles.

"Hurry, Skeeter!"

Cocheta didn't need to urge him again. He'd seen enough to leave his whole throat dry with fear. "Which way did they take her?"

"Through there!" Cocheta pointed to a corridor that led into a portion of the station where new Residential apartments were being assembled, back in another of the caverns in which the station had been built. Clearly, they were taking her where nobody could hear the screams. He was just about to ask Cocheta to get word to someone in Security, preferably Wally Klontz, when someone shouted his name.

"Skeeter! Wait!"

A whole group of down-timers pounded his way, with Kynan Rhys Gower in the lead. The Welsh soldier carried his war mallet. Molly was hot on his heels. Where she'd obtained that lethal little top-break revolver, Skeeter wasn't sure. Maybe she'd brought it with her from London. Or liberated it from Ann Vinh Mulhaney's firing range—or some tourist's pocket. Eigil Bjarneson towered over the whole onrushing contingent of angry Found Ones. He'd managed to reclaim his sword from Security after getting out of jail. Or quite possibly he'd just *broken* out and reconfiscated it? Skeeter wouldn't have wanted to argue with Eigil in this mood, if he'd been working the Security desk, which was probably in chaos anyway, after Bull's arrest . . .

"Cocheta says they took her through there," Skeeter pointed the way.

"Let's go," Kynan nodded, voice tight, eyes crackling with murderous fury.

Skeeter turned to the girl who'd brought him here. He said tersely, "Cocheta, stay here and wait for other Found Ones who might be coming. Send them in after us. Give us twenty minutes to get in there and get into position, then start yelling for station security. By then, the mess at Primary should've settled down enough, Security might actually listen and send someone."

"Yes, Skeeter. The Lost and Found Gang has followed the men who took her. They will tell you which way to go. Hurry!"

He signaled for silence, gratified when his impromptu posse obeyed instantly, and led the way back into the incomplete section of Commons at a flat-out run. They entered the tunnel which led to the new area of Residential and Skeeter slowed to a more cautious pace, silent as shadows chased by a hunter's moon. The concrete floors had already been poured and drywall had gone up in many places. Work lights rigged high overhead cast unnatural pools of light and shadow through the incomplete Residential section, where bare two-by-fours marked out rooms and corridors not yet closed in with wallboard. Skeeter listened intently, but heard nothing. This section of station snaked back into the heart of the mountain, twisting and turning unpredictably.

They found a teenager at a major junction where two Residential corridors would intersect when completed. The boy was dancing with impatience, but remained silent when Skeeter raised a finger to his lips in warning. *That way,* the boy pointed. Skeeter nodded, jerked a thumb over his shoulder to indicate that more hunters were on the way, and motioned for the boy to wait for reinforcements. The boy nodded and settled in to wait. Skeeter stole forward, leading his war party down the indicated corridor. Dust from the construction lay thick on every surface, wood dust and debris from particle board. The chalky scent of gypsum drywall clogged his nostrils as they pushed forward.

Skeeter paused to retrieve an abandoned claw hammer. It wasn't his weapon of choice, but offered lethal potentialities he could certainly make use of, and was better than bare fingernails. When they came to a door marking a stairwell, they found another member of the Lost and Found Gang, a girl of thirteen who stood watch with tears streaming down her face.

"They went down," she whispered, pointing to the stairs. "They had hit her, Skeeter, were laughing about raping her and killing her when they were done . . ."

"We'll stop them," Skeeter promised. "Stay here. More are coming." He glanced at the grim men and women of his posse. "I'd prefer live witnesses to testify against their up-time cronies in the *Ansar Majlis*. Maybe we can crack their terrorist gang wide open. But if we have to spill blood to get Bergitta out of there alive, we'll hit 'em hard and worry about the body count and station management's reaction later. The main thing is, we get her out of there."

Kynan Rhys Gower and the others nodded silently, understanding exactly what he meant and accepting whatever happened. Pride in Ianira's achievement, building this community, flared hot in Skeeter's awareness, pride and a determination not to let anything happen to a single one of his new-found friends.

The girl guarding the stairwell held the door open for them.

Skeeter's pulse thundered as he eased silently down the dim concrete steps. Naked light bulbs glared where ceiling panels had not yet been installed. When they reached the bottom of the stairs, another member of the Lost and Found Gang waited silently. The boy stationed here was only eleven, but had the quick presence of mind to signal for silence. He pointed to the left, mimed following the tunnel around to the right. Skeeter nodded and made sure his entire posse was out of the stairwell before continuing. The rear guard had swelled by three new arrivals, easing so silently down the stairs after them, Skeeter hadn't even heard them join up.

Chenzira Umi, the ancient Egyptian who sat on the Council of Seven, must have been in his apartment when the call went out, because he carried the hunting-dart thrower he'd made for himself. Shaped something like an atl-atl, it could throw a lethal projectile with enough penetrating force to bring down a hippo or a Nile croc. The

Egyptian had brought with him the Spaniard Alfonzo Menendez, who'd liberated a steel-tipped pike from the decorative wall of the restaurant where he worked. Young Corydon, a Greek hoplite of twenty-three who excelled at the sling as a weapon of war, had joined them as well. Corydon clutched an entire handful of rounded stones, still dripping from the goldfish pond he'd stolen them from, and was busy unwinding his sling from under his shirt, where he'd doubtless worn it in honor of the Festival of Mars.

Skeeter acknowledged the newcomers with a brisk nod, then motioned the way and set out in pursuit. And this time, he heard the quarry. Rough male voices drifted through the subterranean corridors, punctuated by distant, feminine cries of pain. He tightened his grip around the lethal claw hammer and eased forward, stealing softly across the concrete floor toward the inhuman sport underway somewhere ahead. Before this business was done, Skeeter vowed, these construction workers would bitterly rue their decision to indulge an appetite for revenge on a member of his adopted family.

As a boy, he'd never been allowed to join a Yakka war party bent on vengeance.

Now he led the raid.

Guide me, Yesukai . . .

The corridor they followed twisted and turned through a maze of partially completed Residential apartments, storage warehouses for equipment, pumping stations to bring water into the new section of station, stacks of dusty lumber, drywall, and cement bags, and tangles of electrical wiring and cables. Skeeter's little band of rescuers, seven strong, now, crept closer to the distorted sounds of merriment from twenty burly construction workers somewhere ahead. God, seven against twenty . . .

They rounded a final corner and found two more Lost and Found members crouched in the corridor, peering anxiously their way. One of the boys, eight-year-old Tevel Gottlieb, had been born on station. Hashim Ibn Fahd, a cunning little wolf of thirteen, still wearing Neo Edo livery, beckoned Skeeter forward, then placed his lips directly against Skeeter's ear and breathed out, "They are in the warehouse just beyond this corner. They have posted no guards."

Skeeter risked a quick look, ducking low to the floor to minimize the chances of being seen by anyone who cast a casual glance their way. The warehouse where they'd dragged their victim was an open bay some fifty feet across, piled high with lumber and construction supplies, coils of copper wire and crates of plumbing and electrical fixtures, preformed plastic sink basins, miniature mountains of PVC pipe. Two walls were solid concrete, marking the boundary with the cavern walls just beyond. The other two were gypsum board tacked to wooden two-by-fours. One of these gypsum walls, which Skeeter crouched behind, had been completed already, awaiting only the installation of electrical outlet covers. The other was only partially complete, with drywall up along half its length. Bare wooden uprights comprised the balance of its span.

Bergitta lay on the concrete floor along this stretch of wall, wrists wired to thick two-by-fours. Another cruel twist of wire, tightened down around her throat, prevented her from lifting her head. They'd ripped her shirt open, had cut away her bra. They hadn't bothered to tie a gag. Her skirt lay in twists around her waist. One of them was busy raping her while others waited their turn, speaking tensely amongst themselves in what looked almost like an argument. Hashim Ibn Fahd, who'd stumbled through the Arabian Nights gate in the middle of a howling sandstorm, having become separated from the caravan he'd been traveling with, pressed his lips against Skeeter's ear once again.

"They argue about bringing the woman here. Some say their brothers in the *Ansar Majlis* will reward them when they have killed this one. Others say raping a prostitute has nothing to do with the cause and the leaders of the *Ansar Majlis* will be angry, for that and for attacking the foreman and others of the faith. They say the leaders came through Primary today and will punish those who take such chances at being caught. The others say it does not matter, because now that their brothers have come to the station, Mike Benson and all who run the jail will die. Soon their brothers will be free again to hunt the Templars who flock to the whore's shrine in Little Agora. Their leader says to hurry with the woman, his balls ache and he wants his turn on her before she is dead from too many men inside her."

The freezing hatred in young Hashim's eyes sent a chill down Skeeter's back. He beckoned the two boys away from the corner, then led his band several yards back further still, well out of earshot. Speaking in the barest whisper, Skeeter outlined his plan, such as it was. "There's too many of them to rush in there the way we are. We'll just get Bergitta killed and maybe us, too. We've got to lure some of them out here, away from the others, split them up. We've got reinforcements coming, but we don't know how many or when. All we can count on is ourselves."

Seven adults and two kids . . .

Not the best odds he'd ever faced.

But it would have to do. God help them all, it would have to do, because they were out of time—and so was poor Bergitta.

They met in a dingy, drab little pub called the Horn of Plenty on the corner of Dorset Street and Chrispin. As he had been the night of Polly Nichols' murder, John Lachley was once again in deep disguise. James Maybrick was proving most useful in procuring theatrical disguises for him, at the same shops patronized by one of Lachley's new clients, a popular actor at the Lyceum Theater where the infamous American play *Dr. Jekyll and Mr. Hyde* was packing in sellout crowds bent on vicarious thrills.

The thrills Lachley and James Maybrick sought tonight were anything but vicarious. Lachley made eye contact with Maybrick across the smoke-filled pub, making certain his disciple recognized him through the false beard, sideburns, and scar, then nodded toward the door. Maybrick, eyes glittering with intense excitement, paid for his pint of bitters and exited. Lachley finished his stout leisurely, then sauntered out into the night. Maybrick waited silently across the street, leaning one shoulder against the brick wall of a doss house opposite the pub.

Lachley's pulse quickened when Maybrick glanced into his eyes. Maybrick's excitement was contagious. The cotton merchant's color was high, even though he didn't know, yet, the identity of the woman they were to kill tonight. The knowledge that Lachley meant to guide him to his next victim was clearly sufficient to excite the man beyond the bounds of reason. The telegram which had summoned Maybrick back to London from Liverpool had read: "Friday appointment. Arrange as before."

That telegram, which had triggered this meeting, would—at long last—culminate in the final episode of Lachley's quest for Prince Albert Victor's eight indiscreet letters. Four obtained from Morgan . . . one from Polly Nichols . . . and the final three would be in his hands by night's end, obtained from Annie Chapman. Three murders—Morgan, Polly Nichols, and Annie Chapman—were already two more than he'd anticipated needing to wind up this sordid little affair. He very carefully did not think about the prophetic words his lovely prisoner had choked out: *and six shall die for his letters and his pride . . .*

He could not afford to indulge doubt on a job of this magnitude, whatever its source. James Maybrick, at least, was a good deal more than satisfactory as a tool to accomplish Lachley's goals. In fact, Maybrick was proving to be a most delightful tool in John Lachley's capable hands. Completely mad, of course, behind those merry eyes and mild smile, but quite an effective madman when it came to dispatching witnesses and blackmailers. What he'd done to Polly Nichols after choking her death with his bare hands inspired awe. The newspapers were still bleating about "The Whitechapel Murderer" and speculation was running wild through the East End's sordid streets. The terror visible in the eyes of every dirty whore walking these streets was music in Lachley's soul. He had more than good reason to wish a calamitous end on such women. Tormenting, small-minded trollops that they were, pointing at him and laughing through their rotting teeth, calling out filthy names when he passed them on the kerb . . .

Lachley wished he'd taken the satisfaction of punishing that blackmailing little bitch, Polly Nichols, himself. He'd enjoyed Morgan's final hours, had enjoyed them immensely, and regretted having allowed Maybrick all the fun in killing the loathsome Polly Nichols. He wondered what it had felt like, ripping her open with that shining, wicked knife, and found that his pulse was pounding raggedly. *This time,* he promised himself, *I'll do the killing myself this time, I'm damned if Maybrick shall have all the fun, curse him for the maniac he is.*

Lachley's lethal little merchant with the unfaithful wife might be dull as a butter knife when it came to social matters, but give him a belly full of hatred, an eight-inch steel gutting blade, and a hapless target upon which to vent that explosive rage, and James Maybrick was a man transformed. A true *artiste* . . . It was almost a pity Lachley had to ensure the man's execution by hanging. Controlling a mind like James Maybrick's was intoxicating, far more satisfying than controlling a dullard like Eddy—even if Albert Victor Christian Edward did have prospects far beyond anything the Liverpudlian social climber could ever hope to achieve.

Men in the baggy clothes of the common factory laborer and women in the shabby dresses of cheap kerb crawlers prowled up and down Dorset Street, intent on enacting mutually attractive financial transactions. Maybrick, Lachley noted, followed the prostitutes with a hungry, predatory gaze that boded ill for Annie Chapman once Lachley turned his killer loose on the owner of Eddy's final letters.

But to do that, they first must *find* Dark Annie.

And that, Lachley had discovered over the course of the previous week, was no easy task. Annie Chapman did not normally travel from doss house to doss house, as many another destitute street walker did, but she had not been seen in Crossingham's—the house she had made her more-or-less permanent home—in well over a week. Lachley *had* seen her during that week, but only twice. And both times she had looked alarmingly ill. During the past two days, he had not seen her at all. Rumor held that she had been injured in a fight with another whore over the attentions of the man who paid a fair number of Annie's bills. He suspected she had spent the two days in the casual ward of Spitalfields workhouse infirmary, since the last time he'd spotted her, near Spitalfields Church, she had been telling a friend that she was seriously ill and wanted to spend a couple of days in the casual ward, resting and getting the medical help she needed.

Her friend had given her a little money and warned her not to spend it on rum.

John Lachley had not seen Dark Annie since.

So he set out down Dorset Street, casting about like a hound seeking the fox, and led James Maybrick into the opening steps of the hunt. And on this night, after many dark and frustrating hours, luck finally returned to John Lachley. He and Maybrick, on edge and all but screaming their tense frustration, returned to Dorset Street shortly after one-thirty in the morning and caught sight of her at long, bloody last.

Annie Chapman was just entering Crossingham's lodging house by the kitchen entrance, badly the worse for drink. John Lachley halted, breathing hard as excitement shot through his belly and groin. He glanced across the street at Maybrick, then nodded toward the short, stout woman descending the area steps to the kitchen entrance of her favorite doss house.

Maybrick slipped his hand into his coat pocket, where he kept his knife, and smiled slowly. Mr. James Maybrick had seen the face of his new victim. Maybrick's face flushed with sexual excitement in the light from the gas lamp on the street corner. Lachley restrained a slow smile. *Soon* . . . They waited patiently across from Crossingham's and within minutes, their quarry came out again, evidently not not in possession of enough money to pay for the room. They heard her say, "I won't be long, Brummy. See that Tim keeps the bed for me." Whereupon she left Crossingham's and turned down Little Paternoster Row, toward Brushfield Street, where she headed out towards Spitalfields Market.

They followed her quietly on the same rubberized servants' shoes they'd worn the night they'd stalked Polly Nichols to her death. It was clear to Dr. John Lachley that Annie Chapman was seriously ill and in a great deal of pain. She moved slowly, but was still successful in collaring a customer outside the darkened hulk of Spitalfields Market, frustrating them in their intention to waylay her, themselves. The man disappeared with her into some refuse-riddled yard full of shadows. Lachley stood in his hiding place, breathing rapidly. Tension tightened down through him until he needed to shout out his impatience. Soon—very soon, now—poor little Dark Annie Chapman would earn a greater notoriety in death than she had ever earned in life. She was about to become the third mutilated victim of John Lachley's ambition. And the second dead London whore in a week. The anticipation of the terror that would explode through the East End was nearly as potent a delight as controlling the fates of his chosen victims.

Playing God was a sweetly addictive game.

John Lachley was well on his way to becoming a sweetly addicted player.

From where he stood in a grimy doorway, John Lachley couldn't hear anything of Annie's encounter with her customer, but twenty minutes later, they emerged, the man breathing heavily and Annie Chapman flushed, her skirts disarranged. They went together to the nearest pub. Lachley and Maybrick entered the pub, as well, finding separate places at the bar, where they drank a pint and watched the woman they had come to kill.

Annie's customer bought her a hearty meal and several glasses of rum, which she downed quickly, like medicine. John Lachley suspected she was using the rum in precisely that fashion, to kill the pain he could see in her eyes and her every slow, awkward movement. From the cough she tried to suppress while in her customer's company, he suspected consumption, which meant she would be suffering considerable pain in her lungs, as well as difficulty breathing. Clearly she hadn't the means to buy proper medications. Doubtless why she had resorted to blackmail, buying Eddy's letters from Polly Nichols. Lachley hid a smile behind his carefully disguised face and wondered how much terror Dark Annie had felt upon learning of poor Polly's violent end?

She remained with her customer from Spitalfields Market for the whole frustrating night, drinking and eating at his expense, disappearing with him once for nearly half an hour, presumably to renew their intimate acquaintance. Then she and her customer sat down to another round of rum, listening to the piano and the pub songs sung by drunken patrons, watching other prostitutes enter the place and find customers of their own and disappear outside again to conduct their sordid business, until the pub closed its doors. When Annie Chapman and her customer left the public house, he took her through the dark streets to what was presumably his own house, a miserable little factory cottage on Hanbury Street, which she entered and did not leave again until very nearly five-thirty in the morning, at which time her customer emerged dressed for work.

He gave her a rough caress and said, "You ought to see a doctor about that cough, luv. I'd give you sixpence if I 'ad it, but I spent all me ready cash on your supper."

"Oh, that's all right, and thank you for the food and the rum."

"Well, I've got to be off or they'll lock the factory yard gates and dock me wages."

They separated, the man hurrying away down Hanbury Street while Annie Chapman lingered at his doorstep, visibly exhausted.

"Well," she muttered to herself, "you've had a good supper and the rum's been a great help with the pain, but you've still got no money for your bed, Annie Chapman."

She sighed and set out very slowly, moving in the general direction of Dorset Street once more. John Lachley glanced quickly along the street and saw no sign of anyone, so he stepped out of the doorway he'd been leaning against and crossed the street toward her. Since he didn't want to startle her into crying out and waking anyone, he began whistling very softly. She turned at the sound and sent a hopeful smile his way.

"Good morning," John said quietly.

"Good morning, sir."

"You seem to be in something of a bind, madam."

She glanced quizzically into his eyes.

"I couldn't help but overhear you, just now. You need money for your lodging house, then?"

She nodded slowly. "I do, indeed, sir. You realize, I wouldn't ask, if I weren't desperate, but . . . well, sir, I can be very agreeable to a gentleman in need of companionship."

John Lachley smiled, darting a quick glance at Maybrick's place of concealment.

"I'm certain you can, madam. But surely you have in your possession something of value which you might sell, instead of yourself?"

Her cheeks flushed, the right one bruised from the fist fight she'd been in with the other whore earlier in the week. "I've already sold everything of value I own," she said softly.

"Everything?" He stepped closer. Dropped his voice to a mere whisper. "Even the letters?"

Annie's blue eyes widened. "The *letters?*" she breathed. "How—how did you know about the letters?"

"Never mind that, just tell me one thing. Will you sell them to me?"

Her mouth opened, closed again. From the distant tower of the Black Eagle Brewery, the clock struck five-thirty A.M. "I can't," she finally said. "I haven't got them any longer."

"Haven't got them?" he asked sharply. "Where are they?"

Misery pinched her face, turned her complexion sallow. "I've been ill, you see, with a cough. I needed money for medicine. So I sold them, but I could get them back or tell you who bought them, only . . . could you give me a few pence for a bed, if I do? I need to sleep, I'm so unwell."

"You could *maybe* get them for me?" he repeated. "*Will* you?"

"Yes," she answered at once. "Yes," she whispered, leaning against the brick wall in visible weariness, "I will."

He dropped his voice to a whisper and asked, "Who's got them?"

"I sold them to Elizabeth Stride and Catharine Eddowes . . ."

Footsteps behind him told Lachley they were not alone. He swore under his breath, careful not to turn his head, and listened with a trip-hammering pulse until whoever it was continued on their way, rather than interrupt what must look to any observer like a whore and her customer in serious negotiations. When the footsteps had died away again in the distance, Lachley took Annie Chapman by the arm, pressed her back against the shutters of the house they stood in front of, bent down to whisper, "All right, Annie, I'll give you the money you need for your bed . . . and enough to re-acquire the letters."

He dug into his pocket and pulled out two shining shillings, which he handed over.

She smiled tremulously. "Thank you, sir. I'll get the letters back with this, I promise you."

The passing of the money between them was the signal James

Maybrick had been waiting for all through the long night. He appeared from the darkness and walked toward them as Lachley caressed Annie's breast through her worn, faded bodice and murmured, "Shall we go someplace quiet, then? You do seem a most agreeable lady on a cold night like this." He smiled down into her eyes. "A mutually delightful few moments of pleasure now, then I'll meet you this evening at Crossingham's," Lachley lied. "And I'll buy the letters from you, then."

"I'll have them," she said earnestly. "There's a nice, quiet yard at number twenty-nine," she added softly, nodding down the street toward a dilapidated tenement. "One of the girls I know oiled the hinges," she added with a wink, "so there's no chance of waking anybody. The second door, there, leads through the house to the yard."

"Lovely," Lachley smiled down at her. "Perfect. Shall we?"

Lachley eased open the door, aware that Maybrick trailed behind, silent as a shadow. Lachley escorted Annie through the black and stinking passage, then down the steps to the reeking yard behind. Very gently, he pressed her up against the high fence. Very gently, he bent, caressed her throat . . . nuzzled her ear. "Annie," he murmured. "You really shouldn't have sold those letters, pet. Give my love to Polly, won't you?"

She had just enough time to gasp out one faint protest. "No . . ."

Then his hands were around her throat and she fell against the fence with a thud, all sound cut off as he crushed her trachea. Her terrified struggles spiraled through his entire being, a giddy elixir, more potent than raw, sweating sex. When it was over, the shock of disappointment was so keen he almost protested the end of the pleasure. Morgan had lasted much longer, struggled much harder, giving him hours of intense pleasure. But they couldn't afford the risk out here in the open, where all of London might hear at any moment. So Lachley drew several deep, rasping breaths to calm himself, then lowered her lifeless corpse to the filthy ground beside the fence. He stepped back, giving her to the impatient Maybrick, who gripped his knife in eager anticipation. The sound of that knife ripping her open was the sweetest sound John Lachley had heard all day.

He bent low and breathed into Maybrick's ear, "Return to Lower

Tibor when you've finished. Use the sewers, as I showed you. I'll be waiting in the secret room."

Then he slipped from the yard, leaving the maniacal Maybrick to vent his rage on the lifeless corpse of Annie Chapman. He was not pleased that he must track down and kill two *more* dirty whores, two *more* potential blackmailers in a position to destroy his future. In fact, as the trembling delight of stalk and strike and murder gradually waned in his blood, he cursed the foul luck that had prompted Annie to sell her precious letters to raise money for medicine, cursed it with every stride he took, cursed Prince Albert Victor for writing Morgan's goddamned letters in the first place, and cursed brainless whores who acquired them only to sell them off for ready cash. Two *more* women to locate and silence! Dear God, would this nightmare never end? *Two!*

His beautiful Greek prisoner had known, somehow; had seen clairvoyantly into his future and known he would not succeed tonight. *Curse it!* He would have to question Ianira more closely about what she had seen in that vision of hers. Clearly, he could do nothing further today. It would be getting light soon and Maybrick had to return to Liverpool today, to meet social and family obligations.

Lachley was tempted to find these women himself, to end their miserable lives with his own hands, without waiting for Maybrick's return. But that was far too risky. Maybrick *must* be involved; that was critical to his plans. He must have a scapegoat on which to pin blame for these murders. *All* of them, including the next two. He narrowed his eyes. Elizabeth Stride and Catharine Eddowes . . . He'd never heard of either woman, but he was willing to bet they were common prostitutes, same as the recently departed Polly Nichols and the even more recently departed Annie Chapman. Which meant they ought to be quite easy to trace and just as easy to silence. Provided the bitches didn't tumble to the truth of what they possessed and run, bleating, with it to the constables or—worse—the press.

It was even possible that someone would connect "Eddy" and Prince Albert Victor Christian Edward. Lachley shuddered at such a monstrous vision of the future. These filthy whores must be silenced, whatever the cost. He made for his own little hovel in Wapping, beneath which was the entrance to the sewers which led to his underground sanctuary. James Maybrick knew the way there, already. Lachley had shown him the route shortly before Polly Nichols' murder, introducing him to Garm, to help him escape detection. Since Maybrick couldn't very well walk around with blood on his sleeves, he'd needed an escape route that was certain. The sewers were the most sure escape route possible.

So he'd showed Maybrick how to find his hideaway where Morgan had passed his last hours screaming out his miserable little life, and had arranged to meet Maybrick there again, after Annie Chapman's murder. Maybrick ought to be arriving there shortly to change his clothes and rid himself of any physical evidence connecting him with the murders, including the knife. He'd left the long-bladed weapon at Lower Tibor after Polly's death and collected again this evening, before setting out in pursuit of Annie. Lachley had *planned* to drug Maybrick after this latest murder, to use his mesmeric skills to erase the merchant's memory of Lachley's involvement, then send the knife and an anonymous tip to the Metropolitan Police's H Division with the instructions that a search of Battlecrease House in Liverpool would yield written evidence of the identity of the Whitechapel Murderer.

Putting that plan into action was clearly out of the question, now, at least until he had obtained the letters from Stride and Eddowes, curse them. It was now September the eighth, nearly two *weeks* since he'd first determined to kill Morgan and finish up this sordid business. Yet he was no closer to ending this miserable affair than he'd been the day Eddy had arrived at his house with the unpalatable news in the first place. He wanted this over with! Finished once and for all!

When James Maybrick finally arrived in his underground sanctuary, only to break the news that he couldn't possibly return to London until the end of the month, due to business and social commitments, it was all John Lachley could do not to shoot the maniac on the spot. He stood there breathing hard, with the gnarled oak limbs of his sacrificial tree spreading toward the brick vault of the underground chamber's ceiling and the smell of gas flames and fresh blood thick in the air, and clenched his fists while James Maybrick changed his clothes, burned the coat and shirt and trousers he'd been wearing, and secreted some hideous package that reeked of blood in an oilcloth sack.

"Took away her womb," Maybrick explained with a drunken giggle. "Threw her intestines over her shoulder, cut out her womb and her vagina." He giggled again, hoisting the grotesque oilcloth sack. "Thought I'd fry them up for my supper, eh? Took her wedding rings, too," he added, eyes gleaming in total madness. He displayed his trophies proudly, two cheap brass rings, a wedding band and a keeper. "Had to wrench them off, didn't want to leave holy rings on a dirty whore's hand, eh? Went back for a second helping of her, took part of the bladder, when I realized I'd forgotten my chalk. Wanted to chalk a message on the wall," he added mournfully. "To taunt the police. That fool, Abberline, thinks he's so very clever . . . not nearly so clever as Sir Jim, ha ha ha!"

Lachley thinned his lips into a narrow line, wishing to hell the maniac would simply shut up. God, the man was sick . . .

"Can't be here next week," Maybrick added, pulling on clean clothes Lachley had laid out for him. "But we will kill the other dirty whores, won't we? You'll let me rip them?"

"Yes, yes!" Lachley snapped. "When *can* you be back, dammit? I'm tired of waiting for you! This business is urgent, Maybrick, dammed urgent! You'd bloody well *better* be here the first day you can get away!"

Maybrick drew on his overcoat, left behind earlier. "Saturday the twenty-ninth," Maybrick replied easily. "You have my medicine ready?"

Lachley thrust the stoppered bottle into Maybrick's hand and watched narrowly as he drank it down. The potent mixture which allowed Lachley to place his patients into such a deep trance was even more critical with this patient, giving Lachley the means by which to accomplish his murderous ends without being mentioned in Maybrick's written record of his deeds. "Lie down on that bench," Lachley said impatiently when Maybrick had finished it all.

The cotton merchant slid up onto Lachley's long work bench and lay back with a smile, clearly pleased with the night's work and equally clearly looking forward to another two repeat performances of the evening's fun. Lachley stared down at the insane insect and loathed him so intensely, he had to clench his fists to keep from closing his hands around the man's throat and crushing the life from him, as he'd crushed it from Annie Chapman. Maybrick's eyelids gradually grew heavy and sank closed.

Lachley took Maybrick through the standard routine to bring about trance, went through the litany designed to abate his physical complaints, then repeated his injunction against ever mentioning or even hinting that Lachley existed when he wrote out his diary entries. "You will wake naturally in several hours, feeling refreshed and strong," Lachley told the drugged murderer. "You will leave this place and go to Liverpool Street Station and take the train for home. You will remember nothing of your visits to Dr. John Lachley, nothing except that he is helping you with your illness. You will not mention Dr. Lachley to anyone you know, not even members of your family. You will remember nothing about this room until the twenty-ninth of September, when you will receive a telegram from your physician informing you of an appointment. You will then come here and meet me in this room and we will kill more whores and you will enjoy it immensely. You will write of your enjoyment in your diary, but you will mention nothing about your London physician or the help I give you. In your diary, you will write of how pleasurable it was to rip your whores, how much you look forward to ripping more of them . . ."

Maybrick, lying there in a drugged stupor, smiled.

Maniacal bastard.

Lachley flexed his hands, clenching them into fists and glared down at the pathetic creature on his work table. *I'll personally certify your death after they've hung you on the gallows. It can't be too soon, either, damn your eyes.*

Two bloody weeks . . . and two more dirty whores to be killed. Preferably, in one night. If he didn't destroy them both on the same night, God alone knew how long it would be before Maybrick could tear himself away from business and family in Liverpool and return to finish this up. Yes, they would have to die on the same night, next time. Bloody hell . . . and they would have constables crawling like roaches through these streets, by then.

But it had got to be done, regardless, too much depended on it. All told, it was enough to drive a sane man into an asylum.

The message arrived on Gideon Guthrie's computer via e-mail.

Trouble brewing, TT-86. Targets have escaped via two separate gates, Denver and London. Senator Caddrick has departed for terminal with entourage, vowing to close station. Please advise your intentions.

It had been relayed through so many servers, rerouted across so many continents, tracing it back to the original sender would have stymied the efforts even of the CIA and Interpol. When Gideon read Cyril Barris' message, he swore explosively. That goddamned, grandstanding *idiot*! He'd *told* Caddrick, dammit, to stay out of this! Did the jackass really *want* to end up in prison?

He sent a reply: *Will handle personally. Do nothing. Timetable still on schedule.*

Then he deleted the original message from his hard drive and blistered the air with another savage curse. God*dammit*! With Caddrick on the warpath, Gideon would have to go there, himself, clean up this whole God-cursed mess the hard way. Time Terminal Eighty-Six . . .

Gideon Guthrie swore viciously and tapped keys on his computer, opening the program which allowed him to make airline reservations. Just as with the e-mail message and its multitude of rerouting server connections, his request for airline tickets hopped the globe before reaching the airlines reservations computer. He typed in the requisite identification information, then calmly assumed the identity of Mr. Sid Kaederman, the name he'd given Caddrick to use as the "detective" hired to trace his missing kid.

Damn that girl! She was a twenty-year-old, wet-behind-the-ears rich-man's brat, with her head stuck in a bunch of history books. Even her boyfriend had played dress-up cowboy, for God's sake, when he hadn't been cozying up to Jenna's film-making friends. But the little bitch had slipped right through their fingers, thanks to Noah Armstrong, and now Caddrick had gone ballistic. The suicidal *idiot*! Trying to play to the press and gain voter sympathy, when the very last thing they needed was Caddrick on *any* warpath.

Once again, Caddrick had failed to use the few brains God had given him, leaving Gideon no choice but to wade in and try to salvage the mess. Therefore, Mr. Sid Kaederman, detective with the world-famous, globe-spanning Wardmann Wolfe agency, would be taking an unplanned time tour. Gideon's lips twisted in a sardonic smile at the notion of posing as a detective from Noah Armstrong's own agency. But he did not find the idea of taking a time tour amusing. He was a fastidious man by nature, fond of his creature comforts, of up-time luxuries. He hadn't done real fieldwork in fifteen years and had vowed never to set foot down a time touring gate, where filth and disease and accident could rob him of everything he'd built over his career.

God, *time touring*!

The only question was, *which* of Shangri-La Station's gates would Mr. Sid Kaederman be touring? Which one, exactly, had Jenna Caddrick disappeared down, and which had Ianira Cassondra and her family gone through? Denver? Or London?

He intended to find out.

With that promise to himself foremost in his mind, Gideon Guthrie started reviewing methods by which he would slowly dismember Ms. Jenna Nicole Caddrick, and began packing his luggage. He was still reviewing delightfully bloodthirsty methods, up to the ninety-ninth and counting, when he snatched up a pre-prepared portfolio with Sid Kaederman's identification, medical records, and credit cards, and headed grimly out the door.

(((Chapter 15)))

Skeeter knew they didn't have much time. The men who'd kidnapped Bergitta would kill her if they weren't stopped, and stopped fast. Making use of what he had ready at hand, Skeeter deployed part of his forces—the closest thing he possessed to shock troops—in an ambush where the corridor turned, forming a blind corner with a partially constructed apartment along one approach and a storage room along the other, providing two doorways strategically positioned for attack.

Skeeter then led his light, mobile infantry—such as it was—back toward the preoccupied construction crew, in what he hoped would be a maneuver worthy of Yesukai the Valiant himself, or maybe Francis Marion, the Swamp Fox. Having selected the least threatening of his troops to accompany him, Skeeter jogged straight into the big open bay warehouse, with Molly and the two kids from the Lost and Found gang hard on his heels.

"There they are!" Skeeter yelled. "Molly, quick! Go call Security!"

Eight-year-old Tevel, playing his role with enthusiasm, taunted, "Boy, are you gonna get yours! They'll throw away the key! Drop you down an unstable gate! Nyah-nyah, you're all going to jail! Come on, Molly, let's tell on 'em!"

Hashim, not to be outdone, was shouting something that sounded scurrilous. Whether it was the teenager's Arabic taunts or Tevel's threats or Skeeter's shout for Molly to call Security, six of the burliest, nastiest, angriest members of the construction crew charged right at them. Screwdrivers and wicked knives glinted in the work lights dangling from the unfinished ceiling. The man in the lead was shouting, "Don't let them get away! Kill them all!"

Skeeter whipped around, bolting back the way they'd come. "*Run!*"

Hashim was still yelling taunts in Arabic as they pounded through a series of twists and turns in the corridor. Molly passed Skeeter, as planned, while eight-year-old Tevel shot into the lead, on a mission of his own. When they plunged through the blind corner, Skeeter turned on his heel and waited, claw hammer clutched in one hand. He could hear the pounding of their feet, could smell the stench of their sweat—

All six of them piled into the blind corner, running full tilt.

"NOW!"

Kynan Rhys Gower lunged through an open doorway, war hammer gripped over his head for a striking blow. The heavy wooden mallet whistled in a short arc. The lead man ran full tilt into it. His skull caved in with a sickening crunch. The man behind him screamed and tripped over the body, trying to dig a heavy Egyptian hunting dart out of his left kidney. A rock whizzed from the doorway nearest Skeeter. It stuck the throat of the man next to the pincushion. The man gave out a gurgling scream and went down, clutching his crushed trachea. Eigil Bjarneson's screaming war cry sent one man racing in retreat—straight onto Alfonzo's pike. Another man screamed and fell to his knees when Eigil severed his hand with a single blow of his sword. A sharpened screwdriver clattered to the floor from the twitching, disconnected fingers. The final man was hit with double blows in the chest, once from a spinning rock, once when a heavy hunting dart embedded itself between ribs.

When Eigil would have finished off the man whose hand lay beside him on the concrete, Skeeter rushed in. "Wait! I want one of 'em alive!"

The man on the floor was pleading for mercy, promising anything, if only they would let him live, if only they'd bring medical help to reattach his hand . . . Rushing footfalls from behind brought Skeeter around in a crouch. But it wasn't an enemy, it was more down-timers, six of them, and the enraged construction foreman, whose face was bruised and scabbed with dried blood.

"How can I help?" Riyad snarled.

"Find out what that bastard knows about the *Ansar Majlis*. Their leaders arrived through Primary today. I want to know *everything* he knows about the *Ansar Majlis* and their plans to invade the station!"

"With pleasure! Get a tourniquet on that arm!" Then he switched to Arabic and Skeeter switched his attention to the rest of his war party.

"Kynan, Eigil, Alfonzo, get moving! Frontal assault. Corydon, Molly, Chenzira, back them up! And somebody get Security down here! Hashim, you're with me!" He scooped up a heavy concrete trowel from one of the dead men. With a blade like a hoe, one which stuck straight out from the handle, rather than bending down at an angle, its edge had been sharpened wickedly. It made a conveniently lethal weapon to back up his claw hammer.

Skeeter sent his troops into the open bay warehouse. He put Molly in the lead, since she had the only pistol, with Corydon and Chenzira Umi backing her up with the other two projectile weapons. Skeeter charged past the open bay's door and raced down the corridor toward the unfinished section of wall where Bergitta lay bound to the uprights. Hashim, too, had confiscated an abandoned weapon: a sharpened screwdriver. They crept past the last of the drywall, then crouched low to peer into the warehouse beyond.

About half of the fourteen remaining men had run toward the doorway, shouting obscenities at Skeeter's attacking troops and charging to the attack. Several others had taken refuge behind stacked supplies, wailing—or so Hashim whispered—that they should never have attacked the crew foreman and brought the woman down here, that they hadn't counted on killing so many people, couldn't they just abandon the whore and run? Only two men had been left behind to guard Bergitta. She was barely conscious, face swollen and bruised, mouth and nose bleeding where they'd hit her repeatedly. Neither guard was paying any attention to her, which meant they weren't looking at the open "wall" behind her, either.

Hashim slipped through first, easing past the two-by-fours on

Bergitta's left, while Skeeter edged past on her right. When Molly started shooting, the guards left with Bergitta moved even further away. That gave Skeeter and Hashim the chance they needed. The down-time boy struck first. He drove the sharpened screwdriver into the nearest guard's back with a snarl of hatred. The man screamed. The other guard whirled, bringing up a knife—

Skeeter slashed with the sharpened trowel. The blow severed fingers. The man screamed and fell to his knees beside the clattering knife. A kick to the man's head sent him sprawling. "Wire his hands!" he yelled to Hashim, who was already crouching low over Bergitta. A twist of Skeeter's claw hammer served to break the wires around her wrists and throat. Skeeter picked her up, then shouted at the embattled construction workers, "I've got your hostage! You might as well give it up and surrender! Security's on the way and there's no way off this station! Surrender now and maybe these down-timers won't kill you like they did your pals just now!"

Hashim translated into Arabic for good measure.

Moments later, it was over. Security did, in fact, arrive in force, led by Wally Klontz and the crew foreman, Riyad, along with several of his enraged crew who'd been jumped and knocked out. They started cleaning up the mess. Skeeter carried Bergitta up to the infirmary, himself, not trusting the job to anyone else. He ran the whole way, while Bergitta lapsed into unconsciousness. He skidded, out of breath, into the infirmary, where battered tourists and the irate Senator Caddrick were being treated for injuries from the riot at Primary.

Rachel Eisenstein, who was busy rinsing tear gas out of Caddrick's reddened eyes, took one look at Bergitta, blanched, and abandoned Caddrick. "What's happened?"

"Some of the Arabian Nights crew dragged her down to the basement, beat her nearly to death, gang-raped her . . ."

"I need a trauma team, stat!" Rachel shoved past the shocked and red-faced Senator, who sputtered an outraged protest at being abandoned.

Skeeter carried Bergitta in Rachel's wake, shoving his own way past the angry Senator, and followed the station's chief of medicine into a treatment room. Skeeter turned Bergitta over to Rachel's care, gratified by the swiftness of the trauma team's arrival, and found himself abruptly trembling from head to toes with the aftershock of battle. He dragged his hands across his face, decided he'd better find someplace to sit down, and stumbled back toward the front of the infirmary.

And ran slap into Mike Benson.

"Jackson!"

He glanced up just in time to see the handcuffs. He was so off balance and exhausted from the fight, from the desperate rush to get Bergitta to a doctor, he didn't even have the strength or presence of mind to slip out of the way. Benson slapped the cuffs around his wrists, cold and terrifying, and tightened them down with a savage twist. "We've got a basement full of bodies, Jackson! And for once, you're not gonna wriggle out of it! Not with Caddrick on station, threatening to shut us down!"

Too badly shaken to do more than stumble, Skeeter followed numbly when Benson hauled him past gaping orderlies, nurses, newsies, and injured tourists. Ten minutes later, Skeeter was in the aerie high above Commons, facing down Ronisha Azzan, Shangri-La's tall deputy station manager. She'd clearly taken over when the feds had dragged Bull Morgan away to jail. Like Time Tours CEO Granville Baxter, Ronisha Azzan claimed Masai heritage and wore richly patterned African textiles done up in expensive suits. At the moment, she towered over Skeeter, glowering down at him from the other side of Bull's desk, while Benson blocked the exit, standing between Skeeter and the elevator doors. Skeeter stood swaying, wrists aching where the too-tight cuffs were cutting the skin, badly shaken and beginning to despair.

Ronisha Azzan said coldly, "We've taken into custody half a dozen down-timers on murder charges, Skeeter. What I want to know is—"

The elevator doors slid open with a soft *ping!* and Kit Carson crashed the party.

"Move it, Mike," Kit growled, facing down Benson when the head of security thought twice about letting him into the aerie. Kit brought one arm up to keep the elevator doors from closing again. "I'm in no mood to play games with *anybody*."

Benson locked eyes with the retired scout, then grunted once and wisely stepped aside. Skeeter sank, shaking, into the nearest chair, having been on the receiving end of Kit's rage once before, but after a moment's utter panic, he realized what Kit's presence here meant.

Kynan Rhys Gower had sworn an oath of fealty to Kit, several months back. The retired time scout had rescued him from Portuguese traders intent on burning the Welshman and Margo as witches on a beach in sixteenth-century East Africa. Kit was therefore obligated to speak on his behalf as the Welshman's liege lord. Kit Carson might, yet, take Skeeter apart for involving his vassal in something as serious as murder, but for the moment, his attention was rivetted on Ronisha Azzan.

Then he spoke, voice flat with anger, and darted a glance at Skeeter's manacled wrists. "Was it really necessary to cuff him?"

Benson snapped, "I thought so! There's half a dozen dead men down there—"

"*And damned near a dead little girl!*" Kit's lean face ran white with barely controlled fury. "That poor kid's been raped and beaten unconscious! Rachel's staff said they're not even sure she'll come out of surgery alive!"

Skeeter blanched.

"Take the cuffs off, Mike! Skeeter's not going to attack one of us. And even if he did, I could throw him through the nearest window without batting an eyelash, which he knows!"

Skeeter knew, all right.

He had no intention of going one-on-one with Kit Carson under *any* circumstances. But thanks to Kit, Mike Benson grudgingly unlocked the handcuffs, freeing Skeeter's wrists. He flexed them gingerly and rubbed the chafed skin.

"Thanks."

Benson just glowered at him and retreated to a watchful stance between Skeeter and the elevator door. Ronisha slowly seated herself in Bull Morgan's chair, studying Skeeter intently. "All right, Kit. He's uncuffed. Now. You want to explain this mess, Skeeter? If I didn't have my phones forwarded down to the war room, I'd have every reporter on station demanding to know why half a dozen construction workers were just murdered on a station totally out of control. Not to mention Senator Caddrick, who's demanded to see me the minute he's released from the infirmary, and I think we can all guess what *he* wants. This isn't going to play well in the press, Skeeter. The station's in very serious trouble, even without Caddrick on the warpath down in station medical."

"Yeah," Skeeter muttered, "that's old news, around here." Kit's unexpected support gave him the courage to say it right out. "Look, I'm not in any mood for games, either. Those bastards timed their hit perfectly, snatching Bergitta during the chaos at Primary. They knew Security would be run ragged, trying to control that mess, and frankly, they were counting on the fact that Bergitta's only a down-timer. She's not Ianira Cassondra, not somebody we'd tear the station apart to find, she's just a worthless, down-timer ex-prostitute, a kid nobody'd miss. If you sit there and tell me you'd have pulled a single security officer off riot duty at Primary to hunt down those bastards or even mount a search for her, right in the middle of this mess, I'll call you a liar, Ronisha Azzan."

Ronisha's brows arched, but the deputy station manager said nothing, merely tapped long, elegant fingernails against the desktop and waited for Skeeter to finish.

Skeeter shrugged. "I figured the only chance she had was the down-timers. It was the little ones, the Lost and Found Gang, who saw them snatch her out of the bathroom she was cleaning. They came for me, ran to warn the others. The kids *heard* those creeps boasting, talking about how they were going to beat her and rape her and then kill her in cold blood when they'd had their fun. When we went in, down there, it was twenty to seven. Twenty, dammit, all of them intent on committing murder. They'd already jumped their own foreman, knocked him out and locked him up along with anybody who disagreed with their idea of fun. And the minute they laid eyes on us, their ringleader started yelling at his men to kill all of us. You tell me what we should've done, under the circumstances. Let them rape to death an innocent girl? Let 'em butcher those kids who led us down there? Tevel Gottlieb is only eight, for Chrissake. Folks around here may not think a helluva lot of me, but goddammit, if you think I was going to stand by with a finger in my ear and do *nothing,* you're as crazy as those idiots out there worshiping Jack the Ripper!"

Before Ronisha Azzan could do more than draw a single breath, Kit Carson said quietly, "I'd have done the same thing, Ronnie. In a second. And I've talked to Mr. Riyad. He supports Skeeter fully."

She glanced sharply at Shangri-La's most famous, influential resident, then sighed and rapped her knuckles agitatedly against the desktop. "Huh. Frankly, if I'd been in Skeeter's place, I might have done what he did, too. Mike, as far as I'm concerned, every one of these people acted in self-defense, saving the life of a station resident. And don't quote up-time law at me, either! I know most of them are down-timers without rights. On this station," she jabbed a finger downward for emphasis, "a resident is a resident. At least they are on *my* watch and I'm pretty sure Bull would back me up, if he weren't in jail with those damned feds holding the keys. So . . . The question is, what to tell those vultures in the press, or that maniac, Caddrick?"

Skeeter's jaw dropped, trying to take in the fact that he wasn't going to jail, after all. Then Skeeter realized he had another ace up his sleeve, one he knew for sure Ronisha Azzan would be interested in. "Well, you might try giving them the story of the week. We've got the key to destroying the *Ansar Majlis,* after all."

"*What?*" The word echoed in triplicate.

Skeeter indulged a brief, satisfied grin. It wasn't every day a guy could shock the likes of *that* trio. Skeeter leaned forward. "The guy who lost his hand? He offered to sing like a caged canary. And according to Hashim, part of what he's offered to sing about is the *Ansar Majlis.* Namely, their plans to invade this station, break their riot-happy Brothers out of jail, and kill off every Security officer in their way and every Templar they can lay hands on, doing it. Their leaders came through Primary today."

Ronisha snatched up the telephone. "Azzan, here. Release every down-timer involved in that fight down in Arabian Nights. Yes, dammit, *now.* And ask that kid, Hashim, and Mr. Riyad to translate for us. Interrogate those construction workers Wally Klontz and Mr. Riyad brought in. I want to know everything *they* do about the *Ansar*

Majlis." Then, to Skeeter, "With a little luck, we may yet blow that terrorist group wide open. Good work, Skeeter. Damned good work, in fact. The station owes you. Go on, get out of here. Get over to the infirmary and see how she's doing."

Skeeter was in such a state of shock, he could scarcely mumble out his thanks. He bolted for the elevator, gratified when Mike Benson merely stepped aside, his own jaw scraping the floor. The head of station security sent an unhappy scowl after him, but that was all. *Good God,* he thought on the way down to Commons, *I'm not going to jail! None of us is going to jail!* Because of Kit Carson. Or was it only that Ronisha Azzan was, in the final analysis, a fair woman, interested in justice? Even though she had to be tough, doing a job like hers, particularly with a whole new stack of corpses to explain to Senator John Caddrick? Skeeter wasn't sure, but he certainly wasn't going to look a gift horse in the mouth.

When he reached the infirmary, he found Wally Klontz there ahead of him, along with Mr. Riyad and Hashim, taking statements from the injured construction workers. Wally glanced up when Skeeter came in. "Hey, Skeeter! Rachel said to tell you. Bergitta's in surgery, but it looks like she'll make it, after all. You got her up here just in time." Skeeter had to lean against the nearest wall, the relief was so profound. "And these birds," Wally nodded at the construction workers he was questioning, "are giving us enough information to arrest the whole up-time *Ansar Majlis* operation. We've already identified their ringleaders and sent out teams to arrest them at their hotels. Seems the leadership decided to come here and supervise the search for Ianira in person, after their underlings screwed up the mission. Once they're in custody, it'll just be a matter of mopping up the cells scattered in various up-time cities. Good work, Jackson."

He couldn't quite believe his ears. Two 'eighty-sixers in a row, *thanking* him!

But the jubilant mood was short-lived. When Bergitta came out of surgery, and Rachel allowed him to step into the recovery room, Skeeter's warm glow of accomplishment drained away so fast, he had to grip the door frame to steady himself. Bergitta was awake, but only just. Rachel had sedated her heavily for the emergency surgery and she was just coming out from under the anesthesia. The injuries looked even worse against the stark white of hospital bed and bandages than they had down in that nasty, half-finished warehouse in the basement. When Skeeter paused, stricken, beside her bed, Bergitta's bruised and swollen eyes focused slowly on his face. "Skeeter . . ." Tears trickled down her blackened cheeks.

"Shh, don't try to talk. You're safe, now. You've just come out of surgery, Bergitta. Rachel says you're going to be all right, but you need to rest, save your strength." Moving gingerly, he took her hand. Heavy bandages covered raw cuts from the wire. Her elbow trailed I.V. lines.

"Thank you," she whispered anyway, throat working to swallow past hideous bruises from more of their damned wire.

"Don't thank me," he insisted quietly. "Thank the kids. They spotted you, when those animals dragged you out of the bathroom. If it hadn't been for the kids . . ." He forced a smile. "But they *did* see you, didn't they? And sounded the alarm. So we got you out of there, thanks to the little ones. And some who aren't so little," he added with a watery smile. "Eigil Bjarneson sent a few to the gods, today."

Her fingers tightened around Skeeter's.

"Listen, you get some rest, okay? Nobody's going to hurt you again, I promise. The ones who aren't dead are under arrest. They'll be kicked off station in handcuffs and tried for attempted murder and ties to the *Ansar Majlis*. You're safe, Bergitta, I promise you are. And Molly wants you to move in with her, when you're stronger, so you won't have to live alone any more." Over at the doorway, a nurse high-signed him. "I have to go now, the nurse says you need to sleep. Close your eyes, I'll come back and see you when you're feeling a little better."

By the time Skeeter extricated his fingers from hers, tucked her hand beneath the blankets, and reached the door, she was sound asleep. He stood in the doorway for a long moment, just watching her, then turned on his heel and headed out into the Commons once again. Bergitta was alive, thank all the Yakka gods of the upper air, and with a little luck, the *Ansar Majlis* wouldn't ever threaten anybody again.

But he still had to find a job, doing *something* to pay for his apartment and groceries, and he still intended to spot and turn in every pickpocket and confidence artist he could find. And somewhere, down one of the station's gates, his dearest friends in the world were hiding for their very lives. Marcus and Ianira and their beautiful little girls . . .

He didn't yet know *how,* exactly.

But Skeeter intended to find them.

And bring them safely home once more.

Jenna Caddrick sat beside the window of her bedroom in the little house in Spitalfields, listening to the angry shouts in the streets outside, as word of the latest murder in Whitechapel spread through the East End. She'd sat in almost this same spot for a whole week, now, exhausted and trying to recover from the gunshot to her skull. Jenna could no longer doubt Ianira's pronouncement that she was carrying a baby, either. Even with the stress of the past few days, she should've started her period by now and hadn't. And she'd never felt so monstrously queasy in all her life, had been feeling nauseated for days, right through the pain medication Dr. Mendel had prescribed. She hadn't wanted anything more than dry toast in days, had been forcing herself to eat, terrified that she'd lose the baby if she didn't choke food down.

Below her window, angry working men shouted at a police constable, demanding better patrols through the area, and frightened women huddled in doorways, clutching shawls about their shoulders and crying while they talked endlessly of the madman stalking these streets. Jenna brought her eyelids clenching down over wetness. *What am I going to do?* She was in disguise as a man, with fake mutton chops and moustaches which the time terminal's cosmetologist had implanted. That false hair would require a cosmetic surgeon to remove. Not a single doctor anywhere in this city would begin to understand if a seemingly male individual showed up ready to deliver a baby, for God's sake. Talk about attracting unwanted attention . . .

And she couldn't go home to deliver her baby, either, might *never* be able to go home. That was something else she'd been running away from, these last few days, sitting in this chair and staring out this window while her scalp wound healed. She didn't want to face the knowledge that the faceless men her father worked with might never stop trying to kill her, even if Noah managed to destroy her father's career and bring down the men paying him.

None of them might ever be able to go home again, not Jenna or Noah Armstrong or Ianira's beautiful, precious family . . . And they didn't even know where Ianira was, or what had become of her in the hands of the lunatic who'd shot Jenna down in cold blood. Jenna's lips trembled and tears came again, a flood of them as bitter anger threatened to choke her. Somehow, her father was going to pay for this. All of this . . . She didn't hear the first knock at her door and only looked up when someone cleared a throat and said, "Hey, mind if I come in?"

Jenna, eyes streaming, looked around. It was Noah Armstrong. The detective, still playing the role of Marcus' sister, was dressed in a plain cotton skirt and worn bodice, leaving Armstrong's gender even more a mystery than ever. Jenna couldn't even bring herself to care. Noah lifted a tray with several slices of dried toast, a hot meat pie, and a steaming mug of tea. "I bought you something to eat."

Jenna swallowed against the nausea any smell of food brought. She wasn't hungry, hadn't been hungry in so long, she'd forgotten what hunger felt like. "Thanks," she made herself say.

Noah set the lunch tray on the table at Jenna's elbow. As she choked down the first bites, the detective rested a hand on her brow. The gesture was so caring, Jenna's eyes stung and the tears came again. She set down her fork and covered her face with her hands.

"Hey," Noah hunkered down beside her, grey eyes revealing a surprising depth of concern, "what's this? I won't let anyone hurt you, kid. Surely you know that?"

Jenna bit her lip, then managed to choke out, "I . . . I know that. It's why . . . I mean . . . everybody who ever cared about me died," she gulped. "Noah, I'm so scared . . ."

"Sure you are, kid," Noah said quietly. "And you've got every right to be. But look at this another way, Jenna." Noah traced the line of fake whiskers down her jaw, brushed limp hair back from her brow, the gesture curiously gentle. "As long as you're alive, as long as your baby's alive, then at least a part of Carl's still alive, too. And that means they've lost. They've failed to destroy the witnesses, failed to destroy quite *everything* you love." Noah took her hand, rubbed her fingers and palm with warm fingertips. "You're not alone, hear? We're all with you in this. And we'll need your help, Jenna. To find Ianira."

Jenna looked up at that, met Noah Armstrong's gaze. The concern, the steely determination to keep her alive gave Jenna a renewed sense of strength. She found herself drying her wet cheeks. "All right," she said, voice low. "All right, Noah. I'll do whatever it takes. Maybe we can try hunting the gentlemen's clubs over in Pall Mall, find some trace of him that way. We have to find her."

"And we will."

"Noah . . ." She bit her lip, half-afraid to broach the subject they'd all been avoiding.

"What?" the detective asked gently.

"When you go back up time with that evidence? I want you to do me a favor, will you?" The bitterness in her voice would have shocked her, once, long ago, at least a week previously, before her father had destroyed her entire world. "*Don't* put a bullet between my father's eyes for me."

Noah's grey eyes showed surprise.

She grated out harshly, "I want to do it, myself."

The lunch Noah had brought, forgotten on the table at her elbow, slowly cooled while Noah gathered her in and let her cry. One day, she didn't yet know how, she *would* make her father pay. She had never been more certain of anything in her life.

to be continued in:
The House That Jack Built

THE HOUSE THAT JACK BUILT

Robert Asprin and
Linda Evans

⟪ Chapter 1 ⟫

Skeeter Jackson wasn't in jail.

And that was so overwhelming a shock, he wasn't entirely sure
what to do with himself. The one thing he *didn't* want to do was hang
around the infirmary, where Bergitta lay in the recovery room after
emergency surgery and where Senator John Caddrick sat bellowing
like a wounded musk-ox, threatening to shut down the station around
their ears. So he ducked past crowds of shaken tourists, wounded in
the riot at Primary, slithered past news crews and the irate, fuming
Senator—who was still taking up a valuable medical technician's time
to wash tear gas out of his eyes—and headed out into the vast crowds
thronging the Commons.

He didn't really know where he was going or what he intended to
do, once he got there. He didn't have a job any longer, and wasn't likely
to find a soul on station to hire him, particularly not with the kind of
trouble Time Terminal Eighty-Six had brewing. Skeeter threaded his
way through the jostling crowds, ignoring the shocked gossip flying
loose through Commons, and wondered for perhaps the fifteen
millionth time what had become of his friends, young Julius, who'd
been born in ancient Rome, and—far more devastatingly—down-
time refugees Ianira and Marcus and both their little girls. Ianira was
the leader of the entire community of down-timers stranded on the
time terminal, Speaker for the Found Ones' Council, and the
inspiration for the fastest-growing up-time religion in the world.

387

Not only major VIPs in anybody's book, but very nearly the only friends Skeeter possessed. They'd all disappeared in the middle of a riot, the first of many to hit Shangri-La Station during the past week, and despite massive searches, not a trace of them had been found. Either they'd managed to escape down one of the open time-touring gates or they'd been kidnapped and smuggled out. Or—and he had to swallow hard at the thought—somebody'd cut them into small pieces and dropped them down an unstable gate. Like the Bermuda Triangle, maybe . . .

"Skeeter!"

He looked around, startled, and found Kit Carson homing in.

Panic struck.

"Don't bolt!" The retired time scout held up a hand as he hurried through the crowd. "I just want to talk."

Skeeter paused, gauging the expression in Kit's eyes—a surprisingly friendly look—and decided not to run. "Okay," he shrugged, waiting. After all, Kit had stood up for him in the station manager's office high above Commons floor, when Security Chief Mike Benson had been chomping at the bit to toss him into the nearest jail cell—or maybe through the aerie's glass window walls. A long shiver caught Skeeter's spine at that too-recent memory. Mike Benson had dragged him up from the station's sub-basement battleground in cuffs, facing murder charges. Neither he nor the station's down-timer refugees had really had any choice *but* fight to the death, trying to wrest Bergitta away from her kidnappers, a group of Islamic *jihad* fighters.

The *Ansar Majlis* had styled themselves after the original *Ansar,* the religiously motivated nineteenth-century "dervishes" of the Sudan, famed for routing British forces and killing General Gordon at Khartoum. The terrorist members of the *Ansar Majlis* had dragged Bergitta down into the station's sub-basement, where they would've beaten her to death, after raping her. But that hadn't mattered a damn to Mike Benson.

If not for Kit's support . . .

He didn't even know why Kit had come to his rescue.

So he shoved his hands into his pockets, suppressing a wince where the cuffs had dug into his flesh, and waited for Kit to catch up. The world-famous time scout actually clapped him on the shoulder, startling Skeeter considerably.

"Come down to Edo Castletown with me," Kit said over the roar of voices on Commons. "I need your help."

Skeeter blinked. "My help? What for?"

Kit grinned at his tone, but the smile faded too quickly. "After you left the aerie, Ronisha ran computer records checks for everyone who entered the station today. I'm afraid the databanks are a mess, thanks to that riot Caddrick started." Kit shook his head and made a derisive sound of disgust. "Half the arriving tourists haven't even scanned their records in properly yet. But Ronisha thinks she's got a line on the *Ansar Majlis* leadership. A couple of businessmen, seemed legit enough. Came to open up a new outfitter's shop for the Arabian Nights sector. They checked into their hotel, nice and quiet, then tried to contact some of your pals from that murderous construction crew. By radio, mind."

Skeeter's brows rose. "Don't tell me, they tried to contact those little radio handsets Benson took off those bodies we left downstairs?"

One corner of Kit's mouth twitched. "You got it. Mike intercepted the call. That down-time kid, Hashim, who helped you with the rescue? He helped us out again, in a big way. He answered the transmission, told them there'd been trouble, but he'd meet them, bring them up to date." Kit thinned his lips. "They're in my hotel, Skeeter. I want them *out*."

"Alive?" Skeeter asked softly.

Kit's eyes blazed, giving Skeeter a dangerous, top-to-toes assessment that left Skeeter sweating despite the bravado of his return stare. "Preferably," Kit said in a low growl. "With as little damage to young Hashim as possible."

"No argument, there. Where'd he agree to meet them? At the Neo Edo?"

Kit nodded.

"When?"

The retired time scout checked his watch. "About fifteen minutes from now."

Skeeter swore. "I'll need a good disguise. Get me somebody's headdress. And a tool belt." He paused. "You're sure you've got the right assholes? Not just a couple of innocent Arab businessmen looking for long-lost relatives?"

"We're sure," Kit said grimly. "They asked Hashim to bring schematics of the station's brig, so they could plan an attack. They aim to break their buddies out of jail."

Skeeter whistled. "That's bad."

"You're not kidding, that's bad. Right now, they're in room Four Twenty-Three, waiting for Hashim to show up with his pals."

Skeeter nodded. "All right, let's get this over with."

A quarter of an hour later, Skeeter and young Hashim ibn Fahd were walking softly down a carpeted corridor on the fourth floor of the Neo Edo hotel, the latter in Neo Edo livery. Skeeter wore a long headdress shrugged down across his shoulders and a toolbelt at his hips. The toolbelt hid an eight-inch Bowie knife and a snub-nosed revolver shoved into a paddle holster inside his trousers. Kit, too, wore a disguising headdress and toolbelt, and carried a sleek little semi-automatic pistol. Security had closed off the corridor at either end, stationing officers in the stairwells and elevator.

The fourth floor was as secure as they could make it without evacuating innocents from adjoining rooms, which they *couldn't* do, not and keep the element of surprise. A bad situation to be sure, but letting terrorists like the *Ansar Majlis* continue to operate was a good deal worse. Five minutes earlier, security had reported the arrival of three additional men from the Time Tripper Hotel, also newcomers to the station. At a guess, the leadership of the *Ansar Majlis* had gathered for a high-level pow-wow. Once inside the room, Skeeter and Kit would probably have only moments before the leadership realized they were meeting with decoys. As Kit knocked, Skeeter told his hands to stop shaking.

The door to room Four Twenty-Three opened just a crack and a low voice spoke in Arabic. Skeeter's heart was pounding. He hoped like hell those incarcerated construction workers in the brig had given Hashim the correct code word to respond with. Hashim answered the challenge, his stance cocky and belligerent. A chain rattled, then the door opened wider. Hashim slipped to one side, out of the line of fire. Kit shoved the door open and strode in. Skeeter followed at his heels, raking the room with his gaze. He found only three men in sight. The door to the bathroom was partially closed. *At least one in there, maybe another in the closet . . .*

A well-dressed man of about fifty stared at them through narrowed eyes. He spat out something that Kit responded to with a gutteral monosyllable. At the doorway, Hashim let loose a voluble flood of Arabic, drawing attention to himself. Then the closet door opened and a new voice spoke sharply. The effect was electrifying. Weapons appeared with terrifying swiftness. The man in the closet grabbed Kit by the arm, clearly demanding to know who the hell he was.

The next instant, he was airborne, flipping arse about head past the end of one bed. A gunshot cracked as Skeeter dove toward the bathroom door, drawing his Bowie knife and slamming it into the unprotected thigh of the man between him and Kit. The man screamed. Another gunshot blasted loose, but Kit wasn't where the bullets impacted. He was across the room, then somebody else screamed and went flying into the mirrored closet. Skeeter kicked in the bathroom door, coming in low to the floor, and heard a yell of pain just as bullets tore through the doorway at head height. The door caught the shooter full in the face and sent him reeling back against the john. Skeeter kicked his feet out from under him. The man went down hard, struck his head against the toilet tank, reeled face-first into the shower stall and lay still. Skeeter disarmed him swiftly, then lunged back out into the hotel room.

Hashim stood on top of the man Skeeter had stabbed, grinding his wrist into the carpet and holding a gun he'd clearly just liberated. Out in the main room, the fight was over. Three men, dazed and bleeding, lay in crumpled heaps where Kit had tossed them. Kit was breathing hard, eyes narrowed down into slits, then let out a bellow that shook dust loose. "*Security!*"

Officers flooded into the room.

Kit stepped aside as handcuffs appeared and dazed men were wrestled into restraints. "Check the room next door," Kit said curtly.

"Make sure nobody was hurt. Bastards got off several shots that went through the wall."

Skeeter stood breathing hard in the bathroom doorway, hardly able to believe it was over so quickly. He turned over his own prisoner from the shower stall, gratefully stripped off the headdress and toolbelt, handed over the borrowed weapons, and gave Security his statement. "Do me a favor, will you?" he asked in a tight, controlled voice. "Find out what they know about Ianira's disappearance." Then, far too wound up from the adrenaline rush to just hang around, he headed out into the corridor, away from the stink of gunpowder and blood, wishing mightily for a glass of something cold to swallow.

"Skeeter."

He glanced up and found Kit heading his way, *sans* disguise. The prisoners were being dragged—or carried—out of room Four Twenty-Three. The door to room Four Twenty-Three was open as officers checked the frightened occupants for injuries and reassured a sobbing woman that the danger was over. "Security will take it from here," Kit told Skeeter. "Hashim's going down with them to translate. Good work. If you hadn't taken those two out, I might've ended up with a bullet in my back. I don't know about you, but I could do with a good, stiff drink and a plateful of hot food. How about I treat you to supper at the Silkworm Caterpillar while we talk?"

Skeeter swallowed surprise—and an involuntary rush of saliva—and was overwhelmed by a sudden flood of hunger, accompanied by a spreading sense of euphoria that he was still alive to *be* hungry. He couldn't recall when he'd eaten his last real meal and didn't want to remember too closely what it had consisted of, either.

"Okay," Skeeter nodded, meeting Kit's gaze. "Thanks."

He wondered what the retired time scout had in mind as they crossed the world-famous Neo Edo lobby, heading for the *Kaiko no Kemushi,* the Silkworm Caterpillar. Kit's restaurant, at least, appeared to have survived the riot at Primary intact, but the hotel lobby bore mute testament to the tear gas and the panic. Hotel employees sponged down silk wallpaper in an attempt to remove the residues. The snarl of an industrial carpet shampooer broke the elegant hush.

Workers were masked against fume exposure to the whitish, powdery film of chemical irritants left behind. What the cleanup would cost . . .

Beyond the lobby, decorative bridges across Edo Castletown's ornate goldfish ponds had been shattered, their railings smashed to splinters during the riot Senator Caddrick and his goons in uniform had instigated. Before the infamous politician's arrival, Edo Castletown had been one of TT-86's most picturesque sectors, with its Shinto Shrine and graceful pagoda-style rooflines. Skeeter clamped his lips as he traced the path of battle scars, broken shrubbery, and smashed ruin that had marred Edo Castletown's fragile beauty.

Too many of his few friends were missing, as a result of station riots.

Kit stood at Skeeter's shoulder, silent and grim as they watched cleanup crews trying to clear away the debris. Shopkeepers sorted through the wreckage of their merchandise. Rachel Eisenstein's medical triage teams, staffed mostly by volunteers since the trained medical personnel were all down at the infirmary, treating the seriously wounded, ministered to those suffering from tear gas exposure and minor injuries. Sue Fritchey's Pest Control crews huddled over a few small, dark shapes lying on the floor, trying to keep prehistoric birds and pterodactyls alive where they'd been tear gassed, trampled, and almost drowned in the goldfish ponds. Sue, tears streaming down both cheeks, was setting the broken wing bones of a crow-sized flying reptile while one assistant held the wing carefully stretched taut and another administered anesthesia and monitored the animal's life signs.

"*Zigsi*," Skeeter muttered under his breath, using one of his favorate Mongolian curses. "Doesn't Caddrick know it's against the law for *anybody* to discharge tear gas on a time terminal? Even law enforcement agents?"

Kit shot him a sidewise glance, mouth hard as marble. "Men like John Caddrick don't care what the law says. And neither do the kind of agents who'd come to Shangri-La with him."

Skeeter shivered, afraid of Senator John Caddrick in spite of—or maybe due to—his rough Mongol upbringing. He recalled with satisfaction trading assaults with Caddrick, back at the leading edge of that riot, but . . . One of these days, Caddrick was going to calm down enough to remember what Skeeter had said and done.

Skeeter knew about powerful men.

Apparently, so did Kit Carson.

"Come on, I need that drink." Kit steered Skeeter past sliding rice-paper doors into the softly lit Silkworm Caterpiller, with its smooth, polished wood floors and delicate porcelain vases and its priceless bonsai cherry trees, bathed in their full-spectrum grow lights and grafted—rumor had it—from cuttings taken from the National Cherry Trees of Washington. The scent of expensive cuisine relaxed Skeeter a degree as he followed Kit toward a private cubicle near the back, threading his way past half a dozen Asian billionaires, two instantly recognizable international singing stars, and a haphazard collection of the merely wealthy, all of them discussing the riot and Senator Caddrick's presence in hushed, worried tones.

Kit motioned him into a chair. "Sit down, Skeeter. You look exhausted." At his signal, a waitress glided up, silent and lovely in a silk kimono and delicate geisha's coif. Kit ordered for them both—in Japanese. Moments later, a steady parade of silk-garbed waitresses materialized, bringing an avalanche of delicate porcelain dishes heaped with the most fabulous food Skeeter had ever smelled and—more importantly—several glassfuls of liquid stress relief. Skeeter upended the first and felt better immediately. As attentive servers brought more whiskey and poured steaming green tea into tiny cups, Kit smiled, the corners of his eyes crinkling into weatherbeaten folds. "Dig in. Enjoy. You've earned it."

Skeeter had no idea what he was eating, but it was all fabulous. Even the stuff that was raw. He'd certainly eaten stranger stuff as a kid, stranded in twelfth-century Mongolia. Kit let him eat in silence, paying attention to his own meal, then glanced up when a bellboy in Neo Edo uniform delivered a heavy leather briefcase. Kit nodded toward a chair and tipped the young man. "Thanks."

Skeeter frowned. "What's with the briefcase?"

"The real reason I asked you here," Kit said, his glance intent.

"Oh, great," Skeeter groused, toying with his chopsticks. "Make me feel better, why don't you?"

"Actually," Kit chuckled, "I hope to do just that."

Skeeter looked up from the dripping bite of whatever wonderful concoction was dangling from his chopsticks and waited, abruptly wary. He did not expect what came next.

"I want to talk about your future," Kit said, sitting back and toying with the edge of his plate. When Skeeter just stared, the grizzled former scout gave him that world famous jack-o-lantern grin and chuckled. "All right, Skeeter. You've been remarkably patient. I'll end the suspense." He dug into the briefcase and dropped a sheaf of computer printouts onto the table. Skeeter looked curiously into Kit's eyes, but the retired scout merely stuffed more of his expensive lunch into his weathered face, so Skeeter picked up the stack and riffled through it. And discovered he was holding copies of the arrest reports for each of the thirty-one crooks Skeeter had put out of business in the last seven and a half days.

Skeeter had, during the past week, managed a feat even he hadn't thought possible. He had stunned the entire 'eighty-sixer population of Shangri-La Station virtually speechless. He'd only had to make citizens' arrests of seventeen pickpockets, five grifters, eight con artists, and a bait-and-switch vendor to do it, the latter peddling fake copies of an inertial mapping system that kept track of a person's movements away from a known point of origin, like a time-touring gate. The real gizmos had saved lives. Substituting fake ones could kill an unwary tourist, fast.

Once La-La Land had recovered the use of its stunned, multi-partite tongue, of course, rumor had run wild. "It's a new scam," went the most popular version, "he's up to something." And so he was. Just not what the rumor-mongers *thought* he was up to. Skeeter had taken his new "job" far more seriously than either of the ones he'd lost, thanks to his frantic search for clues to Ianira's disappearance. To his own surprise, Skeeter Jackson made a profoundly diligent undercover detective.

Judging from the printouts Skeeter now held, that fact was not lost on Kit Carson. He just didn't know what Kit had in mind to do about it.

Kit was grinning at him, though. He leaned forward, still smiling, and tapped the printouts in Skeeter's hands. "Mike Benson, bless him, has been glowering for days over this. If he hadn't been so busy trying to keep this station from exploding into violence, I expect he'd have called you in to explain by now."

Belatedly, Skeeter realized he'd made the head of Shangri-La security look . . . Well, if not outright incompetent, downright foolish. Thirty-one arrests in seven and a half days was a helluva haul, even for TT-86. Kit was studying Skeeter intently, eyes glinting in the indirect lighting. "I must confess to a considerable curiosity."

Skeeter sighed and set the reports down. "Not that I expect you to believe me," he met Kit's gaze, "but with Ianira and her family gone . . ." He blinked rapidly, told himself sternly that now was not the time to sniffle. His reputation for playing on a rube's emotions was too well known. "Well, dammit, somebody's got to make this place fit for the down-timer kids to grow up in! I was thinking about Ianira's little girls the other day, right about the time I saw a pickpocket snatch that Chilean lady's wallet. It made me so flaming mad, I just walked over and grabbed him. Maybe you haven't heard, but Artemisia and Gelasia call me 'Uncle Skeeter.' The last time I was anybody's uncle . . ."

He shut his mouth hastily, not wanting to talk about the deep feelings he still harbored for little Temujin. He'd seen the child born nine months after he'd fallen through an unstable gate, the one that had dumped him at the feet of the khan of forty-thousand Yakka Mongol yurts, or *gers,* as the Mongolians, themselves, called their felted tents. Yesukai had named Skeeter his first-born son's honorary uncle, effectively placing his heir under the protection of the *bogdo,* the sacred mountain spirit the Yakka clan had believed Skeeter to be. He didn't talk about it, much. It was a deeply private thing, standing as honorary uncle to the future Genghis Khan. Skeeter's rescue by the time scout who'd pushed TT-86's Mongolian Gate had caused Skeeter to lose that "nephew." And now the *Ansar Majlis* had deprived him of his honorary nieces.

Ianira's beautiful children . . .

Kit's eyes had darkened; he spoke very quietly. "I'm sorry, Skeeter. We've all searched."

He nodded, surprised Kit had believed him, for once.

Kit pointed to the arrest reports with a lacquered chopstick. "What I'd really like to know is how you managed to catch thirty-one criminals in such a short time."

"*How?*" Skeeter blinked, caught off guard by the question. "Well, jeez, Kit, it was dead easy." He felt the flush begin at the back of his neck and creep up his cheeks. "I mean, I was good at that kind of thing, once. It's not hard to spot the tricks of the trade, when you know 'em as well as I do. Did."

"You realize," Kit said slowly, "a lot of people are saying you pulled the jobs yourself, then planted part of the 'take' on those people, so there'd be a fall guy to blame?"

Skeeter's flush deepened, angry this time. "Doesn't surprise me. Although it's the stupidest thing I've heard in a while. One of those jerks had a stolen money roll with ten thousand bucks in it. If I were still in the business, do you honestly think I'd've turned over ten *grand* to station security?"

Kit held up both hands. "Easy, Skeeter. I didn't say I agreed with them."

"Huh. You must be the only up-time 'eighty-sixer who doesn't."

"Not quite," Kit said softly. "But I have noted the problem. I've also noticed how hard you've been trying to get another honest job. At the same time you've been hauling in all these petty thieves and swindlers." He tapped the sheaf of arrest reports again. "And I know why you've been turned down, too." Kit sat back, then, studying him once more. "Tell me if I'm wrong, but it seems to me you're mighty dedicated to this, ah, new crusade of yours."

"Damn right, I am," Skeeter growled, looking Kit square in the eye. "Mopping bathroom floors never did exactly challenge me. And I don't want the kids on this station growing up where somebody with light fingers can walk off with everything they've worked hard to earn." He added with a bitterness he couldn't conceal, "I never did roll an 'eighty-sixer, you know. Family's family, whatever you think of me."

Kit didn't respond to that, not directly. "So you intend to keep up the vigilance? Continue making citizens' arrests?"

"I do."

The former scout nodded sharply, as though satisfied. "Good. It occurs to me that your, ah, unique talents could be useful, very useful around here. How much did that ridiculous maintenance job of yours pay?"

Skeeter blinked. "Five bucks an hour, why?"

"Five bucks? That's not a salary, that's slavery! Barely enough to pay station taxes, let alone rent. What were you eating, sawdust?"

Skeeter refrained from pointing out that a good many 'eighty-sixers subsisted on less. "Well, I didn't eat fancy, but I got by."

The retired scout snorted. "I can just imagine what you were living on. Tell you what, young Jackson. You take yourself upstairs to my office, fill out the paperwork, I'll put you on payroll for a month, trial basis. Special roving security consultant for the Neo Edo. Set your own hours as you see fit, minimum eight a day, starting at, say, twenty dollars an hour. At the end of a month, if your arrest record justifies it, we'll see about making it permanent."

Skeeter tried to scrape his jaw off the carpeted floor and failed utterly.

Kit's sudden, glittering grin was terrifying. "Know of a better way to catch a con artist than send one of their own kind after 'em? My God, Skeeter, thirty-one arrests in a *week*? That's more than Security caught last *year*. I'm not faulting Mike or his people, but you've got a damned fine point about it being easy to spot the tricks when you've used 'em yourself."

Kit shoved back his chair and stood up. "Come on, Skeeter, I'll take you upstairs, introduce you to the personnel clerk. Robby Ames is a good kid, he'll show you the ropes. Then go home and get some sleep. Tomorrow morning, I'd appreciate a guided tour of Commons. I want to let things cool down out there, before we take a look-see at what we're up against, with Caddrick on station. And frankly, I'd like to watch you work. Maybe we could hit the Britannia crowd when the gate opens in the morning? There's sure to be a pile of pickpockets on hand for that. We'll figure out strategy while we're at it, stuff like should you stick to the Neo Edo proper or follow potential thieves off premises when they follow hotel guests?"

Skeeter still hadn't managed to scrape his lower jaw off the floor.

"Oh, and you'll need a squawky with all the Security frequencies and a training class on codes and procedures. I'll talk to a friend of mine in security about it." He chuckled wickedly. "When Mike Benson finds out, he'll eat nails and spit tacks."

Skeeter Jackson suddenly realized that Kit was not only enjoying this, the offer was serious. For the first time since his return from Mongolia, somebody other than a down-timer *trusted* him. For a long, dangerous moment, he was blind, throat so tightly closed he could hardly swallow. Then he was on his feet, clearing his throat roughly. "You won't regret this, Kit. Swear to God, you won't regret it."

"I'd better not!" But he was grinning as he said it and for the first time since Skeeter had known Kit Carson, the threat didn't terrify him. Kit stuck out a hand and Skeeter grasped it hard, suddenly finding himself grinning fit to crack his face in half.

My God, he thought as he followed Kit Carson out of the Silkworm Caterpillar. *A private eye!* Working for Kit Carson, of all people, the man who'd once threatened to shove him down the nearest unstable gate, minus his privates.

La-La Land would never be the same again.

He wasn't entirely sure Shangri-La Station would recover from the shock.

Jenna Nicole Caddrick had spent a full eight days trapped in a little room at the top of a scrubbed, wooden staircase, staring out the window into the grimy, soot-filled working world of Spitalfields, London. She was too ill to travel even as far as the kitchen. Dr. Mindel's tinctures left her woozy and afraid for the tiny life growing inside her, but the gunshot wound to her head required treatment and she was too deep in shock to protest necessity.

Her strength began to return, however, as the wound healed, and with healing came the restless urge to *do* something. She couldn't spend the rest of her life sitting beside a window, disguised as a Victorian man in a world she scarcely understood. And Carl's blood called out for vengeance, Carl's and Aunt Cassie's, both, murdered by her own father's hired killers. When Jenna woke early on the morning of her eighth day in London, she knew she had to do something to stop her father. She lay staring for a long time at the ceiling, stained where rainwater had seeped through the roof at some point before Noah had paid to have it repaired, and considered where she might begin.

The first thing they had to do, of course, was survive.

But there was plenty she could do, while surviving. And the first thing to enter Jenna's mind was the need to find Ianira Cassondra. The tug of bandages across the side of her head, where Dr. Mindel had shaved the hair close to treat the grazing path of a stranger's bullet, brought a deep shiver. It hadn't been one of her father's hired killers, who'd shot her. A down-timer had done that. A native Londoner who'd saved Jenna's life, then realized what Ianira could do, with her gift for prophetic clairvoyance. Her erstwhile rescuer had calmly shot Jenna in cold blood, then had disappeared into the drizzling yellow rain with the Cassondra of Ephesus.

Eventually, footsteps thumped up the wooden steps outside her bedroom. Jenna sat up, grateful for the lessening of dizziness from concussion, as Noah Armstrong pushed open the door with her breakfast tray. "Good morning." The detective smiled.

"Good morning, Noah." She didn't know, yet, whether the enigmatic private detective was male or female; but it didn't really matter. She owed Armstrong her life, several times over. If Aunt Cassie hadn't hired the best, before the *Ansar Majlis* had shot Cassie Tyrol dead in New York . . .

"You look better this morning," Noah smiled, grey eyes warm and friendly. Dresssed in a Victorian woman's long skirt and a plain brown bodice ten years out of fashion, its perenially high collar obscuring Noah's throat—and therefore any hint of whether or not Noah possessed an Adam's apple—the detective wore what might've been a wig or real hair pulled back into a bun at the nape of the neck. "Are you hungry?"

She nodded. "A little."

"Good."

The cereal was hot and filling, the toast nicely buttered, the bacon fried crisp. Steaming tea sent up a fragrant cloud of steam. "Noah?" Jenna asked softly a few minutes later.

"Yeah?"

"We have to find Ianira."

"Marcus and I are taking care of it," Noah said firmly. "You're staying right here. Where you'll be safe."

"But—"

"No." The detective held her gaze, grey eyes hard as marble, now brooking no disagreement. "You're far too valuable to risk, Jenna. And you had a damned close call, the last time you were outside this house." Noah touched the side of her head. "This is nearly healed, thank goodness. And without infection, which is a small miracle."

Jenna's lips twitched. "I thought it was all the carbolic you keep pouring over my scalp."

The corners of Noah's eyes crinkled slightly. "Cleanliness *is* next to godliness, they say, particularly around here. Be that as it may, I won't risk seeing you shot dead, next time."

She considered arguing. Then realized she was still too weak and shaky to do much of anything physical, anyway, so she subsided, at least for the moment. Maybe she could think of some way to help that didn't require leaving this house? "What are you and Marcus doing?" she asked, instead. "To find her?"

Noah sighed, sitting in a chair beside the window. The corners of the detective's mouth had drawn down slightly. "We know the man who took her is a doctor, and a man of means. Wealthy enough to wear a silk top hat and a good frock coat. He frequents the area of the Royal Opera and Covent Garden, yet he clearly knows the streets of SoHo. Well enough to lose himself in that maze of nasty little alleyways. If I have to, I'll check out the identity of every physician, every surgeon in London." Noah leaned forward in the chair and touched Jenna's cheek gently. "Don't worry, kid. We'll find out who he is and we'll get her back."

Jenna bit her lip. If—no, when, it had to be *when*—they finally did rescue Ianira, she would come to this house expecting a joyous reunion with her family, only to learn that three *years* had passed in her children's lives . . .

Jenna, herself, wasn't over that shock, yet.

Noah had been forced to stay down the Wild West Gate's timeline long enough to catch up to the Britannia Gate's timeline, which ran three years later than Denver's 1885. Would Ianira's little girls even remember their mother? *If* they could even find Ianira . . . London was a depressingly immense and sprawling city, teeming with more than five million people crammed in cheek-by-jowl, inhabiting everything from spacious palaces to ramshackle staircase landings and stinking gutters. The number of places to search would've overwhelmed even a die-hard optimist.

Outside, angry voices in the street were shouting what sounded like abuse at their neighbors. Jenna's startlement gave way to the beginnings of alarm as she stared from the window to Noah. "What's happening?"

The detective moved to look outside and scowled. "Bastards."

"What is it?" she asked sharply, trying to rise.

"A gang of unemployed dock rats, hassling Dr. Mindel."

Ugly taunts and anti-Semitic slurs slammed against the window like hailstones. At least it wasn't the pack of up-time killers looking for *them.* Jenna sank back down against the pillows and shivered. "But why? Dr. Mindel's one of the kindest men I've ever met."

Noah's jaw tightened above the collar of the outdated dress. "Annie Chapman was just found murdered, over in Hanbury Street. Along with a leather apron in a basin of water. Half the East End now thinks a Jewish boot finisher killed her this morning." The detective glanced around at Jenna's involuntary sound and met Jenna's shocked stare. "Get used to it, kid. The East End is set to explode. Anti-Semitism's running wild, because everyone's convinced it has to be a foreigner killing these women. Which is another reason I don't want you outside. You're disguised as a man, Jenna, a foreign-sounding man. Those dock rats down there are going to make life damned dangerous for foreigners in these parts during the next several months. Believe me, it's just too risky out there."

Jenna swallowed hard, listening to the ugly shouts in the street. She wasn't accustomed to such hatred, such naked prejudice. She touched her abdomen, where Carl's baby grew, and realized she couldn't risk herself. Not yet. Someday, her father would pay for what he'd done, wrecking her life, ending Carl's and Aunt Cassie's in a bullet-riddled pool of blood. But for the moment, she had to survive.

She had never hated necessity more.

Ronisha Azzan was a woman with a major-league problem.

Seated in Bull Morgan's office high above the snow-choked valleys of the Himalayan mountains, with her boss in jail and terrorists loose on station, she was preparing for a face-off with the most influential—and dangerous—politician of the era. Ronisha studied Granville Baxter, TT-86's Time Tours CEO, with whom she shared a Masai heritage, and wondered whether or not she had just made the biggest mistake of her career.

"Are you out of your mind?" Bax demanded as the aerie's elevator hummed upwards with its first load of reporters. "Letting a pack of *newsies* into a meeting this critical?"

Ronisha held the Time Tours' executive's gaze steadily, one of the few souls in Shangri-La Station tall enough to meet Bax's gaze eye to eye. "This is one meeting that *has* to be public. And you know why."

The tall executive's lips thinned. "Bull's meeting was public, too!" It came out understandably bitter.

"Yes, it was." She was only too aware of her precarious situation. "Bull's meeting *was* public. But I'm not Bull Morgan. And Bull Morgan is not *me.*"

Almost absently, she flicked invisible lint from her brightly colored suit, its rich African patterns reproduced in silk, rather than plain and ordinary cotton, and shook back over her shoulder three solid feet of intricate braids, most of them her own. Ronisha favored four-inch spike heels to go with her African textiles and elaborate coifs. She hadn't yet met the man she couldn't intimidate, given half a minute's time and a chance to crush his fingers in a handshake while she outmaneuvered him at his own game—whether that game involved matters of the bedroom or the boardroom.

Ronisha Azzan was deeply proud of her Masai heritage and at the moment, that heritage was very nearly her only weapon. The Masai were famed as lion hunters. And the biggest, nastiest man-eating lion in the universe had just strolled into her *kraal.* Ronisha smiled, not at all nicely. As Shangri-La Station's Deputy Manager, Ronisha Azzan was nobody's assistant *anything*—a fact Senator John Paul Caddrick had yet to learn. If she could manage to keep her knees from shaking visibly while she taught him.

Granville Baxter stared hard at her for a long moment, brows furrowed. Then her meaning struck home and he started to grin. A weak grin, given what they had yet to face, but a grin, nonetheless. "Woman, you are wasted in station management. You ought to be a tycoon someplace, rolling in money."

"Oh, I don't think so. Somebody's got to do this job." The elevator doors opened with a faint *ping,* disgorging a cluster of reporters, most of whom stared up at her for a long, disconcerted moment. Newly arrived from up time with the Senator, they hadn't yet met her. She rose from her half-leaning seat against the corner of Bull's desk.

"Welcome to TT-86. Ronisha Azzan, Deputy Station Manager. Yes, set up right there, that's fine, anywhere along here. Glad to assist you. If you have any questions about power connections and cables, my administrative assistant can help you out. Bernie, see to it our guests have what they need. No, I'm sorry, we'll have to wait for the Senator's arrival before I make any official statements . . ."

From a corner of her eye, she saw Bax shake his head and mutter, "Ronnie, I hope you know what we're doing."

Deep inside, where she wouldn't have let anyone see, Ronisha hoped so, too.

Senator John Caddrick arrived ten minutes later. The elevator doors slid open with another soft *ping* to reveal the red-faced enemy, eyes nearly scarlet from the aftermath of the tear gas. Ronisha Azzan narrowed her own eyes as Caddrick halted for just a fraction of a second at the threshold between elevator and office, taking in the glare of lights, the shining camera lenses, and the small forest of microphones. Clearly, the Senator had planned on intimidating a suitably cowed and trembling assistant manager, rather than walking into a live press conference.

As he swept his startled gaze toward Ronisha, the elevator doors attempted to close automatically. He had to jump forward in unseemly haste to avoid the embarrassment of being carried all the way down to Commons again. Behind him, a staffer caught the doors and reopened them as Caddrick stalked forward in silence, leaving his legislative aides and a whole pack of armed, stone-faced federal marshals to trail into the aerie behind him. The Senator made a visible, valiant, and not very successful effort to ignore the electrifying presence of the press corps.

She took that as her cue to launch an offensive of her own.

"Senator Caddrick," she said coolly, "welcome to Time Terminal Eighty-Six. Ronisha Azzan, Deputy Station Manager. This is Granville Baxter, Shangri-La Time Tours CEO. On behalf of Shangri-La Station, please allow me to extend our heartfelt condolences regarding your recent losses. However . . ." and she let a hint of steel creep into her voice, "in accordance with up-time laws governing the safety of time terminals and their official residents and guests, I need to remind you of a few laws regarding conduct on time terminals."

Caddrick's eyes widened slightly, then narrowed with a dangerous glint.

Ronisha plunged ahead. "It is against inter-temporal law to incite riot, or to aid and abet the illegal discharge of chemical agents banned from use on any time terminal, whether by a private citizen or by a member of law enforcement." She flicked a gaze at the marshals, who carried short-barreled riot guns and stared straight through her as though she were vermin. Clearly, they didn't give a damn about breaking inconvenient laws on the other side of a time terminal's Primary.

She faced Caddrick again. "It is illegal, as well, to willfully endanger the lives and property of station guests and residents. Senator, your actions here have put at risk the lives of several hundred innocents on Shangri-La Station. You have also violated several endangered species protection acts by putting at risk the only living population of prehistoric birds and pterodactyls in the world. If any of those animals die, you can be charged with several serious felonies. This station cannot and will not risk a repeat of the incidents you have created since your arrival. Have I made myself clear on these points?" Without giving him time to respond, she added, "Now, then. What, exactly, brings you to my time terminal? Please bear in mind that your answers will be recorded for posterity. Or the courts." She nodded pleasantly toward the utterly enchanted newsies and tried to ignore the terrifying presence of those cold-eyed marshals and their wicked riot guns.

Speaking very softly, which in no way disguised the menace in his voice, Senator John Caddrick said, "Am I to understand you're going to put *me* in jail?"

Ronisha drew herself up to her full height, augmented by stiletto heels, and forced a smile down the full seven inches of her superior stature to the Senator's furious grey eyes. "Not at all, Senator. But you do realize, I hope, that my first concern must be the safety of this station and its residents and guests. I cannot permit *any* situation to threaten human or protected animal lives on TT-86, no matter how well intentioned the action. Surely you, of all people, must understand that?"

She could see it in his eyes, the look of shocked fury that said, *You devious, black bitch* . . . and coldly loathed him. Then he passed a hand across his eyes, a hand that visibly shook, and said in an unsteady voice, "Forgive me, Ms. Azzan, I'm not quite myself today . . . You see, I just received word that the *Ansar Majlis* brought my little girl onto this station. And with the press broadcasting riots and murders on TT-86, naturally we thought it prudent to bring along federal marshals . . ."

Oh-oh. Silent alarm klaxons sounded. If Jenna Caddrick had been dragged through one of TT-86's gates by her up-time kidnappers, Shangri-La Station was in more serious trouble than even she had realized. A man like John Caddrick wouldn't need any additional ammunition to shut them down for good. And he was damned effective at playing to the press.

So she played his game to the hilt, taking the Senator's arm solicitously and guiding him to a chair. "Senator, please, sit down. There's no need for armed warfare between us. Everyone on TT-86 is in deep sympathy with your pain and loss." John Caddrick wasn't the only person in this room who knew the tricks of playing to the press. She wasn't Coralisha Azzan's grandchild for nothing.

Ronisha glanced over one shoulder, looking for her executive assistant. "Bernie, a glass of scotch and soda for the Senator, please." Her assistant handed it over and Caddrick sipped, hand still trembling visibly. Ronisha waited for just a moment longer, keeping her expression carefully concerned, then said quietly, "Now, then, Senator, why don't you fill us in on exactly what you've learned that's brought you to us? Tell us how we can help."

She seated herself in Bull Morgan's chair and composed herself to listen, switching on the digital pad that would send her handwritten notes directly to her computer, as well as turning on the room's meeting-recorder system. Cameras near the ceiling tracked silently, mirroring the swing of press cameras as Senator John Caddrick began to speak.

"Ten days ago," the Senator said heavily, "tragedy struck my family. Again. You must be aware that I lost my wife several years ago to a drunk driver? She was killed trying to get home to my daughter's birthday party. Jenna . . ." He blinked rapidly, eyes reddened and wet. "My daughter and I never got over it, particularly poor little Jenna, she was so young when my wife died. My wife's sister, Cassie Tyrol, became a second mother to her. Jenna Nicole adored her aunt. Wanted to follow her onto the stage, was studying film . . ." He paused, wiped his eyes distractedly with unsteady fingers. "Jenna met her aunt the day Cassie died, at a restaurant in New York. Cassie had flown in from New Hollywood to see her. There was an atrocity . . ."

Ronisha knew all about the terrorist hit in New York. "Yes. I know. The *Ansar Majlis.*"

"This crazy damned Brotherhood!" Senator Caddrick bit out, voice harsh. "They've declared open warfare on the Lady of Heaven Temples. I've tried for years to warn Congress something like this was bound to happen, letting down-timers onto the time terminals in wholesale droves . . ." He shook his head. "Cassie was heavily involved in the Temple, you see, very public in her support. Her last film was about the Temple. It was a smash success and she donated the proceeds to the Templars . . . and now this Brotherhood . . ." his voice was breaking up, his eyes wet.

John Caddrick fought himself under control again with visible effort. "They sent a death squad after poor Cassie. Murdered her, right in the restaurant. Jenna disappeared. Kidnapped by the *Ansar Majlis.* The FBI has been working on it, of course, trying to track down *Ansar*

Majlis ringleaders in New York, but I hired a detective, a good one. Sid Kaederman's been trying to trace my daughter's possible movements after that attack in the restaurant. Mr. Kaederman believes Jenna was forcibly brought to TT-86 by her kidnappers. Jenna's bank account and bank box were emptied, the same day her aunt was murdered."

He looked up, finally, and met Ronisha's gaze. "Some of her friends at college thought Jenna and her roommate had been planning a trip down time, against my express wishes, of course, but they thought she'd made arrangements to buy tickets and a false identity through some underworld mobster, so I wouldn't find out. Jenna's been hyped on film-making all her life, same as her aunt, wanted to make historically accurate films. God knows, it was something she might have done, buying a time-tour ticket to make some idiotic movie. So I put Sid Kaederman to work on the lead.

"When the *Ansar Majlis* forced Jenna to empty her bank account for them, they discovered her tickets and her false identification papers. They forced her to come here, to use them, so they could get out of New York without being detected. But even though we know they came here, and we know the names on the false identities she purchased in New York a year ago, we don't know which down-time gate they might have gone through. None of Jenna's friends knew which gate she planned to visit and we couldn't trace the mobster who sold her the time-touring tickets. She used a different source than she'd used to buy the phony identities and we never traced the ticket-scalper."

John Caddrick drained the rest of the scotch in his glass, then leaned forward in his chair. "What I want, Ms. Azzan, is simple enough. I want my daughter back, alive and unharmed, *whatever it takes.*" The rasp of steel in the Senator's voice sent a chill of genuine terror down Ronisha's spine. "You may believe I've followed the reports of riots, kidnappings, and murders on this station with keen interest. If *anything* has happened to my little girl on this god-forsaken time terminal or down one of its gates, I will use my authority and influence to shut down this entire station. And you may rest assured, Ms. Azzan, these federal marshals *will* shut you down, if the situation warrants it."

Ronisha slipped a hand into her lap and pressed the buzzer under the lip of Bull's massive desk, the one that alerted security headquarters trouble was brewing in the station manager's office. She wanted Mike Benson up here, stat, and kicked herself for not having summoned him sooner.

"Senator," she had to force her voice to steadiness, "I think everyone in this room realizes how serious the situation is. Fortunately, we've obtained a very solid lead on the terrorists you came here hoping to trace. We have several of their henchmen under arrest and are fully informed as to the *Ansar Majlis'* plans. My chief of security has men acting on this information right now, sweeping the station to arrest several of the *Ansar Majlis'* key ringleaders, who arrived through Primary today."

Caddrick's eyes shot wide. "You have information on their plans?" he echoed, voice flat with surprise.

"Yes, we do. Several of the station's resident down-timers discovered the plot and fought a pitched battle against the terrorists, subduing them. Thanks to the down-timers, we have enough information to arrest the entire *Ansar Majlis* operation."

Shock detonated behind Caddrick's eyes. "My God! Why, that's—that's incredible! But that still doesn't tell us where Jenna is." Shock gave way to calculating hostility.

"No, it doesn't," she agreed, stalling for time while thinking fiercely, *Shag your butt, Benson, I need you up here,* and played what she hoped would not prove to be her final trump card. "Because we're dealing with international and inter-temporal terrorism, I don't think it's unreasonable to call in an uninterested third party. To oversee the investigations which will have to be launched. I certainly don't want to give the impression this station has anything to hide. And I'm certain you don't want the investigation to take on the appearance of a personal vendetta."

A few of the reporters suppressed delighted gasps.

Senator Caddrick glared at her while a slow red flush crept up his neck.

"Of course," Ronisha added, "*we* know it isn't anything of the kind. But surely you, of all people, must know how appearances can be deceiving. The public has a right to the truth, obtained in a fair, unbiased manner. Thank you, Senator, for insisting on an independent investigation by an unbiased team. If I recall inter-temporal statutes correctly, that kind of fact-finding mission would fall under the jurisdiction of the Inter-Temporal Court of the Hague. I propose we send a representative of the Bureau of Access Time Functions through Primary at its next cycle and request immediate assistance from an independent team of evaluators appointed by I.T.C.H."

She and Senator Caddrick locked gazes across the desk. She'd just made an enemy for life and knew it; but John Caddrick had walked into this room already a mortal enemy, so no ground was lost by insisting on an unbiased review team. Under normal circumstances, the very last thing *anyone* on station would want was an investigation by the Inter-Temporal Court. Zealous I.T.C.H. officers had been known to shut down station operations over minor violations, putting stations under direct Court control until new management could demonstrate its willingness and ability to comply with the last dotted "i" and crossed "t" of the law.

But these weren't ordinary circumstances.

She was fighting for the life of the station.

Senator Caddrick nodded slow agreement, despite the fury seething in his eyes. "Of course, Ms. Azzan. It was never my intention to conduct an official investigation personally, although I certainly will demand that one be launched immediately. I shall, of course, conduct a fact-finding mission of my own while I'm here."

There being nothing she could do to stop him, short of throwing him into the brig—which would not improve the station's image—Ronisha simply nodded graciously. "Now, then, Senator, you said your daughter had obtained forged identification papers? She and her kidnappers are travelling under assumed names, then. What names? Any information you can give us will be critical in tracing them."

"Yes, of course." The Senator was digging into a pocket for a CM disk, which he held out. Ronisha accepted the disk just as the emergency phone on the corner of Bull's desk jangled, its tones shrill in the hushed office. Ronisha glanced at it with a sinking sensation in her middle. Whoever was on the other end of that line knew what Ronisha was in the middle of, up here, how serious this meeting was.

"Excuse me, please," she said, picking up the phone. "Aerie, Azzan speaking. This had better be good."

"Mike Benson, reporting in!" The security chief had to shout above the roar in the background. "We've got the *Ansar Majlis* ringleaders under wraps."

"Fabulous," she said with a rush of relief.

"Do you still need me to answer that silent alarm?"

"Yes, please."

"On my way."

She hung up the phone and faced the expectant crowd in her office. "Now, then," she said pleasantly, "where were we, Senator? You were about to give us the information on your daughter's forged identifications, I believe."

Caddrick stared at her for long moments, clearly expecting her to explain the interruption. When she didn't, he glowered for a moment, then said coldly, "This disk contains the data we've gathered so far. Mr. Kaederman believes the *Ansar Majlis* ringleader, a notorious intersexual using the alias Noah Armstrong, used one of Jenna's forged identities to bring my daughter here. Jenna's kidnapper was probably travelling under the name of Benny Catlin."

Across the room, Granville Baxter came out of his chair to tap commands into the nearest computer terminal, pulling up Time Tours' records of gate departures.

"Perhaps, Senator," Ronisha suggested, "you might give us some insight into your daughter's interests and habits? Anything we can learn about Jenna, about the way she thinks, what she might do under stress, will increase our chances of locating her."

"Yes, of course. I brought some things with me, besides that disk." Senator Caddrick turned to an aide who hovered nearby. "Hand around those biographical packets, would you? And those photos of that bastard, Armstrong."

While Bax worked at the computer, a sweating senatorial aide passed dossiers around the room, first to Ronisha and the Time Tours CEO, then to the newsies, who struck like piranha. There were several photographs of Jenna Caddrick, all of them recent, as well as a photograph of the *Ansar Majlis* terrorist, Noah Armstrong. Ronisha realized with a start of surprise why the Senator had mistaken Skeeter Jackson for his daughter's kidnapper. From a full-frontal view, they didn't closely resemble one another, but there were distinct similarities of bone structure and coloring. From behind or at an oblique angle, the resemblance was strong enough to understand the mistaken identity. The brief document attached to the photos outlined Jenna Caddrick's habits, manners, routines, interests, and hobbies.

At the other end of the crowded office, Granville Baxter glanced up from the computer screen, looked over the photos, then cleared his throat. "I found Benny Catlin's tour records, but I'm afraid we still have a serious problem facing us—more serious than tracing Benny Catlin in London."

John Caddrick's glare was lethal. "What could possibly be more serious than locating my daughter's kidnapper?"

Bax held up the photograph of Noah Armstrong. "This."

"What *about* it?"

The Time Tours executive paused, then sipped air and looked like he wanted to bolt for the nearest exit. Ronisha Azzan wasn't sure just what the bad news would be, but she was already *quite* certain she wasn't going to like it.

Granville Baxter didn't disappoint her.

"Well, Senator, you see . . ." He held up a snapshot. "This photograph of your daughter's kidnapper . . . This isn't Benny Catlin."

《 Chapter 2 》

Of all the historians, criminologists, and reporters fortunate enough to win spots on the Ripper Watch Team, none was more determined to obtain the truth of the Ripper story than Dominica Nosette. Not one of the other team members had a quarter the professional ruthlessness she possessed in her big toe. The only one who came close was her partner, Guy Pendergast. And Dominica was utterly delighted with Guy, because he had done what no one else had managed since their arrival in London. He had discovered the identity of Jack the Ripper. The mysterious doctor mentoring the irretrievably mad James Maybrick was the guiding genius of the two-man team known to history as the Ripper. And Dominica intended to vault herself to fame and fortune on the coattails of their murderous partnership.

"His name is John Lachley," Guy had said breathlessly as they'd slipped out of Spaldergate House with their luggage, determined to break loose of their time guides' stranglehold. "He's a medical doctor, with training in the occult and ties to the East End. Came up out of SoHo, just west of Whitechapel. He's our man, I'll stake my reputation on it. Calls his house Tibor, mind. The same word our mystery Ripper used the night Polly Nichols died." Pendergast chuckled thinly. "And those fuzzy-brained idiots with me were so busy doting on that Irish poet, William Butler Yeats, they missed the clue entirely!"

John Lachley, they had since discovered, had ties to the royal family, as well, through the queen's grandson, Prince Albert Victor Christian Edward. And John Lachley had been born right in Whitechapel itself, in Middlesex Street, which explained the Ripper's familiarity with the streets. He'd gone to charity school, had John Lachley, and acquired his medical education in Scotland. Once known throughout the East End as Johnny Anubis, séance parlour medium and small-time occultist, Dr. John Lachley now lectured on mesmerism and other occult subjects to large audiences drawn from London's finest families. He was a member of the Theosophical Society, a respected physician with a surgery in Cleveland Street, a model subject of the crown in every way.

That much, Dominica Nosette and Guy Pendergast had managed to discover thus far, working on their own without those repressive, overly cautious Time Tours guides curtailing their every move. But why John Lachley was working with James Maybrick to murder East End whores, and what was in the letters Lachley was slowly tracking down, killing the previous owners to keep some dark and clearly critical secret, Dominica had no idea. She intended to find out.

The video she had already obtained of Lachley was worth a literal fortune, video footage showing him in company with the young prince, footage of him meeting the soon-to-be-notorious Aleister Crowley, and with the founders of the Golden Dawn magical order, Mathers and Waite and the rest. Whether or not these occultists were also involved in the conspiracy of the letters, Dominica didn't know. That, too, she intended to discover.

"We're going to win that Carson Historical Video Prize!" she told Guy Pendergast as they set out from the flat they'd rented in SoHo. "Lachley will strike again September thirtieth. The night of the double event . . ."

"Which means Elizabeth Stride and Catharine Eddowes *must* have possession of the letters he's after!"

"Yes. And Mary Kelly must have another one. Guy . . ." Dominica mused, slanting a glance up at her partner. "How good are you at picking pockets?"

"Picking pockets?" he echoed, brows drifting upward in startlement.

She smiled. "Well, it occurs to me that we could probably unlock the key to this whole thing if we could lay hands on one of those letters. Just long enough to photograph it. Then we slip it back into the pocket you steal it from, long before he kills Stride and Eddowes. All we have to do then is follow him after the double-event murders. Videotape *those*, then collect our Carson Prize. And rather an enormous amount of money," she ended smugly.

Guy Pendergast smiled slowly. "Dominica, my pet, you are brilliant."

"Of course I'm brilliant! I didn't get where I am by being stupid. We'll have to tackle Stride, since Catharine Eddowes is leaving London to head out to Kent, picking hops. It might be interesting to videotape Eddowes out there, working the harvest." She frowned. "You know, it doesn't make sense, that. If she's in possession of something so valuable that Lachley is committing brutal murder to obtain it, you'd think a woman like Catharine Eddowes would try to convert it into cash. She's plagued her own daughter for money so often, the poor thing moves every few weeks around South London, just to keep her mother from tapping her for tuppence. Yet Kate Eddowes walks—*walks,* mind you, in this weather—all the way from London to rural Kent, just to break her back working in wet fields picking hops as a migrant agricultural laborer."

"Maybe," Guy suggested dryly, "she hasn't cashed in on her letter because she can't read it."

Dominica dismissed that as chauvinist nonsense. "Don't be a boor. She was educated in St. John's Charity School, Potter's Field, Tooley Street. And all her friends described her as a scholarly, intense woman. Of course she can read it."

Her partner shrugged. "It was just an idea."

"Well, when we get our hands on whatever Long Liz Stride has, we shall find out, shan't we?"

Guy Pendergast chuckled. "Right."

So they set their faces east and started combing the dismal streets of Whitechapel, looking for one particular Swedish-born prostitute who had barely two weeks left to live.

※ ※ ※

Victoria Station was jam-packed with Ripperoons.

Skeeter, like most of the others jammed in the station's Commons cheek-by-jowl, felt better for a good night's sleep. Memory of the previous evening's riot at Primary was fading in the face of anticipated news from London. After a century and a half of waiting, the world was finally going to learn who Jack the Ripper really was. *If*, of course, and Skeeter grinned to himself, the Ripper Watch experts in London had figured it out.

Tourists who'd appointed themselves lay experts had gathered from all over Commons, surging into Victoria Station and talking nineteen miles to the minute, consulting Ripper-suspect biographies as they argued the merits of various theories. Skeeter, with Kit Carson at his heels, strolled through the madhouse crowd, eyes sharp for any sign of pickpockets or con artists working the throng. Voices like a mile-long swarm of locusts bounced off the girders high overhead with echoes that hurt the senses, expounding favored Ripper theories and wondering what had become of Senator Caddrick's daughter.

"—witness descriptions don't tally well with one another. I mean, they range from a guy in his thirties with fair skin, sandy hair and light brown moustache to a guy in his forties or fifties, dark hair and moustache, dark eyes and complexion, with a 'foreign' look. Personally, I don't think any of the witnesses saw the real Ripper. Except maybe Israel Schwartz, the Jew who didn't speak English. He saw Elizabeth Stride attacked . . ."

". . . whole slew of people claimed they were Jack the Ripper, including a manure collector who emigrated to Australia. Fellow got murderously angry when drunk, at least he did if a prostitute approached. Told his son he was the Ripper and intended to confess before he died, but never did. Confess, I mean. He died, no problem. 1912."

"—they bring I.T.C.H. agents in to monitor this mess, the Inter-Temporal Court will shut us all down!"

"I heard it was Lewis Carroll—"

"The author of *Alice in Wonderland*? The *Ripper*? You gotta be kidding! I mean, so what if he liked to photograph naked little girls?

That's pretty weird, but it doesn't fit the profile of a man who'd rip women open with an eight-inch knife!"

"No, I don't think it was Aleister Crowley, even if he was a sick puppy. Worshipped anything evil and violent, claimed to be the prophet of the anti-Christ. But as a Ripper suspect, I think the evidence is pretty thin . . ."

"—somebody's going to shoot that bastard, that's what I think, and Caddrick's got it coming to him, walking onto this station and tear gassing a crowd full of innocent women and kids—"

". . . convinced the prime minister did it, covering up for the queen's grandson Eddy. Although why he would've married a poor Catholic girl when he was screwing half the women in London, and supposedly several men, as well, is anybody's guess . . ."

"Nuts," somebody else nearby muttered. "We are hip deep in nuts. Sheesh. I need another beer . . ."

And finally, from the loudspeakers overhead: "*Your attention please.* Gate Two is due to cycle in three minutes. All departures, be advised . . ."

Thank God, Skeeter thought. He glanced back at Kit and found the retired scout trailing him half a dozen paces back. Kit rolled his eyes at a mob of sign-carrying loons, chanting the praises of their Immortal Lord Jack and heckling the Time Tours guides trying to organize the outgoing Ripper Watch Tour, then indicated with a gesture, "Okay, hotshot, get busy!"

So he worked the crowd, quartering it leisurely, keeping his gaze sharp. When the immense Britannia finally began its cycle, the roar of voices reached a fever pitch. Wagers rattled like hailstones off every echoing surface in Victoria Station. Skeeter prowled through the surging crowd, alert as a snow leopard and beginning to grow impatient, aware of Kit's presence behind him, watching, judging. He knew his particular brand of prey was out here. His senses twitched, searching for telltale movements, the little signs he knew so well. High overhead, the huge gate dilated slowly open . . . And Skeeter rocked to a halt. His gaze zeroed in, a stooping hawk spotting his next meal. The pickpocket was stalking a man in his fifties whose tanned face, lean build, and expensively casual clothes shouted, *California millionaire.* The pickpocket lifted a fat wallet from the Californian's jacket with a practiced stumble and a hasty apology given and accepted with ease.

Skeeter grinned. *Gotcha!*

The handcuffs he slipped out of his pocket weren't real. He'd picked them up cheap from a station outfitter's bin of discount toys. But they were functional enough for Skeeter's purposes. He slid forward between the Californian and the pickpocket just as the latter slipped the wallet into his *own* jacket. Skeeter tapped the thief on the shoulder. "Hi, there!"

And clicked the cuffs around the guy's wrists before he could blink.

"Hey! What the—"

"Security!" Skeeter bawled, grabbing the guy's jacket lapel. "Got a pickpocket over here! Say, mister," Skeeter got the victim's attention, "this guy just lifted your wallet."

The tourist gasped, hand flying to his extremely empty pocket. "Good God! I've been robbed! Why, you sneaking—"

Security arrived before the irate Californian could take a swing at the struggling pickpocket. "What's going on?" The uniformed security guard sported a bruise down one cheek from the previous day's riot.

"Caught this guy lifting a tourist's wallet," Skeeter explained. "It's in his front jacket pocket. Oh, those cuffs are toys, by the way. Just thought you might want to know."

Skeeter indulged a grin at the look on all three faces, then melted into the crowd, leaving the stunned security officer to deal with the irate tourist and the even more irate pickpocket. He could hear the latter howling his outrage all the way through Victoria Station. Skeeter chuckled. This was almost as much fun as picking pockets, himself. More, maybe. Less risk involved, certainly. He was still chuckling when Kit caught up, grinning fit to crack his face.

"That was impressive. Kids' toys!"

"Yeah, well, sometimes you gotta make do."

"As far as I'm concerned, you won't have to 'make do' with toy handcuffs any longer. You're definitely hired. I was watching close, following your gaze, and I didn't see a thing."

Skeeter's face went hot, but it was a proud flush. He'd done a good job and Kit knew it. High overhead, the returning tour started pouring through the open gate. A Time Tours guide rushed down the stairs, well in advance of the tourists, clutching a heavy pouch. Waiting newsies mobbed him.

"Who is it—?"

"—that a videotape?"

"Has the Ripper Watch Team solved—?"

The grim-faced guide vanished into the Time Tours ticket office and slammed the door, leaving the newsies screaming at sound-proofed glass.

"You know," Skeeter mused, "that guy didn't act like an excited courier carrying the news of the decade, did he?"

"No," Kit agreed, expression thoughtful.

A moment later, the rest of the tour reached Commons floor and word spread like racing wildfire: *Two killers!*

"James Maybrick, after all—"

"Complete unknown! Some doctor, nobody has the faintest idea who—"

"Working *together*—!"

And hard on the heels of that shock, yet another, potentially fatal to the entire station: *Missing tourist!*

"—shot two up-time baggage handlers to death—"

"—said he vanished over in SoHo—"

"Oh, my God," Skeeter groaned. *"Another* missing person!" And another shocking murder spree for TT-86 to explain to the press and the government agencies and Senator Caddrick.

"Who was he?" a woman dressed as a Roman matriarch demanded at Skeeter's elbow.

"I don't know!"

"Someone said he's a graduate student . . ."

". . . heard his name was Benny Catlin . . ."

Benny Catlin?

That name rang alarm bells in Skeeter's memory. Lots of them. Big, fat, warped ones. Benny Catlin was the name on all that luggage Skeeter'd hauled through the Britannia Gate, last time out. What was a graduate student doing with that much luggage? Skeeter hadn't met a grad student yet with enough money to haul five enormous steamer trunks through *any* gate, much less the Britannia. And that trunk Skeeter had almost knocked off the platform had belonged to Benny Catlin, too. Which meant the white-faced, mutton-chopped, short little jerk who'd started screaming at him was their missing man. And a double murderer.

He narrowed his eyes, wondering just what Benny Catlin had stowed in all that luggage. And whether or not the tourist responsible for Skeeter losing his job as baggage porter might look anything like the mysterious doctor in the Ripper Watch video. The thought unsettled him. Not that an up-timer might've committed the murders. That theory had been kicked around so many times, it was old news. But Skeeter might have carried through the murderer's own luggage, had maybe talked to Jack the Ripper, himself, without realizing it.

And *that* was a decidedly uneasy thought. That a serial killer as seriously depraved as the Ripper could pass through society looking and behaving like a completely normal person, while inside . . . Skeeter shivered. And was damned glad he hadn't stayed in London, after all, which he'd planned to do before Ianira's disappearance. If he'd stayed, he'd doubtless have been pressed into searching for the missing Benny Catlin. And hunting Jack the Ripper was not Skeeter's idea of a sane way to pass the time. He'd stick to stalking pickpockets and small-time grifters. Those, at least, he could understand.

He didn't want to understand serial killers.

Not ever.

"Skeeter?"

Kit's gaze was centered squarely on him, brows twitching downward in concern.

"Yeah?"

"What's wrong?"

"I think I saw Catlin, the day the gate opened last week."

"Really? What do you remember about him?"

Skeeter described Catlin, then added, "He had too much luggage for a grad student. Five big steamer trunks. Expensive ones."

"He's not the guy whose steamer trunk almost went off the platform, is he?" Kit asked abruptly, eyes narrowed.

Skeeter blinked in surprise. Then rubbed the back of his neck, embarrassed. "Uh, yeah. I think so. That was the name on the luggage tag. And he was white as any ghost, trying to keep it from falling."

"I think," Kit said in a tight, dangerous voice, "we'd better tell Ronisha Azzan about this, because it looks to me like Catlin may well have been one of the *Ansar Majlis* goons on Armstrong's payroll. I find myself wondering what—or who—was in that trunk. And I'll bet Ronisha Azzan will, too."

"Aw, nuts . . . Kit, I heard she was meeting with Senator Caddrick again this morning, trying to figure out where his kid went. And if he sees me, he's gonna remember I assaulted him, back at Primary. *That* kind of attention, I don't need."

"Nonsense," Kit said firmly. "Nobody's going to jail the guy who figured out where his kid's kidnappers went."

Skeeter had a terrible feeling he would find himself dragged down the Britannia Gate eight days from now as part of the search teams, after all. He wondered briefly if a bullet would've been waiting for *him,* if he'd stayed to haul those heavy steamer trunks to Catlin's hotel? Skeeter sighed, then ran a hand through his hair. Why was it, going legit had turned into the hardest thing he'd ever tried to do? And considering his background, that was saying a lot.

"Well," he muttered, "I guess I'll just have to play it by ear, won't I?"

"That's the spirit!" Kit grinned. "Come on, Skeeter. Let's go find you a security squawky someplace, then maybe by the time we've done that, Ronnie's followup meeting with the Senator will be over?"

Skeeter managed a weak grin of gratitude. "Okay. Thanks."

Wondering if he knew what he was doing, he followed Kit Carson's lead. *Just go with Kit,* he told himself, and tried not to think too closely about where the grizzled old scout would end up leading him. He was *quite* sure he did not want to find out.

Mary Jane Kelly was afraid of the man she'd come to visit. Black magic and demon worship and an appetite for the unholy . . .

Marie Jeannette, as she'd been born, knew the whispers were not just hideous rumour, either, they were terrifying fact. He'd told her so, himself, on his many visits to the high-class West End house where she'd worked at the time, the one she'd been thrown out of shortly afterward for excessive drinking, a habit she'd picked up after becoming this particular gentleman's favorite.

"A whore," he'd smiled down into her eyes, "is my ideal of the perfect unholy woman. A sower of immorality, a merchant of sin. A perfect vessel for wreaking the destruction of prudish social convention and absurd, medieval morals. Don't you agree, my dear?"

Whatever the customer wants, had been her initial response to his blazing eyes and strange appetites. The fear had come later, when he whispered between savage thrusts, mouth half-full of her left breast, "The Second Coming will bring a Great Year to its close . . . and the powers of hell will destroy all the weak and foolish lunacy Christians call goodness. And I . . ." he murmured darkly as he gave her a particularly hard pounding, excitement glittering in his eyes, "I worship those powers of hell. I shall rule upon this earth when the destruction sweeps away godliness and everything it stands for. I shall be the most powerful of men, preparing the way for the anti-Christ . . . Does this shock you, my dear? Or," he laughed and kissed her hard, "does it *excite* you?"

Of all the men who'd paid to use her body, rich men who'd plied her with furs and beautiful clothes and trips to faraway, exotic places like Paris, East End costermongers reeking of gin and dead fish, violent louts who'd blacked her eye, afterwards, and the half-grown boys brought to a certain fancy West End address by their wealthy fathers to learn what to do with a woman, of all those many men, *none* frightened twenty-six-year-old Mary Kelly as deeply as Mr. Aleister Crowley.

But Mary Jane Kelly had been living in fear so deep, she would almost rather have faced Satan, himself, than continue in this terror. So she had brought herself, quaking in her once-fine boots, to Satan's very doorstep, praying that Mr. Crowley's ambitions would cause him to find her plight interesting—and that his dark powers would help keep her alive. The butler who answered the door sniffed irritably, but allowed her to step out of the cold wind into a polished, gleaming hall to wait while he took her message to his master.

Moments later, the butler was ushering her into a study whose bookcases were crowded with hundreds of ancient, mouldering books and manuscripts, and whose shelves were lined with items she decided queasily she didn't really wish to look at too closely. The only crucifix in the room was upside down. It hung above a lit, black candle.

"Why, Mary Kelly, it *is* you! I've missed you enormously, my dear!"

Mr. Crowley had not changed. He came around the desk, hands outstretched, and kissed her cheek, surrounded by a black aura of danger that set her quaking in her boots again. She could still remember gulping down whole bottles of gin, brandy, anything she could lay hands on, trying to forget what it had felt like, with this man in her. *What am I doing here, God help me, I haven't any other choice, they'll kill me, else . . . and the baby, too, can't let 'em kill my baby . . .*

Pregnant, utterly penniless, Mary Kelly had nowhere else to turn.

"Sit down, please." He ushered her to a chair, drawing another up close beside her. "What brings you here? Your hands are like ice, Mary, would you like a brandy to warm you?"

"Please, yes . . ." Her voice was shaking as badly as her hands.

He splashed brandy into a snifter, handed it to her, watched her gulp it down.

"What can I do for you, then?"

She lowered the empty glass to her threadbare lap. "I need . . . I'm in terrible trouble, you see, and I thought . . . I thought you might be interested in . . . the reason why."

He tipped his head to one side, eyes merry. "If you're going to tell me I'm the father of whatever brat you might be carrying, I would point out it's been more than seven months, my dear, and you clearly are not seven months gone with child."

Her face flamed. "No, it's not the baby, that's Joseph's, right enough, and he's been good to me. It's this . . ." She dug into her pocket, brought out the grimy sheets of foolscap which Joseph had brought home for her to translate, after buying them from Dark Annie. Poor Joe, he'd thought these hideous little letters would be their ticket to wealth. But Annie was dead, monstrously so, as was the woman *she'd* got them from, and after reading these letters, Mary was terrified that she would be next, she and whoever else had been insane enough to lay hands on one of these sordid little missives.

He glanced at the writing, frowned. "This is in Welsh, is it not?"

She nodded. "My man . . . he bought them, you see, from Annie, when she needed medicines, asked me to read them out for him. There were others . . ." Her voice had begun to shake again. "Annie had them from Polly and now they're both dead! Murdered and cut apart by this madman in Whitechapel!"

Aleister Crowley was staring at her. "My dear," he said gently, "whatever is in these letters?"

In a low, trembling voice, she told him. Word for word, she told him exactly what the letters said. And he saw it as quickly as she had done.

"My God! Eddy? *Collars and Cuffs?* It must be . . ."

She nodded. "Yes. It must be him. And the queen must have ordered all this hushed up, I can't think why else Polly Nichols would have been killed so horribly, or poor Annie Chapman, who was so sick, she could hardly stand up."

Crowley began to laugh, very softly. "Victoria, order this done? Oh, no, my dear, the queen is entirely too *good* to condone what's been done by our friend the Whitechapel fiend. Oh, she's no fool, and if she knew about these," he tapped the letters in Mary's shaking hand, "she might well try to hush it all up. But order someone to cut the owners of the letters to pieces in the streets? No. She would *not* wish for that kind of publicity, for that sort of scrutiny. The police and the press are simply agog over our friend the Whitechapel Murderer. I must say," he chuckled, "quite a reputation, he's given himself, isn't it? This business must be driving the authorities mad. No, Victoria would never be stupid enough to generate that sort of publicity. Take my word for it, Mary dear, someone else is committing these murders. Someone close to Eddy, no doubt. Someone with a great deal to lose, should Eddy's indiscretions become public knowledge." He sat tapping his fingertips against the arm of his chair for long moments. "Well, now, this is quite an intriguing little mystery you've handed me, my dear. One presumes you want money?"

She shook her head, bit her lip. "I . . . I don't want to be . . . next . . ."

"Ah. Of course you don't."

"I've got a baby coming," she got out in a rush, "and a man who wants to marry me, when he gets another job, even though he knows what I've been. Joseph's a good man, wants to take me off the streets, and he didn't know what this horrible little letter was when he bought it, he was just doing Annie a favor, because she was so sick and needed the money for medicine . . ."

He took her trembling hands in his own and patted them, brought them to his lips. Mary shuddered, fighting more terror than she'd ever known in her young life.

"Here, now, no need for such hysteria, my dear. Of course you're frightened, but you've done exactly the right thing, coming to me for protection." He dried her wet face with his hands, brushed her heavy, strawberry-blonde hair back from her brow, planted a kiss there. "I'll take very good care of you, my dear. Just leave the letter with me, that's a good girl. I've a fair idea who might be profiting from these murders, knowing Eddy as I do, and the way certain men think. Yes, I'll take very good care of you, my dearest . . ."

He was kissing her, unbuttoning her dress, sliding his hand up under her skirt.

He gave her two whole crowns, after, worth half a pound sterling.

Kissed her and told her to buy herself a lot of gin and a pretty new shawl and not to worry, he would see to it that she was never molested by whoever was hunting down Eddy's sordid little letters. When she left the house, pulling her threadbare shawl tightly about her shoulders against the cold bite of the wind, Mary Jane Kelly was trembling far harder than she'd been when she'd arrived an hour previously. *What've I done, letting him do that horrible ritual over me, like that, when he was in me, what in God's name have I done?*

She bit her lip and started for home. Surely, anything was better than being cut into pieces and having her insides strewn across the ground? Surely it was? But she felt dirty and cold and unclean down to her soul, which she never had felt even when letting the meanest, dirtiest louts in the East End spend inside her. She brushed wetness from her eyes and pressed a hand against her belly, where a child was growing. Whatever else, she had to think about far more than just herself, now. Which was why she could have done nothing else, today.

But, oh, God, she was so afraid.

And Mr. Aleister Crowley frightened her only a little less terribly than the rest.

"Kit!"

Kit Carson glanced around, peering into the nervous crowds thronging Commons, many of them wondering in shrill tones what would happen and would their vacations be cancelled and could they get a refund if Senator Caddrick closed down TT-86? He found Robert Li bearing down on him and smiled at his long-time friend.

"Hi, Robert. What's up?"

The antiquarian stared. "*What's up?* You are kidding, aren't you? Kit, are you out of your gate-addled *mind?* Skeeter Jackson, Neo Edo's *house detective?*"

Kit chuckled. "Oh, that. Is that all?"

His friend's expression altered to one of deep pity. "Oh, God, it's true. You have lost your mind."

Kit's lips twitched. "Glad to know you think so highly of me, pal. No, I haven't lost my mind. But you—and just about every other 'eighty-sixer on station—have apparently lost your sense of fair play."

Robert Li blinked, the fair skin of his maternal Scandinavian heritage at odds with features bequeathed him by a paternal Hong Kong Chinese grandfather. "Come again?"

"Skeeter," Kit said gently, ticking off the points on his fingers. "One, that boy never rolled an 'eighty-sixer. *Never.* And if you'd think about it, you'd figure out why. Two, he hasn't been the same ever since that gawd-awful wager of his with Goldie went sour and Marcus ended up in chains down the Porta Romae. Three, Ianira trusted him implicitly. And Ianira Cassondra is no fool." Kit ran a hand through his thinning hair, unable to hide the grief mere thought of Ianira and her missing family brought. "That boy has damn near killed himself looking for them. Lost the only two honest jobs he could find on station doing it, too. And even then, he still didn't go back to picking pockets. The *down-timers* have been feeding him, Robert, because he hasn't had enough cash to buy a hot dog. So what's he been doing? Looking for a job nobody'll give him, tracking down terrorists in Shangri-La's basement, and arresting *thirty-one* small-time crooks in a single week. Without anybody asking him or paying him to do it. So yesterday, when he pulled Rachel Eisenstein out of that disaster at Primary, I decided it was high time somebody around here gave that kid a fair break. He's earned it. Especially with Caddrick likely to press charges for assaulting him, for God's sake. After what Caddrick did, roughing *him* up, that boy is gonna need all the help he can get."

Robert Li closed his mouth. Blinked. "Good God," the antiquarian said softly. Then, slowly, "All right, I'll concede a point when I've been wrong. But you've gotta admit, it's unlikely as hell."

Kit grinned. "Oh, sure it is. And that," he chuckled, "is why I'm having so much fun. What's that you've got with you?" He nodded at the sheet of paper his friend was carrying.

"This? Oh, it's a flier on Jenna Caddrick and that terrorist who grabbed her, Noah Armstrong. Mike Benson's ordered a station-wide hunt, looking for any eyewitnesses who might remember seeing them. I was trying to find you, to ask if you'd seen one of these yet, when I heard the news about you hiring Skeeter."

"No, I haven't seen it." Kit took the flier curiously, glancing at the photos, and ran down the brief descriptions. "I read about Cassie Tyrol. Damned shame."

"What's a shame?" Skeeter's voice asked at Kit's elbow.

He glanced up and took approving note of the security radio he'd sent Skeeter to obtain. "Good, you got the squawky. Cassie Tyrol is what's a shame. She was Senator Caddrick's sister-in-law, poor soul, can you imagine being related to *that*? Have you seen one of these yet?"

Skeeter took the flier curiously. "No." He narrowed his eyes slightly. "Don't know why Caddrick thought this creep was *me*," he muttered, frowning at the photo of Armstrong. "Guy looks sorta familiar, though. Not sure why . . ." The former con artist's frown deepened slowly. Then, seemingly struck by inspiration, Skeeter dug into a pocket and came out with an ink pen. He started drawing over the top of the photograph, startling Robert Li into leaning forward.

"What in the world are you doing?" the antiquarian asked.

"Just an idea," Skeeter muttered. He was sketching in a drooping moustache, sideburns. The pen fairly flew across the page, sketching in a bandana, a sombrero pulled low . . .

"My God," Kit whispered, recognizing the face taking shape. "It's Joey Tyrolin!"

Robert started slightly, swinging his gaze up to meet Kit's. "Joey—? That drunk pistolero we saw the other week, headed to Denver? That was *Noah Armstrong*? We were that close to a murdering terrorist and didn't even know it?"

Another resemblance clicked in Kit's mind. "Joey *Tyrolin!* Skeeter, you genius! By God, I knew I'd hit on a brilliant idea, hiring you! Jenna Caddrick's aunt's name was Cassie *Tyrol*. Jocasta Tyrol—Joey Tyrolin!"

Skeeter wasn't smiling, however. In fact, he wasn't even standing beside them, any longer. He'd bolted through the crowd. He came back with another flier, one he'd ripped off the nearest concrete post. Kit had seen those fliers plastered up everywhere, with photos of the station's missing down-timers. Skeeter was sketching over Julius' photo. Skeeter's lips thinned to a grim line as he drew in long hair pulled back into a bun beneath a wide-brimmed calico bonnet. Then he held up the altered sketch of his missing young friend. "And this is the woman Joey Tyrolin tangled with at the Wild West ticket kiosk. The one Tyrolin's porter dropped a trunk on. I worked that gate departure, looking for some trace of Ianira and her family, and dammit, I didn't even recognize that boy!"

Kit remembered the incident clearly. "You're right." He took the altered sketches and scowled down at them. "Miss Caddrick must have used the name Joey Tyrolin on that fake I.D. she bought in New York. And Armstrong simply appropriated the I.D. and her tickets. If Armstrong was in that departures line, you can bet Jenna Caddrick was, too."

"Probably *in* one of the suitcases that porter dropped," Skeeter growled. "What I want to know is, how the *hell* did Julius get tangled up with terrorists? I know that boy. He wouldn't get involved in something like that, not without a damned good reason."

Robert Li said slowly, "Those *Ansar Majlis* leaders you caught are denying it, but it's pretty clear they paid Armstrong to hit Jenna Caddrick. So it's a good bet Armstrong masterminded the hit on Ianira, too. If I remember right, Julius disappeared about the same time her whole family vanished, didn't he? But surely the boy wouldn't have helped the *Ansar Majlis* voluntarily?"

Kit glanced at Skeeter, reading murderous hatred in the younger man's eyes and the set of his jaw. The one-time con artist said through clenched teeth, "If Armstrong blackmailed him with a threat to Ianira's life, he would've done anything that pack of cutthroats demanded. And waited for a chance to slit *their* throats, later."

A chill shivered its way up Kit's spine. This was a side of Skeeter he'd never witnessed, the side that had survived twelfth-century Mongolia and the worst childhood any 'eighty-sixer on station could lay claim to. Slowly, Kit nodded agreement. "Yes, I think you're reading this situation very clearly, Skeeter. Julius would've done anything to save Ianira, if Armstrong had kidnapped her as well as Jenna Caddrick. Armstrong's pals in the *Ansar Majlis* might well have been holding the boy prisoner with Marcus and the girls, probably forced him to help them all escape the station. And my bet is, Armstrong sent at least one of his men down the Britannia with the fake I.D. Jenna Caddrick's roommate was supposed to use. Benny Catlin wasn't anything more than a decoy, to make us think her kidnappers had gone to London, when they planned to take her to Denver, all along."

Robert Li swung his gaze from Kit back to Skeeter. "Okay," he grinned suddenly, "I'm convinced! Damned smart move is right, hiring this genius. Question is, what do we do now?"

Kit eyed Skeeter narrowly. "How well do you ride a horse?"

Skeeter Jackson's sudden, lethal grin blazed like a noonday sun. "If it's got hooves, I can ride it."

"In that case, we visit Time Tours, Incorporated. Because your new boss just came out of retirement. It's been a while since I visited Denver."

Robert Li's mouth dropped open. Then the antiquarian started laughing. "Oh, my God! Wait until word gets out! Goldie Morran, for one, may strangle from simple shock. Kit Carson and Skeeter Jackson, *partners in crime?* I just wish I could get away from the studio long enough to go with you!"

Kit clouted him across one shoulder. "The price of being the only IFARTS. agent on station. But there is something you could do . . ."

"Why do I have the feeling I ought to be counting my fingernails and locking my safe?"

Kit grinned. "You wound me. Head over to Connie's, if you don't mind? We've only got six days before the Wild West Gate re-opens, which means we should've started outfitting last week, not to mention all the training Skeeter needs before we step through. I'd head straight to Connie's, but Skeeter and I have to break the news to Ronisha. And the Senator."

Skeeter visibly lost color.

"Well, since you put it that way," Robert said hastily, "I'd rather ask Connie for favors than go near Caddrick, any day of the week."

"Thought you'd see it my way. C'mon, Skeeter. The Senator's not going to throw you in jail, not when you're the genius who figured out where his little girl disappeared to."

Skeeter swallowed once. "Well, okay."

"C'mon, Jackson. Time's wasting."

Skeeter's grin was a little forced, but it was a brave effort.

Personally, Kit could hardly wait to beard this particular lion. One thing he had very little tolerance for was a cocky politician. Particularly one threatening to shut down *his* station. Senator John Caddrick didn't know it yet, but he'd made the worst enemy of his life. Kit fully intended to enjoy his revenge.

(((Chapter 3)))

Ianira Cassondra wasn't sure how long she'd been imprisoned.

The man who'd brought her to this room had kept her drugged for endless days. She knew only that she was somewhere in London, separated from the only people who could help her, and that her life remained in far too much danger from up-time threat to risk returning to Spaldergate House and its Britannia Gate, to seek help from friends on the station. She was as much on her own as she'd been in Athens, married to an inhuman merchant who valued her only for the male children she had been unable to produce. Her first husband had terrified Ianira. But the man who held her captive now . . .

He was mad, this Dr. John Lachley. He was also the ruling half of a killing team the up-time world knew as Jack the Ripper. John Lachley could not come within touching distance of her without Ianira slipping into shock and the most monstrous visions she had ever suffered. When she heard footsteps on the stairs outside her imprisoning bedroom, Ianira broke into a cold sweat and uncontrollable tremors. But the door opened to reveal only the manservant, Charles. He carried a meal tray. "Mrs. Seddons sent up your supper," he said gently, his warm regard filled with pity.

The food would be drugged, of course.

It always was.

"Thank you," Ianira whispered, voice hoarse.

Outside her bedroom window, twilight settled over the rooftops and chimney pots of London. She stilled shaking hands, having waited and planned for this moment, terrified that something would go wrong, now that it had come. Charles set the tray on the little table beside her bed, then settled into a chair to watch her eat. They did not leave her alone at mealtimes, making sure she swallowed the drugged food that kept her witless and utterly helpless in their hands. The manservant and the cook, Mrs. Seddons, had been told Ianira was in deep shock and suffering from delusions. She no longer even tried to speak with them. What John Lachley had done to her after her first attempt to enlist the servants' aid . . .

Ianira shuddered under the bedclothes. There wasn't enough hot water and soap in all of London to wash away what he'd done to her. Afterward, Ianira had planned a different route to freedom. So she sat up, trembling violently, and reached for the tray. Which she promptly dropped, spilling the contents across the carpets with a crash and clatter of broken china and tumbled silver.

Charles lunged to his feet with a dismayed cry, making certain she was unharmed first, then eased her down against the pillows and said, "Let me clear this away and bring another tray for you . . ."

The moment Charles left the room, Ianira lunged out of bed. She flung herself to the window, dragging up the heavy wooden frame, and scrambled out across the sill. Her bedroom was three floors up, but it faced the back of the house, overlooking a dismal, wet garden. The sloping roof of the rear porch broke her fall when she let go, jumping down in her nightdress and nothing else.

She landed with a grunt and a thud, rolled helplessly across slick, wet roofing slates, and grabbed for the metal drain at the edge. She hung for a moment by both hands, bruised and shaken, then dropped the rest of the way to the ground. She fell sprawling into shrubbery and wet grass with a spray of water from the soaked branches. Ianira lay stunned for a long moment, then managed to roll to hands and knees and lifted her head, looking up through wild, fallen hair. She could hear shouts inside the house and the pounding of running footsteps. With a whimper of terror rising in the back of her throat, Ianira came to her feet and ran across the wet grass, limping on a bruised hip.

The garden had to be escaped, whatever the cost. A high wall surrounded it on all sides. So Ianira ran for the front of the house, slipping and stumbling through mud that squelched beneath her bare feet, hiking her nightdress up to her knees. She found a gate and shoved at it, managed to find the latch and wrenched it open. She flung the heavy wooden gate back with a solid whump and ran down a carriage drive, past a small carriage house where she could hear a horse shifting in a wooden stall, kicking the side of its home in rythmic boredom. *A horse . . .*

She didn't know how to ride, but surely a horse could take her farther and faster than she could run on bare, bruised feet? Ianira lunged into the carriage house, groping through near darkness to the stall where the animal snuffled through its feed trough, looking for stray oats. Teeth chattering, Ianira forced herself to calmness, found a lead rope hanging from a peg, and slipped open the stall door. "Hello," she whispered to the startled creature. "Let us go for a ride, we two."

She clipped the lead rope to the horse's halter and led him out past the dark silhouette of Dr. Lachley's carriage. She clambered awkwardly onto the animal's back by means of the carriage's running board. Then she guided him with a soft nudge and whispered words of encouragement, bending low as they clopped through the carriage house door. She turned toward the street—

"There!"

The shout came from the garden behind her.

She thumped muddy heels against the horse's flanks and the startled animal jumped forward, breaking past the front edge of the house at a jogging trot. She clung to the mane and gripped the horse's sides with bare legs, clinging for dear life. A dark shape loomed directly in front of them. Someone shouted and flung something straight at them. The horse screamed and reared, trying to shy away from the sudden threat. Ianira lost her grip and plunged backwards with a ragged scream of her own. She hit the ground with a sickening thud and lay winded, unable to move. The horse clattered away, riderless.

Then he was on top of her, grasping her wrists, checking for broken bones.

Ianira struck out wildly, trying to rake his face with her nails. *"Don't touch me!"*

"She's delirious again, poor thing." John Lachley dug his thumb into the hollow of her throat, silencing her and cutting off her air. Ianira struggled until darkness roared up to swallow her awareness. When she could see and breathe again, he was carrying her up the stairway to her prison once more. She could feel the rough texture of his woolen coat against her cheek, could feel the dampness where he'd just come in from the raw night. Ianira clenched her eyelids down over burning wetness. Another five minutes . . . Had she only been given another five minutes . . .

"You're sure she's taken no injury?" A man had spoken, somewhere behind her captor. She didn't know that voice, tried to stir, was held savagely still against Lachley's chest. She moaned softly as he answered his unknown companion.

"I'll examine the poor thing at once, of course, Crowley. Dreadfully sorry to've brought you slap into this."

"On the contrary," Crowley said with a hint of delight in his voice, "I am amazed and intrigued. Who the devil is she?"

"So far as I've been able to ascertain, a foreigner who fell prey to footpads the moment she set foot on English soil. Poor thing's been raving for over a week, out of her mind with terror and delusions. I've had to sedate her to keep her from doing herself a mischief in her delirium."

"Seems devilishly determined to escape, I'd say."

"Yes," Lachely said dryly, carrying her back into her room. "The footpads were brutalizing her. She hasn't been in her right mind since, poor child. Imagines we're all footpads, intent on finishing what they started. I'm determined to see her through the crisis, learn who she really is, perhaps make some sort of amends for the wretched abuse she's suffered at English hands."

"Rather a striking child, isn't she? Mid-twenties, I'd guess. Has the look of the East about her."

"Indeed," Lachley placed Ianira in her bed once again, "she speaks Greek like an angel. Now, then . . . Ah, Charles, good man. You've brought it."

Ianira struggled to escape the needle. "No, please . . . I will tell no one, please, just let me go . . ."

It was no use. He injected her easily, holding her down until the drug roared through her veins, leaving her limp and helpless. With the drug came the visions, terrifying, of the women who had died under this man's brutal hands, of the knife in the other man's hands, striking in the darkness, directed by her captor . . . And the ghastly chamber beneath the streets, which reeked of stale blood and decaying flesh . . .

Crowley's voice came from far away. "Poor thing's raving."

"Yes. The way she babbles like that, I can't help wonder if she didn't escape this hideous Whitechapel fiend, only to fall prey to footpads."

"She's no common streetwalker," Crowley's voice said, roaring dimly in her ears.

"No. But how are we to know the Whitechapel murderer won't attack ladies, as well as common slatterns, given the opportunity? She's clearly only just arrived from the docklands, after all, and if she was separated from her family in the crush of the crowd and didn't know how to summon help . . ." Lachley's voice was fading in and out of Ianira's awareness. She managed to open her eyes and found him leaning down over her. Lachley smoothed her hair back from her brow and smiled down into her terrified gaze, promising dire punishment for what she'd attempted, tonight. Ianira shuddered and turned her head away, closing her eyes again over despair. What he would do to her if she tried to warn Crowley that Lachley *was* the Whitechapel murderer . . .

The horror of it was, Crowley wouldn't believe her.

No one would.

She sank, helpless and despairing, into darkness.

Ronisha Azzan had already been in the war room for an hour that morning, hard at work on the Jenna Caddrick abduction case, when security escorted the Senator up from the Time Tripper Hotel. He arrived flanked by staffers carrying briefcases, intimidating by themselves, but the federal agents were conspicuously absent. That unexpected pleasantness allowed Ronisha to relax a fraction—but only a fraction, because the Senator's grey eyes blazed with a look that boded ill for her immediate future, leaving her to wonder if he'd spent a bad night or if he woke up every morning in a foul temper.

Bax arrived on the Senator's heels, carrying a sheaf of printouts and a CM disk. If the bags under his eyes were any hint, the Time Tours CEO had definitely spent a bad night, working as hard as Ronisha had. She nodded Bax toward the coffee; he poured himself a deep cup before sliding into a chair at the war room's immense conference table. Ronisha turned her attention to their unwelcome guest. "Good morning, Senator. I hope you slept well?"

Caddrick scowled. "As a matter of fact, a bunch of goddamned maniacs kept me awake all night, in the room under mine. Am I to understand that you actually permit lunatics on this station to worship Jack the Ripper as their personal god?"

Ronisha shrugged. "Last time I checked, we still had freedom of religion, Senator. As long as they don't actively threaten anyone, they can worship whomever they like."

Caddrick flushed. "So you have no intention of protecting the public safety? Or of enforcing public disturbance laws?"

His staffers began scribbing notes.

Ronisha bristled. "I will enforce whatever laws and policies are necessary to keep the peace on this station, Senator. As a number of federal agents have already discovered. Now, since the issue of the Ripper cults is not germane to the business at hand, I suggest we tackle the subject of your daughter's possible whereabouts."

"That suits me!" Caddrick snapped. "And let me make one thing very clear. If you don't produce my little girl, alive and uninjured, I will personally see to it that your career is over! You will never work again, not in the time-touring industry, not anywhere else. And don't think I can't do it. I've destroyed far more important careers than yours!"

An ugly silence fell, into which Granville Baxter, at least, copiously perspired.

Ronisha had been expecting it, of course, but anticipation of such a threat didn't lessen the impact. The bottom of her stomach turned to solid lead. "Senator," she said softly, refusing to roll belly up at the first tightening down of political thumbscrews, "I want you to know that's a mud-ugly road you're walking down. You just take a good look at who's sitting in the station manager's chair right now. Then you think real hard about it. *Real* hard. You are not the only person on this station who can bring out the big guns. The last five politicians of your caliber to tangle with the African-Origin Business Women's Caucus did not fare well at the polls, their next election bid. Not well at all. And since we both share the same goal, finding your daughter and returning her safely to this station, there's no need to head down that particular road, now is there?"

Dust could be heard falling onto the tabletop.

Bax actually looked sick and the Senator's staffers turned white as ice.

John Caddrick stared at her for long moments, his expression a shuttered mask, grey eyes narrowed into calculating slits. She did not back down under that cold, thoroughly reptilian gaze. When the mask unfroze just enough for one corner of his mouth to quirk in a sardonic, unpleasant little smile, she knew her warning had been heeded. She'd have to watch her back; but he wouldn't try anything else heavy-handed. Not for a while, yet. And if she could produce one live and kicking kid, maybe not ever. Caddrick might be a thorough-going bastard, but he wasn't stupid.

"I'm glad we understand one another, Senator. Now, I would suggest we study your daughter's profile for clues, hers and her kidnapper's, and track each potential gate they might have used."

"That's the best suggestion you can make, after an entire night to work on this? Next, I suppose, you will magic Jenna out of a silk top hat?" The scorn in his voice relegated Ronisha to the back of the intelligence bus.

Ronisha narrowed her eyes and bit down on her tongue. *You will eat yours one day, Senator, and choke on it raw! I just hope I'm there to watch.* "Right now, we're doing what can be done, regardless of how little you may like it. Since we have not been able to identify either Jenna or her kidnapper from tour records, I suggest we take a look at Jenna's most active interests." She ran down Jenna's dossier. "Historical re-enactment, horseback riding . . . She keeps two horses in a stable on Long Island?"

The Senator nodded. "Her aunt pays for them. Paid, rather, before the shootings."

Bax cleared his throat reluctantly and leaned forward, steepling his fingertips. "Well, horsemanship skills would stand her in good stead down Shangri-La's gates. Horses were the primary means of land transport for thousands of years, after all. Jenna's kidnappers will doubtless take advantage of that, since most up-timers know very little about horses. Some of the tour gates, however, are better choices for your daughter's kidnappers than others."

"Meaning?" The Senator's scowl boded ill for Bax's future.

The Time Tours executive, however, was made of stern stuff. Holding a job like his, he had to be. "Well, Senator," he cleared his throat again, "Athens in the age of Pericles, for instance, is not a likely choice. Neither Jenna nor her abductors would have the language skills to blend in and disappear, not without help from temporal guides. The majority of Philosopher's Gate tourists are wealthy Greek tycoons, artists, and classics scholars. You've got the same problem with Porta Romae and its destination, Claudian Rome—neither your daughter nor her kidnappers are likely to speak classical Latin. Or Greek or Aramaic or any of the other dozen or so languages spoken in Rome.

"That's not to say they couldn't easily lose pursuers, choosing Rome, they could. But it would create a whole list of problems for them to overcome. Like, how the money works, where to find living space, how to earn a living, obtain food and clothing, avoid all the pitfalls Rome offers the unwary and ignorant visitor."

Caddrick's continued withering glare brought beads of sweat to Bax's forehead, but he kept gamely at it. "According to this profile, your daughter favors more modern history, particularly the periods after the use of gunpowder in personal arms became widespread." He frowned slightly, pursing his lips and tapping them with doubled forefingers, clearly thinking through some chain of surmised options.

"Spanish Colonial South America is closer to her period of interest, but it wouldn't be a good choice for her kidnappers, either. One presumes they'll be armed, which could pose problems for them down the Conquistadores Gate. Under the Spanish colonial system, firearms were tightly restricted to the upper classes. Very few

Conquistadores tourists opt for the role of peon, for obvious reasons. Your daughter's kidnappers, however, would have difficulty passing themselves off as Spanish nobility, again because of language difficulties. Most Conquistadores Gate tourists are of Hispanic descent, with the balance taken up mostly by Amer-Indians."

"I don't give a damn about Amer-Indian tourists!" Caddrick snapped. "What about the other gates?"

Bax started down the list. "The Mongolian Gate is out of the question. It hasn't cycled in months. Same with the Colonial Williamsburg Gate. The Anachronism's timing is off, too, and besides, a Society for Creative Anachronism tournament is the last place your daughter's kidnappers would try hiding." When Caddrick gave him a baffled look, Bax explained. "The SCA is a tightly knit organization of people who recreate the Middle Ages, complete with jousting, knights battling in homemade armor, trained hunting falcons, you name it. They're very clannish and you have to be a member in very good standing to go on a tournament through the Anachronism Gate. Outsiders wouldn't stand a chance of slipping through undetected."

Senator Caddrick's expression made it clear that he considered tournament-bound medieval knights in homemade armor to be unstable lunatics, fitting in with the rest of Shangri-La Station's environment. Bax made an aborted movement to blot his glistening brow, then plowed steadily through the rest of his list. "The Shogun's Gate into medieval Japan is completely out of the question, of course. The Japanese under the Tokugawa Shogunate actually killed any occidental unfortunate enough to be shipwrecked on Japanese shores. Firearms were outlawed too—any mere peasant could kill a samurai with one, which made them too dangerous to have around. Firearms hadn't been invented yet at the time of Thor's Gate, of course, and the Viking age would also present insurmountable language barriers. Did Jenna speak any foreign languages?"

Before the Senator could comment, the Security channel sputtered with static. "Hey, would somebody let us through the mess out here? We need to see Ronisha Azzan, ASAP."

Ronisha stared at the speakers. Skeeter Jackson was the last person she'd expected to hear on a Security channel. She leaned over and punched the intercom that patched her into the security network. "Skeeter? What are you doing on a security squawky?"

"Later! Listen, would you tell these goons down here to let us through? We need to meet with you. I wouldn't interrupt, but it's important. Real important. Kit Carson's with me."

Ronisha scooted her chair back. "I'd better see what this is about," she said a trifle grimly, nodding to the Senator and Bax. "Skeeter, I'll meet you at the aerie. Bax, see what you can do with that profile while I'm gone." She dialed Mike Benson's code and told him to let Kit and Skeeter through, then climbed the stairs to the fifth-floor manager's office. Two security agents followed, making her feel a little better about walking into a potential trap set by disgruntled federal marshals. They hadn't taken kindly to her order to lock down their weapons, a precaution she'd taken to safeguard visitors and residents. After what those agents had done with their tear-gas cannisters, she did not want a bunch of uniformed thugs running around with riot guns, stirring a hornet's nest that had already been shaken several times. The last thing they needed was some trigger-happy fed opening fire on somebody like the Angels of Grace Militia.

Trying to shove that ghastly image aside, Ronisha emerged into the glass-walled office just as the elevator from Commons hummed to life. Moments later, Skeeter Jackson and the world's most famous time scout stepped onto the thick carpet. They'd come alone. Kit Carson was all but bouncing on his toes, eyes alight with a wild kind of exultation. "Hi, Ronnie. Got a minute?"

"Good God, Kit, what *is* it? You know what we're in the middle of, here." She'd never seen the ex-time scout so excited.

"It's Jenna Caddrick's kidnapper. We found him! Skeeter did, that is. I had the good sense to put Skeeter on the payroll as a detective for the Neo Edo—which is why he's got a squawky, since you asked—and the first thing he did was solve the mystery of where Noah Armstrong went."

"*You found Armstrong? Where?* My God, Skeeter, say something!"

La-La Land's most notorious miscreant—Neo Edo's *house detective?*—smiled wryly and handed over a couple of improvised sketches. He'd drawn over the top of a flier with Noah Armstrong's photo. "That's what Armstrong looked like when he went through the Wild West Gate. Dressed as a pistolero named Joey Tyrolin. Pretended to be drunker than a British lord, stumbled around bragging about how he was going to win a shooting competition. Now for the bad news. Our missing down-timer, Julius, went through with him. Posing as a woman and probably under duress. You ought to be able to pull the gate records to find out which name Julius was using. He was dressed as the woman Joey Tyrolin's porter dropped a trunk on." He handed over a second sketch.

She stared from one altered photograph to the other, mind racing back to the events at the Denver Gate's last opening; then pivoted on one stiletto heel and headed for the telephone. "Good work, Skeeter, very good work. Denver opens—" she peered through the windows to the nearest chronometer hanging from the Commons ceiling "—at nine-fifty A.M., six days from now. Be there. You're joining the search team. If I remember right, you've been down the Wild West Gate before and you're good in a scrap. And clearly, you've got more than laundry fuzz between your ears."

Kit said drolly, "Better make that two reservations for Denver, Ronnie. I'm going, too."

Telephone halfway to her ear to arrange for Skeeter's gate pass, Ronisha aborted the motion mid-air. She stared, mouth coming adrift. Kit and Skeeter started laughing. "Okay," she muttered. "You're going, too." She punched the direct-line intercom to the war room. "Bax, outfit a search team through the Wild West Gate, stat. Skeeter Jackson and Kit Carson have located Noah Armstrong. He's posing as Joey Tyrolin, in company with those kids headed for the Colorado pistol competition. And I've got a sketch up here to match against photos of all the women who went through on that tour. I want you to put a name to one of them. The one Tyrolin's porter dropped a trunk on. You remember the incident? That lady was our missing down-time teenager, Julius. Looks like Armstrong forced the boy to help him escape by threatening Ianira and her family."

Startled sounds came over the speaker, then Bax replied strongly. "I'm on it."

Ronisha closed the open circuit and jabbed a lacquered fingernail down onto one of the phone's memory buttons, linking her to security. "Mike, send somebody to every outfitter on station. Jenna Caddrick's abductors went down the Wild West Gate. They had to pull together an outfit for Denver, so somebody on Shangri-La ought to remember them. Get somebody on it. Several somebodies."

"On the way."

"Skeeter. you and Kit get busy outfitting. I'll join you—where? Connie Logan's is your favorite outfitter's, isn't it, Kit? I'll authorize the expenditures from station coffers. Kit, you're priceless. With a little luck, we may yet keep Shangri-La open for business."

"That is," Kit said dryly, "the basic idea. C'mon, Skeeter. Did I say twenty an hour? Make it fifty."

Skeeter looked like a man in deep shock.

Ronisha sympathized.

Skeeter and Kit, the latter grinning like the devil's own favorite imp, sauntered into the elevator, Kit whistling merrily as the doors slid closed. Ronisha stared after them for a long moment, still nearly speechless, herself; then she was on the telephone again, tracking down every Wild West guide who'd ever worked the gate, for somebody to guide the search team out to the site of that black powder shooting competition.

Six days wasn't much of a head start to plan a time tour, when the so-called tour was a search-and-rescue mission into dangerous country by horseback, on the trail of armed terrorists holding hostages. If he'd had time, Skeeter might have panicked. Fortunately, Skeeter Jackson had plenty of practice in falling slap into unexpected little "situations" and landing more or less on his feet. Nor had he truly panicked in quite a while. At least, not since encountering that enraged gladiator, Lupus Mortiferus.

An hour after leaving the aerie, Connie's staff was busy packing away his new wardrobe and Skeeter was bent over a table in the infirmary, getting a backside full of needles. He'd already received the necessary immunizations once before, of course, having been down the Denver gate on a trip wheedled out of a rich mark. But his records showed a need for several booster shots, so he dutifully reported to the infirmary, where he listened to some tourist complain bitterly about the sting as injection after injection went in. Rachel Eisenstein's voice floated in, calm and unsympathetic. "If you'd followed the instructions in your tour-planning immunization schedule, you could have had this over with weeks ago, one at a time."

"But I'm going to be too sore to sit in a saddle!"

"That is not," Rachel said briskly, "my problem."

Skeeter grinned as unhappy curses, centering mostly around the sadistic bent of doctors in general and women doctors in particular, issued from the cubicle, interspersed with complaints about the waste of paying good money for a tour the price of the Wild West Gate if one had to spend the entire trip as a walking, talking pincushion.

"Tourists," Skeeter grimaced. "You'd think they'd remember to bring their brains along, when they leave home."

"You just said a mouthful," the nurse behind him agreed. "There, that's it. Last one. Six boosters, all guaranteed to keep you from coming down with a full-blown case of what ails you. Get going. Kit's chewing nails, waiting to drag you over to the library."

"Oh, God . . ."

The next six days passed in a blur of frantic activity. Kit Carson put Skeeter through the most rigorous training he'd ever endured. He learned that speaking "Old West Slang" was not as simple as imitating John Wayne movie dialogue, which was what he'd done in the cathouses and gambling dens of Denver on his last trip—major portions of which he preferred not to recall too closely. And loading bullets for black-powder guns, even replica models made of higher quality steel, with closer tolerances, was nowhere near as simple as shoving a cartridge into a six-shooter and pulling the trigger. Not if you wanted to hit what you were shooting at when the six-shooter went bang. And Skeeter had never even heard of "balloon head cartridges." The only thing he really comprehended was that you could get slightly more black powder into them, which was fine by him. More bang for the buck was a great idea, in his opinion, going after the *Ansar Majlis* down time.

He also learned how to reload them. And while he measured bullets and sorted them out by weight and discarded those with any slight flattened spots or surface bumps, Kit taught him Old West Slang. He learned why a man should never bake a bang-tail before bedding-down the remuda and why a gentleman never called a lady a Cypriot. If he did, the lady's husband or father might shoot him over it. Might as well just come right out and call her a whore.

And so it went, until Skeeter thought his brain would burst.

He spent two entire days at the firing range, where Ann Vinh Mulhaney put him through hours of shooting lessons, both live-fire and inside the computer simulator she'd built, a room-sized Hogan's Alley affair with three-hundred-sixty-degree rear-projection screens and plenty of real props to use as cover. He spent most of the first day in the computer simulator, working on target acquisition skills and reacting to armed threat and finding out just how many ways one can miss with a firearm at close range under stress. The second day was less fun than the room-sized shooting gallery, but just as instructive. Skeeter could hold his own in a knife fight, but he'd never fired a gun. Ann doled out electronic earmuffs, which allowed her to continue the lecture, while filtering out the sharp, damaging reports of guns discharging the length of the weapons range. "I had to kick a tourist off the line and he wasn't happy about it," she said, dragging him toward an empty lane. "Kit wants you on this firing line all day, Skeeter, which means we've barely got time for adequate weapons selection, load selections, firing procedures, shooting practice, and cleaning lessons."

"Cleaning lessons?" Skeeter blurted, genuinely startled.

Kit nodded impatiently as they joined him at the firing line. "The priming compounds used in 1885's black-powder cartridges were corrosive and black-powder's residue attracts moisture. There's a reason those old time gun slingers were fanatical about cleaning their weaponry."

"Wouldn't it make more sense for me to carry what I'm familiar with? Like a big Bowie-style knife? I'm pretty good with a fighting knife, but what I know about guns wouldn't fill a teacup."

"We'll see Sven before we leave the weapons range. But we're going up against armed terrorists holding hostages. Believe me, if things get rough down that gate, you'll want the ability to reach out and punch somebody well beyond arm's length."

"What are you carrying?" Skeeter asked, eying the pile of weapons Ann had set out on the shooting bench.

"I've always favored the S and W Double Action Frontier. I lost a light-weight model called a Wesson Favorite in the Silver Plume, Colorado, fire of 1884, just about a year before the time we're going to. *This* one," he held up a revolver, "is in .38-40 and has a six and a half inch barrel. Some folks might call it a horse pistol, because it's almost as big as the pistols from before the War Between the States, and most people carried it in a strap over the saddle horn. I'll wear it on my belt, though."

Kit picked a small handgun from the pile on the bench. "For a hideout, I'll be taking my little five-shot S and W .38 double action. The second model with a three-and-a-quarter inch barrel, for concealability. And for a long gun," he hoisted a rifle, working the action with a sharp metallic clack to demonstrate its mode of operation, "I'll bring a Winchester 73 rifle, in .38-40 caliber, same as the big Smith and Wesson. It won't be good out beyond two hundred yards or so, but my eyes aren't what they used to be, so something like a Sharps would be a waste of time for me. And you don't know enough to bother with one, either."

"Why don't you just put a good scope on it?" Skeeter asked, brows twitching down. Then, answering his own question, "Because it's an anachronism, right?"

Kit chuckled. "Actually, rifle scopes were in use as early as the Civil War, a good twenty years before the Denver Gate's time period. But we won't be taking period-scoped weapons. They had too many problems to bother with them. They were so hard to see through, shooters of the day compared them to peering through a rusty pipe. And they weren't very well sealed, so if you carried one around on a hot, muggy day, the minute the temperature dropped, at night, for instance, moisture would condense inside the scope. Very bad for scopes. And they were fragile. Most of them used black-widow spiderweb silk for cross hairs, which broke very easily, and steel wire cross hairs were more prone to breakage than spider silk."

Ann fished out a couple of ordinary telescoping spyglasses made from brass tubing, just like the ones in old movies about sailing ships, and a couple of pairs of early-style field glasses. "These gather light much more effectively and offer better magnification, too. You should do just fine with the iron sights on the firearms and one of these for distance reconnaisance."

The first gun they armed Skeeter with was one of Ann's Royal Irish Constabulary Webleys. "Unlike the later military-issue Webley," Ann said briskly, "which was a clunky monster of a top-break pistol like Kit's Smith and Wessons, the RIC is a good concealment gun, with a solid frame and a loading gate more like the big Colt you'll also carry. It's bigger than Kit's .38, and it shoots a bigger cartridge, which is a distinct advantage for an amateur shooter. You might find it easier to handle because of its size, plus bigger bullets might make up for some of your lack of expertise with handguns."

The Webley had a tiny, stubby little barrel, only two and a quarter inches long, but the thing had plenty of heft when Skeeter accepted it. When he swung it around to see how the gate at the side of the cylinder opened, Ann grunted in exasperation and grabbed his wrist, levering the barrel around so that it faced downrange, not at her midsection.

Skeeter reddened to his undershorts. "Oops. Sorry!"

"*Always* point a firearm downrange. Even if you're absolutely positive it's not loaded. Imagine a laser beam coming out the end of that barrel. Anything that laser touches is at risk for having a hole blown through it, if you have an accidental discharge. Now, then, let's put you through the paces for loading, firing, and unloading."

Skeeter learned how to use that little Royal Irish Constabulary Webley better than he'd ever dreamed he could. Ann was a crackerjack teacher, patient and thorough and very clear in her instructions. After more or less mastering the Webley and overcoming his movie-instilled desire to "throw" bullets by jerking his hand forward, Skeeter graduated to a big six-shot Colt Double-Action Army in .38-40 with a four-and-three-quarter-inch barrel, which Ann referred to as the "The Thunderer."

"This one uses the same cartridge Kit will be using in his belt revolver and his rifle, so you guys will have at least some ability to interchange ammunition."

"But why the shorter barrel?" Skeeter asked. "Kit's other gun has six and a half inches!"

"So you can draw it faster," Ann explained. "You're not as experienced with this as Kit, so don't argue. You need a weapon you can draw, point, and shoot fast and easy, without needing a lot of drilled-in practice on sight pictures and target acquisition techniques. I'm not going to turn you into a champion marksman, never mind Kit's equal, in the time you have before the gate goes, Skeeter. I'm going to teach you the point-shoulder technique, which ought to work pretty well out to ten yards or so, and you don't need a long barrel to do that. We're not comparing your anatomy, here, we're trying to keep you alive. So a four-inch barrel is what you get, my friend."

Skeeter reddened again and opted to keep his mouth shut.

For a long gun, Skeeter discovered he would be carrying a twelve gauge double-barrel shotgun, which he learned how to use with buckshot. It felt a little—granted, a *very* little—more like shooting a bow, which he knew how to use, than the handguns had. As long as his target was within fifty yards, Skeeter stood some chance of success with the shotgun, if he remembered to cock the hammers first. "I hope," he muttered to himself, after hours of practice with each gun, "we won't have to rely on my marksmanship to get out of this alive."

Kit, who had been steadily punching neat, absurdly tiny groups of holes in his paper targets, glanced over at Skeeter's dismal ones and grimaced. "I hope not, either. Keep practicing."

Skeeter felt a great deal better about the pair of Bowie knives Sven Bailey presented him with, one to wear openly in a sheath and one that was somewhat smaller, like a camp knife, to carry concealed under his shirt. "This is more like it," Skeeter nodded, far more at home with a blade in his hand. "And much better quality than what I grew up using in Yesukai's camp."

"Just try to bring them back undamaged," Sven glowered. The bladed weapons instructor was no taller than the diminuitive projectile weapons instructor, but broader and heavier boned. The epithet "evil gnome" had been hurled Sven's way more than once, although usually not to his face. Sven Bailey was widely acknowledged the most dangerous man on TT-86, which was a considerable accomplishment, given Kit Carson's presence on station.

"I'll take care of them," Skeeter promised with a gulp and a hasty retreat from Sven Bailey's armory.

Skeeter's final lesson of the day, after another intensive round of firing practice, involved properly cleaning a black-powder firearm in the field, using 1885 techniques and equipment. "Clean your firearms after every use," Ann explained as Skeeter learned how to disassemble each of his borrowed weapons, "or you'll end up with a rusted, corroded piece of junk. That can happen fast, in a matter of days."

"What do you use?" Skeeter asked dubiously, eyeing the stack of filthy firearms.

"Soap. Not detergent, mind, but *soap* and water. Modern shooters usually use one of the liquid-formula soaps or even chemical cleaners that don't require water, but you won't have that luxury down the Wild West gate. You'll carry soap flakes or shave thin strips from an ordinary soap bar, dissolve them in hot water, and scrub the disassembled pieces with gun brushes. Then you oil every piece thoroughly to prevent rust. You'll carry a small flask of a modern substitute that looks and feels like sperm-whale oil and works even better, without killing an endangered species." She nodded to the heavy little flask Skeeter held.

Kit grunted softly, scrubbing hard at his disassembled Frontier Double Action with a stiff, soapy brush. "Beats what I've used, on occasion. A lot of shooters in the Old West carried strips of leather wrapped around lumps of lard. It works, but man, oh, man, does it smell."

Skeeter chuckled. "Hot iron, burnt powder, and rancid pig fat? Yeah, I'll bet it does. Of course," he added wryly, "I did grow up with people whose idea of *haute cuisine* was *tsampa* and *kvess. Anything* rancid smells bad, take my word for it. Okay, show me how to shave soap flakes and disassemble these babies."

Once Kit and Ann were satisfied that Skeeter could load, shoot, disassemble, clean the pistols and shotgun, then successfully reassemble them in working order, Ann loaded him down with ammo and cleaning supplies, gunbelts and holsters, all the miscellaneous gear he'd need for carrying the weapons down the Wild West Gate. Then, and only then, did Ann and Kit consent to let him leave the gun range. Reeking of burnt gunpowder and gun oil and reeling on his feet, Skeeter took the elevator up with Kit, who clapped him on the shoulder and told him he was doing fine, just fine, then got out on a different floor and left Skeeter to make it home under his own steam.

The hot shower he crawled into felt marvellous. As water sluiced over his skin, carrying away sweat and the reek of burnt powder, Skeeter discovered he couldn't shake the feeling that something important was eluding him, niggling at the back of his mind, something that didn't quite fit.

He cast back through his memory to the day of the first station riot, the day Ianira Cassondra and her family had vanished without a trace. He finally put his finger on what was bothering him. If Jenna Caddrick's abductors had kidnapped them, who had rescued Marcus and the girls at the daycare center? *Somebody* had shot dead two terrorists attempting to snatch the girls. It just didn't make sense that the *Ansar Majlis* would've killed two of their own, did it? The terrorist leaders he and Kit had nailed were hotly protesting the kidnapping charge, claiming they'd never touched Jenna Caddrick.

Nobody on station believed them, of course, but given what had happened during that first station riot, it was just possible they were telling the truth. What if someone else *was* involved? Someone who'd known those murderous fanatics were planning to kill Ianira and her family? It was certain that *somebody* had broken up the attempted kidnapping at the daycare center—there'd been plenty of terror-stricken witnesses. Where was that somebody now? And who had he been? And if the *Ansar Majlis* hadn't snatched Caddrick's daughter, who had?

Skeeter narrowed his eyes and slicked back wet hair, scrubbing at his hide with soap while he went over the whole thing in his mind again, from the first sign of trouble to the disastrous end of the first station riot. Come to think of it, there'd been *two* people involved in the initial attack on Ianira, neither of whom fit the profile of terrorists carrying out a hit mission. There was that wild-eyed kid who'd shot the construction worker—one of the same crew that had later tried to kill Bergitta—and somebody else, who had knocked Skeeter and Ianira to the floor.

At the time, Skeeter had thought that second person had shoved them out of the way to keep the wild-eyed kid from killing Ianira, but now he wasn't so sure. Killing that construction worker might've been accidental, if the kid had been aiming at Ianira. But maybe that kid had been aiming at the construction worker, instead? Who'd been standing right behind Ianira? If *that* were true, they might *not* be looking at a relatively simple case of kidnappers running with a hostage and setting up a hit against Ianira on their way through the station.

Not at all.

A scowl tugged the edges of Skeeter's mouth down as spray cascaded down his chest. The Senator's hired detective hadn't mentioned anything like this in his report. Skeeter narrowed his eyes, trying to recall every detail of that first riot. He'd glimpsed the wild-eyed kid brandishing a black-powder pistol, right about the time someone crashed into Skeeter and Ianira, sweeping them to the floor. And the kid had yelled something, too. The word "no," and a cry of fear, all slurred together like, "No! Ahh—"

Skeeter gasped and swallowed a mouthful of water.

Not *"No, ahh—"*

Noah! Noah Armstrong!

Skeeter blinked water out of his eyes, mind whirling in sudden confusion. Noah Armstrong was the terrorist leader who'd grabbed Jenna Caddrick. The *Ansar Majlis* killer who wanted the Lady of Heaven Temples destroyed. But why would a terrorist's hired gun intervene to stop his own hit, when that hit was about to be successfully carried out by his own minions on station? A coil of ice-cold fear slithered its way into the pit of Skeeter's belly despite the hot water cascading down his skin. Just what had they stumbled into the middle of, here?

If Noah Armstrong had been trying to *stop* Ianira Cassondra's murder . . . Then the information the Senator had given them about Noah Armstrong and his plot to kidnap Jenna was suspect. Which meant the FBI and the Senator's paid detective were wrong, too, dead wrong. He'd have to tell Kit, warn him about what they might be walking into, down the Wild West Gate. But not here, not on station. Not within reach of Senator Caddrick's electronic ears and eyes. Skeeter muttered under his breath and finished his shower. *More trouble we need like a white rhino needs Chinese horn hunters.*

But if Skeeter was right, more trouble had landed squarely in their laps. Even worse, it looked like Skeeter was going to have to get them out of it. And that made for a very long and sleepless night.

(((Chapter 4)))

The man travelling under the name Sid Kaederman knew something had gone seriously wrong the moment he stepped into Time Terminal Eighty-Six. While children shrieked and zoomed in and out of line, parents burbled enthusiastically about which gates they planned to tour, bored couriers waited to haul through deliveries of critical supplies, and newlyweds cooed, glued together at lips and palms, Sid Kaederman focused his entire attention on the angry, close-mouthed station security and BATF agents scrutinizing new arrivals and their identification papers.

By the time his own turn for scrutiny came, Sid Kaederman—whose real name and face were a far cry from the ones he currently carried—was sweating blood and planning out in exquisitely barbaric detail exactly what he would do to John Caddrick and his missing offspring when he finally caught up to them. The time terminal's public address system blared non-stop, belting out messages in half-a-dozen different languages until Sid's eardrums ached and his temper approached breakpoint. He bit down and held it, though, not daring to draw attention to himself.

He shuffled forward in a long, snaking line, as thick and variagated as a reticulated python, and cleared various checkpoints: baggage handling, ticket verification to validate his Primary Gate pass, medical stations where his records were scanned in and checked against his identification paperwork. Sid had no real qualms about the quality of his I.D. He could afford the best in the business. It was the other security arrangements that worried him. Adding insult to injurious invasion of his accustomed privacy, Sid Kaederman found himself, along with every other in-bound tourist entering the station, subjected to the most thorough search of luggage and person conducted in the history of TT-86.

Station officials were clearly trying to prevent contraband weaponry or explosive devices from entering the embattled station. Fortunately, Sid possessed a cover story that gave him a perfectly legitimate reason to be armed: a private detective in Senator John Caddrick's employ. He showed his paperwork for the firearms he'd brought along and received his clearances from Time Tours and BATF security, then stalked into TT-86 nursing a silent, volcanic rage.

Shangri-La Station, for all its vaunted fame, was little more than a fancy shopping mall with hotels and bizarrely dressed patrons playing dress up in outlandish costumes. The station itself didn't much impress him, beyond its apparent lunacy of construction, with stairways to nowhere and steel platforms hanging midair for no apparent reason. What got Sid's immediate attention, however, was the *feel* of the station. The mood of Time Terminal Eighty-Six was explosive. If that seething anger had been aimed at the proper target, Sid would've been delighted; his plans called for riots and mayhem directed at specific, carefully chosen groups and individuals. But the meticulously planned fury his operatives were orchestrating against down-timers and time tourism, a campaign of terror and intimidation which formed a critical piece of Sid's long-term plans, was notably distorted on TT-86.

People were angry, all right. Murderously angry.

At exactly the wrong target.

"Who does Caddrick think he is?" a slender woman in expensive Victorian attire demanded, voice as strident as the colors of her costume. "That creep waltzes in here with a pack of armed thugs like he owns the place. Teargasses half of Commons and tries an armed takeover of the whole station . . ."

". . . keeps it up, somebody's gonna shoot that son of a bitch! And I'll dance on his grave when they do!"

". . . heard Caddrick can't even leave his hotel room. He's terrified the Angels of Grace will break his neck. And for once, I agree with that bunch of lunatics . . ."

". . . hear about his fight with Kit Carson? The Senator demanded a suite at the Neo Edo. Kit turned him down flat! God, I wish I could've seen his face. Jackass had to settle for the *Time Tripper,* because everybody else was full up for the Ripper Season! I hope Orva puts stinging nettle in his bedsheets . . ."

The running commentary dogged Sid's heels from the precinct surrounding Primary clear through the sprawling insanity of the station, all the way to the lobby of the Time Tripper Hotel, a modest hostelry that clearly catered to tourists on a limited budget. Smiling tightly at the thought of Caddrick's well-earned discomfiture, he placed a call to the Senator's room from the lobby's courtesy phone. Ten minutes later, Sid found himself in a tawdry little hotel room littered with empty liquor bottles, facing down the disgruntled Senator. John Caddrick's air of calm self-assurance faltered slightly when Sid allowed the steel to show in his gaze. The staff weenie who had escorted Sid up from the lobby hesitated nervously.

"That'll be all," Caddrick snapped.

The man fled. The moment Caddrick's aide closed the door, Sid exploded.

"*What the goddamned hell do you think you've been doing?*"

Caddrick backed up a pace, eyes flickering in visible dismay. Sid advanced on him. "Are you *trying* to get us all electrocuted? My God, Caddrick, what possessed you to walk in here with *federal marshals,* trying to take over the whole goddamned station?"

"Now, listen just a minute—"

"*No, you listen!*" Caddrick actually jumped, then closed his mouth, lips thinning as his face lost color. Sid jabbed a finger at the nearest chair. Caddrick thought about arguing, thought better, and sat. Sid stood glaring for a long moment, wrestling his temper under control.

"You are out of your mind, Caddrick, stirring up a hornet's nest like this. Grandstanding for the press will earn you a one way stroll to the gas chamber, if you're not damned careful. And I, for one, am *not* taking that walk with you. Get that very clear, right now! I'm here to contain the damage as best I can. It was bad enough your kid slipped through the net we threw up around New York. But now you've got the *Inter-Temporal Court* diddling in the middle of our business. I heard the station courier sent through placing the call the instant he came through Primary into the up-time lobby. Do you have any *idea* what an investigation by I.T.C.H. means?"

Caddrick had enough intelligence, at least, to lose an additional shade of color. "Yes." He swallowed hard enough to bounce his Adam's apple like a nervous bird. "I do know. That goddamned bitch of a deputy manager—"

"No! Don't lay this one on the station, Caddrick. You're responsible for this mess. Haven't you figured out by now, there are some people you can push and bully and others you have to slip up behind with a silenced gun, if you want to neutralize them? Didn't you even bother to do a little basic personnel research? That deputy station manager you're bleating about is the granddaughter of Coralisha Azzan!"

The Senator had the grace to blanch, widening his eyes in alarm.

"Yes, you begin to see just how badly you've stepped in it, don't you? That woman is not going to back down, not for you or God or anybody else. And word out there is," he jerked his thumb toward the station Commons, "you've also managed to piss off Kit Carson. For God's sake, Caddrick, you'd better not buy that drivel about Kit Carson being a washed up has-been, playing hotel manager and hiding from the world. That bastard is one dangerous old man. And he's just as likely as the Inter-Temporal Court to start poking into your affairs, just to get even for threatening his station."

"But—"

"*Shut up, dammit!*" He had to grab his temper in both hands to keep from cracking the idiot across the mouth with the back of his hand. "I *told* you to lay low, Caddrick, *told* you to keep your nose out of this! Playing choked-up Daddy for the press cameras up time is one thing. Throwing your weight around TT-86 and threatening an armed takeover of a major time terminal . . . Jeezus H. Christ, Caddrick, I think you've actually started to believe your own biographers! Nobody, not even John Paul Caddrick, is *that* invincible."

"What the hell was I *supposed* to do?" Caddrick snarled. "Sit around with my thumb up my ass while Jenna and that putrid little deviant Armstrong slipped back through this station with their evidence and took it straight to the FBI?"

Sid just looked at him, unable to believe the man's colossal stupidity. "Slip back through the station?" he repeated softly. "Are you out of your mind? No, you have to be in possession of a mind, first, to be out of it. For your information, Armstrong and your misbegotten little girl won't risk setting foot back on this station for the next *year*. Armstrong is nobody's fool, Caddrick. That bastard's given us the slip three times, already. There was never any danger of Armstrong *or* Jenna slipping back through this station with their evidence. Not before we could trace them and shut them up for good. Time was on *our* side, not theirs. But no, you had to stick your big, fat foot right in the middle of the biggest hornet's nest I've ever seen, and smash it for good measure."

"All right!" Caddrick snapped. "You've made your point! But things aren't nearly as grim as you seem to think. We know where Armstrong took Jenna *and* that down-timer bitch, Ianira Cassondra. They went through the Denver Gate. The station's mounting a search-and-rescue mission, naturally. It leaves in three days. All we have to do is put you on the team. Armstrong and Jenna won't live to testify, not to Kit Carson or anyone else on the search team."

"Kit Carson?" Sid echoed. "What does he have to do with it?"

"Carson," the Senator muttered, unwilling to meet Sid's eyes, "took it upon himself to lead the damned search mission."

Sid Kaederman counted twenty. Twice.

"All right," he finally grated out. "What other nasty little surprises do you intend springing on me?" Sid listened in appalled silence as Caddrick related the state of affairs on TT-86. When the Senator finally wound down, Sid promised himself to see Caddrick's career down in flames. "What's done is done," he muttered. "And as much as it pains me to say it, I would suggest you throw your excessive weight around the station manager's office one more time, because I don't think there's a chance in hell Kit Carson is going to allow me on that search-and-rescue mission without threats from you to put me there."

Caddrick glared at him, hatred burning in those famous grey eyes, but he picked up the telephone and dialed. Sid found the hotel room's wet bar, downed a full tumbler of scotch, and waited.

Kit Carson was too busy to watch Primary go through its antics. With only three days until the Denver Gate cycled, he was putting Skeeter through as much cram-session training as possible. Nor did Kit have any intention of being caught near the start of another potential riot. Skeeter Jackson, sweating and swearing where he'd just fallen to the gym floor's protective mat yet again, victim of Kit's smooth Aikido, wiped wet hair out of his eyes with the back of a sweaty arm and glared up at him.

"Hey, boss?"

"Yes?" Kit balanced lightly on the balls of his feet, waiting.

"You *are* gonna let me live long enough to walk through the Wild West Gate, aren't you?"

Kit just grinned, which left Skeeter muttering under his breath again. Kit understood enough basic Mongolian to catch the gist of what he'd just said, if not the specific details. "Good God, Skeeter, where'd you pick up language like that?"

The newly fledged Neo Edo house detective grunted and heaved himself back to his feet. "Pretty little thing named Houlun."

Kit blinked in surprise. "Yesukai's captive bride?"

It was Skeeter's turn to stare. "Good grief. You're the only person besides Nally Mundy who's ever heard of her."

Kit found himself laughing. "I've forgotten more history than Doc Mundy ever knew, bless him. And he would've made a fine time scout, if his health hadn't been so frail. So, Houlun could swear like a sailor, could she?"

Skeeter rolled his eyes. "Oh, man, could she ever. Well, she did have reason to be pissed off. Yesukai kidnapped her right out of her wedding procession to a guy from another clan. I was there when it happened. After I'd learned enough Mongolian to figure out what she screeched at him all the way back to Yakka Clan territory, I turned red for a solid week. I was only eight, after all."

Kit chuckled. "Someday—" and Skeeter's headlong rush toward

Kit transformed itself into an abrupt need for the ex-thief to become airborne "—I'd love to hear the whole story."

"*Oof . . .*" Skeeter knew, at least, how to land, which made Kit feel better about the younger man's chances in a fight. He groaned and rolled over onto hands and knees. "No way. I ain't gonna live long enough."

"You're just soft from easy living. Now, let's try it again—"

"Hey, Kit!" Sven Bailey poked his head out of his office. "Phone! Ronisha Azzan. And she doesn't sound happy."

Kit and Skeeter exchanged startled glances.

"Now what?" Skeeter muttered.

"We'll find out. Take five." Kit jogged over to Sven's office, where the bladed-weapons instructor had gone back to sharpening a *gladius.* Kit grabbed the phone left lying on the desk. "Kit Carson."

"We've got trouble."

Echoing Skeeter, Kit said, "Now what?"

"You'd better get up here. Skeeter, too. We're adding somebody to the search team. And you're not going to like it."

"With Denver cycling in three days, I already don't like it. Who?"

Ronisha said very dryly, "A detective. Senator Caddrick's. He just arrived through Primary. He and the Senator are in the aerie, demanding to see you."

Hoo, boy . . .

"We'll be there in five." Kit didn't plan on showering first, either; honest sweat never hurt anybody and the Senator deserved it, thrusting some up-time detective down their throats, without adequate time to prepare him for down-time work.

"What's Caddrick done now?" Sven asked, glancing up from a whetstone, where he was putting a keen edge on the thrusting tip of his favorite Roman short sword.

"Saddled us with some up-time detective."

"Oh, great. That's all you need."

"You're telling me. I'll see you later. If Caddrick doesn't toss us in jail for telling him what I think of his idea."

Sven snorted. "Yeah, right. Bull Morgan's one thing. *Kit Carson,* not even Caddrick's stupid enough to tangle with."

Rarely—very rarely—world-wide fame had its advantages. Kit grinned, then headed out at a jog. "Skeeter, heads up, we got trouble. We're going to the aerie."

Skeeter, rubbing gingerly at bruises, whipped around. "The *aerie?*"

"Come on, I'll fill you in on the way."

"But, Kit! I smell worse than my last pony at the end of a Mongolian summer!"

Kit's grin blazed. "Good."

Skeeter, bless his quick mind, chortled and fell into step beside him. "Caddrick, huh? Now what?" Kit told him. Skeeter rolled his eyes. "Oh, God, do me a favor, huh? This detective, whoever he is, make *him* spend six whole hours weighing and sorting bullets while learning how not to bake a bang-tail, will you?"

Kit chuckled all the way to the aerie.

Once they arrived, however, all desire to smile fled. Senator John Paul Caddrick was in the middle of a tirade, demanding to know where the search team was, did they think he had nothing better to do than cool his heels, waiting, when there was work to be done and if Ronisha Azzan wanted to keep her job, she'd better produce them in the next sixty seconds or less . . .

"Save your threats," Kit growled as he left the elevator where Skeeter was visibly gulping for courage. "They don't impress me. Now what's this garbage about adding somebody to my search team?"

John Caddrick rounded on him, mouth opening for something doubtless intended to be earthshattering. Then he rocked back on his heels and thought better of it. "As I live and breathe . . . Your manners always were atrocious, Carson."

Kit ignored the insult and came straight to the point. "What's this about saddling me with a detective you want to tag along?"

Caddrick started to reply, then evidently caught a whiff of Kit's gym-clothes perfume, because the Senator stepped back a pace, nostrils pinching shut, as Kit advanced. It was a minor psychological victory, forcing the Senator to give ground, but it served to put Caddrick slightly off-stride and that was exactly where Kit wanted him. He pressed his momentary advantage.

"You do realize how stupid it is, how dangerously stupid, sending somebody without down-time experience on a mission like this? And with only three days' worth of prep time? We're not heading for New Hollywood, Caddrick. People who don't know what they're doing can get themselves killed all sorts of messy ways in 1885, even *without* chasing armed terrorists."

"I would point out," Caddrick said coldly, "that Wardmann-Wolfe agents are the most experienced in the business. Sid Kaederman has more than impressed me with his credentials. He's the man for this job and I insist he be added to the search team."

Kit flicked his gaze to the man seated behind Caddrick, a serenely unruffled man with dark hair and fair skin who looked to be in his mid-thirties and might have been as much as ten years older. Or younger. He was already dressed for the Denver Gate, in a fancy-cut Eastern gentleman's suit with an embroidered silk vest. He sported a silver-headed cane that doubtless concealed a lethal sword. *Christ, he looks like a riverboat gambler. That's all we need.* Short, compact, probably well muscled under that fancy costume, he had the kind of face that would've looked equally at home in a Wall Street brokerage firm, on a fishing trawler in the North Sea, or cutting through a bank vault with acetylene torch and plastic explosives. His gaze, as he returned Kit's appraising stare, was direct enough, yet hooded and wary as any predator's faced with an unknown opponent.

"Mr. Carson," he said softly, rising with abrupt, easy grace that spoke of superb conditioning, but probably not much martial arts training, "Sid Kaederman's the name."

He offered a hand. Kit shook it, detecting in the process a slight roughening of callus along the pad of his index finger, suggesting long hours of practice on a firing range, using a trigger with grooves cut into it. "Mr. Kaederman. How many temporal gates have you stepped through? And how well can you handle a horse?"

A tiny smile came and went. "I've never been down a time gate, actually. I confine my work to the up-time world. And rarely indulge in vacations. As for horses, I've never had any trouble dominating lesser creatures. I can ride well enough to suit even you."

Kit ignored the veiled insult. "A search-and-rescue into the Rockies of 1885 on the trail of known terrorists with hostages isn't a quick jog down a bridle trail at some dude ranch or urban riding club. And I won't be putting you on the back of a well-trained hack used to beginners. The Old West doesn't bear much resemblance to the up-time urban world where Wardmann-Wolfe agents pick up most of their clients. Just exactly what *does* qualify you for a mission like this? If you don't mind?"

A glint that might have been humor—or something else entirely— appeared in Kaederman's dark eyes. "Apart from anything else, I'm going because my employer will shut down this station if I'm not on the team. Senator Caddrick has made it quite clear that he doesn't trust any effort put forth by this station. More to the point, we're dealing with *Ansar Majlis*. Terrorists, I *do* understand. Very thoroughly."

Caddrick had them over a barrel and Kit knew it. Worse, he knew that Sid Kaederman knew it, too, and was amused. Kit shrugged, conceding defeat in the only way possible. "If you're thrown by your nag the first time it steps on a rattler or hears a puma scream, you're on your own. As team leader, I won't take the time to nursemaid an injured greenhorn back to the Denver gatehouse. If you don't have an acceptable kit thrown together by the time the gate cycles, too bad. You'll either miss the gate or find yourself on your own to furnish it down time, because I won't wait for you to buy or rent items you should've been acquiring days ago."

"I'll do my best not to disappoint." Dry, self-assured, amused once again.

Kit snorted. "Frankly, Kaederman, I don't give a damn whether you disappoint me or not. Do your job or you'll be looking for another one. Senator," he glanced at Caddrick, "since you insist on including Mr. Kaederman on the search-and-rescue team, you can pay the bill. Send him to Ann Vinh Mulhaney for appropriate historical arms. I'd suggest a Remington suite," he added, glancing at the fancy cut of Kaederman's clothes.

The Senator blinked. "A what?"

Caddrick, who had introduced some of the most draconian anti-gun legislation in the history of Western civilization, clearly had no idea what Kit was talking about.

Kit glanced directly at Kaederman. "As a Wardmann-Wolfe

detective, you doubtless know how to use modern guns. But you won't have the slightest idea what to carry for 1885."

"Black-powder firearms can't be any more challenging than service-rifle competitions."

Kit raised his brows. "You've done long-distance shooting, then? All right. We'll start you out with, say, the Remington Model 1875 single-action revolver in .44-40 and a Remington Number Three rifle in .45-70, the Hepburn falling-block model. Tell Ann to put Creedmore sights on it, and if you take the time to learn it, that'll give us a half-mile range if we end up in a long-distance shootout with the *Ansar Majlis*. And put a .41 Remington derringer in your fancy coat pocket, Mr. Kaederman, if you want a hideout gun. Just be careful you don't blow your foot off with it. Those derringers don't have safety mechanisms and the firing pins are longer than the breech faces. Drop one hammer down, it'll blow a .41-caliber hole in your gut. Get Ann to show you how to safely load and unload it. Tell her to bill the Senator. Meet me in the station's library first thing after dinner. You've got a lot of research ahead, if you want to go on this mission. Now, if you'll excuse us, Mr. Jackson and I have some unfinished business waiting."

Senator Caddrick sputtered, "Now, wait just a damned minute—"

Kit narrowed his eyes and held Caddrick's gaze coldly. "Those are *my* terms, Senator. You hired him. So don't try to blackmail the station into paying his expenses. Those are *your* problem. Mr. Kaederman," he nodded curtly, "I'll see you at the library, six-thirty sharp. Don't be late."

Skeeter all but tripped over his own feet, rushing into the elevator ahead of Kit. Senator Caddrick was still sputtering. But as the elevator doors slid shut, Sid Kaederman gave Kit a small, satisifed smile and a tiny flick of the fingers at his brow, acknowledging a minor victory in the murderous little game in which they were embroiled. Skeeter Jackson rearranged sweat on his forehead with a glistening forearm. "Sheesh, Kit, you really do like to live dangerously, don't you?"

"Skeeter," he sighed as the elevator carried them down toward Commons, "there's only one thing infinitely worse than running a luxury hotel on a time terminal."

"What's that?"

"Not having a time terminal to run that hotel *on*."

To that, Skeeter had no reply whatsover.

Catharine "Kate" Eddowes generally enjoyed her annual trek out to the fields of Kent to work the harvest. Picking hops wasn't as difficult as some jobs she'd done and the Kentish countryside was almost like a great garden, full of flowers and green fields and fresh, crisp air. Moreover, John Kelly, with whom she had shared a bed more or less continuously for seven years, almost always benefitted from the change to the countryside, where the cleaner air eased his constant cough.

But this year, things were different.

Late September was generally warm and beautiful. But the whole summer had been unseasonably chilly and full of rain. By the time they arrived in Kent, the late September weather was raw. Working sunup to sundown in wet, cold fields, John Kelly's health deteriorated alarmingly.

"It's no use, John," she finally said. "We can't stay the season, this time. You'll catch your death, so you will, and then what'll become of me, luv? I need you, John Kelly."

Tears of defeat and shame caused him to turn aside, but by nightfall, his cough had grown so alarmingly worse, he agreed to abandon the hop harvest, even though it meant giving up money they both needed. They had no choice but return to London, where they could at least find a dry room for Kelly to sleep in at night. It was a long walk from Hunton, Kent back to London, but they hadn't any money for a train, so walk it they did, in the company of another couple they'd met working the same fields.

"We're off for Cheltenham," their newfound friends said as they came to the turning for London, "so we'll say goodbye and luck to you. Kate, look here, I've got a pawn ticket for a flannel shirt up there in London, why don't you take it? It's only for twopence, but the shirt might fit your old man, there, and I'd say he needs a bit of a warm shirt, what with that cough of his."

"Thank you." Catharine accepted the crumpled pawn ticket gratefully. "I worry about John's health, with the cold weather coming and us with no money. It's good to us, you are." She slipped the ticket into one of her pockets, next to the wrinkled letter she'd bought from Annie Chapman, poor soul, the letter she'd been too terrified to have translated, after what had happened to poor Annie. And Dark Annie had confessed to buying the letters from Polly Nichols, who was also brutally dead.

Maybe the smartest thing would be to get rid of the letter altogether?

Just throw it away or burn it, never even try to have it translated?

As they waved goodbye and set out walking again, taking the fork in the road that would lead them back to London, Catharine stole worried glances at John. His color wasn't good and his breathing was labored. His kidney complaint had flared up again, too, given the number of times he had to stop along the roadside and from the way he rubbed his side and back from time to time, when he thought she wasn't looking. They needed money for a doctor and medicine, just as poor Annie had, and they'd very little left to sell or pawn to obtain it. They'd so counted on the money from the hop harvest to see them through the winter and now there wouldn't be anything in reserve at all, with the coldest months yet to come.

I'll have to find out what's in the letter, Kate realized with a shiver, *I'll have to find who wrote it, if I want my John to live 'til spring. Too bad them coppers won't put up a reward for that Whitechapel murderer what's done in Polly and Annie.* She didn't want to try blackmailing the author of the filthy thing, not after what had become of its previous owners, but she didn't know what else to do.

Well, she told herself, *there are plenty of Welshmen in the East End, so there are, surely one of them can tell me what's in this precious letter of Annie's. Pity John doesn't speak Welsh, then I wouldn't have to worry about sharing the money with whoever translates it for me. Maybe I can pawn the flannel shirt somewhere else and use the money to pay someone to read it out for me in English?*

Her stomach rumbled, as empty as the pocket she reserved for cash when she had any. John Kelly, striding gamely along despite his labored breathing, glanced over and smiled briefly. "Heard that, luv," he chuckled. "Hungry, are we?"

"I could stand a meal," she admitted, aware that he would be just as hungry as she and in greater need of food, what with fighting off two kinds of illness. "Don't fret about it John Kelly, we'll get to town all right, even if we're hungry when we get there, and you always manage to earn a few pence, luv, so we'll have ourselves a hot supper soon enough."

And she could always earn a few pence, herself, if it came to that. She only resorted to selling herself when their circumstances became truly desperate. But whenever he fell ill, they had to have money, and Kate Eddowes was not too proud to earn fourpence any way she could. And her daughter, doubtless prompted by her new husband, had taken to moving about the south end of London with such frequency, Kate often found it difficult to trace the girl and ask for tuppence.

She'd try to find her daughter again when they got to town, first thing after securing a bed at their old lodging house, down to 55 Flower and Dean Street. They'd pawn something to raise the money for food and the bed, then she'd find her little girl and try to get more cash, and if that didn't work, then she'd jolly well find some drunken Welshman who wanted a quick fourpenny knee trembler and trade herself for a translation of Annie Chapman's letter. Once she had that, there'd be plenty of money for John Kelly's medicines and her own gin and as many warm, dry beds as they wanted, for the rest of their lives. And whoever had butchered Polly Nichols and Annie Chapman would find himself dangling from the end of a gallows rope. Kate Eddowes had once made a fair living, writing and selling cheap books of lives at public hangings. She suppressed a wry smile. Wouldn't it be ironic, now, if she ended up making her fortune from a little gallows book about the Whitechapel Murderer?

A fierce sky shimmered like an inverted bowl of beaten bronze. Dust, hot and acrid, bit Skeeter's throat despite the bandanna tied across his lower face. Skeeter shifted his weight in the saddle once again, nursing a blinding headache and a prickle of heat rash under his dirty, grit-filled clothes. The constant shift and sway of his horse under aching thighs reminded Skeeter forcefully how long it'd been since he'd done any sustained riding. He was a good rider. Skeeter had, in a different lifetime, felt at home on anything a saddle could be thrown across. But after years of easy living on Shangri-La Station, he was simply—sadly—out of practice. And thanks to Sid Kaederman's irritating, smug presence, somehow contriving to be constantly underfoot without ever becoming downright intrusive, Skeeter hadn't found even three seconds alone with Kit to air his suspicions about Noah Armstrong.

Why couldn't Armstrong have picked January to go on the lam, rather than July? Heat fell like water down into the narrow draw where their string of ponies clattered and clopped along a so-called trail. *And why couldn't that pack of black-powder enthusiasts have picked a spot closer to civilization for their Wild West shootout?* He and Kit had figured Armstrong would ditch the time tour first chance, heading for someplace crowded. San Francisco, maybe. Chicago or New York, if he really wanted to get lost. Searching an entire continent for Noah Armstrong and his hostages had not been Skeeter's notion of a good time, although he cheerfully would do just that, to catch up to Ianira and her family.

But Armstrong hadn't done that. Travelling in the guise of Joey Tyrolin, drunkard and braggadocio, Armstrong hadn't even ditched the black-powder competition tour. Instead, the terrorist ringleader had ridden up into the mountains with the rest of the eager shooters, presumably with his hostages still under duress. Why Armstrong had stuck to the competition group, not even Kit could figure. And Sid Kaederman, who had boasted so suavely of understanding terrorists, offered no explanation at all, merely shrugging his shoulders.

So Kit and Skeeter and the Wardmann-Wolfe agent followed their trail, which meant they took the train from Denver down to Colorado Springs, then saddled up and headed west toward Pikes Peak for the distant, abandoned mining camp where the competition was underway. Kurt Meinrad, the temporal guide detailed to their mission by Granville Baxter, had rounded up a short train of pack mules to haul their supplies. An hour onto the trail, Sid Kaederman began to shift ceaselessly in his saddle, obviously suffering from the unaccustomed activity. He finally urged his horse up alongside their guide's. "Why did that pack of idiots come clear out here to hold some stupid competition? Why not just stay in Denver? There weren't any gun-control laws in effect yet, so why come out to the middle of nowhere?"

Meinrad, face weathered to old leather by years of guiding time tourists through these mountains, turned easily in his saddle. "They wanted the feel of a real Old West event, which isn't possible in Denver. The city's too grown up, too civilized. Millionaires who made their fortunes in the gold and silver booms have turned Denver into a miniature copy of cities back East, with fancy houses, artwork imported from Europe, and some of the most snobbish society you'll ever meet. *Nouveau riche* are always edgy about proving how superior their cultured manners are and the Denver Four Hundred are among the worst."

Kaederman just grunted and shifted again, trying to get comfortable.

"What they wanted was an abandoned mining town back in the hills, with plenty of old buildings and rusting equipment lying around to be shot at and hidden behind. The trouble is, not many camps are abandoned yet. The big strikes started in the 1850s, at places like Central City, with more coming in the '70s, at Animas Forks and Apex and Leadville. They're all boom towns, full of miners and drunken hopefuls and prostitutes and enterprising merchants making fortunes selling supplies at outrageous prices. You can't hold this kind of competition in a boom town, so we decided on Mount MacIntyre." When Kaederman gave him a baffled look, Meinrad chuckled. "The town's been deserted for years. In fact, the legendary Cripple Creek strike was actually ignored for twelve years, because of Mount MacIntyre."

Skeeter, intrigued despite Kaederman's irritating presence, asked, "How come? Even *I've* heard of Cripple Creek. I can't believe gold-hungry miners would ignore a strike that rich for twelve whole years!"

Meinrad grinned. "Well, a guy name of Chicken Bill claimed he'd struck ore that assayed out at two thousand dollars to the ton—quite a motherload, even for this area. Trouble was, the whole thing was a hoax. Miners flooded in and ripped the countryside to shreds, looking, and all they found was dust and bedrock. Folks got to calling it the Mount Pisgah Hoax, through a mix-up in locales, so when drunken old Bob Womack found ore worth two hundred dollars a ton at Mount Pisgah back in '78, nobody would believe it. They still don't. It'll be another five years, 1890, before a German count by the name of Pourtales proves Womack right. Then, of course, Cripple Creek becomes a legend, particularly after the fires of '96 burn the whole town to the ground. By 1902, they'll be bringing twenty-five million a year out of Cripple Creek's gold mines, but right now, the whole region is deserted, thanks to the Mount Pisgah Hoax."

Skeeter chuckled. "Which really happened at Mount MacIntyre. Sounds like the perfect place to hold a black-powder competition. And if folks do a little prospecting on the sly, down toward Mount Pisgah, who's going to complain?"

Meinrad laughed. "Certainly not the BATF. They'll get their cut of any nuggets brought home. Anyway, there's enough local color to give our competitors all the Old West they can stomach." He glanced at the unhappy detective, who was shifting uncomfortably in the saddle again. "Don't worry, Kaederman, you'll survive, although your thighs might not thank you for it. You shouldn't develop saddle galls, that only happens when your clothes and your gear don't fit proper, but if you do, you can smear them with a salve I always bring along for the greenhorns." He grinned and tapped his saddle bags. "Antiseptic, antibiotic, and plenty of anesthetic to deaden the pain."

The thought of the insufferable Mr. Kaederman smearing saddle galls in his fancy backside cheered Skeeter no end. Kaederman's performance for the press at their departure had been enough to earn Skeeter's enmity for life, standing there sucking up to that overweening toad, Caddrick, calmly assuring the newsies that he would personally see Jenna Caddrick safely back to her father's care, a job clearly beyond the capabilities of the station's search team.

Skeeter would've given a great deal to jab a straight pin in the man's rump during that so-called press briefing, just to watch him yelp. He already dreaded the hullaballoo waiting for their return. The *next* newsie who stuck a microphone in Skeeter's face and shouted, "Is it true you're running a con-game on the Senator, taking advantage of his bereavement?" would get a mouthful of unpleasantness, courtesy of the nearest object not fastened to the floor.

Meanwhile . . .

There were two ways to reach the dud mines at Mount MacIntyre, from Colorado Springs. They could loop around to the north, through Woodland Park Divide then down through Florissant toward Cripple Creek, or they could ride south past Victor, then swing north around the flank of mountains in the way. Either route would take time, but the northern trail was longer, so Meinrad chose the route down past Victor. They'd left the Colorado Springs rail station near mid-morning, moving at a steady lope that wouldn't put too great a strain on the horses. By the time the sun was low over the shoulders of the Rockies, Skeeter was bushed, far worse than their tough mountain ponies. The canyon they'd been following finally opened out into a moonscape of blasted, barren hillsides where nothing but scrub grew along deep, eroded gullies. *Gold mining country.*

They straggled along in a stretched-out line, rounding enormous mounds of broken rock and silt left to bake in the hot sun, and came at length to a ridge above a ramshackle town. The mining camp sprawled between piles of tailings, sluice flumes, open-pit mine works, boarded-over mine shafts, and the meanders of a sparkling river which caught the hot sun in diamond flashes. Water rippled and spilled its glittering way over and around immense boulders which had been blasted down from the surrounding mountainsides.

A sharp report cracked on the still air, prompting Skeeter's pony to shift under his thighs. He controlled the uneasy animal with his legs, settling it down to blow restively and champ its bit. A long, dry wooden flume teetered its way a good three hundred feet down a barren hillside to the valley floor. Down beside it, a cloud of blue-grey smoke puffed out onto the hot afternoon air. The smoke hung above the flume's broken sides for a moment before gradually dissipating. A hundred feet away, another puff of smoke appeared as a second shot was fired from the vicinity of a ramshackle livery stable.

Then a galloping horse burst out of the stable and shot across a broad stretch of open ground at a dead run. The rider, leaning low over his horse's neck, drew smoothly from a right-handed hip holster and fired at the side of the flume. Smoke bellied out and hung on the still air. Dust swirled up from thundering hooves as the rider holstered his six-gun, then reached across to his left hip and pulled a second enormous pistol from a cross-draw. He fired again as the galloping horse shot past the flume. He reholstered at full gallop and raced down to a shack at the edge of the clearing.

The sweating rider pulled up hard on the reins and hauled his mount to a slithering stop. Then he drew from his right-hand holster again and twisted around, firing a shot at the flume over his shoulder. Kicking his horse into motion, he reholstered once more as the animal swept around the shed and galloped back toward the rickety wooden watercourse. Another cross-draw shot from the left-hand hip and the horse raced past the flume to the livery stable. A sharp whistle sounded as the horse galloped back inside, hidden by a cloud of dust.

"Time!" a man's voice rang out from one of the abandoned houses. Then, "Reset! And . . . Next shooter up!"

This time, Skeeter saw a man crouched behind the flume, positioned several yards uphill from the mounted rider's target. The guy at the flume ran downhill and yanked targets from either side of the dilapidated wooden structure, hastily tacking up new ones for the next contestant. He ran back uphill and jumped into a pit which protected him from flying lead. He then drew a revolver and fired into the air. At that signal, another shot rang out from the livery stable.

This time Skeeter saw the puff of dust fly up from the dry, brittle wood as lead struck a target. Then a second galloping horse shot out into the open, the second rider also leaning low. This contestant wore his six-guns butt forward. The rider fired both shots at the flume as his horse, a big paint with brown splotches down its flanks, raced past. Again, the rider galloped to the shed, where he pulled up hard, his single-leather reins hooking down under his belt buckle as he snugged his horse's head back for the sliding stop. He fired the over-the-shoulder shot and reholstered, then urged his mount forward, letting the reins slide forward.

The single leather strap hooked itself under his second, butt-forward pistol, and dragged it out of the holster neat as anything. The gun flipped midair and landed in the dust with a disastrous thunk.

The rider froze in dismay for a long, penalizing second. Then he scrambled out of the saddle and retrieved his piece, lunged back into the saddle again with a one-footed dancing hop, and urged his mount around the shed. He had to circle it again, to give himself time to reholster his gun and draw it correctly for the shot on the return gallop.

Skeeter chuckled. "I'll bet that guy's cussing a streak by the time he gets back to the livery stable."

Kit glanced around. "Yes. And if that was a real shootout, down there, he'd probably be an embarrassed corpse right about now."

Skeeter sobered. "Point taken."

The judge in the abandoned house called, "Time!" and Kurt Meinrad put hands to lips and gave out a loud, drawn-out whistle. Then he yelled, "Halluuuu!" For a moment, all was still in the abandoned mining town; then doors were flung open and abruptly the place swarmed with life. Men in faded, dusty denim work pants and checked shirts or fringed buckskins came out of hiding from a dozen buildings. Women, too, some clad in buckskins like the men, others in long prairie skirts and frontier-rugged dresses, with wide-brimmed bonnets to shade their faces from the fierce sun, came running excitedly from seemingly abandoned structures. Down beside the disused ore flume, the target changer waved up at them and returned Meinrad's vigorous greeting.

"Move out," Meinrad called.

Kit Carson's thump of heels to his pony's sides was almost as weary as Skeeter's own. The retired scout hadn't been in a saddle any more recently than Skeeter had—and while Kit was as lean and tough as old belt leather left too long in the sun, he wasn't getting any younger. The sight of the toughest man Skeeter knew, just as whacked out as he was, cheered Skeeter a little. They rode silently into "town" while the re-enactment shooters assembled in front of the ramshackle livery stable. Someone had refurbished the stalls and corral sufficiently to house several dozen horses, but only a dozen or so were in sight. He spotted drifts of smoke from the chimneys of several tumble-down houses, their windows long since broken out by storms and wild animals.

A thickset man in his thirties, holding a Spencer repeater propped easily across one shoulder, blinked up at their guide. Skeeter recognized the man vaguely as one of Time Tours' Denver guides, who spent most of his career down time. The guide was staring at them in open puzzlement. "Kurt Meinrad! I didn't figure they'd send *you* out here! Weren't you supposed to be on vacation by now? Not that I'm sorry to see you. I told that courier we needed the best help there was. You must've been sitting in the Denver gate house, to get here this fast."

Skeeter swung himself out of the saddle as Meinrad and Kit, the latter all but unrecognizable under gritty dust, dismounted. The ground was hard under Skeeter's boot soles, baked dry by the blazing summer sun. The town smelt of woodsmoke, sulphurous gun powder, hot sunlight on dust, and human sweat. Skeeter reeked of overheated horse.

"Courier?" Kit asked sharply. "What courier? We're not here because of any courier."

The Time Tours guide with the Spencer glanced at Kit, then did a classic double-take. "Good God! *Kit Carson?* No, they certainly wouldn't have sent you to answer my call for help. What in God's name are *you* doing here?"

Kit shook his head. "Never mind that now. Why'd you send out a courier? What kind of trouble did you need help with?"

"Two murders, is what," the man grunted, spitting tobacco juice to one side with a brown splat. "Two stinking murders and four disappearing tourists." When Skeeter groaned under his breath, the man glanced from Kit to Skeeter to Sid Kaederman and shot a worried look at Kurt Meinrad, then held out a meaty hand to Kit. "Orson Travers. Let's get you settled in before I give you the details. It's hot as blazes out here and you men look to need a good, cold drink before we start poking into this mess."

Kit nodded, clearly impatient with the delay, but acknowledged their need to slap the dust off and slake their thirst and care for their horses. "Pleasure to meet you, Mr. Travers. This is Skeeter Jackson, Neo Edo house detective. And Mr. Sid Kaederman, private detective with the Wardmann-Wolfe Agency."

"Gentlemen," Orson Travers said gravely. "My drovers'll see to your ponies and settle your pack mules. We'll go up to the saloon and talk things out. I got a funny feeling our trouble's related to whatever you're doing here with two detectives."

So did Skeeter. And from the look on his face, so did Kit. What Sid Kaederman thought, Skeeter didn't care. John Caddrick's pet snoop could jump over the nearest cliff, if he wanted to do something really useful.

"Saloon is up that way," Travers pointed.

Shortly, Skeeter found himself in a mended wooden chair sipping cool water from a chipped enamel cup. Tourists crowded into the ramshackle saloon to listen. Skeeter didn't see a single face in that crowd that could possibly have belonged to Noah Armstrong or Jenna Caddrick, let alone his missing friends. He was seriously worried that he knew exactly who was dead and who was missing.

"All right," Kit said quietly when the last of the tour group had crowded in. "You say you've lost six people. I'm betting your bad news will tie in with ours. We're here on a search-and-rescue mission. One that will either keep Shangri-La operational or see the station closed down, depending on how well we do our jobs." He studied the whole group closely. "I don't see Joey Tyrolin anywhere. Or Cassie Coventina."

Orson Travers ran a hand across his sweat-soaked face and hair. "No, you won't. That's the trouble I mentioned." Travers grimaced. "There was an ambush, out on the endurance course. Two tourists dead, shot to death by God only knows who. One of their horses, too. And another tourist lit out during the confusion, just skied up with everything he owned. Took his porter with him, the porter *and* his kids, who weren't even supposed to be out here. Bull Morgan and Granville Baxter will have my job," he added glumly, "losing six members of my tour group in one day."

Skeeter hardly dared breathe. Who was dead and who was on the run? The porter with the children could be nobody but Marcus, with Gelasia and Artemisia. Only who was with them? Ianira? Might his friends be safe, after all, running for their lives out in the mountains? But two people were dead—and there'd been six hostages. Quite abruptly, Skeeter needed to know just who had died, up here. He found himself on his feet, voice grating harshly through the dust and weariness. "Show me the bodies."

Travers hesitated. "There's more to this than you realize, Mr. Jackson—"

"*Show me the goddamned bodies!*"

Kit was on his feet, as well. "Easy, Skeeter," he said, voice low. Then, to Travers, "You'd better show us. I take it you didn't send the bodies back with the courier?"

"I thought I'd better wait until the search party got back. I was hoping to find our deserters and send them back together, but the trackers haven't shown up yet, so I sent a rider on ahead to Denver. I wanted him to get there before the gate cycled, but if you didn't run across him, he obviously didn't make it." Travers nodded toward a doorway at the rear of the room. "We embalmed 'em from the medical kits and put 'em in body bags, back in the saloon's storage pantry. It's the most secure place in town. Didn't want the local wildlife getting to them, after all. Our surgeon went with the search team, just in case."

"Paula Booker?" Kit asked sharply.

Travers nodded. "After what happened on the trail, there was no stopping her. Said she could've saved one of 'em, if she'd gotten to him in time. I've never seen a woman so upset in all my born days."

Kit sighed, weariness etched into his grizzled features. "Open it up, please. Let's get this over with."

Skeeter and Kit followed Travers into the next room, leaving Kaederman to bring up the rear. None of the tourists volunteered to go with them. A sickening, sweet stench met them when the heavy door groaned open. A moment later, zippers went down on the body bags and Skeeter found himself staring at two dead men. One was a stranger, thank God. The other . . .

Even expecting the worst, Skeeter lurched, the shock took him so hard. The dusty room, the sun-baked mountains beyond the broken windows, swooped and dove for a long, dizzy instant. Skeeter clutched at the open doorframe. He heard his voice, distant and strange, saying, "I'm gonna break the neck of the bastard who did this . . ."

Julius had been gut-shot. He'd clearly survived the fatal wound long enough to reach camp and Paula Booker, because someone had taken stitches before he'd died. Kit's hand settled on Skeeter's shoulder. "I'm sorry, Skeeter." The scout's voice had filled with a compassion that would've touched him, had the pain not been so sharp and terrible.

"Dammit, Kit! That boy wasn't even seventeen yet!" Skeeter jerked around, half-blind and not wanting Kit to notice. He was set to stride out of the monstrous little room, to get outside, to breathe down some fresh air, when he noticed Sid Kaederman. The detective had come up quietly behind them to peer past their shoulders. Even through Skeeter's blinding grief, Sid Kaederman's sudden deathly stillness brought Skeeter's instincts to full, quivering alert. He'd seen that kind of lethal tension before, in one or two of Yesukai's most deadly warriors, men who would've cheerfully slit a friend's throat for looking crosswise in their direction. The look in Kaederman's eyes set the tiny hairs along Skeeter's nape starkly erect.

Kaederman was staring down at the bodies. And for one unguarded moment, Skeeter glimpsed a look of naked shock in his cold eyes. Skeeter followed Kaederman's gaze and realized he wasn't staring at the murdered down-time teenager, but at the other corpse, a man who'd been shot several times through the back, by the look of the wounds. Kaederman's sudden stillness, the stunned disbelief in his eyes, set inner alarms ringing.

Without warning, Kit had Skeeter by the arm. "Easy, Skeeter, you're awfully white around the mouth. Let's get you outside, get some fresh air into your lungs. I know what a terrible shock this is . . ." The former scout was literally dragging him across the saloon's warped floor, past the gawking tourists, outside into the hot sunlight where the air was fresh and a slight breeze carried away the stink of death. An instant after that, the scout thrust a metal flask into his hand and said a shade too loudly, "Swallow this, Skeeter, it'll help."

Whatever Kit was up to, Skeeter decided to play along, since it had taken them out of Kaederman's immediate presence for the moment. Whatever was in the flask, it scalded the back of his throat. Skeeter swallowed another mouthful as Kit steered him down toward the livery stable, one hand solicitously guiding him by the arm, as though taking a distraught and grieving friends away from curious eyes. When they were far enough from the saloon, Kit muttered, "What the hell did you see in Sid Kaederman's face, Skeeter, that caused you to come out of shock so fast? One second, you were falling apart, ready to bawl, and the next you looked like you were ready to kill Kaederman where he stood."

Skeeter glanced into Kit's hard blue eyes. "That why you hustled me out of there so fast?"

Kit snorted. "Damn straight, I did. Didn't want Kaederman to notice the look on *your* face. Left him staring at the bodies."

"Huh. Well, that's exactly what stopped me in my tracks. The way he was looking at those bodies. Got any idea why the Senator's pet bloodhound would go into shock, looking at a dead drover? Because for just a split second, Sid Kaederman was the most stunned man in this entire camp. Like he knew the guy, or something, and didn't expect to find him dead on a pantry floor."

Kit let out a long, low whistle. "I find that mighty interesting, don't you?"

"Interesting? That's not the half of it. There's something screwy about Caddrick's story, all that guff he fed us about Noah Armstrong. Either Caddrick's lying, or somebody fed *him* a line, because I'm starting to think Noah Armstrong didn't kidnap anybody. And maybe he's not a terrorist, at all."

Kit halted mid-stride, his lean and weathered face falling into lines of astonishment. Grimly, Skeeter told him, all of it. About the wild-eyed kid who'd shouted Noah's name. "And I'm willing to bet," Skeeter added, "it was Noah Armstrong who shot the *Ansar Majlis* gunmen in the daycare center, when those bastards tried to grab Ianira's kids. They lit out through the Wild West Gate, came up here, and after somebody murdered Julius, Noah Armstrong went on the run with Marcus and the girls. Only . . . Why was Julius posing as a girl?" That part bothered Skeeter. It didn't fit anywhere.

"I wonder," Kit mused softly, "just who Julius was supposed to be? Why, indeed, pose as a *girl*? Unless, of course, he was acting as a decoy for someone."

"*Jenna Caddrick?*" Skeeter gasped.

"Isn't any other candidate I can see. But why? And if Noah Armstrong isn't *Ansar Majlis,* then who the hell is he? And how did he know there would be an attack on Ianira and her family?"

"I've been asking myself those very same questions," Skeeter muttered. "Along with the name of that wild-eyed kid in the crowd."

"You said he was carrying a black-powder pistol?"

Skeeter nodded.

"It would be very interesting," Kit said, scratching the back of his neck absently, "to know if that gun had once been registered to Carl McDevlin."

Skeeter stared. "You mean—that kid might've *been* Jenna Caddrick? Disguised as a boy?"

Kit's grimace spoke volumes. "She disappeared in the company of Noah Armstrong, whoever he turns out to be. And we know Jenna's a Templar. That gives her a powerful motive to protect Ianira's life. Jenna would certainly be in a position to suspect Ianira's life was in danger, after the attack that killed her aunt and roommate."

Skeeter whistled softly. "I don't like this, Kit. Not one stinking little bit."

"Neither do I," Kit growled, kicking savagely at a dirt clod under his boot toe. It exploded into a shower of dust. "But then, I already didn't like it, and I've never had any reason to trust a single word that came sideways out of John Caddrick's mouth. The question I want answered is what motive Caddrick would have for lying about Noah Armstrong. Surely the FBI would be able to corroborate or disprove his claim that Armstrong is a terrorist?"

Skeeter said uneasily, "Maybe Caddrick *bought* the FBI? It's been done before."

Kit shot him an intense, unreadable glance, then swore in a language Skeeter didn't recognize. "Skeeter, I really hate it when you say things like that. Because I have this terrible feeling you may just be right."

"Great. So what are we going to *do* about it?"

"First," and Kit's face closed into a lean, deadly mask, "we find out just what happened in this camp that left two men dead and Marcus on the run for his life, with his kids. Then, we track down Armstrong and our friends. Before another pack of *Ansar Majlis* killers beats us to it."

As they headed back for the dusty saloon, Skeeter wondered uneasily about yet another mystery: just what Sid Kaederman's role in this lethal mess might be.

(((Chapter 5)))

John Lachley laid a sheet of blotter paper gently across the glistening, blood-red ink of the missive he'd just finished, then held the newly penned letter up to the light to read it again, judging the effect. It hadn't been easy, writing in the style of Maybrick's disjointed ramblings. He'd worked very hard to sprinkle the man's irritating Americanisms into the language. But he was proud of the results.

"Dear Boss . . ." the letter began.

I keep on hearing the police have caught me but they wont fix me just yet. I have laughed when they look so clever and talk about being on the *right* track. That joke about Leather Apron gave me real fits. I am down on whores and I shant quit ripping them till I do get buckled. Grand work the last job was. I gave the lady no time to squeal. How can they catch me now. I love my work and want to start again. You will soon hear of me with my funny little games. I saved some of the proper *red* stuff in a ginger beer bottle over the last job to write with but it went thick like glue and I cant use it. Red ink is fit enough I hope *ha. ha.* The next job I do I shall clip the ladys ears off and send to the police officers just for jolly wouldn't you. Keep this letter back till I do a bit more wo7rk,

then give it out straight. My knife's so nice and sharp I want
to get to work right away if I get a chance. Good luck.

                                          Yours truly,
                                          Jack the Ripper

Dont mind me giving the trade name.

P.S. Wasn't good enough to post this before I got all the red
ink off my hands curse it No luck yet. They say I'm a doctor
now. *ha ha*

John Lachley dated the letter September 25th and blew the final
line of red ink dry, then chuckled to himself. He'd instructed Maybrick
to bring his diary to London during his last visit, and had read the
depraved drivel scrawled in it with avid curiosity. He'd copied the
madman's way of writing, including his insane insertions of the words
ha ha and other underscored phrases here and there. When
Maybrick's diary was discovered in Liverpool, this letter would help
to hang him.

Perhaps he'd write out a few more letters and cards, drop them in
the post over the next few days? After all, once he'd recovered Eddy's
wayward missives from Stride and Eddowes, he would no longer need
Maybrick for anything save a weight at the end of a gallows rope. He
grinned down at the bloody signature line, intensely proud of the
appellation he'd thought up. *Jack the Ripper* . . . Poor James, who
referred to himself in his diary as Sir Jim. He'd protest innocence of
writing this all the way to the drop. Yes, Lachley smiled, he would
write out a few more letters, perhaps scrawl one or two across a
newspaper article, something with the word Liverpool in it . . .

A tap at the study door roused him from delightful musings. He
hastily slid the letter into his desk drawer and locked it. "Yes? Come!"

His manservant bowed in the doorway. "You asked to be notified
when your patient woke, sir."

"Ah, yes, thank you, Charles. I'll see the young lady directly."

"Very good, sir."

Lachley climbed the stairs while planning where to send his

traitorous little missive. The editor of the *Daily News,* perhaps, a respectable newspaper with a large circulation and a keen appetite to solve the mystery of the Whitechapel Murderer. Or maybe the Central News Agency. He wished he might see the face of the editor when that letter landed on the gentleman's desk. Chuckling at his own joke, Lachley entered the room of his comely young captive.

"Good afternoon, dear lady!"

The girl was awake, listless from the effects of the drugs he fed her daily. A spark of terror flared in her eyes as he sat beside the bed. He took her hand, felt the chill of her fingers. "Now, then. Let us chat, Miss Ianira."

A shudder, very faint, ran through her.

He patted her hand. "I have seen what you are capable of, my dear. I intend to make excellent use of your skill." He brushed hair back from her brow, stroked her ashen skin. "How pale you are, today. Come now, you must surely see the advantages of a connection with me? I can give you all of London, all of Britain's power and wealth." He stroked her hand again. "I've obtained the license, you know. Special dispensation." He chuckled. "Knowing Eddy really is such a tremendous help. It isn't easy, getting a special license from the dear old C. of E. Clergy are such ruddy sticklers for details. However," he smiled brightly, "you will soon be Mrs. John Lachley and I will strew pearls of gratitude at your feet."

A choked sound escaped pale lips. "No . . ."

He frowned. "No? Of course you shall marry me, dear girl. I cannot have you living under my roof, unmarried. People will talk and talk is one thing I cannot afford."

She was struggling to speak. "My husband . . . children . . ."

Astonishment swept through him. "Married? You are *married?*" Then he began to laugh. "Widowed, you mean. I shot your dear husband dead in the street. Put a bullet into his head."

She strained away from him, dark eyes wide with revulsion. "No! Not Jenna . . . *Marcus.*"

Lachley frowned again. "The man I shot was not your husband?"

The girl lay trembling, tears sliding down her face. She had given him only one name to call her by, despite the drugs he'd fed her, refusing against all efforts he'd made thus far to reveal her full name.

"What is your husband's surname, girl?"

She shook her head. "What . . . what is a surname?"

"A last name!" he snapped, growing impatient. "Dammit, I know they use surnames even in Greece!"

"Not Greek . . ." she whispered. "Poor Marcus, sold in Rome . . . He'll be frantic . . ."

She was babbling again, raving out of her head. He gripped her wrists, shook her. "Tell me your last name, girl!"

"Cassondra!" she shrieked the word at him, fighting his hold on her. "I am Ianira, Cassondra of Ephesus!"

"Talk sense! There is no city of Ephesus, just a ruin buried only the ancients know where! How did you come to London?"

"Through the gate . . ."

They were back to that again. The sodding *gate,* whatever the deuce that was. She babbled about it every time he questioned her. Lachley changed his line of attack. "Tell me about the letters. Eddy's letters."

Her eyes closed over a look of utter horror. "Lady, help me . . ."

Losing patience, Lachley poured the drug down her throat, waiting for it to take effect, then put her into a deep trance. She lay without moving, scarcely even breathing beneath the coverlet he straightened over her. "Now, then," he said gently, "tell me about the letters."

Her lips moved. A bare whisper of sound escaped her. "Eight letters . . ."

"Tell me about the eight letters. Who has them?"

"Morgan . . . down in the vaulted room with the tree and the flame that always burns . . ." A shudder tore through her despite the grip of the strong medication. "Polly is dead . . . and poor Annie, who could scarcely breathe . . . Stride carries Eddy's words beneath the knife . . . Kate fears the letter in her pocket, picks hops in the countryside, afraid to touch it . . . and the pretty girl in Miller's Court, she'll die cut into pieces, poor child, for a letter she learned to read in Cardiff . . ."

"*What girl in Miller's Court?*"

Ianira's eyes had closed, however, so deep in the grip of the drug that no amount of slapping would rouse her. Lachley paced the bedroom in agitation. *What girl in Miller's Court?* Annie Chapman hadn't mentioned any such person! He narrowed his eyes, thinking back to that last conversation with the doomed prostitute. They'd been interrupted, he recalled, just as she'd been telling him who she'd sold the letters to, mentioning Elizabeth Stride and Catharine Eddowes. He'd thought she was finished, after giving those two names, but wondered now if perhaps that interruption had kept him from learning the name of a third person in possession of Eddy's incriminating letters?

He swore savagely, wondering what in God's name to do now.

The bitch must be found, of course, found and silenced.

She lived in Miller's Court, Ianira had said. He knew the place from his childhood. Miller's Court was not a large space, after all. How many girls from Cardiff could there be, living in that dismal little square? He closed his eyes against such a monstrous spectre. A Welsh girl, in possession of Eddy's Welsh letters . . . Had she already sent a blackmail demand to the palace? Were Eddy's power and position in mortal peril, after all? Because Annie Chapman, the stupid bitch, had neglected to mention a third recipient of her letters?

He drew a deep, calming breath. Surely no blackmail demand had been sent, yet. Eddy would've come to him in a high state of panic, if one had. Hopefully, Polly and Annie's grisly fate had frightened the Welsh tart too deeply to act. Still, she had got to be found and done away with, the sooner the better. God, would this nightmare never come to an end? With yet another woman to trace and destroy, perhaps Lachley ought not send his damning Ripper letter to the press, after all? A moment's consideration, however, convinced him to risk it, anyway. Maybrick would be in London at the end of the week, so this girl in Miller's Court could be eliminated on the same night as Stride and Eddowes. Three women in one weekend was a bit much, true . . .

But he hadn't any real choice.

He spared a glance for the mysterious Ianira, pale and silent in her bed. "You," he muttered aloud, "must wait a bit. Once this business is done, however, I *will* discover the identity of your husband."

Christ, yet *another* murder to be undertaken.

This mess occasionally bade fair to drive him insane.

The silence in the dusty little Colorado mining town was so utterly complete, Skeeter could hear the distant scream of an eagle somewhere over the sunbaked mountains. The scrape of his chair as he dragged it harshly around and sat down caused several women to jump. Julius' too-young face, waxen with that ghastly, bluish color death brought, floated in his mind's eye, demanding vengeance. The dark look he bent on Sid Kaederman went unnoticed, because the detective was busy glaring at Orson Travers. Clearly, the Time Tours guide had stalled him off until Kit and Skeeter's return. The silence lay so thick, the creak of wooden floorboards as tourists shifted sounded loud as gunshots.

The moment Kit settled into an easy stance beside Skeeter's chair, Sid Kaederman growled, "All right, Travers, you want to tell us just what's been going on?"

"Yes, let's have the details, please," Kit agreed. "This is messier than you can possibly guess."

Orson Travers, an unhappy man made monumentally unhappier by Kit's pronouncement, cleared his throat. "There wasn't any hint of trouble on the way up here. Oh, it was a rowdy enough bunch, lots of high spirits. We packed our gear in by mule from Colorado Springs, whipped the town into shape for the competition, refurbished a couple of houses to bunk down in, built the target stands and laid out the course of fire for the running action events. All that prep work was part of the package tour, using nineteenth-century techniques to build the competition course and refurbish the camp. And we planned the wedding, of course—"

"Wedding?" Kaederman interrupted, startled.

A pretty girl in a muslin gown blushed crimson and leaned against a tall, gangly kid in buckskins. He grinned. "Got ourselves hitched proper, brought a preacher with us and all, held the ceremony over at the trading post last week."

"Oh, it was so wonderful!" his bride put in excitedly. "There were real Indians and mountain men and everything! And the silliest salesman you ever saw, selling ordinary crescent wrenches, called them a new high-tech invention out of Sweden, patented only three years ago. People were paying outrageous prices for them! It was amazing, I'd never seen anything like it, fur trappers and miners buying crescent wrenches!" The blushing bride was clearly determined not to let the tragedy of a double murder mar her honeymoon.

Kit smiled. "Congratulations, I'm sure it was a wedding to remember. Now, *what the hell happened?*" He swung his gaze back to the Time Tours guide.

Travers sighed. "The action and endurance course runs through the hills and gullies around town. The idea is, you stalk and shoot every full round of the course over a period of several hours, to test your endurance and accuracy under pressure. Well, Cassie Coventina, or rather, the kid we *thought* was Cassie Coventina, was moving steadily through it on horseback, just as planned. We put spotters out along the route to act as judges and scorekeepers, but she—I mean he—never made it to the first target. Let me tell you, it was one helluva shock, when Dr. Booker stripped that kid off and we discovered Cassie Coventina was a teenage boy in drag!"

Skeeter bridled. Kit pressed a restraining hand against his shoulder. "Never mind that, Travers, just tell us what happened."

The thickset guide shifted uncomfortably. "Someone ambushed him. Killed the kid *and* his horse. We found it on the trail, later. Joey Tyrolin claimed he and his porter followed the kid out onto the course. They weren't supposed to be out there, but Tyrolin was always so damn drunk, he pretty much did what he pleased. Guy claimed all he wanted to do was watch. Said he and his porter rode up right after the kid was ambushed. Tyrolin gave chase and killed the attacker—one of the drovers," Travers added unhappily. "A tourist who signed up to work the tour, so he could get a cheaper ticket."

"And Tyrolin killed him?" Kaederman asked softly.

An underlying tone in the man's voice, a tone Skeeter would've sworn was agitated anger despite those curiously chilly eyes, brought Skeeter's hackles up again.

"Oh, yes, Tyrolin killed him. Was bold as brass about admitting it, too. Said the man shot at him when he gave chase, so he fired back. Killed him stone dead. I'd have said it was a case of self-defense, if Tyrolin hadn't bolted out of camp with his porter and those kids, right after. While everybody was rushing around trying to set up an emergency field surgery, they just packed up their gear and rode off. We sent riders after them, of course, and half the tour group volunteered to help search. Not that we let anybody but guides and regular Time Tours drovers out of camp, after what happened with Tyrolin and that tourist. And the kid, poor bastard."

"I don't suppose," Kaederman put in, "you happen to have a photograph of Tyrolin and his porter?" The tension in his voice caught Skeeter's attention once more. Kaederman wanted that picture badly.

"Never mind the photo just now," Kit overrode him. "I presume you dispatched your courier to inform Denver of the double murders? After sending out the search party on Tyrolin's trail?"

"Yes. I'm the only guide left in camp right now. I sent everyone else and half the drovers out after them. Along with Dr. Booker. She insisted on going, in case her surgical skills were needed." Travers sighed. "So that's what happened on our end, but you haven't told us why *you're* up here, looking for Joey Tyrolin, too. Don't tell me he was a wanted criminal, up time?"

Kaederman said coldly, "You might say that. A terrorist, to be exact."

Gasps broke from the tourists. A couple of the women let out tiny shrieks.

Kit said a little wearily, "We've got troubles of our own on station just now. *Big* troubles."

"He's not kidding, either," Skeeter muttered. "Senator John Caddrick's on station. Threatening to shut us down if we don't bring back Joey Tyrolin. Among other things."

"*Caddrick?*" Orson Travers' face washed white.

"Yes," Kit nodded. "And it gets better. Joey Tyrolin's real name is Noah Armstrong. A member of the *Ansar Majlis,* that terrorist cult out of the Middle East. They murdered Cassie Tyrol in New York and kidnapped Caddrick's only child. Not to mention kidnapping Ianira

Cassondra and her entire family. Between the Templars and the cult crazies flooding into the station and starting riots, we've had several critical injuries and nine murders. And if we don't find Jenna Caddrick and bring her back safely, her father will shut down Shangri-La for good. The Inter-Temporal Court's been called in, as a last-ditch measure to try and keep the station operational. Mr. Kaederman, here, was hired by the Senator to help search for his daughter."

Travers looked like a slight breeze would've knocked him over.

Someone from the back of the crowd whispered, "Oh, my God. And we let the terrorist responsible get away!"

"Yes," Kaederman said with enough frost to freeze every cup of water in the room, "you did. And we're here to find him. Now, does anyone have a photo of Tyrolin and his porter? I want to make a positive identification of that bastard before we ride out after him and his hostages."

"I have a photo," a woman spoke up, pushing her way to the front. "I should have several, in fact." She ignored Kaederman, addressing Kit, instead, which left the Wardmann-Wolfe agent bristling. "Ellen Danvers, Mr. Carson, professional photographer. Hired to do the wedding party. I've been taking pictures steadily with a digital camera. I can bring all the disks for you to study, if you like."

Three minutes later, Skeeter found himself staring at a photograph of Marcus on the miniature screen at the back of Ellen Danvers' digital camera. He was clearly in disguise, but a guy didn't live through what Skeeter'd lived through, trying to rescue his friend from slavery, without getting to know that friend's face well enough to recognize him under any circumstances. The only reason he'd failed to spot Marcus at the gate's opening was Joey Tyrolin's masterful performance, drawing attention away from everything else within a thousand paces.

Ellen Danvers scrolled through shot after shot. "Joey Tyrolin was camera shy, considering how drunk he was all the time. I didn't get many shots of him. In fact, I had to work hard to get any photos of his face at all, and my client specifically asked for candids of the entire competition group." She'd used up dozens of disks taking pictures of just about everything but the horse dung.

"There," Miss Danvers paused the scroll, freezing a frame for them to look at. "That's them. Joey Tyrolin and his porter. And these are the porter's little girls. Beautiful children, both of them." The photographer's gaze was troubled as she glanced up at Kit. "We had no idea they were Ianira Cassondra's daughters, or that the porter was her husband. Are they really hostages?"

Sid Kaederman answered, voice still colder than spiked icicles. "They most certainly are, if they're even still alive. This," he tapped Noah Armstrong's photo, "is one of the most dangerous men in the world. Or rather, one of the most dangerous *people*. Armstrong's an intersexual, neither male nor female, able to assume any disguise he pleases. Armstrong's the cleverest, deadliest bastard I've ever run across. God help those kids, in the clutches of a monster like that."

Skeeter peered sharply at Kaederman, wondering about the level of venom. Was Kaederman that prejudiced against intersexuals? Lots of people were, Skeeter knew, although Kaederman didn't strike him as the type who would hate without reason. He could be playing some other game, however, painting Armstrong as the one thing Skeeter was beginning to suspect he wasn't: a terrorist.

Ellen Danvers, of course, with no reason to suspect Kaederman's motives or honesty, had paled, her expression stricken. "Those poor little girls! Can you find them?"

"We'll give it our best shot," Kit said quietly. "Let's check our gear and rations. I want to ride out within the hour."

Skeeter stayed where he was until Kit and the Wardmann-Wolfe agent had left the room. As the meeting broke up and the tourists milled around outside, trying to help and mostly dithering and getting in everyone's way, Skeeter took Ellen Danvers quietly aside and asked to see her photos again.

"All of them?" she asked.

He nodded, studying each of the shots in turn, looking carefully at every digitally recorded face. "You're sure you took pictures of every single person in the group?" he asked at length.

"Yes, quite sure."

"And there wasn't any way they could've been hiding someone else? In their luggage, say?"

"No, I don't think that would've been possible. Not an adult, anyway. The porter smuggled the children in his trunk, but they're such little things. I can't imagine how anyone could have stuffed an adult into one of those trunks."

"But they took their luggage with them? Steamer trunks, pack horses, all of it?"

Puzzled, she nodded. "Yes. Why?"

Skeeter merely shook his head. "Just a theory. Nothing I want to discuss, yet." He wondered if Kit had noticed, or Kaederman, for that matter, that the one face missing from Ellen Danvers' impressive collection of photos was Jenna Caddrick's? Nor did Ianira Cassondra appear in any of her shots, which struck Skeeter as both ominous and profoundly odd. If neither Jenna nor Ianira had come with Armstrong and Marcus, just where had the two women gone? Were they, in fact, hidden away in the steamer trunks? Or buried somewhere in a shallow grave? Skeeter's gut churned queasily. He didn't want to share those particular thoughts with anyone just yet, not until he could get Kit alone once more. He said only, "Thanks for letting me look through these again."

"Of course. Do you think there's much chance you'll be able to find them?"

Skeeter hesitated. "We'll do the best we can. I'm a good tracker. So's Kit. But they've got a good lead on us and it's a big country, out here. Frankly, I'm not holding out much hope. And I've got more reason than most to find them. Marcus is the closest friend I have in the world."

Ellen Danvers' eyes misted. "I'm sorry, Mr. Jackson."

"Thanks." He handed back the camera. "I'd appreciate it if you didn't mention this conversation."

"Of course." She hesitated. "You don't trust the Senator's detective much, do you?"

Skeeter's laugh was as colorless as the burnt sky overhead. "Does it show that much? Would you trust a man working for Senator John Paul Caddrick?"

She bit one lip. "Well, no, not as far as I could throw him, which isn't very far. Good luck, Mr. Jackson. And be careful."

Her concern surprised Skeeter. He hadn't realized ordinary people could care so much. "Thank you, Miss Danvers. I appreciate that, more than you know."

He left her peering at the screen on her camera, studying the photos, clearly wondering what, exactly, he'd been looking for. Ellen Danvers was a smart lady. He wouldn't be at all surprised if she didn't tumble to it on her own.

If she did, he hoped she kept it quiet as a tomb.

Elizabeth Stride was known throughout the East End for her stormy temper and her explosive relationship with her lover, Michael Kidney—a violent relationship she wasn't particularly ashamed of, any more than she was ashamed of the way she made her living. When Liz's younger lover drank, which was frequently, Michael grew abusive. And when she drank, which was even more often, Long Liz Stride grew belligerent. And when they quarelled, which was nearly every time they drank, Liz usually ended by slamming Michael's door behind her—if he hadn't padlocked her in again to keep her off the streets.

On Wednesday, September twenty-sixth, after another violent and drunken row, Long Liz Stride found herself on the streets once more, fuming and furious and looking for a bed at her favorite lodging house, 32 Flower and Dean Street. The kitchen was filled with more than a dozen women and girls of all ages, most of them cold and frightened and in various stages of drunkenness. All of them whispered about the shocking murders which had struck down so many women just like them since Easter Monday.

"—scared to let a man touch me, I am," one girl of seventeen was whispering miserably, "but I got to eat, 'aven't I? What's a lady to do, when she's got to eat and there ain't no other way to put bread in 'er Lime'ouse Cut, but lift 'er skirts for whatever man'll pay 'er to do it?"

Liz had, until recently, entertained her own ideas about the infamous Whitechapel Murderer, as the newspapers had taken to calling him. She had spent a hard-earned shilling to buy a short, blunt knife to carry in her pocket as protection, after what had happened to Polly Nichols and Annie Chapman. Ever since Dark Annie's murder,

Liz had been terrified to do anything about her own letter. But surely, if Annie had been killed because of these letters, the killer would have dragged out of the poor woman the identity of everyone she'd sold the letters to? Logically, a killer looking for those letters would've found that out first thing, then come after anyone who'd bought one. But nearly two weeks had passed and no one had come knocking on her door, so the newspapers must be right and poor Annie had simply fallen victim to a madman, same as poor Polly Nichols, a week before.

Besides, there were those other women killed, Martha Tabram on August Bank Holiday and Emma Smith on Easter Monday, and *they* couldn't have had anything to do with Annie Chapman's letters, which, by her own admission, she'd had from Polly, rest her soul. Still, Liz bought that knife, and she was careful not to approach any potential customers resembling the descriptions of the killer.

As Liz hesitated on the doss house's kitchen threshold, a woman she'd met during her last visit called out a greeting. "Why, Liz," Catharine Long exclaimed, gesturing her to a vacant chair beside the hearth, "I haven't seen you here in three months! Whatever's happened?"

Liz joined her, grateful for the warmth of the coal fire. The weather outside was blustery and wet, cold enough to turn her ungloved fingers red. "Oh, I had words with my man, is all. I'll let him cool his temper for a few days, then he'll see the error of his ways and I'll go back to him, drunken fool."

"But will he take you back, Liz?"

She smiled a little grimly. "Oh, yes, Michael will take me back." She patted her pocket, where several folded sheets of foolscap rested, down beneath that sharp little knife. Surely it must be safe to do something about her little investment now? And with the blackmail money she would obtain, Michael would certainly take her back, temper or no. All she had to do was find a Welshman in one of the ironworks sprawled through the vast shipyards to translate her letter and she would be rich. More than rich enough to tempt any man she wanted.

"Yes," she said again, her slight smile at odds with the atmosphere of terror and misery in the kitchen, "Michael will take me back, Catharine. So tell me the news, it's been an age since I saw you."

"Oh, I'm fine enough, Liz. But these killings . . ." Catharine Long shuddered. "And the police are such hopeless fools. You heard what Sir Charles Warren's done?"

Liz shook her head, not particularly interested in what the head of the Metropolitan police force did. As long as a woman kept moving and didn't try to stand in one place, coppers generally didn't bother her. "No, I haven't heard."

"He's taken every single East End detective off the beat! Assigned them to patrol *west* London. And he's switched about the West End detectives to patrol Whitechapel and Spitalfields and the docklands. Have you ever heard of suchlike? Why, the detectives out there don't even know the street names, let alone the alleyways this madman must be using to escape!"

A woman seated beside them moaned and rocked back and forth. "They don't care about us, so they don't! All they want is to show the ruddy newsmen they've put a few coppers on the street. Not a man Jack of 'em gives a fig for the likes of us. Now if it was fine ladies he were cuttin' up, they'd have a policeman in every house, so they would . . ."

Liz and Catharine Long exchanged a long, silent look. It was only too true, after all. Despite the show of putting extra men on the beat, both women knew they would have to defend themselves. Liz clutched the handle of her knife through her worn skirts and held back a shiver. Perhaps she ought to just burn the letter?

That won't do you any good if he comes after you, she told herself grimly. *Might as well get some money out of it, then leave London, maybe go across to America.*

She'd find someone to translate the sheets of foolscap for her, get out of this hellhole, live decently for a change. Meanwhile, she'd do a bit of charring to earn her keep, maybe offer to clean some of the rooms in the lodging house for a few pence. She might even ask around the Jewish community to see if anyone needed a charwoman for a few days. She'd done a great deal of char work for Jewish businessmen and their plump wives. They knew her to be dependable when she could get the work. And not a lot of charwomen would work for a Jew just now, not with these Whitechapel murders being blamed on a foreigner, same as that Lipski fellow last year, who'd poisoned that poor little girl, barely gone fifteen.

Long Liz didn't care how many people in the East End hated Jews or called them dirty, foreign murderers. Work was work and she certainly didn't mind cleaning houses, if it came to that. Charring was better than selling herself and she'd done that enough times to keep body and soul together, not only here in London, but back in Sweden, too, so what was a little thing like charring for a few Jews? Besides, she wouldn't need menial work much longer, would she? Not with money to be made from Annie Chapman's legacy.

"Say, Catharine," she asked quietly, leaning close to her friend so as not to be overheard, "do you know any Welshmen?"

Her friend gave her a startled glance, then laughed. "Oh, Liz, you are a piece of work! Quarrelled with your man this morning and looking for a replacement tonight! Try the Queen's Head pub, dearie, I've heard there's a Welsh ironworker from the docks with money in his trous, likes to have a drink there of an evening."

Long Liz Stride smiled. "Thank you, Catharine. I believe I will."

By week's end, Elizabeth Stride intended to be a rich woman.

The trail Armstrong had taken out of camp did not lead south, along the shorter route to Colorado Springs and the railway station. Armstrong and Marcus had fled north, the long way up toward Florissant. By nightfall, Skeeter, Kit, and Sid Kaederman, along with their guide, were deep in the Colorado Rockies, following the path the other Time Tours guides had already taken. They camped overnight in a sheltered nook of rock out of the wind, then set out at first light, covering ground rapidly along a trail Skeeter, at least, could've followed blindfolded. He'd hunted with the Yakka Clan often enough to learn what spoor to follow through rough country. "It hasn't rained for a while, at least," Skeeter muttered, studying the fading trail which sporadic wind gusts had partially obliterated in the more open spots. "Fortunately, their trail was protected in low-lying areas like this." He pointed to faded hoofprints. "They were in a tearing hurry, too. The Time Tours guides who came through after them weren't moving nearly as fast as Armstrong and Marcus."

"How do you know that?" Kaederman demanded.

Skeeter shrugged. "I've tracked quarry through broken country before. Look," he dismounted and crouched down alongside the trail, pointing to a mishmash grouping of hoofprints. "These are the oldest prints. They're nearly a blur from the wind filling them in and the mud's completely dried out. And look how far apart the stride is." He paced off the distance between hoof prints. "They were moving at a fast canter or a slow gallop, depending on the height of their ponies. Given the weight their pack horses are carrying, that's a gruelling pace to keep up. These other prints, the fresher ones from the search party, are a lot closer together. They're trotting, at best. They'll never catch up if Marcus and Armstrong keep up the pace they've been holding, pushing their ponies that fast."

"But they'll wear out their horses in no time!"

"Not if they're smart and careful," Skeeter disagreed. "I've been studying these prints all morning. They slow to a walk periodically to give the horses a breather, probably more for the pack animals' sake than the riding mounts. And I've spotted a couple of places where they dismounted and let the animals rest and graze. But when they're in the saddle, they're moving fast. Judging from those photos Ellen Danvers took, Armstrong can't weigh much more than one-thirty, one-forty, and Marcus is slender, too. He and Ianira never had the money to indulge overeating. Even with the children, he's probably lighter for a pony to carry than I am and I'm not exactly massive, myself. Armstrong is obviously no fool. I'd say he knows exactly what he's doing. As long as they're careful with the pack animals, or don't care about abandoning their baggage, they won't founder those horses. And wherever they're going, they'll get there a lot sooner than any of us will."

The big question Skeeter *couldn't* answer from these tracks, however, was whether or not any of the Time Tours guides or drovers searching ahead of them might be in the pay of the *Ansar Majlis*. If he'd been part of a terrorist cult dedicated to murdering someone like Marcus and Ianira, he would've sent more than one hit man through the Wild West Gate. Which left Skeeter wondering just how many killers they might yet run into on this trail—or how much use Sid Kaederman would be, if they did. He kept his eyes and ears open and hoped they didn't stumble into an ambush somewhere along the way.

By their third day of hard riding, they'd swung around the north flank of Pikes Peak and were moving east toward the rail line again. They had to call a brief halt when Kaederman's pony pulled up lame. The detective dismounted stiffly and watched unhappily as Meinrad showed him how to check his pony's hooves for stones, lifting each foot in turn to check the soft pad known as the frog. They were prying loose a sharp rock from his near forefoot when Skeeter heard it: a faint, sharp report that echoed off the mountains. Another distant crack reached them, like a frozen tree splitting wide open, then a third, followed by a whole volley. The sound fell into an abruptly familiar pattern.

"Gunfire!"

Lots of it.

Kit jerked around in the saddle. "Jeezus Christ! There's a war breaking loose out there! Kurt, we don't have time to wait, nursemaid him when you've got that pony's hoof cleared! Skeeter, move it!" Kit clattered off at a gallop just as Skeeter jerked his shotgun out of its scabbard. Skeeter put heels to flanks and sent his mount racing after Kit's. He leaned low over his horse's neck, his double-barrel clutched in one hand like a war spear, and snarled into the teeth of the wind. Even above the thunder of hooves, he could still hear gunfire popping ominously ahead. He couldn't imagine locals producing that much gunfire. But the *Ansar Majlis* easily could. Had the Time Tours guides found Marcus and the girls after all, bringing them back toward camp, only to ride into the fusillade of an ambush?

Kit crouched so close above his horse's neck, he looked like a fluid statue cut from the same flesh as the racing animal. The retired scout surged ahead, splashing through a shallow, rocky creek and switching with consumate skill around outcroppings, tumbled boulders and loose piles of scree. Skeeter's horse slipped and slid through the jumbled heaps of weather-fractured stones, then drew up nose to tail behind Kit's, nostrils distended and running flat out. This was bad country for a full-bore charge. If either nag put a foot wrong at this speed . . .

A sudden silence ahead robbed him of breath. Then the staccato pop of gunfire rattled again in the harsh sunlight, sporadic but closer than before. *Somebody had to reload. Several somebodies. Both sides, maybe.* Which meant there was a chance the *Ansar Majlis* were using period firearms, rather than modern stuff smuggled through the gate. Against black-powder guns, even replica models, his friends might stand a halfway decent chance. Given the sound of that shooting, whoever was under attack was firing back, giving at least as good as they were getting.

Then Kit was reining in and Skeeter pulled up hard to slither to a halt beside him, both horses blowing from the run. Kit held up a warning hand, then pointed down into a narrow little arroyo. Two riderless horses pawed the dusty ground uncertainly, skittish and laying their ears back each time gunfire tore through the hot sunlight. Their riders lay pinned between an outcropping of stone and a jumble of boulders, firing up toward a knife-edge ridgeline that lay to Skeeter and Kit's left. Skeeter dragged his field glasses out of his saddle bag, the brass warm with the scent of hot leather, and peered toward the ridgeline while Kit studied the riders pinned below.

"That's a Time Tours guide," Kit muttered. "And Paula Booker!"

"*Shalig!*" Skeeter snarled under his breath. "There's at least six gunmen up there." He pointed toward the narrow ridgeline. "Counting puffs of smoke, at least six, maybe more."

"*Six?*" Kit shot back, brows diving toward his nose. "That's too many for Armstrong's crew."

"Maybe. How many guys did he plant with those drovers?"

Kit swore. "*Shalig* is right. Let's get around the back side of that ridge, come at them from behind."

They had to abandon the horses halfway up, the slope was so sharp. Skeeter panted for breath and scrambled for handholds, climbing steadily, shotgun gripped awkwardly in one hand. Kurt Meinrad and Sid Kaederman, arriving late, struggled to climb the same slope in their wake. Skeeter gained the top and bellied forward, lying flat so he wouldn't skyline himself and make a visible target above the ridge. Kit slithered out beside him, grunting softly and peering through his own field glasses. Kurt Meinrad arrived just as Kit began surveying the scene below. Skeeter handed the guide his own field glasses and jerked Kaederman down when the idiot just stood there, standing out like a neon sign flashing "shoot me." Skeeter waited in a swivet, using the naked eye to mark spots where gunmen lay hidden in the rocky outcroppings of the ridge. Meinrad gave a sudden grunt.

"Huh. That's no pack of terrorists, Carson."

Kit swung a sharp look on the Time Tours guide. "Oh?"

"That's the Flanagan brothers. With a couple of their low-life pals. Irish railroad men who took to holding up trains after they finished laying track. Small-time thugs, temporal natives. We've had trouble with them before, roughing up a couple of the tours. They like holding up stage coaches, too, and robbing campsites."

"They may be small time, but they've got your guide and Paula Booker pinned down neat as any trap I've ever seen," Kit shot back. "And if they're down-timers, we don't have any guarantee they *can* be killed, even if we shoot amongst 'em."

"Maybe not," Skeeter said, misquoting a favorite mid-twentieth-century television show he'd watched endlessly in reruns, "but I'll bet you credits to navy beans I can put the fear of God into 'em."

Before Kit could reply, Skeeter let out a war whoop and charged down the precipitous slope, yelling and cursing in twelfth-century Mongolian and loosing off rounds as fast as he could jam shells into his scattergun. Six astonished faces swung up toward him. Skeeter let fly another round of buckshot and heard Kit scrambling down the slope after him, yelling in some unknown, bloodcurdling language that left Skeeter's hair standing on end. Kit's Model 73 barked with a roar like thunder. Lead whined off rock so close to a Flanagan brother's ear, the man jumped six inches straight up and landed running.

When Kurt Meinrad joined the insane plunge, shooting and shouting on Kit's heels, it was too much for the Flanagans. They all broke and ran, heading for ponies concealed in the brush. A clatter of hooves rattled away in a boiling swirl of dust, then Skeeter slithered to a halt, panting and sweating and wondering if he'd completely lost his mind, pulling a stunt like that. But he hadn't felt this alive since returning to civilization at the age of thirteen—with the possible exception of fighting for his life in the Circus Maximus.

Kit Carson, hair dishevelled, jaw unshaven, pale eyes alight with an unholy look that might've been fury or glee, stalked toward him. "Skeeter, you *lunatic!* What possessed you to pull a bone-headed piece of insanity like that?"

Skeeter grinned. "Got rid of 'em, didn't it?"

Kit's mouth thinned. "Yes. And I could be piling rocks over what was left of you, too."

"Well, hell's bells, Kit, I never yet met a bully who wouldn't back down when confronted."

One corner of Kit's lips twitched. "Next time, wait for instructions."

Skeeter sketched a sloppy salute. "Yessir!"

"Huh. Thank God you were never in the army, Skeeter, you'd have ended in Leavenworth inside a week. All right, let's go find out what that Time Tours guide is doing out here by himself with Paula Booker. Besides playing bait for every outlaw in the territory."

Wordlessly, they headed down into the rocky defile.

《 Chapter 6 》

Time scout in-training Margo Smith was so keyed up she was very nearly shaking as she and her fiancé—freelance time guide Malcolm Moore—eased open the gate beside the International Workingmen's Association. A lively concert was underway, spilling Russian music out into the streets. Malcolm held the gate as Margo slipped into the long alleyway leading back to Dutfield's Yard. The Ripper Watch Team followed silently, carrying miniaturized equipment they would use to film Long Liz Stride's brutal murder. Their satchels were heavy, carrying three times the equipment needed for the previous two murders. This was only the first stop of three the team would make tonight, placing low-light cameras and microphone systems in Dutfield's Yard, on a certain stairway landing in Goulston Street, and in Mitre Square.

While Margo and Malcolm stood guard, the team members placed their tiny cameras, hiding them where they would not be discovered by the police, some at the entrance to the alley and others back in the yard. Margo glanced every few moments at the windows of the crowded hall, convinced someone would spot them and demand to know what they were doing down here, but no one noticed. It gave Margo an insight into how the Ripper had been able to strike so frequently in the heart of a crowded slum. The people of Whitechapel, like those in many another overpopulated city, turned their attention inward to their own business and feared to pry too directly into the business of neighbors, particularly with a deranged killer walking the streets.

Margo drew a deep breath of relief when the Ripper Watch Team finally finished and she was able to lead them all back to the street once more.

"Very good," Malcolm said quietly, easing the wicker pedestrian gate closed, "that's the first one. Now, Mitre Square is this way."

Malcolm led the way toward the soon-to-be infamous site that Margo and Shahdi Feroz had first visited only two weeks previously. They had noticed, during their study of the killing zone, that the Ripper had left his fourth victim within sight of both a policeman's house and a Jewish synagogue. Tonight, Catharine Eddowes would walk straight into that killing zone, where her life would end violently. Margo shivered in the darkness and thrust away memories of her own mother's brutal murder, concentrating instead on their surroundings and her primary task of guarding the Ripper Scholars from footpads and gangs.

The overwhelming sense of Whitechapel by night was a region of utter darkness punctuated randomly by brightly lit pubs which drew residents like moths. Their attraction was due as much, Margo suspected, to the cheerfulness of the light and the sense of safety it gave, as to the gin and ale. They walked down entire city blocks without passing a single working gas lamp, skirted past alleyways and side streets which loomed like black caverns in the night, inhabited by God alone knew what. Sounds came drifting to them, scuffles and muffled arguments. Children lurked underfoot by the hundreds, crowding into doorways and open landings of stairwells, their eyes following the Ripper Watch Team with hungry intent.

Pubs were packed with rough workmen and drab women carrying hungry-eyed children, all swilling alcohol and talking uproariously, faces puffed and reddened from drink. Outside the pubs, women walked endlessly up and down, pausing only briefly in the doorways, drifting from one pub to another soliciting customers at the Britannia, the Princess Alice, The City Darts and the Alma, at King Stores and the infamous Ten Bells, Mary Kelly's favorite haunt for plying her trade.

Stepping out onto Commercial Road was a shock, by comparison.

From where they stood on the corner, all the way down to Mile End highway, stretched a raucous hive of bright-lit pubs, shops with dim gaslights still flickering, street preachers surrounded by heckling crowds, a waxworks displaying reproductions of the latest Whitechapel murder victims—children with pennies clutched in grubby fingers struggling to gain admittance—a suit salesman pitching the quality of his wares to a crowd of avid listeners, and drifts of sailors up from the docks, swilling gin and ogling the women. Despite the lateness of the hour, the Saturday night street stunned Margo with its noise and throngs of merrymakers, intent on forgetting the horror stalking the lightless roads nearby.

One of the Watch Team's experts, Dr. Shahdi Feroz, studied the street carefully as they pushed their way west, toward the border with The City of London and Mitre Square. Margo edged closer to her. "Is it usual for people to pretend like nothing's happening?"

Shahdi flicked her gaze up to meet Margo's. A slight vertical line appeared between her brows. "It is not surprising. It has been two weeks since the last killing, after all. People with no choice but to stay in this place persuade themselves the terror is over, or at least they drink and pretend it is. You have noticed the darker streets are nearly empty?"

"Yes, I was just thinking about that. Frightened people are drawn to the light and bustle." She nodded down the roaring thoroughfare. "I guess they're hoping to find safety in numbers. Not that it will do any good."

"For most, it will. Very few of these people will be up and about between one and two A.M., when the murders will occur. And even the prostitutes are trying to be cautious," she motioned with one slim, Persian hand, "staying near the lighted pubs or Saint Botolph's Church."

Margo shivered. "Not even buying a knife will help poor Liz."

"No."

They pushed past the end of Commercial Road, gaining Adgate, and turned off for Mitre Square. Once again Margo and Malcolm stood watch at each of the two ways into the secluded little square, while the Ripper Watch Team rigged their miniaturized equipment behind a temporary construction fence which closed off one interior corner of the square. Catharine Eddowes would die just outside that fence. Margo watched closely through the dark alleyway known as Church Passage, which ran beneath an overhanging building, turning the little lane into a tunnel between Mitre Square and the street beyond. Rough workingmen could be heard laughing and singing at pubs. Women's voices drifted past, some openly brazen, accosting potential customers. Others were hushed with fear as they whispered about the killer, wondering what to do to protect themselves and their families.

Most of the women in the East End weren't prostitutes, any more than most of the men were pickpockets and thieves; but these women had no way of knowing the killer loose amongst them wouldn't be attacking "honest women." They were all frightened, as unaware as the police of the psychology that drove psychotic serial killers like James Maybrick and his unknown accomplice. Who that man was, the team hoped to learn tonight. They also hoped to discover which of the killers was the rabid anti-Semite.

As soon as the equipment was in place, Malcolm led the way once more, moving north and east again, across Houndsditch and past Middlesex Street, over to Goulston Street and the landing of the Wentworth Model Buildings. The tenement was noisily occupied, which made the installation hazardous. Malcolm slipped up the dark staircase past the landing and stood guard above while Inspector Conroy Melvyn worked alone to fix the tiny, button-sized camera and transmitter in the upper corner of the landing. A raucous burst of voices from above sent both the up-time police inspector and Malcolm plunging back down to street level, sweating profusely.

"Got it," Melvyn gasped out, voice shaking slightly.

"I would suggest we leave the area at once," Malcolm said urgently, glancing back as several men and women burst from the staircase, locked in a bitter argument that threatened to turn violent momentarily.

"Agreed," Melvyn nodded, heading back for Middlesex Street at a brisk walk.

A clock from one of the many breweries in the district, Margo wasn't sure which one, tolled the hour. Midnight. An hour before the first murder, plus another forty minutes until the second one. Moving in utter silence, the Ripper Watch Team headed for Leadenhall Street and the Bank of England, where their carriage would be waiting to take them back to Spaldergate. Margo glanced once over her shoulder into the dark maze of alleys that formed the Ripper's killing ground and held back a shudder.

Jack the Ripper had already posted his first letter to the editor. Tomorrow morning, the *Daily News* would publish it.

Skeeter reached the bottom of the bone-dry gully slightly behind Kit. Before either of them could call a greeting, Paula gave a glad cry. She came hurtling out from behind a sheltering boulder and threw herself straight into Kit's arms. "Oh, God, Kit Carson! I've never been so happy to see anybody in my whole life! And Skeeter Jackson!"

"What's happened?" Kit asked tersely, fishing for a clean bandanna. Paula dried her eyes with it, gulping to control tears of sheer relief at her rescue.

The Time Tours guide with the surgeon answered through clenched teeth. "Bastards jumped us from cover, when Paula's horse threw a shoe. I was trying to reshoe the nag when they started shooting."

"Then you haven't caught up with Joey Tyrolin, yet?" Kit asked sharply.

Paula shook her head. "No. And we won't, either. Mr. Samuelson and I were bringing back the bad news."

"Too right," Samuelson growled. "Little bastard and his porter *emigrated* on us! They jumped a train before we could catch up and headed east. The drovers and other guides are trying to trace them, but they bought a ticket for Chicago, so they could jump off anywhere between here and Illinois. Or keep going, switch trains in Chicago and head for the East Coast."

Skeeter kicked disgustedly at a clod of dirt. "Great. Now what, Kit?"

The grizzled scout shoved his hat back and wiped sweat from his brow. "We hold a council of war."

Skeeter certainly didn't have any better ideas.

✖ ✖ ✖

Dominica Nosette was so excited she could scarcely stand still. *At last!* John Lachley and James Maybrick together on the same street! The night was windy, full of rainshowers and sudden gusts that whipped Dominica's skirts against her ankles and rattled her bonnet around her ears, but Dominica scarcely noticed. Her tiny video camera rode next to her ear, mounted underneath the concealing brim of her bonnet. The lens recorded everything in front of her, whichever way Dominica turned her head, and the camera was specially fitted with low-light and infrared technology to record video signal in even the darkest alleyways. An infrared light source in the fake fruit fastened to her bonnet illuminated a wide fan in front of her, switched on whenever she pressed the plunger inside her pocket. She'd been holding it down steadily for the past five minutes, eyes riveted to the two men who conferred briefly under a grimy street lamp, one of the few scattered through the East End. The directional microphone in her bonnet picked up their low-voiced conversation and broadcast it to her earplug.

"The woman lives in this house," Lachley's voice said. "Eddowes is her name, Kate Eddowes, a dirty whore."

Maybrick's voice, breathless with sick excitement, answered. "I want her, John, I want to rip her . . ."

"Not until I have my letters."

"Of course . . ."

Dominica finally knew what was contained in the letters John Lachley sought. She and her partner had managed to make a photocopy of Long Liz Stride's priceless missive, telling her precisely why John Lachley was stalking these women to death. The queen's grandson, the firstborn son of the Prince of Wales, in the direct line of succession, had been indiscreet. Highly indiscreet. With a male prostitute, no less. If proof of that indiscretion fell into the wrong hands, Eddy would be ruined, possibly even jailed. And John Lachley's career as Eddy's spiritual advisor would come to a disastrous end. Classic motive and response. Except, of course, that Lachley was a psychopath and was using another psychopath as a weapon to rid himself of all witnesses.

Poor Kate Eddowes. She and her lover had returned to London on Friday from Kent and the hop harvest, a return Dominica and Guy had videotaped.

"I'll get a room over at the casual ward, Shoe Lane, luv," Eddowes had told Kelly. "We won't be apart long. You rest, now, and see to that cough."

Dominica had followed her down to Shoe Lane, capturing for posterity her fateful conversation with the casual ward's superintendent. "Oh, I'll get money, right enough. I know the Whitechapel murderer, I do. I'll collect that reward being offered by the newspapers!"

But if Kate Eddowes knew, she'd done nothing about it, contacting neither the police nor the newspapermen who were offering rewards of up to a hundred pounds—a literal fortune to someone like Catharine Eddowes—for information on the Ripper. She avoided constables, shunned reporters, and walked the streets as always, drinking what she earned and staring into shadows, clearly trying to drink her way through her terror or perhaps trying to drink her way to enough courage to finally act. Dominica thought pityingly that she was doubtless too frightened to come straight out and say, "Look, here, I've got a letter from the queen's grandson in my pocket and I think he's your killer . . ."

Prince Albert Victor was, of course, safely away in Scotland with his grandmother, just now, providing him with an ironclad alibi for the murders of Stride and Eddowes. Dominica doubted the prince even knew what Lachley was doing, although he might guess. Perhaps that was why he'd fled to Scotland, leaving his spiritual advisor behind in London.

When the night of September thirtieth arrived, Dominica and Guy followed Lachley from his home in Cleveland Street, then lost him for more than an hour in the teeming streets of Wapping. "Where the deuce did he get to?" Guy Pendergast muttered as darkness descended over London's rooftops.

"Where the devil does he always get to? Wherever it is, I intend to find out!"

"To do that, pet, we'll have to find him again. Of course, we can always pick him up at Dutfield's Yard."

"I plan to videotape much more of his activities this evening than that! We'll go to Catharine's doss house," Dominica decided. "Surely he'll show up there?" And that was exactly where they caught up to him, in the company of James Maybrick, at long, bloody last.

"We'll find Eddowes, first, if we can," Lachley muttered, his voice whispering electronically in Dominica's ear. "She's too bloody dangerous to leave wandering the streets any longer."

Lachley and Maybrick set out, stopping at public house after public house, searching for the doomed Kate Eddowes. Dominica, of course, knew exactly where Eddowes was—at least, where she'd be at eight o'clock, or thereabouts. Lachley wandered, by chance, directly into her path just in time to see events unfold in Aldgate High Street. He watched in open-mouthed disbelief and rising fury as two police constables incarcerated the woman he had waited two entire *weeks* to kill.

Catharine Eddowes was drunk. So drunk she could hardly stand up. Wailing like a fire engine and giggling, one would've thought her a girl of twelve. The sight of a forty-six-year-old prostitute whooping her way into Bishopsgate Police Station, carrying a letter in her pocket that could destroy everything Lachley had worked for, had *murdered* for, very nearly put the man over the edge. He stood across the street from the police station, hidden in shadows, soaking wet from the gusting rain, and closed his gloved hands into fists so tight, his hands trembled. The look of murderous rage in his face left Dominica momentarily shaken. When he stepped close to Maybrick, the words he hissed at his accomplice sent a shiver up her back.

"*They can't keep her there forever, God curse her! And if she shows them that letter, I'll set fire to the whole bloody police station, blow up the bleeding gas main under it!*" He jerked his black cloth cap down further over his brow, all but concealing his face, even from Dominica's low-light camera. "We'll find Stride, follow her as we did the others, wait until she's drunk, then I'll approach her and secure my letters. You can have her, afterwards."

"Yes . . ."

"You remember the code, James, that we agreed upon, should anyone come upon us while we're about our business?"

"Yes, yes," Maybrick said, his voice a trifle impatient now, "if you see someone, you'll cry *Lipski!* and I'll do the same if I spot anyone."

Lipski . . . The name of a poisoner who'd triggered a wave of anti-Semitic hatred in these streets the previous year. That hatred was sickeningly alive and well in the wake of the Ripper's murders. John Lachley and James Maybrick were deliberately fanning the flames of anti-Semitism, throwing the police even further off their trail, by using a word like Lipski as a coded warning. Anyone hearing that particular name would automatically assume it was aimed at a foreign Jewish murderer, rather than a warning between conspirators.

No wonder the constabulary had never caught the Ripper. Diabolically clever, these two. But hardly a match for Dominica Nosette. She smiled to herself as they returned to Flower and Dean Street, heading to the doss house at number 32 in search of Elizabeth Stride. And this time, they hit paydirt straightaway. The kitchen entrance opened, spilling light and warmth into the blustery night. Elizabeth Stride paused in the doorway, speaking to someone in the kitchen.

"Look, Thomas, luv, I've got sixpence! The deputy gave it to me. I'm off for a drink, but I'll be back!" Long Liz sailed cheerfully out into the evening, chuckling to herself as she passed Maybrick and Lachley, hidden in the darkness. "I'll be back, all right, but not 'til I've found me a jolly Welshman!" She laughed aloud at that, then headed briskly in the direction of Commercial Road where the kind of trade she sought would be plentiful on a night like this.

From her shadowy place of concealment, Dominica Nosette watched James Maybrick and then John Lachley set out in pursuit, moving at a leisurely pace, entirely silent on what must have been rubberized shoes, to have made so little noise against the wet pavements. She hadn't thought of that and kicked herself for not considering it. Normally she wore rubber-soled trainers for undercover work like this, but they would've garnered instant attention in the down-time world of Victorian London. Too late now to remedy the lack.

Pulse pounding, Dominica waited until both men were well ahead; then she gathered up her skirts and stepped softly out onto the rain-puddled street and glanced across the road. Guy Pendergast emerged from another cramped and dark little nook. They exchanged a brief glance, then Dominica smiled and set off. She was about to land the story of a lifetime.

Their council of war didn't last long. Despite Skeeter's urgent desire to follow Marcus' trail as long and as far as possible, they had other considerations to think of, not the least of which was Jenna Caddrick's conspicuous absence from Armstrong's party.

"Their luggage couldn't have had anyone stuffed inside it," Willie Samuelson said glumly. "We bribed the station manager to tell us everything he could remember. He said their luggage must've been almost empty, it weighed so little."

"Which means Jenna Caddrick was never with them in the first place," Kit sighed. He dragged his hat off and ran a hand through sweat-soaked hair. "Much as I hate to say it, it looks like we've been hoodwinked by Armstrong's sleight of hand. I suggest we abandon the hunt for Noah Armstrong and his porter. Either Jenna's already dead or she never was with Armstrong."

"In other words," Skeeter muttered, "the little bastard deliberately sent us on a wild goose chase."

"If you were a terrorist leader running for your life," Kit said in a disgusted tone, "with up-time authorities bound to be on your trail, wouldn't *you* try to set up a false trail to follow? Remember, Julius was dressed as a girl, so he must have been acting as decoy for whoever was bound to follow Armstrong. The names Cassie Coventina and Joey Tyrolin have been bothering me for quite a while. We were meant to follow Armstrong, presumably so whoever took Jenna Caddrick and Ianira Cassondra could slip away quietly someplace else."

Kaederman muttered under his breath. "But *where,* dammit?"

No one had an answer to that question. Skeeter rubbed the back of his neck and said under his breath, "I do *not* look forward to telling the Senator how Armstrong tricked us. Christ, this is all we need. Riots all over the station, that jackass Benny Catlin missing in London—"

"Benny Catlin?" Paula echoed, staring. "You mean that nice young kid is *missing?*"

Kit jerked his gaze up. "You *know* Benny Catlin?"

Paula blinked, started by the sudden intensity of the stares levelled at her. "Well, yes. I mean, it isn't every day I give a whisker job to a girl."

Kit's lower jaw came adrift.

Sid Kaederman actually grasped her arm. "*What?*"

"Take your hand off me!" Paula snapped, yanking herself loose.

Kaederman flushed and apologized. She shrugged her shoulder, rubbing her bicep, then asked Kit, "I take it you didn't you know Benny Catlin was a girl? She told me she wanted to disguise her gender, which was a big disadvantage in London. It's not that unusual, actually, I've just never done a whisker job on a girl that pretty."

"My God!" Skeeter matched the face in the Senator's photo to one in his memory and came up with an unpleasant, inescapable conclusion. "*Benny Catlin is Jenna!*"

Sid Kaederman swore in tones that caused several horses to lay back their ears. "God *damn* it! Armstrong duped us again! That stinking little bastard ordered his men to take her to *London . . .*"

"Yeah," Skeeter agreed, "but how did they get tickets? The Britannia's been sold out for nearly a year!"

"Jenna and her roommate must've bought Britannia tickets from that up-time scalper," Kit said slowly. "A year ago, when they first planned to go down time. There would've been plenty of Ripper Tour tickets floating around the black market, a year ago."

Skeeter groaned, "The Senator said she wanted to film history. She must've planned to videotape the Ripper terror."

"Yes. And landed right in the middle of the *Ansar Majlis* terror, instead." Kit scrubbed at his lower face with one sweat-begrimed hand. "We have to get back to TT-86. We'll sleep here tonight, set out first thing in the morning. I'm afraid we'll be riding hard, to make it back to Denver in time to catch the gate. Can you keep up?" He glanced from Paula to Kaederman.

Paula Booker thinned her lips. "I'll cope. The last thing I want to do is stay *here*. I've had about as much vacation as I can stand, this year."

Kit turned his attention to Kaederman. "I'd suggest you try pain pills for those muscle cramps, or we'll leave you behind."

"I'll take the pills," Kaederman growled. "And when this is over, I am never setting foot down another gate in my life! I hate it!"

"Suits me," Skeeter muttered.

Kit's hard-eyed gaze met Skeeter's. "Well, Jackson, looks like you'll be going to London, after all."

"Great," Skeeter groused. "Jack the Ripper *and* the *Ansar Majlis*. Just my cup of tea. Anybody want to place a bet on what the Senator has to say about all this?"

He didn't have a single taker.

(((Chapter 7)))

The stalk was in James Maybrick's blood, hot fire that only the red stuff of a life pouring out across his hands could quench. The wild night, with its gusting rainshowers and biting cold winds, spoke to the demons raging in his soul. It called them forth, hungering and slavering, until they ran barefooted through the flames of his own private hell. *She shall pay! By God, the bitch shall pay, her and her whoremaster both! All London knows my work, now, and she trembles with fear when people speak of Sir Jim's deeds. Soon, I will pay her the same as I gave the others, whores all . . . and my knife will drink the bitch's blood, as well . . . Maybe I'll take her before I rip her open . . . take her while her whoremaster watches, then rip them both, God damn them!*

James Maybrick held in his mind the face of his beautiful, stupid wife, who had whored herself again and again with that fool Brierly. He summoned up the memory of the terror he'd inflicted on that prostitute in Manchester, the even more delicious terror of Polly Nichols and Annie Chapman here in London, painted that same wild-eyed fear across his wife's vapid face . . . and smiled as he watched his mentor close in on the common streetwalker chosen as Maybrick's next victim. Maybrick's blood pounded in anticipation.

The potent medicine Lachley gave him each time he visited London left James absolutely invincible, stronger and more sure of himself than he'd felt in his entire fifty years of life. He laughed behind his moustaches, laughed at the notion of Abberline and those bumbling idiots in the Metropolitan Police Department actually *catching* anyone, let alone Sir Jim and his personal god. So many constables and fine inspectors, wasting their time searching for a foreign Jew to hang!

The game delighted him. That leather apron left in the basin beside Annie Chapman had been a most diverting clue. It had sent the idiots of Whitechapel's H Division chasing after the wrong sort of man. They'd actually arrested a fellow over that lovely apron, so they had! A dirty Jewish boot finisher they'd desperately wanted to be guilty.

Too bad he'd had an alibi, an unshakeable one, at that. Not that they'd have believed him guilty for long, when other filthy whores had to be punished, had to be ripped with his shining knife. No, they wouldn't have held Mr. Pizer forever, certainly not past tonight. Tomorrow, all London would quake in its shoes at the work he would perform, he and John Lachley. A clever cotton merchant from Liverpool and a doctor of occult medicine from London's own SoHo, playing them all for the fools they were . . .

Rain spattered down from dirty skies, black and cold as last winter's ashes. The whore they'd been following for almost two hours, now, was a filthy foreigner. Lachley had told Maybrick about her. She frequently went begging at the Swedish parish church, spinning lies about a non-existent husband and children. She'd supposedly lost them ten years previously, when the saloon steamer *Princess Alice* had collided with the steamship *Bywell Castle* in the Thames, killing nearly seven hundred people. Lachley's inquiries, quiet but thorough, had revealed that the bitch's real English husband had died of heart failure only four years previously, in 1884, not in the famous steamship collision. Children, she had apparently never had.

The one thing about Liz Stride that fretted Maybrick was her nephew, or rather, the late John Stride's nephew, who was a member of the bloody Metropolitan Police Force, of all things. But that didn't worry James too much. Clearly, the nephew couldn't care overly much for his aunt, not if Liz Stride were living in Whitechapel, charring for Jews and mending their garments for them, selling her body to whatever man would have her. He must remember to leave some nasty little clue on the streets, tonight, pointing the finger of suspicion at the foreign Jews again, he really must. He'd remembered to bring his chalk, this time, too.

But he couldn't write out any messages until his knife had drunk its fill.

After witnessing Catharine Eddowes' arrest for public drunkenness, they spent hours searching pubs for Stride and finally caught up to her shortly before eleven P.M. on Settles Street, at the Bricklayer's Arms Public House. Alarmingly, they found her in the company of a short, well-dressed man she laughingly called Llewellyn. *A Welshman!* Maybrick darted a glance at Lachley, who watched the couple narrowly from the shadows.

The whore and her Welshman stood in the doorway of the pub, waiting for the driving rain to slacken. Her customer was eager enough for it, kissing her and carrying on like some low sailor, rather than the respectable tradesman he clearly was, probably some arse of a merchant up from Cardiff on business, slumming in the East End where a man could have whatever he wanted for the price of a glass of cheap gin.

Two workmen, also taking refuge from the rain, ordered ale and watched the antics in the doorway, clearly bemused. One nudged the other. "Hey, Liz, why don't you bring your fella in and 'ave a drink, eh?" The tall woman glanced around, laughter shaking her strong-boned face, then whispered something to her customer. The man shook his head, intent on pawing at her bosom under her drab coat. The man who'd invited them in snorted knowingly. His friend called over the noise of laughing, swearing, singing voices, "Better watch out, Liz, that's Leather Apron trying to get round you!"

Laughter greeted this assessment, since the man clearly was not an Eastern European Jew. He was obviously too new to town even to understand the reference. James Maybrick smiled into his own ale glass, delighted. *Leather Apron, now there's a lovely joke, indeed! Little do they know Leather Apron's sitting right here, watching, waiting for that bastard to finish, so Sir Jim can have his own chance at her.* Not that Sir Jim would actually taste her dirty wares. That wasn't what he was here for. Sir Jim could take a whore anytime he wanted, just by bedding his wife.

Shortly after eleven, Liz Stride and her importunate Welshman left the Bricklayer's Arms, heading out into the rainy night for a tryst in a dark stairwell on Goulston Street. From his place of concealment at the foot of that stairwell, Maybrick could hear her asking the man to read a letter for her, one she had in her pocket.

"Read a letter for you?" he gasped out, clearly giving her the business while she asked her question. "Are you daft?"

"It's in Welsh."

The man grunted. "I didn't come to London to read somebody else's letters. And only the lower classes bother learning to *read* Welsh. Good God, woman, if a Welshman wants to rise above the handicap of being born Welsh, he'd better scrap everything *Welsh* he can. Coarse brown bread, coarse Welsh language, all of it. Great Christ, woman, hold still, I haven't finished yet!"

James Maybrick, hat pulled low against the cold wind and rainsqualls, smiled behind his moustaches. Long Liz's customer didn't know it, but his lack of ability to read his own native language had just saved his life. Clearly, Elizabeth Stride was none too pleased that her Welshman's sense of inferiority had turned him into a greater English snob than most Englishmen.

When she emerged at last from the stairwell, her color was high and so was her temper. "Ta very much, luv," she snapped, pocketing a few coins.

The Welshman, looking bewildered, watched her storm away down the street, muttering, "What the devil is it these creatures really want? Now, where's my hotel, I wonder . . ." He peered about him, squinting into the rain, then set off briskly, heading west.

What Elizabeth Stride wanted, at any rate, was clear. Over the next thirty minutes, James Maybrick and his mentor shadowed her across most of the East End, from Whitechapel down through Wapping, east into Poplar, a wretched stretch of dockside gambling dens and gin palaces where—so rumor had it—Long Liz and her late husband had once run a profitable little coffee shop, but never once catching her alone. She was being careful, obviously, to stay in the well-crowded streets. It was in Poplar that Stride picked up the sailor. He reeled out of a pub in the company of several of his mates, singing off-key about his long-lost and sorely missed Cardiff. By eleven forty-five, she and her sailor, a young man in a cutaway black coat and ubiquitious sailor's hat, were strolling down Berner Street, back in Whitechapel, where they paused in the doorway to number 64, waiting out another brief rain shower. A passerby glanced up and noticed them kissing, but failed to notice either Maybrick or Lachley where they stood across the road in the shadows, watching and listening.

"You would say anything but your prayers," the sailor laughed, voice carrying across Berner Street. And a moment after that, when the passerby had turned onto Fairclough Street and was out of earshot, "How about it, then? Will you?"

" 'Course I will, there's a nice quiet spot just down the street, Dutfield's Yard, where they used to make carts. Nobody uses the yard at midnight, luv. Mr. Dutfield moved his cart-making business over to Pinchin Street and the sack maker's shop next to it's closed this time of night. And there's a dry stable in there, empty now the carts have gone."

"Ah . . . Sounds perfect, then. Lead on, angel."

When they emerged from the doorway to number 64, the young sailor's black trousers bulged noticeably in front. Maybrick, hand thrust deep into his pocket, gripped his knife and breathed harder. Dutfield's Yard . . . He knew the place. It *was* perfect. Completely closed in, only one way in or out, and that through a narrow alley eighteen feet long. The yard could only be reached through a pair of wooden gates set into the street between a row of terraced cottages, occupied by cigarette makers and tailors, and the Jewish International Working Men's Club on the opposite side of the alleyway.

A meeting of some kind was in progress at the Club. Maybrick could hear voices speaking half a dozen different languages, English, Russian, Hebrew, French, Italian, something Slavic that might have been Polish or Czech . . . They came from halfway across Europe to this miserable little meeting hall where upwards of two hundred working-class louts and their women crammed themselves in to give plays and musical concerts, all of them hideously amateur, not to mention the radical meetings that attracted troublemakers from all over the East End. Maybrick detested them, agitators with wild notions about the manumission of the labouring classes. Why, they and their kind would bring down the Empire, so they would, them and their dirty whores, the ruination of decent British morals . . .

Elizabeth Stride, as foreign a bitch as the workers in the lively hall opposite, was taking her time, back there in Dutfield's Yard. Was the sailor reading out the letter for her? Maybrick caressed his knife. He didn't give a damn about the sailor, although he would have to die, too, if he'd translated Dr. Lachley's letter for the dirty screw. Christ, they were taking their time about it! He eased his pocket watch out, peering at the crystal face in the dim light filtering out through the Workers' Club windows opposite. Bloody near twelve-thirty A.M.! He was cold and tired and wet, had spent five miserable hours on a train today, just getting here from Liverpool, and they'd had to walk across the whole bloody East End since his arrival.

Get on with it! He snapped shut his watch with a savage motion, thrust it back into his waistcoat pocket. Impatience was making him edgy. Once already tonight, he'd primed himself to strike, only to have the chance snatched away, thanks to Catharine Eddowes' drunkenness. By the time Stride finally emerged, James Maybrick was ready to do a violence worse than anything he'd unleashed to date. By God, the moment Lachley had his letter, he would knock the bitch into that alleyway, throttle her, then slash and slash until the fury was finally spent . . .

"Sorry about the note in your pocket, darlin'," the sailor was saying as they stepped out of the black little alleyway. "I can read me own name, just about, but not anything else. Never went to any school."

"Oh, it isn't your fault," she said, voice peevish. Clearly, she was no happier about this customer's lack than the previous one's. "I'm beginning to think there's not a Welshman in all of Britain can read his own language!"

The sailor laughed. "Give me a kiss, then. I'd better be off and find me mates, they'll wonder where I've got to."

If Maybrick hadn't been so feverishly furious to strike, he'd have laughed aloud. Poor, dirty whore, had a letter in her pocket worth a king's ransom—literally—and she couldn't find a soul to read it to her. The sailor gave her a lusty kiss, then strode off toward Poplar and the docks. Maybrick stepped forward, seething with impatience, only to curse under his breath when a young man in a dark coat and deerstalker hat left the Workman's Club, carrying a newspaper-wrapped parcel some six inches high and eighteen inches long. He was moving fast, eyes clearly not yet adjusted to the darkness beyond the club, because he very nearly ran her down.

"Oh, I am sorry!" he exclaimed, steadying her on her feet. His accent marked him as a foreigner.

"Give me a fright, you did," she gasped, managing a smile for him.

"You are not hurt, then?"

"No, I'm fine, honest. I don't suppose you'd know anybody hereabout who reads Welsh?"

The young man looked startled, but shook his head. "No, I'm afraid I do not. I am Hungarian, have not been long in England."

"Oh. Well, maybe you might walk me back to my rooms, eh? It's not far and I'm that nervous, with this madman walking about the streets . . ."

"Of course, madam."

He escorted her across the street, straight toward Maybrick's hiding place. Maybrick all but crushed the handle of his knife under his fist and shrank back into the darkness of the doorway he stood in. God above, would this lousy whore never spend two minutes alone? If she made it all the way back to her doss house with the blasted Hungarian, they'd never have a chance at her! Then *another* set of footsteps coming along the pavement sent Maybrick even deeper into the shadows. *Holy Christ, it's a bloody police constable!* Pulse thundering, he stood paralyzed, watching the constable approach Stride and her Hungarian. The constable frowned at her, moustaches twitching. " 'Ere, now, move along, Liz, none of your dirty business along 'ere."

Liz Stride drew herself up, drunk and beginning to show the effects of her own night's frustration. "I never asked this gentleman a thing like that! He nearly knocked me down, coming out that door." The Hungarian doffed his hat nervously and muttered something about getting home, then fled down Berner Street in the opposite direction from the constable. The policeman shrugged and moved on, leaving Stride to mutter a curse after him.

"Well, at least I got enough for the doss house. Bloke might not've been able to read, but he had money in his trous, sure enough." She sighed, then headed back across Berner Street, clearly intent on giving up her quest for the night.

And finally, God, *finally,* she was alone.

Across the street, John Lachley moved in fast, stepping out of his concealment and hurrying toward her. "Madam? I say, madam, I couldn't help overhearing you just now." He was speaking in a very low voice, but Maybrick, senses twitching, heard every breath drawn, every syllable uttered. "You said you were looking for someone who reads Welsh?"

Liz Stride paused, taken by surprise. "Welsh? Why, yes, I am."

He doffed his rough black cap, gave her a mock bow. "I'm Welsh, as it happens. What were you looking to have read?"

Eagerness flooded across her face and she reached toward her pocket, then she paused, sudden wariness stealing across her features. "You couldn't help overhearing?" she repeated nervously. "How long have you been watching me?"

"Why, madam, not long at all. Here, do you want me to read this letter out for you or don't you?"

She backed away from him, toward the alleyway to Dutfield's Yard. "I never said it was a letter."

Anger flushed Lachley's face. He was as impatient as Maybrick, maybe more so, having waited two full weeks for this moment, while Maybrick had been busy with his work in Liverpool and the children and a household to run. "Of course it's a letter! What else would it be? Oh, for God's sake, just hand the bloody thing over!"

"I've got to go, have a friend waiting for me at the pub down the street, there . . ."

She started to step away and Lachley's temper snapped. He grabbed her by the arm, flung her back toward the alley. "Give me the letter, you stinking whore!" When she tried to break free, Lachley slammed her to the muddy ground. A tiny scream broke loose from her throat, then two more. She was trying to scramble to her feet, digging for something in her pocket. Maybrick, pulse racing, reached for his knife, started out into the open, then heard footsteps coming and swore under his breath. He fumbled out his pipe instead, lit it with shaking hands just as Lachley glanced up.

"*Lipski!*" The warning burst from Lachley, galvanizing the short, dark little man approaching. Already in the act of crossing the street to avoid the altercation at the gate, the heavily bearded man, obviously Jewish from the prayer shawl visible under his coat, started walking much faster. Maybrick went after him, so furious at yet another interruption he was ready to slash anything and anyone who got in his way. The Jew broke into a run and Maybrick pelted after him, chasing the interloper all the way down to the railway arch. He finally realized that Lachley would be back at Dutfield's Yard, securing his letter. Chasing a damned interfering Jew wasn't why he was out here tonight, wasn't why he'd spent the whole stinking night in the cold rain.

Maybrick turned and hurried back to the alleyway, where Lachley had finally snatched his letter from the whore's pocket. He'd forced her back against the gate, one hand across her mouth, his arm pressed against her throat, cutting off her air and trapping her against the gate. Murderous rage had twisted Lachley's face—and mortal terror had twisted hers. Her eyes rolled as Maybrick approached, hope flaring wildly.

"Not in the street!" Maybrick hissed as he came closer. "That bloody constable might come back any moment! Get her into Dutfield's Yard . . ."

Keeping her safely throttled, they dragged Elizabeth Stride back into the blackness, down the eighteen feet of blind alleyway and along the wall in the yard beyond. She fought them with every scrap of strength in her brawny frame, giving them a dreadful time, subduing her. Lachley, wheezing and panting, finally threw her against the brick wall and pinned her with one arm across her chest, bruising her while his hands closed around her throat; Maybrick held a gloved hand clamped across her mouth while Lachley strangled her, to keep her screams from alerting the crowd in the hall just above their heads.

"I want her!" Maybrick hissed.

"When I've bloody well finished!" Fury cracked through Lachley's voice. She was struggling, but more feebly now, losing consciousness. Maybrick had his knife out, shaking with need. At length the struggles ceased, her life fading away with a harsh rattle in her throat; then Lachley was shoving her down into the mud. "Got to make it look like she was back here for the sex," he was muttering, voice a bare whisper. Maybrick could hear the doctor searching her pockets. "Ahh . . . that's grand, a packet of Cachous . . ."

Ahh, indeed . . . Maybrick smiled. Pills used by smokers to sweeten the breath. When the constables found her, they would think she'd taken them out to chew before servicing her customer, never dreaming she'd been strangled to death and cut open for the letter Lachley was stuffing into his coat pocket. On the heels of that thought, Lachley swore. "Christ! The bitch had a knife in her pocket!" He came up holding a short, wicked little blade Maybrick could just make out in the near blackness. "Bloody bitch! All right," the doctor hissed at last, "she's yours! Make it fast!"

"Give me her knife!" Maybrick gasped, wanting to do her with her own blade. Lachley handed it over and Maybrick crouched down, delighting in the shock against his hand as he slashed through the throat. He reached for her skirts, wanting to rip at her gut—

And the gate at the end of the alleyway rattled open.

A horse's hooves struck the bricks sharply, heading straight toward them. Maybrick stood up so fast, he went dizzy. Lachley grabbed his arm, dragged him deeper into the yard, back toward the stable. Maybrick's heart thudded, heavy and hard and terrified. Hot blood trickled down his hands, which shook wildly out of control as the pony cart clattered right into the yard with them.

Dear God, we're going to hang for this goddamned slut!

The pony nearly trod on the bitch's body. The animal snorted and shied at the last moment, obviously having caught the scent of blood, and tried to avoid the bundle on the ground.

"What's got into you?" a man's voice muttered, heavily accented. "What did I do with that whip? Eh, is there something on the ground?" They could hear the man scraping and probing downward into the blackness. "Who's this? Are you drunk? Get up, you're blocking the way." Then, voice suddenly uncertain. "Maybe she's ill." He jumped down from his cart, hurried back down the alleyway. "I must fetch help, get a lantern, it is black as pitch in here . . ."

Oh, my God, he's leaving!

"Quick!" Lachley's voice hissed into his ear.

Maybrick needed no second prompting. His legs shook violently as they made their escape, silent on their rubberized servants' shoes. Thank God Lachley had thought of using them when this business began, they'd have been overheard leaving the yard for certain, without them. He still couldn't quite believe they were going to make their escape. He shoved both knives into his coat pockets as they hurried down Berner Street, while the cart driver entered the noisy Working Men's Club behind them.

"What is it, Diemschutz?" a man's voice floated to them.

"A woman, collapsed in the Yard. Get a lantern . . ."

The man's name burned in Maybrick's mind. *Diemschutz!* Another stinking *Jew!* He would hunt the bastard down, so he would! Slit his goddamned throat, how dare he interrupt like that? He'd had no time to do more than cut her throat, curse it!

"Keep your hands in your pockets," Lachley hissed. "They're covered with blood. We'll have to get underground as fast as possible."

"But I didn't get to rip her!"

Fury blazed in his mentor's eyes. *"I don't give a bloody damn what you didn't get to do!* You sodding maniac, we were damn near caught! And the whole East End is going to be crawling with constables inside a quarter of an hour!" Lachley's cheeks had gone ashen.

"I know we were almost caught, blast it!" Maybrick hissed, gut churning with frustrated rage. "But we *weren't,* were we? And the bloody buggers won't be looking for *us,* they'll be looking for a lone man. A stinking foreign Jew, walking by himself!"

Lachley's breaths slowed perceptibly. His jaw, knotted with anger, gradually relaxed. "Right. All right, then, we walk along together. Just a couple of jolly mates, 'aving a bit of a bobble on a Saturday night, out for a quick one down to boozer."

Maybrick blinked in surprise. "Good God. You really *have* lived in these streets before, haven't you? I didn't quite believe . . ."

"Of course I have, idiot!" Lachley hissed, moving down the pavement at a more leisurely pace. "How the bloody hell do you think I know the sewers so well?"

"Oh, I hadn't thought of that, really . . ."

"Just shut up, James, for God's sake, just *shut the bloody hell up!*"

He considered arguing, but one look into Lachley's eyes told Maybrick that his mentor was in no mood for trouble, not even from him. He walked along in broody silence, the blood on his hands drying into a sticky mess. When they passed a gutter with a broad puddle, he paused and glanced both directions down the street, then crouched and rinsed off his hands and his whore's knife. Her blade was sticky with its owner's lifeblood. His hands were still unsteady as he shook the muddy water off and thrust the prostitute's knife back into his other coat pocket, opposite his own, longer-bladed weapon. He shoved his hands into his pockets to hide the bloodstains on his white cuffs.

"I want to get right out of Whitechapel," Lachley muttered, moving steadily west. "Forget about your rooms in Middlesex Street. If there's an inquiry, if that bloody Jew on Berner Street identifies us to the constables, I want to be out of Metropolitan Police jurisdiction, fast."

They were already in Commercial Road, walking steadily west toward the point where Commercial Road took a sharp bend toward the north to become Commercial Street. Once past Middlesex Street and the Minories, along Aldgate, they would be in the jurisdiction of The City of London, with its own Lord Mayor, its own city officials and—ah, yes, Maybrick smiled, clever Lachley!—its own constabulary. As they passed a nasty little alley, they nearly stumbled over a drunk, who lay snoring in the gutter. Lachley paused, cast a swift glance around, then stooped and pulled the drunken sailor deeper into the alley.

"Well, don't just stand there! That miserable Jew can describe these clothes!"

Lachley was stripping off his dark coat, peeling off the sailor's jacket and grimy shirt. "Here, put this shirt on, your cuffs are bloody."

The idea of putting on a filthy sailor's unwashed shirt did not appeal to James Maybrick. But neither did the gallows. He stripped off his shirt in haste, switching his blood-stained one for the sailor's. Lachley had appropriated the man's jacket for himself, dropping his own coat over Maybrick's arm. Maybrick slithered into it, then dumped his coat, the sleeves spattered with Stride's blood, across the drunk's naked torso. When they stepped back into the light, Lachley wore a grey cap instead of the black one he'd left behind, a salt-and-pepper grey jacket, too loose for him, and a red kerchief knotted around his neck, nautical fashion.

"You don't look the same man at all," Maybrick said softly, studying Lachley with a critical mein. Then, wistful and frustrated, "You don't suppose those sodding constables at Bishopsgate have let that drunken bitch Eddowes out yet?"

Lachley stared at him, then gave out a short, hard bark of laughter. "Great God, you do enjoy dangerous living, don't you? One wife in London, another wife *and* a bloody mistress in Liverpool, every week you swallow enough arsenic to poison all Bethnal Green, and now you want to stop at the police station and ask if the nice whore they arrested for impersonating a fire engine has sobered up enough to go home!"

"What I want," Maybrick growled, "is what I didn't get with the whore in Dutfield's Yard."

Lachley, equilibrium restored by their semi-miraculous getaway and a change of disguise, laughed again, harsh and wild as the rain-lashed night. "All right, damn your eyes, we'll just go along and see! The fastest route from here," he peered at their surroundings, "would be down Houndsditch from Aldgate."

As they were currently in Aldgate High Street, it was a matter of perhaps two minutes' walk to reach Aldgate proper, then they swung sharply northward up the long reach of Houndsditch, moving away from the Minories to the south. The clock on a distant brewery up in Brick Lane chimed the half-hour. One thirty A.M. and his blood was high, the terror of having nearly been caught now transformed into a feral sort of euphoria. Pure excitement flowed through his veins, hot and electrically charged, as though he'd just taken a dose of his arsenic. Sir Jim was invincible, by God! All he asked was to get his hands on that other bitch he'd been promised. He'd cut her with all the wildly charged strength in him, rip her to pieces and leave some jolly little rhyme for the City Division's bumbling fools to puzzle over. His brother Michael, who could rhyme like anything, sat in his lovely rooms over in St. James' writing songs the whole sodding country was singing. If Michael could do it, so could he. He'd think up a right saucy little rhyme to tantalize the police, maybe stir up more trouble with the Jews. Yes, a truly fine way to cap off the evening . . .

As they approached Duke Street, a short, auburn-haired woman emerged from that narrow thoroughfare, moving with angry strides and muttering to herself. A dark green chintz skirt with three flounces picked up the light from a distant gas lamp, revealing yellow flowers of some kind in the cloth. Her black coat had once been very fine, with imitation fur at the collars, cuffs, and pockets. A black straw bonnet trimmed with green and black velvet and black beads was tilted rakishly on her hair. The woman was strikingly familiar, Maybrick couldn't immediately think why.

". . . lousy bastard," she was growling to herself, not having seen them yet, "give you two whole florins, I will, he says, if you can get me to spend! How was I to know he was so sodding impotent, he hadn't managed it in a whole year . . . Half a damned hour wasted on him and not tuppence to show for it! I've got to find somebody who can read that blasted letter of Annie's, that's what, get some real money out of it. The newspapers will give me a reward, that's what I told the superintendent of the casual ward, and I meant it, by God! If I could just get a reward, now, maybe I could take John to a regular hospital, not a workhouse infirmary . . ."

Lachley closed his hand around Maybrick's wrist, halting him. Recognition struck like a rolling clap of thunder. *Catharine Eddowes!* Wild exultation blasted straight through him. Lachley hissed, "I'll lure her down to Mitre Square, in City jurisdiction . . ."

Yes, yes, get on with it! His hand already ached where he gripped his own long-bladed knife. Maybrick faded back into the shadows, leaving Lachley to approach the angry prostitute, whom they'd last seen so drunk she could scarcely stand up. Clearly, the evening's stay in jail had sobered her up nicely. *Good!* Her terror would be worse, cold sober.

" 'Ello, luv," Lachley said with the voice of a rough sailor, a voice that matched his stolen jacket and cap and neckerchief. "You're a right comfy sight, so y'are, for a bloke wot's far from 'ome."

Catharine Eddowes paused, having to look up a long way into Lachley's face. She was barely five feet tall, nearly seven inches shorter than the man smiling down at her. "Why, hello. You're out late, ducks, the pubs have all closed. I know," she said with a wry smile, "because I wanted a drink tonight and couldn't get one."

"Well, now, I can't say as I could 'elp you to get boozey, but a body don't need gin to 'ave a good time, now does a body?" Lachley dug into his pocket, came out with a shining coin. "Just you 'ave a butcher's at this, eh? Sixpence, shiny an' new."

Catherine's eyes focused sharply on the coin Lachley held up between gloved thumb and forefinger. Then she smiled and moved closer to him, rested a hand on his chest. "Well, now, that's a pretty sixpence. What might a lady have to do, to share it?"

Further along Duke Street, where lights blazed in a local meeting hall known as the Imperial Club, three men emerged into the wet night, glancing toward Lachley and Eddowes. They moved off in the opposite direction, giving the woman and her obvious customer their privacy. James Maybrick watched them go and smiled in the darkness from his hiding place on Houndsditch.

"Let's take a bit of a stroll, shall we?" Lachley suggested, following the men who'd just left the Imperial Club, but moving at a far more leisurely pace to give the talkative trio plenty of time to lose themselves in the streets ahead. "Find us someplace nice an' comfy to share?"

Her low laughter delighted Maybrick. The song she started singing left him laughing softly to himself. The silly screw had perhaps ten minutes left to live, at best, and here she was, walking arm in arm with the man who was going to kill her, singing as though she hadn't a care in the world. Maybrick laughed again.

Soon enough, she *wouldn't* have.

After two solid weeks in a saddle, short of sleep and in dire need of a shower, Kit Carson was in no shape for a face-to-face with Senator John Caddrick and half the newsies in the northern hemisphere. But he didn't have much choice. They were waiting as soon as he stepped into the station through the Wild West Gate. Guides bringing back Julius and the murdered tourist followed on his heels. Screams and a roar of voices broke out, a solid wall of noise.

"Jenna!" Senator Caddrick's voice cut through the chaos. The Senator was bolting past the ropes . . . "*Jenna!*" A Time Tours employee caught the Senator and held him back. His expression twisted through a whole range of emotions.

"Senator Caddrick," Kit told the ashen politician, "it isn't your daughter. Neither of them is."

Visibly shaken, Caddrick, gasped out, "Not my daughter? Then where is she? Why isn't she with you?" Sudden fury crackled in the Senator's eyes. He shook off the hands holding him back and advanced menacingly. "What are you doing back if you haven't found her? Explain this immediately!"

"She isn't with us because we didn't find her."

Newsies were crowding against the lounge's velvet-rope barriers, shouting questions. Barricades fell with a crash, spilling newsies into the chaos as the returning tour reeled back into the station. Skeeter Jackson, gaunt from hard riding, came through the open gate just ahead of Sid Kaederman and Paula Booker. A steady stream of returning tourists and guides began to pour through the gate as Senator Caddrick dragged his gaze from the body bags to his exhausted detective and back to Kit's face. "Didn't find her? Why not?"

"Because we have excellent reason to believe your daughter never left TT-86 through the Denver Gate at all. I'd rather not say more until we've spoken in private." Kit glanced toward shocked Time Tours employees. "Could someone notify Ronisha Azzan we need a meeting with her? Thanks. No, I'm sorry, there will be no further comments at this time."

He waded against the tide of shouting newsies and shaken tourists, heading for the aerie, then decided he didn't want to risk the kind of fireworks that would explode if he took the entire search team with him. So he shoved his way through the chaos in Frontier Town and muttered, "Paula, get out of here. Kaederman, go with Skeeter to Connie Logan's. Start outfitting for the Britannia."

"Right, boss!"

"You got it, Kit."

Skeeter peeled off so fast, news crews were left stammering in the vacuum. Paula took advantage of their surprise to haul Sid Kaederman away in his wake.

"What's going on?" Caddrick demanded.

"I'll brief you at the station manager's office," Kit growled.

"But—"

Kit left him standing in the midst of an unholy, shrieking mob of newsies. The Senator, trailing reporters like a school of noisy fish, caught up and stalked along in thin-lipped silence. At the aerie's elevator access, Kit threw a body check to hold out the crowd on their heels and mashed the button for the top floor. The elevator rose swiftly toward uncertain sanctuary. When the doors slid open, Kit discovered just how uncertain that sanctuary was. Along one glass wall, lined up like so many gargoyles, sat three stone-faced men and women from the Inter-Temporal Court of the Hague, their uniforms glittering with brass officialdom. Like it or not, I.T.CH.'s grand inquisitors had arrived.

Kit held back a sigh and entered the glass-walled office anyway. The I.T.C.H. agents were stiff in their spotless uniforms, while Ronisha Azzan stood in cool elegance behind Bull Morgan's immense desk, which left Kit feeling even dirtier, grittier, and wearier than before. He rearranged grime on the back of his neck, then stalked over to the nearest chair and promptly folded up into it. Tired as he was— and stolid as the Grand Inquisitors were—Kit didn't miss the slight shuffle in chairs as his pungent perfume, the accumulation of fourteen days on a horse, wafted across the office.

"Welcome home, Kit," Ronisha Azzan greeted him quietly. "If I could have your report, please?"

Kit told the Deputy Station Manager what they'd found in the mining camp, bringing everyone up to date in a few brief sentences. When he finished, utter silence held the glass-walled aerie. Senator John Caddrick's expression was a study in lightning-fast realizations: shock, dismay, anxiety, and oddly, triumph. Then Caddrick's face went slowly purple as anger—or something approximating it—won out over the other emotions. "*Benny Catlin?* Do you mean to tell me you've wasted two entire *weeks* chasing the wrong tourist? When my daughter has been lost down your godforsaken Britannia Gate this whole time?"

"It wasn't wasted!" Kit snapped. "We know a great deal more than we did two weeks ago. One of our residents was *murdered,* down the Denver gate! That boy hadn't even turned seventeen, Caddrick, and he took a bullet *meant for your daughter!*"

Caddrick had enough sense, at least, to shut up. He sat breathing hard for long moments. Ronisha Azzan sat back in her chair, looking abruptly tired and grey around the lips and nostrils. Kit sympathized. He felt grey all over. Ronisha shoved herself to her feet and poured out three stiff scotch-and-sodas. Caddrick's hand was shaking as he lifted his drink, nearly sloshing it down his expensive suit jacket. Kit drained his own glass at one gulp. "Thanks, Ronnie. God, I needed that. So . . . What we're trying to determine now is our best chance of tracing Benny Catlin in London. Dr. Paula Booker is probably the best bet we've got for identifying Jenna, since she's the surgeon who gave Jenna a new face."

"I want to see this doctor," Caddrick growled. "I want to know how my little girl was when she came through this station, who was holding her prisoner, why the surgeon didn't report any of this—"

"Dr. Booker didn't report it for the simple reason there was nothing to report. Your daughter came in voluntarily, alone, claiming to be a grad student. Paula gave her a set of false whiskers, surgically implanted. The very next day, Paula left for her own vacation down time. You're damned lucky, Senator, to have any witness at all. When we caught up to Dr. Booker, trying to trace Armstrong and his prisoners, she and her guide had been bushwhacked by a gang of local bandits. If we hadn't come along, Paula might well have been murdered in cold blood."

Caddrick glared at him, his mouth tightened into a thin white line. "Live witnesses won't do any good if Jenna's already dead in London! For your information, Carson, my daughter was nearly killed her first night there. Twice! Then she disappeared, leaving two dead men behind her. And now you tell me you've got two *more* men murdered in cold blood down the Denver Gate? Not to mention a known international terrorist who escapes with three hostages—and you don't even bother to *follow?* My God, mister, of all the careless, irresponsible—"

"*That is enough!*" Kit Carson had the lungs to be heard when necessary.

Caddrick slammed the scotch glass down, knuckles white. "Don't you dare use that tone with me—"

"*Gentlemen!*" Ronisha bellowed, towering over both of them. "Senator! You will remain civil or you will leave this meeting! Is that understood? Kit Carson has just risked his life, not to mention two weeks of unpaid time away from his business, looking for your little girl. In my book, you owe Mr. Carson a very serious apology! As well as whatever humble thanks you can muster up as a parent. You ought to be dancing for joy he's discovered as much as he has, considering what he was up against, out there!"

Caddrick clearly didn't intend to dance for anybody, much less for joy. He sat glaring at Ronisha for a long, dangerous instant, then glowered at Kit, obviously waiting for further explanations. Kit considered walking out, then considered unemployment and life as suffered up time. Speaking coldly, he said, "Suppose you tell me just what I was supposed to do, Senator? Spend the next five years combing the North American continent for Armstrong? When we had a positive lead on your daughter's whereabouts? The Time Tours guides we left in Colorado are still searching for Armstrong and his hostages, will be for months to come, down the Wild West Gate. But *this* search and rescue mission was charged with finding your little girl. And that's exactly what it's going to do. Find your daughter. In London. Ronnie, what's the news from Spaldergate House?"

Ronisha sighed. "We know Benny Catlin was involved in two fatal shootings, leaving two baggage handlers dead and a carriage driver wounded. Malcolm's been searching, of course, but no one in London has any inkling that Benny Catlin is Jenna Caddrick."

Kit grunted. "Sounds to me like Jenna's managed to escape, which means our searchers will have to split up to locate Jenna and whoever took her through the gate. I pity the searchers. They'll have a helluva time, covering London for two separate targets with a three-week lead on them."

"*They*?" Caddrick echoed. "What do you mean, *they*? You're the team leader, Carson! I insist you continue to lead this mission!"

"I can't," Kit said bluntly, rubbing sweat and grit from his brow. "And it's got nothing to do with your lack of gratitude or my pressing business interests, so forget the protests. I already exist in September of 1888. I'd shadow myself and die instantly if I attempted to enter London during the next four months. Someone else has to head up search-and-rescue operations there. I'd suggest Skeeter Jackson, working closely with Malcolm Moore. Skeeter's already—"

"Now, wait just a minute! I've done some checking on this Jackson. Not only is he the same little creep who assaulted me at Primary, I've heard more than enough to know I don't want a con-man and thief heading up the search for my little girl!"

Kit silently counted ten. "Skeeter Jackson is not conning anybody, Senator. I hired him as my own hotel house detective and believe me, it takes a helluva lot of trust to hire somebody for that job. As for the so-called assault . . ." Kit swallowed the words poised on the tip of his tongue. "Just be forewarned. If you press assault charges against him, I'll be damned sure he countercharges you with criminal battery."

John Caddrick's entire face went white.

Even the I.T.C.H. inquisitors shifted in their chairs.

When Caddrick started to sputter, Kit overrode him. "Forget it, unless you really want the fight of the century on your hands. We've got photographic evidence of the whole incident, Senator. I, for one, will *not* allow a personal vendetta against Mr. Jackson to cripple this search mission. There's too much riding on the outcome. Skeeter's more than proven himself. Virtually every breakthrough in this case has been made by Skeeter Jackson, whereas *your* detective is virtually useless. I told you Sid Kaederman wasn't qualified for a down-time mission, whereas Skeeter's already experienced down the Britannia Gate. And he'll be working with Malcolm Moore, who specializes in London tours. Jackson and Moore head up the London mission, whether you like it or not, Senator. Unless, of course, you *want* your little girl killed?"

Senator John Caddrick's normally florrid jowls faded to the color of old wax. He opened his lips several times, but no sound came out at all. He glanced once at the I.T.C.H. inquisitors, then swallowed and sat motionless in his chair for long moments. The only sound in the room was the whir of the air-conditioning fans. Caddrick finally managed a faint, "All right. I don't see that I have much choice." His voice strengthened into a low growl. "But I will not be browbeaten and threatened, is that clear?"

If he stayed, Kit knew he would say something the entire station regretted. So he stood up, heading for the elevator. "Quite. Now, if you'll excuse me, we have a lot of work to do before the Britannia opens again. And frankly, I need a shower and a shave before I do any of it. And a cold beer."

Kit stalked into the elevator before Caddrick could protest.

On his way down toward the howling mob of newsies, he thought bleakly of Margo, already in London, and of poor Julius, no older than his granddaughter, who lay dead with a bullet in his gut. Kit wondered with a chill just how many of the searchers on this hunt were likely to come out alive?

(((Chapter 8)))

Dominica Nosette was cold and wet where she stood shivering in the darkness. Rain was falling again, as dirty as the grimy brick walls along Whitechapel's narrow streets. Sudden gusts sent torrents skating across the cobblestones like rats scurrying for shelter. Soot ran black in the gutters where the occasional gaslight illuminated swirls and foul-smelling rivers of refuse on their way to the sewers. It was a hideous night to be alive, a worse one to die in.

Dominica had seen far too much death this night to have stomach for any more. She prided herself on a tough professionalism, a hard core of indifference under layers of thick callus that had made her one of the most ruthless and successful photojournalists in the business. Watching the death of Polly Nichols on video from the vault beneath Spaldergate House in Battersea had been very much like watching an ordinary movie. It was easy to disconnect the reality of it and watch dispassionately, even though it had been frustrating for her professional sensibilities. She would've obtained far better video footage by filming the whole thing on site, using more creative camera angles, better audio equipment.

Elizabeth Stride's murder in Dutfield's Yard had been harder to witness, with the immediacy of sight and smell and sound and the knowledge that only the complete blackness of the closed-in yard and the concealing half-walls of a disused stable stood between her camera lens and the man crouched over Stride with a gutting knife, nearly severing her head with a few powerful slashes. But even there, it had been only a murder, after all. At least Stride had been dead when the knife struck, strangled by that other lunatic, Lachley.

But Catharine Eddowes . . .

Tough as she was, Dominica did not relish the death waiting in this square for poor Kate Eddowes. Mitre Square resembled a miniature amphitheatre in brick. Along one edge ran a solid, three-story brick structure comprised of vacant cottages, jutting out like a peninsula perpendicular to Mitre Street just beyond. Along the short, squat end of this peninsular "cottage" ran a tiny, short jog of road and pavement giving access to the square. The pavement zagged back in a loose Z-shape from the Mitre Street access, with the Sir John Cass School running slap up against the vacant cottages. The resulting interior corner, like the crook of an elbow, was isolated, with a broad pavement that stood nearly three times wider than a normal walkway.

Beside the school rose a tall warehouse belonging to Kearly and Tongue. Opposite, facing the warehouse and school, stood another Kearly and Tongue warehouse, the Orange Market along King Street, and a house belonging to Police Constable Pearse. Along Duke Street, the fourth border of the square, stood the Great Synagogue. Narrow, lightless Church Passage—a covered alleyway—led into the square from Duke Street, past the southern edge of the synagogue.

The tiny "square" thus formed, a secluded island cut off from the busier streets surrounding it, was where Lachley and Maybrick would lead their second victim of the night. There was a sickening symmetry, Dominica realized, to their revolting anti-Semitism. They were murdering Eddowes within view of a synagogue. And given their narrow escape from Dutfield's Yard, these men possessed a terrifying confidence, to kill her within plain view of a policeman's home not half an hour after nearly being caught dead to rights. That alone shook Dominica as she and Guy Pendergast fled Dutfield's Yard before Mr. Diemschutz could bring help. She and her partner sped along side streets, running to get ahead of the murderous Ripper duo, literally racing the whole distance to Mitre Square to get into position for the best vantage point to film Eddowes' death.

In front of the school, a waist-high iron railing partitioned off half the available pavement. Because of minor work being done, a much higher temporary fence had been erected along the line of that railing, effectively cutting the broad pavement in half and sealing off the entire corner of the elbow. It was behind this temporary fencing Dominca and Guy chose to conceal themselves, less than six feet from the spot where Catharine Eddowes was slated to die.

Five minutes after they went into hiding, Constable Watkins appeared in Church Passage, doing his rounds and peering dutifully into the square. And not two minutes after Watkins retreated down Church Passage again, John Lachley appeared, escorting the unsuspecting Catharine Eddowes. Dominica held her breath, trembling slightly in the cold, wet air. Lachley and Eddowes paused within whispering distance of Dominica's hiding place, while James Maybrick slipped up silently behind them, knife already out of his pocket.

Dominica knew what was coming. But the shock left her trembling when John Lachley smashed Catharine Eddowes to the pavement, strangling her right in front of them. The woman struggled, flailing her arms and kicking helplessly, while Lachley snarled into her face and crushed her throat under his hands. Kate Eddowes finally went limp, arms falling lifelessly to the pavement at her sides. Lachley rifled her pockets for his letter even as the slavering Maybrick struck with his knife, too impatient to wait any longer.

And it was that, watching the infuriated and massively frustrated Maybrick, which finally broke through Dominica's tough professionalism and left her trembling and sick behind the high, temporary schoolyard fence. This was no make-believe movie, no documentary on ordinary little murders. Not even the impersonal blowing apart of a solider by an artillery round. This was a frenzy of psychopathic hatred, a man who was no longer fully human, slashing at an innocent woman's face, cutting an inverted "M" straight through the flesh of her eyelids, hacking off ears, nearly severing the head from its neck. And when he jerked up her skirts . . .

Dominica couldn't watch, squeezed shut her eyes and swallowed hot bile, tried hopelessly to force away the image of him snatching out Catharine's intestines, tossing them across her shoulder, cutting part of them loose and arranging them beside her. *Don't gag, don't heave, they'll hear you, oh, dear, God, the smell* . . . Guy Pendergast's hand was bruising her shoulder, the fingers digging in and flexing as he, too, fought to remain silent during the ghastly ritual Maybrick and Lachley were enacting beyond the fence. She could hear low voices, almost whispers, and didn't want to distinguish individual words.

When at last their footfalls moved away, she opened her eyes. She tried not to look at the mangled shape lying huddled in front of the empty cottages. Dominica was violently atremble, dizzy and light-headed. She wasn't sure she'd be able to take a single step without collapsing. "They're gone," Guy whispered directly against her ear, to prevent the sound from carrying. She nodded. *Time to leave. Get the hell out of here, Dominica, because Police Constable Watkins is going to walk into the Square down Church Passage in about two minutes, discover the body and raise all bloody hell . . . come on, legs, move it!*

She'd taken one step, no more, when racing footfalls thudded back into the Square. Her vision greyed out for just an instant and only Guy Pendergast's grip kept her on her feet. Maybrick had jogged back to the body, was hacking at it again, tearing away part of her apron and wrapping up something . . . oh, Christ, something he'd cut out of her, he was carrying part of her insides away with him . . .

"*James!*" An all-but-silent hiss of fury broke through the shock. It was Lachley, white-faced. "Get the hell away from her! Come on, man, before a copper strolls in here. They do a patrol past the Square every few minutes and they're bloody well *due!*"

"Forgot my dinner," Maybrick said calmly.

If Guy hadn't been behind her, propping her up, Dominica might well have fallen against the fence, giving them both away. The pistols she and her partner had concealed in their pockets were utterly useless against these two. The men out there arguing over the remains of Catharine Eddowes literally could not be killed, not by anyone from up time. Maybrick wouldn't die until 1889, of arsenic poisoning, and until Mary Kelly was murdered more than a month from now, neither of these men could be so much as harmed.

But Dominica certainly could be.

"If you want to make off with her kidney and uterus, fine!"

Lachley snapped. "But I'll be damned if I go walking along with you while you carry them! I'll meet you back at Lower Tibor, as usual."

The two halves of the team that comprised Jack the Ripper split up, Lachley pale with anger, Maybrick flushed and euphoric. Lachley uttered one short curse, then strode off through the broad opening to Mitre Street, vanishing to the southwest, walking fast. Maybrick thrust his bloody prize under his coat, shoving the knife into a deep pocket. Something dark fell out as he pulled his gloved hand free again. It landed with a dull sound against Eddowes' mangled body. Something small, made of leather . . . Dominica had to stifle the wild, hysterical impulse to laugh as Maybrick strode jauntily down Mitre Street, following Lachley's route at a more leisurely pace. Maybrick had dropped a red leather cigarette case, the one experts had puzzled over for a century and a half. It was far too expensive for a destitute woman like Catharine Eddowes to have been carrying. She'd have pawned it for cash in a heartbeat. It lay, now, amidst the contents of her rifled pockets, which Maybrick had set out neatly beside her body.

Then Maybrick's footfalls died away and they had scant seconds in which to make their own escape, before the momentary arrival of PC Watkins stirred this whole neighborhood to a frenzy. There were only two ways out of Mitre Square and the constable would be arriving through Church Passage. They had no choice but to follow on the heels of the killers.

"Well, come on, then," Guy hissed, dragging her toward the exit to their hiding place. "You're the one who wanted to follow those damned lunatics!" His anger stung her pride fully awake. She jerked away from his supporting grasp and stalked out from behind the temporary fencing. After what she'd been through tonight, Maybrick had better not give her the slip! Concentrating fiercely on Carson Historical Video Prizes and million-dollar movie advances, Dominica Nosette eased past the pitiful remains of Catharine Eddowes and set out down Mitre Street. *I can still find out how they pull that disappearing act, in the middle of a crowded city . . .*

As they slipped down Mitre Street, a police whistle rose shrilly behind them.

Maybrick's bloody legacy had just been discovered.

⊠ ⊠ ⊠

Skeeter supposed he should've seen it coming, at least where Goldie Morran was concerned. But he was so tired and still so shaken by Julius' murder, he didn't, not until it hit. The Duchess of Dross spotted him through her shop windows and shot out the door like a javelin going for the gold. "Skeeter! Just the person I've been looking for!"

He stopped dead, about as eager to talk to Goldie as he was to spend the night in Senator Caddrick's hotel room. "What do you want, Goldie?"

"A bit of . . . mmm . . . professional advice."

Skeeter's glance came up sharply. "*You* want advice from *me*?"

Purple-tinted hair glinted evilly; so did her faintly sharp teeth. "Why, yes, Skeeter. You do have a certain amount of useful knowledge tucked away in that bony head of yours."

"Really? And what makes you think I'd go out of my way to accept a cup of coffee from you, never mind give you advice?"

She glanced around nervously, wet her lips. "Well . . . Since you ask, it concerns a mutual acquaintance."

Skeeter narrowed his eyes. "I've been helping Kit Carson arrest most of our mutual acquaintances, Goldie. Going to bribe me to look the other way when one of your cronies comes through? Forget it. Besides, you must've heard? I'm leaving through the Britannia in a couple of days. I'm busy."

For just an instant, real anger flickered through her eyes. "I'm talking about Jenna Caddrick!" she hissed, voice carefully modulated not to carry.

"What about her?"

"Not here. Too many ears."

"Huh." With I.T.C.H. crawling all over the station, never mind Caddrick and his staff goons and all those disgruntled federal marshals, that was no lie. "All right. Where?"

"My shop. In back. It's sound-proofed."

Figures. "As long as you make it quick. I've got about a thousand hours of library work ahead of me before I go to bed tonight."

She sniffed autocratically and led the way into a shop completely devoid of customers. Tourists, wary of the violence that kept breaking out, were staying in their hotel rooms unless a gate was actually cycling, abandoning Commons to the loons and the protestors, all of which had hit station entrepreneurs hard in the cashbox. Goldie hung up the "Out to Tea" sign—a ruse to gain privacy, since mere tea never passed Goldie Morran's lips—then turned the lock. She led the way into the back, past a solid steel door that clearly served to secure her vault. It thumped as she closed it.

The large room beyond was divided, one part lined with small, metallic drawers floor to ceiling, labelled neatly as to semi-precious contents. The balance formed a cozy corner where she'd rigged a sitting room of sorts with a comfy sofa, a table stacked with trade magazines, a small wet bar, and a beautiful porcelain birdcage. Skeeter did a classic double-take. Inside sat two birds which very few people now alive had ever seen outside a museum's stuffed collection. Lovely grey with bright splashes of yellow and white and orange, the breeding pair of Carolina parakeets chirped cheerfully above the sound of quiet music.

He wondered how many viable eggs she'd sold to smugglers already.

"Now," she said briskly, "let's get down to business. Would you care for anything?" She was opening a scotch bottle.

Skeeter was parched, but shook his head. He had his standards. "What have you got to say, Goldie? That you didn't tell Security when they came calling?"

She smiled slightly. "My, my, testy, aren't we?" She poured a drink, neat, and sipped delicately, then came around the end of the bar to settle into her sofa, waving Skeeter to a seat. "I need your help with possible . . . legal entanglements that don't necessarily need to come to light."

Skeeter remained standing and just looked at her.

Something in his expression caused her to sit up straighter. "You do recall, Skeeter, I did save your life once. Lupus Mortiferus would've chopped you into mince if I hadn't interfered. You owe me."

Dammit, she was right. For once. He did owe her, despite the savagery they'd done one another during that idiotic, near-fatal wager. "All right, Goldie. I'm listening."

"I didn't tell Security about this, for reasons you'll understand in a moment. That tourist who went missing in London, Benny Catlin? He came in here to exchange some currency just a few minutes before the Britannia cycled. He was a very nice young man. Quiet, a little scatter-brained, it seemed. It was idiotically easy, really. And if Benny Catlin had been an ordinary graduate student instead of Jenna Caddrick . . ."

"Christ, Goldie, what did you do?" He was afraid he already knew.

Goldie didn't disappoint him. "I, er, passed some counterfeit bank notes. Someone stiffed *me* with them, returning from a Britannia tour. Which should tell you how good they are. I didn't give her *all* counterfeit notes," she added hastily, "but enough that if Jenna Caddrick has been spending them, well . . . She's been down the Britannia long enough, now, it could get her into serious trouble if they're detected. They're good fakes, quite good, but I didn't intend for anyone to spend months down the Britannia with them. I mean, nobody expected Benny Catlin to go missing—"

"Or turn up as Senator Caddrick's kidnapped daughter!"

Goldie flushed.

"God, the messes you scheme yourself into . . ." He was tempted to tell her she could just scheme herself right back out again; but he wanted to know the rest. "So just what do you want me to do about it?"

Again, she wet her lips. "Well, you see, it occurred to me that Jenna Caddrick might be missing because she's been, well, jailed. For counterfeiting. I mean, if she got away from her abductors the way everybody's saying, that would certainly explain why nobody's been able to trace her. Searchers wouldn't think of looking in a Victorian prison, after all, for a terrorist's hostage. Probably not even the terrorists would think of that."

Reluctantly, Skeeter had to admit she had a point. "So you want me to check all the London jails, looking for a woman disguised as a man, arrange a prison break, then sneak her out through Spaldergate while whoever's trying to murder her isn't looking, then convince her not to press charges against you for passing her counterfeit banknotes in the first place? Jeez, Goldie, you don't ask much."

"It isn't just getting her out of jail," Goldie said quickly. "I mean, there would be a considerable, ah, sum of money involved to compensate her. For legal expenses in London. Inconvenience experienced. That sort of thing."

"You want me to *bribe* her? My God, Goldie! We're not talking about some addled half-wit tourist, here! Do you honestly think you can bribe your way out of this with *Senator Caddrick's kid?*"

"Well, it's worth a try! I'll pay you, too," Goldie added venomously. "Don't worry about that. Cash advance for half my offer, with the balance on delivery of one live and kicking, close-mouthed kid!"

"I don't want your money, Goldie. If I do find Jenna Caddrick, maybe I'll pass along your message. Then again, maybe I won't. If you did get her tossed into some Victorian hellhole of a jail, just pray real hard she doesn't have the same capacity for holding a grudge her father does."

He left her sitting, mouth ajar, and heard a forlorn chirp from the caged parakeets as he swung the vault door open and stalked out. He was tempted to head for the nearest bathroom just to wash his hands. Instead, he headed for Kit Carson's office. Kit needed to know about this. As he headed down through Urbs Romae and Victoria Station toward Edo Castletown, having to push his way through a crowd of chanting protestors, it occurred to Skeeter that Jenna Caddrick might not even *be* in London any longer. Particularly not if she'd discovered her money was no good. Hiding in London would be expensive, which meant she was likely running short of funds already.

Caddrick's story was even more full of holes now than it had been before. If Jenna Caddrick had been a hostage, she wouldn't have simply waltzed into Paula Booker's surgery *or* Goldie Morran's shop unaccompanied, looking to alter her face and change currency. But Benny Catlin had done just that, then had climbed the five flights of stairs to the Britannia platform and chewed Skeeter's backside over a steamer trunk that had very nearly skidded over the edge. There hadn't been anyone up there with Benny Catlin. Nobody holding a metaphoric gun to Jenna Caddrick's head. She was on her own, in London. The guys she'd shot and killed must have been London counterparts of the bastard who'd murdered Julius. Who'd been doubling for her, as a decoy. And since it was clear that Armstrong was helping Marcus and the girls, Jenna Caddrick must be helping Ianira Cassondra . . .

Skeeter actually went so dizzy, he staggered, rocking to a halt so fast, the protestor behind him ran slap into his back. Skeeter caught his balance, ignoring a flurry of angry mutters from the sign-carrying loon, and stood there with his eyes narrowed to slits, thoughts racing, then groped for the nearest wrought iron bench and collapsed onto it, shaking.

"My God," Skeeter whispered aloud. "*Ianira was in the trunk!*" No wonder Jenna Caddrick had been so badly shaken! He shut his eyes for long moments, trying to blot out the image of that trunk sliding off, falling the long, fatal way to the Commons floor . . . Then shoved himself to his feet and stalked through the jostling horde of lunatics rampaging through Victoria Station, carrying signs and howling out protests he barely heard, furious with himself for not tumbling to it sooner. "Kit'll have my badge, overlooking a clue that big," he muttered under his breath.

When Skeeter reached the Neo Edo Hotel, he found Kit in his palatial office, bent over his computer. Skeeter paused just long enough to kick off his shoes before stepping onto the pristine *tatami* rice mats. "Where's Kaederman?" Skeeter asked tersely, searching the corners of Kit's office with an uneasy gaze. "I thought he was coming up here."

Kit glanced up. "Kaederman," he said flatly, "went to bed. That man is the laziest detective I've ever met."

"How'd we luck out? At least he's nowhere around to hear the news."

"What news?" Kit leaned forward, eyes abruptly glittering.

"Ianira's in London. She went through in a steamer trunk. One of Benny Catlin's. I'm sure of it. You remember that pile-up of luggage at the platform, when one of the trunks nearly slid off."

"Yes, you mentioned it belonged to Benny Cat—Oh." Kit could out-swear Yesukai the Valiant. Then he grimaced. "Skeeter, you had no way of knowing, not at the time."

"Maybe not," he muttered, pacing from the enormous desk to the withered landscape garden of raked sand and carefully placed stones to the wall of television monitors which kept Kit abreast of events all over Shangri-La Station. "But if I hadn't been so damn muddled, I'd have figured it out a lot sooner. And the trail wouldn't be so cold!"

"Well, beating yourself up over this won't do Ianira any good," Kit pointed out gently. "At least we have a pretty good indication Ianira was alive, inside that trunk, given Jenna's reaction. I begin to wonder if *anyone* from the *Ansar Majlis* was with that girl when she went through the Britannia," Kit mused. "Other than a couple of hit men who died messily? And since she went through on her own, that really makes me wonder where Marcus and Armstrong went after hopping their train in Colorado. Once Armstrong eliminated the man who shot Julius, they certainly lost no time hightailing it out of there." Kit frowned slowly as he sat back in his chair. "Unless," he mused, "they weren't running *away* at all."

Skeeter halted his pacing. "Huh?"

"Maybe . . ." Kit tapped steepled fingertips against his lips. "Just maybe, they were running *to* something."

Skeeter stared, trying to figure out what he was driving at. "Running *to* something? What? Where? There's nothing in 1885 they'd *want* to go to!"

"No. Not in 1885. But in *1888* . . ."

Skeeter felt his eyes widen. "*London?*"

"Makes sense. A lot of sense. Hide out for three years, make damned sure nobody's on their trail, cross the Atlantic to meet Jenna and Ianira when they come through the Britannia. Armstrong could easily have set up a base of operations in London, complete with false identity, a good occupation lined up, so money's coming in steadily. They could hide out for months, years, if necessary. With damned little chance of the *Ansar Majlis* ever finding them."

"Or anybody else, for that matter," Skeeter added bitterly.

"A definite plus, when one's marked for murder. And they'll have the children to think of," Kit added gently. "Surely you can see that?"

He could. All too clearly. "So you think we shouldn't look for them, after all?"

"No, I didn't say that. Shangri-La Station's still in mortal danger.

And something tells me none of our fugitives will be safe until we get to the bottom of this. Too many pieces of this puzzle are still missing. Like that guy who killed Julius, for one. He was certainly no down-time Arabian *jihad* fighter. So who hired him? The *Ansar Majlis*? Hiring a paid killer isn't their style. Crazies like the *Ansar Majlis* do their own killing. So, if not them, who?"

Skeeter didn't like the road Kit was walking down.

"Yes, you do see it, don't you? I'm getting very itchy about the safety of this search team. If someone *besides* the *Ansar Majlis* is trying to kill Jenna, then merely looking for her could be as dangerous as finding her. The question is," Kit mused softly, "how, exactly, to begin the search once you get to London? I'd rather not risk Paula's life any more than necessary, but she ought to go along, to make a positive identification."

Skeeter snorted. "That part's easy."

Kit blinked. "Oh?"

He told Kit about Goldie's counterfeit banknotes. Kit whistled softly.

"So, you'll start by looking for angry merchants who've been ripped off? Hmm . . . It might work. There was a fairly large trade in counterfeit banknotes and coins, especially near the waterfront, where the fakes could be passed to unwary newcomers, people unfamiliar with English currency, but it's certainly the best lead we've got so far." Kit's grin was sudden, blinding, and terrifying. "Grand idea, Skeeter. Let's have you pose as a Pinkerton agent. Say you're after a Yank from New York, who's been counterfeiting money in the States, tell our angry London merchants you think he's moved his operation to London. We'll get Connie to whip up Pinkerton identification papers for you."

"Good grief. First a house detective for the Neo Edo, now a Pinkerton agent? Who'd a-thunk it? *Me,* a private eye!"

"And a pretty good one, so far," Kit grinned. "Get over to Connie's. I'll call her, give her a head's up. You'd better collect a few of those counterfeits from Goldie, too, so you'll have samples with you in London, as part of your cover story. And Skeeter . . ."

"Yeah?"

Kit's smile was positively evil. "Let's not tell Sid about this?"

Skeeter started to laugh; then felt a chill, instead, straight down his spine.

Margo was not keen to watch the murders of Stride and Eddowes. Rather than join the Ripper Watch Team in the Vault, she changed clothing, requested a cup of hot tea from one of the Spaldergate House maids, and curled up beside the fire in the parlour. There she stayed, sitting on the floor in front of the hearth, chin on knees, watching the flames dance across the coals. Malcolm came in shortly after two A.M., looking for her. He paused in the doorway.

"There you are. Well, it's over, down there. Maybrick turns out to be the one who chalked the graffiti in Goulston Street. And you'll never guess who we caught on tape? Those idiot reporters, Dominica Nosette and Guy Pendergast. They're following Maybrick and Lachley. Shadowed Maybrick to Goulston Street and photographed the graffiti after he left, then started trailing him once more."

"Great. We should've staked out the murder sites, ourselves, and waited to nab those idiots."

"Perhaps, but the chance is gone now. We've sent out Stoddard and Tanglewood to try to locate them, but they'll be long gone before either man can get close, I'm afraid." Malcolm crossed the parlour toward her, navigating his way around heavy furniture and tables full of bric-a-brac. "Whatever have you been doing, sitting here alone in the dark?"

"Trying not to think about what's going on in Whitechapel."

He settled on the carpeted floor beside her and wrapped an arm around her shoulders. "You're trembling."

"I'm cold," she muttered. Then, betraying the lie, "You don't think I'm too weak for this job, do you? Because I can't watch?"

Malcolm sighed. "There's a fairly large difference between running slap into something you're not expecting and going out of your way to watch something grisly, particularly when others are on the job to do it, instead. No, I don't think you're too weak, Margo. You extricated several people from that street brawl at the examination of Polly Nichols' remains, didn't you? Doug Tanglewood said he'd never been more thoroughly frightened in his life, yet you pulled them safely away, even Pavel Kostenka, when that lout was intent on beating him senseless."

"That wasn't so hard," Margo shivered. "I just charged in and did the first thing that came to mind. He wasn't expecting Aikido, anyway."

"Then you did precisely what a budding time scout should do," Malcolm murmured, stroking her hair gently. "Between the Ripper Watch and searching for our missing tourist, I haven't had the time to say how proud of you I've been. You've nothing to be ashamed of, nothing at all."

She bit her lip, wondering if now was a good time to talk about the past, which had been troubling her ever since she'd come to London. Her mother's descent into prostitution had been Margo's shameful secret for a long time, one she'd feared at first would drive Malcolm away; but she'd had time to think about it and wondered now if she'd misjudged him, unfairly assigning to him the same prejudices she'd encountered in Minnesota. He knew about her being raped by a gang of fifteenth-century Portuguese, after all, and still wanted to marry her. Surely he wouldn't mind what her mother had done to make ends meet, if he didn't mind the other?

Malcolm lifted her face, his expression deeply concerned. "What *is* it, Margo?"

She leaned against his shoulder and told him. All of it. Her father's drinking. Her mother's desperation to pay the bills, when her father spent his paycheck and her mother's both, buying the booze. What her mother had done . . . and what her father had done, when he'd found out. "I never meant to say anything, because it would kill Kit, to learn how his little girl died. But I thought you ought to know. Before you married me."

"Oh, Margo . . ." His voice shook. "I wish to God I could go back and undo it all. No wonder you fight the world so hard. You've had to, just to survive . . ." He brushed his thumb across her cheek, across her unsteady lips. "You're so beautiful, so full of courage, it makes my heart stop. If your father hadn't died in prison, they'd have to hang me for him."

Margo's mouth twisted. "They don't hang people anymore, Malcolm."

Then he was holding her close and nothing else in the universe mattered.

Dominica watched in astonishment as James Maybrick unlocked the door of a filthy hovel in Wapping and disappeared inside. Gas light appeared briefly through the windows and a ferocious barking erupted, then subsided just as abruptly. A moment later, the gas went out, leaving the house dark again.

"What on earth?" she wondered aloud, startled. "What d'you suppose should we do now?" she whispered.

"I'm going 'round the back, see if I can get a look inside."

"Be careful!"

Dominica waited impatiently while her partner vanished into the inky blackness. Rain spat at her, cold and miserable. She huddled deeper into her coat and shifted from one foot to the other, trying to keep warm. She'd been waiting for perhaps five minutes when snarls and savage barking erupted again from the house. A single gunshot split the wet night.

"Guy!" Dominica ran across the street, just in time for the front door to be thrown wide. Guy snatched her wrist and pulled her inside. "Come on! There isn't a moment to lose!"

"What—"

"Shh!"

He dragged her through the dark house into a central, windowless room where a gaslight burned low. A massive black dog sprawled across the bare wooden floorboards, dead in a puddle of spreading blood; Guy had shot it through the skull. In the center of the floor rested a heavy trap door, which Guy pulled up cautiously. Beneath, they found steps leading down into a cellar. "He's nowhere in the house," Guy whispered urgently. "He had to go through here. There's nowhere else he could have gone."

Dominica dragged out her own pistol, aware that she was trembling violently.

"There's no lantern," she muttered, eying the black hole uneasily.

"He had one. Must have. It's pitch black, down there, but we'll hear him at the very least, follow the sound."

Yes, she thought, *and he'll hear us, as well.* But they'd come this far and she wasn't giving up on the story of the century so easily. She gripped her pistol with damp fingers and followed Guy into the cellar, which proved to be no cellar at all, but rather a tunnel through the sewers beneath Wapping. *So this is how he did it! Simply popped home to Wapping and vanished beneath the streets!* Then, faint with distance, they heard it: the splash of footfalls through the filth in the tunnels. She and Guy, pausing at the base of the stairs, exchanged glances. Then Dominica hiked up her skirts and waded cautiously forward.

She was *going* to get that Carson prize. And all that lovely money, which her video would fetch in the up-time world. Dominica Nosette intended to be the world's most famous photojournalist ever. And nothing was going to stop her.

⟪ Chapter 9 ⟫

John Lachley had just finished burning Elizabeth Stride's letter in the flames of his altar beneath the streets when a woman's high, ragged scream echoed out in the sewer. A man's angry snarl and a volley of gunshots roared through the tunnels, followed by a thud of colliding bodies, a grunt and sudden masculine cry of pain. Then James Maybrick's voice, maniacal: *"Lipski!"*

Over and over again, *"Lipski! Lipski! . . . LipskiLipskiLipski . . ."*

The ragged chant jerked Lachley across the room and out through the open iron doorway. The Liverpudlian was on his knees in the muddy water, his lantern thrown aside, hacking and stabbing at a motionless form. The thing lying on the sewer floor had, before Maybrick's violent assault, been a man. Blood had spurted and sprayed across Maybrick's face and chest. It dripped and spattered down his chin and hair from the arterial bleeding Lachley had warned him against when stalking the prostitutes. But a more terrible sound, by far, than the slam of Maybrick's knife into dead flesh came to Lachely's ears: running footsteps, receding into the blackness, unsteady and desperate.

The woman who had screamed.

Lachley left Maybrick to his grisly pleasure and raced after her. He had to stop her. Had to silence her. *Whoever* she was. It didn't matter a damn *who,* he had to catch her. She was slipping on the wet bricks ahead. Scrabbling up to run again. Blind and deaf and crashing into walls in the darkness. He could hear the scream of her breath. Shallow. Ragged. Wild. Could hear the scratch of her shoes. The splash of puddles under her staggering feet. Could smell the terror. Thick. Sexual. Delicious.

When he caught her, she screamed. Fought him. Writhed and clawed at his hands, his face. He backhanded her into the bricks. Caught a fist in her hair. Forced her head back. Found the death grip at her throat . . . And ghostly red light flickered in his eyes, eerie and startling. Lachley reeled back a step, bringing up one arm defensively. Her head moved and the light vanished. Then a gunshot split the darkness. The bullet whined off bricks behind him. Lachley backhanded her again, fist clenched. The gun discharged, blinding him. They struggled for the weapon and she fired until the gun clicked, empty. He struck her a third time, knocking her to the floor, this time. She splashed into the muck at his feet and lay still. A faint moan escaped her. Lachley caught her under the arms, grasped her jaw, tilted her head—

And the flicker of dull red light came again.

Badly startled, he searched along her neck, up toward her ear, and touched slick, alien cords of some kind, something glassy, an odd tube of some kind, what felt like tiny wires . . . *What the bloody devil?*

He gave a practiced heave and tossed her across one shoulder. Her head trailed down his back, arms loose, unjointed. Lachley strode back through the darkness, guided by the light pouring from Lower Tibor's open door. Maybrick was still hacking at the dead man.

"James!"

When the sharp sound of his voice failed to break the maniac's slavering frenzy, Lachley shoved him off balance with a booted foot. Maybrick sprawled sideways, splashing into the water, then snarled like an animal, knife flashing at the ready.

"James! Put the sodding knife down! He's dead!"

The cotton merchant blinked slowly and, as the wildness faded gradually from his eyes, he focused on Lachley's face. "Sorry," he whispered, voice shaking, "I'm sorry, Doctor, didn't realize . . ."

"You did well, James, killing that bastard. Drag him inside, now, and we'll see who our visitors might be."

"Yes, of course." He hauled the dead man up by the arms, dragging the body out of the filthy water, and pulled him into Lower Tibor.

"Leave him by the door, James, and find his sodding gun." Lachley dumped the unconscious woman across his work table and bound her wrists efficiently with a twist of rope. He found a cup and calmly poured out a dose of the drug he always gave Maybrick when they returned after a successful hunt through Whitechapel. "Ah, you found the pistol. Very good. Put it there. Now, James, you're shaking, badly in need of your medication. Here, swallow this down. Then take off your coat and the rest of those clothes. Burn them, you're covered in blood."

Maybrick drank the powerful drug without question, then stripped off the blood-caked garments and dropped them on the altar for burning. Lachley heard water splashing as he cleaned himself up at the tiny basin. Satisfied that his mad cotton merchant was under proper control once more, Lachley turned his attention to the mutilated body lying beside the door. He opened the coat, torn and hacked through in two dozen places, searched the pockets, emptied the contents of his waistcoat and trouser pockets, as well. Then frowned slowly at what he found. Crouched beside a perfectly ordinary corpse, John Lachley found himself confronted with objects he could not comprehend.

The man's pockets contained a handful of shillings, florins, a few half crowns, plus a wad of bank notes, a surprisingly large number of them. Nearly two hundred pounds, in fact. But the other items . . . He found a stiff, rectangular card of some sort, made of a substance Lachley had never encountered. Neither paper nor wood nor metal, it was nevertheless shiny and brightly colored, with a series of dark stripes down the back, formed of some other unknown substance which could not be scratched off easily with a fingernail. It reminded him of gutta-percha, obtained from the milky sap of a tree native to Malaysia, which like latex hardened on exposure to the air, forming a stiff substance somewhat like this, useful in cements, insulations, and so on. This card was not gutta-percha, however; attempting to dissolve it with oil of turpentine and naptha had no effect whatever, which proved it to be some other substance. Nor was it caoutchouc, which was not even as strong as gutta-percha and certainly nothing like as strong as this substance. Frowning, he put the little card aside and studied the other mysterious object he'd found: a tiny cylinder covered with a soft, spongy substance, with trailing wires coming out of it, coated with something slick and flexible. The wires plugged into a compact, heavy box. This was made of some other unknown substance, its feel similar to the stiff card, yet completely different, bent into a virtually seamless shape with tiny buttons and a hinged lid. This boasted a transparent cover of something that was not glass. In fiddling with the buttons, he pressed one that caused a faint, whirring sound to emerge from the box. Startled, he mashed other buttons, trying to get the sound to stop . . .

And James Maybrick's voice spoke from inside!

He dropped the thing with a shocked yell, toppled straight over onto his backside and stared at the box which lay there talking to him, like some parlour medium's trick with ventriloquism or the tiniest Victrola phonograph imaginable; but there was no one here except Maybrick and himself, and Maybrick stood on the other side of the room, gaping, mouth dropped wide to hear his own voice coming from a box the size of Lachley's hand. Lachley could not imagine anyone making a phonograph *this* small.

"*What is it?*" Maybrick's voice shook violently.

"I don't know!" Lachley picked up the box and shook it gently. Maybrick's voice kept talking. Then he heard another voice and recognized with a jolt of shock what he was hearing. "*James!* Get the hell away from her! Come on, man, before a copper strolls in here. They do a patrol past the Square every few minutes and they're bloody well *due!*" This was followed by Maybrick's calm, prosaic, "Forgot my dinner . . ." and his own furious, "If you want to make off with her kidney and uterus, fine! But I'll be damned if I go walking along with you while you carry it! I'll meet you back at Lower Tibor, as usual."

He stared, open-mouthed now, himself. This little box had somehow captured their conversation of one hour previously, when they'd stood over the gutted remains of Catharine Eddowes. "It *is* like a phonograph or a miniaturized telephone," he whispered, awestruck, "one that *records* voices, rather than transmitting them across a wire!

My God, how is this accomplished? Where is the mouthpiece? Both a telephone and a phonograph's recorder have a mouthpiece to capture the voice and transmit it, but there's nothing except these little wires and this tiny thing at the end. And what powers it?"

"They must be police!" Maybrick gasped out, shaking with furious terror. "Filthy coppers, following us, they're onto us—"

"London coppers do not have devices like this!"

"*Then who are they?*"

Lachley stared from Maybrick to the dead man and back, considered the box in his hand and the unconscious woman, stared at Maybrick again. Under other circumstances, the tableau they presented might have struck him as enormously funny: a naked man with blood in his hair, dripping water down his face and chest, a corpse in possession of a talking box, and a woman with bound hands lying sprawled across his work table. "I've no idea who they are," Lachley said at last, pushing himself to his feet and fiddling with the box until the voices stopped. "But I intend to find out. Get dressed James, you're bollock naked. And rinse the blood out of your hair before it dries to a clotted mess."

The madman ran a hand through sticky, thinning hair and grimaced, then bent over the basin again and washed his balding head clean. He recovered the clothes he'd worn on the train down from Liverpool and dressed himself silently. The drug was beginning to take hold, thank God, leaving him calmer and quieter. Lachley searched the unconscious woman, finding even stranger things secreted about her person than he had on the man. He had no idea what to make of the tiny, lenslike device hidden in her bonnet, nor could he comprehend the other device, which emitted the dull red light he'd seen in the dark sewer. Footsteps roused him from his frowning reverie. Maybrick had come to stand behind him.

"What's that?" he asked quietly, pointing to the little tube the light came from.

"I've no idea. It emits a pale, red-colored light."

"I don't see anything."

Lachley shone it at his eyes. "There, see it?"

"No."

Even when the cotton merchant stared directly into the device, he could not see the dim reddish light that was plainly visible to Lachley. Curiouser and curiouser . . . The lenslike affair and light emitter were connected via slick-coated wires to a heavy, very dense gadget hidden under the woman's coat. It resembled the voice recorder only in the sense that both were housed in compact boxes of some unknown material. Her device had metal parts, however, buttons and levers, and a strangely textured surface along one side that resembled a dark window, but there was nothing to see through it. In fact, it wasn't even transparent, the way the hinged lid of the voice recorder was.

Lachley found another of the stiff, strange cards in her pockets, along with a surprising amount of cash, a tiny mirror and other personal grooming implements, and a variety of oddments to which he could ascribe no purpose whatever. Her clothing was perfectly ordinary stuff: a cheap if substantial coat, heavy woolen skirt and bodice, worn over petticoats and combinations. Knitted stockings, stout and well-made shoes for walking. A heavy chemise under the bodice . . .

And under *that,* a garment the likes of which he'd never seen. Straps and smooth cups of some stretchy black substance, fastened snugly around her breasts, clearly meant to support her anatomy in a fashion superior to any female garments he'd ever seen, and he'd had enough sisters, growing up, plus several hundred female patients who visited his surgery, to know whereof he spoke. "What the devil is it made of? It isn't latex rubber, yet it's very *like* rubber, and exceptionally well crafted."

"C'n I rip her?" Maybrick's voice came from nearby, dulled by the drug, sleepy.

"No, James. She's mine." He glanced around to find the drugged merchant swaying on his feet. "Come here, James, you'd best lie down and rest." He dragged the unconscious, half-naked woman to one side, making room on the long work bench for Maybrick to stretch out. Ignoring the woman for several minutes, Lachley concentrated on taking Maybrick into a deep trance to erase any possibility of Maybrick's mentioning him or the bizarre devices they'd found tonight, when he returned home and scribbled out his diary entries.

"When will you be able to return to London, James?" he murmured.

"Not sure . . . long time . . . business . . ."

"Dammit, we have to find the Welsh woman in Miller's Court and eliminate her," Lachley muttered, "the sooner the better. Very well, James, the next time you return to London, you will locate a woman in Miller's Court for me, one who speaks Welsh. She is the woman you will kill next."

Maybrick's drugged face changed, coming alive with a hunger Lachley recognized very well, now. "I want to rip her . . . I'll slash her face, the faithless whore, cut off her breasts, kiss them when I've cut them off . . ."

"Later, James! You may do all of that, the next time you return to London." Maybrick's eyes were closing again, his breaths deepening. "Later . . ."

"Sleep, James," Lachley muttered. "When you wake, you will return to Liverpool. You will have no memory of me at all, not until I send you a telegram. Only then will you recall my name, this place. Sleep, James, and dream of ripping the whore in Miller's Court . . ."

The drugged merchant slept.

That nasty little chore out of the way, Lachley returned his attention to the woman at the other end of his work bench. It was time his mysterious prisoner woke up. He needed to question her, but she would not be likely to cooperate with the men who'd killed her companion. The dead man probably wasn't her husband, given the absence of any wedding ring on her hands, but they were clearly connected somehow, so he would have to take steps to ensure her compliance. He prepared another draught of the drug he'd given Maybrick, then roused her with water splashed into her face and gentle slaps across the cheeks.

"Wake up, now . . ."

She stirred, moaned softly. Gaslight glinted along her dark blond hair and fair complexion. She was a pretty little thing, with wide and frightened blue eyes that gradually opened. For a long moment, confusion held those eyes perfectly senseless. Then memory stirred sharply and an indrawn shriek broke loose. She focused on him, cowered away, tried to get her hands under her, and belatedly discovered the ropes on her wrists.

"Hold still," Lachley told her, "before you fall off the edge of the bench."

A tiny whimper broke free. He lifted her head and felt tremors ripping through her as he pressed the rim of the cup to her lips. "Drink this."

"No . . . please . . ."

"Drink it!" She struggled feebly, no match for his strength. With the simple expediency of pinching shut her nostrils, he forced the drug down her throat. She coughed, gagged, then swallowed it. Lachley stroked her hair gently. "There, that wasn't so bad. Don't bother to fight me, pet, you're not going anywhere. I haven't poisoned you," he added with a wry smile.

She trembled, biting a lip, and tried to hide her face. "Please, don't kill me . . ."

"Kill you? Oh, no, my dear, I've far more interesting things in mind for you." The shuddering gulp of air she dragged down left him chuckling. "Now, then, my dear, the drug I've just given you will make you very sleepy. By the way, would you mind terribly telling me your name?" She lay trapped against him, shaking, and didn't answer. He drew a fingertip down her wet cheek. "All right, then, we'll wait a bit, until the drug's taken hold. Terribly sorry about your friend, you know. James was quite beyond himself this evening." The woman's tears came faster and her breaths went ragged. Curiosity prompted his next question. "Was he your lover?"

She shook her head. "No."

"Your brother, perhaps?"

"No . . ."

"What, then?"

"B-business partner." Her eyelids had begun to droop.

"What sort of business, my dear?"

"Journalists . . ." A faint sigh of sound.

Lachley frowned. *Journalists?* Penny-dreadful *journalists?* What was the world coming to, when women presumed to enter a sordid profession like newspaper muckraking? The entire world was unravelling these days, with women demanding suffrage and entering medical training at university, becoming doctors, for God's sake, setting themselves up with typewriting machines as secretaries, a fine and estimable man's profession. Women would turn the job of personal secretary into a mockery, offering their sexual services, no doubt, breaking up the homes and marriages of perfectly respectable businessmen. Society was disintegrating and *women* were largely at fault. "What newspaper do you work for? Or do you write for some absurd women's magazine?"

"Newspaper . . ." Her eyes had closed completely. "*London New Times.*"

New Times? He'd never heard of it. Hardly surprising, though, new penny dreadfuls hit the market every month, competing for readership and advertisements. "What were you doing in the sewer?"

"Following you . . ."

A chill chased down his back. Well, of course she'd been following him, how else would she and her partner have found their way down here?

"What did you come here for?"

A tiny, fleeting smile. "Going to win the Carson Prize . . . in historical photojournalism . . . nobody else had the guts to try it, following the Ripper . . ."

For a long moment, Lachley stood dumbstruck. The *Ripper?* She knew of the letter he'd sent out? The one the Central News Agency had not yet made public? He'd expected the newspaper to print the Dear Boss letter immediately, but the dratted editor had clearly held it back and might well have sent it to the police. Perhaps she'd seen the letter at the Central News Agency office, spying for her own publication? Then the rest of what she'd said sank in. *Historical photojournalism?* He'd never heard of such a profession, any more than he'd ever heard of a Carson Prize, whatever that was. Clearly, winning it was important enough to risk her life for it. "Historical photojournalism?" he echoed blankly. "Are you a photographer, then?"

Perhaps that device she'd been carrying was some sort of camera?

"Oh, yes, a very good photographer. Dominica Nosette, most famous photographer in the world . . ."

Lachley indulged a wry smile, at that. He'd never heard of the bloody bitch.

"Videotape's going to make me rich," she sighed. "Fools on the Ripper Watch Team, all those famous criminologists and historians, they don't know anything . . . too cowardly to try what I did."

Ripper Watch Team? This sounded deuced ominous. "What did you try?" he asked softly.

Another fleeting smile. "Hid in Dutfield's Yard, of course, waited for you to bring Liz Stride there. And we hid again in Mitre Square, behind that high fence. They put their hidden cameras up and filmed it from the vault, but you can't get a decent story hiding in a cellar halfway across London. You have to get right out where he's going to strike next . . ."

The room spun as the implications of her babbling story sank in. *She'd known exactly where to hide! Had known where to watch them kill Stride and Eddowes! Had known in advance!* It wasn't possible, how could anyone know where he and Maybrick were going to be, when they hadn't known, themselves, where they would encounter the prostitutes? They hadn't even realized Catharine Eddowes had been released from Bishopsgate Police Station, not until they'd run across her on Duke Street. Yet *others* knew, she'd said, had put up cameras in advance, to photograph him and Maybrick . . . others who sat in a vault of some sort halfway across London . . .

John Lachley seized her chin, shaking her hard. "Explain! *How did you know where I would be?*"

She blinked slowly. "Everybody knows. Ripper's a famous case. Most famous murder mystery in the last two centuries . . . and I'm going to solve it, *have* solved it! When I go back to the station, to my own time, I'll be famous, and rich, I've got videotapes of Jack the Ripper . . . both of them . . . who'd have guessed it was two men?"

Lachley stood shaking. She was babbling, out of her head. Had to be . . .

"All those idiots," she was murmuring, "thinking it was Prince Eddy or his tutor, or that barrister who drowned himself or Sir William Gull. They've been arguing over who it was for the last hundred-fifty years . . . even thought it might've been some time traveller using the Britannia Gate . . ."

John Lachley stared at the raving woman, seriously considering whether she had taken leave of her senses or if he had taken leave of his. Time traveller? A *century and a half,* arguing over his identity? She wasn't a journalist, she was an escapee from a lunatic asylum somewhere on the fringes of London . . .

Then something she'd said hit home.

The gate! Ianira, the woman who had known so much about him, had babbled endlessly about a mysterious gate. Was she, too, some sort of traveller in time, who had come to hunt him? He reeled at the implications. His gaze rested on the heavy box he'd taken from her coat, with its trailing wires and tubes and cylinders hidden in her bonnet, and frowned. He picked it up, then shook the woman. "Look at this." Her eyelids fluttered for a moment before opening. "Tell me what this is."

"My camera. Digital videocamera, best in the business . . ."

*Video*camera? Latin for *I see?*

"Show me how it operates!" He loosened the ropes on her wrists, braced her in a sitting position and leaned her against him. She fumbled the camera into her lap and fiddled with controls. "See? This is what I recorded tonight." She tried to hold the camera up, but couldn't lift her arms. He took it from her—and let out a yell. The strangely textured surface along one side was *moving.* Pictures flickered across it, in color, showing Maybrick bent over Catharine Eddowes, hacking her to pieces . . .

Dear God! How the devil could such a tiny little box have captured them in pictures like this, color pictures, *moving* pictures? He pressed the controls she had manipulated and the box whirred softly, the pictures flashing with such speed he couldn't follow the motion. People racing backwards, colors flashing and rippling across the surface, a blur of sight and confusion. When he fumbled at the controls again, hands shaking, the motion slowed abruptly. He found himself staring at a place straight out of nightmare. Vast open rooms, with whole buildings inside, hundreds of tiny people moving about the floor and climbing staircases made of metal, insanely colored lights glowing in strange shapes. "What is this place?" he demanded, voice shaking.

She blinked slowly and focused on the camera he held. "Shangri-La Station," she murmured. "The time terminal . . ."

Lachley drew a whole series of deep breaths, gulping down the damp air, gradually steadied his shaking nerves. "You," he said slowly, enunciating each word with care, "are from my future?"

"Had to come down time, through the gate, to catch the Ripper, to photograph him . . ."

He didn't really believe it, didn't want to believe it, such things were fantasy, the maunderings of popular authors like that Frenchman Jules Verne. Yet he was holding a camera that no craftsman in the British Empire could possibly have constructed, made of things Lachley had never seen or heard of, and the bitch was drugged, *couldn't* be lying, not with what he'd given her. Excitement stirred to life, with tantalizing glimpses of a world which could offer him more power than anything he'd dreamed possible. "Eddy," he whispered, "tell me about Eddy. Prince Albert Victor. When does he become king?"

"Poor Prince Eddy," she sighed, eyes closing again. "Only four more years . . . so young . . . 1892 . . ."

Lachley began to tremble in a wild excitement. *Four years?* Eddy would be crowned king in only four more years? Dear God, what was going to happen, that would kill both Queen Victoria and the Prince of Wales? Bertie was healthy as an ox and Victoria, herself, likely to live for another decade. "What happens?" he demanded, breathless now, "What happens in 1892?"

"Influenza. Epidemic of '91–'92. Poor Eddy, he'd just been engaged to be married, named Duke of Clarence, whole life ahead of him, and he's killed by influenza. Victoria was heartbroken, his parents inconsolable . . ."

The room lurched under his feet, swaying and whirling in mad circles. *Dead of influenza? Never crowned?* It couldn't be, he'd worked too hard, invested *everything*, spent five weeks in hell, tracking down Eddy's God-cursed letters to protect him, to ensure the ascension to the throne. Had done murder after stinking murder to keep Eddy safe, so he could become king, to ensure himself the power Lachley craved, the safety of wealth and control over the political future of an empire . . .

And Eddy was to be killed by a *stupid influenza epidemic?*

Lachley began to laugh, the sound wild and high, echoing off the bricks of the vaulted ceiling. He gripped the impossible camera in both hands and laughed until the sound choked him, until he could gasp out, "How do you get back? To your own time?"

"Through the gate," his drugged victim answered in a sleepy, reasonable tone.

"Gate? What gate? Where?" He was still laughing, the sound of it edged with mania, a mind giving way under the stresses.

"The Britannia Gate. In Battersea, Spaldergate House. But it doesn't open for days, not until the second of October, only opens every eight days . . ." Her head was lolling. "Won't go through it, though, not 'til Mary Kelly's murdered on November ninth . . . I'll take my videotapes back, then, I'm sure to win the Kit Carson Prize . . ."

Another spate of laughter broke loose. Mary Kelly? She must be the bitch in Miller's Court. What the bloody hell did he care about a scheming little whore with a letter written by a dullard who wouldn't even survive to wear the crown? Oh, God, it was too funny, here he stood in a satanic sanctuary devoted to the accrual of political and psychic power, with a dead time traveller on the floor, a drugged maniac on his work bench, and a babbling journalist planning to photograph a murder he no longer had any earthly reason to commit, with a total of *four* whores dead and cut to pieces for no reason whatever, and the decaying head of an adolescent Nancy-boy glaring at him from across the room and laughing at his shattered dreams . . .

Only this woman had brought him a glimpse of something new, something which fired his imagination even more passionately than Eddy's prospects had done. A whole, immense new world to explore, in which to control little minds and live as a king, himself. He laughed again and stroked the woman's hair. Thoughts of Eddy fell away like flakes of rust from fine Damascus steel. Dominica, the self-important photojournalist, had done him a greater favor than she dreamed, tracking him through London's sewers.

He left her tied to the great iron hook on his sacred oak tree, drugged into a stupor, and deposited the equally stupified James Maybrick on the floor of the sewer outside, then locked the door to Lower Tibor and began walking through the dark tunnels beneath London, laughing softly and wondering what he ought to wear when he carried Dominica through the Britannia Gate two days from now, dying of the wounds he would inflict shortly before arriving in Battersea?

Sometime early in the morning hours, Ianira Cassondra woke to gibbering terror. Dr. John Lachley had crashed into her bedroom, rousing her from drugged sleep with slaps, bruising her arms and shaking her. "Tell me about the gate!" he demanded, cracking his hand across her face. "Wake up, girl, and tell me about the gate! And the station! Where are you from?"

Ianira shrank away from him, weeping and trembling. "I came through the Britannia Gate! From the station! Please . . ."

"What station? What's it called?"

"Shangri-La," she whispered, her bruised face aching where he'd struck her. Her wrists, crushed in his hard hands, were slowly purpling under his grip. "Time Terminal Eighty-Six—"

"*Eighty-Six*? My God, are there so many of them? Tell me about your world, woman!"

She shook her head, desperate and confused. "I live on the station. I am not permitted to leave, for I am a down-timer—"

"A *what*?" His face, looming so close above her own, had twisted into an unholy mask of madness. She shrank back into the pillows, but he jerked her up again, roughly. "Explain!"

"I was born in Ephesus!" she cried. "Came to the station through the Philospher's Gate! From Athens . . ."

He went very still, staring down at her. Voice quiet, now, he said, "Tell me again where you were born. And when."

"In Ephesus," she whispered. "We did not reckon the years in the same way, but the Philosopher's Gate opens into what the up-time world calls 448 B.C., in the time of Pericles . . ." She trailed off at the look of naked shock in his eyes.

"My God," he whispered. "It's true, then. Of course you kept saying you were born in Ephesus, when the city doesn't exist any longer."

Ianira blinked up at him, terrified and confused. Clearly, he believed her. Why, she couldn't imagine. Something had obviously happened tonight . . . Ianira's eyes widened. The Ripper Watch! He must have encountered someone from the Ripper Watch tonight, must've seen something that had left him convinced of the reality of time travel. John Lachley's wild eyes focused slowly on her bruised face. He smiled, stroking her hair possessively. "My dear, tell me about the people trying to kill you."

She tried to explain about the up-time world's Lady of Heaven Temples, the *Ansar Majlis* terrorists who had sworn to destroy the Templars and her family, about Jenna's murderous father and the men he'd sent to butcher his own daughter.

"Then you are quite important," Lachley mused. "Far more important than that brainless bitch I left in Lower Tibor. A woman journalist, whoever heard of such a thing?" Ianira closed her eyes to shut out horror. He'd not only encountered members of the Ripper Watch Team, he'd kidnapped them. "Yes," he was murmuring, "I do believe you're far more important than Miss Nosette. Very well, my course is clear. I'd better do that bloody lecture tomorrow night, curse it, to lull suspicion. I shan't risk drawing attention to myself over those wretched murders on the eve of stepping into the future!" He shook her again. "Tell me about the gate. What time it opens. That Nosette woman said something about Spaldergate House, in Battersea."

"I don't know what it looks like," Ianira quavered, straining away from him. "They smuggled me out of the station in a steamer trunk. I know the gate opens in the garden behind the house, but I don't know what time. It is in the evening, always, every eight days."

"Ah. Miss Nosette can tell me precisely when, before I dispose of her. Very well, my dear," he pressed a kiss to her brow. "I do believe," he said quietly, "you had best be moved for safekeeping. I don't wish to risk having you escape, my pet. Eddy has proven himself worthless as dross, but you, my dear, will take me into a place of power beyond anything I imagined."

She gasped, staring up into his mad grey eyes. "You can't go to the station!"

He laughed softly. "Nonsense. I'm John Lachley, I can do anything. The police haven't a clue that I've helped butcher four destitute whores in the East End, controlling Maybrick's pathetic little mind. Miss Nosette tells me your world has puzzled over my identity for a century and a half. If I can accomplish that in London, with no more than I've had to work with, I will become a god on your station!" He smiled at her through dark, insane eyes. "And you, my pet, will be my goddess . . ."

She fought him when he drugged her again.

And wept hopelessly when he carried her down the stairs, wrapped in a cloak, carrying her toward the nightmarish room she had seen in visions, the brick room beneath the streets where he had carried out at least one murder and had planned so many others. Somehow, she must find a way to stop this madman before he reached the station. Down-time men whose minds were sound and whole sometimes went mad when they first entered a time terminal and confronted the shocking realities of the up-time world. What John Lachley would do, once he reached TT-86 . . .

She faded into unconsciousness, still trying to discover some way to stop him.

Jenna tried to ignore the ugly roar of voices in the street just outside their little house, but there was no escaping the angry sound of brawling out there. The bells of Christ Church, Spitalfields, sounded bleak and hopeless this morning, calling worshippers to a rainy Sunday service, while the grim news flashed like wildfire from house to house: two women butchered within half an hour of one another, confounding the police of two separate jurisdictions and shocking the entire city of London, this time, not just the East End. And that at a time when most residents here had believed themselves beyond further shock.

Noah had gone out to buy fresh-caught herrings for their breakfast, refusing to let Jenna set foot into the angry mob outside. Jenna was determined to cook breakfast today, however, so she bent over the monstrous, coal-fired stove in the kitchen, trying to take in Marcus' instructions on how to operate it, when Noah Armstrong rocketed into the house.

"I've got a lead," the detective said without preamble, dumping a wrapped packet of fish onto the kitchen table with a thump.

Jenna and Marcus jerked around. "What lead?" Jenna demanded breathlessly.

"There's to be a lecture tomorrow night at the Egyptian Hall, on Theosophy and the occult sciences. The speaker's a doctor, claims to be a mesmeric physician. I ran across a man talking about him when I was coming back from the costermonger's. It seems the doctor who's giving the lecture came up from Whitechapel, was born in Middlesex Street, turned to mediumism and the occult. I don't know if this is our man, but the doctor who attacked you, Jenna, reacted violently to whatever Ianira said in trance. So maybe he had occult connections. We're certainly running out of leads, trying to trace ordinary doctors. And with the Ripper terror coming to a boil out there, I'm not sure it's entirely safe just now, asking about physicians and surgeons. The police are looking for a doctor connected to the Ripper, after all, and poor Dr. Mindel has barricaded himself into the house, terrified of the mobs. Frankly, I think it's worth a shot, going to see this Lachley fellow."

Jenna's mouth had dried out like thistle-down, all the liquid in her body rushing to her palms, which she wiped unsteadily on her trousers. "Yes. I agree. I'm coming with you, Noah." The detective started to protest. "No, hear me out! I can identify him faster than you can. If he's giving a lecture, there'll be a crowd, which means I can watch without him noticing me. If he's the right man, we can trace him to where he lives, maybe even find Ianira there."

Noah's lips thinned. Clearly the detective wanted to argue. Then a sigh broke loose. "You're right, dammit. But I don't like putting you in harm's way for any reason."

"I'll go armed," Jenna muttered. "For bear."

"I, too, will go," Marcus interjected. "Mrs. Mindel has offered to watch the girls if I ever need to leave them alone. Ianira is my wife. I *will* go to search for her."

Again, the detective clearly considered arguing, then gave in. "All right," Noah groused. "If things do get sticky, another gun hand will be welcome. God knows, you learned quickly enough when I gave you those shooting lessons after that mess in Colorado."

"You taught me well," Marcus said quietly. "I have not forgotten how to use the revolver I bought in Chicago."

Noah nodded. "We'll *all* go armed. And we'll need better clothes than these. The Egyptian Hall is a respectable place. If we show up in East End castoffs, they might not even let us through the door."

Jenna frowned. "The only good suit I've got is what I was wearing the night the gate opened. It's got bloodstains all over it. The last thing I want to do is show my face in public with blood on my clothes. Somebody'll take me for Jack the Ripper. I had decent stuff in my luggage, but I had to abandon all my baggage at the Piccadilly Hotel."

"The lecture's not until tomorrow night, so there's plenty of time to pick up new clothes. For all of us, if it comes to that. Fortunately, it's market day in Petticoat Lane, so there'll be plenty of new suits to pick and choose from."

Jenna nodded. "Good. I'll get my money belt out. I changed a lot of currency at the station. We can use that to pay for everything."

"Very well. Let's get over to Petticoat Lane, before the best bargains are gone."

Wordlessly, they set out to buy yet another set of disguises.

《 Chapter 10 》

Margo had never placed a wire tap before.

Watching Inspector Conroy Melvyn work that morning in near darkness, her admiration for the up-time Scotland Yard detective's skill soared. He placed the tap into the telephone lines leading into the Home Office in a very short time, then rejoined her on the pavement. "Got it," he grinned. "Now when the queen telephones the Home Office this afternoon from Scotland, expressing shock over the double murders, we'll get a recording of it."

"That's great!" Margo grinned, wondering how much money the residuals for up-time broadcast of the historic phone call might land in her bank account. "What's next?" Whatever it was, it wouldn't be nearly as hair-raising as recovering their hidden equipment from the murder sites had been. Thank God the Victorian police hadn't yet carried the forensic science of crime-scene evidence very far. Not only had they failed to put a quarantine on the murder scenes, they'd allowed surgeons and coroners to disturb the bodies, wash away the blood, and Sir Charles Warren had even erased the chalked graffiti over on Goulston Street after Maybrick had slashed it across a stairwell landing. Margo could almost understand the reasoning behind the erasure, given the anti-Semitic slur Maybrick had written and the already-explosive mood of the East End. To their credit, the City Police had argued about it, hotly, finally forced to give in to the Metropolitan Police decision to erase it before it could be seen or even photographed, since Goulston Street lay in Metropolitan Police jurisdiction.

"What next, indeed?" Inspector Melvyn mused scratching his chin thoughtfully. "I think, my dear, I'd like to be on hand at the Central News Agency when the Saucy Jack postcard arrives."

"Do you want to try videotaping Michael Kidney when he shows up at the Leman Police Station, accusing the PC on duty for his lover's murder?" Margo sympathized with the man. Poor Michael Kidney. He really had loved Elizabeth Stride, despite their stormy relationship.

"Might be a bit of a risk," the inspector frowned.

"More risky than recovering that equipment from Mitre Square?" Margo laughed nervously. "Or tapping the Home Office telephone lines?"

The inspector grinned. "Well, now you mention it . . ."

"All right, we'll try to get a video of Mr. Kidney. I'll change into East End togs before we go."

"Right."

They set out at a brisk walk for Spaldergate House. Malcolm was already in the East End, with Pavel Kostenka and Shahdi Feroz and Doug Tanglewood, studying the crowd dynamics on the streets. Margo shivered, remembering the explosive riot the day Polly Nichols' mutilations had been discovered, and was selfishly glad Malcolm had assigned her to Conroy Melvyn, rather than the Whitechapel group.

The sun rose while they walked westward down Whitehall where, tomorrow morning, a decapitated, legless, armless woman's torso would be discovered in a vaulted cellar beneath the New Scotland Yard building, still under construction. Tonight, Malcolm and Conroy Melvyn would try to place miniaturized camera equipment in the cellar to see if they could catch the perpetrator of the so-called Whitehall torso mystery and settle once and for all whether that anonymous victim had also fallen prey to the Ripper's knife.

As they walked westward, early-morning paper criers were already on the streets, hawking the morning's shocking news. Church bells tolled from St. Paul's Cathedral, from Westminster Abbey and churches Margo didn't even know the names of, the sounds of the bells deep and sonorous and inexpressibly lonely in the early light. They paused and bought copies of the papers, listening to the gentlemen who gathered on street corners, men who spoke in hushed, angry tones about the horror in Mitre Square, taping the conversations with hidden microphones and the miniaturized cameras in their scouting logs.

"The *Financial News* is offering a three-hundred-pound reward for this fiend's capture," one gentleman muttered as they passed.

"The Lord Mayor's offering five hundred pounds," another said, his heavily jowled face flushed with anger. "The government jolly well should've done so ages ago, before six women were cut to pieces, four of them in as many weeks! That Lusk fellow, with the Whitechapel Vigilance Committee, asked just yesterday for a reward to be offered, officially, by the government. And they turned him down! Now we've two more women dead . . ."

"Sir Alfred Kirby telephoned me to say he planned to offer one hundred pounds sterling and fifty militia men to help apprehend the beast, asked if I would volunteer. My wife had a fainting spell at the notion of me hunting such a madman, wouldn't hear of it . . ."

"—said he'd heard a chap named Thomas Coram found a bloodstained knife in Whitechapel Road. Ruddy thing was nine inches long! You could put a knife like that straight through a woman, God help the poor creatures. Sir Charles Warren's at his wit's end, trying to investigate, what with the City Police demanding cooperation and frothing at evidence destroyed . . ."

Conroy Melvyn murmured, "Poor Sir Charles. I feel for the chap, I do. Trying to tackle a thing like the Ripper killings, without the faintest notion of psychopathic serial-killer profiling or decent forensic science. This case breaks his career. I shouldn't want to try investigating such a thing in *my* jurisdiction, I can tell you that."

"I wonder what the coroner will do at the inquest for Elizabeth Stride?"

He shook his head grimly. "Not enough, clearly. Still, I intend to be in Cable Street when the inquest opens. Vestry Hall will be jam-packed, right enough."

Margo sighed. *Another* inquest. With descriptions of wounds and witness testimony . . . She'd almost rather be with Malcolm in the explosive East End, than trapped in a room full of shouting reporters after the gruesome details of murder and mutilation. "You know, one thing has me puzzled," she said at length. "Someone wrote an entry in the Swedish Church Parish Register that Elizabeth Stride had been murdered by Jack the Ripper. They dated the entry September thirtieth, the morning she was killed. Yet the name Jack the Ripper wasn't released publicly until today, October the first."

"I know," Melvyn sighed. "Pity we can't be everywhere, isn't it? But even with a team of us working and you lot of guides helping, we can't solve *every* mystery connected with the Ripper."

"Maybe someone who worked at the Central News Agency, who'd seen the Dear Boss letter, wrote it?"

"Or someone backdated the entry by a day," the police inspector mused. "But we'll never know, eh? What drives me batty is not identifying this bloke working with Maybrick. We've come up empty handed at every turn, trying to trace the blighter."

"Well, somebody's got to know him. Dominica Nosette and Guy Pendergast figured out who he is, I'm willing to bet on it. Whatever William Butler Yeats and his friend said, that night at the Carlton Club, Pendergast figured out who the mystery doctor was."

"Or maybe he just saw the bloody chap and followed him," Melvyn muttered, flushing with embarrassment over the affair. The police inspector had not taken it well, that a reporter had given him the slip while he'd been focused on a famous poet.

"Maybe. That might mean he could have an occult connection, if he was there on the night of the Theosophical meeting. Or even if he wasn't there, because Malcolm said you were discussing Celtic religions and other stuff that would interest someone like Yeats."

"Bloody hell . . ." The inspector's footsteps faltered as a look of surprise crossed his face.

"What?" Margo asked. "What did I say?"

"Perhaps nothing. Perhaps everything." The policeman was staring at the newspaper they'd just bought. "It's this." He tapped the newspaper, then opened it hastily, skimming one finger down the newsprint columns. "There was a lecture notice on the front page . . ."

he muttered. "Jumped out at me just as you spoke about Celtic religions. There! Got it."

He held the newspaper open so she could see the article.

"Dr. John Lachley," Margo read out loud. "SoHo scholar of the occult, mesmeric physician . . ." Her eyes widened. She clutched at the policeman's sleeve. "He keeps a surgery in Cleveland Street, *in a house he calls Tibor.*"

Conroy Melvyn stared at her, mouth coming adrift. "My God! The same place our chap told Maybrick to meet him!" Then he frowned. "Cleveland Street, though? That's a bit of a distance to walk, with bloodstains on one's sleeves. Still, it's a ruddy good clue. Good job, eh what? Jolly well done, Miss Smith!"

She grinned. "You saw the article, not me."

"Which I would have failed to notice if you hadn't been reminding me of what I'd heard that night in the Carlton Club. I say, let's get back to Spaldergate post haste. I can hardly wait to spring the news on the rest of the team!"

Margo laughed. "Me, either. And wait until Malcolm hears!"

"Mr. Moore," Conroy Melvyn said, stepping to the kerb and hailing a hansom, "will quite likely insist on attending tonight's lecture."

"Hah! You couldn't keep him away with wild horses. Me, either!"

"Well said. Now, then . . . Battersea, cabbie," he said, handing Margo up into the cab which had drawn to a halt beside them, "Octavia Street. And no tricks, my good man, I've consulted Mogg's for the fare!"

"'Ere, now, guv'nor," the cabbie protested, "I'm an honest man, so I am!"

Margo settled in with a grin. She'd learned the hard way to consult Mogg's map of cab fares, to avoid being cheated blind by the cabbies. Then they were rolling down Victoria Embankment at a rush, headed West for Battersea Park and an unexpected break in the Ripper case. She couldn't take full credit for the discovery, but glowed nonetheless. Just wait until Malcolm heard! And Kit!

Maybe she was cut out for this job, after all!

❅ ❅ ❅

By the following evening, Jenna had been transformed, as had Noah and Marcus, by the acquisition of decent quality gentlemen's clothing, the sort a middle-class businessman might wear. They left the girls in the care of Mrs. Mindel, making certain that Dr. Mindel was armed and knew how to use a revolver, in case of trouble from the mobs, then walked to Threadneedle Street, the financial district in the heart of The City, to find a cab. It was impossible to hire a hansom cab anywhere in Spitalfields—not only were the residents too poor to afford the fares, cabbies were leery of robbery from East End gangs. They finally found a cab rank near the Bank of England and hired the conveyance at the front of the line. Jenna crowded in with Marcus and Noah for a jolting ride up to Piccadilly and shivered at the memory of her last visit to those environs. She'd very nearly died, that night in Piccadilly. *No sense dwelling on it,* she told herself firmly. *Even if I am looking for the man who shot me in cold blood.* She couldn't quite suppress a shiver, however, and earned a long, worried look from Noah, which she returned with a forced smile. When the cab finally halted, Jenna climbed down on shaking legs, hoping no one recognized her as the individual who'd jumped from a window in the Piccadilly Hotel after a bloody shootout. It was one thing, hiding in anonymous Spitalfields. It was far more frightening, coming into a part of London where she'd nearly been murdered—twice.

"There's the Egyptian Hall," Noah said quietly.

The building was tall, its face decorated by elaborate stonework, including a winged scarab above a tall, rectangular window which was crowned by an ornate pediment. A sign above the door proclaimed the premises to be the Egyptian Hall, museum and meeting room. Down the street, on Piccadilly's south side, she could see the immense facade of Fortnum and Mason's famous store, and down the other way, the imposing edifice which housed the Royal Institute of Painters in Water Colours. Along the north side stood the Burlington Arcade, bustling with fashionable shoppers going home for the evening. Shopkeepers were busy closing up for the night; the building loomed above them, dark and forbidding in its shadows next to Burlington House Mansion. Jenna swallowed nervously as fine carriages rattled past, drawn by well-groomed, shining horses flinging their hooves out smartly. Wealthy gentlemen strolled the pavements. Silver-headed canes gleamed in the twilight, silk top hats nodded like mobile chimney stacks, and heavy gold watches and fobs glinted as their owners checked the time. The ladies on their arms wore thick silks and fur-trimmed coats over swaying bustles; ostrich and egret feathers drooped from exquisite hats and fur muffs in fox, mink, and black sable protected their hands from the cold air. In this exquisitely upscale area, Jenna felt very downscale, drab and vulnerable in her middle-class wool and fake mutton chops.

Then Noah was leading them into the Egyptian Hall, buying tickets to the lecture and the exhibits. Signs explained the origins of the collections, which had belonged to naturalist and antiquarian William Bullock, who had built the hall in 1812. Faded photographs of General Tom Thumb, the American dwarf who had come here for a wildly popular exhibit, hung on the wall near the entrance. Other gentlemen were arriving for the talk, accompanied by a few intrepid and curious ladies. A sign with the subject of the evening's lecture directed them to the meeting room, where they found a fair crowd gathered. Voices washed through Jenna's awareness as she peered anxiously at faces, but she saw no one resembling the man who'd tried to murder her outside the Royal Opera. She consulted the thick, silver-plated pocket watch she'd purchased earlier in the afternoon, and frowned. The lecture was due to begin at any moment . . .

"Where the deuce is Lachley?" a man just behind her complained. " 'Tisn't like him to be late!"

"Perhaps," another man's voice drawled, "he's preoccupied with that ravishing creature he took in, the other week? If I'd rescued a girl that lovely and had taken her into my home, I might be a bit distracted, as well!"

"Is it immoral liaisons you're insinuating, Crowley? Of Dr. Lachley?" The speaker's voice held a thick Irish lilt, tinged with anger.

Jenna turned to find several gentlemen watching the two speakers. The first speaker, Crowley, shrugged. "Men will be men, after all. I don't doubt the good doctor's intentions in trying to help the poor creature. But what a comely little thing she was, even if she was half-crazed. It would be a simple enough, after all, to take advantage of a lady in such distress."

The other man, in his twenties, perhaps, with a fire-eaten look to his eyes, glared at Crowley. "You, sir, are contemptible! In Dublin, you would be publicly shamed for such slanderous sentiments!"

"Easy, Yeats," another young man muttered. "Crowley's infamous for baiting people with his depraved ideas. Ignore him. We do."

Crowley's eyes glinted with amusement. "Only a fool ignores the devil, sir."

The young man shrugged. "You may bill yourself as the prophet of the anti-Christ, Mr. Crowley, but you're no devil. Unless, of course, it's you ripping up these poor souls in the East End? Hardly your style, I should think. Reading a black mass over them is more in your line."

Several listening gentlemen gasped aloud, faces paling in shock, but Crowley merely smiled. "Perhaps you might join me, next time? No? Pity. Ah . . . Here's Lachley, at last."

Jenna turned quickly toward the front of the meeting room . . . and lurched. For a long, terrifying moment, the entire room circled like a washing machine on spin cycle. She knew the man who'd appeared, who stepped up to the tall lectern. The last time she'd seen him, he'd levelled a pistol at her head and pulled the trigger. Her mind reeled, partly with the implications of the conversation they'd just overheard. *If that's Lachley and Lachley's holding a young lady in his house, she can't be anyone but Ianira Cassondra!*

Dr. John Lachely was in a high state of agitation, Jenna realized as the spinning room steadied down. His color ran high and his dark eyes glinted with a touch of madness that left the fine hairs along Jenna's neck and arms standing erect. She clutched at Noah's arm. "*It's him!*"

The detective gave her a sharp stare, then gripped Marcus by the arm and forcibly held him back. Ianira's husband had started forward, fists clenched. "Not here!" Noah cautioned sharply. "We'll sit through the lecture. Then we'll follow him home."

Marcus, his own eyes a trifle wild, glared at Noah; then he glanced at the room full of eyewitnesses and subsided. "Very well," Marcus growled under his breath. "But if he has hurt her, I will kill him!"

"I'll help you," Jenna muttered. "I owe that bastard a bullet through the skull!"

"Keep your voice down!" Noah hissed. "And take a seat, for God's sake, the lecture's starting."

Jenna found herself in a chair next to the young Irishman with the fire-eaten eyes, Mr. Yeats. The name was familiar, somehow, from long ago, she couldn't quite place where or why. Yeats sat glaring across the aisle at Crowley, who listened calmly to the opening of the lecture and ignored the Irishman's furious stare. Jenna sat wrapped in her own feverish thoughts, hardly paying attention to what Lachley said, and only stirred when Yeats' friend, the other dark-haired Irishman, muttered, "What on earth can be wrong with him? I've never heard such ramblings. He doesn't make proper sense, half the time."

Yeats murmured, "I'm sure I don't know. I've never seen Dr. Lachley in such a state."

Jenna frowned and concentrated more fully on what Lachley was saying.

". . . the Classical writers were notorious for confusing all things Celto-Gaelic with all things Germanic. I have been to Germany, to Hungary and places north. The taking of trophy skulls . . . drinking from them . . . rites of blood on oak trees . . ." Lachley's eyes were wild, his hands shaking visibly on the edges of the podium. He drew back from some hideous thought with evident difficulty and cleared his throat. "These sacrifices, yes, ancient Roman writers consistently erred. Attributed human sacrifice to ancient Celts, when such rites should more appropriately be laid at the feet of their savage and bloodthirsty northern neighbors. These Germanic tribes gave Caesar enormous difficulty, it is to be remembered. And Germanic rites and customs of the Viking period, it should be noted, included such barbaric practices as the blood eagle. A man would cut out a living victim's lungs and drape them across his back like an eagle's wings . . ."

Several women in the audience emitted cries of horror. Up at the lectern, Lachley's eyes, shining and wild with a sort of unholy pleasure, widened slightly at the shocked sounds coming from his audience. He calmed himself a little, settling into a more lucid frame of mind. "I beg pardon, ladies, but the subject is a most indelicate one. So, I cannot help but conclude that classical sources for Celtic barbarism and human sacrifice *must* be suspect. Their traditional enemies, the Romans, wished most profoundly to rule the Celts and thus cannot be trusted to have painted them with anything approaching honesty.

"The Celtic peoples therefore have been seriously maligned for the past two thousand years. They have been held up to the world by their Roman enemies as barbarians who would slaughter an innocent victim, simply to read the oracles in his death throes. Maligned and slandered, the Celts have ever since been painted villainously, when their history and many accomplishments in law and the arts prove that their rightful place in history is among the most civilized and learned peoples of the world. Their ancient magical wisdom was very nearly destroyed by systematic genocide waged against the Celts' intellectual class by their conquerors.

"This wisdom has now been recovered through the wood-carved ogham script, from hundreds of 'library sticks' bundled to form whole books, hidden away in Irish attics and cellars, and is revealed in its astonishing depth and power. This magical legacy of the Celtic peoples will certainly prove to the world at large that we, as Theosophists and students of the psychic sciences, owe a profound debt to the original inhabitants of the British Isles. We who look to the occult for spiritual guidance walk in the footsteps of true greatness and surely shall rule the world for centuries to come!"

Lachley was trembling at the podium, eyes glowing with a hideous passion that left Jenna queasy and cold. He surveyed his audience, then gave a mocking little bow. "Thank you, this concludes my lecture for the evening."

The applause was thunderous, the entire hall surging to its feet in a spontaneous ovation. Dr. John Lachley bathed in the glory of the moment, bowing and stepping back from the lectern, raising his hands in a show of humility which he was clearly far from feeling. His smile was almost manic as he stepped down and shook hands with luminaries from society and the arts, bowed over the hands of great society matrons and ladies of more dubious reputation, mystics and mediums who had come to hear him speak on the popular subject of Celtic occultism, allowed himself to be congratulated by journalists who wished to interview him . . .

Jenna felt sick, trapped in the same room with him. "Noah, we have to find out where he lives."

At her side, the young Irishman named Yeats gave a start and turned toward her. "Are you ill, sir?" he asked at once. "Dr. Lachley keeps a surgery in Cleveland Street, of course, but I daresay I wouldn't go near it. The man's raving, tonight. I've never seen him in such a state."

Jenna took a risk. "Do you know anything about the girl that man Crowley was talking about?"

Yeats frowned, his intense eyes turning frosty. "No. And I don't care to discuss filth with you, sir."

Noah spoke up. "You misunderstand. Our friend, here," he nodded toward Marcus, "is searching for his wife. She was the victim of foul play. This gentleman," the detective nodded toward Jenna, "was escorting her from the docks the night of her arrival in London and was set upon, shot nearly to death. We are merely hoping that Dr. Lachley may help us. We've reason to believe he witnessed the lady's abduction. Cleveland Street, you said? Thank you, sir. We'll meet the good doctor there, no need to bother him now, while he's busy with the lecture audience."

Noah hustled them out of the hall, rushing Jenna and Marcus through the darkened museum, its collection of oddities and antiquities looming like something out of a horror flick. They finally reached the street. Piccadilly was brightly lit, jammed with carriages as the fashionable and wealthy of London took to the streets in search of diverting entertainment. "We'll have to reach his house before he returns," Noah said grimly. "She must be there. We'll break in and carry her out by force if the servants object. Hurry, there's a cab rank further along."

Please, let this work, Jenna prayed. *And let Ianira be all right . . .*

After three weeks in Dr. Lachley's mad care, Jenna didn't see how she could be.

Malcolm Moore enjoyed dressing to the nines, particularly when

Margo was able to dress the part as his lady companion. She looked stunning in watered silk the color of pale lilacs, with several yards of skirt trailing down over a swaying bustle and her fiery hair augmented by a hairpiece from Connie Logan, which allowed her to imitate the upswept coiffeurs popular with stylish ladies.

"My dear," he murmured as he handed her down from the gatehouse carriage to the pavement of Piccadilly, "I shall be the envy of every gentleman who sees you."

She blushed. "Nonsense, sir," she said, glancing toward Shahdi Feroz.

Behind them, Inspector Conroy Melvyn was handing down the Ripper scholar, whose exotic beauty was so striking, she captured the attention of several passing gentlemen; but Dr. Feroz held far less appeal for Malcolm than Margo's fresh enthusiasm and sparkling, lively green eyes. "Nevertheless," he offered his arm, escorting her toward the Egyptian Hall, which stood opposite Bond Street's terminus, where their carriage had dropped them, "you are quite a fetching sight. Inspector," he turned to the policeman, "Madame Feroz, the lecture awaits."

"Well," Margo smiled, glancing at Shahdi Feroz as they crossed Piccadilly through heavy carriage traffic, "it is a relief from East End rags, isn't it?"

Dr. Feroz chuckled. "Indeed, Miss Smith. A welcome relief."

The police inspector grinned as Malcolm purchased tickets for the lecture. He and Melvyn escorted the ladies inside, where a sizeable crowd had already gathered. Frock-coated gentlemen and elegant ladies murmured pleasantries while they waited for the speaker to put in appearance. Malcolm steered the way toward a far corner, where he and Margo could watch newcomers while remaining unobserved, themselves. Conroy Melvyn and Shahdi Feroz strolled through the room, circulating through the crowd, speaking to such luminaries as Madame Blavatsky and filming the event through concealed cameras. They had been waiting for perhaps six or seven minutes when Margo clutched at Malcolm's arm, denting his fine woolen sleeve with her nails. "*Look!*" She was staring toward the entrance, where three gentlemen had just appeared. "My God, *it's Marcus!*"

He frowned. "Surely you're mistaken?" One of the trio did, indeed, look very much like Ianira Cassondra's missing husband. Yet there was too much grey in his hair and he'd aged in other ways, with a deep-set look of fear and frustration etched into his features. Then Malcolm noticed the mutton-chopped gentleman at his side and stiffened. "Great Scott! That may or may not be Marcus, but the chap with him is most certainly Benny Catlin!"

"It is, too, Marcus," she insisted stubbornly. "If somebody were trying to kill me and my whole family, I might've gone grey overnight, too! But what's he doing in London with Benny Catlin? And who's that guy with them?"

"You do have your camera running, don't you?" Malcolm whispered, referring to the tiny digital videocamera hidden beneath Margo's elegant bustle, its wire snaking up her back to a miniature lens concealed in her brooch.

"I turned it on while we were still in the carriage." When Malcolm started to move closer, she grasped his arm. "*No!*"

He glanced down, surprised.

"If Marcus spots you, wanna bet he'll bolt? He could've called on friends for help while he was still on the station, but he didn't. After everything that's happened, he'll be too terrified, Malcolm, to trust anyone."

"Anyone except Benny Catlin," Malcolm growled. "I'd like to know the reason for that."

"So would I. If they're in London, want to bet Ianira and the girls are, too?"

"No bets," Malcolm shook his head. "But how the deuce did they slip through the Britannia without tickets?"

"That Time Tours driver who was shot, up at the Piccadilly Hotel, said Benny Catlin smuggled a woman through in his luggage. We've been assuming she was another student who couldn't get a ticket, or maybe that she and Benny were actually reporters. But what if that woman was Ianira Cassondra? And maybe Marcus and the girls were in some of the other trunks and got out before the police opened the luggage?"

"However they got here," Malcolm said quietly, "the main question is why they would come with two gentlemen they hardly know. It doesn't look to me like Marcus is here against his will."

"No, it doesn't look that way to me, either."

"Oh, bother!" Malcolm said abruptly, noticing another newcomer. "That's all we need, tonight!"

"What?"

"Those gentlemen who just came in? Mr. William Butler Yeats and Mr. Bevin O'Downett. Poets over from Dublin. I know them both, slightly. Met them at the Carlton Club the night Guy Pendergast and Dominica Nosette vanished. Mr. O'Downett and I have scraped acquaintance before. I certainly don't want them to recognize me and draw attention while Marcus and Catlin are standing right there!"

"Then sit down," Margo said reasonably. "You're less conspicuous in a chair than you are head-and-shoulders above me."

Malcolm seated himself with alacrity, turning slightly in the chair so that he sat with his back to the group near the door. It was frustrating, having to sit there, unable to see what was happening, but Margo's eyes were sharp and she was recording the entire evening. She murmured, "Looks like Mr. Yeats is getting into an argument with somebody."

Malcolm risked a quick glance. "Aleister Crowley. Good God, and there's Robert Donston Stevenson. Is the entire occult community of London here tonight?"

"Wouldn't surprise me," Margo muttered. "Not to mention a real convention of Ripper suspects." Then she dug fingers into his shoulder. "Look!" She was staring raptly toward the front of the room. The speaker had just arrived to take the lectern.

Malcolm gasped, staring at Jack the Ripper. "*My God!*" he whispered, voice hushed. "It *is* him!"

"Don't look now," Margo hissed, "but Benny Catlin looks like he just saw a ghost!"

Malcolm glanced around cautiously, just in time to see the unknown gentleman with Catlin grasp Marcus by the arm, holding him back forcibly. The ex-slave's fists were clenched. A look of murderous rage had swept his face.

"What the devil is going on?" Malcolm wondered. "Why would

Marcus be so angry with . . . Oh, dear God." He saw the possibility in a sudden tightening of his gut.

"Oh, no," Margo protested, voice cracking slightly. "*Not Ianira?*"

At the front of the room, Dr. John Lachley began his lecture. Margo sat down hastily as the rest of the assembly settled into chairs. Malcolm scarcely took in what Lachley was saying, as his mind was racing down unpleasant corridors of conjecture. How had Marcus and Ianira run afoul of Jack the Ripper? They must be living somewhere in the East End. Yet Ianira was not among the Ripper victims, all of whom were frightfully well known.

Perhaps he'd killed her and they'd discovered the body, maybe buried her themselves, rather than risk the public scrutiny of a police investigation? Or perhaps—and he swallowed hard, at the thought— perhaps the Whitehall torso, due to be discovered on October third, was Ianira? He tried to shut out such a vision, even in imagination, but he couldn't think what other reason Marcus might have for wanting to murder Jack the Ripper.

A swift glance toward Margo prompted him to settle his arm about her shoulders. She was crying, silently, wiping away the tears with trembling hands. Clearly, her thoughts had wandered down the same hideous corridors his had just done. She looked up and tried to smile, then her face crumpled and she covered it with both hands, trying to compose herself. Malcolm clenched his jaw and stared coldly at Dr. John Lachley, loathing him with a far more personal hatred than he could ever have mustered for a mere psychotic serial killer. If this man had truly destroyed Ianira Cassondra . . .

With a bleakness like death, Malcolm realized there wasn't a great deal anyone could do about it. Jack the Ripper could not be killed. Not until Mary Kelly had died, if then. It gradually occurred to Malcolm to wonder why Dominica Nosette and Guy Pendergast weren't here. Surely the reporters would've tried to film such a historic lecture, given by the Ripper? Blast those two! They'd trailed Maybrick last night, wandering into camera range at all three key sites: Dutfield's Yard, Mitre Square, and Goulston Street. Had they met with misfortune in the process of tailing Maybrick and Lachley?

He narrowed his gaze, wondering abruptly why Dr. Lachley

seemed so manic, up at the podium. Perhaps he was always a disjointed, rambling speaker? A glance at the crowd suggested otherwise. Several listeners looked puzzled, even concerned as they watched Lachley, who was literally trembling behind the lectern. A few were whispering among themselves, clearly wondering about it.

Mysteries on top of mysteries . . .

Lachley ended the lecture abruptly, a wild look in his eyes as the audience applauded, giving him a standing ovation that was, perhaps, out of line with the quality of his oration, but which was a strong testament to the popularity and power of the Celtic revival sweeping through nineteenth-century British society. Malcolm surged to his feet, as well, trying to keep Lachley in sight as the man stepped down into the crowd, shaking hands. Malcolm caught sight of Shahdi Feroz speaking briefly with Lachley and knew a moment's worry for her safety, despite Conroy Melvyn's presence at her side, then glanced back to where Marcus and the others sat . . . and swore aloud.

"*Bloody hell!* They've gone!"

"What?"

"Marcus and Catlin! They've gone!"

Malcolm shoved his way impatiently through the audience, trying to reach the door. Margo struggled gamely behind him. Malcolm reached the street well before she did, but Catlin and his group were nowhere in sight. Margo, out of breath from running in her form-fitting watered silk, skidded to a halt beside him. "I'm sorry!" she wailed. "I was too short to see over everybody's heads and didn't notice them leave!"

He stood breathing hard for a moment, wrestling his anger under control, then said, "Let's get back inside, blast it! The least we can do is trace Lachley!"

"Malcolm, it isn't your fault."

"No, but it is, too. We were charged with locating Catlin as well as tasked with identifying the Ripper. And the future of the station is far more seriously affected by Catlin's disappearance than any of our work verifying the Ripper's identity."

"I know," she said in a small voice. "At least we know Catlin's alive, now," she said with grim determination, "which is better news than we thought we might end up with, after following that horrible blood trail across London. You know," she said suddenly, frowning in concentration, "if Benny Catlin and Marcus have it in for John Lachley, they might try to ambush him at his house."

Malcolm shot her a startled glance. "Good God, Margo. You're onto something, there."

"So what do we do about it?"

He frowned. "We collect Madame Feroz and Chief Inspector Melvyn before we do anything. Then perhaps we'd best follow Lachley home? If Catlin and Marcus *are* there, they'll be in far greater danger than Lachley will, because *he* jolly well can't be killed."

Margo's face, already pinched with worry, drained white in a single heartbeat. "Malcolm, we have to find them!"

"Get back inside, warn Madame Feroz and Inspector Melvyn that we may need to leave in a hurry. The Spaldergate carriage isn't due to collect us for another thirty minutes. I'll find some sort of transport to hire, so we can follow Lachley."

"Right." She hurried into the Egyptian Hall, lifting her skirts to make running easier. Malcolm swore under his breath, then headed down Piccadilly in search of a cab that would hold all four of them. He worked very hard to dispel the vision of what would happen if Marcus tangled with Jack the Ripper. He had a sinking feeling that neither Dominica Nosette nor Guy Pendergast would ever be seen again. He didn't want that happening to anyone he called friend. If he'd thought he could persuade Margo to return to Spaldergate, he'd have packed her off immediately. But he knew only too well the futility of trying, so he set his jaw and vowed to do what he could to ensure that no more of his charges ended up missing or dead.

So far, in this lethal little game they played, Jack the Ripper had won every round.

Jenna stood in the shadows beside the garden wall behind Dr. John Lachley's house in Cleveland Street, clutching the Beale's revolver she'd brought with her from New York, and waited in a swivet for Noah to reappear. The detective had forced a window casement at the rear of the house and was searching quietly for any trace of Ianira

Cassondra. Across the street, Marcus waited to give the alarm, should Lachley arrive before Noah finished the search.

Come on, she breathed silently, *what's taking so long?* She expected Dr. Lachley to return at any moment, expected to hear a scuffle break out inside, terrified that Lachley's manservant, whom they'd spotted in the front parlour, would hear Noah's footsteps and go to investigate. *If he's got a telephone in there, he might even summon the police!* That's all they'd need, to be arrested by London's constabulary for thievery of a respected physician's home.

When Marcus' whistle of warning came, Jenna's heart thundered into her throat. She melted back into the high, walled garden as a carriage rattled and clattered into the drive, coach lanterns gleaming in the darkness. Jenna trembled as she flattened against the inside of the wall, pistol clutched in one fist. *He's back! Oh, God, he's back and Noah's still inside!* She heard Lachley's voice, giving instructions to his coachman to stable the horse, then the carriage-entrance door opened and closed with a rattle and thump and Lachley was inside. She waited, not even breathing, for the shouts to erupt as Noah was discovered . . .

"Hsst! Come on, kid! Let's move!"

She swallowed a scream and nearly went to the ground as Noah materialized from the darkness of the garden. "Noah!"

The detective grasped her arm and led her rapidly through the gate, which they eased closed, then jogged down the carriage drive, slipping past the open stable door. They reached Cleveland Street without being spotted and headed for Marcus. Jenna glanced over her shoulder toward Lachley's home, where lights were coming up in various windows, as Noah began to speak, voice lowered to a whisper. "It's quite clear Ianira was held in an upstairs room for some time. Not only are there toiletries for a lady and clothing of Ianira's size, there are long, dark hairs matching Ianira's, caught in the hairbrush. She is not, however, in the house now. He's moved her. Where, we must discover."

Jenna's heart sank. Marcus' face ran pale in the light from a distant gas lamp. Then Jenna started. "Look! He's coming out again."

They glanced around quickly, even as Noah herded them all into the darkness of a neighboring yard. Lachley had, indeed, emerged through the carriage-drive entrance. Dressed in rough clothes, with an old felt hat pulled low over his brow, hiding his face in shadow, he set out on foot, walking swiftly down Cleveland Street, then turned and headed toward the distant river.

The moment he vanished from view, Noah darted across the road. Jenna and Marcus exchanged glances, then ran after the detective at top speed. They passed a carriage where two gentlemen were involved in a domestic dispute with their wives over a stray muff, then moved steadily eastward, leaving behind the fashionable districts. They came out on a street Jenna recognized as Drury Lane, the same street Noah had carried her down the night Lachley had shot her.

They followed Drury Lane for its entire length and burst out eventually onto the Strand, where they plunged into a maelstrom of shoving, shouting men and boys on Fleet Street. Gradually, they angled toward Bishopsgate and the East End. Jenna wasn't used to so much walking and struggled gamely to keep up, crossing busy Commercial Street into the heart of Whitechapel, then moving south down Brick Lane, past breweries that left the air smelling of spilt beer, past brick-making factories where giant kilns glowed hellishly in the darkness, fire-curing bricks by the millions. They headed down toward Flower and Dean Street, where women strolled the streets mostly alone, a few walking in pairs or small clusters, their eyes bright with fear and misery, soliciting rough-dressed men who emerged from pubs and gin palaces and gambling hells.

Past Flower and Dean, Lachley took them into a narrow alleyway between ramshackle doss houses. A stink of urine rose like a miasma. Jenna closed her hand around the butt of her pistol, which she'd thrust deep into her coat pocket. They moved steadily down the narrow way, boots squelching in mud and God alone knew what else. Jenna certainly didn't want to know. Halfway along, Lachley interrupted a streetwalker and her customer in the midst of the transaction for which she was being paid. Mercifully, Jenna caught only a glimpse of white thighs under the woman's hiked up skirts as Lachley shoved past, with curses flung after him.

"Sod off, y'bloody feather plucker, or I'll shove me beetle crusher up yer Kyber Parse!"

To which Lachley flung back, "Don't threaten me, y'stroppy brass nail!"

Fortunately, the angry prostitute was far too occupied—and so was her client—to offer any real trouble, not even when Noah plunged past, leading the pursuit. Lachley stalked steadily southward, toward the distant river, down past garment factories where gaslights burned to illuminate rows of sewing machines. Tailors and sweat-shop seamstresses worked in such factories for twelve and sixteen-hour shifts, six days a week, churning out ready-made clothing for an empire. Jenna thanked God they hadn't been forced to take up such work to keep from starving.

What's a respectable doctor like John Lachley doing skulking around the East End? Unless . . . Jenna blinked in sudden, startled conjecture. *Unless he's Jack the Ripper! Oh, my God, the facts fit! Poor Ianira! Is she even still alive?*

They barrelled through a crowd of men gathered on a street corner, talking loudly about what ought to be done about the maniac stalking women on these streets. "Sorry," Noah doffed his hat as angry protests rose on all sides, "don't want any bother, we're on the trail of a missing lady . . ."

"Ah, gwan, y'sozzled face-ache," one of the angry men flung after them, "better keep goin' clappers or I'm like to put me bunch o' fives in yer mince!"

As Jenna shoved her way through in Noah's wake, one of the other men muttered, "Button it, Albert, an' lay off the gin, you're drunk as a boiled owl. It's clear they got trouble, all right, Gawd 'elp if it's this bleedin' Ripper again . . ." A block further on, a Salvation Army quartet blared away into the damp night while a frowsy woman with three children half-hidden in her skirts listened intently to the singers. The music sounded like a spiritualized rewrite of an old drinking song, "What Can You Do with a Drunken Sailor?" but included the unlikely refrain, "Anybody here like a sneaking Judas?"

Further along, a shouting match broke out between two very drunken sailors and the badly dressed women who accompanied them. One of the girls, who couldn't have been above thirteen years of age, was pulling a long swig from a gin bottle. Jenna wanted to avert her gaze as they rushed past, but she'd seen worse since arriving in the East End—and was afraid she'd see far worse, yet, before this night ended.

As Noah took them around a corner, an angry roar of voices erupted behind them. Jenna glanced back to see an immense crowd of men burst from a side street and utterly engulf the sailors, their hired girls, and the Salvation Army quartet. They were shouting about the Ripper, making demands and ugly threats that left Jenna intensely grateful they'd missed being swept up with the rioters. She turned and hurried after Noah. Lachley, still oblivious to their pursuit, led them down into Wapping where they encountered two neatly dressed, earnest young men with American accents. The Americans were speaking with a group of women and ragged children.

"No, ladies, the golden tablets of Moroni don't set aside the Bible, not at all. They are only Christ's revelation of His word in the New World, translated by His prophet Joseph Smith. Here, let me read from this pamphlet, it will help explain the new gospel . . ."

They passed the Mormons, still moving south, and walked all the way to Pennington Street, where enormous brick warehouses lined the road. Jenna could smell the stink of the river. Just beyond the warehouses lay the great London Docks, with the enormous Western Basin closest to them now. The smaller and older St. Katharine's Docks lay to their immediate west, cut into the reeking earth of Wapping, so that streets ended abruptly at the waterside, with immense ships pulled up like cars parked along the kerb. Lachley ignored the docks and led them east, deeper into Wapping. *Did he take her on board a ship?* Jenna wondered. *What would be the point? Unless he's leaving England?* Fear skittered through her nerves.

They left Pennington Street three blocks further along, winding back into filthy, crowded alleyways north of the warehouses. Sailors thronged the streets, shoving their way roughly into stinking pubs and gambling dens, brawling in the middle of the road, singing boistrously in as many as five languages within two blocks' distance. Hollow-cheeked, dull-eyed children sat along the kerb, begging for a few pence. And still Lachley led them back into the maze, past groups of furtive men who eyed them, considered it, then thought better after weighing the odds.

And finally, at one of the sagging, broken-windowed houses along a street where gaslights were as rare as police constables and chickens' teeth, Lachley finally stopped. He unlocked a door and vanished into a tumble-down brick house with filthy, broken glass windows. These were dark. The house was silent, seemingly deserted. Jenna glanced at Noah, then Marcus. "What now?"

Noah was frowning thoughtfully at the door. "If we annouce ourselves, it might provoke him into panic-stricken, drastic action. I don't want to give him time for that."

The detective tested the door gently, then backed up and smashed his booted foot against the heavy panel. The lock splintered on the second try. Jenna dragged her pistol out of her pocket and rushed in on Noah's heels. Marcus brought up the rear. They found a cheerless room empty of anything save bits of refuse and appalling drifts of filth along the floor. A swift search, downstairs and up, revealed only one inhabitant: an enormous black hound chained in a room near the back of the house. The dog had been dead for a couple of days, judging from the stench. Beside the hideous, putrifying corpse lay a rug someone had turned back. And under the rug could be seen the outlines of a trap door.

"Right," Noah said briskly, pulling up the trap.

Marcus helped lift the planks while Jenna gulped back nausea. Stone steps, damp brick walls, the smell and splash of water . . . They could hear Lachley's footsteps receding quickly and Jenna caught a faint flicker of light at the bottom of the hole, which vanished a moment later. Noah glanced up into Jenna's eyes. The gun in Noah's hand looked like part of the detective's arm, an organic piece that had grown there, like the fine hairs on the back of Noah's wrist and the chipped nails that tipped short, strong fingers. "I'd feel better if you stayed here."

"I ain't no weed," she muttered, quoting the girl who delivered their milk every morning. "And if you tell me to stay here, well, then, same t'you, wiv brass knobs on . . ."

Noah frowned. "You're picking up the slang pretty well, aren't you?

But that doesn't make you a match for a thing like Lachley. He's a bloody dangerous bastard. Stay behind me."

"No argument, there," she muttered.

Marcus found a stub of candle in a battered tin holder beside the bed and a wooden box with matches, printed with the trade name Lucifers. Marcus lit the candle and handed it to Noah, who led the way down the narrow stone steps. Marcus pocketed the matches and Jenna edged down the steps next, leaving Marcus to bring up rear guard. The stink of decay and filthy water clouted her nostrils well before her feet touched the wet floor below. There was no cellar, as Jenna had been expecting. They were standing in a brick tunnel, its arched roof clotted with cobwebs and stained with poisonous patches of mold and lichen. Water trickled and dripped in the distance.

"What kind of place is this?" Jenna breathed.

"Sewer tunnel, I'd guess," Noah answered, the whisper harsh and strained. "Lachley knows his way around, that's clear." They couldn't see Lachley's lantern, but his footsteps came with a faint echo from further along the sewer tunnel. Jenna stared into the pitchy darkness, then swallowed as Noah set out with soft-footed stealth. She cast a doubtful glance at Marcus, whose eyes were tortured. But they hadn't much choice. Jenna clutched her revolver, the grip solid and reassuring against her palm, and eased forward, trying to walk without her footsteps splashing. Jenna strained to catch the faintest echo of sound in the clammy darkness, but heard only the distant rush of water and Lachley's sharp, clattering footsteps far ahead. The sound ran away down the tunnels, leaving Jenna biting her lip.

"Hsst!"

At that sharp sound from Noah, Jenna froze. Her lungs rasped in the silence and her heart slammed against her ribs. Sweat, cold and dank as the putrid air, clung to hair and skin and eyelashes. She listened . . .

"*Bloody bitch!*" A man's voice echoed through the sewers, fierce with some nameless rage that left the tiny hairs along Jenna's nape and arms starkly erect. Her fingers tightened of their own volition around the butt of her gun. A bloodcurdling scream, high and ragged, pierced the blackness. A woman's scream . . .

The woman was sobbing out, "Don't kill me, please, I won't tell anyone you're the Ripper, please, just let me go home!" The woman's voice, clearly British, shook on a wild note of despair.

"That is not Ianira," Marcus breathed.

"*What time does the gate go?*" Lachley's voice . . .

"I don't know!"

"What time was it when you came through, then?"

A choked-off cry of pain floated through the sewer tunnels. "About—about eight o'clock, I think . . . it was just dusk . . . oh, God, please . . . *no!*"

She screamed again, high, ragged. The sound cut off hideously. Jenna stood trembling, torn between the need to stay hidden and the need to rush forward, to stop whatever ghastly torture was underway. A moment later another sound drifted through the sewers, a sound Jenna couldn't identify at first. Heavy, rhythmic thumps, a grating, scraping sound, like someone hacking apart a cow's carcass. Jenna covered her mouth with the back of one shaking hand. Then they heard footfalls and a heavy thump that echoed like a door closing.

Someone was moving through the sewers toward them, splashing quickly through the water. For a long, horrible moment, Jenna thought he was coming back toward them. Noah blew out the candle, plunging them into a terrifying darkness. Lachley's footsteps approached to within a frightful distance, accompanied by a lantern's dim glow, then faded once more, moving away down another route and disappearing back into the maze of sewer tunnels.

Jenna discovered that she was shaking violently. Minutes crawled past in the utter blackness of the stinking sewer while doubt and fear banged around the inside of her skull like screaming, imprisoned monkeys. The echoes of Lachley's footsteps had long since faded, but still they didn't move, scarcely daring to breathe. At last, Noah shifted. The detective whispered, "Marcus, let's have a lucifer, please." A match flared and Marcus relit the candle.

Light sprang up, yellow and warm and glorious, revealing ashen faces. Jenna swallowed hard, hands trembling visibly. "Wherever he was torturing that poor woman, it's not far."

"He closed a door of some kind," Noah mused. "Perhaps another trap door. We'll try to find it and see if he's hidden Ianira down here with his other captive."

A cross-tunnel intersected their own. Noah turned left, opposite the direction Lachley had taken. Jenna cast worried glances back over her shoulder every few seconds, terrified the monstrous killer behind them would turn and come back, having heard their footsteps. Her hand sweat on the grip of her pistol despite the chill in the foetid air. Jenna knew her gun was useless against Jack the Ripper. He *couldn't* be killed tonight, not before Mary Kelly died, more than a month in the future. But it was all she had and just holding it made her feel slightly less panic-stricken.

"Well, blow me for a game of soldiers . . ." Noah muttered.

The low-voiced exclamation brought Jenna around. "What is it?"

"An iron door! Locked tight as a drum."

The low door had been set back into an alcove. Clearly, John Lachley had come from behind that door. Jenna tested it, searched for a lock, realized that without a key, they would never get in. The hinge-pins were on the inside, so they couldn't even lift the door off. "What we need is a key."

"We'll have to make do with a lockpick," Noah muttered. "I've cultivated the habit of carrying a set, during the past three years. With your father's killers on our trail, we've occasionally needed a fast entrance into a hiding place. Fortunately," the detective fished into a coat pocket, coming out with a set of burglar's tools and crouching before the door, slipping them expertly into the keyhole, "Victorian locks are generally large, clumsy, and easy to open." Marcus held the candle close to the lock, giving Noah the best light available. The lockpicks scraped and scratched inside the iron door, then something grated and clicked.

"Got it!"

The sudden silence was thick with tension.

The heavy door swung noiselessly open, which spoke of constant oiling and maintenance in this damp environment. Surprisingly, the room beyond was not dark. Gas jets in the floor lit a scene from someone's private version of hell. Jenna's skin crawled as she stepped across the threshold, following Noah. She choked the instant she was inside. The sickly odor of rotting meat struck her like a physical blow. The stench permeated the air, foul and thick. When she saw what lay on the floor, Jenna realized with a shock of horror what the stink actually was.

"*Oh, my God!*"

Somebody had spilled a great deal of blood in this room. And pieces of at least two fresh corpses had been stacked up beside the door like cordwood. Arms, legs, gobbets she couldn't readily identify. And two severed heads, a dark-haired man's and a blonde-haired woman's. They rested on a work bench which stretched beneath cupboards along one long wall, sightless eyes staring at the door, faces set in ghastly expressions of terror and agony. White robes hung from a hook set into the bricks. Dark brown stains were visible across the sleeves and front. A stone pedestal that looked very much like an altar stood in the middle of the room. On top was another severed head, its flesh and hair still rotting off the bones. From what little remained, it looked like it had once belonged to a young boy, a teenager. An enormous tree trunk, with many of its major branches intact, took up at least half the space. Iron brackets and bands held the tree together where it had been sawn apart to get it into the room. Ianira, hands bound above her head, hung naked from an iron hook set into one enormous branch, limp and unconscious, her ribcage barely lifting with her shallow breaths. Gas jets at the base of the tree shone across her skin.

"Oh, sweet Mother Mary . . ." Noah whispered, voice harsh.

Marcus had already whipped off his coat, was lifting Ianira down and wrapping her nude body gently in its folds. Jenna, keeping her jaw tightly clenched, found a knife on the work table and used it to slice through the ropes on Ianira's wrists. Marcus was smoothing hair back from his wife's brow, trying to rouse her.

"She's been drugged," Noah said tersely. "I can smell the chloroform."

"Bastard!" Marcus snarled. "I will put a bullet through him!"

Noah said tersely, "Just now, our business is getting the hell out of here before the maniac who owns this place comes back."

The detective stepped to the door and peered into the darkness while Jenna pressed one hand against her mouth, struggling desperately not to throw up. The blonde woman must have been the one who'd screamed. And they'd just stood there, listening, while he hacked her apart . . . She bolted past Noah into the darkness of the sewer tunnel and threw up in the murky water against the far wall. The slight current washed the mess away, even as she shuddered and choked again. Noah bent over her shoulder. "You all right?" the detective asked worriedly.

She nodded, and finally managed to straighten up. "Sorry," she whispered, wiping her mouth. "Couldn't help it."

"God, no," the detective managed through clenched teeth. Noah looked very near to being ill, as well. Marcus carried his wife out of the stinking chamber. Noah closed the door and fiddled with the lock again. "Think I'll leave it the way we found it. Let him sweat, wondering how a drugged victim got out of a locked room. Ought to bother the hell out of him."

"If it's all the same to you," Jenna said through chattering teeth, "I'd just as soon not go back through his house in Wapping. I don't want to meet him coming back, not for anything in this world."

Noah's glance was keen. "I couldn't agree more." The detective peered both ways down the tunnel through narrowed eyes. "We must be near the river. We weren't all that far from London Docks when we climbed down those steps. With the distance and direction we came, the Thames must be close by, off that way." Noah pointed at the wall behind them. "Western Basin's probably off that direction, so I'd say we need to go that way." Noah nodded down the tunnel opposite the direction they'd come.

"Let's go, then," Marcus said quietly. "We need to get Ianira to safety and have Doctor Mindel look at her."

It was a silent and tense group that set out through the maze of sewer tunnels beneath the East End's filthy streets, searching for a way out.

(((Chapter 11)))

John Lachley carried Dominica Nosette's hacked up torso a long way through the sewer tunnels. The bundle he'd slung over one shoulder was heavy and he paused frequently to shift it, but Lachley never considered simply dumping it and turning back. He wanted to leave her somewhere appropriate and had tumbled to just the perfect spot. When he finally reached the place, he paused, listening to the rumble of carriage traffic through a grating overhead, then smiled and turned off into a freshly broken opening in the sewer. The vaulted space in which he found himself was destined to become part of the cellar of New Scotland Yard. The police headquarters, still under construction, was directly overhead.

Lachley smiled to himself and dumped the butchered remains of his pathetic little journalist where workmen would find her, then tipped his cloth hat. "Ta, luv." He grinned, using the voice of his childhood. "I'm obliged, Miss Nosette, that I am."

Then he set out the way he'd come, whistling jauntily to himself. The tunnels he followed to reach Tibor snaked and twisted in multiple directions, following gas mains and sewage flows and underground streams bricked over, odd corners and chambers formed out of the remnant cellars of sixteenth- and seventeenth-, even eighteenth-century warehouses and wharfside pubs, all connected like gladiator tunnels beneath an ancient fighting arena. As he walked, he planned exactly what he would do when he carried Ianira to Spaldergate House.

He'd kept the identification papers and cards he'd found in Miss Nosette's possession, as well as those from the recently deceased Mr. Pendergast's pockets. Lachley was quite confident that no one would notice the switch in a dark garden. He would rush in, carrying Ianira, claim to be Pendergast and babble out some story about being attacked by the Ripper, then simply carry her through into the station. He could hardly wait to see what the station was really like. With Ianira in his power, there was no limit to what he could do in such a place.

When he reached Lower Tibor, John Lachley was in exceedingly high spirits.

He set his lantern down with a faint splash. The iron key from his pocket grated in the lock, which clicked open. He slid the key back into his coat, then stooped to retrieve his lantern. The door opened silently at his touch, swinging back on its well-oiled hinges. Light from the perpetual flames burning in the gas jets at the altar welcomed him home again . . .

And John Lachley froze halfway through the door.

She was gone.

He literally could not take it in, could not comprehend the emptiness his senses told him existed in the room. He had left her hanging from the iron hook in the great branch above the altar, the hook he'd dangled Morgan from, the night that miserable little sod had died, had left her hanging as naked as he'd left the boy, bound and drugged senseless. There was no humanly possible way she could have freed herself from the ropes and the iron hook, much less escape from a brick vault with only one door in or out. And that iron door had been firmly locked, the lock not forced in any way he could see. Yet she was undeniably gone.

Nothing in this chamber could have provided hiding space for a child, let alone a full-grown woman. He stood there with his hand uplifted against the cold iron of the open door, gaze jerking from shelf to cabinet to altar and up to the massive tree trunk and back to the shelves again. *How had she gotten out?* The key in his pocket was not a standard iron skeleton key. It would've taken a master locksmith to slip this lock. Or a duplicate key. Or an extremely talented thief. Had someone broken in here, then, and carried her off? *Who?*

He could not conceive of a master locksmith having sufficient motive to pick his way through a maze of sewer tunnels until stumbling across this one particular alcove, to open a locked iron door. It simply wasn't *reasonable*. Common locksmiths didn't have the imagination to attempt such a thing! And why would a thief have ventured here? There'd been nothing in that entire house in Wapping worth stealing, if a thief had come down that way. A duplicate key, then? That was even more absurd than the other possible explanations. Take a wax impression, create a mould, cast a key, all in a single hour's time, with the owner of this door likely to return at any moment, irate and possibly murderous?

The longer he pursued a sane explanation, the faster sanity ran through his fingers like the dirty water under his feet. Lachley's drugged captive simply could not have gotten out. But she had. And Lachley's greatest refuge, the result of years of labour and intensive study—his very *life* if this place were connected with the deaths of the whores—everything he had built was now threatened, because the bitch had *gotten out!*

The explosion jolted the very bedrock of his sanity.

Fury was an expanding fireball inside him, an anarchist's bomb, a Fenian detonation that sent him plunging across the room, hands so violently unsteady he dropped the lantern with a crash of broken glass and spreading lamp oil. He searched places too small for a mouse to hide, but found no trace of her. A knife had been moved from his workbench and used by *someone* to cut through the ropes on her wrists, ropes he found abandoned on the floor. Someone must have followed him down, picked the lock while he was out.

Lachley swore savagely. He had been so careful, confound it, so bloody careful . . . Had someone recognized him, after all? Recognized the heavily moustachioed man in seedy clothes as the thin and seething boy he'd once been in these streets? Lachley had barely gone twenty when he'd last walked Wapping and Whitechapel, passing himself off as parlour mediumist Johnny Anubis. But who else *could* it have been, if not some god-cursed tea leaf who'd grass on his own loving wife, if a reward might be involved?

He halfway expected to find all of Scotland Yard crouched in the tunnel beyond the open door to Tibor, billycocks at the ready. What he found was a black expanse of dripping brick tunnel, silent and cold as a tomb, just as he'd left it. Lachley stood motionless, gazing at the ruin of his sanctuary, breathing hard and trying to think what he should do. Going home might be fatal. Whether an East Ender had recognized him as Jack the Ripper or the girl's husband had trailed him down here, whoever had taken Ianira had discovered enough to hang Lachley from the nearest gallows. He had to get out of London. Before the police *did* trace him. Well, the gate into the future would open near dusk tomorrow evening, which meant he had to elude capture for only twenty-four hours.

Dominica Nosette's severed head stared blindly at him from his work bench, unable to tell him its secrets. He'd have to take the head with him, he realized slowly. Tell them he'd been trying to locate his partner and had found her hacked to pieces in the sewers, that he'd been able to recover only her decapitated skull. Yes, that's what he would do to gain admittance to the gate, he'd shock them all with her bloody head, then step through while they bleated about what ought to be done.

Moving with calm deliberation, Lachley found a wooden box beneath the work bench and dumped out the implements inside, then replaced them with Miss Nosette's head. He packed away a few other items he'd want along, shoving them into a leather satchel, mind racing. *Can't bloody well go home, I might find the coppers waiting for me. I'll have to stop at the bank tomorrow, secure funds to buy some decent clothing. Best not withdraw too much, don't want to tip my hand that I'm leaving. Better sleep the night in a hotel room or better yet, a doss house. Fewer questions to answer, that way, arriving without luggage . . .*

Decision made, Lachley stripped off his bloodstained clothing and shoes, changed into spare garments he kept on hand for just such emergencies, then carried his satchel and wooden case outside, locking the door to Tibor one last time. He'd never dreamed the day would come he'd leave the sanctuary for all time. But his fate was sealed and his plans were made. He would get onto that station, come hell or high water or the damned souls of all eternity, trying to bar the way.

He literally had nowhere else to go.

Malcolm had been to Cleveland Street before, with wealthy tourists who wanted to visit the famous art studios, hoping to buy canvases or commission fine souvenir portraits. He'd never guided tourists to the street's other, more infamous destinations, of course, although a number of zipper jockey tours did, in fact, include stops at Cleveland Street's homosexual brothels. Malcolm found it somewhat ironic that Jack the Ripper had chosen to live sandwiched between London's higher and lower arts and wondered if John Lachley's unstable personality had been affected by the proximity of the brothels.

They had trailed Lachley's carriage halfway across London, following at a discreet distance. When Lachley pulled into a drive and halted, Malcolm asked the cabbie to pull up to the kerb a full block short of Lachley's home. "I think it would be wiser to leave the ladies here and scout this out on foot, Mr. Melvyn."

"But—" Margo protested.

"No. I will not unnecessarily risk either you or Dr. Feroz." He spoke in a whisper to prevent the driver from overhearing, and would brook no argument. "We came here to discover why Marcus is trailing him, not to put either of you ladies in the path of Jack the Ripper. And there's Marcus now, across the street there." He pointed to the dark hedge sheltering the ex-slave from view of Lachley's house. Marcus watched Lachley enter his home by the side entrance and gave out a warning call, a clear and piercing bird's trill in the gathering dusk and gloom. "Want to bet his friends are inside, searching the house?" Margo pouted and favored him with one of her famous stationary flounces, refusing to honor his friendly wager with an answer, but gave him no further trouble. "Driver," Malcolm said a little more loudly, "please be kind enough to wait here with the ladies while we determine whether or not our acquaintance is at home."

"Right, guv'nor."

Conroy Melvyn joined Malcolm on the pavement. "D'you want to go right up and talk to your friend?" the inspector asked quietly, nodding slightly toward Marcus.

"It is tempting, as Marcus appears to be alone."

"What's your plan, then?"

Malcolm was about to reply when someone left Dr. Lachley's house at a brisk walk. Poorly dressed, he would have looked more at home in Whitechapel than Cleveland Street. Whoever the man was, he was headed straight toward them. Malcolm's eyes widened when he realized who it was. "Bloody hell," Malcolm hissed, "it's *Lachley.*" He turned at once to the carriage, leaning inside to murmur with the ladies as Lachley approached. Conroy Melvyn also turned to the carriage and said for Lachley's benefit, "Confound it, ladies, we shall be quite late! We haven't time to return and fetch your muff! If you'd wanted it, you should have secured it before calling for the carriage!"

Lachley strode past without a second glance.

Malcolm peered over his shoulder and caught a glimpse of Marcus, who had been joined by Benny Catlin and the other man from the Egyptian Hall. They trailed Lachley straight past the carriage, Marcus and the others passing literally within touching distance. Margo was wailing, "But I must have my muff, Geoffrey, I simply must! Oh, you beastly man, I cannot face Lady Hampton without it, after that dreadful creature showed me up last Saturday with her ermine . . ."

The moment Marcus and his companions had passed, Malcolm handed both ladies down. "We dare not follow in the carriage," he murmured, securing coin to pay the driver. "I fear you ladies are not dressed for hiking, but there's no help for it."

Margo said cheerfully, "I'll worry about blisters on my heels after I've got 'em."

The driver was shaking his head, mystified, as he drove off. Malcolm set out briskly, feeling some affinity for the tail end of a freight train as they whipped through the streets in pursuit. Lachley, far ahead, was moving rapidly. Both Margo and Dr. Feroz had difficulty keeping up. Their fashionably tight skirts and heeled shoes forced them to trot along with mincing little steps.

"Where the devil is he heading?" Inspector Melvyn wondered aloud as they moved steadily eastward, angling down toward the river. "It's the wrong night for another Ripper strike."

"Maybe he's hunting for Mary Kelly?" Margo suggested.

"Without Maybrick? Deuced unlikely, I should think. He kills to a pattern."

"Perhaps," Shahdi Feroz mused, "he works alone to locate the women, then strikes with Maybrick as his weapon?"

Margo put in suddenly, "Maybe the Whitehall torso *is* one of his victims? Somebody he meets tonight? The torso will be discovered just two days from now, after all."

"Another of these unfortunates in possession of his letters?" Inspector Melvyn frowned. "Blast, I wish we knew what these letters were!"

"You said a mouthful," Margo muttered, struggling to keep up.

As they trailed their double quarry steadily eastward, into increasingly poorer districts, Malcolm's misgivings increased just as steadily. They were dressed to the nines, all of them, and Lachley was leading them straight toward the East End, where gentlemen in fancy dress coats and ladies in silk evening gowns would stand out like beacon fires, inviting attack by footpads. Lachley took them down Drury Lane, echoing another night's anxious search, when they'd trailed Benny Catlin with bloodhounds. Tonight, at least, Catlin was in plain sight. They emerged, as they had that previous night, onto the Strand. Lachley headed down through Fleet Street, moving briskly.

Malcolm plunged into the crowds thronging the jammed pavements, trying to keep the others in sight. As the heart and soul of the British printing industry, Fleet Street was clogged by literally hundreds of newspaper reporters, ink-stained printers' journeymen and apprentices, bootblacks, newsboys scurrying along with stacks of the latest editions piled high, and women of dubious status all jostling elbows as they fought for space in the pubs, comandeered hansom cabs, and paid street urchins to run errands for them—all struggling to outwit one another in the business of keeping the Empire apprised of the latest news. From here, reports of the shocking, double Ripper murders had raced outward by telegraph to claim massive headlines across the length and breadth of the British Isles and far beyond.

From out of pubs with names like Ye Olde Cheshire Cheese wafted the multitudinous smells of cheap sandwiches, greasy fried potatoes, and enough alcohol to inebriate several herds of elephants. Malcolm wondered fleetingly just how many journalists affiliated with newspapers like the prestigious *Times* and the *Star* or penny dreadfuls with lofty-sounding titles like the *Penny Illustrated Paper and Illustrated Times* or the *Illustrated Police News* were combing the East End tonight, looking for leads to the Ripper case? Given the number of men and boys crowding these pavements, only a fraction of those he'd expected to cover the case. Fleet Street *seethed*.

"The ladies can't keep up!" Conroy Melvyn called above the roar of voices and bar songs, the rumble of carriage wheels, and the neighing of several hundred, snorting horses in the street. Margo and Shahdi Feroz were struggling through the thick crowds, falling farther and farther behind. Malcolm craned for a glimpse of Benny Catlin and Marcus. "Blast it, we'll lose them! Margo, we can't afford delays. Hire a cab and take Dr. Feroz back to Spaldergate. Let them know what's happening."

"But—"

"No argument! We haven't time!"

"Oh, all right!" she snapped, cheeks flushed with temper as well as brisk walking. "Come on, Shahdi, let's go home like good little girls!" She stormed off in search of a cab for hire, taking the Ripperologist with her.

"I shall pay for that, presently," Malcolm sighed, hurrying after their escaping quarry. The Scotland Yard inspector gave him a sympathetic glance as Lachley led them down past Shoreditch into the heart of Whitechapel, moving steadily eastward and skirting his way closer to the river.

"He isn't going anywhere near Miller's Court, is he?" Malcolm muttered.

Before the inspector could reply, a roar of angry voices erupted from the street just ahead. An immense crowd of angry men spilled out into their path, shouting demands for better police patrols, more gaslights, for a reward to be offered by Her Majesty's government for the Ripper's capture . . .

"Hurry!" Malcolm cried, darting forward. He shoved his way into the mass of shouting workmen who were still spilling out onto the street, unable to push his way through. "Mr. Lusk!" someone was shouting at his elbow. "Mr. Lusk, is it true you asked the authorities to offer a reward for information on the Ripper's accomplices?" The man shouting the question held a notebook and a stub of pencil, trying to scribble down information as he was jostled by the swarm of angry Vigilance Committee members and loiterers swept up in the crowd.

"They told me t'bugger off!" Lusk shouted back, whipping up a roar from the crowd. "Aren't goin' to pay blood money, they said, t'catch nobody!" The head of the Whitechapel Vigilance Committee was furious, justifiably so. As a prominent East End businessman, Lusk had to live and work here, wondering which of his friends or family members might be butchered next, while police officials like Sir Charles Warren sat safe and insulated in their headquarters and stately homes to the west.

Malcolm fought his way past angry tradesmen, struggling to reach the far street corner where Marcus and the others had vanished. Several men flung curses after him when he shouldered past and one beefy lout swung at him, but by the time the punch landed, Malcolm had dodged past. Shouts erupted in his wake, then he was finally through the mass of seething protestors. Conroy Melvyn struggled out on his heels, panting. "Where'd they go?" the inspector gasped.

"I don't know! Dammit, I can't see them anywhere!" Malcolm plunged down the street at a run, heedless of stares, but within three blocks, they had to admit defeat. Marcus and Benny Catlin and the other gentleman trailing John Lachley had vanished into the maze of dark alleyways, swallowed alive by the black gloom which lurked just beyond Whitechapel's major thoroughfares. Malcolm kept hunting, stubbornly, for nearly an hour, while Conroy Melvyn questioned passers-by in search of clues, running into suspicion and close-mouthed wariness again and again. Not even the lure of shining crowns—coins worth more than a month's good wages in these streets—shook loose any information.

"Well," the inspector muttered, pocketing the last of his crowns, "looks like they've given us the slip, all right. What now, Moore?"

Malcolm grimaced, eying a knot of roughly dressed men loitering near the entrance to the Kings Stores Pub at the corner of Widegate Street and Sandy's Row, a building once famed as Henry the Eighth's arsenal. Several of the loafing roustabouts were buying roasted chestnuts from a poorly dressed woman who'd stationed herself outside the roisterous public house. Several of the men were staring speculatively in their direction. "Much as I hate to admit it," Malcolm muttered, "we'd best return to Spaldergate House. We're attracting entirely too much attention to ourselves. The longer we remain in these streets, the more likely we are to be attacked, particularly dressed as we are. It's getting late and blokes like those won't hesitate for long, looking for easy pickings."

Conroy Melvyn glanced around. "I agree, but where the deuce are we? Ah, yes, there's the Kings Stores. Been there myself, a time or two, when I was still walking a beat. Good God, that must be Mrs. Paumier!"

"Who?" Malcolm asked, glancing over his shoulder as he turned and headed west, moving briskly to put them out of easy striking distance of the men on the corner.

Inspector Melvyn caught up hastily. "Lady who claimed she spoke with a man in a dark coat, carrying a black bag. Chap asked her if she'd heard of a murder in Miller's Court, the morning Miss Kelly was killed. Claimed she had, indeed, and the bloke told her that he knew more about it than she did. She was standing right outside the Kings Stores, selling chestnuts. Pub still trades on the claim that Jack the Ripper was last seen outside its doors."

"I didn't realize that. It's been an age since I visited *our* London." He laid a slight emphasis on the possessive. "I wonder if the lady spoke with our good friend Dr. Lachley or his accomplice from Liverpool?"

"We'll find out, come November the ninth."

"If we survive so long," Malcolm muttered, glancing back. The men from the Kings Stores pub had followed them. "Step lively, we've got company."

The inspector swore under his breath and speeded up. Malcolm homed in on the roar of shouts from the Vigilance Committee's angry street meeting, steering the Ripperologist back into the chaos in an effort to shake off pursuit. They swept off their high top hats, which stood out like signposts, and edged their way through the mob, taking their time and avoiding any further altercations with the shouting vigilantees. By the time they reached the other side, someone had picked Malcolm's pocket, absconding with all his ready cash, but they'd shaken their more dangerous pursuers in the crush.

"Afraid they cleaned me right out, as well," the police inspector said with a grimace of disgust, searching his own pockets. "Got my pocketwatch, as well. Looks like we'll have to hoof it, eh?"

"I fear so. I haven't even tuppence left."

Malcolm did not look foward to arriving at Spaldergate with the news that he'd discovered the identity of Jack the Ripper *and* located both Marcus and Benny Catlin, only to loose them all in the chaos of a street meeting. Margo would spit like an Irish wildcat, after he'd dismissed her from the search back on Fleet Street. And the Ripper Watch Team's work was not yet done for the night, which loomed endlessly ahead of them. They still had to stand watch over the Whitehall torso mystery, to determine whether that unfortunate victim could also be laid at Jack the Ripper's doorstep. Malcolm resigned himself to yet another stressful night of short sleep and kept walking.

Jenna unlocked the door to the little house in Spitalfields with shaking fingers, then stepped back to give Marcus room to pass. He and Noah carried Ianira upstairs, fumbling for the treads in the darkness while Jenna hunted for the gaslight. Once she'd lit it, they made better progress up the stairs. Noah called down, "I'll change clothes and pick up the girls from the Mindels."

Jenna nodded wearily. Shortly, Noah left the house in disguise as Marcus' sister once again, returning with the children and Dr. Mindel, who hurried upstairs to treat Ianira. Jenna followed, dreading Ianira's return to consciousness. She found Dr. Mindel bent over the *cassondra,* making worried noises, while Artemisia and Gelasia clung to their father in the far corner, eyes wide and frightened as they gazed at their mother for the first time in three years.

"Drugged, you say?" Dr. Mindel muttered, peering under her eyelids. "Such a hideous thing to do to a helpless lady. Her pulse is strong, though, and her breathing is regular. She should sleep quietly until the drug wears off." He rummaged in a satchel and came out with a small jar of salve, which he smoothed onto her wrists where the ropes had roughened her skin. "There is no way to guess how long the dose will last. When she wakes, please come for me."

"Thank you, Dr. Mindel," Noah said quietly. "We will."

The doctor left and Jenna met Noah's gaze. "There isn't much else we can do, is there?"

"No."

Marcus took the children across the narrow hallway to their little room and put them to bed. Noah rested a hand on Jenna's shoulder. "You'd better get some rest, Jenna. You're exhausted and you don't want to risk the baby."

Jenna nodded. There wasn't really anything else anyone could do, except wait for Ianira to regain consciousness and pray she was sane when she did. Jenna left the room blinking back tears and went quietly to bed, where she couldn't get the image of those dismembered bodies out of her mind, or that blonde woman's head sitting on a work table beside a dark-haired man's skull, left lying as casually as last week's empty milk bottles.

She wished she'd paid more attention to the various theories about the Ripper's possible occult connections. Clearly, Dr. John Lachley was a practicing occultist, not just a theorist and scholar. There'd been symbols painted on those hideous brick walls, symbols of occult magic, satanic ritual, God knew what else. Lachley was a renowned physician and lecturer, a member of the Theosophical Society and a man of means, with royal connections. No wonder the police couldn't find Jack the Ripper. They were searching for some depraved East Ender, a foreigner, not a well-respected member of society.

She could all too easily imagine Inspector Abberline's reaction or Sir Charles Warren's if anyone told the police they were up against a madman with ties to the royal family. A man who had perverted all notions of ancient Druidic rites, including the taking of trophy heads. Jenna shuddered, recalling his hideous lecture and the monstrous excitement in his eyes when talking about such things. And she had actually planned to film the Ripper murders! She and Carl, both. What innocents they'd been. Foolish innocents.

The world was full of madmen like John Lachley, killers looking for power, men like John Caddrick, her father. Jack the Ripper had built himself a hideous house beneath the streets, filling it with death. Jenna curled protectively around her abdomen, where Carl's baby was growing, and vowed that her child would never become a victim of the slaughterhouse her father had built. Jenna would see his monstrous construction torn to the ground and her father dead, first. Even if she had to pull the trigger.

Weeping softly in the blackness of a Spitalfields night, Jenna Caddrick listened helplessly to the hushed whispering from Ianira's room across the hall.

As John Lachley's cab rattled its way up the approach to Battersea Bridge, his thoughts rushed and tripped across one another like spawning fish. He was eager to reach the end of the journey and discover what really lay beyond the "gate." Despite the images in the dead woman's fantastical camera, he could not truly imagine the world which had produced such marvels. Anxious and impatient, he tried to steady his hands, but they would not remain decently calm. He gripped more tightly the case hiding Miss Nosette's severed head and craned forward to see how much farther it was to the end of the bridge. *Soon . . .*

God grant him patience, for *soon* could not come quickly enough.

Full dark settled inexorably across London's rooftops and chimneys as the cab jockeyed for position in the long queue of carriages and wagons crossing the river. On the far shore, Lachley could just make out Battersea Park's miniature lake where, on summer days, children chased ducks and swans or floated little armadas of handmade boats. There were no children in the park tonight, nor anyone else, for that matter, save a few modest carriages and the occasional hansom or barouche for hire. Black smoke pouring from Battersea's chimney pots snaked its way upward to merge with the ominous darkness of yet another rainstorm threatening to the east. Low clouds raced all along the southern bank of the river. From their vantage point on Battersea Bridge, lightning flared and flashed across the distant rooftops of Surrey and Bermondsey and damp wind slashed at Lachley's coat and hair through the open carriage, threatening to rip his hat loose. He secured it with an irritable jerk and checked his pocketwatch impatiently. It was now nearly eight and the journalist had guessed the "gate" would go at about eight-fifteen.

The cab finally tilted down the descent from the bridge and swung past the dark dampness of Battersea Park, cutting off in a right-hand turn which took them toward the long, lazy river bend which formed Battersea's western border. Once they reached Octavia Street, it wasn't difficult to suss out which house was Spaldergate. Carriages and hansom cabs lined the kerbs, disgorging elegantly dressed ladies and immaculate gentlemen and their servants, dozens of people arriving for what neighbors must imagine was an elegant dinner party.

He ordered the cabbie to stop well back from the line of arriving carriages and paid the man, waiting until the battered cab had rattled away down the street before moving toward Spaldergate, himself. Hidden in the shadows, he watched the arrivals through narrowed eyes. If people were still returning to the house, the gate couldn't be open yet. He settled his back against a tree trunk, biding his time, more than anxious to step through the gate but forcing himself to wait until the last possible moment. He did not want to risk being detained by the gate's operators. At length, a final carriage arrived, disgorging its passengers, a portly gentleman who was saying to the lady with him, "Hurry up, Abby, we'll miss the gate!"

At last!

Lachley stole softly down the pavement in their wake, then slipped into Spaldergate's side yard and found a wooden gate set into the high wall. Beyond, he discovered a vast and overgrown garden. Lachley eased into a clump of shaggy rhododendrons and peered into the garden, expecting he knew not quite what, a miniature version of a railway station, perhaps, with a gate leading into somewhen else, or perhaps the iron hulk of some inexplicable and infernal machine. The high stone wall ran right round the sprawling garden, its far reaches just visible in the gaslight from lamps spaced evenly along a patterned stone walkway. His brows rose at the extravagance, so many gaslights illuminating a mere garden, and one that was improperly maintained, at that. The walkway ended abruptly at the rear wall, as though some fuedal war lord had erected a fortress keep straight across an ancient Roman highway. Had that bitch Nosette lied? Was there no "gate" after all? No route into the distant future?

Yet something was clearly afoot, for milling about in a state of high agitation were more people than Lachley—in his own state of high-strung, sweating eagerness—could readily count. Upwards of seventy-five, at least, plus piles and haphazard stacks of luggage and porters swarming like angry mosquitoes, as though this garden were St. Pancras Station, that fantastical castle of brick and iron and glass with its bustling thousands. Most of the strange guests in Spaldergate's garden carried parcels or ladies' toiletry and jewel cases, bulging valises, carpet satchels with ironwood grips, all in a colorful and meaningless jumble of haste and nameless excitement.

Lachley felt the sting and ache of jaw muscles rigidly clenched, of teeth too tightly ground together. The confusion of voices scraped against his very nerves, until he had to close his fists to stop himself taking the nearest chattering bitch by the throat and squeezing until his knuckles collided in the center. The need to move, to do something besides huddle in the shrubbery, clawed at him, shrieked until the very substance of his skull vibrated with an agony like broken bones grating together. He reached for his throbbing temples, wanting to clutch at his head and hold the fury forcibly inside the cage of his fingers.

The vibrating pain had become a shriek when he noticed with a distant surprise that others in the garden were doing exactly the same thing. Some actually clapped hands across their ears, as though to shut out an inaudible noise. The unnerving sensation was not his imagination, then, nor the manifestation of multiple stresses on his overwrought nerves. He frowned, trying to comprehend what it might be—

—and a hole of utter, midnight blackness opened in the center of the stone wall, right above the flagstone path. Lachley sucked air down, a sharp gasp. The hair on his arms came straight up and his back muscles tried to shudder and crawl away down his spine, intent on running as far and as fast as possible, with or without the rest of him.

The gate . . .

It pulsed open with a silent thunder, gaping wider, swallowing up more of the garden wall, which simply ceased to exist where that blackness touched it. The edges scintillated in the glow from the gaslamps, shot through with irridescent color, like a film of oil spilled from steamship bilges across Tobacco Basin's darkened waters. The fascination of it drew him, repulsed him, left him trembling violently. What power did these people possess, to open such a thing out of sheer air and solid stone?

Ancient names and half-recalled incantations stumbled through his broken, sliding thoughts, names of power and terror: *Anubis, destroyer of souls, guardian of the underworld's pitchy gates . . . Heimdall of the shattering horn, watching for any who dared to cross the glinting rainbow bridge . . . Kur, the coiled serpent of the fathomless abyss, destroyer of the world in flood and thunder . . .*

The outward shudder of the gate's receding edges finally came to a halt and it hung there, silent and terrible, beckoning him forward while his senses screamed to run in the opposite direction and never glance back. Then, as though such a thing were the most ordinary occurance in the world, the men and women in the garden stepped calmly through it, vanishing from sight like a cricket ball whacked solidly with the bat, rushing away to dwindle down to nothing. They were rushing through, hurrying, crowding on one another's heels. How long would the monstrous thing remain open? He took one step toward it, then another and a third, then rushed forward, impatient with his own gibbering terror, determined to step through, to discover for himself what horrors and delights might lie beyond.

Working himself into a state of frenzy, electrically aware of the risk, Lachley pulled Nosette's dismembered head from its carrying case and rushed forward into the puddle of light from the nearest gaslamp. A well-dressed lady in watered silk saw him first. She let go a high, piercing scream. Lachley was abruptly engulfed by a stinging cloud of liveried servants and distraught gentlemen. "I tried to stop her . . ." Lachley gasped out, waving Miss Nosette's ghastly head about, her streaming blonde tresses clotted with blood. Summoning tears, Lachley gripped a white-faced gentleman by the arm. "She wanted to follow that madman in the East End, to photograph him! By the time I got to her it was too late, he'd cut her to pieces, oh, God, all I could bring away was this . . . this little bit of her. Poor, stupid Dominica! I just want to go home, please . . ."

People were shouting, calling for someone. Lachley started toward the gate, not caring to wait. Just behind him, a woman's voice shrilled out, "My God! It's John Lachley!" He jerked around and focused on a woman who stood not ten paces away, a dark-haired woman of extraordinary beauty, who looked vaguely familiar to him. She was staring straight at him, eyes wide in recognition. Scalding hatred rose in his gorge, threatened to peel back his skin and burst out through his fingertips. *She knows me! By God, she'll not stop me!* Lachley whirled and plunged toward the gaping black hole. Behind him, the woman shouted, "*Stop him! That's Jack the Ripper!*"

Screams erupted on his heels . . .

Then he was inside. Falling, rushing foward with dizzy speed. He yelled. Then staggered across a metal grating, into a railing at waist height. He looked up—

John Lachley screamed.

It was a world inverted. Stone for sky, pendulous glowing lights hanging from iron beams and girders, booming voices that echoed and rolled, more terrifying than any thunder, speaking out of the air itself, a maze of twisting confusion that fell away at his feet, at least five full stories below, as though he stood at the top of Big Ben's clock tower or the highest point of St. Paul's arching dome. Wild displays of light in alien colors hurt his eyes.

People moved in crowds far below, like flotsam caught in the eddy of the docklands' swirling waters. Down a rampway, down endless metal steps, down and further down still, the people who had come through the gate ahead of him wound their way toward the distant floor, while a few yards away, suspended on ramps and metal stairs in a mirror image, crowds of nattily dressed men and women pressed their way upwards, toward the very platform where Lachley stood.

At the base of the metal stairs, confusion reigned. A screaming mob shouted questions, inchoate with distance. Men dressed as guards shoved and pressed the crowd back. Lachley realized with a start that a number of those guards were women, women wearing trousers as though they had renounced their sex and thought themselves the equal of any man. Eddies moved sharply through the crowd as a fight broke out, unmistakably riot, brutal as any mob of drunken dock hands demanding pay higher than the handful of shillings a week they deserved . . .

Someone lunged through the gate behind him, shouting his name.

He whirled. The vaguely familiar woman had rushed through with two men, who dove straight at him across the platform. Lachley hurled aside Dominica Nosette's head and drove an elbow into an unprotected gut, then slammed the heel of his hand against a nose, felt bone crunch. Both men went sharply down, barely stirring. The woman's eyes widened as she realized her abrupt danger. She opened her mouth to scream and tried to lunge away from him. Lachley snatched her back by the hair. She fought him with unexpected ferocity. Her nails caught his face and her knee slammed into his thigh with a sharp flare of pain, narrowly missing his groin.

"Bitch!" He slugged her, putting his entire body into the blow. It caught her brutally across the temple. She collapsed, a boneless weight in his grasp. Someone was shouting from the stairs, where several shrieking women stood in ashen shock and one narrow-eyed, dangerous-looking man was rushing right toward him. Lachley couldn't fight the whole bloody station!

He snatched up the unconscious woman as a hostage, heaving her across his shoulder, and plunged down the steps toward the distant floor. He skidded down flight after flight, one hand balancing the inert burden on his shoulder, the other gripping the railing as he slung himself around corners at each landing. A glance below revealed several uniformed men charging up from the floor, trying to cut him off. He snarled aloud, but Lachley was only a flight and a half up, so he vaulted across the rail, dropping a full ten feet into the middle of the rioting crowd. He landed on someone's back and felt bone crunch under his feet as the man went brutally down. Lachley stumbled to hands and knees, dropping his hostage in the melee. Someone kicked him aside, sent him spinning and rolling under running feet. Bruised and shaken, Lachley finally skidded into a momentary pocket of clear space and shoved his way to his feet. He thrust himself past intervening bodies, reeled from a punch against his unprotected side, turned with a snarl and broke the bastard's neck with a wrenching heave and twist—

Then he was clear of the riot. Lachley found himself staring at cobblestoned walkways and park benches and wrought iron lamps, even a pub that reminded him incongruously of Chelsea. The riot surged behind him, shoving Lachley straight past a line of stunned security guards, who were busy to distraction searching the rioting mob for him. He bolted, determined to discover some way out of this madhouse. He needed to find a quiet place to think, to sort out what to do next. He was very nearly clear of the chaos when a group of wild-eyed men brandishing placards rushed at him.

"*Lord Jack!*"

"Lead us, holiest one!"

"Command us! We are your servants!"

Lachley opened his mouth, not entirely sure what might emerge. Behind him, someone shouted, "There he is!" He glanced wildly back toward the platform, where the two men who'd rushed through the gate on his heels were stumbling down the stairs under escort, pointing right at him. Lachley whirled on the placard-carrying lunatics, who were plucking at his very coat sleeves in fawning, worshipful attitudes.

"You want to help me? I need shelter, curse it!"

"At once, Lord Jack!" the nearest cried eagerly, tugging at his arm. "Anything you desire! We have awaited your coming . . ."

They surrounded him, rushed him away from the shouting guards who were shoving rioters aside, trying to reach him. Lachley ran with the madmen, insane sycophants who gibbered at him from all sides and hid his face with their hand-scrawled signs. *Am I doomed to rely on madmen all my days?* He'd traded Maybrick's lunacy for a whole crowd of insanity. But sheltering with madmen was preferable to hanging, should the wardens of the gate catch up to him.

His unanticipated escorts brought Lachley eventually to a place that—despite its overwhelming strangeness—appeared to be a hotel of some kind. The men who'd appointed themselves his adoring acolytes rushed Lachley across a brightly lit lobby, where a desk clerk glanced up only briefly, then ushered him straight into what proved to be a lift. They rose with startling speed and quite delightfully, the controls were automated, eliminating the need for a lift operator who would have to be eliminated for witnessing his flight. The lights overhead were strange, far too bright, and he couldn't determine what the translucent panels covering them were fashioned from. Then the doors slipped quietly open with a soft bell chime and he found himself in a luxuriously carpeted corridor. One of the madmen produced a small, stiff card, which he inserted into a metal box on one of the numbered doors. The panel opened to his touch.

Lachley stepped warily inside, finding two neatly made beds, a strange box with a flat glass front perched on a low table, several odd lamps, ugly artwork framed on white-painted walls, and just to the left of the door, a lavatory fitted with a large mirror and the strangest water closet he'd ever seen.

"Christ, but I need a drink . . ." he muttered, scrubbing at his face with unsteady hands.

"At once, Lord!" The man who had unlocked the room hurried across to a small cabinet, procuring a bottle of amber-colored liquor which he opened and poured while the other madmen crowded inside. Lachley knocked back a surprisingly good whiskey, then considered the men who stood in a huddle near the door, gazing at him with the intensity of utter reverence.

"Who are you?" Lachley demanded.

"Your Sons, Lord Jack. We have long awaited your coming. Command us. We are your chosen."

He narrowed his eyes as he considered the implications of that patently absurd answer. Were all the inhabitants of this world completely insane? No, not all, he frowned, thinking back to those guards at the gate. Lachley wondered what to ask first and finally decided on the simplest question in his mind. "What year is it?"

None of the madmen seemed at all surprised by such a question. The one who'd given him the whiskey said, "By station time, Lord, it is 1910. Beyond Primary . . ."

"Station time?" he echoed, startled.

"Yes, Lord. The station exists well over a century in our past and some thirty years in your future."

Lachley's mind reeled. Sanity slipped and lurched beneath his feet. He groped for it, finding, instead, the bed, which he sank onto simply to prevent a nasty fall. "Do you know the bitch who followed me through the gate?" he asked harshly. "The one I lost in the crowd?"

"Yes, Lord. She's a Ripperologist, one of the Ripper Watch Team, Dr. Shahdi Feroz. She went to study your great works in London."

Ripperologist? Lachley narrowed his eyes. She'd come to London to study *him?* The journalist had said as much, but he hadn't believed her. The unlamented Miss Nosette would have said anything to persuade Lachley to release her unharmed. Lachley shut his eyes for long moments, trying to place where he'd seen that Feroz woman's face before. The familiar features finally clicked in his mind. The lecture. She'd attended the lecture at the Egyptian Hall. Had spoken with him briefly, afterwards. Lachley frowned. Had she known all along, then? Known that he was responsible for the deaths of the whores in the East End? She must have. Hadn't she cried out that he was Jack the Ripper, back in the garden behind Spaldergate? Lachley narrowed his eyes coldly. That woman's testimony could see him hanged.

"I must find her," he growled. "Find and silence her."

"Do you want a knife, Lord Jack?"

The question jolted him. He blinked in surprise. "A knife?"

"Yes, Lord. To kill the whores on the station, once you have killed Dr. Feroz?"

The leader of the madmen was opening a leather case. He took from it a long, shining blade, nine inches of sharpened steel edge, with a thick wooden handle. The lunatic held it out to Lachley, balancing it across both palms, presenting it like a royal sceptre. He went to one knee, offering the weapon as a token of fealty. "My Lord, we are your humble servants. Take our knife, Lord, and command us."

Lachley picked it up slowly, realizing it was a far better tool than Maybrick's. Better, even, than his Arabian jambala, with its thick, slightly curved steel blade, nearly as wide as his palm. Better even than the scramasax—a weapon much like an American Bowie knife with a hook at the end—which he'd used as a sacramental blade in Lower Tibor to take Morgan's trophy head. *This* blade, held out so reverently, was a delight to behold.

Command us, his followers offered, madmen from a hellish, sunless world he did not yet understand. *'Tis better,* the blind poet's words rumbled through Lachley's memory, boulders crashing down a mountainside in a thundering avalanche, *'tis better to reign in hell . . .* John Lachley began to laugh, a sound so dark and wild, it brought a sharp gasp from those worshippers still huddled near the door. The leader, holding out the knife across his palms, met Lachley's gaze and smiled slowly. Glorying in his newfound power, Lachley accepted the knife from his faithful disciple's hands . . . and gave the orders to kill his first victim: the dark-haired, petite, and lovely Dr. Feroz.

(((Chapter 12)))

Skeeter Jackson had never minded crowds.

But the packed mob in Victoria Station would've been enough to discompose the pope and his entire College of Cardinals. Skeeter hadn't even reached the rope barricade of the departures lounge when waiting newsies swarmed all over him, shouting questions and shoving microphones and cameras into his face with scant regard for damage inflicted.

"Mr. Jackson! Is it true you're leading the search team over the protests of Senator Caddrick—"

"—tell us your plan to locate the Senator's missing daughter—"

"—how much they're paying you to risk your life, bringing terrorists to justice—"

Skeeter, lips thinned down to a tight, white line, had never been gladder in his life to reach a departures lounge. He fled past the barrier, gate pass in hand, leaving them to howl in his wake. Paula Booker had taken refuge in one corner, notably seating herself as far as possible from Sid Kaederman. The detective glared sourly at Skeeter and snapped irritably at a Time Tours employee who'd just brought coffee. Skeeter headed the other way, having no desire to renew his acquaintance until absolutely necessary.

"Coffee, Skeeter?" The voice came from the farthest corner of the lounge, startling him. He found Kit Carson leaning against one of the steel beams supporting the long flights of stairs and departures platform.

"Kit! What're you doing here?"

"Seeing you off, of course. Coffee?"

"Oh, man, how I need a cup! Thanks, boss." Skeeter gulped, while scratching his itching thigh surreptitiously and mentally castigating the British for insisting on woolen suits. He wasn't quite allergic, but misery was relative. He should've put on that synthetic bodysuit Connie had offered, which helped reduce the itch, rather than stuffing it into his luggage.

Kit refilled his coffee cup from a thermos flask and said, "There's just time to go over the use of your new scout's log." He handed over a satchel tucked under one arm. "I've been working on it for the last three hours, getting it set up for you."

"My scout's log?" Skeeter echoed, abruptly excited. He dug open the satchel with eager fingers. The computerized device nestled inside was, Skeeter knew, a mandatory piece of equipment for any time scout. "How come you're giving me a scout's log? I'm not a time scout."

"You've always relied on the time cards before, I know. But it occurred to me this morning, this search-and-rescue mission might just become far more temporally complex than anyone planned. You may well need a more substantial record of when and where you've been, to prevent potential accidents in the future. Don't worry, I'm not taking it out of your pay." The grizzled former scout chuckled, eyes glinting with wicked amusement. "I chalked it up to Senator Caddrick's account."

Skeeter grinned. "Bet he flips when he gets the bill." Skeeter peered curiously at the device. He'd seen time scouts carrying them, of course, but had never managed to lay hands on one, not even in the days when he could've turned a tidy profit snitching a new one and selling it on the black market. He would never have stolen a used one, of course, even if 'eighty-sixers hadn't been off-limits as prey. Ripping off someone's record of their gate travels would've been tantamount to premeditated murder. But he'd wistfully dreamed of the money a new one could bring, had spent many a pleasant hour drooling over the stuff he could buy with that kind of cash.

"Now," Kit was saying, "you haven't been down as many gates as the average tour guide, let alone a time scout, but you've done enough time travelling to cause potential trouble. Particularly since the Wild West Gate and the Britannia can be lethal, if you don't watch which direction you're moving through them. So you'll use this. I've already programmed in the two weeks we spent in Colorado. You'll want to add the time you've spent down other gates, as well. Your first trip to Denver, your previous trip to London, plus the brief minutes you spent there as a Time Tours porter. And your stay in Claudian Rome, of course, finding Marcus and bringing him back. When you get to London, turn the log on immediately and take your first set of readings. Before this search is over, God knows how many time zones or gates you'll have to jump through, particularly if Armstrong has left London for healthier climes."

"Aw, man, don't even suggest it!"

Kit grimaced, rearranging a whole ladderful of weathered lines. "Sorry, that's my job. Now, then, open it up. Like that, yes. You're going to learn how to use this thing in your sleep. Malcolm and Margo can help, they know the drill cold."

"Believe me," Skeeter said fervently, "the last thing I want to risk is shadowing myself." Dying instantly by stepping into a time where he already existed was not Skeeter's idea of a smart career move. "Okay, show me how this thing works."

Kit put him through drills right up to the two-minute warning, when Time Tours guides urged the departing tour to start climbing the stairs reserved for departures, so they would be ready to step through the Britannia the moment the returning tour cleared the gate. Kit gripped his shoulder in a friendly fashion. "You're doing very well, Skeeter. You catch on fast." The retired scout chuckled. "Margo took much longer, her first few tries, but she by God knows it now. You won't need an ATLS, but it wouldn't hurt to have her and Malcolm show you theirs, run you through the process of taking star fixes and geomagnetic readings when you get to London. Keep the log running as you step through the gate, so you won't forget to turn it on."

Skeeter fiddled with controls, then closed up the log and slid it into the trademark satchel Kit had been the first to design. "I'll check in with Malcolm right away. Thanks, boss."

Kit held out a hand and Skeeter shook it solemnly.

"Good luck, Skeeter," Kit said quietly. "Try not to get yourself—or anyone else—killed on this mission."

Skeeter held his gaze solemnly. "I'll do my best."

"I know you will. Scoot, then. Send word periodically with the returning guides, so we'll know what's happening."

"Right." Skeeter gulped the rest of his lukewarm coffee, then hurried for the stairs, giving Paula a high-sign. Kaederman was still sipping coffee. Caddrick's pet snoop finally began the long climb as Skeeter rounded the first landing and started up the second flight. Baggage handlers were already fiendishly at work on the high platform. In a dizzying moment of *déjà vu*, Skeeter halfway expected to see Benny Catlin barrelling through the piles of steamer trunks and portmanteaus. Then the gate rumbled open with a skull-splitting backlash of subharmonics and the returning tour staggered through, jabbering animatedly.

"—that poor woman, decapitated, they found nothing but her torso!"

"—left the body in the cellar tunnels beneath the new Scotland Yard building—"

"The Ripper Watch Team said Jack the Ripper left the body there, himself! Poor Miss Nosette, if only she'd stayed with the Ripper Watch Team instead of striking out on her own, like that—"

Skeeter edged closer to the front of the platform, aware of his conspicuous place at the head of the departing tour. The press corps had trained cameras on him from five stories down. The gate was nearly clear, tourists down to a trickle and baggage handlers staggering through under heavy loads, when a wild-eyed man Skeeter vaguely recognized plunged through the gate. Whoever he was, the guy let out a bloodcurdling yell and went rigid, staring down into Commons. Then Skeeter noticed what was clutched in his hand and stiffened in shock. *A decapitated head!* A woman's head, severed with what must've been an axe. The grisly thing swung by the hair from the man's white-knuckled grip. Screams erupted from the women near Skeeter just as he recognized the dead woman: Dominica Nosette, the Ripper Watch photographer. Then two men Skeeter didn't know rushed through the open gate, with Dr. Feroz on their heels. The Ripperologist was shouting, "There he is! It's Dr. Lachley! Stop him!"

The man at the platform railing spun around—and attacked with single-minded fury, flinging the severed head aside. He hit both men like a pile driver; they went down hard and didn't stir. Then Lachley grabbed Dr. Feroz. She fought back, even as Skeeter shoved his way toward them, past screaming women and shocked Time Tours guides and baggage handlers, who stood with mouths gaping. "Don't just stand there!" Skeeter shouted. "*Stop him!*"

Lachley cast one wild-eyed glance in their direction, then slugged Dr. Feroz so hard her head snapped around. He threw her across one shoulder and bolted down the stairs for the Commons floor. Skeeter lunged after him—and one of the men Lachley had knocked down came to his knees right in Skeeter's path. Skeeter sprawled and they both crashed to the platform floor. A pile of luggage upended and fell straight off the edge. Screams erupted somewhere far below. Then Skeeter grunted and heaved himself up to look. The luggage had crashed to the floor, knocking half a dozen people flat. A panic-stricken riot was spreading through the crowd. Dr. Lachley was almost to the floor, running hard, with Shahdi Feroz dangling over one shoulder like a broken doll.

"Skeeter!" Paula Booker was shouting his name. He glanced back and saw the departing tour rushing through the gate. The Britannia had already begun to shrink back in on itself. A Time Tours guide had bent to help the injured. Paula was waiting at the very edge of the gate. "Hurry, Skeeter! The gate's going! Kaederman's already through!"

Whoever Dr. Lachley might prove to be—and Skeeter had a sinking sensation he might just be Jack the Ripper—Skeeter wasn't about to miss this gate and give Sid Kaederman eight solid days to search for Jenna Caddrick by himself. Skeeter plunged into the shrinking gate, grabbing Paula by the wrist on his way through. They skidded into the dark garden behind Spaldergate House and landed smack in the center of utter chaos. Time Tours guides were racing toward the gate and hysterical women were sobbing. Porters stumbled through into the garden, literally shoved through the rapidly closing gate by station-side Time Tours employees. One of the women was screaming, "My luggage! He knocked off my luggage! I must have my medicine!" Another, less sympathetically, was howling about her jewelry, presumably strewn all over the Commons floor.

"What's going on?" Skeeter demanded of a passing Time Tours guide, who completely ignored him. A tourist nearby gasped, "They said it was Jack the Ripper! He's crashed the Britannia!"

Paula gasped. "*What?*"

"That man who came through! That was Jack the Ripper! Burst into the garden, shouting something about one of the Ripper Watch reporters, said the Ripper had cut her to pieces . . ."

A final porter struggled through the rapidly closing gate, dragging five steamer trunks hastily roped together, then the Britannia shrank to a point of darkness and vanished, leaving only a tangle of vines and shrubbery along the high garden wall. For better or worse, TT-86 was sealed up tight as a drum. With Jack the Ripper inside.

"*Skeeter?*" a familiar voice jerked his attention back around. "Skeeter Jackson? What on God's green earth are you doing in London?"

Skeeter blinked up at Malcolm Moore, who had burst into the Spaldergate garden at a dead run. Margo, hot on his heels, slithered to a halt as lightning flared overhead, deepening smudged purple shadows under her eyes. "Skeeter?" she gasped. "And Paula Booker? What's going on? What are you doing here?"

"Uh . . ." Skeeter said helpfully. He struggled to pull his scattered thoughts together. "Was that really Jack the Ripper?" He gestured vaguely toward the now-vanished Britannia Gate. "Crashing the gate?"

Malcolm's lips thinned to near invisibility. "I'm afraid so, yes. Dr. Feroz recognized him and gave chase with some of the guides—"

"I've got bad news, then," Skeeter muttered. "He overpowered 'em. And took off with Dr. Feroz. Knocked her cold and hauled her down the stairs. The gate was going, or I'd have chased them down."

Malcolm's mouth worked for a long second before any sound emerged. "*My God!*" he finally erupted, voice cracking in unmodulated fury. "*What in hell could be more important than letting Jack the Ripper escape into TT-86?*"

Skeeter blinked. Then said unhappily, "Finding a pack of terrorists who kidnapped Senator John Caddrick's little girl and hauled her through the Britannia. She was in disguise. As Benny Catlin."

Malcolm's anger faded faster than an image from an unplugged television. The guide stood blinking for a full sixty seconds, then whispered, "Oh, dear God . . ."

"You said it. We gotta talk. Somewhere quiet." Women were still sobbing hysterically over the severed head the Ripper had hurled at the departing tour, lamenting their lost baggage and the cash they'd left in their trunks, cash they needed for the trip.

"Yes, the sooner the better," Malcolm said thinly. "Margo, my dear, please ask Mr. Gilbert to meet us in his study. With a very large decanter of bourbon."

Margo shot toward the house, threading her way nimbly through wailing tourists and staggering porters. Malcolm asked, "How many men have you brought to search, Skeeter?"

"All the porters who came through are on search detail if we need 'em. Dr. Booker's come through to help make an identification. She gave Caddrick's kid a new face. Benny Catlin's. And there's a detective you're just gonna love. Caddrick hired him."

Paula Booker peered through the crowd anxiously. "I'd better find Mr. Kaederman. We don't want him slipping off on his own."

Malcolm followed her progress with his gaze, then turned to Skeeter, waiting expectantly. "Long story," Skeeter sighed. "Very long."

"Then the sooner we're inside, the sooner you can begin telling it." Malcolm ushered him through the chaos in the garden, steering him past the back door, which one of the servants had chocked open, leading him to another door farther on. They entered Spaldergate through a scrupulously maintained conservatory replete with hothouse flowers and overly green smells. From there, they followed a carpeted corridor toward the front of the house, bypassing the bulk of the arriving tour. Darkened, silent rooms closed away from public view for the night lay just off the hall, while the parlour, at the front of the house on the ground floor—rather than the more traditional first-floor arrangement found in London town houses—blazed with light. The whole front of the house was filling up with distraught refugees from the shaken tour.

Malcolm turned off the corridor well before they reached the parlour, entering a decidedly masculine room dominated by hundreds of leather-bound books and the unmistakable scent of beeswax and turpentine, used to polish the mahogany furniture. Margo had reached the room before them and stood in the corner, pouring bourbon from a decanter. A film of coal dust dulled every white surface to grey, despite scrupulous cleaning by the house staff. The feel of smooth wood under Skeeter's hand, the thick, rich carpet, and the mustiness of the air were all familiar from his previous visit. Like half-remembered ghosts, they filtered through his awareness while Malcolm headed for the bourbon. Margo handed over generously filled tumblers and Skeeter gratefully upended one.

"Thanks. God, I needed that." He refilled the tumbler and sipped more judiciously, this time. Paula Booker found her way into the room, lamentably in the company of Sid Kaederman, who thrust out his hand for the bourbon as though Margo were a mere servant. Margo handed him a tumbler, eying him curiously. Kaederman gulped, ignoring Margo and fixing his attention squarely on Malcolm Moore. Skeeter noticed that Kaederman's hand was slightly unsteady as he drained his drink. Skeeter decided he'd better make the introductions.

"Mr. Sid Kaederman is a detective, hired by Senator Caddrick to search for his daughter. Malcolm Moore is a freelance temporal guide in charge of the Ripper Watch arrangements. Margo Smith is a trainee time scout and is assisting the Ripper Watch Team, as well."

Kaederman shot Margo a surprised glance, then said, "Would someone care to explain how the hell you people let a thing like Jack the Ripper get into your station? Don't you put any security around your goddamned gates?"

Malcolm bristled. "It is not my gate, Mr. Kaederman. Time Tours has charge of the Britannia and I do not work for Time Tours. Neither does Miss Smith. Now, then, Mr. Jackson, will you kindly explain your remarks about Senator Caddrick's missing child?"

Marshall Gilbert appeared in the doorway before anyone else could comment. "What in the world can possibly be so urgent—" He rocked to a halt. "*Skeeter Jackson?* And Paula Booker? What on earth—?"

Skeeter smiled wanly. "Evening, Mr. Gilbert. Hope you don't have plans for tonight."

The gatekeeper frowned. "I don't believe I care for the sound of this. What's happened?"

"Benny Catlin, is what." Skeeter sank into in a leather-covered chair, took a long pull at his bourbon, then explained what had happened and why they were here. Sid Kaederman and Paula Booker sat opposite Skeeter, listening to his terse explanation. "So, after we got back from Colorado," Skeeter finished up, "Senator Caddrick threatened again to shut the whole station down if we don't find his daughter and this terrorist, Noah Armstrong." Skeeter passed around photographs. "And after what he did to Bull Morgan, with all that cockamamie crap he used to throw Bull in jail, we're taking him damned seriously."

"Good God!" Malcolm gasped, staring at the photos. "That *is* Benny Catlin! We saw him just last night! And this Armstrong chap was with him."

"You saw them?" Skeeter sat forward quickly.

"*Where?*" Kaederman had surged to his feet.

"At the Egyptian Hall. They were attending a lecture by the man we identified as Jack the Ripper. In fact, they were following him, for reasons we have yet to ascertain, although I suspect it has something to do with Ianira Cassondra. We trailed them right across London into the East End, but a street meeting jammed our way and we lost them in the crush."

While Skeeter's imagination betrayed him with monstrous visions of what Jack the Ripper would do to Ianira Cassondra, Sid Kaederman bellowed, "*You lost them?* My God! What a bunch of incompetant jackasses! I don't care what that interfering old bastard Carson said, I'm taking over this search operation—"

"Like hell you are!" Skeeter snapped. "Last time I checked, nobody had appointed you God."

"You insufferable little—! How dare you talk to me that way! I've a good mind—"

"*Enough!*"

Coal dust settled in the aftermath of Malcolm Moore's bellow.

Malcolm pinned Kaederman with his gaze. "You will please be good enough to refrain from further outbursts, Mr. Kaederman. And we can do without the barbed remarks, Mr. Jackson."

"Huh. You weren't stuck for two weeks in Colorado with this pompous—"

"Enough!"

"Oh, all right," Skeeter muttered. "Shutting up." He sprawled deeper into his chair, wishing to God he'd never agreed to come in the first place.

"That's better. Now, then. We'll take this one at a time, gentlemen." Malcolm glanced at Kaederman, who returned his gaze coldly.

"Where are you going to search?" Kaederman demanded. "And just how, exactly, did you manage to lose track of Miss Caddrick and her abductor?"

"As you have not been to the East End, do not presume to judge conditions there. Street meetings are always disruptive and frequently violent. The Ripper murders have sparked riots and serious violence, particularly against foreigners, for the past three weeks. We were caught right in the thick of one. It cut us off from Dr. Lachley and the group following him. Including your terrorist and Miss Caddrick. Not to mention Marcus, Ianira Cassondra's husband. We suspect Ianira is somehow involved, because Marcus had to be restrained from attacking Lachley during the lecture."

Skeeter caught a glimpse of Margo opening her mouth to ask something, then she thought better of it and scooted back in her chair again, brow furrowed slightly. From her corner, she levelled a slow, suspicious gaze at Kaederman. *Good.* With luck, she'd just picked up on the inconsistency in Kaederman's story. Namely, that Jenna Caddrick wouldn't be running around London voluntarily with Armstrong if she were his prisoner. Until Skeeter could get rid of Kaederman, he wouldn't be able to tell Margo and Malcolm the real story—or, at least, his suspicions.

Skeeter caught Malcolm's eye. "Yes, Ianira's involved, I'll stake my reputation on it. She was inside a steamer trunk I carried through, one of Benny Catlin's. Catlin chewed my ass when it nearly fell off the departures platform. Cost me a job with Time Tours."

Malcolm's mouth twitched. "Pardon the frankness, but that's no great loss." Malcolm was famous for his long-standing feud with Time Tours, which he held accountable for the suicide of a long-ago employer. "Well, this is quite a sticky wicket you've handed us, Skeeter."

While Skeeter was wondering what, precisely, a sticky wicket *was*, Kaederman said, "Is that all you've got to say? When are you going to get off your damn dandified butt and *do* something about it?"

Malcolm shot an intent stare at Caddrick's detective. "Mr. Kaederman, there are ladies present. Kindly refrain from vulgarities."

"You're kidding?"

"No, I am not, sir. You will please refrain from swearing in the presence of ladies. Unless you wish to provoke some gentleman on the streets into correcting your manners forcibly? You are investigating a kidnapping. And the London outside those windows," he nodded toward heavy damask curtains falling thick as honey down the long windowpanes to close out the rising storm, "is nothing like the London of our own time. You cannot safely behave as though you were in New York or even up-time London, not if you wish to escape serious injury. Now, you have raised the question we all must answer: What to do next. I feel constrained to point out that neither you nor Mr. Jackson nor Dr. Booker is particularly qualified to search Victorian London. I daresay the baggage porters have more experience down the Britannia than any of you."

Paula said hastily, "Leave me out, please. I had enough searching in Denver to last a lifetime. I agreed to come along because I can provide a positive ID on Miss Caddrick. And Kit thought it would be a good idea to have two surgeons in residence at Spaldergate, with the team going up against armed terrorists."

Malcolm's expression made it clear that he questioned the wisdom of sending through such an inept team, but he merely said, "You say Armstrong went through the Wild West Gate? I suppose he must have arrived in London conventionally enough, by steamship from New York to Liverpool or London, bringing Marcus and the children with him. They'll have had ample time to set up a hideout anywhere in the city, which means they'll be devilishly difficult to trace. On the other hand, we know that Miss Caddrick was wounded—"

"*What?*" Kaederman lunged out of his chair a second time.

Malcolm blinked. "I thought you'd been thoroughly briefed?"

The detective thinned his lips. "That particular detail was left out."

"I see. Well, the dog we used to trace Benny Catlin followed a blood trail away from the Royal Opera House. Not a great deal of blood, but clearly Benny Catlin's. Or rather, Miss Caddrick's. We don't know how seriously she was injured in the fight at the Opera, but we saw her just two days ago, quite recovered, so the wound was clearly not a life-threatening one. We'd been searching the hospitals and workhouse infirmaries without turning up anything, so I would suggest we now broaden the search to private physicians. We'll begin by contacting all the private doctors and surgeons in the region of the Strand, then spread out in sectors from there, trying to trace where Miss Caddrick received treatment for her injury. The baggage handlers can assist with that."

"You've got to be joking?" Sid protested. "That could take months!"

Malcolm favored him with a mild look. "Indeed. Your time might be well spent compiling lists of names and addresses to contact."

Margo leaned forward. "If they've set up housekeeping somewhere in London, they're likely to need a staff, even if it's a small one."

"Not necessarily. Servants gossip. Armstrong won't want to risk that."

Margo looked abashed. "I hadn't thought of that."

Malcolm smiled wanly. "You aren't accustomed to servants, yet, my dear. It's entirely possible Armstrong has chosen to hide in the East End, as the least likely place anyone would search. Conditions in Bethnal Green or Spitalfields, for instance, aren't quite as desperate as they are in, say, Stepney, Whitechapel, or Wapping, never mind Poplar and Limehouse. And Marcus' accent would blend in rather well with the European immigrants in Spitalfields. Whereas it would be quite remarkable in more homogenously English districts, even those as relatively poverty stricken as SoHo or Cheapside. Consider their position for a moment. Armstrong's group includes at least one Yankee gentlemen, or rather, a young lady posing as one, which is dangerous, in itself, plus a man with a decidedly Latin accent, two small children, and attendant guards. That would be extraordinarily memorable in the better London neighborhoods. Enough so, were *I* running from up-time legal authorities, I wouldn't risk that sort of attention."

"Okay," Skeeter nodded, "that makes sense. So we comb the East End, same as half the cops and reporters in London. And check out all the doctors." He wished Kaederman would leave, so he could tell Malcolm the rest of the story. "When do we start?"

"I suggest you begin by settling into rooms and unpacking your cases. Then you and I, Mr. Jackson, will spend a long evening at the Vault's computers, planning the search and assigning personnel to various sections of the city. Mr. Kaederman, you shall begin by working on your list of physicians."

"The sooner I get these goddamned wool pants off, the better."

Margo chuckled. "Better not say that, Mr. Kaederman. Not around here."

"Say what?" Kaederman asked, blinking in confusion.

"In London, the word 'pants' refers to underwear. Call them trousers, unless you want the locals to laugh at you."

The look Kaederman shot her told Skeeter he planned to stay as far from the locals as humanly possible. Which suited Skeeter just fine. The Wardmann-Wolfe agent muttered, "If that's all, I'm tucking it in for the night." He stalked out. Paula pleaded weariness and also left.

"You know," Malcolm remarked to no one in particular, "I'd say that chap doesn't enjoy time travel."

"You don't know the half of it. That man is a major pain in *everybody's* backside. Now that he's gone, though, there's a few little things you need to know . . ."

Malcolm's glance revealed a surprising amount of dread.

Skeeter sighed. "This is the part where this mess gets really complicated. Although I think Margo's already tumbled to part of it."

Margo sat forward, eyes blazing with green fire. "You mean, if Jenna Caddrick's a prisoner, what was she doing at the lecture with Noah Armstrong? Running around London, free as a bird?"

"Exactly."

Malcolm shot his fiancée a startled glance. "I hadn't considered that. Yes, that does complicate things a bit."

Skeeter nodded. "You may not know it, but I was right beside Ianira when she was kidnapped. Armstrong knocked Ianira flat, swept her and me straight to the floor, just as Jenna Caddrick burst out of the crowd and shot a terrorist behind us. An armed one, about to murder Ianira. I started wondering why Armstrong would've knocked her out of an assassin's way, if he was trying to kill her, then I realized the kid who'd shot that terrorist couldn't be anybody but Jenna, herself. They hustled Ianira out of danger and pulled Marcus and the girls out of another terrorist hit at the daycare center. Then Armstrong and Julius took Marcus and the girls down the Wild West Gate—"

"And Jenna came here," Margo finished. "With Ianira."

"Right. And the hit men who went through the Wild West Gate killed Julius, thinking he was Jenna Caddrick."

Margo sat up very straight. "Then the men Benny Catlin killed were *hatchet men*? The one she shot at the Piccadilly Hotel and the one who chased her all the way to the Royal Opera?"

"It certainly seems probable," Malcolm frowned. "But what game is Kaederman playing?"

"That," Skeeter answered softly, "is what I intend to find out. Somebody's lying. Either Kaederman is or the Senator is."

"Or both," Margo muttered.

"Or both. So we've not only got to find Armstrong and Miss Caddrick, but we don't dare let Kaederman know, if we do locate them. Not 'til we know more about his game and why he's playing it."

"Skeeter," Malcolm sighed, "you have a distressing knack for handing out problems it would take Sherlock Holmes, himself, to untangle."

Skeeter grinned and dug out Goldie Morran's counterfeit banknotes and his Pinkerton badge. "Maybe so, but this time, I've got an ace or two up my sleeve . . ."

Kit Carson had narrowly avoided death hundreds of times during his career as a time scout. But no one had ever tried to crush him by shoving luggage off a five-story platform. The man who'd crashed the Britannia scored a first in Kit's life. Kit saw the big cases slither over the edge of the platform, slither and topple and fall straight toward him, where he stood trapped in the middle of a sardine-packed crowd.

He did the only thing he could. "*Look out!*"

Then shoved aside three women, knocked down two reporters, and lunged sideways, himself, trying to get as many of them as possible out of the way. People screamed and bolted, trampling one another in a rising panic. Then he was down, sprawled flat under running feet, as the enormous steamer trunks revolved in a slow-motion tumble . . .

Steel struck sparks when the first trunk smashed into the lobby floor. Catches burst and contents exploded as the other four trunks and a deadly rain of portmanteaus cannoned into the wild crowd. One of the smaller cases bounced, cracking down one whole side, then rebounded like a grenade into a hapless tourist just above Kit. The blow struck the man's arm so hard, all that broke loose was a sick gasp.

A woman in high heels ran straight across Kit's back, digging divots through his ribs. Kit dragged himself under the rope barricades into the departures lounge, away from the outward rush of fleeing spectators. He'd no more than pulled himself under the nearest staircase when the man who'd crashed the Britannia leaped over the railing, landing atop the hapless tourist with the shattered arm. The man went down with a scream. The gate crasher staggered, going down under the weight of the woman slung over his shoulder, then someone slammed against him and he dropped his hostage. The woman slithered, unconscious, to the floor as the gate crasher disappeared under the feet of the wild throng.

Kit scrambled out from under the stairs, running toward the abandoned hostage, who lay ominously still. He checked gently for broken bones and tested the pulse at her throat, unable to reach her wrist under its tight Victorian sleeve. She lay crumpled on her stomach, long dark hair falling in disarray across her face, obscuring her features. Kit was afraid to move her until he was certain there were no broken bones. Very gently, he eased her hair back . . . and gasped sharply. *Shahdi Feroz!* What was the Ripperologist doing back in TT-86, weeks too early? She'd followed the gate crasher through, leading the efforts to capture him. Kit didn't care for the ominous implications.

A nasty bruise was swelling and purpling along her temple. She needed medical attention. Kit searched the confusion of screaming, running tourists. Half a dozen fistfights were in progress and a medi-van was just arriving at the edge of the riot zone.

"Medical!" The roar of the seething melee swallowed his shout as though he'd barely whispered. The only people who heard were a handful of vultures who'd descended on the spilled luggage, carting off cash and valuables. The nearest looter glanced up, looked right at him, then ran for cover, pockets stuffed with spoils. Kit cursed roundly. He'd have to go find someone.

Kit bolted through the chaos, heading toward the arriving medi-vans. He reached the nearest and flagged down a team. "Medical! Dr. Shahdi Feroz is back there, unconscious. The gate crasher knocked her out."

The emergency technician said, "Sorry, we're under a triage emergency. We're transporting critical cases first. There's already been one outright murder. Someone snapped a tourist's neck like kindling." The technician was stooping to work feverishly over a tourist whose broken leg lay at a ghastly angle, with bone protruding from the skin and blood spurting from a severed artery. The tech had tightened down a tourniquet and was trying to stabilize the break enough to transport for surgery.

"Do what you have to," Kit shot back, "but somebody'll want to talk to her ASAP, ask her why she came running through the gate after that maniac, and why he tried to snatch her."

The tech shot him a startled glance, finished strapping the leg brace over the tourniquet, then grabbed his squawky while others lifted the tourist into the back of a medi-van. "We need an assist, pronto, with Dr. Shahdi Feroz. Station manager's gonna want her story the minute she's awake. She's near—" the tech asked with a glance and Kit pointed "—the gate platform stairs."

The radio crackled. "Roger, we've got somebody on it."

"Thanks," Kit nodded.

He was pushing his way back toward Dr. Feroz when the entire station shook to the thunder of emergency sirens. Kit jerked to a stunned halt as the pattern of the maddened wail registered. "*Code Seven Red! Repeat, Code Seven Red!* Clear the Commons! All visitors to Shangri-La Station, clear the Commons immediately! Visitors are hereby restricted to hotel rooms for their own safety. Station residents, please assist security in clearing Commons. Repeat, Code Seven Red, Zone Three . . ."

"*Code Seven Red?*" Kit gasped.

That particular code hadn't been invoked in the entire history of Shangri-La Station. And Zone Three was right outside the infirmary, in Little Agora. Kit bolted, heading for the trouble zone, intent on finding out what had just broken loose inside the station. He met the answer at the door to the infirmary. Ann Vinh Mulhaney, bleeding badly, was being rushed toward surgery by station security. A gash ran down her shoulder, shallow enough, thank God, not to prove instantly fatal, but her collar bone had been laid bare by the slashing attack. She held one of her Irish Royal Constabulary Webley pistols in a white-knuckled death grip. From the look in her eyes, it would take an act of God to pry it loose again.

Rachel appeared at a dead run. "Get her onto a gurney!" she ordered, ripping open the remains of Ann's blouse to apply direct pressure with both hands. "Compresses, stat!"

A nurse ran for the supply cabinet.

Ann Vinh Mulhaney's lips were moving as the gurney rushed past Kit, on a direct course for surgery. "Bastard was on me before I knew he was there. Almost got my stomach. Dropped to the floor to get out from under his knife. Pulled my Webley, shot at him. Missed, God *damn* the son of a bitch . . ."

The Code Seven Red made abrupt, horrifying sense. Kit knew, without anyone having to confirm it, who their gate crasher had been and why Shahdi Feroz had bolted into the station on his heels. Kit shut his eyes for a long, horrified moment.

Jack the Ripper.

Loose on Shangri-La Commons.

And with Mary Kelly still very much alive in London of 1888, it was high odds he couldn't even be killed. History could not be changed. Jolly Jack had to survive long enough to cut that poor girl into mangled pieces. Kit began to curse, starting in English and moving through Portuguese, German, Latin, Old Norse, and every other language he'd ever learned. If the petite weapons instructor hadn't been so well trained, if she hadn't been the kind of woman who went armed everywhere but bed . . .

Station sirens slashed through the infirmary once more.

"*Code Seven Red, Zone Five! Repeat, Code Seven Red, Zone Five!* All resident time scouts and guides, report to station security immediately for emergency duty. Clear the Commons at once, this station is hereby under martial law. Code Seven Red, Zone Five . . ."

Kit bolted toward the door, glancing at the television in the infirmary lobby, tuned to Channel Three, which was permanently hooked into the Commons' extensive security-camera system. Station security, pest control, even BATF agents herded terrified and angry tourists toward their hotels, using riot batons to push them along when necessary.

"Caddrick is gonna eat this up like a hog in heaven," Kit groaned, abandoning the television and heading out the door at a dead run. He had barely cleared the entryway when it came again. "*Code Seven Red! Zone Six!* All Shangri-La shop owners, lock down and secure your areas. Any visitors not clear of the Commons in three minutes will be arrested on sight. Repeat, Code Seven Red, Zone Six . . ."

Security rushed past carrying a woman with long, dark hair. She'd been gashed from navel to groin. A badly shaken security officer was holding her abdomen closed, keeping direct pressure on with hands gloved in blood, while two others carried her. Kit started rounding up shaken, confused tourists. "Clear the Commons!" he roared above the wailing sirens. "Get to a hotel!"

"But we're in the Neo Edo!"

"I don't care if you're camping out in the basement! Get to the nearest hotel and stay there!" He herded them toward the Time Tripper, which was closest. They could sort out who was supposed to be where later, after the innocents had been gotten out of harm's way.

Within five minutes, Commons was nearly clear, echoingly empty. Scores of tourists huddled in shop entryways and restaurants, ashen and trapped, unable to reach their hotels. Security and Pest Control officers, even BATF, rushed through the station, driving remnant crowds toward safety. At the edge of Little Agora, Kit could just see two more ashen, grey-lipped security officers carrying the bloodied remains of yet another petite woman with long, dark hair. This one hadn't survived. Her throat had been slashed to the bone, her abdomen ripped and gashed.

Kit cursed long and harshly, driving his last charges into the Time Tripper's crowded lobby, then headed for the nearest security team to offer his services for the manhunt. Wally Klontz' radio crackled just as Kit jogged up.

"We need a medical team in Valhalla, stat! Massive coronary at the Langskip Cafe."

"On it!" a harried voice responded.

"What can I do?" Kit asked as Wally sent a team of Pest Control officers bolting toward the emergency.

"Kit, thank God. Try to find someone from the Council of Seven, get the down-timers organized. We need a station-wide manhunt. Jack the Goddamned Ripper crashed the Britannia and the Ripper Cults have gone mad, attacking every petite, dark-haired woman on station."

Kit's eyes widened. "My God! They're trying to kill Shahdi Feroz."

"What?"

"Shahdi Feroz! She came through the Britannia after the Ripper. He tried to kidnap her, but dropped her in the riot. I left her lying unconscious at the departures lounge, waiting for medical treatment."

Wally Klontz keyed his radio. "Alert, Signal Eight-Delta, repeat, Signal Eight-Delta, missing person, Dr. Shahdi Feroz. Expedite, condition red. We need a location on Dr. Feroz, stat. She's the Ripper's target."

The radio crackled and sputtered, then someone said, "Roger, Signal Eight-Delta, Shahdi Feroz."

Kit said tersely, "I'm heading back to Victoria Station to look for her."

Wally nodded as his radio crackled again. Kit broke into a run as Wally flagged down a pair of BATF agents. Commons had never been so echoingly deserted. A score or more of injuries, an outright murder during the Britannia riot, and three women slashed by the Ripper cults, sparking three Code Seven Reds in damn near as many minutes . . . How many more people would die before they could stop this maniac and his worshippers? *If* they could stop him? John Caddrick would have a field day with this, curse him. And God alone knew what those damned I.T.C.H. agents would do, faced with fresh disaster. Shangri-La Station needed a miracle.

Kit was very much afraid they'd just run out of grace.

(((Chapter 13)))

Ianira Cassondra woke slowly from a long, blurred nightmare to the sound of rumbling wagons, bright voices speaking incomprehensible English, and the laughter of small children at play. She stirred beneath warm quilts and turned her head toward the sounds, deeply confused. The presence which had waited like a monstrous, ravening wolf, swooping down across her each time she had awakened from drugged stupor, was gone without a trace. For long moments she could not bring herself to believe that, even when her eyelids fluttered open to reveal a shabby, well-scrubbed room she had never seen before.

Someone moved close beside her and she focused her gaze slowly on a familiar face. She knew him at once, but the change in those familiar, beloved features shocked her speechless. Marcus' face was lined, his hair greying at the temples, and a terror of long standing burned hot in his eyes. His smile was radiant as the sunlight, however, as he took her hand. "You are home, Ianira. Safe."

She lifted a trembling hand, touching his face, finding wetness under her fingertips. "How—?"

"We followed him. He gave a lecture and we followed him when he went beneath the streets. We found you after he had gone, took you out of his horrible little room and brought you home. We're in London, beloved, in Spitalfields, hiding with Noah and Jenna. The girls are safe with us."

She began to cry, from sheer relief and the release of pent-up

639

terror. Marcus held her close and she clutched him tightly, revelling in the touch of his hands and lips. "I tried to escape," she whispered, "but he caught me. Kept me drugged. Marcus, he wanted to use me, to gain power . . ."

"He is mad," Marcus said roughly.

"Yes. He is the Ripper."

Marcus' arms tightened protectively. "You will never see him again. This, I swear."

When the first storm of emotion had finally passed, Ianira tipped her head back and gazed into her husband's wet eyes. "I want to see our children, husband."

Marcus hesitated

Ianira touched the grey in his hair. "Tell me."

"We had no choice," he began, voice agonized. "They came after us, in Colorado. Julius . . ." He faltered. "Julius died, beloved. Their gunman murdered him. Noah and I took the girls away, ran for the train and fled east."

The grey in his hair, the lines that had aged his face, his reluctance to call the girls made abrupt sense. "You did not return to the station," she whispered, shaken. "It has been three years for you, hasn't it?"

He nodded. "Please forgive me . . ."

She could not stop the tears, but lifted a trembling hand and placed it across his lips. "No, there is nothing to forgive. I have seen what war does to people. Ephesus was fighting for her independence. Was not my marriage to an Athenian part of that war, with me as a sacrifice? You and I have been caught in another war, Marcus. We are under attack from these men who seek Jenna's life. They use madmen like the *Ansar Majlis* to destroy and terrorize. In such a war, losing three years of your company, three years from my children's lives is nothing. Nothing at all, compared to losing *you*."

The terror faded from his eyes, replaced by a flood of tears. He kissed her gently, as though she were made of fragile alabaster, and smoothed back her hair where long strands clung to damp cheeks. Then he went to the door and called in their children. Artemisia had grown into a tall, beautiful girl of seven, with wide, dark eyes and a curiously adult air of watchfulness and restraint. Gelasia clung to her sister's hand, eyes bright and inquisitive as she studied Ianira.

Little Gelasia spoke first. "Are you really my mamma?"

Ianira's throat closed and Artemisia said in a voice tinged with distinct British tones, "Of course she is, don't you remember?" Then Misia rushed across the room, flinging herself into Ianira's arms. "I missed you, Mamma!"

"Oh, my darling . . ."

Little Gelasia was more than willing to accept the return of a mother into her life, snuggling up to Ianira and telling her solemnly about her new doll and the lessons Noah had been giving them. "I can read!" she said proudly. "Papa and Noah taught me!"

"You have always been a clever girl," Ianira smiled. "You and Misia, both." She ruffled her older daughter's hair affectionately. "What do you study, Misia?"

"English and Greek and Latin," she answered promptly, "with Papa, and history and mathematics and geography with Noah and Jenna." A shy smile came and went. "And we study the future, too. Noah has a little computer, like a time scout's log, so we will understand science and technology when we go home to the station."

Home to the station . . .

"You miss the station?" Ianira asked softly.

Artemisia nodded. "Sometimes. I miss the school and the television and the music. And I miss Uncle Skeeter. Do you remember when we fed the big pterodactyl and the bucket of fish spilled down his shirt? I can just remember that. We laughed and laughed."

"We all miss Uncle Skeeter," Ianira agreed. "When it is safe again, we will go home."

Artemisia's eyes told Ianira that her daughter remembered the violence of their last day on the station only too clearly. "Yes, Mamma. When it is safe again. If the bad men come here, I will help Noah and Jenna and Papa kill them."

Ianira shivered. Another casualty of war: innocence.

"Then we must hope," Ianira said gently, "that the bad men never come, because I will never let anyone harm my beautiful little girls."

As she hugged her daughters close, Ianira could sense danger beyond the walls of their house in Spitalfields. It was not the same danger she had felt in John Lachley's presence. This was a cold, implacable danger which threatened from the future, from the world beyond the station's Primary Gate. Somewhere nearby, the killers who had sought Jenna's life in New York and their own lives on the station were searching for them in the dismal, rain-drenched streets of London.

Skeeter was up at the crack of dawn and on the street very shortly afterward, with Margo as a guide. They left Spaldergate House in company with a mass of Time Tours baggage handlers, groomsmen from the stables, even a couple of the housemaids, all detailed to the search team.

"We'll spread out through SoHo first," Margo briefed them in the dimly lit stable. "We'll search street by street, combing the clothiers shops. We're looking for a merchant or merchants who've been robbed with counterfeit banknotes. Strike up casual conversations, see what you can turn up. If you stumble onto a hot lead, get word to Skeeter and me. I'll be wearing an earpiece under my hat, so you can signal me by radio." She handed around miniaturized transmitters, which vanished into coat pockets. "I'd advise taking umbrellas, since it looks like more rain. And here are the photos Mr. Gilbert reproduced last night." She handed out thick, card-backed "tin-type" prints of Noah Armstrong, Marcus, and "Benny Catlin" as they'd appeared at the lecture, taken from Margo's scout log. "Any questions? All right, then, let's move."

A Time Tours carriage drove Skeeter and Margo to Regent Street, an ultrafashionable thoroughfare lined with ritzy tailors' establishments, fine bootmakers' shops, ladies' milliners, every sort of fashionable emporium a Londoner might want to visit. At this hour, Regent Street was very nearly silent, the shops deserted and the streets clear of traffic. "We won't actually be searching Regent Street," Margo told Skeeter, carefully holding her skirts and long umbrella aside as Skeeter handed her down to the pavement. "But Regent Street forms the western border of SoHo, which is jam-packed with the kind of shops middle-class businessmen frequent. These," she waved the tip of her umbrella toward the expensive establishments along Regent

Street, "won't even open for a couple of hours, but SoHo gets up with the birds, same as its clientele."

She was right about that. As Skeeter escorted her eastward, activity and noise picked up sharply. Delivery wagons groaned through the streets, their heavy drays straining against harness and collar, heads thrust forward and hooves ringing against the cobbles with the sharp sound of iron on stone. Shop keepers rattled open doors, jangling tiny brass bells against the glass, while clerks arranged window displays to their liking and called greetings to the draymen or dickered over prices and freight charges with delivery men. Shop girls, neat as pins in their starched dresses and aprons, bustled to greet early customers. A tantalizing drift from a bakery's open door set Skeeter's mouth to watering.

"Let's start there," Margo decided, nodding toward a respectable looking shop advertising gentlemen's suiting off the rack.

Skeeter held the door, escorting Margo inside. A middle-aged clerk in a well-made if inexpensive suit greeted them. "Good morning. How may I assist you?"

Margo gave the clerk a surprisingly cool smile, causing Skeeter to glance more sharply at her. "Good morning," she inclined her head politely. "My name is Smythe, sir, and this is Mr. Jackson, of America. We're hoping you might be of some assistance in a rather difficult situation. Mr. Jackson is a Pinkerton man, a sort of private police agency. He's come to London on the trail of a counterfeiter, a man who's deprived me of a considerable sum of money I could ill afford to lose."

"Counterfeiter?" Genuine alarm showed in the clerk's guileless eyes. "D'you mean to say we've a counterfeiter working in SoHo?"

Skeeter produced a sample of Goldie's fake banknotes. "These are some of the forgeries recovered from Miss Smythe, here. I have reason to believe the men producing these banknotes are passing them somewhere in SoHo. This young lady is not the only vicitm they have damaged. I've traced this gang from Colorado to New York to London and I mean to locate them, sir."

The clerk's eyes had widened in sympathetic surprise. "I should hope so! I'll check the cash drawer at once!" The clerk searched carefully, but located none of Goldie's fake banknotes, nor could he recall having seen any of the gentlemen in the photographs Skeeter produced. The clerk frowned over them, shaking his head. "No, sir, I'm afraid I don't recognize any of them. But I'll certainly be on my guard and I shall inform my employer immediately to be wary of any fivers and ten-pound notes we receive."

"My card," Skeeter handed over the first of several dozen Spaldergate's staff had run off for him the previous night, "if anything should turn up."

"Deeply obliged, sir," the clerk said earnestly, "for the warning. I'll keep your card right here in the cash drawer."

Skeeter tipped his hat as Margo thanked the clerk, then they headed for the next shop. And the one after that, moving from street to street, until Skeeter's feet ached and his throat burned and the skies poured miserable, sooty rain down their collars. He and Margo hastily opened thick umbrellas against the downpour and checked the time on Skeeter's pocket watch.

"One o'clock. No wonder my feet are killing me."

"And my stomach's about to have a close encounter with my spine," Margo said ruefully. "Let's find something to eat, then keep searching."

The afternoon was no more profitable than the morning had been, just wetter. By the time Margo admitted they'd struck out, the sun was already below the rooftops and the chilly evening wind was biting through Skeeter's overcoat.

"I'm afraid there's not much more we can do today," Margo sighed.

"Maybe someone else found something?"

"They would've contacted us," she said with a slight shake of her head. "Let's get back to Spaldergate. We'll cross check with everyone else and come up with a new plan of attack for tomorrow."

"My feet aren't even going to speak to me by tomorrow," Skeeter groaned, flagging down a ratty-looking hansom cab.

The two-wheeled, open carriage slithered to a halt at the kerbside. "Battersea," Margo called up as Skeeter handed her into the cab, "and I've consulted Mogg's!"

"Why, I'd never cheat a lady, miss!"

The cabbie flicked his reins and they set out at a jolting trot.

"What's Mogg's?" Skeeter asked, hanging onto his seat and struggling with his stubborn umbrella.

"Mogg's maps." She pulled a little booklet from her handbag and passed it over. "Study it carefully. It lists the fares for every conceivable route through the city. Otherwise, cabbies will cheat you blind."

"I'll remember that," Skeeter said as the horse jolted around a corner and swung smartly into heavy traffic, nearly colliding with two carriages and a drayman's wagon and eliciting rude commentaries from cabbies they narrowly avoided while rounding a traffic circus Skeeter didn't recognize. "If we survive so long. Man, not even New York traffic is this nuts!"

Margo just grimaced and held on.

True to Margo's prediction, nobody else had found a trace of counterfeit banknotes, nor had anyone located a witness who could identify Armstrong, Catlin, or Marcus. Skeeter was feeling massively discouraged when he eased his aching, blistered feet into a basin of hot water in his bedroom. Maybe they hadn't bought their clothes in SoHo? Or maybe they'd lucked out and used genuine banknotes when making the purchase? What else would they have to buy, which could be paid for with Goldie's counterfeit banknotes? Food, of course, and coal for the cookstove and fireplace. But they weren't likely to pay for any of *that* with five- and ten-pound banknotes.

"Well," he mused aloud, "they have to live somewhere, don't they?" Had they brought enough cash between them to buy a house or were they reduced to renting? Probably the latter, unless Armstrong had found lucrative employment somewhere. According to Goldie's records, she hadn't changed enough currency for "Benny Catlin" to buy a London house, not even a really ratty one. But if they were renting, they might well use larger denominations to make the payments. "I wonder how somebody goes about renting a house in London?"

He asked that question at dinner, since Kaederman had announced his intention of taking all his meals in his room. Malcolm toyed thoughtfully with a spoonful of turtle soup—the mock variety, since no one in Spaldergate House would buy sea turtle, even if the creatures wouldn't be endangered for another century. As he pushed around bits of mock turtle meat, Malcolm's brow furrowed slightly.

"We hadn't pursued that avenue of inquiry, Skeeter, because finding one man in all of London by knocking up every leasing agency in the city is an even longer shot than checking infirmaries and hospital wards. But we're not looking for Benny Catlin on his own, any longer, we're looking for a rather conspicuous group, aren't we? Yes, we might do well, at that, searching for some trace of such a group. One leases a house through a variety of means, generally via agencies which maintain lists of properties to let. Quite a few such agencies also have telephones, these days. We could put someone on it from Spaldergate while the rest of us continue to search along other lines. And there will certainly be agencies we shall have to check in person."

Miss Tansy, Spaldergate's capable administrative assistant, offered to compile a list. "I'll begin telephoning when the agencies open tomorrow."

"Thanks," Skeeter said, flashing her a grateful smile.

When he finally crawled into bed, he dreamed of endless shopfronts, their windows streaming with sooty grey rain, and of endless, babbling voices and blurred faces reflecting only puzzled bafflement as he posed question after question. When Skeeter finally woke, aching and tired with the unfair exhaustion that comes of too many stressful dreams, he roused into consciousness with an immediate awareness of a renewed throbbing from his feet, a gradual awareness of watery light and the spatter of rain falling against his window, and the unhappy knowledge that he would have to coax his swollen and protesting feet through several more miles of London's mazelike collection of storefronts. He sighed, eased gingerly out of bed, and got ready for another day of searching.

Surely there had to be an easier way to go legit?

Shahdi Feroz knew she was lucky when she woke up on the Commons floor. She was alive. Frankly, she hadn't expected to wake up again. She tried to move and bit her lips over a gasp of pain, then opted for lying very still, instead. A station riot had erupted as far as her swollen right eye could see. Given the shocking bruises she could feel the length of her body, Shahdi suspected panic stricken tourists had stepped on her, multiple times. John Lachley's single, if somewhat devastating, right cross to her temple couldn't begin to account for her stiff, unresponsive limbs and aching back muscles.

At the moment, she could only give profound and shaken thanks that John Lachley had dropped her at all. What he would've done to her . . . She shuddered, recalling the sight of Dominica Nosette's severed head clutched in his hand. Poor, stupid reporter. The rest of her lay in the basement of New Scotland Yard on Whitehall; they'd watched Lachley drop off the mutilated torso and bid her a flippant farewell, via the camera hidden at the construction site. Shahdi was gingerly flexing her fingers, trying to decide whether or not her body would accept being pushed to hands and knees, when someone literally dragged her to her feet. Blinding light caught her square in the eyes and the world erupted into a chaos of shouting voices.

"Dr. Feroz—"

"—comment—"

"—really Jack the Ripper—"

"—how could you allow that monster—"

She stumbled and swayed sharply, and would've fallen again if she hadn't collided with someone far taller and heavier than herself. The man grasped her by the shoulders, keeping her on her feet, then a new voice thundered into her awareness.

"By God, you're going to answer for this!"

Before she could even blink her vision clear, Shahdi was dragged forward, tottering off balance, literally hauled through the chaos by a man whose grip added another layer of bruises. Still half-stunned from Lachley's blow, she couldn't even offer a struggle for the first hundred paces. By the time her head was clear enough to realize she'd just been assaulted—again—and had been kidnapped by some new maniac, there wasn't a security officer in sight.

Shahdi dug in her heels. "Let go of me!"

She wasn't sure whose face she expected to swing furiously into focus.

Senator John Caddrick hadn't even made her list of possibilities.

She gasped, then wrenched her arm free. "Who do you think you are? Take your hands off me at once!"

"Oh, no you don't!" Caddrick snarled, dragging her forward again. "You and I have an appointment with federal authorities. I want some answers!"

She twisted free once more, ready for combat. "Touch me again and I will have you jailed for assault and battery!"

Before Caddrick could reply—or grab her wrist again—a howling mob of reporters descended, screaming questions and thrusting cameras and microphones into their faces. From somewhere out of the confusion, a uniformed BATF agent appeared.

"Thank God! You found her!" the agent cried, speaking briefly into her radio. "Secure from Signal Eight-Delta, I have Dr. Feroz, unharmed."

"Roger, bring her in."

"Dr. Feroz, please come with me immediately. Your life is in danger."

Another security patrol rushed toward them, flanking Shahdi and pushing back reporters with a certain callousness that shocked her.

"What's going on?" Caddrick demanded.

"Dr. Feroz is being taken into protective custody. The Ripper Cults have targeted her for murder."

While she tried to take in the implications of that shocking statement, the security agents hustled Shahdi through the station, leaving Caddrick and the reporters to trail after them, shouting questions nobody answered. They literally dragged Shahdi through the doorway into security headquarters, with the Senator and fifty screaming newsies on their heels. The lobby was in chaos. Agents scrambled past them, swearing and shoving reporters aside with scant regard for broken equipment. Telephones shrilled for attention between deafening hoots from the station's emergency sirens. Dispatchers shouted instructions into radios, scribbled information from the reports crackling over the speakers.

John Caddrick stood staring at the confusion, then strode toward the main desk, mouth thinned to near invisibility. Shahdi was escorted past the uncertain haven of the dispatcher's desk where a harried woman was shouting into a radio. A moment later, Shahdi found herself in a nearly empty corridor lined with closed doors. "This way, Dr. Feroz," her escort said, steering her around a corner. They cannoned straight into someone at least two feet taller than Shahdi was. She staggered and fell against the wall, then found herself staring up at Ronisha Azzan, Shangri-La's Deputy Station Manager.

"Dr. Feroz?" Ronisha Azzan blinked. "Thank God, I was told you'd been located. Come with me, please. I was just coming down to meet you."

Behind the tall Deputy Station Manager, a squat, fire-plug shape was storming down the corridor like a torpedo fired at a battleship. Shahdi blinked in surprise. Bull Morgan was out of jail. Caddrick rounded the corner at just that moment, then stood sputtering. "What's he doing out of jail?"

The squat station manager growled, "What the hell is he doing here?" reminding Shahdi of an angry pit bull.

Caddrick flushed, nostrils flaring with barely controlled anger as he stared up at the tall deputy station manager beside Bull Morgan. "Azzan, I will have your head for this! Letting a known criminal out of jail before—"

Bull Morgan shouldered him aside. "Get out of my security headquarters. You're obstructing an emergency operation during a declared state of martial law. Leave right now or pick out your cell in the detention block. The one I've been using is free."

"How dare you—"

The security agents who'd escorted Shahdi to safety produced handcuffs and startlingly effective grins. The nearest said with a chuckle, "Mr. Morgan never bluffs, Senator. And neither does the BATF."

Caddrick sputtered for an instant longer, then turned on his heel and strode away. Bull bit the end of a cigar he'd magicked out of a pocket. "Better give that schmuck an escort back to his hotel. God knows, we don't want anything happening to him out there."

Security pelted after him as Bull appropriated his deputy manager's radio. "*Benson!* Report, goddammit!" He strode off before

Shahdi could hear the reply. Ronisha Azzan stalked after him, drawing Shahdi along.

"Ms. Azzan," she said, wincing as the rapid pace jolted her bruises, "I don't know what a Code Seven Red is, but I do know Jack the Ripper is loose on this station and right now, I know more about Dr. John Lachley than anyone else on TT-86. I'd like to help."

The tall deputy manager nodded her thanks. "Doctor, you just got yourself a job."

Moments later, she was at ground zero of the biggest crisis in the history of time tourism, wondering what on earth she was going to tell the harried, white-faced security officers looking to her for answers.

By the end of his first week in London, Skeeter Jackson had begun to think Jenna Caddrick and Noah Armstrong had made their own clothes. Or that Noah had bought their entire wardrobe in the States and brought it over by ship. Hundreds of tailors' shops and ready-made clothing stores, scattered throughout SoHo, had yielded not so much as a trace of the missing Senator's daughter and her companions. Even the inquiry into leasing agents had drawn a blank. None of the agents they consulted had found any counterfeit banknotes, nor could they identify the photos Skeeter and the other searchers circulated.

At Malcolm's suggestion, they turned their attention to the East End, a far more dangerous territory to search. Teams consisted of three searchers minimum, for safety's sake. Also at Malcolm's suggestion, Sid Kaederman remained at Spaldergate, supervising the teams fielded to question private physicians and surgeons; the actual questioning was done by Spaldergate staff and Time Tours porters.

Skeeter's first run into the East End was supervised by two seasoned pros: Malcolm and Margo, who wanted to be sure he knew the ropes before turning him loose with a couple of groomsmen. Whitechapel, with its dismal, dirty streets and its stench of rotting refuse in the gutters, was open for business well before Skeeter arrived, less than an hour past dawn.

Immense wagonloads of freight groaned their cumbersome way down Houndsditch, Aldgate High Street, and Commercial Street.

Heavy drays with chipped, ponderous hooves and shabby coats of hair growing in thick for winter, strained against worn leather harness and collars. The big draft horses carted vast tonnages of export goods to the docks for shipment across the face of the world, and brought out staggering amounts of raw lumber and bales of cotton arriving from foreign shores, huge bundles of animal hides and fur for the leather and garment industries, ingots of pig iron and copper and tin for the smelting plants and iron works which belched their stinking smoke into Whitechapel's skies. The high whine and rasp of industrial saws poured from open factory windows, like clouds of enraged wasps spilling furiously from a nest shaken by a foolish little boy.

And everywhere, the people: dirty to the pores with coal smoke and industrial grime no amount of scrubbing with harsh lye soap could remove. Women in frowsy dresses ran bakeshops, trundled basketloads of fish and flowers, plied meat cleavers against stained butchers' blocks in grimy little storefronts whose back rooms often hid the misery and desperation of illegal abortions. Men hauled butchered carcasses over their shoulders or gutted fish in stinking open-air markets where feral cats and fat, sleek rats fought for discarded offal and fish heads.

Other men hauled handcarts piled high with bricks and building stone or carried grinding wheels on frayed leather harnesses, calling out in roughened voices, "Knives to grind!" as they wandered from shop to doorstep. Boys ran urgent errands, clutching baskets of vegetables and heavy stacks of newspapers, or trundled rickety wheelbarrows spilling over with piles of red, coarse brick dust which they sold in little sackfuls. One boy jogged along with a ferret in his arms, leading a bright-eyed spaniel on a worn leather leash.

"Good grief, is that a pet ferret?" Skeeter turned to stare.

Malcolm followed his glance. "Not a pet. That boy's a rat-catcher. 'You maun have a ferret, to catch a rat,'" he added in what sounded suspiciously like a quotation. "He'll spend the day over in the better parts of town, de-ratting some rich woman's house. The ferret chases them out and the spaniel kills the sneaky little beasts."

"And the boy gets paid a small fortune by some hysterical housewife," Skeeter guessed.

Margo shook her head. "More likely by some frantic housekeeper who doesn't want to lose her place because rats have broken into the cellar or littered in the best linens."

"There is that," Skeeter admitted as the boy dodged past, heading west. Then he spotted a long, shallow wooden trough where girls appeared to be dunking handfuls of dried leaves into stinking dye. "What in the world are they doing?"

"Dying tea leaves," Malcolm said drolly.

"*Dying* them? What for?"

Margo chuckled. "There's fortunes to made in the tea-recycling business. Housekeepers in wealthy households sell used tea leaves for a tidy sum, then girls in the tea trade dye the leaves so they look new and sell them in the poorer parts of town."

"Remind me not to buy tea anywhere around here. What's in that stuff they're using? It smells horrible."

"Don't ask," Malcolm said repressively.

"You don't want to know what's in the food around here, either," Margo added. "They keep passing laws against putting in the worst stuff. Like brick dust in sausages, as filler."

"Remind me to skip lunch. And I'm not a squeamish eater." A guy couldn't spend five years in Yesukai the Valiant's tent and stay finicky, not if he wanted to survive. But he'd never eaten brick dust—of that, at least, he was morally certain. They passed the Ten Bells, a public house strategically poised on the corner of roaring Commercial Street and Fournier, within sight of the gleaming white spire of Christchurch, Spitalfields. Rough-dressed men loitered near the entrance, eyeing tired women who walked slowly past, returning the interested stares with calculating glances. A shabby woman selling roasted chestnuts beside the door paid the prostitutes no attention, reserving her efforts for paying customers. One woman who'd stopped to rest against the pub's wall was driven away by a nearby constable.

"Move on, there, or I'll take you in, so I will!"

The woman's reply was not precisely in English, baffling Skeeter with a sharp spate of incomprehensible syllables, but she moved farther down the street. Skeeter scratched his neck. "What was that all about?"

Malcolm said quietly, "They aren't allowed to pick a spot and solicit. They have to keep moving. Women walk from pub to pub, or simply circle a building like Saint Botolph's Church, known locally as the 'prostitutes' church,' for the women walking in dreary circles around it, hours at a time. They often stake out little territories without ever stopping long enough to get themselves arrested. Mary Kelly patrols the area around the Ten Bells pub, there. Rumor is, she's very jealous of her beat. Of course, that may just be sour grapes from the other women. She's very pretty and vivacious. She likes to sing and the men like her."

Margo put in, "Women like poor Liz Stride would've hated her for it."

Skeeter had seen enough pictures of Long Liz to know she'd been a mannish, horse-faced Swede, missing half her teeth, poor creature. Word was, her lover had been utterly devastated by her death. "Well," Skeeter cleared his throat, "where do we start? I hadn't realized the East End was so big."

"Huh, this is nothing," Margo put in. "You ought to see the docklands. They stretch out to forever."

Malcolm cast a jaundiced eye at his fiancée. "I fear Mr. Jackson will have ample opportunity to tour the docklands before this business is done. Now that you've seen something of Whitechapel, Mr. Jackson, and have a feel for the territory, I would suggest we repair to Middlesex Street. If they're supplying their wardrobe from the East End, it's the likest spot to search."

"I'm following you," Skeeter said ruefully.

Malcolm led the way past Christchurch, which rose in startling white purity from the grime, and walked briskly down to Fashion Street, then cut over to Middlesex, a long block to the west. The Sunday cloth fair which had given the street its famous nickname was conspicuously absent, but shops selling ready-mades of a cheap cut, mostly stitched from mill-ends cloth, were open for business. Malcolm pushed open the door of the nearest, leaving Skeeter and Margo to follow. As the door swung shut with a solid thump, a well-scrubbed shop girl in a worn dress eyed them, taking in their fine clothes with a dubious, narrow-eyed stare.

"Wot you 'ere for?" she asked suspiciously. "You never come round 'ere t'buy togs, not the likes of you, wiv yer fancy city suiting."

Malcolm doffed his hat. "Good morning, miss. No, indeed, you're very sharp. We're hoping you might be able to help us. We're looking for someone."

"I ain't like to grass on nobody, I ain't," she muttered.

Malcolm produced a shining shilling and said casually, "The gentlemen we're looking for are foreigners, miss, foreign swindlers and thieves. They have cheated this young lady of a substantial sum of money by passing counterfeit banknotes and they have robbed me of quite a sum the same way, passing their filthy money at a game of cards last week."

Margo spoke up in a voice Skeeter scarcely recognized. "Give me a fiver, 'e did, miss, said 'e 'adn't got nuffink smaller, an' I give 'im near four quid change for it, when it weren't worth the paper the cheeky blagger printed it on 'is own self."

The girl's eyes widened, her suspicion dwindling under the twin onslaughts of Margo's East End voice and alarmingly serious complaint. Skeeter stepped forward with one of Goldie's sample banknotes. "My name is Jackson, ma'am, from America. I've trailed these criminals all the way from New York, where they were counterfeiting dollars. This is one of their forgeries." He handed over the banknote and let her peer curiously at it, then produced the photographs. "Have you seen any of these men?"

The shopgirl took the heavy cardstock photos and gazed at them carefully, shuffling through them. "No," she said slowly, "never clapped me minces on any blokes wot stood for these 'ere likenesses. But I'll look sharp, so I will. Some tea leaf passed me a bad fiver, I'd just about as well shut me doors an' walk the streets or starve." She handed the photos and the fake banknote back with a grim, angry look in her eyes. "Mark me, I'll keep a sharp butcher's out, so I will."

Malcolm handed her a small white card. "If you do see them, here is where you can reach me." He handed over the shilling, as well, which she pocketed hastily, along with Malcolm's card. He put his hat on again, tipping the brim. "Good day, miss."

They tried the next shop on Middlesex Street, then the one after that and the next in line, with Malcolm sometimes initiating the questions and occasionally Skeeter stepping in to fill that role. They had reached the end of the lane, having covered every shop in Middlesex Street, when a voice rose behind them.

"Mr. Moore, sir! Wait a bit, mister!"

They looked around to see the first girl they'd questioned, running breathlessly toward them. They waited, hope suddenly an electrifying presence in their midst. The girl reached them and gasped out, "Cor, but I'm glad you 'adn't gone yet! Mistress just come into the shop, y'see, it's 'er shop, like, and I told 'er what you said. She thinks she knows of 'em, mister."

Skeeter exchanged startled glances with Margo as Malcolm said, "By all means, let us speak with your employer."

A moment later, they were showing the photographs to a stout, sallow-cheeked woman with white hair and poor teeth. "That's 'im, I don't doubt," the woman said, pointing to Noah Armstrong's photograph. "Of a Sunday, when the market's in the street, me sister-in-law sets up a stall just outside, there. Sold a fistful of suits, Sunday last, to a bloke wot give 'er a fiver. An' it weren't worth no more'n me shoelaces, come the time she went off t'spend it. I remember the bloke, as I was set up next ter Sally an' she were that excited, she were, t'get a fiver when she needed the money so desperate. Like to put 'er in the work'ouse, bastard did, 'an 'er a war widow wivout no 'usband nor child t'look after 'er in 'er age. It's me own profits, small as they are, wot's paid 'er rent an' put food in 'er Limehouse this week past."

"Do you remember anything about him that might help us locate him? Did he say anything about where he was staying?"

"That 'e didn't, or I'd 'ave sent a copper after 'im."

"My dear lady," Malcolm said, producing two five-pound notes from his wallet, "you have been of incalculable service. Please see that your sister-in-law's losses are replaced."

The old woman's eyes shot wide at the sight of so much money. She took the banknotes with a shaking hand, turned them over and over, staring at them. Wetness spilled over and traced down both cheeks as she closed wrinkled hands around the money. The crackle of crisp paper was loud in Skeeter's ears. Voice trembling, she said to her shopgirl, "Go an' fetch Sally, luv, tell 'er God sent a right proper angel t'look out for us. God bless you, mister."

The girl's eyes were bright, as well. She dropped a brief curtsey and ran out the back way. A door thumped, marking her exit, then Malcolm tipped his hat. "Good day, madam. Thank you again. If you hear anything else, your girl has my card."

They left her clutching the money to her bosom.

The moment the door swung shut behind Skeeter, Malcolm said, "They are here, then, as surmised. It remains to locate their hiding place. It occurs to me that they cannot be staying anywhere in the immediate area, or the shopkeepers hereabouts would have recognized them as neighbors."

"Well, they have to eat, don't they?" Skeeter pointed out.

Malcolm's eyes glinted. "Which means they must procure victuals from a chandler."

"Remember what you said, Malcolm?" Margo said thoughtfully. "If you were going to hide in the East End and knew you would be marked as a foreigner, you'd find a place with a high concentration of immigrants, so you wouldn't stand out so much. Like Spitalfields and Bethnal Green. Let's try the Chandler's Shops up there."

"Indeed," Malcolm glanced north. "A capital idea. Let us begin at Spitalfields Market, shall we?"

They walked rapidly north and jogged west to Bishopsgate, which they followed north again through the bustle and crowds of carts and groaning freight wagons and strolling vendors calling their wares. The market, when they arrived, was a vast confusion of Cockney voices singing out in rhyming patter that echoed with a roar of alien sound.

Fresh flowers spilled a heady perfume into the wet morning air, thousands of blossoms tied in dripping bunches. Flower girls piled them high into heavy baskets and trays for sale in better climes. Fresh vegetables heaped in mounds lent a more sober note to the riot of hothouse flowers. Fishwives haggled over the price of mussels and eels and ragged urchins bartered for coarse-ground flour while their harried mothers counted out pennies for bricks of tea.

"If we can't find a trace of them here," Malcolm shouted above the roar, "I shall be very much surprised. Mr. Jackson, why don't you take the right-hand side of the market. Miss Smith, try the left-hand way and I shall tackle the middle."

They split up and Skeeter approached the first stall, where a sweating woman in her fifties manhandled huge rounds of cheese, hacking off wedges for sale. He gave her the pitch, holding up a shilling to catch her attention.

"Ain't seen 'em," she said shortly, pocketing Skeeter's money.

He tried again at the next stall, where re-dyed tea sold briskly. The negative response cost him another shilling and several elbows in his ribs from customers anxious to buy a brick of tea for tuppence. He moved on to a flower vendor who gave him a suspicious glare over the nodding heads of pure white daisies, their centers yellower than the sun over Spitalfields' grey sky. The woman shook her head impatiently and pocketed the coin. Skeeter glanced around, searching for Margo and Malcolm, making their grim, determined way through the stalls. He turned back with a sigh and tried the next vendor, where slabs of fatty bacon hung from meathooks.

"Why d'you ask about 'em?" the man behind the counter demanded sourly, eyes narrowed as he peered at the photographs.

"We believe they're counterfeiters. They've cheated a young lady who runs a shop up in Bethnal Green, gave her a counterfeit banknote that nearly landed her in the workhouse, unable to pay her bills. I've followed them all the way from America, where they printed dollars instead of pound notes." The man hesitated, giving Skeeter cause to hope. He fished out a glittering half crown coin. "I realize you don't like to grass on anyone," Skeeter said, holding up the coin, "but these men are cheating women who can't afford the loss. An elderly war widow in Middlesex Street lost five pounds to them."

The man's jaw muscles bunched. He spat to one side, then tapped the photograph of Marcus. "I seen 'im, lots o' times. Lives wiv 'is sister and some chap who come over from America. And a pair of sweet little girls, God 'elp 'em, wiv a father like that. Comes 'ere regular, like, t'buy bacon an' flour, 'e does, along wiv 'is sister."

Skeeter handed over the half crown and produced a full sovereign, glittering gold in the light. "Where do they live?"

The man jerked his head to the east. "Be'ind Christchurch, someplace along Fournier Street, is all I know."

"Thank you," Skeeter said quietly, handing over the sovereign and retrieving his photographs. "More than you can know."

He hurried through the mob, finding Malcolm near the end of his own row. The guide wore an expression of frustration. Skeeter waved him over. "Malcolm! I've got a solid lead! Behind Christchurch, on Fournier!"

Malcolm's eyes came violently alive. "By damn, Jackson, good work! Where's Miss Smith?"

They found Margo deep in conversation with a woman selling flour by the scoop. Malcolm caught her eye, but she lifted a hand, so they waited. When the woman finished talking, Margo handed her a whole sovereign and turned toward them, cheeks glowing with excitement.

"You've found them, too?" Malcolm said without preamble.

"Yes! Fournier Street, seventh house on the right. Mr. Anastagio," she tapped Marcus' photo, "and his sister and their friend, Mr. Dillon, from America."

"All I got was Fournier Street," Skeeter admitted wryly.

"Cockney women," Margo chuckled, "love a good gossip. Especially when there's money in it. Let's go beard Mr. Anastagio in his den," she added, eyes bright with excitement.

"By all means," Malcolm agreed, heading out of the crowded market. "And let us pray that Mr. Dillon and Miss Anastagio do nothing rash before we convince them we are Marcus' friends."

Skeeter's heart was triphammering as they turned into Fournier Street and passed poor but well-scrubbed houses where stout women called to one another in Yiddish. At the seventh house on the right, they found shuttered windows and a closed door, but flowers grew in pots along the steps and smoke curled upwards from the chimney. Inside, Skeeter could hear the squeal and laughter of children's voices. His throat tightened. Artemisia's voice . . . teasing her sister . . . Malcolm and Margo waited expectantly, gazes locked on him. Skeeter nodded once, then climbed the stone steps and knocked on the door.

The voices inside cut off sharply, then footsteps hurried their way. Margo joined Skeeter on the top step, just as an unknown voice called out, "Who is it?"

Margo glanced at Skeeter, winking, then raised her voice to carry through the door. "Eh, luv, you got a dog?"

"What?"

"I ast, 'ave you got a dog? There's a bitch wot's littered pups on yer front steps."

The door opened quickly and Skeeter found himself staring at "Benny Catlin"—Jenna Caddrick in the flesh, wearing woolen trousers and a heavy flannel shirt. Wide eyes swept down, looking automatically for the mythical puppies. Suspicion and wild terror leaped into Jenna's eyes and she tried to slam the door in their faces. Margo shoved her foot against it and said, "It's no use running, Miss Caddrick. We're here to help."

At that instant, a childish voice squealed from the dim interior. "*Uncle Skeeter!*"

An instant later, Artemisia had flown into his arms.

Skeeter buried his face in her thick hair to hide the tears.

(((**Chapter 14**)))

Kit Carson arrived at the security office complex with a mob of screaming reporters on his heels. As Kit fled through the doors, someone in a BATF uniform looked around at the howling noise. "Oh, God, who let *them* in?"

Irritated time scouts joined forces with security personnel to bodily shove the horde of newsies back out the door. Several cameras and more than one face failed to survive the process. A cordon of armed guards was hastily thrown into place in front of the doors, pulled from off-duty shifts called in for riot control and search teams.

"What can I do to help?" Kit asked the nearest harried desk jockey, who was manning five phones at once and handing out search assignments. The officer glanced up and three phones shrilled at the same time. She lunged for the nearest, listened, jotted notes, grabbed the next one without bothering to hang up the first. Then swore and grabbed a microphone.

"*Code Seven Red! Zone Nine!* All visitors on station are hereby ordered to seek the nearest available shelter. Repeat, Code Seven Red, Zone Nine!"

Somebody else was snarling, "I don't care who the hell you are, get off this channel! We're in a state of emergency, here . . ."

Kit ground his teeth and waited for somebody to tell him how he could help. He was still waiting when Bull Morgan, slightly thinner than the last time Kit had laid eyes on him, arrived. Bull had already managed to scrape up a cigar someplace, despite the fact he couldn't have been out of his own jail more than five minutes. The station manager was busy masticating the end of it into a pulpy, wet mess that indicated his current level of stress. Kit wondered who'd had the audacity to unlock his cell door. Ronisha Azzan, no doubt. With Jack the Ripper loose on station, she very well might have thrown the federal marshals into jail, just to keep them out of everyone's hair.

Bull caught Kit's eye and waved him over. "Kit, I need someone to hustle downstairs to the weapons ranges and open up the arsenals, Ann's and Sven's, both. We don't have enough arms for our security officers. And I want a couple dozen Found Ones deputized as security to search the subbasements. You know the Found Ones, and they trust you. Give 'em weapons from Sven's lockers, they'll know how to use bladed weapons. And if we had some clubs . . ."

"What about those 1880's style baseball and cricket bats the outfitters stock?"

"Good idea. Get 'em. Every Ripper cult on station has gone nuts, killing women. We need all the help we can get, stopping this mess."

"I'll organize the men in the Found Ones, put together sweep teams."

"Make damned sure the women stay out of harm's way. Especially the dark-haired, petite ones, who look like Dr. Feroz."

"Has anyone seen her?"

Bull twitched the unlit cigar to the other side of his mouth. "She's back with Ronnie, right now, telling us what she knows about this maniac. If he wasn't totally insane before he got here, chances are, he is now. Even the most balanced down-timers go a little bit nuts when they first arrive on station."

The coldness in the pit of Kit's belly deepened. At least the Ripperologist was safe.

"Kit, why don't you join the briefing Dr. Feroz is giving our sweep teams before you organize the Found Ones. You can pass along what she has to say. The briefing is back in Mike's office."

Kit found Shahdi Feroz speaking tersely to a group of security officers, Pest Control units, and BATF. Even the I.T.C.H. agents had put in appearance, listening intently and recording notes of their own.

The Ripperologist was just answering a question. "Yes, that would fit the pattern of a psychotic serial killer. They usually kill to a pattern. If you can unravel the pattern, you can go a long way toward stopping the killer. Unfortunately, in John Lachley's case, it is not so simple. He was killing women in possession of letters which he was desperate to recover. What sort of letters, we still do not know. Clearly, he didn't come to Shangri-La Station looking for them, which suggests he has abandoned whatever plans he'd made, which these letters threatened. I believe he has come forward in time looking for bigger game. Power is what lures him. He rose from obscure beginnings in the East End and pursued a medical degree as a means to greater power. Occult scholarship was another tool he used. Aleister Crowley studied under him and Lachley succeeded in positioning himself as personal advisor to the queen's grandson, Prince Eddy."

A nearby scout muttered, "Now there's a scary thought. The man who bills himself as the prophet of the anti-Christ, studying Satanic ritual under Jack the Ripper."

"What about the Ripper cults?" a BATF agent asked worriedly.

Dr. Feroz thinned her mouth. "That is part of the bad news. Lachley has already begun to wield immense power through the Ripper cults. We must deprive him of his new worshippers, quickly. Isolate him in a time he does not yet understand, while he is still vulnerable to technology which baffles him."

One of the I.T.C.H. agents spoke up. "You can isolate him all you like," the woman said coldly, "but it won't do any good if he can't be killed."

The Ripperologist surprised Kit—and everyone else—with her answer. "We have no guarantee he cannot be killed. After all, Jack the Ripper was two men. It is entirely possible James Maybrick will act alone in the murder of Mary Kelly. The girl looks enough like his adulterous wife to send the man into a frenzy. In crime scene photographs taken the day of her murder, there are initials visible in blood on the walls, an F and an M, suggesting the name Florie Maybrick.

And Catharine Eddowes, poor woman, had an M carved through her eyelids, another clue to Maybrick's identity, had the police realized it. With Lachley out of the picture, Maybrick is on his own, without a mentor to guide or goad him into repeated murders. If one studies Maybrick's diary, one finds a startling change of tone and attitude after Mary Kelly's murder. It is almost as though Maybrick had roused from a murderous stupor of some sort, returning to sanity and remorse.

"Importantly, Lachley is a mesmerist of some note. I would not be at all surprised to learn that Lachley had used that skill to gain control of Maybrick, using hypnotic suggestion to bring his hatred of prostitutes boiling over to critical levels, then pointing him at the victims Lachley chose. Without Lachley to reinforce the hypnotic suggestions, Maybrick might well come to his senses after the butchery of Mary Kelly and look back on what he has done with the very shock one reads in the diary. Given all this, with Maybrick quite probably acting alone in the Kelly murder, we *cannot* assume that Lachley is impossible to kill. Not based on the assumption that he must be present for Mary Kelly's death."

Kit was impressed. Maybe there was hope, yet?

Mike Benson spoke up quickly, however. "We're going to play it safe and assume the worst, just the same. I don't want anyone tackling this guy alone. We've cleared Commons, which has robbed Lachley and his worshippers of easily available victims, but his fury will make him dangerously unpredictable. He may well go to ground somewhere. Or he may start breaking down doors, looking for Dr. Feroz or the next best substitute. There may be no way to stop his killing spree, short of evacuating the station."

"You can't be serious!"

"My God, Benson—"

"*Quiet!*" The bellow came from behind Kit's shoulder. He jerked around to find Bull Morgan striding into the briefing room. "I'm *not* evacuating this station, get that clear right now. One, it's impossible to do, not in time. There is no physical way to get everyone on this station through Primary during its next cycle, not to mention trying to herd every man, woman, and child in Shangri-La down to Primary precinct in the next three minutes, just to make the gate opening."

Glances at wrist watches caused a miniature sea of bobbing heads, a flock of guinea hens popping up and down in tall grass. As though on cue, the station announcer came on, the sound muted through the walls: "Your attention please. Primary is due to open in three minutes. Be advised, all station passes through Primary have been revoked for the duration of the station emergency. Remain in your hotel room or your current place of shelter with the door locked. Do not make any attempt to reach Primary . . ."

Bull Morgan waited for the echo to fade, then said grimly, "I've ordered a total lockdown of this station, including cancellation of Primary passes, so he can't slip out with panic-stricken tourists the way he crashed the Britannia. I want everyone on a search team to stay in radio contact. Work in teams of at least three and never lose sight of your teammates. If your team doesn't have a radio, see Mike Benson. That's it people, move out and comb this station like it's never been combed before."

The nearest I.T.C.H. agent collared Bull. "What do you intend to do with Lachley when you find him?"

"Since you ask, I hope to God he can be killed, because I have no intention of taking Jack the Ripper alive and then ending up stuck with him for the rest of his natural life. Up-time law says we can't ship him home and we can't send him to an up-time prison, either, because that same law prevents us from sending any down-timer through Primary. And frankly, there's not a cage I could build on this station that a psychopath couldn't eventually break out of. We're not equipped to hold a thing like that in a cell for the next forty or fifty years."

"What happened to trial by jury?" the I.T.C.H. agent demanded, her glare icy.

Bull Morgan chewed his cigar to shreds. "I'll tell you what, lady. You answer me this. What happened to four gutted women? And a man with a broken neck, who was unfortunate enough to simply be in Lachley's way? We have a station cram full of potential victims, here, and it's my job to see they don't become statistics. And just in case you've forgotten, down-timers don't *have* any legal rights, the honest and decent ones any more than some psychopathic butcher. And I didn't write *those* laws, either. I'm just stuck enforcing 'em. I'm not real happy about it, but, by God, I *will* protect innocents. This ain't New York, lady, and it ain't the Hague, and you're not in charge. You don't like it, get the hell off my station."

The I.T.C.H. agent gave Bull a combative glare, but she backed down. They might be stuck in the middle of the worst situation any station had ever faced, but Bull Morgan wasn't going down without a fight. Kit felt like cheering.

"Okay," Bull said briskly, "I want sweep teams out, combing the lower levels, and I want every searcher armed with a knife, bare minimum, and a pistol for the up-timers. Ronisha, organize the new teams by zone. And get the word out to teams we've already fielded, same rules. Let's find this bastard before anybody else dies."

A rush of footsteps brought Skeeter up from his crouch, holding Artemisia in one arm. She leaned her head against his shoulder, arms wrapped around his neck as the door was thrown wide. Jenna Caddrick vanished as someone thrust her aside. An instant later, Skeeter found himself staring at the wrong end of an enormous revolver.

"Put her down!"

It was Noah Armstrong, dressed in women's clothing. There was no mistaking the cold, murderous rage in Armstrong's grey eyes. Behind Noah's shoulder, Marcus appeared, ashen. When he caught sight of Skeeter, the former slave's mouth fell open. "*Skeeter?* And Margo! And is that Malcolm? What are you doing in London?"

Skeeter shifted Artemisia to his other arm. "Looking for you, of course. You might tell your friend, there, to put the gun down."

"Noah, these are my friends! From the station!"

Armstrong didn't even blink. "I don't care if they're Santa's elves. Anyone could've followed them here!"

"Sure, anyone could've," Skeeter agreed, "*if* they'd known where we were heading today. Which they didn't. And I'll put Misia down when you put that pistol away. If anybody's got some explaining to do, it's you, Armstrong. And you'd better start talking fast."

Armstrong's eyes narrowed over a cold glint, then backed up and gestured with the barrel of the gun. "Inside. All of you."

As Skeeter stepped past, Marcus said quietly, "They are my

friends, Noah. Skeeter risked death in the Circus at Rome to free me from slavery. He is one of the Found Ones, a trusted friend. My children call him uncle. Malcolm is a freelance guide, friend to Kit Carson, and Margo is to marry him. She will be the first woman time scout, when her grandfather has trained her fully. We can trust them, Noah." Marcus turned to Skeeter, then, his face twisting in an expression that hurt to witness. "I am sorry I did not come to you on the station. Please try to understand, Skeeter. We could not risk it, then. Men were trying to kill us and I could not put my children in jeopardy, not to contact anyone."

"I figured that out," Skeeter said softly. "It's all right."

Marcus' eyes gleamed wet for a dangerous moment, then he managed to say fairly steadily, "I am glad you have come. Ianira needs to return to the station. So do our children. We must end this long terror and go home."

"You found her, then?" Margo asked sharply. "Did Lachley have her, after all?"

Surprise lit Marcus' dark eyes and Jenna Caddrick blurted, "How did you guess?" Even Noah Armstrong was momentarily taken aback.

Margo eyed the revolver still levelled at them, then answered Jenna's question with a faint smile. "We went to the lecture at the Egyptian Hall, of course. Malcolm and I did, that is. Skeeter wasn't in London yet. We're guides for the Ripper Watch Team and we'd finally figured out that Dr. Lachley must be Jack the Ripper, so we staked out the lecture—and saw you. We tried to follow when you left, but lost you in the crowd. Where was Ianira? Not in Lachley's house, surely? You left there without her."

Marcus' eyes darkened with grim memory that set Skeeter's skin to crawling. "In the sewers," he said harshly. "He had a place in the sewers, a room where he kept Ianira and other things, pieces of people he had butchered, a terrible place . . ."

"Good God," Malcolm breathed, eyes going wide as realization dawned, "the *sewers*! Of course no one could catch the Ripper. He was using the sewers to escape!"

"To hell with Jack the Ripper!" Armstrong said in a cold, hard voice. "How did you find us?" The revolver still tracked Skeeter's chest.

Footsteps on the stairs distracted everyone but Armstrong, who said sharply, "Get back upstairs!"

An instant later, Ianira rushed past Armstrong and flung both arms around Skeeter's neck, tears streaming, as she hugged him, Misia and all. "Skeeter! You are safe . . . We have missed you!"

She kissed Skeeter's cheek, then hugged Margo and Malcolm in turn, eyes brilliant with the tears streaming down her face. "It is good to have old friends among us again! But how *did* you find us? Noah and Jenna have been very careful and our hiding place was well chosen."

Skeeter handed Artemisia to her father, lips twitching into a faint smile. "We tracked you through your money, actually."

"Our *what*?" Jenna gasped.

Skeeter grinned. "Your money. The banknotes you picked up on station when you exchanged your up-time currency."

Her brow wrinkled above the ludicrous mutton chops Paula Booker had given her. "Banknotes? How in the world could you trace me through banknotes?"

"They're fakes."

Jenna stared, shaken so badly out of her composure her face ran dead white. Even Armstrong, who had finally put the revolver away, blanched. Clearly, they understood the implications of Victorian prison as well as Skeeter did.

"Believe it or not," Skeeter spoke into the shocked silence, "Goldie Morran admitted it before I left the station. She was terrified you'd been arrested in London for passing counterfeit banknotes, which would explain why nobody could find Benny Catlin. The last thing she wants is your father breathing down her neck, so she came clean, spilled the whole thing to me. They're not all fake, but she slipped you enough counterfeits to cause trouble. You bought some suits with a counterfeit five-pound note and we traced you through that. Once we knew you were in the East End, we started showing people your photographs until we'd tracked you down."

Jenna's ashen face ran ice pale this time and she swayed sharply, prompting Armstrong to steady her. "Oh, my God. You didn't? We can't stay here!"

"Perhaps," Malcolm said quietly, "you would be good enough to explain why not? The only information we have, your father supplied, through his own sources and from the detective he's hired. And we have reason to suspect that gentlemen's credentials, thanks to Skeeter."

Armstrong said brusquely, "Let's go into the parlour. I could use a drink and Jenna had better sit down."

Marcus brushed his daughter's hair back from her brow. "Misia, please go upstairs and finish your lessons with your sister."

"Okay." She kissed her father's cheek as he set her down, then ran to Skeeter and hugged him tightly before clattering up the stairs, hitching her dress up to her knees.

Jenna Caddrick brushed past, moving woodenly into the parlour, followed by Noah Armstrong. Jenna stood near the window, staring silently into the street, while Marcus and Ianira took seats on the worn upholstery of a high-backed sofa with carved mahogany legs and arms. Armstrong followed them into the parlour, stopping near the hearth, where a coal fire blazed cheerfully, then hesitated. "It's clear that Marcus and Ianira trust you. Very well, I'll give you the full story." Armstrong swept off a woman's hairpiece, revealing short, dishevelled brown hair which didn't quite reach the high Victorian collar of Armstrong's dress. Without the wig, it was abruptly difficult to tell whether Armstrong was a young man in woman's clothing or a young woman with short hair. "It's a very long story, but the upshot is, I'm a detective. I was hired to protect these people." Armstrong nodded toward Jenna, Marcus, and Ianira.

"*You're* a detective?" Skeeter blurted, then narrowed his eyes. "Who hired you?"

"Cassie Tyrol."

Skeeter's mouth dropped.

Margo gasped out, "*Cassie Tyrol?*"

"My aunt," Jenna said in a choked voice. "She hired Noah before they murdered her. They would've killed me, too, if Noah hadn't dragged me out of the restaurant. They killed my fiancé, Carl, at my apartment." Her voice began to quake as wetness spilled over from her eyes. "I was talking to him on the phone when they shot him, so I wasn't at the table when they shot Aunt Cassie. I'm . . ." she bit her lip and pressed a hand against her abdomen, protectively. "I'm going to have Carl's baby. It's all I have left. I can't even call on my family for help," she added bitterly, "because it's my *father* who's trying to kill us."

Mouths sagged open, even Malcolm's. The silence was so profound, Skeeter could hear a clock somewhere out in Spitalfields strike the hour, its ghostly notes singing through the cold October air. Then Jenna swayed and Noah Armstrong hurried to help her to the nearest chair, guiding her with a tender look and gentle hands. Clearly, Noah Armstrong was anything but a murderous terrorist. Skeeter found his voice first.

"Miss Caddrick, your father is threatening to shut down the station unless you're brought back."

Shocking hatred blazed from her eyes. "If I could, I'd put a bullet through his skull!" Even as she spoke, fury transmuted into terrible grief. Jenna covered her face with shaking hands and began to cry, raggedly and very messily. Ianira produced a handkerchief and sat down beside her, sliding an arm around her shoulders. Jenna groped for the handkerchief and struggled to regain her composure. "I'm sorry," she whispered through hiccoughs. She finally blotted her cheeks, then looked up, shoulders slumped, face haggard with too much fear and far too little sleep.

Malcolm suggested gently, "Why don't you tell us your story, Miss Caddrick? I suspect Mr. Jackson, here, knows more of it than the rest of us do, but Miss Smith and I know enough to realize that we're facing a very serious threat."

Jenna rubbed reddened eyes with the backs of her hands, clutching Ianira's sodden handkerchief, then drew a deep, unsteady breath. "Yes. I literally don't know how many people have already died because of what we know. Noah and I, that is. And now Marcus and Ianira." She drew a second watery breath and met Malcolm's gaze. "Guess I ought to start with proper introductions? This is Noah Armstrong, a private detective with the Wardmann-Wolfe Agency."

Skeeter swung a sharp stare at Armstrong. "*You're* a Wardmann-Wolfe agent? Why, that lying, scum-sucking, low-life *bastard*!"

"I take it," Armstrong said grimly, "my reputation has been compromised?"

Skeeter snorted. "You might say that. Senator Caddrick's telling the whole world you're *Ansar Majlis*."

The look that passed across Noah Armstrong's face set Skeeter's hair on end.

"I see," Armstrong said very softly. "I suppose it's fitting, after all, since he put them on our trail in the first place."

"Senator Caddrick?" Malcolm asked sharply. "In league with the *Ansar Majlis*?"

"It's true," Jenna whispered, her watery eyes haunted with terrible shadows. "Daddy ordered his hit men to dress like *Ansar Majlis*."

"I was sitting right beside Cassie Tyrol when they burst in through the door, shooting," Noah Armstrong said heavily. "She was dead before I even had time to draw my pistol. If I hadn't thrown the table in their faces, they'd have shot me down, as well, then they'd have found Jenna and killed her. They did kill dozens of people standing near us as we escaped the restaurant. Caddrick and the men paying him off have stirred up the real *Ansar Majlis*, as well. Fed them money, munitions, transportation, names and locations of targets, helped them to attack Ianira on the station."

Margo was frowning. "Wait a minute. Am I the only one confused, here? I know I've been in London for quite a while, but what possible connection is there between Jocasta Tyrol and Ianira Cassondra? Would you mind starting at the beginning? Because this isn't making much sense to me."

Noah Armstrong spoke quietly. "Miss Tyrol came to me three years ago; at least, it was three years ago for Marcus and the girls and myself, just a few weeks ago for Jenna and Ianira." Grey eyes flicked toward the Senator's daughter. "Miss Tyrol was curious about some very ugly things she had uncovered about her brother-in-law, Jenna's father. She hired me and also helped a young friend of hers get a job in Senator Caddrick's office. An actor doing role research. The boy stumbled across some very nasty evidence. He sent it to her, but was murdered for it. I'd been doing my own investigations, along the same lines, and as soon as Mr. Corliss was killed, I persuaded Miss Tyrol to go into hiding until we could take the evidence to the authorities."

Jenna said bitterly, "Aunt Cassie tried to warn me. She slipped away from Noah and called, arranged to meet me. *I'm* the reason she's dead! Aunt Cassie and Carl, both . . ." Tears tracked messily down her face, dripping into her surgically implanted sideburns. "Carl McDevlin was going to marry me, in spite of my father's nasty habits and the chaos of the press following everything we Caddricks do. And my doting *father* gave the order to murder him, just on the chance I might have told him something."

Armstrong brushed wet hair back from Jenna's face, the gesture eloquent of the trust that had grown between them. "Miss Caddrick and I managed to get into TT-86," Armstrong sighed, "with the tickets for London she and her fiancé were planning to use, but the assassination squads followed. Two of them almost killed Miss Caddrick the night she arrived."

Jenna shivered. "I managed to shoot my way out of the Piccadilly Hotel or I'd be in a morgue someplace. And so would Ianira."

Malcolm said very quietly, "I hope you have proof?"

"Yes." Jenna whispered. "Noah does."

The Wardmann-Wolfe detective nodded wearily. "There've been quiet rumors for years about Senator Caddrick's association with organized crime. The evidence Alston Corliss gathered is enough to hang Senator Caddrick and several of his cronies, particularly a paid enforcer named Gideon Guthrie. And Guthrie works for Cyril Barris, who has mob connections on three continents, just for starters. Ties to the Yakuza and the Russian mafia, you name it, he's diddling in it. Barris has been paying off John Caddrick for a couple of decades. Unfortunately, Alston Corliss was a total amateur up against seasoned killers. The pieces were found in several different locations."

Margo shuddered.

"What Alston Corliss found," Noah added, "were payoff records made through companies the Senator owns, monies deposited into accounts only he had access to, as majority shareholder and CEO. Construction companies, mostly, both in the States and abroad, Asia and Japan, in particular."

This finally started to make sense to Skeeter. In the aftermath of the orbital accident that had formed the time strings, the whole Pacific Rim had been hard hit by earthquakes and tidal waves. The rebuilding had been going on for most of Skeeter's life.

Malcolm was nodding, as well, face set in weary lines. "And the construction industry in Japan is controlled by the Yakuza gangs, has been for centuries. The Senator allied himself with these gangs?"

"Yes. There and in the States, in South America, anywhere the Yakuza gangs were active. In the States, particularly on the west coast, local gangs of American thugs started affiliating themselves with the Asian gangs coming in, running drugs, prostitution, and gambling. Years back, even before he launched his political career, the Senator had ties to a local mafia boss in Los Angeles, a man who later affiliated his gang with a prominent Yakuza family. It turned out to be a very profitable affiliation. For all parties concerned. It certainly financed the Senator's campaigns."

"Yes," Margo frowned, "but how does Ianira tie into all of this?"

Jenna's mouth thinned to a bitter line. "Think about it. You know what she was responsible for starting. The Lady of Heaven Temples are the fastest growing international religion in the world. What better way to smuggle drugs halfway around the planet, launder money, ship American girls out to Asian brothels—"

"Ianira's not involved in that kind of garbage!" Skeeter snapped.

Jenna was crying again. "No. I never said she was. But my father is. He's using the Temples as a cover. Several congressmen have been calling for an investigation of Templar possessions and financial activities, something Daddy couldn't risk. So he decided to turn the Templars into martyrs, so public sentiment would crucify anyone who dared investigate Temple finances."

Skeeter swore aloud. It made abrupt, sickening sense.

"I see you've tumbled to it," Armstrong nodded, holding Skeeter's gaze. "Miss Caddrick's father also knew he was being investigated by one of the best detective agencies in the business and he knew Miss Tyrol had put us on his trail. But he couldn't order an ordinary gangland hit on a woman as widely popular as Cassie Tyrol. There'd be far too much press, not to mention police asking questions, if he simply had his regular paid thugs kill her. His one piece of luck was that both Jenna and Miss Tyrol were prominent Templars, and so was Miss Caddrick's fiancé. Miss Tyrol donated her share of the profits from *Temple Harlot* directly to the Temple."

Skeeter's blood ran cold. "So he used the *Ansar Majlis*. Of course. They were a perfect front."

"Yes. They made it look like a terrorist hit. Only the bastards in that restaurant were never part of the actual *Ansar Majlis*. Neither were the hired killers who came after us on the station. They activated real *Ansar Majlis* moles already in place on TT-86, of course, so the riots on station would look like the genuine thing. The Senator targeted Ianira as one of his primary public martyrs, since the *Ansar Majlis* exists specifically to destroy everything she's responsible for starting. He knew very well what public sentiment would be if the deified prophetess of the Temple were murdered, along with her entire family." The bitterness in Armstrong's eyes was terrifying. The shame in Jenna Caddrick's was infinitely worse. Silence spun out like filaments of glass, waiting to be shattered.

"So that's the whole, sordid story," Noah finally shattered it. "We're in hiding, with Miss Caddrick posing as a gentleman and me posing as Marcus' sister, trying to stay alive long enough to put Senator Caddrick in prison where he belongs."

Malcolm rubbed the bridge of his nose for a moment, eyes bleak when he met Armstrong's gaze again. "According to Skeeter, there have been multiple riots and murders on TT-86, with a number of cults, including the Angels of Grace Militia, at odds with supporters of the *Ansar Majlis*. Now we know why. Everything we've built on TT-86 is at enormous risk. The Senator is making threats, very serious threats, to close down the station."

Jenna said in a low, hard voice, "He's been looking for a way to shut down-time tourism for years."

"He doesn't even need to do it, himself," Skeeter muttered. "The riots and murders alone are likely to shut us down. He brought federal marshals with him and arrested Bull Morgan, the station manager, on trumped-up tax charges. I.T.C.H. has been brought in to investigate and God knows where that will end. The Inter-Temporal Court has shut down stations before, replaced their whole management operations. And with Bull Morgan and Ronisha Azzan out, only God knows what would become of the down-timer community on station. I.T.C.H. sure as hell doesn't care—down-timers have no legal rights to protect and not enough financial clout to influence a gnat, never mind the Inter-Temporal Court."

Malcolm added heavily, "Down-timers on other time terminals I could name live like animals, compared with TT-86. Most 'eighty-sixers have no idea how fortunate our down-time population really is."

"We must stop this!" Marcus cried, moving protectively to Ianira's side.

"Yes, but *how*?" Margo wondered, frustration burning in her eyes. "You're a detective," she swung abruptly toward Armstrong, "and you say you've got proof. What do *you* suggest we do? You can't hide forever and you certainly can't expect *us* to sit and bury our heads in the sand like a bunch of ostriches. Marcus and Ianira are our friends. We won't sit around and do nothing!"

Noah's lips thinned. "No, clearly we *can't* just sit here, not now. The Senator and his assassins know we're in the city, since they sent you through to look for us. Hiding in London was only a stopgap measure, we knew that from the start. All we've done by coming here is buy ourselves time. We would've been gone before now, if Ianira hadn't been kidnapped her first night in London. It took us days, tracing and rescuing her. What has to be done is simple. I have to go back with the proof. Make sure the Senator and his gangland bosses are arrested and stand trial for murder." Armstrong frowned. "Getting the evidence to the authorities is going to be a major battle, even if someone else takes it to them. And you know what mafia trials are like. Clearly, the Senator has taken pains to ensure I'm shot on sight as a dangerous terrorist, so I won't live to testify." With a bitter twist of lips, Armstrong added, "I really do appreciate your not shooting me out of hand and asking questions later."

"I started wondering about Caddrick's story even before we went chasing halfway across Colorado on your trail," Skeeter muttered. "I was standing next to Ianira when that first riot broke out. What I saw didn't tally with the line Caddrick fed us."

"For that, I am deeply grateful, Mr. Jackson. I also suspect," the detective added darkly, "there will be at least one hired killer in London trying to trace us."

"Oh, yeah," Skeeter said softly. "There is, all right. And I know his name. At least, the name he's been using. Mr. Sid Kaederman. The Senator's so-called detective. A Wardmann-Wolfe agent, so he says."

Noah Armstrong's brows twitched downward. "Sid Kaederman? There's no Wardmann-Wolfe agent by that name."

"You know them all?" Malcolm asked quietly.

"I'd better. The agency's founder, Beore Arunwode, is my grandfather. I know that agency and its employees better than most people know their own kids. Part of my job was running security clearances on every agent we hired."

"Great," Skeeter groused. "I *knew* there was something wrong with that guy, I just couldn't figure out what."

Malcolm favored him with a faint smile. "I've never known your instincts to fail, Mr. Jackson. It seems they were right on target, once again. The question is, how to deal with Mr. Kaederman? If he's a hired gun, the proof you have, Mr. Armstrong, isn't likely to incriminate *him*. At least, not directly. Which means we need to trap him into committing a crime we can hang him for. Or I should say, trap him into *trying* to commit that crime."

"Like what?" Jenna asked bitterly. "The only thing he's here for is to murder me. And Noah. And Ianira and her family."

The answer skittered across Skeeter's mind in a jagged lightning strike, a notion so wild, he actually started to laugh.

"Skeeter Jackson," Margo asked sharply, "what are you thinking?"

"He wants Jenna Caddrick and Noah Armstrong. So, let's give him what he wants."

"*What?*" Jenna came out of her chair so fast, it crashed over. "Are you *insane?*"

"No," Skeeter said mildly, "although I know a few people who might argue the point. When your father showed up, he mistook me for Noah. And Paula Booker's here in London with us. Kit insisted she come along."

Margo gasped. "*Skeeter!* You're not thinking what I *think* you're thinking?"

Malcolm moved sharply. "You *do* realize the risk?"

"Oh, yeah," Skeeter said very softly. "But do you have a better way to trick him into trying to commit murder, without risking the real Noah Armstrong's life? Not to mention Marcus and Ianira and the children, and Miss Caddrick, here. Noah's got to testify. He's the only one who can put a noose around Caddrick's neck. We can't risk *Noah,* but we can sure as hell hand Sid Kaederman a life-sized decoy. If you have any better ideas, I'm all ears."

Malcolm didn't. Neither did anybody else.

"All right," Malcolm said tersely. "I'll have to get him out of the road long enough for Paula to work her magic on your features. When Kaederman tries to murder you, we'll nab Kaederman, dead to rights, with enough evidence to hang him."

"Where do we spring the trap?" Margo asked, brow furrowing slightly as she considered the problem.

"Someplace open enough to give him a shot at Mr. Jackson," Malcolm mused, "but not so open he could give us the slip too easily. A public place, with plenty of witnesses, but not a crowd so large he can lose himself in it."

"Train stations are out, then," Margo frowned. "Victoria Embankment or maybe Chelsea Embankment?"

Malcolm shook his head. "Access to the water taxis is too great. He could jump into a waterman's boat and be gone before we could lay hands on him. It'll have to be someplace he wouldn't expect a trap. A place we could tell him we've found a clue to Armstrong's whereabouts and have him believe it without question."

"What about the Serpentine? Or Boating Lake in Battersea? We could say he's been seen there with Ianira and the children."

"I've got a better idea," Skeeter said suddenly. "We tell Kaederman you've discovered the counterfeit banknotes, which is something Kit and I kept secret. So we tell him you're running short of cash. Kaederman already knows you're in disguise as a man, Miss Caddrick, and we also know that Noah Armstrong can assume any disguise he feels like, male or female. So the two of you have been hitting the gentlemen's clubs, gambling, as a way to dump the counterfeits and make up your losses, fast."

Jenna frowned. "Gambling? But why would we do that? Gambling is a good way to *lose* money."

"Not—" Skeeter grinned, abruptly merry as any imp, "—if you cheat."

(((Chapter 15)))

The tunnels beneath Frontier Town were a maze of immense glass aquaria, ranks upon tiers of them, which had been empty the last time Kit had searched Shangri-La Station's basement. Now they held all the live fish the station could import through its gates. Between the flock of crow-sized pterodactyls and toothed, primitive birds and the enormous *pteranodon sternbergi,* whose wingspan rivalled that of a small airplane, pest control had been hard pressed to import enough fish. Sue Fritchey had turned the corridors and tunnels beneath Little Agora and Frontier Town into a miniature biological preserve where pterodactyl lunches swam by the thousands.

In this dim-lit world of glass walls and gleaming fish scales and the patterned reflections of water on tunnel walls and ceilings, the caged *sternbergi's* weird, primordial cries vibrated eerily against the stacked aquaria, each cry drifting through the basement corridors like the soundtrack from a bad horror flick. The noise set teeth on edge as once-extinct screams echoed and reverberated for hundreds of yards in every direction, distorted by distance, inexpressibly strange.

Kit hunted the alien terrain with a team of four: Sven Bailey and Kit out front with riot shotguns, Kynan and Eigil behind them with bladed weapons and a couple of old-style wooden baseball bats, to reduce the chances that an attack would put friends in the line of fire. They had searched about a hundred yards of cluttered corridor, finding no trace of Jack the Ripper or his manaical worshippers, when they came to an intersecting tunnel. Kit held up a hand. "Stay back until I've had a look."

He had just eased to the corner when they came boiling out of hiding, at least a dozen of them, brandishing knives and hurling murderous threats into Kit's teeth. Kit fired into the thick of them. Men screamed and went down as Sven, too, loosed off a load of buckshot. A baseball bat smashed into an aquarium at Kit's elbow. Water and wriggling fish flooded the corridor floor, stained red where several attackers had fallen, gutshot and screaming. Kit fired again, trying to drive the madmen back. Eigil was shouting in Old Norse; the Viking *barsark* was lopping off limbs and smashing more aquaria to the floor. Screams and moans echoed amidst the shattering noise of smashing glass. Then the Ripper cult broke and ran, with Sven and Kit hard on their heels. Eigil and Kynan, their borrowed weapons dripping blood, were right behind.

Pounding footsteps echoed, distorted by the piled aquaria. Kit put on a burst of speed, rounded a corner on Sven's heels, and piled into the middle of a seething mass of bodies. The Ripper cult had turned at bay, blocked by the massive bulk of the *pteranodon sternbergi's* cage. Kit slammed into a would-be killer and they reeled against the cage. The gigantic pterosaur screamed, shattering eardrums, and lunged in a state of maddened agitation. The immense beak, longer than a man's body, shot between the bars as Kit flung himself aside. The Ripper cultist screamed, impaled on a razor-sharp beak. The *sternbergi* reared backwards, scraping the body off against the bars. Kit staggered off balance, buffeted by the backdraft of immense leathery wings. One of the cultists snarled and slashed at his throat. Kit dropped to the floor, under the blow, and fired his riotgun upwards into the man's gut. Kit's attacker reeled backwards against the bars, then screamed and dropped his knife as the pterosaur struck again, its wicked eye gleaming like a poisoned ruby. Its beak snapped shut with a clacking sound like two-by-fours cracking, taking off the man's arm at the elbow. He screamed and went down in a puddle of arterial spurts.

Kit rolled, trying to come to his feet, and heard Sven's shotgun roar. More screams rose, then a group of men burst around the corner and slammed full-tilt into the battle. Kit caught a glimpse of flying burnooses and grim, dark Arabic faces, then Mr. Riyad, foreman of the Arabian Nights construction crew, was fighting his way to Kit's side. A group of his workmen, proven innocent of terrorist affiliations, mopped up the remnants of resistance. Kit staggered to his feet, wiping sweat and someone else's blood, and met Mr. Riyad's gaze.

"Am I glad to see you," he gasped out.

"We came as quickly as we could, when we heard the screams and the shooting."

"Thank God."

They'd taken five men alive, having left a trail of nine dead and wounded behind them. Kit fumbled with his radio. "Code Seven Red, Zone Eleven. We've got prisoners and a helluva mess, down by the *sternbergi's* cage."

"Roger, Zone Eleven. Sending reinforcements."

"Better get a medical team down here and tell Sue Fritchey to bring a tranquilizer gun. The *sternbergi's* out of control." The immense pterosaur was still screaming and trying to attack anything that moved near its cage.

"Copy that, we'll do what we can. We've got casualties all over the station."

"Roger, understood. Anybody find Lachley yet?"

"Negative.

"He's not with this group, either. We'll keep searching once we've turned these guys over to security. Kit out."

"Roger, security out."

As Kit clipped the radio to his belt, Pest Control arrived with a dart gun. They shot three separate tranks into the immense pterosaur, which gradually ceased hurling itself against the bars. Its wings and head drooped to the cage floor, its baleful ruby eye heavy lidded and closing. Security arrived a moment later, taking charge of prisoners with rough efficiency. The battered cultists stumbled off in handcuffs and shackles, too dazed to protest. Pest Control agents opened up the cage and began treating lacerations on the *sternbergi's* hide and wings. A weird grunting moan issued from the pterosaur's immense throat, then its wicked little eyes closed completely and it lost consciousness.

"We'd better regroup and keep searching," Kit sighed.

The construction foreman nodded. "Yes. We should perhaps search together, this time? These men are completely mad," Riyad gestured at the dead Ripper cultists. "They fight like demons."

Sven Bailey, who was wiping blood off Kynan's gladius while Kynan wrapped a shallow cut in his ribs with makeshift bandages, muttered, "You just said a cotton-pickin' mouthful. Never saw anything like it."

They sorted themselves out, then spread into a loose fan, moving down the corridor past the open cage. As they searched, grim and silent, Kit couldn't help worrying about Margo's safety in London and cursed himself for not asking Dr. Feroz. He'd have to wait, now, because he couldn't clutter up security channels with a personal request. Besides, he needed to focus his entire attention on this lethal search for the Ripper and his maniacal followers. So Kit thrust the worry aside as best he could, telling himself that she was in good company with Malcolm and Skeeter, and kept hunting.

"You want me to *what?*" Paula Booker stared.

Skeeter grinned. "I want you to make me look like Noah Armstrong."

She blinked at him, eyes still blank with astonishment. "*Here?* In Spaldergate House?"

"Yeah. Here. Tonight, after everyone has gone to bed. Mrs. Aldis, the housekeeper, will let us into the vault, that's no problem. It's a little crowded right now, because the Ripper Watch Team is down there, but we won't be in their way. They aren't using the surgery, in any case, just the computer facilities. The surgery's modern, has all the amenities. And Mrs. Aldis is a surgical nurse, assists Dr. Nerian all the time."

"I know that," Paula said impatiently. "I've been down there already. But . . . *Tonight?*" The request had clearly thrown her off stride. Clearly, she thought Skeeter had taken leave of his senses.

He let his grin fade away. "Paula, we learned something tonight that . . . Well, let's just say I'm not going to sleep very well 'til this is over. Sid Kaederman isn't what he's pretending to be. If we don't trick him into giving himself away, he will literally get away with murder.

And if we don't stop him, it'll be Ianira and Marcus on his hit list, them and their kids. And that's just for starters. This is one helluva mess we're stuck in, Paula. Believe me, I wouldn't ask you to rearrange my face with a scalpel if it weren't necessary. I happen to like my face, whatever anyone else thinks of it."

Paula Booker's eyes widened. "*You found them, didn't you?*"

"Shh!" he motioned frantically to keep her voice down.

She darted a worried glance at her closed bedroom door. Like Skeeter, she was on the third floor, bunking in the servants' quarters. Sid Kaederman, as a VIP, had been given the last available room on the "family" floor, one level down and at the opposite end of the house, overlooking Octavia Street rather than the rain-choked gardens at the back.

Paula whispered more carefully, "You *did* find them today, didn't you?"

Skeeter nodded. "Yeah. They're mostly all right. Once you're finished rearranging my face, though, Malcolm wants to talk to you. He wants you to run a checkup on everyone, make sure no lasting damage has been done. Particularly Ianira. She's had a rough time in London. Malcolm will explain all that later. Right now, I need that new face, so we can lay a trap for Kaederman. The sooner he's in cuffs, the sooner we can all go home."

Paula sighed, pushing back her hair in a weary gesture. "All right, Skeeter. I don't have everything I'd like, not to do a face job of that magnitude, but I think we can do a creditable job of making you look like Armstrong. Enough to suit, anyway. Fortunately, your bone structure and coloring are very similar, as you've pointed out. And we do have good photos of Armstrong to work from. That'll help. Let me get my medical bag. I brought through a lot of instruments and medicines to supplement Spaldergate's supply. You realize, this is going to put you out of commission for about a week? It'll take that long for the swelling and bruising to fade and the stitches to heal where I nip and tuck."

"Yeah, we figured it would take a while. That'll give Malcolm and the others a chance to lay the trap for Sid. And it'll give you time to work with Ianira, too."

"All right, Skeeter. We'll have to tell Sid something so he won't grow suspicious about your absence."

Skeeter nodded. "We'll spread the word I was hit by a carriage or a wagon and had to be rushed into surgery."

"That should work. Let's go down to the Vault, then, and get started."

Eight hours later, Skeeter woke up in recovery to a dull throb of pain all through his face and the muffling, claustrophobic feel of bandages. As he swam toward full consciousness, with the sounds of a heart monitor beeping somewhere beside his ear, his gaze focused slowly on Margo, who sat beside his bed.

"Hi," she said quietly. "Don't try to say anything, Skeeter."

He wouldn't have moved his face on a dare.

"Sid bought the story about you being hit by a freight wagon. The creep actually chuckled and said it was about time you got your comeuppance. Malcolm was extremely rude to him."

That surprised Skeeter, even as it warmed his heart. He still couldn't get used to the idea that Malcolm Moore and Margo Smith were giving him their friendship. Margo smiled. "Paula's gone to Spitalfields to check up on Ianira and the others. They're all moving to Malcolm's flat in Belgravia, just in case there's trouble about the counterfeit banknotes."

Skeeter regretted the necessity of ruining his friends' down-time cover.

Margo patted his hand gently, taking care not to disturb the I.V. leads. "Rest for now, Skeeter. We've got everything under control. I'll visit again tonight, after Paula gets back." She gave him a cheery smile, then vanished from his line of sight. Dr. Nerian appeared and spent several moments fussing with his I.V. lines, then injected something into the heplock. Whatever it was, it eased the deep ache in his face and left him drifting.

Skeeter fell asleep wondering what he really would look like, a week from now.

Goldie Morran was having the worst week of her life. I.T.C.H. agents had been prowling through her books, finding discrepancies she would have to explain, and Interpol agents had been breathing down her neck, curious in the wake of the Inter-Temporal Court's investigation. She would have been deeply thankful for the reprieve brought about by the Ripper, but for one detail. The entire station was locked down, leaving her trapped for three solid days in her shop, which she'd had the foresight to equip with a well-stocked back room, including a convertible sofa bed, a wet bar, and plenty of food.

But all business was suspended for the duration of the search, which meant she was losing thousands of dollars, same as every other merchant on station. So Goldie sat in her back room in splendid solitude, listening to her Carolina parakeets chirp, tried to straighten out her books, and brooded over what news might arrive about Jenna Caddrick when the Britannia Gate opened again.

Skeeter, thank God, had kept his mouth shut about the counterfeits, but Goldie was terrified she would end up facing charges over them. She hadn't done anything so *very* wrong—she hadn't printed them, after all. She'd simply tried to recoup some of her own losses, passing them to that idiot, Benny Catlin. Goldie cursed her luck and poured another brandy from her rapidly dwindling supply. Who'd have dreamed that moronic little graduate student would turn out to be Jenna Nicole Caddrick, in disguise? Making an enemy of Senator John Caddrick was a dreadful business move. Worse, even, than attracting the attention of Interpol agents and the Inter-Temporal Court.

Her nerves were so frayed, when the telephone rang she actually dropped her brandy snifter from nerveless fingers. She left it lying on the carpet and lunged out into the shop where the telephone sat. "Goldie Morran!" Her voice came out breathless and unsteady.

"Goldie? Mike Benson, here. No wonder we didn't get an answer at your apartment. How long have you been trapped in your shop?"

"Since that maniac arrived, of course!"

"We're conducting a room-by-room search of the station. You're alone, I take it."

"Of course I'm alone! Did you think I'd be giving wild parties, back here? I want out of this shop, Mike. Send somebody over here to escort me home, for God's sake."

"I'll send someone," Benson retorted, "to search your shop, then your apartment."

"Thanks for the royal treatment!"

"Don't mention it, Goldie. Be ready to unlock your door."

"I'll be waiting," she promised grimly.

Five minutes later, a young BATF officer arrived, security radio in hand. Goldie unlocked her doors and stood tapping one foot impatiently while he searched her shop. She followed him into the vault to be sure he didn't appropriate anything.

"Nice birds," he commented with an avaricious twinkle in his eyes. "Carolina parakeets, aren't they?" He scribbled something into a notebook. "Mr. Wilkes will be very interested. He loves birds, you know." The arrogant booby was laughing at her.

Goldie seethed. It was perfectly legal for her to have them on station. But Monty, curse him, would be watching her like a hawk from now on, curtailing her profitable sideline in viable egg smuggling.

"All right, you can lock up, now," he said, snapping his notebook shut and pocketing it. She closed the vault door while he radioed in that her shop was clear. "I'll escort Miss Morran to her apartment and clear that, as well."

"Roger."

They left through the front door, which she bolted, then she rattled down the big steel mesh doors and locked them, as well. "I can't tell you how much I'm looking foward to a hot shower and a real bed," she muttered.

"You think you've had it rough," the BATF officer complained. "We've been running on two hours of sleep a day since that maniac got here. And things were no picnic before he crashed the Britannia."

They hurried across Valhalla, the fastest way to reach the section of Residential where Goldie lived. The emptiness of Commons was downright eerie. Their footsteps echoed. She could hear other security patrols in the distance, mostly when their radios sputtered where patrols reported in. "How much of the station has been searched?" she asked uneasily as they started around the end of the big wooden ship housing the vacant Langskip Cafe—

They ran slap into someone coming the other way. Goldie staggered under the impact. She had only a split second to register wild, inhuman eyes in a narrow, darkly Eastern-European face, then a wicked knife flashed and the BATF officer went down, throat cut to bone. Goldie drew breath to scream and he slammed her against the wooden hull of the ship. She hung there, stunned, while he pressed a gore-covered hand across her mouth and nose. She choked on the stink of blood.

"*Do you live here?*" he hissed.

Goldie nodded, so terrified she could barely keep her feet. He dragged her away from the ship, shoved the knife against her ribs, and stooped to secure the dead BATF officer's radio and pistol. He then marched her rapidly across Commons toward a Residential corridor. "My followers have told me much about your Primary Gate. Unfortunately, your guards have deprived me of my acolytes, so *you* will have to assist me through that gate. Take me there. And hurry up, bitch! The gate goes in ten minutes."

She glanced despairingly at her shop, safe behind its locks and steel-mesh doors. If she could get to the shop, she could trip the silent alarm, summon help. And she kept a pistol in the shop. When she tried to change direction, he pressed the knife against her ribs again. "Not that way! I saw him take you from your shop. I shan't allow you to summon help, woman, a fact you had better learn *now*. Take me to Primary, by a safe route. If you do not oblige me quickly, I will find someone else." The blade cut through her blouse. "Do you understand me?"

She nodded, still half-choked by the bloodstained hand pressed across her mouth. The entire left side of her face ached, where he'd slammed her against the side of the Langskip, and her eye was starting to swell closed. Senses whirling, Goldie took the nearest route into Residential, moving woodenly along with the Ripper's knife under her ribcage. Goldie staggered frequently, but her captor made no offer to assist her. He simply held the knife against her ribs and hissed, "Cry out and I will kill you where you stand." She guided the killer through twisting corridors until they reached a passageway that emerged at the junction between Edo Castletown and Primary Precinct.

She pointed toward the gate, since he hadn't freed her mouth.

He eased to the corner and peered around, surveying the stretch of open Commons beyond. Goldie, too exhausted even to try running, hung in his grip and waited to die. Tremors threatened to send her to the floor even sooner. As she sagged against the wall, waiting, the public address system blared to life.

"Your attention, please. Primary is due to open in three minutes. Be advised, all station passes through Primary have been revoked for the duration of this emergency. Remain in your hotel room or your current place of shelter with the door locked. Do not make any attempt to reach Primary . . ."

The Ripper jerked Goldie around to face him. "*Explain this!*" He laid the sharp steel against her throat and drew his hand away from her mouth.

She shook her head in a stupor. "They've shut down the station," she mumbled, voice shaking. "Locked down all the gates, so no one can leave. They'll have security officers swarming all over Primary, to keep anyone from coming in or going out."

Goldie could, in fact, see a whole cordon of security officers blocking the gate access, armed to the teeth with riot guns. The Ripper swore savagely, then gazed down at her through cold, implacable grey eyes. "You said you live in this insane place?"

"Yes—"

"Where?"

"Back—back that way."

"Take me there!"

Goldie's heart sank. Tears blinded her. "Please don't kill me . . ."

"Stop snivelling, you stupid harridan! If I had intended to kill you, I would have cut your throat already. Since my worshippers have been killed or taken prisoner by your station guards, I require shelter and someone to explain the operation of this infernal place! Now take me to your flat or I'll find another hostage!"

Goldie limped toward her distant apartment, hardly able to keep to her feet. By the time they reached it she was weaving so badly, all that kept her on her feet was his monstrous grip on her arm. She stumbled to a trembling halt in front of her door.

"Open it."

She fumbled with the lock, turning the key from her pocket, then he kicked the door farther open, dragging Goldie inside and shutting the door with a slam that echoed. He hunted through the apartment swiftly, then shoved Goldie into the bedroom. He threw her onto the bed and tied her to it, leaving her shaking in a film of sweat.

"Have you a name?"

"G-Goldie Morran . . ."

"What trade are you in?"

Humor him . . . that's what they always say, humor a madman . . .

"I change currency," she quavered out. "Up-time money for whatever a tourist needs down a gate . . ."

"Tell me how to operate this device." He held up the stolen security radio.

"You press the talk button," she gulped. "Then someone from security answers."

He pressed the button. The radio sputtered. "Security."

"I've searched Goldie Morran's rooms. There's no one here."

"Roger."

Even if she'd dared scream for help while the radio was live, he gave her no chance, switching it off immediately and setting it down on her dresser. He considered her coldly where she lay sprawled, bound hand and foot to her own bed. "Where might I find a map of this accursed place?"

Goldie swallowed down a dry throat. "The computer would be best."

She had to show him how to use it. He tied her to the bed again, afterward, then returned to the living room and spent hours sitting in front of Goldie's computer. She heard keys clicking, listened numbly through a haze of terror to his soft-voiced verbal commands, not really taking in anything he said. Then the living room fell silent. Goldie strained to hear, trying to catch any hint of movement beyond the open bedroom door. Nothing came to her ears except the hum of the air-conditioning fan.

How long she lay rigid on the rumpled bedspread, Goldie wasn't sure. She couldn't see a clock from her angle. Pain and fright began taking their toll of her strength. She was nearly unconscious when the sound of footsteps jolted her back to full awareness. *Oh, God, he's back, he's going to hack me to pieces . . .*

The Ripper smiled down at her. "You've done very well, my dear. Now, then, show me how to operate the devices in your kitchen. I could use a cup of tea."

"I'm in pain," Goldie whimpered. "I can't feel my feet and hands and my eye is swelling shut."

He frowned slightly, then pulled loose her bonds. He examined her ankles and wrists, then traced the extent of the bruising along her face with surprising gentleness. "Mmm . . . A bit swollen and there will be a bad bruise, I fear, but you're in no danger of losing the eye. Beg pardon for handling you so roughly. Have you an icebox?"

Goldie stared, trying to comprehend the shift of attitude. "What?"

"An icebox. You need a cold compress to bring down the swelling. And a tincture of laudanum would ease the discomfort. I fear I left my medical bag in London."

Goldie managed to whisper, "I don't keep any laudanum. You need a prescription for something like that. There's ice in the freezer. In the kitchen."

He tied her to the bed again, although less tightly than before and he wrapped her wrists and ankles first with scarves from her closet to keep the skin from chafing, then headed for the kitchen. She heard rummaging sounds as he searched through cabinets and finally tried the freezer door. "Ah . . . What an ingenious device! How is it powered, I wonder?" She heard the clink and rattle of ice cubes, then the hush of running water. A moment later, he was back in the bedroom, carrying a wet towel packed with ice cubes. He laid it carefully against her face, stroked her hair back from her cheeks and tested her pulse. "You've suffered a shock, dear lady. We really must bring the pain level down."

"In the bathroom," Goldie whispered. "Aspirin . . ." Nausea and pain were setting the room to lurching like a capsized boat.

More sounds of rummaging drifted to her, then he forced something between her lips and held a water glass to her mouth. She choked and swallowed a handful of aspirin tablets. He covered her warmly with her own blankets and checked the icepack, as though genuinely concerned for her welfare. Goldie closed her eyes as he searched her closets and bureau drawers, whistling contentedly to himself. "Have you been through many gates?" he asked at length, rousing her from near stupor.

"No. I don't go down time." Not since that disastrous trip to New Orleans a few years back. The gate had gone unexpectedly unstable, forcing her to leave behind a young historian she'd taken with her. She'd felt worse pangs of guilt, trapping him there, than she'd ever felt in her life, but there really hadn't been anything she could have done, or anyone else, for that matter. "I stay on the station and run my shop," she added with a shiver.

"Ah. How soon before Primary opens again?" he asked at length.

"Three days."

"In that case, my dear Mrs. Morran, make yourself comfortable while I learn the vagaries of your ingenious cookstove."

Goldie lost consciousness to the sound of rattling pots and pans.

Six days after Skeeter's surgery, on the tenth of October, Malcolm baited the trap. Sid Kaederman had made no secret of his disgust with the lack of modern amenities and repeatedly criticized the search efforts in scathing terms when Malcolm and Margo returned to Spaldergate each night to report their "lack" of progess. When Skeeter's new face was finally healed and ready, Malcolm returned to Spaldergate with news of a major and unexpected "break" in the case: Armstrong had been spotted.

"Who saw the bastard?" Kaederman asked eagerly. "*Where?*"

"An inquiry agent," Malcolm said smoothly. "We ran across the chap this afternoon. Runs a small agency out of Middlesex Street. He's done work for hire before, on behalf of Spaldergate."

"What did he say? How did he find Armstrong?"

Malcolm poured brandy as he explained. "Essentially, he was hired by an irate merchant to discover who'd been passing counterfeit banknotes."

"Counterfeit banknotes?" Kaederman's brows twitched upward in startlement.

"Indeed. It seems the money changer he used on station was somewhat less than scrupulously honest. She slipped a number of counterfeit banknotes in amongst the genuine article. Just before Skeeter Jackson left the station, the money changer asked Mr. Jackson to look into it for her. She was afraid Jenna Caddrick might have been arrested for passing counterfeit money. We'd hired this particular inquiry agent before, looking for Benny Catlin, so this afternoon I hunted him up. Mr. Shannon had been hired recently by a local merchant, trying to trace a foreigner passing fake banknotes. The merchant was irate, wanted to find the counterfeiter to recover substantial losses."

Sid Kaederman laughed quietly, utterly delighted, judging from the glint in his eyes. "Imagine Armstrong's shock when he discovers he was swindled by a money changer!"

Malcolm frowned. "You appear to misapprehend this situation. Counterfeiting is a serious charge, Kaederman. If we don't get to Armstrong before the police, he will be in more trouble than we'll be able to get him out of—and God knows what that will mean in terms of recovering his hostages. We must move quickly. Mr. Shannon has identified him and only a substantial bribe kept him from reporting what he's learned to his client and the police."

"Where's he hiding?"

"He *was* staying somewhere in the East End, but moved out of his lodgings very suddenly, with his entire family—or rather, obviously, his hostages. According to Shannon, Armstrong has discovered the difficulty with his cash supply and may well have passed counterfeits to his landlord without realizing it. Clearly, he wanted to disappear before his landlord could create trouble. Shannon managed to locate him again and saw him purchase a fancy suit and silk top hat. Armstrong subsequently wrangled an introduction at one of the Pall Mall gentlemen's clubs and has been gambling at the gaming tables. Loses here, wins big there."

"Sounds like he's trying to get rid of the counterfeits without having to go to a bank."

"Precisely. Which means we should be able to lay hands on him tonight, when he returns to the gaming tables. Shannon overheard him make an appointment with some of his new acquaintances for the Carlton Club tonight. Unfortunately, when Armstrong took the underground railway out of Blackfriars Station, Shannon lost him in the crush of the crowds, so we still don't know where he's moved the hostages."

Kaderman ignored that last piece of information, eyes glinting with feral excitement as he latched onto the useful item in Malcolm's story. "Tonight! The Carlton Club, where's that?"

"Pall Mall, just west of Waterloo Place. All the fashionable gentlemen's clubs are found in Waterloo Place and Pall Mall. It's an ideal setup to pass counterfeit banknotes. So much money changes hands at the gaming tables, a man would be hard pressed to determine just who had passed the counterfeits. Are you a gambler, Mr. Kaederman?"

A small, secretive smile came and went. "Often."

"Might I suggest, then, that we arrange to play cards this evening?"

Kaederman chuckled. "With pleasure."

"I'll arrange for a hansom cab to take us down at eight o'clock, then."

"I'll be ready."

Malcolm wondered if Kaederman would wait until they approached "Armstrong" at the Carlton Club's gaming tables or if he'd try a hit from some distance, before his victim could realize Kaederman was there. They hadn't been able to search Kaederman's luggage—he kept both his room and his cases locked—so he could easily have any number of modern weapons stashed away. They were putting Skeeter in body armor, which Kit had thoughtfully sent along, but Malcolm still worried over the problem like a Staffordshire terrier with a soup bone. He hoped Skeeter knew what they were all doing. Far too many lives were riding on the outcome of this trap, Margo's and Malcolm's own, among them. With a final worried glance at Sid Kaederman, Malcolm arranged for the hired carriage and settled down to wait for showtime.

Skeeter fiddled nervously with his watch fob as he climbed out of the Spaldergate barouche into the elegant bustle of Pall Mall. He was a man transformed. His formal black jacket was the forerunner of the modern tuxedo and his diamond horseshoe stick pin, high collar, and heavy gold watch and chain marked him as a man of considerable wealth. The expensive macassar oil that slicked his hair back glinted in the dying light of sunset as his reflection wavered in the Carlton Club's windows. He did an involuntary double-take—his new face startled Skeeter every time he glanced into a reflective surface.

At least the swelling had gone down where Paula had tugged and snipped his flesh into a different shape, and the bruises had faded. He could even talk without pain and had finally graduated to solid foods after nearly a week on liquids, unable to chew without the aid of opiates. As the Spaldergate House carriage rattled away, returning to the gatehouse, Skeeter told the butterflies in his belly to settle down and behave. Any other night, he would've been thrilled beyond measure to play the role of wealthy gambler in one of London's finest gaming establishments. But springing a trap on Sid Kaederman left Skeeter scared to the bottom of his wild, adopted-Mongol heart. He'd accepted the risks when he'd set this in motion, but that didn't stop every monarch and swallowtail butterfly in the northern hemisphere from doing a rumba under his ribs.

Douglas Tanglewood, the Time Tours guide assigned to Skeeter for the night, flashed him a wan smile. "Feeling a bit keyed up?"

"A little."

"It's to be expected," Tanglewood said with forced cheeriness. The guide had been pressed into service with a critical role to play. He would provide Skeeter with the necessary introductions at the Carlton Club, since Malcolm had another mission tonight. Malcolm was bringing in Kaederman. As they crossed the pavement toward the Carlton Club's doorman, Tanglewood kept darting glances at Skeeter, clearly disturbed at seeing him wearing another man's features.

The entrance to the Carlton Club was crowded with laughing gentlemen, opportuned on all sides by unfortunates who made their living—such as it was—off the spare change flowing like wine through Pall Mall. Bootblacks and eel-pie vendors jostled shoulders with flower girls, all crying their wares while newsboys hawked the latest shocking reports out of Whitechapel. Skeeter spotted Margo in heavy disguise as a bootblack boy, diligently polishing some gentleman's shoes in the glow from the club's gaslights. Her unsuspecting customer had stepped up with one foot on her overturned wooden box, reading his newspaper while Margo darted quick looks through the crowd.

Margo caught his gaze and nodded imperceptibly. Skeeter nodded back, then followed Tanglewood into the opulent interior of the Carlton Club. The Time Tours guide greeted the liveried doorman by name as the man opened massive mahogany doors. "Good evening, Fitzwilliam. I've brought a guest this evening, Mr. Cartwright, of America."

Fitzwilliam accepted a small tip from Tanglewood's gloved hand. "Good evening, sir." The doorman spoke politely, his accent as carefully cultured as his gleaming livery. "Welcome to the Carlton Club."

"Thank you." The instant Skeeter stepped across the threshold, he knew he had just walked into *money*. The game rooms were in full swing with lively conversation and gambling activities, the air thick with cigar smoke and the smell of wealth. Skeeter and his guide checked their overcoats and wandered through the busy rooms to acquaint themselves with the club's floor plan, then paused at a craps table where Skeeter tossed a few rounds, just to "keep the hand in." He paid his losses with a polite smile, then, as they walked off, muttered, "Don't play that table. I tossed four sets of dice and every one of 'em was loaded."

The Time Tours guide shot him a startled stare. "*What?*"

Skeeter chuckled. "Never try to con a con. He'll spot you every time. The first ones I tossed were weighted, probably with a mercury tumbler inside. Did you notice how that portly guy with the mutton chops kept tapping them? Dead giveaway. It's why I asked for a new set. Second pair was shaved on the edges. I could feel where they'd been rounded off on all corners but two. That means a better chance they'll roll until they hit a true squared edge, skewing the odds."

Tanglewood was gaping at him.

"Then there was a set where they'd shaved a few of the faces just slightly convex, causing 'em to tumble more readily along the bulged sides. The one concave face creates just the tiniest vacuum against the table's surface, causing the die to land on that face. Wouldn't happen every time, of course, but over a long enough period of throws, you'd get a consistent win. Or loss, if you're trying to prevent sevens or elevens from showing."

"And the fourth pair?" Tanglewood asked, visibly astonished.

"Weighted again, very subtle, though. The paint didn't quite match on all the dots. Your basic slick operator made those. Used heavy lead paint on the dots for the sixes on that pair, so they'd consistently end up on the bottom." Skeeter gave the gaming room they'd just left a disgusted glance. "I didn't say anything, because we're not here to create a scene and I didn't particularly feel like getting involved in a duel of honor with some stiff-necked British lord. But I think I'll avoid the craps tables from now on, thank you."

"Good God, Jackson. Where do you learn such things? No, don't answer that. I'm not sure I want to know. Ever consider a career as a detective?"

"As a matter of fact," Skeeter chuckled, "Kit Carson hired me to work security for the Neo Edo."

Tanglewood let out a low whistle. "I am impressed."

Ten minutes later, Tanglewood had introduced him as "Mr. Cartwright, of New York City, America" at the card tables and Skeeter found himself wallowing happily in a rip-snorting game of stud with the scions of several noble houses, all of them happy as clams to be playing "cowboy poker" with a genuine Yank. In the third hand, one of the players lit a thin, black cigar and gave Skeeter a friendly glance. "I was in America, once, had business in San Francisco. Met a fellow there who played this game very well, indeed. Perhaps you know him, if you've played cards widely over there?"

Skeeter glanced up. "What was his name?"

"Kiplinger. Mr. Kiplinger."

Skeeter sat back in his chair. "*Kiplinger?* Why, yes, I have heard of him, although we've never met." The corners of his lips twitched. "Quite a gambler, Mr. Kiplinger." Skeeter's eyes twinkled as a positively wicked mood stole over him. "Do you suppose you'll ever be going back to San Francisco, sir?"

The card player smiled. "No, Mr. Cartwright, I think it exceedingly unlikely. An uncle of mine had gone out there during the Gold Rush of '49, you see, made a fortune selling whiskey and victuals to the miners. Parlayed it into an astonishing sum, buying shares in mining operations. When he died last year, I went out to see to the estate, since I was named in his will. He'd never married, poor old Uncle Charles, left a fortune with no heirs but a nephew. Black sheep of a very fine family, let me tell you. But he added ten thousand per annum to my baronetcy when he passed on. Quite an astounding country, America."

Skeeter grinned. "Well, since you don't plan on going back, mind if I let you in on Mr. Kiplinger's secret? Quite a scandal it was, too. Happened just before I came over here." The other gentlemen at the table leaned foward, abruptly intent. Even Tanglewood, whose job was to keep watch for Malcolm and Kaederman, listened with keen interest. "Mr. Kiplinger," Skeeter warmed to his subject, "is what's known as a machine man."

"A machine man?" the baronet frowned. "What the deuce is a machine man?"

"In short, a cheat, a swindler, and a fraud. Maybe you've heard the term 'ace up your sleeve'? Well, what Mr. Kiplinger did was invent an ingenious little machine that fit around his forearm and wrist. It had a little clip in the end of it, to hold a playing card or two, and it could be extended down along the inside of his wrist, like so," Skeeter pointed to his own forearm, "or pulled back again, to hide whatever cards he'd slipped into the clip. He tied a string to the end of the sliding arm of his machine, ran it down his coat and inside his trousers, to a little mechanism at his knees."

The gentlemen had forgotten their own cards, staring in open-mouthed delight.

"The devil you say! How did it operate?"

"The string was attached to a tiny little hook sewed to the inside knee of his other trouser leg. If he wanted to slide the arm of his machine down to his wrist, so he could palm a hidden card into his hand, he squeezed his knees together, which took the tension off the string and lowered the sliding arm with the cards clipped to it. When he wanted to sneak a card up his sleeve, all he had to do was pull his knees apart and presto! Away went the card, slick as a whistle. He practiced with that little contraption until he got so good at it, he could slip three or four cards into that clip during the course of a round of poker and nobody was the wiser."

The gentlemen at their table were gasping, both delighted and scandalized.

"Eventually," Skeeter chuckled, "he got greedy. About two months ago, it must've been, he decided to enter a really high-stakes poker game in San Francisco. And he kept winning. Every single hand. There were a number of very fine card players in that game, professional gamblers, all of them, and several of these professional gentlemen started to get just a little suspicious of Mr. Kiplinger and his phenomenal run of luck at the cards. So at a prearranged signal, they jumped him, dragged off his coat, and found his little machine with three aces and a queen clipped into it."

"Good God! Did they shoot him on the spot?"

"Oh, no." Skeeter grinned. "Not to say that didn't cross their minds, of course. Men have been shot for cheating less seriously than that. No, what they did was tell Mr. Kiplinger he had a choice. He could either die, right then and there, or he could earn his life back."

"How?" That from a heavy-jowled gentleman whose peerage earned him the right to wear a jewelled coronet in the presence of the sovereign. He'd told them so, within five minutes of their having joined the group.

Skeeter sat back, grinning triumphantly. "All he had to do was build one of these machines for each and every one of them. Which he did."

Laughter and exclamations of astonishment greeted the pronouncement.

"But I say, Cartwright, however did you find out about this?"

Skeeter laughed easily. "One of those fellows was my uncle. Black sheep of *my* family. Hell of a card player." He winked. "One hell of a card player."

Doug Tanglewood joined in the laughter as Skeeter scooted back his chair, gracefully slid off his coat and removed his cuffs, revealing no trace of Mr. Kiplinger's infernal contraption, then replaced cuff and cufflinks and evening coat and resumed his seat.

"All right, gentlemen, let's play poker, shall we?"

Kit was jolted from sleep by the insistent shrill of his telephone. He groped, bleary-eyed, for the receiver. "Mmph?"

"Kit? Are you awake?"

"No." He started to fumble the receiver back onto its cradle.

"Kit! Dammit, don't hang up, it's Bull Morgan. I need you in the aerie."

Kit hadn't slept more than ten hours during the last five days. In fact, he had just spent four of those days combing the station for Jack the Ripper, placating and browbeating by turns panic-stricken, infuriated tourists in the Neo Edo, and working gate control to keep any in-bound tourists from coming back into the station. Tours had backed up not only in New York, where in-bound tourists were refused admittance, but also in every down-time location TT-86 operated, leaving literally hundreds of tourists stranded down time, unable to return until the station neutralized the Ripper threat. Having just fallen into bed after nearly twenty hours of non-stop work, Kit told Bull Morgan exactly what he thought of the station manager's latest request. In graphic and shocking detail.

Unfortunately, Bull didn't speak medieval High German, which was Kit's favorite language for cursing. The moment he wound down, Bull said maddeningly, "Good. I'll see you in ten minutes. Caddrick's on his way with I.T.C.H. They're shutting us down, effective today, unless we can figure a way to stall 'em off."

"Oh, God . . ." Kit propped his eyelids open. "If I'm not there in ten, send an ambulance."

"Thanks, Kit. I owe you."

"You sure as hell do. I'll collect on this one, too, just see if I don't."

The line went dead and Kit crawled out of bed, feeling a certain kinship with a recently squashed garden slug. He dragged on the first clothes that came to hand, staggered in search of footgear, and finally stumbled out onto Commons, heading at a drunken pace for the aerie. He was halfway there, repeating to himself, *I will not fall asleep on my feet* every few seconds, before he woke up enough to realize he wore nothing but a loosely belted kimono that covered entirely too little of him and house slippers that had been new when Queen Elizabeth the First had taken the English throne. He'd stolen them, himself, from an Elizabethan house he'd entered under very unhappy circumstances.

"Ah, hell . . ." He pulled the belt tighter, which at least kept the more private bits of him from showing, and scowled at his hairy shins. No time to go back and change, now . . . He couldn't even stop somewhere and beg a pair of jeans. Commons remained eerily quiet, shops and restaurants resembling darkened caves behind their steel security-mesh doors. Scattered patrols of security, BATF, and Pest Control officers stood guard over major gates due to open, to be sure no one got into or out of the station. After that dead BATF officer had been found beside the Langskip Cafe, a few days back, not even Commons security forces made the rounds without partners along. A slow, door-to-door search of every hotel room and Residential apartment on station was underway, looking for both Lachley and a handful of Ripper cultists still at large, but the search was taking forever, with no guarantee that the Ripper wasn't simply changing lodgings to a room already cleared.

By the time Kit reached the aerie, he was almost asleep again, leaning against the elevator doors for the ride up from Commons. The elevator doors slid open, dumping Kit unceremoniously into the room. He staggered, recovered, and hitched the kimono around with an irritable twitch, then met the astonished gazes of John Caddrick, three armed bodyguards, and five I.T.C.H. agents impeccably attired—respectively—in six-thousand dollar suits and neatly pressed uniforms. Kit scratched absently at a thick growth of stubble, yawned, and wove his way toward a chair, where he promptly collapsed.

Caddrick glared. "You're drunk!"

"God, I wish," Kit muttered. "I just haven't been to bed in about five days. Thanks for waking me up. Now, what's this bullshit about closing Shangri-La?"

Caddrick glanced at the highest-ranking I.T.C.H. officer. "Agent Kirkegard has agreed to shut down this station. TT-86 is dangerously out of control, thanks to gross incompetence among the managerial staff."

Kit just looked at him. Then switched his attention to the immaculately groomed Kirkegard, her blond hair pulled back into a severe knot at the nape of her neck. "You wouldn't mind, would you, if I toss this jackass through the window?"

"This is not a time to joke!" she snapped.

"I'm not joking," Kit growled. "The only thing wrong with this station is John Caddrick's butt, sitting on it."

Bull Morgan stood up hastily, clearing his throat. "Kit, I know how hard you've been working during this crisis. I asked you to join this meeting to present your case as a station resident and business owner, before I.T.C.H. makes its final determination."

"I see. Tell you what," Kit leaned forward, holding Agent Kirkegard's gaze. "You people have been probing around in our books and our private vaults and auditing our tax returns until you've dug down to Himalayan bedrock. I'd like to issue you a *real* challenge."

"A challenge?" Kirkegard echoed, her Nordic brow creasing briefly.

"Yep. A real barn-burner. I'd like you to figure out why John Caddrick, here, would lie to the press, the FBI, Interpol, and I.T.C.H. about the circumstances of his little girl's disappearance."

For a long moment, utter silence reigned in the aerie. Every mouth in the room had dropped open, including Bull Morgan's. Kit was beyond caring if he'd just signed the station's death warrant—not to mention his own. He was simply too tired to keep pussyfooting around what he knew about Jenna Caddrick's vanishing act, and he was fresh out of other options. And it looked to Kit like he'd struck paydirt, with this one.

Senator Caddrick's face had utterly drained of color, leaving him virtually transparent for long instants. Then a scarlet flush darkened toward purple. He came out of his chair, snarling. "Why, you miserable, drunken, washed-up *has-been*! How dare you insinuate any such thing!"

"Sit down," Kit growled, "before you step close enough to call it assault and I retaliate in ways we'll all regret."

"Don't sit there and threaten me!"

"All right." Kit stood up. "I'll stand here and do it. Maybe you'd care to explain a few facts. You say your daughter's so-called kidnappers came to this station and tried to murder Ianira Cassondra, but we've got eye witnesses who'll swear in court that your daughter came into this station of her own free will. Moreover, she came armed with a loaded revolver she used to *kill* the terrorist about to murder Ianira. Or what about Noah Armstrong, who's supposed to be a ringleader of these same terrorists? Armstrong shoved Ianira to safety, just as the man Jenna killed tried to shoot her. And why did Julius, not to mention Marcus and his children, voluntarily run to Denver with Noah Armstrong in disguise, smuggling the girls out in their luggage and setting up Julius as decoy for your daughter? For that matter, why was Jenna, who was supposed to be held hostage, allowed to wander around this station at will, changing money all by herself in Goldie Morran's shop just minutes before the gate departure? Furthermore, she strolled into Paula Booker's cosmetic surgical studio and paid for a new face, again totally on her own. She was all by herself when she stepped through the Britannia Gate, too—we've got witnesses who'll swear to that, too, in a court of law. Nobody forced that girl through any gates on this station. How about it, Caddrick?"

Caddrick's cheeks faded to the color of dirty ice. "*This is preposterous!*"

"Is it? Your story doesn't add up, Caddrick. I wonder what we'd find out about Noah Armstrong if we went back up time and started digging? The man can't be an *Ansar Majlis* terrorist, not when he's kept Ianira's whole family from being murdered by *Ansar Majlis* operatives, and he can't be a kidnapper since he let Jenna and Ianira walk through the Britannia Gate without armed guards. She was seen on the departures platform by one of the baggage handlers. There wasn't anybody close to her who could've been holding a gun on her. And she walked out of Spaldergate House in London with no escort except a Time Tours driver. No kidnappers in sight, nothing. She was followed, of course. Two men who trailed her out of this station, working as baggage handlers, tried to kill her at the Piccadilly Hotel. Only Jenna shot both of them, with the same revolver she used to kill the *Ansar Majlis* gunman on station, killed both men and got away clean. Personally, Caddrick, I'd like to know why your story doesn't wash with the facts."

"*I will not stand here and be slandered!*" Caddrick shouted, causing dust to jump on the surface of Bull's immense desk.

"Good!" Kit shot right back. "I'll personally escort you to Primary and kick your butt through, the second it re-opens!"

Ms. Kirkegard stepped between them, holding up an imperious hand in either direction, forestalling whatever shattering curse was about to erupt from Caddrick's mouth. "Silence! All of you! Mr. Carson, these are very serious allegations."

"You bet they are. Believe me, I know exactly how serious they are. I wouldn't risk making such accusations lightly, because too many people who thwart John Caddrick's plans end up conveniently dead."

"I will sue you for every goddamned cent you own!" Caddrick snarled.

Kit grinned into Caddrick's teeth. "Like to see you try it. We're outside American jurisdiction, here. You'll have to convince the Inter-Temporal Court, if you want to sue my butt."

Agent Kirkegard said forcefully, "I want to see these witnesses, immediately."

"Sorry. They're in London. Looking for Jenna Caddrick. And keeping a very suspicious eye on the Senator's private detective, Mr. Sid Kaederman. Caddrick rammed him down our throats with threats to shut us down if we didn't send him along. The man had never stepped through a single gate, was monstrously unqualified for a down-time search mission. I spent a couple of weeks in Sid Kaederman's company, on horseback in Colorado. Maybe the Senator, here, can explain why Mr. Kaederman recognized the man who murdered one of our station residents in an abandoned Colorado mining town? Recognized him and didn't expect to find him dead? That man had committed cold-blooded murder of a sixteen-year-old boy, I might add, who went to Colorado as decoy for Jenna Caddrick."

"There are perfectly good reasons why Kaederman might not say anything," Caddrick began.

"Really? If Kaederman were legit and had recognized one of the terrorists, he'd simply have said so. But he didn't say anything. In fact, he took pains to make sure no one realized he'd recognized the man. Why? Mr. Sid Kaederman's story doesn't add up, either, does it? We sent him to London to avoid having your federal goons shut us down, but I sent Skeeter Jackson and Paula Booker through to keep an eye on him. Skeeter knows this case better than anyone—he's been at hand when every key piece of this mess has unfolded. And when it comes to Ianira Cassondra, Skeeter's the only man on this station I can guarantee no amount of money will buy off. A boy doesn't get adopted by twelfth-century Yakka Mongols without adopting their moral codes. For Skeeter, clan is sacred, and someone's already killed one member of his adopted station-side clan and tried to murder several others. Believe me, Caddrick, that boy will kill to protect Ianira and her family, if he has to. And he *will* find Jenna and Noah Armstrong. The question is, what will they tell him when he does?"

"You're mad!" Caddrick shouted. "Completely insane! My God, Carson, is this the only way you can find to keep your precious pocketbook from being shut down around your ears? By making wild accusations and threatening me?"

"Why don't we let Jenna settle it?" Kit smiled coldly into Caddrick's eyes.

The Senator swung on the I.T.C.H. agents. "Are you going to listen to this garbage? I insist you do your job! Shut down this station right now, before any more lives are lost! As for Carson," he flung a pitying look over his shoulder, "it's clear he's cracked under the strain. Up-time hospitalization is what he needs."

Agent Kirkegard frowned. "Senator, I cannot believe Kit Carson has gone raving mad in the space of one week. Not when he has worked so heroically to save lives on this station. No, do not interrupt!" she snapped, as Caddrick started to protest. "Grave charges have been made, charges which must be investigated. If what Mr. Carson says is true, your actions on this station must be considered highly suspicious. Until this delegation is satisfied that no evidence exists to prove these accusations, my fellow agents and I must take them seriously. You will return to your hotel, Senator, and you will not leave it unless you are summoned by this delegation. Is that clear?

Mr. Morgan," she turned her attention to Bull, leaving Caddrick sputtering in naked shock, "I believe your security system records events on Commons?"

"It does," Bull nodded. "We recycle the tapes on a weekly basis, but we've kept the footage of every riot on station, for legal purposes."

"Very wise. I hereby subpoena all security tapes showing the disturbance surrounding Ianira Cassondra's disappearance."

"But she's a down-timer without rights!" Caddrick protested.

Kirkegard turned an icy gaze on him. "Indeed. But if your daughter and Noah Armstrong are shown in that tape doing what Mr. Carson claims they were doing, your entire story will come under serious suspicion. And they are not down-timers, but up-time citizens with full legal protection. Therefore, that tape is critical evidence. Mr. Morgan, if I may suggest it, the Senator should not be privy to any further discussions this commission has with station management, until such time as these charges are proven or dismissed."

"You can't be serious!" Caddrick blustered.

She levelled a cool stare back into his seething grey eyes. "I would suggest you remove yourself to your hotel, Senator. Or I will have you removed."

Caddrick stood sputtering for several incoherent moments, then stalked to the elevator. His stunned bodyguards hurried in his wake, exchanging worried glances. The elevator swallowed them down and took them mercifully away. Kit ran a hand through badly disheveled hair. "Thanks. And now, if you don't mind, I'm going back to bed. You can subpoena me to testify later."

And without waiting for a by-your-leave, he stalked to the elevator and followed Caddrick's abrupt exit. Ten minutes later, he was sprawled in bed once more, his last conscious thought a worried one, wondering what he'd just unleashed on them all.

《 Chapter 16 》

The cold night wind chilled Margo through her thin bootblack's disguise. She shivered and wished she could walk through the ornate doors to the Carlton Club, just long enough to get warm. Instead, she danced in place, hugging herself for warmth, and called out to passing gentlemen, "Shine, guv'nor? Farthing for a shine?"

She had just secured a customer and was diligently blacking his boots when Skeeter and Douglas Tanglewood arrived in a rented hansom. They nodded imperceptibly in her direction and vanished into the warmth of the club. Margo worked briskly, as much to keep warm as to maintain her disguise. The pistol inside her trousers was held snug against her abdomen by a belly-band holster and the dagger in her boot rubbed her calf as she moved about. She kept close watch on the arriving carriages, impatient for Malcolm to arrive with Sid Kaederman. More than a quarter of an hour passed without a trace of them, leaving Margo more and more uneasy. She was busily blacking another gentleman's boots when a hansom cab rattled to a halt some distance from the kerbside and a well-dressed gentleman swung himself down.

"Driver," he called out, "my friend wishes to continue on to London Docks, to catch his steamer."

Even as he spoke, he thrust his arm back into the dark cab, which jolted slightly on its high wheels. Margo slowed her strokes with the buffing brush, puzzled. The cab started down the street and the gentleman turned, heading toward the club entrance. Margo gasped. *Kaederman!* He strode past, nodding to the doorman. "I shall be joining friends this evening, a Mr. Cartwright and his companions."

"Very good, sir."

Margo dropped the buffing brush, abandoning her astonished client. She darted after the hansom cab, terrified of what she might find. It took her half a block to catch up and she only did so then because the cab was caught in a jam of carriages trying to turn into Waterloo Place. Margo flung herself onto the step and lunged up, ignoring the driver's startled demand to get out of his cab.

"Malcolm!"

He lay slumped against the side of the carriage, cheeks ashen in the gaslights from nearby club windows. "Margo," he whispered in a terrible, weak voice. "Sorry, love, took me by surprise . . ." He had fumbled one hand beneath his coat, was holding himself awkwardly. Blood had spread across his shirt, was dripping down his arm and spreading across the back of his hand. "Get back to . . . Carlton Club . . . warn the others." He sipped air. "I'm not hit bad. Managed to fling myself aside . . . when he told the driver to go to the docks . . . would've had me through the heart, otherwise."

Even as Malcolm was explaining, Margo was ripping his coat and shirt off, using her dagger to cut the shirt into bandage strips. She wound them around Malcolm's chest, folding a couple of thick pieces to act as compresses over the wound. Her hands shook violently, but she managed to tie them off snugly.

"Go, Margo," Malcolm wheezed. "I'll take the cab to Spaldergate. Go!"

She swore aloud, recognizing the necessity. "Driver! Your passenger's been shot! Take him to a surgeon! Battersea Park, Octavia Street! And hurry those horses!"

The driver let go a voluable flood of invective and cracked his carriage whip, urging his horses up onto the pavement to bypass the crush of carriages in the street. Pedestrians scattered, cursing, as Margo shoved her knife back into her boot sheath and flung herself down to the street, pelting toward the Carlton Club once more. She dodged carriage wheels and horses, gained the pavement, and slung herself around startled gentlemen strolling from club to club. She finally gained the Carlton and hurled herself at the doors—only to be snatched back by Fitzwilliam.

"Here, now, where d'you think you're going? This is a gentleman's club! Take yourself away, you filthy bootblack!" He dragged Margo by the back of her shirt collar and shoved her roughly to the pavement, where she landed in an undignified sprawl.

"Listen to me!" she shot back to her feet. "I have to get a critical message to Mr. Tanglewood and Mr. Cartwright! Send a message, yourself, if you won't let me in! Tell them Kaederman shot Mr. Moore and he's going to kill Mr. Cartwright! They're in terrible danger—!"

"Take yourself off before I summon a constable, you little lunatic!"

Margo darted past, but Fitzwilliam was quick. He trapped her between his body and the wall, pinning her like a bug on display. He boxed her ears so soundly, Margo's head rang and her eyes streamed. She swore in gutter langage, then bit his hand, flinging herself around him and running toward the now-unguarded door.

"Stop that boy! Stop him, I say!"

A group of startled gentlemen just leaving the club made a grab for her. She slithered past, cursing them, and dragged out her pistol— then someone seized her shoulder and spun her around and pain exploded through her head, sending her sprawling across the pavement like a ragdoll.

Goldie rapidly discovered that John Lachley, while certifiably mad, was nevertheless no fool. Killing her was thankfully the furthest thing from his mind. She spent most of her captivity tied to the chair in front of her computer, teaching him everything he demanded to know about the up-time world. He needed her—for a while, anyway. And that gave her the courage to hope she might somehow survive.

"This," Lachley demanded, touching a finger to the glowing computer screen, "is the schedule for the various gates, then?"

Goldie nodded. "Yes." Her left wrist was bound to the chair, her right tied to the desk with a short length of rope, just enough to operate the mouse.

"Three different dates are given for each gate," he frowned.

"There have to be three. One is the time-frame of the up-time world, where the tourists come from, one is the time-frame of the station, and one is the time-frame of the tour destination beyond the gate."

He studied the readings for a moment. "This one has only two dates."

"That's Primary, of course. Gate One."

"Ah, of course . . . The way into the up-time world which your guards have so churlishly denied me. Of course there would be only two dates given. Yes. Show me how one obtains a proper gate pass for your Primary."

Goldie bit her lip nervously. "I can't. You get one in New York. When you come into the station. And a down-timer *can't* get one. Down-timers are never permitted to step through Primary. It's against up-time law."

Lachley scowled. "Deuced awkward. I shall simply have to obtain one from a tourist or station resident, then. No matter. A trifling detail. Make this machine show me what your up-time worlds looks like."

Goldie explained how to put in a CD encyclopedia which contained photographs and movie clips, since she couldn't reach the shelf where they were stored, then clicked into various files to show him what he demanded. As he frowned at the screen, she suggested nervously, "You'd get a better idea, watching videotaped movies on television."

Ten minutes later, Goldie sat bound hand and foot on her couch, while John Lachley sprawled at his leisure beside her, watching Goldie's movies. He exclaimed often, sitting forward with interest whenever cars or jets or cityscapes appeared, took particular note of new machinery and gadgets, and demanded explanations of everything he saw until Goldie's mind whirled in exhaustion. He watched videotapes until she fell asleep in her bonds and when she woke again, stiff and aching, he was still watching. He also spent hours at her computer, reading station library files, and studied every book on Goldie's shelves. Lachley's growing knowledge of the up-time world terrified Goldie. He correctly identified every item in the videos, explained each item's proper use, and had picked up modern slang and idiom with an ease that left her shaking. If he got loose in New York . . .

She couldn't see any way to stop him, short of reaching a telephone to cry for help, and since he was already familiar with their use from London, he hadn't allowed her near one—once he'd recognized hers for what it was; it bore no resemblance whatsoever to an 1880's telephone. When operating the computer, she wasn't even able to send an e-mail to station security. He'd grasped the e-mail concept with terrifying rapidity and had forced her to delete the programming from her hard drive.

Goldie knew the entire station was being turned upside down, searching for him, but no one had come to her apartment, thanks to his trick with the dead BATF officer's radio, and no one had called her, either, not even to commiserate over lost profits. It hurt to realize that in such a crisis, not one of the station residents had thought to check on her, to see if she was alive or dead. People she'd thought of as friends had completely ignored her. Bitterness choked Goldie, but there was nothing she could do except wait and hope that her captor grew careless just long enough to scream for help.

Every day's passing, however, left Goldie sinking further into despair. He never relaxed his vigil for even a moment and Goldie entertained no doubts about what he'd do if he caught her trying to telephone. Lachley would cut her to ribbons so small, there wouldn't be enough to fill a casket. On the other hand, if she didn't anger him, he would probably let her live, at least until he made the attempt to crash Primary outbound. And he couldn't try that as long as Bull Morgan kept the tourists in their hotel rooms and refused to let anyone through. Goldie's greatest terror was that Lachley would simply kill her, waylay a security agent and steal his uniform, then slip through Primary that way.

As days passed, the intolerable situation left John Lachley deeply impatient, forced as he was to sit through two cycles of Primary without anyone allowed near it. He paced agitatedly, muttering under his breath, then finally snatched up another videotape from her rapidly dwindling supply. Lachley poured himself a generous brandy from the last bottle in the cabinet and slid in Goldie's copy of *Temple Harlot,* which she had just recently acquired through a video pirate. When the pre-movie interview of Ianira Cassondra flickered across the screen, Lachley jerked so violently, he knocked the glass to the floor. He stared at the screen and ripped off a shocked oath. "*God's blood!* It's her!" He turned a wild-eyed stare on Goldie. "Who is that woman?" He stabbed an unsteady finger toward the television.

"Ianira Cassondra. One of the station's down-timers. A member of the Found Ones, the down-time community of refugees. She sits on the council as their speaker."

He ran the tape back to listen to the interview in its entirety, then stopped the video and demanded a full explanation. Goldie told him everything she knew about Ianira, her flight from a murderous husband in Athens, her arrival on station, her marriage to Marcus, the adoring acolytes who had named her their prophetess, hailing her as the Goddess incarnate. "They flock to the station," she quavered. "When she was kidnapped, they went berserk. Staged protests and started brawls with the *Ansar Majlis* and half the station. The Angels of Grace Militia has sworn to defend Templars from harm until Ianira is restored." Goldie wanted to ask why he was so abruptly interested, but couldn't find the courage to open her lips again.

Lachley sat staring into empty space for long moments, mind clearly racing. At length, he murmured, "It is possible, then, to wield that much power, even in this strange world . . . If a mere chit can be taken for a goddess, then I shall certainly rule as a god." He smiled, laughed softly to himself, eyes twinkling. Then untied Goldie from the couch and hauled her unceremoniously into her bedroom, where he dumped her onto the mattress and tied her down again. He stroked Goldie's wild, unwashed hair back from her face and smiled down at her. "You have done very well, my pet. According to the time tables on your computer, Primary opens again tomorrow evening. You and I shall be ready, dear lady. Whether they permit it or no, I *will* step through that gate."

Goldie was too exhausted, too numb to ask how. She hadn't forgotten how he'd created his last diversion—or the severed human head he'd flung down into the crowd, its plunge caught vividly on

SLUR-TV's cameras. It had been a woman's head, with once-beautiful blonde hair. Goldie knew in her creaking bones he would cut *her* to pieces, too, if he could find no other way through Primary.

Despite Goldie's soul-deep weariness, sleep was a long time coming.

Skeeter was winning the latest round of poker, hands down, when a liveried servant carrying a folded slip of paper on a silver tray entered the card parlour. "Message for Mr. Cartwright!" He spoke just loudly enough to be heard, without disrupting conversations under way over the cards. The servant was peering around the room, trying to locate the recipient. At the sound of his assumed name, Skeeter jerked his glance up.

"What is it? What message?"

"Ah, Mr. Cartwright? A message, sir." The man handed Skeeter the folded slip of paper and waited for the tip Skeeter produced, then departed with a slight bow. Skeeter glanced at Doug Tanglewood, who was frowning already, then opened the note. Every droplet of blood drained out of his face. *There's serious trouble at home, come at once, someone's taken the children . . .*

The table flipped over with a crash. Cards and money went flying. Skeeter hit the floor running and took the stairs five at a time, leaving Tanglewood to follow in his wake. Skeeter was ruthless with elbows and shoulders. "Let me through, damn your eyes!"

Shocked gentlemen scattered out of his path, staring after him. Then he was on the ground floor, retrieving his coat, rushing toward the door. He was nearly there when a voice at his ear said, "Where's the fire, Armstrong?" He jerked his gaze up, startled, to find Sid Kaederman at his elbow. An instant later, something hard, cylindrical, and terrifying jabbed his ribs, as luck would have it, between the front and back panels of his hidden body armor.

"Make any noise at all and I'll blow a hole through your liver," Kaederman hissed. "Outside, Armstrong. We're going have a friendly little chat someplace quiet. About your friends."

Shaking with fury at his own stupidity, Skeeter walked into the cold October night. The jaws of the trap had slammed shut, all right—

only Skeeter was the one caught and where the hell was Malcolm? Nothing was going down the way it was supposed to! How had Kaederman gotten the drop on them all, leaving Skeeter off balance and everyone out of position? Kaederman pushed open the door and shoved Skeeter through, gun still jammed into his ribs. Skeeter raked the pavement with his glance, searching for familiar faces and not spotting any. Kaederman was lifting a hand and whistling for a hansom cab when Margo appeared, running toward them.

"Kaederman!"

The killer stiffened—and the damned, interfering doorman grabbed Margo by the shoulder, slugging her so hard, she sprawled across the walk. Her little .32 top break clattered across the pavement and into the street. Men were shouting, calling for a constable, and someone cried, "Good God! The boy had a gun!"

Kaederman shoved Skeeter away from the fracas, toward a hansom cab waiting for a fare, the horse's head bent low, the cabman bundled against the cold wind. Skeeter's fury faltered into the beginnings of real fear.

"I say," a familiar voice said from behind them, "did you drop this, sir?"

Kaederman started to glance around, an instinctive response to the polite inquiry—and Doug Tanglewood kicked Skeeter's feet out from under him.

He went down with a startled yell, no more expecting that sudden move than Kaederman. A brief, sharp scuffle exploded above him. The muted *clack!* of a silenced pistol reached him. The scent of burnt powder and hot metal filled the air as the gun discharged almost soundlessly. Tanglewood gripped Kaederman's gun wrist with both hands while swearing savagely, oblivious to the hole through the loose side of a once-fine Prince Albert coat. The crowd of gentlemen on the steps stood like spectators at a sporting event, thinking this was an ordinary brawl; not one of them recognized the anachronistic, suppressed semiautomatic pistol as a dangerous weapon.

Skeeter kicked out and managed to clip Kaederman's ankles with one thrashing foot. Kaederman tripped, flailing for a moment off balance. Tanglewood suddenly had his opponent's full weight slipping through his hands and only slowed Kaederman's fall enough for the assassin to control it, leaving Tanglewood the one off balance and Kaederman rolling back up. Skeeter scrambled to his feet just as Margo rushed in low, under Kaederman's gun arm. She prevented his second shot from catching Tanglewood between the shoulderblades. The gun fired wild as Kaederman tried to avoid her. A giant's fist punched Skeeter in the chest and sent him sprawling, saved from the bullet by the Kevlar panel under his fancy dress shirt. Margo was still struggling with Kaederman. Shrill whistles sounded, police whistles, and someone shouted, "Constable! Over here!"

Tanglewood lunged at them just as Kaederman punched Margo in the solar plexus. She doubled up with a gagging sound and he dragged her back with the gun to her head. "Get back, damn you, or I'll kill her!"

Skeeter tried to crawl to his feet, stunned and gasping against pain to his ribs, bruising pain from that shot to his body armor. Kaederman kicked him in the gut, dumping him to the ground again, and dragged his hostage into the street where he flung her into a cab. Then Kaederman lunged up and shouted at the driver, who sped away with a clatter, swerving into traffic at a reckless pace. Skeeter and Tanglewood bolted in pursuit—and found their way blocked by two burly constables.

"What's going on, here?" the taller policeman demanded.

"That man's a killer!" Skeeter gasped, pointing at the vanishing hansom cab. "He's taken a girl hostage! We have to stop him!"

Tanglewood dashed into the street, scooping up Margo's revolver in one fluid movement while flagging down another cab. "Skeeter! Come on!"

The constables grabbed for him and missed. A moment later, the cab driver was racing down Pall Mall in pursuit. Skeeter clung to the side of the rocketing hansom to avoid being flung out as they whipped between carriages at a reckless pace. Douglas Tanglewood was swearing nonstop. "Goddammit, what a bloody *mess!*"

"What'm I gonna tell Kit?" Skeeter groaned, closing his eyes against the very thought. "What in the world am I gonna tell Kit? And the others . . ." He could hear the voices already, could picture the freezing contempt. *And where were you, Skeeter, when Margo was abducted by that killer? Ah, gambling . . . Well, of course you were, Skeeter, who could expect anything better of you . . .*

He had to find her. Before Kaederman tortured her to learn where Jenna was. Skeeter wouldn't give a plugged nickle for her life, once Kaederman knew. Skeeter clenched his jaw. He vowed to hunt Kaederman to the ends of the world, if necessary.

And kill him.

(((Chapter 17)))

Primary was due to open at eight-fifteen P.M., station time. Goldie spent the day in a mute daze, watching John Lachley prepare his escape. He had raided Goldie's wardrobe, finding a pair of her jeans and a sweatshirt that fit him reasonably well. He carefully studied the identification papers and cards in her wallet, requiring Goldie to explain the purposes of each. He knew, now, about the BATF kiosks and medical stations he would be required to pass, with identification in hand. Goldie didn't see how he could possibly fool anyone with her ID, but he clearly had a plan and that scared her even more thoroughly. If he used her ID, he wouldn't need her.

Lachley also tucked into her wallet all the loose cash Goldie had left in the apartment. He'd already appropriated her private stock of jewelry, gemstones, and rare coins, some of which she kept separate from her shop inventory in case of robbery or other disaster to her storefront. She reflected bitterly that the one contingency she hadn't planned for was kidnapping and armed robbery by Jack the Ripper. He was packing Goldie's suitcase, chatting almost gaily about the up-time world and his plans, when the buzzer sounded at her apartment door.

Goldie jerked her head up from the mattress. Lachley whipped around, transformed in the blink of an eyelash to a cold-eyed, ruthless killer. He snatched up his knife and advanced on her with a terrifying, soundless movement, a snake that had abruptly sprouted legs. The door buzzer sounded again, followed by an impatient pounding.

Lachley dragged her from the bed and hauled her, trembling, into the living room. He laid the razor-sharp blade at her throat and whispered, "Call through the door. Say you're ill and can't open it."

"Hello?" Goldie called, voice cracking with terror.

"Security!" a man's voice came back through the door. "Mind if we check the place again, Goldie? We sent you an e-mail, but you never answered, so we thought we'd check on you."

"Could you come later?" she choked out, shaking so violently the knife knicked her throat in a thin red line. "I'm not well. I slipped and fell and can't move around much."

"Do you need a doctor?" the security officer called back, sounding worried, now. "I'll send for someone . . ."

Lachley pressed the steel tighter against her jugular. "No!" Goldie cried. "I'm fine! Just bruised and shaken, is all."

"Open the door, Goldie," the man demanded maddeningly. "We'll let the doctor decide. And I have to search the apartment, no exceptions allowed."

Lachley cursed under his breath, then shifted the tip of the knife to Goldie's spine and slid around behind her. "Open it," he hissed.

Goldie's hands trembled violently as she reached for the locks and the doorknob. Lachley stood hidden from sight as the door swung open. She shuffled aside for the security team. Wally Klontz and a BATF agent stepped inside, the BATF officer entering first. Wally had barely crossed the threshold when Lachley shoved Goldie brutally to the floor. Lachley sank his knife into the BATF officer's throat in a lightning attack, leaving Goldie screaming and covered with spatters of blood. Wally flung himself at the killer, but Lachley twisted aside and slashed out. The blade tore Wally's shoulder to the bone, sending the security officer reeling back in shock and pain. Then Lachley was out the door and running. Wally fumbled with his radio while blood poured down his arm and spread across the front of his shirt.

"*Code Seven Red!*" he screamed. "Goldie Morran's apartment! Lachley killed Feindienst and laid my shoulder open, then bolted!"

Goldie dragged herself to Wally's side and tried to stanch the bleeding with her hands. The radio crackled. "Roger, security teams are responding. Medical's on its way. Did he kill Goldie?"

"Negative, but she's pretty shaken up."

Goldie's hands trembled violently against Wally's torn shoulder.

The radio sputtered. "Roger. Sit tight, help's on the way."

Ten minutes later, Goldie lay strapped to a gurney in the back of a medi-van, headed for the infirmary. Wally Klontz occupied the gurney next to hers, where EMTs worked over his gashed shoulder and threaded an I.V. into his elbow. Goldie still didn't quite believe she had survived. As terror finally dropped away, Goldie's mind gradually came back to life again, presenting her with several startling, lucrative possibilities. After all, very few people could claim to have survived a week as Jack the Ripper's prisoner. Why, there might be television appearances in this, exclusive magazine and newspaper stories, books, perhaps even a movie . . .

Feeling more like herself than she had in a full week, Goldie settled down to enjoy her notoriety.

For long moments, shock held Margo motionless on the floor of the cab. The driver had whipped his horse to a gallop, urged on by Kaederman's shouted promise of reward. By lifting her head, she could just see over the footboard. It was dark beyond the open side of the hansom, which swayed and jolted badly as they rattled over uneven paving, but as they whipped around a corner, she caught a glimpse of the Atheneum gentlemen's club. They'd turned onto Waterloo Place, then, which meant they now raced northward along Regent Street.

The long, gentle curve of Nash's Quadrant left her slightly queasy as the windows and street-level doorways flashed past. A dizzy swing through Piccadilly Circus sent them plunging past the County Fire Office into a broad, sliding turn down Shaftesbury Avenue. They rattled down Shaftesbury at a terrific clip, the SoHo district flying past on their left hand, then the cabbie swung sharply into a skidding right-hand turn that left them racing down High Holborn.

Margo was beginning to recover her breath, at least, despite the terrific jouncing against her ribs as she was jolted around on the floor. Her wits returned, as well, stirring into anger. She was alive and if she wanted to stay that way, she'd better do something fast. She'd lost her pistol, thanks to that idiot doorman, but she might still have the boot-knife, if all that thrashing around hadn't knocked it out of her boot sheath. He hadn't searched her yet, which was a small miracle. If she hoped to use that dagger, she'd have to do it quick. His silenced pistol frightened her, his prowess with it even more so, but they were in a flying cab with her sprawled across the floor, supposedly stunned and terrified out of her wits, so he probably wouldn't expect her to try anything yet. She groped cautiously toward her boot with one hand, trying to brace herself with her other arm to reduce the bone-shaking jar of the ride.

Cor, I'll 'ave bruises from me thri'penny bits to me toes . . . she thought sourly, lapsing into the Cockney she'd been speaking almost more than standard English, this trip. Margo stole her hand into her boot and closed her fingers around the grip of the little dagger Sven had given her. It wasn't a large one, only four inches or so of blade, thrust into a leather sheath sewn to the boot lining, but it was a weapon and she certainly knew how to use it, after all those lessons with Sven Bailey. Just closing her hand around the stout wooden handle lifted her flagging spirits. Kaederman shouted up to the driver, "Turn south! And you can slow down, now. We've shaken the bastard following us!"

"Can't turn, guv," the driver called down, "we're on the Viaduct, no way to turn 'til we come to Snow Hill an' Owd Bailey!"

The Viaduct! Margo's hopes leapt like bright flames. Built to eliminate the treacherously steep drop along Holborn Hill, the Viaduct was essentially a bridge fourteen hundred feet long, with shops and even a church built down the length of it. Where the Viaduct's single open space of visible ironwork crossed Farringdon Street—itself the covered-over course of River Fleet—there was a sheer drop of some fifteen feet. No carriage could get off the Viaduct anywhere between Charterhouse Street and Snow Hill, with the Old Bailey Criminal Court just beyond.

But a lone person on foot could.

Stone steps descended to Farringdon on either side.

The trick would be to create such confusion, he couldn't shoot her. She considered—and swiftly rejected—three separate plans of attack before settling on the one likeliest to work. It was also the riskiest, but she wasn't afraid of risk. If she didn't escape, Kaederman would kill her. Probably after torturing her for Jenna's location. So, as the cabbie slowed his horse to a swaying trot past St. Andrews' Church, she quavered out, "P-please, can I g-get up? I'm hurt, down here . . ." She slid the dagger out of her boot and held it tight in the hand farthest from him.

Kaederman muttered under his breath, "Try anything and I'll put a bullet through you." He grasped her wrist and levered her up. She swayed, losing her balance deliberately—which wasn't hard to do. Hansoms were notoriously tippy contrivances and they were still going at a fair clip. She slipped sideways with a gasping, frightened cry. She flung out one arm to catch her balance, which put the knife exactly where she wanted it.

Right over the trotting horse's rear quarters.

She slammed the blade home, hilt deep.

The horse screamed, a tearing, jagged sound of pain. It kicked and reared violently, sheering wildly to the right. The cab flung sideways. The maddened animal was kicking, lunging, trying to get the steel out of its flank. The whole carriage crashed sideways. Margo grabbed for the edge of the roof above her head as they went down. She lost her grip when they slammed to the street. The force crushed Margo back across the seat, with Kaederman under her. She kicked anything that moved and dragged herself up over the lip of the toppled hansom. The driver was yelling from his seat at the rear of the cab. From the sound of it, he was pinned by the weight of the carriage.

Then she was out and running, with no time to be sorry for the driver or the horse and no time to recover the dagger. Kaederman was shouting, cursing hideously. The iron railings over Farringdon Street flashed past, then she was skidding in a desperate lunge for the nearest of the step-buildings flanking Farringdon, plunging down the steep steps, clutching at the railing for balance. She heard thudding footfalls above, pounding in pursuit across the bridge and down the stone staircase on her heels. *Oh, God, help me, please . . .* She expected a bullet to slam through her back any moment. Margo reached the street and cut back toward Shoe Lane and St. Andrew Street. If she could just reach Holborn again, she wasn't far from the Old Bell. The ancient coaching inn would be busy, with lots of people coming and going. Famous along all the old coaching roads, the Old Bell beckoned as her only safe haven. The proprietor and his customers would help her and there might even be a constable, in for a bite of supper. She flew up St. Andrew, gasping for breath at the steep climb back up Holborn Hill.

Just short of Holborn Circus, a heavy hand closed around her shoulder. Kaederman spun her against the side of a closed shop, snarling and backhanding her brutally. Margo punched and kicked, screaming bloody murder—and a shrill whistle sounded, practically on top of them. A constable pounded down Holborn Hill, straight toward them, shouting at Kaederman to halt immediately. Kaederman swore and ran, instead, vanishing down a side street. Margo staggered and slid down the side of the shop toward the pavement, reeling with the shock of her near escape.

"Are you hurt, boy?" the constable cried.

She sat on the cold stone pavement, shaking violently. "N-no . . . He was going to kill me . . ."

The constable crouched beside her, than said in a surprised voice, "Cor, it's a girl!"

She glanced down and realized Kaederman had torn her shirt open during the struggles. She blanched and clutched the edges closed, hands shaking violently.

The constable's eyes widened abruptly. "Dear me, miss, was he—was that the *Ripper*?"

Margo's head whirled for just a moment. She found herself giggling shrilly and fought to get herself under control. "I don't . . . I dunno," she gulped, deciding she'd better stick with Cockney, given her current appearance. "Said 'e would give me somefink to eat, but 'e never. Just tried to kill me. Dragged me into 'is cab, only I got away an' run down the steps from 'igh 'olborn t'Farringdon. The cab tipped over, y'see, an' I think the driver's 'urt, up there on the Viaduct."

"You're all right, then, miss? Truly?"

She nodded. "Just shook, is all. You'd better go an' see about that cabbie, mister."

"Stay here, please. I'll see you're taken someplace warm and I'll certainly want a description of your attacker."

She nodded again, leaning against the shop wall while the bobby hurried up the steps toward the Viaduct. The moment he was out of sight, she dragged herself to her feet and headed the opposite way, walking as fast as she could push herself. Margo was still badly shaken, but she had to get away before that constable returned and started asking questions she didn't want to answer. She had to report Kaederman's escape, too, and Malcolm was injured, on his way to Spaldergate for treatment. She groaned aloud. It was a long way from Holborn to Battersea, which left her with far too much time to worry about Malcolm on the way. He had to be all right! Just had to be . . .

I blew it, Kit, she wailed silently, *I really messed up! Worse than South Africa!*

Castigating herself every step of the way, Margo walked faster.

At Skeeter's harsh insistence, they moved Jenna Caddrick and the others into the vault beneath Spaldergate House within half an hour of the attack at the Carlton Club. Spaldergate's vault was, at the moment, quite literally the safest place in all of London. "Kaederman's got Margo hostage, which means he'll find out exactly where you're hiding," Skeeter had said ruthlessly, overriding Noah Armstrong's objections. The detective, shaken at seeing his own face mirrored in Skeeter's newly rearranged one, reluctantly agreed, even handing over the damning proof that would condemn Senator Caddrick. They packed up and moved yet again, returning to the gatehouse only to find another crisis underway. Malcolm had arrived twenty minutes earlier by hansom cab, shot through the chest and barely conscious. Both Dr. Nerian and Paula Booker were in surgery, working to save his life. Skeeter tightened jaw muscles over a whole spate of curses and carried his honorary nieces down the stairs leading to the vault.

The Spaldergate housekeeper took charge of Ianira, Jenna, and the others, settling them down on sturdy cots in one corner, but nothing Skeeter said would induce Noah Armstrong to stay in the vault, as well.

"No!" The detective glared at Skeeter, expression haggard. "Dammit, what kind of coward do you think I am, to hide down here when he's holding Miss Smith hostage! God knows what he'll do to her! I've only stayed in hiding this long because of *them*," he jerked his head toward Jenna Caddrick. Ianira and Marcus sat on one of the temporary cots, holding their frightened little girls close.

"What you've done for my friends . . ." Skeeter said quietly. "Nothing I do will ever repay that. Except, maybe, catching this bastard. But if Kaederman kills you while we're chasing him, you won't be able to testify and all of this will have been for nothing."

In the brief silence, while Noah Armstrong ground molars together, the vault's telephone shrilled. One of the housemaids on duty with the Ripper Watch Team answered. Her eyes lit up as she gasped, "*Margo's back?* But we thought she was a hostage!"

Skeeter ran for the stairs, Armstrong pounding right on his heels. They found Margo in the parlour, where Hetty Gilbert was fussing over her, wrapping a quilt around her shoulders and putting an icepack to her bruised face, while Mr. Gilbert brought a generous brandy and forced it between her teeth. She was shuddering, from cold or shock or both. "Malcolm's really all right?" she was asking anxiously as Skeeter and Armstrong burst into the room.

"He's in surgery, dear," Hetty Gilbert soothed, brushing back Margo's hair with one hand. "Doing fine, they said. Hold that ice *on* the bruise, child."

Margo noticed Skeeter and bit her lips, startling him when tears welled up. "I'm sorry, Skeeter. Kaederman got away."

"Thank God *you* got away," Skeeter said fervently, collapsing into the nearest chair and upending the brandy Gilbert poured for him. "*Shalig*, what a night! How in the world did you escape?"

She told them succinctly, glossing quickly over any details that might have betrayed her own terror during the experience. Margo was one tough cookie, all right, for all that she was barely seventeen. Malcolm was luckier than he knew, to have a girl like Margo. She sighed, at length, nursing her own brandy and shifting the icepack on her cheek. "When that constable shouted, Kaederman ran off and disappeared down a side street. I sent the constable up to check on the poor cabbie, pinned under the wreckage, then got out of there as fast as possible and came back here."

"Quick thinking," Marshall Gilbert nodded approvingly. "Very quick thinking. You not only saved your life, you kept the authorities from asking uncomfortable questions that might have led them here. And God knows, we've been under enough official scrutiny as it is, thanks to Benny Catlin's shooting spree at the Piccadilly Hotel."

Margo nodded and leaned her head back against the chair, drained and pale, but her hand on the icepack was rock steady. "They'll assume it was the Ripper, I suppose. That's what the bobby thought, anyway, and I didn't disabuse him of the notion. Look, we've got to find Kaederman. And we have to get Ianira and the others to safety—"

"They're in the vault," Noah said, attracting her attention for the first time.

She did a double-take, then laughed weakly. "God, that's startling. You really do look like twins, now."

"Do you have a photo of Kaederman?" Noah asked, voice grim. "Something we can duplicate and use, the way you traced us?"

Skeeter nodded and rescued his scout's log from his room, replaying their arrival through the Britannia Gate. Noah swore. "Good God! That bastard really must be desperate!"

"You know him?"

Armstrong tapped the screen on Skeeter's log. "That's Gideon Guthrie. Provides security for the L.A. gangland boss who's been doling out Senator Caddrick's payola. For Guthrie to be handling this personally, they're running *scared*. He hasn't actually dirtied his own hands in years. Maybe," Armstrong mused darkly, "he simply ran out of hit men to send after us?"

"And now he knows we're onto him," Skeeter growled. "Want to bet he bolts? Jumps on the nearest ship and runs?"

Armstrong shook his head. "He's got a helluva lot to lose, if he just ditches."

"Yes," Skeeter countered, "but he's gotta figure Caddrick will do time, over this, and maybe his own boss, as well. There's no way he can get back onto the station, not without somebody putting him in cuffs.

So he's down to just a couple of options. He can run for it and start over, in this time period. And surely a guy like Kaederman has enough experience to set up shop someplace like New York or Chicago, even San Francisco, maybe, put together a sweet little gang of thugs with all the up-time tricks he's accumulated. Or he can do what Marcus and you did, getting *here*. He can hot-foot it to New York by the first trans-Atlantic steamer, board a train headed for Denver, and slip through the Wild West Gate in disguise, try and get back through Primary to New York."

"Will the Denver gate still be operational in 1888?" Armstrong asked quietly.

Mr. Gilbert answered. "I don't see why not. The Wild West Gate is very stable, has been for years, or we wouldn't be using it as a tour gate. I can't imagine it going suddenly unstable and closing."

"Then our boy might try it," Skeeter mused. "All he'd really need to do is mug a Denver tourist for his ID to get through the gate."

Armstrong gave him a grudging glance. "Not a bad point. So, we comb the steamship ticket offices?"

Margo eased the icepack into a new position as color returned to her cheeks. "It's a start," she nodded. "And we'd better put one of the groomsmen in each major railway station, in case he tries to catch a train for another port city. Liverpool did a lot of trans-Atlantic shipping, passenger as well as cargo." She grimaced, wincing slightly under the icepack. "James Maybrick certainly shuttled back and forth between Liverpool and the States for years. In fact, he met his wife on one of the crossings, poor woman. I wonder how many trains leave tonight? Or how many ships are scheduled to sail? It's going to be a long night."

Fortunately, the Gilberts were able to produce a table of scheduled ship departures from the day's newspapers. Hettie Gilbert copied them out while her husband retrieved a map of the docklands. He spread it out across his desk, then turned up the gaslight for better illumination. Skeeter stared in rising dismay at the immense stretch of land to be searched. Wapping, the Isle of Dogs, Poplar and Limehouse and Shoreditch, not to mention Whitechapel, of course, and Shadwell. St. Katharine's Docks, London Docks, Wapping Basin, Shadwell

Basin, and the Old Basin below Shadwell. And there was the great West India Docks complex and the smaller Junction Dock, Blackwell Basin, and Poplar Docks. And east of there stood the *East* India Docks, the Royal Victoria and Albert Docks, and south of the Thames, the vast Surrey Commercial Docks . . .

Skeeter groaned aloud. Hundreds of acres, tens of thousands of people to question if the ticket offices didn't pan out, and very few of those teeming thousands likely to part with a word of information without palm grease of some sort, even if it were only a pint of ale or a glass of gin. "My God," he said quietly, "we'll never cover all of that."

"It isn't quite hopeless," Marshall Gilbert insisted. "Look, we can probably discount this whole complex, and this one," he swept a hand across the map. "They're cargo facilities only, no passenger services offered. And these, too, no point in searching naval shipyards. No commercial traffic, just military vessels. I'll get Stoddard in to help, he knows the docklands better than anyone else on staff. And we'll put Reeves on it, as well as all the groomsmen, footmen, drivers, and baggage handlers. I would imagine," he added, glancing from Skeeter to Noah Armstrong and blinking mildly at their startlingly matched faces, "Miss Smith will be keen to assist, as well."

"You'd better believe it," she muttered.

Twenty minutes later, Hettie Gilbert handed over her finished list. "There's only one ship scheduled to sail tonight, leaving in an hour, but a dozen are due to sail tomorrow."

Skeeter nodded. "We'll just have time to reach the docklands, if we leave right now."

Groomsmen and gardeners and footmen were already clattering out of the stable yard on horseback, dispersing for every train station in the city. A woman in a housemaid's dress was leading more horses from the stable, saddled and ready as riders were assigned. Iron-shod hooves rang against the paving stones. Skeeter mounted in silence as Margo, who had changed into warmer clothing, hurried out of the house and took her own horse, still in masculine disguise but looking now like a young man of the middle classes, rather than a ragamuffin bootblack.

"All right," Skeeter said tersely, "we'll follow your lead, Margo."

They set out in silence.

Kit was in his office at the Neo Edo Hotel, trying to placate outraged tourists and worrying about the rapidly dwindling supply of foodstuffs in the hotel's larder, when word came: Lachley had been spotted at Goldie's apartment. The security radio he carried everywhere crackled to life with a generalized call to every member of the volunteer security force.

"*Code Seven Red, Residential Zone Two.* Lachley's on the run, last spotted heading into the sub-basements. All teams are hereby reactivated. Report in for a zone assignment."

Kit clattered the phone down in the middle of a wealthy dowager's tirade and snatched up the radio. "Kit Carson reporting."

"Kit, take Zone Seventeen again, same search team and pattern."

"Roger."

He picked up the telephone and started calling members of his team. They met on Commons, which stretched away in an echoing, empty vista of deserted shops and restaurants, the floors scattered with refuse no one had yet cleaned up. Alarm sirens hooted at intervals and lights flashed overhead, red and malevolent. Sven Bailey arrived first, followed by Kynan and Eigil. To Kit's intense dismay, Molly and Bergitta were with them, both women moving with a determined grimness that boded ill for reasoning with them. "We aim t'help," Molly said without preamble, "an' nuffink you say will stop us."

Bergitta, who had finally recovered from a terrible beating and gang-rape at the hands of the *Ansar Majlis*, gave an emphatic nod. "I will not stay hidden when this man attacks our home. We will help drive him out."

Molly added, "We got Viking ring-mail shirts on, underneath." She plucked at her loose-fitting dress. "Connie give us the loan. Didn't 'ave no other armor would fit under a frock, so she didn't. B'sides, I know somefink about this 'ere bloke, might be important."

Kit rocked back on his heels. "You *know* him? John Lachley?"

Molly shrugged. " 'Corse I knows 'im. Come up out of Whitechapel, 'e did. Called 'imself Johnny Anubis. Read fortunes and suchlike. Nasty little blagger. Wot's more, 'e ain't a normal man, so 'e ain't. I walked them streets, 'eard wot the girls said about 'im. They said 'is male parts weren't made right. Were 'alf woman, 'e were, wiv an Hampton Wick small as your little finger and wot a lady's got, besides, only that ain't made right, neither. A couple of girls wot laughed at 'im ended floating in the Thames wiv cut throats. Never could prove nuffink, but I say 'e done 'em, 'is own self."

Kit frowned. Had John Lachley been born an intersexual? He had to force aside quick pity. It didn't matter—couldn't be allowed to matter—what Lachley had suffered in London's East End, growing up with a blurred gender. Too many people had died already. Kit said quietly. "Whatever he once was, John Lachley is now Jack the Ripper and it's our job to end his career. All right, ladies. You just might help us flush him out, acting as bait. I know Bergitta started training with you, Sven, after that *Ansar Majlis* attack, and I'd trust Molly in any scrap. Bergitta, you and Molly take the middle. Sven, you and I will take point, Kynan and Eigil, bring up rear guard. We're searching Zone Seventeen again."

Sven grunted. "Just remember to stay away from that damned pterosaur's beak. I don't want any of *us* skewered."

"Amen to that," Kit muttered, leading the way.

They moved warily past barricaded shops and restaurants, past ornamental fountains and ponds and secluded alcoves formed by shrubbery and statuary and mosaic tile floors. They'd just reached Little Agora when the overhead sirens screamed.

"*Code Seven Red!* Zone Thirteen . . ."

"That's just downstairs!" Sven yelled above the ear-splitting howl of the siren.

Kit jammed his radio against his ear, trying to hear. "Down-timers have spotted him! He's in the tunnels under Frontier Town!"

They rushed down the stairs, sprinting past stacked aquaria where idling fish watched curiously as they raced past. Someone was screaming, a high and hideous sound that brought Kit's hair on end. Garbled shouts echoed and floated down the long, twisting corridors, then Kit burst around a curve and skidded to a halt. Two down-timers lay twisted on the floor, one man's neck obviously broken, another gutted and lying with sightless eyes. A third, the young Greek hoplite,

Corydon, clutched at a gash across his arm, which had been laid open to the bone.

"He ran . . . that way . . ." Corydon gasped, nodding with his head. His radio lay on the floor, sputtering with static. "I called . . . security . . ."

Bergitta dropped to her knees beside him, ripping her own skirt and using a comb from her pocket to form a tourniquet band just above the massive wound. "Go!" she snapped. "I will watch Corydon until medical comes!"

Kit keyed his radio even as he pelted in the direction Lachley had taken. "Medical emergency, Zone Thirteen. Two dead, one serious casualty. Tell medical to shag butt, Corydon's nearly lost an arm!"

"Roger that. Medical's on the way."

Kit slowed when the corridor branched off in three directions. "We don't dare split up, Lachley'd just gut us one by one," he muttered, listening for any sound of footfalls. All he heard was echoing silence and an occasional, distant mutter and weird cry from the immense pteranodon's cage. "We'll take the left-hand fork," he decided, "and come back if we run into a blind alley without finding him."

They did not run into a blind alley. In fact, they ran into a deep maze of tunnels twisting through the bowels of the mountain, past doors where machinery chugged and hummed and rumbled and a distant rush and tumble of water could be heard through pipes and fittings. Kit marked the corridors they'd searched by scrawling on the walls with an ink pen, trying to sort out the tangle of passageways. Storage rooms were locked tight, but the heating and cooling plants, the sewage works, the generator pile all had to be searched painstakingly. Which they did, as time piled up in their wake.

The gigantic pteranodon was asleep when they eased past its cage, wicked red eyes shut inside their whorls of brightly colored, leathery skin. Bloodstains still marked the concrete floor from the pitched battle fought with the Ripper cultists, but they found no trace of John Lachley.

"He can't have vanished into thin air," Kit muttered as they pressed on past the pterosaur's cage. He'd begun to feel a superstititous prickle of sympathy with those befuddled London constables.

Kit glanced at his wristwatch and scowled. Upstairs in Commons, security would be preparing to turn back the incoming tour from Denver as the Wild West Gate dilated open. If they could just find Lachley *before* the gate opened, they could end this monstrous blockade and get the station back to normal.

"Molly," he frowned thoughtfully. "You told me Lachley grew up in the East End. Is there something we could use to drive him into the open, maybe goad him into attacking?"

Molly's eyes began to glitter. "I can't flush 'im out, nuffink ever will." Molly drew a deep breath and let go a flood of Cockney gibberish. "C'mon, then, let's 'ave yer 'ideous Cambridge an' Oxford out where we can 'ave a butcher's, eh? I grassed on you, so I did, Johnny Anubis! You an' your disgustin' Kyber, 'ope you like it in a flowery, corse yer lemons 'as done caught up wiv you, so they 'ave!"

Sven cast a dubious glance at Molly. "Do you really think any of that's going to flush him out? Somehow I don't think he cares about the crimes he's committed."

Molly's eyes flashed with irritation, but she changed her approach. "Eh, Johnnie, you got no cobbler's t'show yer ugly boat to a frog-chalkin' fanny like meself? Shouldn't wonder, you weren't born wiv none, was you, Johnny Anubis? An' you ain't pinched none from them fancy friends of yours, neither, 'ave you? I shouldn't wonder you *don't* show yer Kingdom Come! Corse you bloody well can't chalk, wiv as bad a case of Chalfont St. Giles as ever you saw, wot you got off lettin' a toff like yer lovin' Collars an' Cuffs run 'is great Hampton up yer bottle."

"This isn't working," Sven muttered.

"You got any better ideas?" Kit shot back.

Molly was still trying to goad Lachley into the open. "I don't give an 'orse an' trap, so I don't, Johnny Boleslaus, not for you nor your tea-leafin' ways, takin' a starvin' woman's last 'apenny an' tellin' 'er t'bend over again so's you can tell 'er she's fore an' aft, wivout a brain in 'er loaf. Gypsy's kiss on you, an' you'd better Adam an' Eve *that,* so you better. An' yer bubble an' squeak friends, 'ere, says the same to you!"

"Kit, Molly's just wasting her breath—"

He came in low and fast, lunging from a dark alcove where the corridor snaked around in a tight twist. Molly screamed and went down. Lachley's blade flashed in the dim light even as Kit whirled, trying to bring his pistol to bear on the struggling figures. Sven's gun shattered the silence. The bullet whined off the concrete wall. Molly was in Kit's line of fire, kicking and screaming at Lachley. Eigil waded in as Lachley rolled to the top, knife slashing again at Molly's unprotected throat. The Viking *barsark* snatched him up by the neck. Lachley rammed his knife into Eigil's gut and the Viking went down with a sharp grunt of pain. Kit fired, but Lachley was already moving again, slamming the point of the knife toward Sven. The blade just grazed the weapons instructor as Sven flung himself down and back, away from the knife's arcing path. Sven's pistol went clattering and slid into the pteranodon's cage. Kynan was dragging Molly away, sliding her across the floor on her back. Kit might have gotten another shot off, but Eigil was in his line of fire, clutching at his belly while blood poured out between his fingers. Kit lunged past, trained his pistol on the maniac—

And Lachley was away and running, knife in hand, twisting around a corner and vanishing even as Kit fired. The bullet shattered a door at an oblique angle, driving splinters outward. Kit swore and shouted into his radio, "*Code Seven Red! Zone Seventeen!* Converge on my signal! And get a Medical team down here, we've got casualties, bad ones!" Kynan was already stripping off his own shirt and shoving it as a compress against Eigil's gut wound. Molly was bending over Sven, saved from worse injuries, herself, by the chain mail under her dress. That steel-ringed undershirt had done exactly what ring-mail armor was designed to do: deflect the slashes of a bladed weapon. *Connie Logan, I'm gonna buy you a whole* case *of champagne, maybe even a keg of Falernian through the Porta Romae . . .* The boom and rumble of the station's public address system came echoing eerily down the open stairwells to the tunnels.

"*Code Seven Red, Zone Seventeen, repeat, Code Seven Red, Zone Seventeen!* Station medical personnel, report to Zone Seventeen, stat, for transport and emergency triage. Please be advised, Gate Three cycles in seven minutes. All tour passes are hereby revoked until the station emergency has ended. Repeat, all visitors are required to stay in their hotel rooms until further notice. Shangri-La Station is operating under martial law. Code Seven Red, Zone Seventeen . . ."

Sven was muttering under his breath and brushing Molly's hands away. "It's just a scratch, dammit! I can't believe I let him get that close to me in the first place!"

"You were a little distracted," Kit grunted, wiping his brow with a sweating arm. "We've got to trail him. Sven, can you move?"

"Hell, yes," the weapons instructor growled, coming to his feet to prove it. Kynan, shirtless and holding compresses against Eigil's gut, handed up his borrowed gladius. "Kill that son of a bitch, please."

Sven saluted him with the blade.

Kit muttered, "We'll give it our best shot, Kynan." He didn't add what he was thinking: *We shot at that maniac from close quarters and missed. Maybe he can't be killed, after all. God help us . . .*

Then they whipped around the corner, following the Ripper's bloody footprints.

(((Chapter 18)))

Grey dawnlight spilled like dirty bilge water across thousands of chimneys jutting up from factory roofs, refineries and foundries, from ironworks and shipyards as Skeeter entered the docklands, accompanied by Margo, Noah Armstrong, and Doug Tanglewood. Their search the previous night had turned up no trace of Sid Kaederman, either at the train stations or the docks near Wapping Old Stairs. Skeeter carried a list of ship departures scheduled for today, convinced Kaederman would be on one of them.

A forest of masts stabbed skyward, dark silhouettes against clouds which promised more rain before the morning grew much older. Furled sails and limp rigging hung like dead birds on all sides, marking the berths of hundreds of sailing vessels used mostly as cargo transports, now, too antiquated and slow for passenger service. The heavier, stubby iron snouts of steamship funnels jutted up alongside passenger quays, cold and silent until coal-fired boilers were heated up for departure.

Douglas Tanglewood led the way toward the main offices of St. Katharine's Docks along St. Katharine's Way, Wapping. Carts and draymen's wagons bumped and jockeyed for space on the crowded roads. Surrounding the dockyards lay a jumbled maze of factories, foundries, food processing plants, icehouses, shipbuilding yards, and shops that fed, clothed, and supplied thousands of industrial workers.

"St. Katharine Docks," Tanglewood said quietly, "is the oldest and now one of the smallest dock complexes. More than twelve hundred homes were razed to build it. Left eleven thousand Londoners homeless and destroyed some of the oldest medieval buildings in the city." He shook his head, clearly regretting the historical loss. The dockyard gate, an arched entrance of stone, was surmounted by elephants on pedestals. Immense brick warehouses abutted the waterfront across from berthed ships. "On these small docks, like this, there's no room for transit sheds between water's edge and the warehouse doors. That gives our quarry fewer places to hide. It'll be much worse, if we have to search the other dockyards."

Skeeter watched a confusion of sweating stevedores off-loading valuable cargoes into vast, echoing warehouses, then asked, "Where do you buy tickets?"

"The Superintendent's office and transit offices are this way," Tanglewood nodded, pointing out the buildings beyond a stone wall that separated the dockyards from the street. "Mr. Jackson, please come with me. Perhaps Miss—ah, Mr. Smith and Mr. Armstrong could ask around for word of an American trying to buy passage."

Margo and the enigmatic Noah Armstrong, both decked out in middle-class businessmen's wool suits, moved off to talk to the dock foremen. Skeeter followed Tanglewood into the transit office.

The clerk glanced up from a ledger book and smiled a cheerful greeting, his starched collar not yet wilted under the day's intense pressures. "Good morning, gentlemen, how might I help you?"

Tanglewood said, "We're hoping you might be able to assist us. We understand there is a ship scheduled to leave St. Katharine's this morning at six-thirty, a cargo ship. Do you know where we might discover if a certain man has tried to book a passenger berth on her? Or maybe hired on as shiphand?"

The clerk's smile reversed itself. "You're trying to find this man?" he asked cautiously.

"We are. He is a desperate criminal, a fugitive we're trying to trace. He kidnapped a young lady last night and shot a gentleman, leaving him nearly dead, and we have proof that he is responsible for several other deaths in the recent past. The young lady has escaped, thank God, made her way to safety last night. We have reason to believe he'll try to book passage on any ship that will have him, to escape the hangman. This gentleman," Tanglewood nodded to Skeeter, "is a Pinkerton Agent, from America, one of the Yanks' best private inquiry agencies."

Skeeter dutifully produced his identification.

The transit clerk's eyes had widened in alarm. "Dear God! Have you contacted the Metropolitan Special Constabulary, sir? The river police should be notified at once!"

"If this ship proves not to be the one we're looking for, we certainly shall. But it's nearly six already and the ship sails in half an hour, so there's hardly time to go and fetch them."

"Yes, of course. Let me check the books." He was opening another stiff ledger, running a fingertip down the pages. "The *Milverton* is the ship you want, just two years old, so she's new and fast for an iron sailing vessel. Western Dock, Berth C, opposite East Smithfield Street, north of the offices. Go along the inner perimeter at water's edge, is best. You'll have to go right round the basin, there's no way across the inlet on foot. Watch your step when you're out by the warehouses, we're very busy this season, and the stevedores will cause trouble if you get in their way. As to a passenger . . ." He was consulting another ledger. "There's no record of anyone booking passage on the *Milverton* this crossing, but a desperate man might well approach the captain privately, rather than risk transit office records or the presence of river police." The clerk shook his head, frowning. "Plenty of men are still shanghied off the streets round here, by commercial captains desperate for shiphands. A man asking for a berth or offering to work for his passage wouldn't even be questioned."

"Wonderful," Skeeter muttered. If Kaederman offered to work his way or paid a tidy sum the captain wouldn't have to report to the ship's owner, not a captain in the docklands wouldn't jump at the offer, no questions asked.

"You've been very helpful, sir," Tanglewood thanked the clerk, slipping him a half crown for his trouble. The young man pocketed the coin with a nod of appreciation and returned to his ledgers. Tanglewood opened the door and stepped quickly outside.

"We'd best hurry. They won't welcome interruptions at this late hour."

They hailed Armstrong and Margo, who stepped smartly out of the way when sweating stevedores cursed at them. The *Milverton* was a sleek ship, her iron prow and bowsprit jutting so far out over the wharf, the tip end of the bowsprit nearly scraped the warehouse opposite. Men bustled across her, shouting commands and unfurling her great sails in preparation for departure. Loading was still underway, stevedores by the dozens manhandling huge casks and crates out of the warehouse along her port side, hauling them up into her vast iron holds. Skeeter kept a sharp watch for Kaederman. The captain, when Skeeter and the others climbed the main gangplank, was not amused by the interruption. "Get the bloody hell off my deck! I sail in a quarter hour and we're behind schedule!"

"This won't take long," Tanglewood assured him, producing a conciliatory five-pound note and holding it up. "Have you taken any passengers aboard in the past twenty-four hours? Or a new crew hand, a Yank?"

"I bloody well have not and if you don't get off my deck, I'll toss you into the basin!" He snatched the five-pound note and stalked off, shouting at a hapless crewman who'd snarled a coil of rope leading from the capstan to the mainsail, which rattled lopsided in the rising breeze.

They searched the ship anyway, dodging irate ship's officers, but were finally forced to admit that if Kaederman were aboard, he'd stowed away as cargo. They jumped back to the quay with minutes to spare before becoming stowaways, themselves. Standing on the quay, they watched until the *Milverton* pulled slowly and majestically across the basin toward the river, under tow by steam-powered tugs. They held vigil to make sure Kaederman didn't show up at the last minute, but he remained a no-show. When the ship passed through the locks into the river, Skeeter pulled a rumpled list from his coat pocket and scratched off the *Milverton*'s name.

"London Docks," he said quietly, "a ship called *Endurance*. She leaves Wapping Basin at seven."

London Docks, down in the heart of Wapping, dwarfed little St. Katharine's. The immense, double-armed Western Dock alone was larger than all the basins of St. Katharine's, combined. The smell of tobacco was strong in the air, coming from the central basin and its warehouses. When Skeeter mentioned it, Tanglewood nodded. "That's Tobacco Dock, of course. Rented out by Her Majesty's government to the big trading companies. You said the *Endurance* leaves from Wapping Basin? This way, then."

The appalling noise overwhelmed the senses. Beneath the level of the quays Skeeter could see vaulted cellars where stevedores trundled great casks of wine and brandy. Transit sheds stood between waterside and warehouses, temporarily sheltering a vast tonnage of goods and providing a maze in which one man could hide almost indefinitely.

Lock-keepers worked incessantly, regulating the flow of ships in and out of the great basins, while draymen arrived with wagonloads of luxury goods for export to Britain's far-flung mercantile markets. The stench of raw meat and blood and cooking vegetables mingled with the smells of coke-fired furnaces from vast food-packing plants. Whole wagonloads of salted sea-turtle carcasses rolled past, off-loaded from a ship out of the Caribbean basin, destined for the soup canneries and luxury manufacturers who made combs, hair ornaments, boxes, ink-pen barrels, and eyeglass rims from the shells.

Past the canneries were great icehouses, bustling with men and boys loading ice into insulated wagons. Every time the doors opened, cold rolled out in a wave across the road. Skeeter began to realize just how overwhelming London's docklands really were as they passed the Ivory House, with its immense stockpiles of elephant tusks, and warehouses where eastern spices and enormous pallet-loads of exotic silks were trundled off the quays. The number of places Kaederman might hide was distressing; to search all of it would take a small army.

The *Endurance* proved to be a squat little tramp steamer, its days as a passenger boat eclipsed by vastly larger luxury ships. The hectic pace of loading was no less frantic than it had been aboard the *Milverton*. The captain was no less harried, either, but was slightly less brusque. "A Yank? No, I haven't laid eyes on a Yank today nor yesterday, neither, and not a paying passenger the last three crossings. New crew hired? Not a single hand, no, sir, I've a good crew, treat 'em right. They've turned down offers of more money working for harsher masters and that's a fact . . . No, no! The deliveries for the galley go into the center hold, not the bloody prow! You'll break every egg in that crate, storing victuals in the bow, that's where she takes the brunt of the waves!"

And off he went, correcting the error, leaving them to question crew hands. No one had laid eyes on anyone answering Kaederman's description.

"Strike two," Skeeter Jackson muttered, crossing the *Endurance* off his list. "Next stop, Regent's Canal Dock, Stepney."

Rain began falling in earnest, plastering Skeeter's hair to his forehead and horses' manes to their necks. Draft horses strained against their harness collars and slipped on the wet streets. Drivers shouted and cursed and wagon wheels churned piles of dung into a foul slurry carried into the nearby river and the sewers underfoot. They struck out at Regent's Canal Dock, as well: the *High Flyer*, sailing for Hong Kong, produced no trace of Kaederman.

Perhaps it was only the grey and dirty rain soaking through his coat and snaking in runnels down his collar, but Skeeter began to think the task of finding one murderous lout in this overcrowded, reeking maze of humanity and bustling commerce was impossible. He tried to protect the ink on his slip of paper from spatters of rain gusting in beneath the broken eaves of a pub where they'd taken momentary shelter. "Next ship departs out of Quebec Dock."

"Where's that?" Noah Armstrong asked, rubbing hands together absently in an attempt to warm them. The October rain was cold. Keening wind cut through their trousers and coats.

"Surrey Docks, that's south of the river," Margo said, shivering. "We'll have to cross at London Bridge, there isn't any bridge closer. Which is why Tower Bridge is being built, to shave miles off the round trip from London Docks to Surrey Docks, for the draymen. But it's still just an iron shell, doesn't even span the river, yet. We'll have to backtrack. When does the ship go?"

Skeeter consulted his pocket watch. "Three-quarters of an hour from now."

"We'd best not walk it, then," Tanglewood muttered, "that's a bloody long way from Stepney to Rotherhithe and Bermondsey.

There's a tram line nearby, we'll catch the next tram heading west. When do the other ships go, Jackson?"

He used his cap to protect the ink on his list. "Eleven o'clock, Blackwell Basin, West India Docks. Two P.M., Import Basin, East India Docks. Seven o'clock this evening, Royal Albert Dock."

"He might try for a later ship," Margo mused as they located the tram stop. "Just to give himself time to pull together the kit of goods he'll need. Money, clothing, sundries, a packing case or duffel bag to hold them in."

"We might get lucky at the secondhand shops, if the transit offices don't pan out," Noah Armstrong said quietly. Armstrong didn't say much, but listened with an almost frightening attentiveness and the detective's ideas were always sound. The tram arrived a moment later, glistening a wet, cheerful red, its sides covered in advertisements. They managed to secure seats on the lower level, where they could sit out of the rain. Passengers on the upper deck sat huddled under the open sky, with rain pouring down their collars despite umbrellas that turned the top of the tram into a lumpy, domed canopy. The horses snorted, shaking their great, dappled heads against the downpour, and chewed at their bits, jingling their harness bells and tugging at the reins, then the tram rumbled into motion along the tracks.

They crossed the Thames, its grey water choppy in the storm. Hundreds of river taxis and sailing ships bobbed like forlorn, waterlogged birds. Steamers chugged and churned their way through the leaden water, spewing coal smoke into the dark sky. Rain spattered against the tram's windows, bringing Skeeter's spirits even lower as he caught sight of the vast Surrey Commercial Docks on the southern shore of the river. Surrey was exclusively commercial, offering no passenger service, which meant security would be tighter.

Skeeter spotted only a few gates along the access roads, used by draymen and their wagon teams. It occurred to Skeeter that Surrey Docks could become a trap to anyone caught inside, if a security force could be thrown across those few gates. The four of them, however, did not comprise such a force, and they clearly couldn't involve the river police. How would they ever find one man, in all that immense sprawl? Surrey was bigger, even, than London Docks.

Entering the Surrey complex was like walking straight into a foreign land. Spoken English was in the minority, with half a dozen Scandinavian languages battling for dominance over harsh Russian and garrulous French as fur traders and timber importers argued tariffs with stolid dock foremen. And permeating it all came the scents of raw lumber and cured animal skins and dark, dirty water lapping and slapping against the sides of iron hulks tied up at the quays.

They entered through Gate Three, out of Rotherhithe, and found the Superintendent's office. "Berth 90, Quebec Dock," the clerk read from the ledger. "The clipper ship *Cutty Sark*. Yes, they've registered a new hand, galley cook from America, name of Josephus Anderson. He signed on as crew this morning after the regular cook took suddenly ill. Says he can't read, but he signed his name on the books." The clerk showed the signature, a laborious scrawl that was nearly illegible.

"Could be trying to disguise his handwriting," Skeeter said thoughtfully as he and Tanglewood rejoined the others. "Make himself look less educated than he is, so he won't attract as much attention. He wouldn't need to know a thing about sailing to work as a galley cook. And it would be just like him to drug or even poison the real cook, so they'd have to hire a new one in a hurry. Josephus Anderson sounds like Kaederman, all right."

When Skeeter told Armstrong and Margo which ship they were looking for, Noah Armstrong gave a start of surprise. "My God, the *Cutty Sark?* Bastard has a real sense of style, doesn't he? Haven't they retired her by now?"

Tanglewood said, "Oh, no, she's a few more years of work left in her career. The *Cutty Sark*'s days as a trading clippership are numbered, of course. She might've been the fastest to make the tea run in her day, but they'll put her in drydock in a few years, never fear."

A passing trader who overheard the remark laughed heartily. "Drydock, eh? What on earth would you put a useless ship in dry dock *for?* Charge sixpence a tour?" He continued on his way, laughing and shaking his head.

Tanglewood chuckled. "Well, that *is* what becomes of her, thank God. Imagine, ripping up a ship like her for scrap!"

Skeeter led the way past the end of Canada Dock basin, toward berth 90. Rain pelted down harder as they headed down Redriff Road, dodging heavy wagons and piles of dung and sodden masses of sawdust heaped into ruts and holes. Mud spattered their trousers and squelched underfoot. Wet lumber towered in stacks higher than their heads; stevedores were throwing tarpaulins across piled crates in the shadows of those lumber stacks. French Canadian sailors grumbled and groused about the foul weather and asked for directions to the nearest pubs and whores. Near the immense warehouse beside berth 91, casks marked *Black Powder, Explosive!* formed a squat pyramid under the transit shed. A ship's officer was giving instructions to the stevedores.

"We've got an iron hull, boys. I don't want any man jack of you striking sparks or you'll blow my ship and half this dock sky high. Black powder is shock sensitive and friction sensitive and we're packing three tons of it into those holds. Thank God for this rain, it'll dampen down static electric charges. Be damned sure your men are wearing leather-soled boots, no steel heel plates, no hob-nails, no copper-toed work boots, have I made myself clear . . ." Skeeter edged past the massive pyramid of powder kegs, where unhappy stevedores were already grumbling about having to change footgear in the middle of a driving rainstorm thick enough to put out hell's own fires.

Berth 90 stood in Canada Yard South, opposite Bronswick Yard, Greenland Dock. The two yards were separated by Redriff Road, which snaked and twisted its way between Surrey's various basins. They found the captain on the quay, deep in discusssion with dock officials regarding fees the captain insisted were sheer piracy. One look at the captain's wrathful countenance and Tanglewood suggested, "Let's try one of the crew hands first, shall we? I'd say that chap's in no mood for polite inquiries."

A crewman passed them, headed up the gangplank toward the *Cutty Sark's* beautiful decks, and Margo darted forward. "Hey, wait a second, could I ask you a quick question?" Money changed hands, then Margo waved them over. "This gentleman," she nodded at the puzzled crewman, "will escort us down to the galley to meet Mr. Anderson."

Skeeter pressed elbows against ribs, where his pistols lay concealed in twin shoulder holsters: the Royal Irish Constabulary Webley he'd carried to Denver and a larger Webley Green borrowed from Spaldergate, a commercially popular revolver predating military models carried by British army officers. And snug against the small of his back, in a sheath worn sideways beneath his coattails, rode one of Sven Bailey's Bowie knives. Going after Kaederman, he would've felt happier carrying a Maxim machine gun, as well.

As they climbed the gangplank and crossed the holystoned decks, Skeeter's pulse kicked in at triple time, jumping savagely in anticipation of Kaederman's violent reaction. Then they were climbing down into the ship's dark interior, following the narrow passageway to the cramped galley. Skeeter stole his hand into his coat and gripped the butt of his Webley Green, fully expecting trouble to break out the instant "Anderson" caught sight of them.

"Hey, Anderson!" the sailor poked his head into the galley. "You got company, mate!" He then sauntered away on his own business, jingling Margo's coins in his pocket.

"I comin', suh, I comin' . . . can I help you all, somehow? I got work to do . . ."

Anderson's voice was soft, respectful, almost obsequious. And the moment Skeeter caught a glimpse, his spirits plunged toward despair. Their new galley cook was a Yank, all right. A very black one, at least sixty years old, with grizzled white hair, missing half a tooth in front. He spoke in a broad, drawling dialect that sounded like the deep South. Anderson proved to be a former plantation slave who'd signed as cook aboard the first ship out of Savannah after his manumission. Said he wanted to see something of the world, have a few stories to tell his grandchildren.

While Tanglewood thanked the cook and apologized for interrupting his work, bitter disappointment sent Skeeter striding back topside, fists clenched as he reached the rain-slick deck. A ship's officer sporting a vulcanized rubber rain slicker was telling someone, "Your bunk's below, stow your gear and report to the quartermaster for a uniform. Then shag your arse back topside and find the first mate, he'll tell you what your job's to be."

A man with a heavy sea duffel across one shoulder turned to locate his new bunk below decks . . . and Skeeter gasped. Then yanked loose his big Webley Green revolver, aiming for Sid Kaederman's heart. "Don't move! Don't even breathe, Goddamn you!"

Sid froze in astonishment. The officer in the rain slicker was staring at the Webley, slack-jawed. "Here, what's the meaning—"

"*Tanglewood!*" Skeeter shouted. "Get up here! He's on deck!" Running footsteps sounded below. The deck officer started forward, plainly furious. "What is the meaning of this outrage? Put away that pistol, sir, or I'll have you put in irons!"

"Stay back!" Skeeter shouted. But it was too late. The officer had stepped straight into Skeeter's line of fire. Kaederman dropped the heavy duffel with a thud and raced across the rain-slick deck, heading for the gangplank. Skeeter lunged around the officer and fired. Splinters flew as lead struck the ship's rail. Kaederman plunged down the gangplank and hit the quay running. Skeeter cursed and followed as Armstrong and Tanglewood ran across the wet decks of the *Cutty Sark* at full tilt, guns drawn. Tanglewood fired, as well, missing the fleeing Kaederman clean. Tanglewood skidded wildly across the slick decking and Skeeter's feet did a creative skid of their own, slowing him down so badly, Armstrong beat them both to the gangplank. The detective plunged down toward the quay on Kaederman's heels. Douglas Tanglewood was swearing as he scrambled up from the deck. Margo appeared just as Skeeter rushed down the gangplank in pursuit, shoving aside shocked stevedores and ship's crew to reach the quay.

Skeeter glimpsed Kaederman ducking through the transit sheds alongside berth 91. Armstrong plunged in after him, shoving his way past angry stevedores trying to shift heavy casks from a dwindling pyramid. A scant instant later, the detective came racing back Skeeter's way, white-faced and shouting. "*Get down! Get down!*"

A massive explosion rocked berth 91. Fire belched outward in a solid wall of destruction. The concussion hurled Armstrong to the ground. The shockwave knocked Skeeter flat, crushing the breath from his lungs. Heat seared his sodden coat as he flung both arms over his face. Then rain was pouring over him again, slashing down at the mass of flames that had, seconds before, been an immense transit shed. Blazing timbers and tin shingles crashed to earth in a deadly rain. The rigging and sails of the ship at berth 91 were on fire. Stunned sailors were already struggling aloft with buckets and heavy knives, chopping at the ropes, trying to put out the inferno before it reached the holds.

"Armstrong!" Skeeter yelled, scrambling to his feet. The detective stirred sluggishly, but staggered up. Skeeter braced the Wardmann-Wolfe agent when Armstrong nearly fell, again, reeling and dizzy on his feet.

"Was Kaederman in that shed?" Skeeter shouted, barely able to hear his own voice.

"What?" Armstrong shouted back, voice tinny and distant through the ringing in his ears.

"*Kaederman!* Was he in there?"

"No! Saw him bolt for Redriff Road, right after he broke open one of those casks. Struck a match and threw a damned blazing rag right onto the loose powder, then ran out the other side!"

"*Black powder?* Good God!" No wonder the whole transit shed had gone up like a bomb. Unlike modern, smokeless powders, black powder was genuinely explosive, deadly as hell in that kind of mass. *How many stevedores were killed in there?* Skeeter wondered as he dodged and jumped across burning timbers and twisted, smoking tin shingles.

He reached the terminus of Redriff Road and searched wildly for any trace of Kaederman. He swore . . . Then heard shouts and curses drifting down from the direction of Greenland Dock. Any disturbance was a good bet. Skeeter raced that way and pelted slap into an angry group of Scandinavian sailors, cursing to make a Viking raider proud. A whole stack of crates had been knocked down, breaking open to strew their contents of valuable furs into the mud, white ermine and sleek mink and glorious black sable. Then Skeeter caught a glimpse of Kaederman far ahead, running down Plough Way through Commercial Yard on a direct course for Gate Eighteen.

And Kaederman's diversionary tactics abruptly backfired right into his face. He hadn't quite reached the gate when a whole squadron of irate constables burst through, inbound. London's river police, responding to the emergency. Kaederman, clutching an up-time pistol in one hand, skidded to a halt. For an instant, Skeeter thought he meant to shoot the entire police squadron. Then he doubled back, instead, and raised his gun directly at Skeeter.

Shit—!

Skeeter ate mud. He skidded face-first on his belly and tried to bring up his own pistol. There were too many innocents in his line of fire. He spat filthy muck and rolled frantically as Kaederman dodged past, firing at him on the way and shoving aside the furious sailors busy rescuing their sodden furs. Kaederman fired at Armstrong, Tanglewood, and Margo, too, as he ran toward them. The hail of bullets sent all three headlong into the mud. Then he raced along the very rim of the quay at water's edge and reached Redriff Road again before they could turn their weapons on him.

Swearing and spitting, Skeeter propelled himself to his feet, covered head to foot in slimy, foul mud that carried a rank stench into his sinuses. He didn't want to consider what might be *in* that mud. Armstrong was in the lead as they burst out of Commercial Yard in pursuit. Kaederman was a sizeable distance ahead, but even Tanglewood and Margo were gaining ground and Skeeter, abruptly in the rear thanks to the about-face, was steadily catching up.

Kaederman headed this time for Gate Three, the principle entrance to Surrey Commercial Docks. And once again, his delaying tactics with the black powder backfired. A horse-drawn fire engine, bells clanging madly, charged through, followed closely by four more. The fire engines completely blocked the way as they swung into the dockyards. Trapped inside the walls, Kaederman turned north toward the warehouses alongside Albion Dock. River police had taken up the hue and cry, as well, shouting at the fire officials to send word for another squadron.

"We've got us a bloody arsonist!" a policeman behind Skeeter yelled, fury lashing his voice. "Damned Fenian bomber, blew a shed of gunpowder to hell! Try and head him off at Gate Two . . ."

Rain slashed down across Skeeter's face in blinding gusts and unpredictable squalls. The mud under his boots sent him slipping and sliding for purchase in the choppy mess. At least it washed the reeking stuff off his face. Kaederman didn't try any delaying tactics at Albion Dock. He passed the warehouses and a gang of startled stevedores at full tilt, racing for Gate Two and escape. They charged past another huge basin in a straggling, strung-out line, then Skeeter caught up to Doug Tanglewood and Margo. They ran—as he did—with guns clutched in wet, muddy hands.

"If he gets out of this dockyard, we're sunk!" Skeeter gasped.

"Looks like we're sunk, then!" Margo spat back.

Kaederman had just slipped through Gate Two, with Armstrong hard on his heels. Skeeter put on a burst of speed and drew ahead. By the time Skeeter shot through Gate Two, a second squad of river police had put in appearance, running north from the direction of Gate Three. They were still in the distance, however, nowhere close to Kaederman. He was just visible on Rotherhithe Street, dodging past startled pedestrians on the pavements, cutting around large groups by ducking into the street. Horses flung their heads up and reared, shrilling a sharp protest at his erratic flight. Skeeter had just caught up to Armstrong when Kaederman cut sharp south again, leaving Rotherhithe Street.

"Where the hell is he going?" Skeeter gasped. "The river police are down that way!"

For a long moment, Armstrong didn't answer, too busy dodging past a protesting carthorse and its cursing driver. Then a startled expression crossed the detective's face. "Surely not?"

"What, dammit? Where's he heading?"

"The *tunnel?*"

It took a few seconds for Skeeter to call up his mental map of the area, memorized before leaving the station, then he had it: Isambard Kingdom Brunel's Thames Tunnel, connecting Rotherhithe and Wapping. Twelve hundred feet long, it had taken eighteen years and countless lives to build. It was also the only way to get from Rotherhithe's Surrey Docks to Wapping without detouring to London Bridge—or swimming.

"Isn't that a railway tunnel now?" Skeeter asked as they ran, heading helter-skelter straight for the tunnel's entrance.

"Yes! Trains from London to Brighton, owned by East London

Railway Company. But the railway uses only one of the tunnel shafts! The other's still a pedestrian tunnel!"

"Aw, shit, you *are* kidding, right? If he makes it to Wapping . . ."

Unfortunately, Armstrong was not kidding.

He was also correct. Sid Kaederman plunged into the circular structure that housed the Rotherhithe entrance to the Thames Tunnel and vanished from view. They followed at a run, clattering past startled men and women in working-class garb. Skeeter and Armstrong pounded their way through the vast entrance, with Margo and Doug Tanglewood on their heels.

The entrance was a circular shaft at least fifty feet across. Skeeter peered past wrought-iron railings as they plunged down the broad, double-spiral stairs. The shaft was a good eighty feet deep and Kaederman was already halfway down, plunging three and five steps at a time. Skeeter's muddy boots skidded on the stone treads. Down and around, in a broad, lazy spiral, a dizzying gyre that would prove fatal if he put so much as one foot wrong. *Down, down to goblin town . . .*

He was beginning to pant for breath when they finally reached the landing where the double spiral came together. Half a turn more and they were on the ground, paving stones clattering underfoot. The Thames Tunnel loomed before them, a double-barreled shotgun nearly a quarter of a mile long. The air was dank, foetid, cavelike. The tunnel walls exuded a chilly sweat, moisture running in tiny rivulets like the condensate on a beverage glass. Twin tunnels receded into infinity, dimly lit at regular intervals with gas lamps. Railway tracks ran down the center of one side.

"Which tunnel?" Skeeter gasped as Tanglewood and Margo bounded down the last few steps to join them. "Which one did he go down?" They listened intently at each entrance for the echo of footfalls. The chugging of water pumps growled and echoed. They couldn't distinguish anything like a sound of running footsteps against the background noise.

"That one!" Armstrong finally decided, pointing to the pedestrian tunnel. "I doubt he wants to risk meeting a train. He's no coward, but he's no fool, either."

Dank, chilly air closed in as they pelted down the echoing brickwork and stone tube in pursuit. A few handcarts loaded high with coal and wooden crates jockeyed for space in the narrow tunnel. Gas lamps gave plentiful if rather dim light the length of the shaft, which had been constructed as a series of connective arches beneath the river. Nearly forty-five years old, the long pedestrian tube remained the province of footpads, thieves, and innumerable prostitutes who led a troglodyte's existence beneath the river. They passed sleeping drunks huddled in the brick archways, women who'd set up stalls at which tawdry goods and cheap jewelry could be purchased. Ragged children begged for money. A pair of roughly dressed men eyed them as they shot past, then thought better.

A train deafened them as it roared past on the other side of the brick supporting wall. If Kaederman had chosen the other route—or if they had—they'd have been crushed under the wheels. Then they were through, emerging on the Wapping side of the river, somewhere to the east of the great London Docks. The eighty-foot climb up the dizzying double-spiral of the Wapping shaft, a twin of the Rotherhithe entryway, winded Skeeter badly halfway up. He staggered on with a stitch in his side and cursed Kaederman with every upward step of burning thigh muscles. They caught a glimpse of him from time to time on the way up, moving doggedly toward the street high above.

The raucous noise of workaday Wapping drifted down in distorted echoes and clangs, human voices and riverboat whistles and the slam of cargo being offloaded at the docks. The rumble and clatter of freight wagons mingled with the roar of the train chugging through the tunnel far below. Then they reached the street. Sunlight, dim and watery, replaced the gaslights of tunnel and shaft. Rain was still pouring in wind-blown gusts. A vast throng of people and horses and overloaded carts clattered wetly through the narrow streets, past ships parked at dead-end roads.

"Where *is* the son of a bitch?" Armstrong gasped, face contorted with frustrated anger. "We'll never find him in that stinking mess!"

Skeeter was too busy dragging down enough air for his starving lungs to answer. They started asking passers-by and finally obtained a lead from a ragged and muddy girl of twelve, totting bunches of bedraggled flowers in a basket over her arm. She pointed down Wapping High Street. "Cor, 'e went that way, mister, knocked me down an' never said nuffink, spilt me flowers all over the frog, 'e did, ruint' the lot, and never 'pologized, neither . . ."

Skeeter tossed a couple of shillings into her basket, eliciting a soprano squeal of astonishment, then pelted down Wapping High Street through the driving downpour. They finally caught a glimpse of Kaederman—just as he made a flying leap at a cart rattling smartly northward. He caught the tailboard and dragged himself in. The cart shot forward at twice, three times the speed a man could run. Cursing, Skeeter and the others lagged farther and farther behind, searching for some transport of their own. For an entire block, Skeeter staggered along with a butcher's knife of a stitch in his side, beginning to despair. Then a shopkeeper who'd clearly arrived a short time earlier came out to back his horse and cart up onto the pavement, unloading a pile of crates directly into his shop.

Skeeter dove toward the horse with a gasping cry of relief. A quick snatch at the Bowie knife concealed under his coattails, a few slashing blows at harness straps, and the startled horse was free, front hooves coming up off the pavement as it tried to stand on rear legs. "Whoa, easy there . . ." Skeeter stepped up onto the cart pole, its front end digging into the street, and threw a leg over, clutching the grip of the fighting knife in his teeth until he could slide it back into the sheath. The shopkeeper shouted just as Skeeter urged the horse forward with knees and heels.

"Hey! Wot you doin', that's me 'orse!"

Skeeter kicked the nag into startled motion even as he dug banknotes out of a pocket and tossed them onto the street as payment. "Come on, let's go . . ." Obedient, if puzzled, the horse slanted an ear back to catch the sound of Skeeter's voice and broke into a shambling trot, probably its top speed while harnessed. A solid thump of heels sent the horse into a surprised canter, stiff-legged and jolting from the unaccustomed gait. Skeeter gained ground rapidly on Kaederman's cart, while the shopkeeper screamed curses after him.

A swift glance revealed Noah Armstrong halting a hansom cab at gunpoint. Margo and Doug Tanglewood piled in. Then Skeeter gave all his attention to guiding his aging carthorse through the crowded street, cutting and weaving between high-piled wagons, shabby cabs for hire, even a few gentlemen's carriages. Businessmen or merchant traders, probably, come to check on arriving cargo or oversee outgoing shipments. Gaping pedestrians and liveried drivers stared at the sight of a carthorse lumbering past at its top, stiff-kneed speed, trailing harness straps and the end of long reins which Skeeter was looping and pulling in to prevent their being caught in a passing wagon wheel or carriage axle. He had no desire to end his ride that abruptly.

Skeeter pushed his shaggy mount to a rumbling gallop. The carthorse burst past the boundary between Wapping and Whitechapel, steadily gaining ground on Kaederman. The cart made a right-hand turn, swinging smartly into Whitechapel High Street, which was jam-packed with hay wagons, oxen pulling loads too heavy for horses, and fast-moving hansoms. There was a near-collision that sent Sid Kaederman sprawling against the side. Skeeter saw his mouth move and the cart's driver turned his head sharply. The driver started shouting, then turned to crack his cartwhip at the stowaway. Kaederman's answer was to pull loose his pistol and fire at the irate driver, point-blank.

Either the jostling spoiled his aim or the driver was one of those down-timers who couldn't be killed, because Sid missed him clean from a distance of twelve inches. The driver, white-faced and still yelling, performed a diving roll that landed him on the cobbled street, spitting curses and running for his life. The carthorse picked up speed without a guiding hand on the reins. Kaederman's transport careened out of control down the congested road. Kaederman, thrown violently from side to side as the carthorse dodged and shied away from other wagons and horses, crawled awkwardly over the seat, trying to reach the reins. Skeeter leaned low over his horse's flying mane and urged the draft animal to greater speed. *If I can just catch up while he's distracted . . .*

They raced down Whitechapel High Street in a grim, jolting chase. Kaederman's cart plunged into Whitechapel Road, careering past screaming women on the pavement and cursing draymen who swung violently wide to avoid collision. Children scattered like ants, shouting curses after Kaederman's runaway horse. Truant boys and chimney sweeps scooped up mud clots and pieces of broken brick, hurling them in Kaederman's wake.

The inevitable disaster struck just as Skeeter pulled alongside. A heavily laden team of drays, moving ponderously down the middle of Whitechapel Road, couldn't swerve fast enough. The driver tried. Tried hard, in fact. He succeeded in pulling his team broadside to the onrushing cart.

The shock of collision drove Sid's horse slam against the other team's harness poles. Wood splintered. Horses screamed. The heavy wagon toppled. Its driver and a stack of crates six feet high were hurtled under the wheels and hooves of other wagon teams. A human scream tore the wet morning air. The horses were still screaming, crashing down as wood splintered like shotgun blasts.

Sid's empty cart jacknifed around, airborne. It smashed down across the upturned drayman's wagon. Crates broke open under the force of the cart's landing. Hundreds of shoes and ladies' skirts, cheap dresses and steel bustles, men's trousers, and warm woolen coats spilled out into the mud. Sid, thrown violently airborne by the cart's twisting gymnastics, landed asprawl in a heap of dark, wet skirts on the other side of the broken wagon. The spilled garments cushioned his fall, probably saving his life.

Then Skeeter's galloping horse, presented with an impassable barrier, jumped the upturned wagon. The horse's rear hocks clipped the top boards, then they landed roughly on the cobbles beyond and slipped on the wet stones. The horse skidded and went to his knees with a ringing scream of pain. Skeeter was thrown forward across the horse's neck. His superb riding skills—mastered on wild, half-broken Mongol war ponies—and a desperate grab at the harness collar kept Skeeter from smashing face-first onto the cobbles. His horse neighed sharply again, a sound of pain and fright, then heaved and scrambled up, bleeding down both torn knees. Skeeter, badly shaken, slid down the horse's forequarters and landed on the wet street.

Poverty-stricken children, shrieking women, and idle louts from nearby gin palaces descended on the wreckage, a swarm of devouring locusts intent on carrying off as much as they could cram into their arms, toss over their shoulders, stuff into gunny sacks, or simply pull on over their own clothes. Hundreds shouted and cursed and scurried for the choicest pickings, using prybars to open unbroken crates or simply hauling them off, contents unseen.

Kaederman's horse, badly wounded, was lunging, trying to climb over the backs of the toppled drayman's horses. All three animals were down, kicking and neighing shrilly, trying to regain their feet. Harness lay tangled, fouling their legs, which kept them from scrambling up. A man in a blood-stained leather apron hacked at the harness leather with a broad meat cleaver, trying to free the trapped animals. Wagons and carts, blocked by the wreckage, piled up on either side, their drivers shouting curses or jumping down to help shift the broken cart and wagon out of the way. Someone mercifully shot Sid's mortally wounded carthorse, ending the agonizing, bone-grating screams. Skeeter—limping where metal harness fittings had torn a gash through his trousers and thigh—hunted through the wreckage for Sid.

Kaederman had regained his feet, bleeding from cuts down his face and arm. His coat was torn, smeared with mud and dung slurry from the street. The hired killer stumbled, visibly dazed, through the crowd of riot-happy scavengers, then drifted erratically toward the edge of the road. He staggered at every step, clearly having wrenched a knee on landing. He was still running, though, moving raggedly and glancing over one shoulder to locate Skeeter. At least with a bad leg, he couldn't run fast or far.

Skeeter abandoned his own injured horse and fought his way on foot through the near-riot. A hansom cab shoved and clawed its way forward along the crowded pavement, scattering irate pedestrians into the jam of wagons and carts on the street. It halted six feet behind Skeeter's limping carthorse, which an opportunistic girl of fifteen was leading swiftly away. The cab disgorged Margo, Douglas Tanglewood, and Noah Armstrong; the latter tossed a wad of bank notes to the driver before jumping down to join the pursuit.

"He's heading that way," Skeeter pointed as they slithered through the crowd of spectators and fighting scavengers. "Hurt and limping, but still on the move." The up-time killer had reached a three-story, eighteenth-century structure that might have once been a grand house, built of grey-painted stone and mellow brick. Coal smoke and soot had stained wide windows and trim a dingy grey. Kaederman peered through the windows, clearly trying to decide whether he should bolt inside or continue down the street. A semicircular, cross section of metal from what might have been the rim of a wagon wheel or maybe a large bell, had been mounted above the door.

Kaederman spotted them and thought better, limping past the entrance and rounding the corner to parallel a whole series of longer and lower, grey-painted buildings attached to the rear of the main structure. Skeeter and the others had already reached the corner when Kaederman found a set of double doors into the third building back, a three-story factory of some kind, judging from the noise and the smoke bellying up from a forest of chimneys. A wagon and team of horses stood in the open doorway where men drenched with sweat were loading heavy crates. Kaederman sidled past and plunged into the dim interior beyond.

Despite his own limp, Skeeter was at those wide double doors in a flash. On his way through, he caught a fleeting glimpse of a sign painted in neat white letters: *Whitechapel Bell Foundry, est. 1420, these premises since 1570, home of Big Ben, Bells of Westminster, the American Liberty Bell . . .*

The appalling noise and stench of a nineteeth-century smelting plant struck Skeeter square in the face. Intense heat rolled outward in a visible ripple, distorting the foundry's interior for just a split second. Then he was inside, breathing the fumes of molten metal and burning charcoal. Rows of windows high up did little to dispel the gloom. The vast, clangorous room, fully three stories tall, remained in near darkness, aided and abetted by the wet, cloudy day outside.

Men shouted above the crash and slam of immense machines, heavy conveyors, and the boom of newly cast bells being tested for trueness of sound. Molten bronze—and possibly iron and silver and brass, judging from the color of the ingots on those conveyors— glowed in immense vats, surging like volcanic rock, seething and malevolent in the near darkness. Enormous, pulley-driven crucibles of liquified metal swayed across the room some eight feet above the foundry floor, moving ponderously down from the smelting furnaces to row after row of casting molds, some of them six and seven feet high. Filled molds were jammed and crammed to either side, forming narrow aisles—canyons in miniature—stacked high to cool.

Men with long, hooked poles tipped the crucibles to pour their glowing, gold-red contents into the open snouts of bell molds, every pour sending cascades and showers of sparks and molten droplets in a deadly rain that sent foundry workers scattering back for safety. Others used heavy iron pincers to lift smaller, filled molds aside for cooling, making room for new, empty molds beneath the I-beam pulley system on which the crucibles rode. Catwalks hung like iron spiderwebbing above the smelting furnaces. Conveyors brought heavy ingots up to be tossed by sweating men and half-grown boys into the fiery furnaces. They dumped ingots, secured returning crucibles from the pulley line for refilling, regulated the temperature in the huge furnaces, and fed charcoal from enormous mounds to keep the fires burning hot enough to melt solid bronze for pouring.

And straight down the middle of that hellish inferno, Sid Kaederman was limping his way toward escape. Skeeter plunged in after him, tasting the stink of molten metal on his tongue and in the back of his throat. *We could die in here*, he realized with a gulp of sudden fear. *Every one of us.* If Kaederman succeeded in ducking out of sight long enough to go to ground, he could use the darkness and that ear-numbing noise for cover, lay an ambush and pick them off one by one with that silenced pistol of his and nobody'd even hear the bodies hit the floor.

"Split up!" Skeeter shouted above the roar as Kaederman dodged and ducked past startled foundrymen, darting into the maze of miniature canyons. "Try and cut him off before he can get out through a back door—or go to ground and lay in wait someplace nasty! And for God's sake, be careful around those furnaces and crucibles! Go!"

Tanglewood and Armstrong turned right and jogged warily into the near-blackness. Their shadows flickered and fled into the surrounding darkness as they passed a backdrop of fountaining sparks from another massive pour. Margo followed Skeeter. "Are you all right?" she shouted in his ear. "You're limping!"

"It's nothing, just a shallow scratch! Stings a little is all!" He'd suffered worse as a boy, learning to ride in the first place. Skeeter had the big Webley Green out, held at the ready, up near his chest, elbows folded so Kaederman couldn't knock it out of his hands should he come around a corner where the killer was hiding. Leading with a gun, sticking it out in front of you with locked elbows, was a fast way to disarm yourself and end up seriously dead. Only idiots in the movies—and the idiots who believed them—were stupid enough to lead with a firearm.

Skeeter and Margo edged their way into the wood-and-iron ravines between cooling bell molds. They worked virtually back to back as they advanced, moving one haphazardly strewn row at a time. Molds of differing sizes and shapes jutted out unpredictably, threatening knees, elbows, shoulders. Heat poured off the stacks like syrupy summer sunlight, deadening reflexes and hazing the mind. It was hard to breathe, impossible to hear above the din of the foundry floor. Down the room's long central spine, bright gouts of light shot out at random, throwing insane shadows across the stacked molds to either side.

Skeeter moved by instinct, hunting through the alien landscape. Sidle up to a junction, ease around for a snap-quick glance, edge forward, check the floor for droplets of blood, peer along the rows down either aisle for a hint of motion . . . Then on to the next junction, row after row, sweat pooling and puddling, the wool of uncreased trousers raw on bare skin and stinging in the wound down his inner thigh, hands slippery on the wooden grips of the pistol . . . Another fast, ducking glance—

The bell mold beside Skeeter's head splintered under the bullet's impact. Iron spalled, driving splinters across his cheek and nose. Pain kicked him in the teeth, then he was dodging low, firing back at the blur of motion three rows down. The big Webley kicked against wet palms, the noise of the foundry so immense he barely heard the sharp report. Skeeter blinked furiously to clear his vision, waved Margo back and down. Wetness stung his eyes, sweat mingled with blood burning like bee-sting pain from the jagged slivers in his cheek where the bell mold had spalled. He blinked and scrubbed with a muddy, torn sleeve. When he could see again, he dodged low for another look, down at hip-height, this time. Sid Kaederman was leaning around a stack, waiting to shoot him, but he was looking too high. Skeeter fired and a wooden pallet splintered six inches away from Kaederman's chest. Skeeter cursed his blurring, tear-blocked eyes, and the sweat that had let the gun slide in his hands, and his lousy aim . . .

"Go!" Skeeter yelled as Kaederman ducked back. They rushed forward and ran flat-out, gasping hard for breath in the stinking, steaming air. Down three rows, risk the peek . . . Kaederman was running, stumbling every few strides on his injured leg. Skeeter sprinted after, gaining fast. The paid killer glanced back, but failed to fire at him.

He's out of ammo! Skeeter realized with a rush of adrenaline. There was no other rational reason for Kaederman not to whirl and fire dead at him. A surge of confidence spurred Skeeter to draw ahead of Margo, relentlessly whittling down Kaederman's lead. The hit man ducked down a sideways aisle, vanishing from view. Skeeter swore and closed the distance, ducked low through his own skidding turn. Harsh, sulphurous light flared, momentarily blinding him. The smelters were dead ahead. Workers with iron poles nearly four feet long, hooked on one end, and men with heavy prybars snagged a big crucible and tip-tilted it, pouring its blazing contents into the mouth of a bell mold four feet across, using the prybars to control the angle of the tilt.

Sid Kaederman reached the newly filled mold and started waving his gun at the stunned foundrymen, shouting that he would shoot them if they didn't get out of his way. The men stumbled back, away from the apparent lunatic. Then Kaederman ran along the line of pulleys, toward the far end of the foundry where access doors led to the street. Blistering hot crucibles, just filled with molten metal, swayed down from the smelters toward another big bell mold waiting to be filled. Kaederman glanced back, realized Skeeter was gaining . . .

He whirled around and snatched up a long iron pole from the floor where a terrified bell caster had abandoned it with a clatter. Kaederman dropped his useless pistol and reached with the hooked pole, instead. He snagged the lip of a brimming crucible swaying its way toward him, a big one that must've held a bathtub's worth of blazing liquid metal. Pulling hard, Kaederman slammed the rim down and ran. Molten bronze flooded out across the floor. Liquid metal splashed and crested in a wave of destruction, spreading across the entire narrow space between stacked, newly cast bells, an inch deep and still flooding outward. There was no way around it and no way to climb those red-hot iron molds to either side. Skeeter's forward momentum was too great to avoid the deadly lake in his path.

So he jumped straight toward it.

Toward it and *up*. He stretched frantically, reaching for the massive iron I-beam of the pulley system overhead. *It's too high, I'm gonna miss it, oh Christ, don't let me miss . . .* He dropped the Webley, needing both hands free. It fell with a splash and vanished into the scalding, hellish glow. Then his palms smacked against the I-beam and he grabbed hold, swinging his feet up in a frantic arc. He clamped arms and ankles tight, then just hung there, slothlike, panting and sweating so hard he was terrified his grip would slide loose. Uncurling his fingers long enough to wipe first one hand, then the other, against his coat took a supreme act of will.

Then he wriggled himself around, managed to crawl up and over the top of the narrow iron beam, and balanced on hands and knees, all but prone above the hellish puddle. A black crust had formed along the top, a thin scum of solid metal that seemed to breathe as it cooled. The molten metal beneath flashed and flared in a scaly pattern like the scutes on a crocodile's back. Kaederman had turned to run, dropping the long iron pole into the edge of the molten flood splashing back toward him, but he wasn't moving very fast, clearly tottering at the last of his strength. Margo, thank God, had dodged the lethal flow, ducking sideways into another canyon between bell molds.

Breath regained and balance secured, Skeeter moved forward along the beam in a scooting crawl that was taking far too long. Swinging himself cautiously down once more, he passed hand over hand above the heaving mass of cooling metal, moving apelike along the beam, swinging up again only to avoid pendulous crucibles.

Kaederman, who'd managed to stumble maybe a dozen paces beyond the far edge of the puddle, glanced back . . . and tripped, sprawling flat. His mouth moved soundlessly as he scrambled up again.

Then Skeeter was across and jumping down to face him. Kaederman lunged forward, snarling curses and giving him no time to draw his other gun. They grappled for long moments, gouging and punching.

A blow from Kaederman's knee grazed the cut along Skeeter's thigh. Pain shot through the abused flesh. Skeeter staggered back a step and tangled his feet over the iron pole Kaederman had used to tilt the crucible. His stumbling footsteps kicked its far end askew, out of the puddle of molten bronze, trailing lethal beads across the foundry floor. Skeeter danced a wild jig-step and finally righted his balance, just a boot heel shy of the malevolent lake. The cool end of the long pole rolled and bumped into Kaederman's foot, a weapon ready for the snatching. Kaederman's face twisted in triumph. An unholy laugh broke loose. Before Skeeter could fling himself forward to stop him, Kaederman stooped and snatched up the pole in a two-handed grip—

By the wrong end.

Glowing and still half-molten, the pole dripped liquid bronze which flowed over both of Kaederman's hands. A terrible scream burst loose. He tried to let go. Kaederman staggered back, away from the puddle, face contorted, still screaming. The stench of cooking hair and meat struck Skeeter's nostrils. Then Kaederman's damaged fingers unclenched enough to let the pole drop. The skin of both hands sloughed away with it. Kaederman's knees gave way. He hit the floor and nearly splashed headlong into the glowing, syrupy-thick bronze. Skeeter snatched him back, dragging him bodily out of danger, and shoved him to the floor. Then held him there. Skeeter smiled down into stunned grey eyes.

"Hello, Sid."

He'd stopped screaming. Broken, gasping sounds tore free in their place. Shock was setting in fast, leaving him shaking and clammy under Skeeter's hands. Skeeter shook him slightly to get his attention. When that didn't register, he used the bastard's real name and shook him again. "Gideon! Hey, Guthrie! Look at me!"

Dull eyes focused. His mouth moved, but nothing came past his lips except those strangled, hideous whimpers. "Listen, pal. You got a choice," Skeeter slapped his face gently to keep his attention. "You listening?"

He nodded, managed to force out a single coherent word. "W-what?"

Skeeter fished out his little RIC Webley and let Kaederman see it. "What I *ought* to do is shoot you where you lie, pal. You don't rate the oxygen you're breathing. But I'm gonna offer you a choice. Your pick all the way. If you like, I'll step away and let you crawl out of here, free and clear. No charges for murder. No prison time. No gas chamber. Of course, with the state of medical care around here, you'll lose both those hands for sure. And even if you didn't, you'd probably die from shock and infection and gangrene."

Kaederman's eyes had glazed. "Wh-what's the—?"

"What's your other choice?" Skeeter's grin sent a shudder through the injured man. "Why, you get to come clean. Tell the cops everything they want to know about your boss. Hand them Senator Caddrick and his mafia cronies on a silver platter. Give us enough to send *them* to the gas chamber, instead of you."

Ashen lips moved, mouthing the words. "Goddamned little bastard . . . should've killed you on sight, Armstrong."

Skeeter grinned down into Kaederman's glazed eyes. "Too bad, ain't it? What'll it be, then? I'll trade the medical care you need to save your hands, trade you a surgeon and a burn-care unit, for Senator Caddrick in prison. That's a fair trade, I think. One of those new prisons he helped fund, a no-frills, maximum security cage without television or libraries or anything to distract a guy except Bubba's hard-on in the next cage over. Couldn't happen to a nicer bastard, don't you agree? Maybe you'll even get a reduced sentence for turning state's evidence. How about it? We'll keep you out of pain, stabilize your hands for you, keep you alive long enough to get you to a burn specialist. Otherwise, I'll just leave you here."

He jerked his thumb at the stench of the Victorian-era foundry. As the ashen killer shuddered, rolling his eyes at the grimy room, Skeeter added off-handedly, "Oh, and by the way. *If* you decide to stay here, and *if* you manage to survive shock and infection and amputation of those hands, I'm told Scotland Yard still hangs a murderer. And I know a couple of folks who'd be delighted to rat on you."

Kaederman didn't answer for a long moment, just lay there

sprawled on his back, trembling and sweating, his skin grey and his hands curled into meaty, scorched claws. He glared up at Skeeter while making horrible, strangled sounds and bit his lips until they bled. His body twitched spasmodically, his whole nervous system overloaded with the pain of the burns.

"Okay," Skeeter shrugged, rising from his crouch and sliding his RIC Webley back into his shoulder holster. "Have it your way. Maybe you can actually crawl to the door. Dunno what you'll do once you're outside, though, with all that manure in the streets to drag yourself through and Whitechapel's toughs kicking you into the mud, just for chuckles . . ."

Skeeter started to step away.

Kaederman lunged up onto an elbow. "*Wait!*" He shook violently, eyes wild and desperate. "For God's sake, Armstrong . . . wait . . . Go ahead and take your revenge, curse it, kick my ribs in, smash my teeth, do whatever makes you happy—*just don't leave me to die in this hellhole!*"

Skeeter stood glaring down at him, drawing out the man's terror with cold, calculated loathing. How much pity had this bastard shown any of his victims? When Kaederman fell back, eyes closing over a moan of despair, Skeeter finally decided he'd had enough.

"Okay," he said softly, crouching down again. "But you're gonna have to walk out of here on your own pins, Sid, because I'm not carrying you." He tugged the man by his coat lapels, levering him up to his knees and bracing him under one armpit. Noah Armstrong and Doug Tanglewood, their faces flushed from the intense heat of the bell molds, skidded up just as he got Kaederman onto his feet. Margo was close on their heels, having gone around the long way to avoid the puddle of cooling bronze. Skeeter glanced up. "Hi, Noah. Got a present for you. Sid, here, is going to teach us all a new song. Goes like this: 'All I want for Christmas is my boss in jail . . .' "

Sid Kaederman stared from Noah Armstrong's face to Skeeter's matching one and back again, eyes widening as the import of their ruse set in. Then his eyes turned belly up and his knees went south and Skeeter ended up carrying him out of the bell foundry, after all.

(((Chapter 19)))

Kit hurled through Shangri-La's basement corridors, Sven Bailey pounding along in his wake, both of them grim and silent. John Lachley's footsteps echoed up ahead. He didn't have much of a head start. Kit flung himself around a twist in the corridor and caught sight of the quarry down a long straight-of-way, maybe fifty yards ahead. Easy shot. Kit fired—and missed. Three times. Sven's gun was back in the pteranodon's cage, in a spot nobody wanted to retrieve it from. Lachley whipped into a side corridor. Kit and Sven reached it seconds later. They were gaining on him. Kit lined up the pistol sights as best he could while running full tilt, and tried again.

He succeeded in blowing out the sides of four aquaria in rapid succession.

Water and fish flooded across the floor as Kit spat curses. "Goddammit! I shouldn't have missed! Not *seven times!*"

"Maybe he's got to go back to London, after all?" Sven growled. "And you're out of ammo, by the way."

Kit glanced down. The slide had locked back. He'd shot the pistol dry. When he groped in his shirt pocket, he discovered nothing but emptiness. The spare magazine had fallen out during the fight and he hadn't noticed. *Careless is stupid,* he snarled at himself, *and stupid can be fatal.*

He mashed the send button on his radio.

"Kit Carson reporting. We're in pursuit, heading into Zone

Eighteen! Sven and I are both out of ammo—looks like the bastard can't be killed, after all!" Either that, or he was phenominally lucky.

"Copy that, we have search teams triangulating on your location." In the background, he could hear the station announcer again. *Gate Three is opening in three minutes . . .*

"Set up blockades out of Zones Seventeen and Eighteen," Kit gasped as as they skidded around a corner. He slammed one shoulder into a ten-foot wall of stacked aquaria, which shifted with an ominous groan. Water slopped out of the topmost layer. A door slammed back and Lachley's footsteps receded upward. "Oh, hell, he's gone up a *stairway*!"

"Come again?" the radio sputtered.

"He took the stairs, heading for Commons!"

"Copy that and relaying."

Why was Lachley headed for Commons? Just running blind, heading *up*, same as many another fugitive, or was he planning something . . .

Kit's eyes widened. "Holy—Sven, *Gate Three*!"

He mashed the transmit button again. "I think he's headed for Gate Three! And even if he isn't, leave a corridor open, try to herd him into it!"

"*What*?" the radio sputtered. "Right into the middle of an *incoming tour*? Kit, are you out of your—Oh. Roger that. Kit, you are one devious bastard."

"So give me a medal—if this works. Sven, be ready for anything. I'm going to try something dangerous."

"Chasing Jack the Ripper *isn't*?"

He had a point, there . . .

How much time? Kit wondered frantically as they plunged up the stairs four at a time. *Christ, how much time's left*? They burst out onto Commons at the edge of Frontier Town. Chronometer lights flashed steadily overhead. The vast open floor lay deserted, as empty of life as a midnight cemetery. Their footsteps slapped and echoed off the distant girders high overhead. Kit jumped a decorative horse trough filled with goldfish, which Sven whipped around, too short to go over it.

He knew they were close when he felt the savage backlash of subharmonics from the gate. The sound that wasn't a sound vibrated through the vast, echoing stretch of Commons. A security team stood waiting at the entrance to the Wild West Gate's departure lounge, charged with keeping the in-bound tour from re-entering the station. Behind the security officers, the massive gate dilated slowly open, right on schedule. Lachley, running flat out, ran straight toward the rapidly widening black chasm which hovered three feet above the Commons floor and whipped through the open lanes snaking outward from the departures lounge. He clearly intended to shake pursuit by jumping through the moment it opened wide enough.

Kit shouted into the radio, "Get those security officers away from the gate! For God's sake, move 'em out before he veers off!"

Too late! Lachley had seen them. He skidded sideways, trying to vault over a row of chairs. Kit charged, frantically trying to recall where he'd been in early August of 1885. It didn't really matter. He was the *only* one in position to take out the Ripper. Kit's flying tackle caught Lachley's knees—and sent them both reeling straight through the gaping black hole of the Denver Gate.

They fell headlong down the dizzying drop. The station end of the tunnel lay at the end of a spyglass inverted, far away and shrinking. Lachley brought the knife up even as they fell like doomed meteors. The Denver end of the gate loomed huge. Kit tried to brace himself, wondered what it felt like to die ... Then jarred his back. He sprawled, badly winded, across the dirt floor of the Time Tours livery stable. John Lachley snarled above him, teeth bared, knife poised to strike—

And almost made it to the floor.

His whole body wavered like candle smoke and vanished, a shadow eaten whole by a moonless night. For just an instant, a lingering look of shocked surprise floated where Lachley's face had been. Then his blood-stained knife clattered to the dirt beside Kit's ear and a heavy pouch thumped down beside it, inside a flutter of stolen, up-time clothes.

Sven thudded into the stable at Kit's feet, grunting on impact.

Kit lay flat, just gulping air, oblivious to the shocked demands erupting on all sides. Furious guides tried to calm hysterical tourists who had just watched a man die, shadowing himself. Several women were sobbing, abruptly too terrified to go anywhere near the open gate. Kit shut his eyes for long, shuddering moments, trying to convince his own muscles that it was safe to move, now.

He was still alive.

Jack the Ripper was finally dead.

Slowly, wincing at pulled muscles and bruises, Kit picked himself up and dusted himself off and gave Sven a hand up, as well. Tour guides were shouting above the general roar. Kit picked up Lachley's knife, plucking it out of the dirt with trembling fingers, and managed to retrieve the heavy pouch. He said to the nearest guide, "It's safe to bring them into the station, now. Quarantine was just lifted." Then he jerked his head once at Sven, turned his back on the whole shouting mob, and stepped back through the open Wild West Gate to go home.

Once there, he intended to get quietly, massively drunk.

I must be crazy . . .

Jenna Caddrick couldn't believe she'd agreed to this. Couldn't believe she'd just stepped through the Britannia Gate to confront her father in front of half the world's television cameras. Camera flashes and television crews lit up the whole departures lounge, illuminating a sea of spectators beyond the velvet-rope barricades. A sniper could be lurking anywhere in that vast, heaving mob. Noah Armstrong, silent at her side, descended the stairs with eyes narrowed, intent on the business of keeping them alive long enough to testify. She rubbed her chin nervously, wishing Paula Booker had left her muttonchop whiskers in place. But Noah had inisted the surgeon remove the implanted disguise and restore Jenna's face to her own appearance, for the benefit of the cameras. Jenna felt naked, defenseless.

Below them, Malcolm Moore's gurney had nearly reached the Commons floor, followed closely by Sid Kaederman's—or rather, Gideon Guthrie's. The man who'd trailed her from Colorado to London, bent on murder, was unconscious, his burnt hands cradled in special harnesses above his chest. Margo Smith walked beside her fiancé's gurney, holding his hand as they carried him down to the station's medical crews. Jenna's throat closed at the thought of what these people had risked for her sake. Malcolm had nearly been killed and Skeeter Jackson had undergone plastic surgery, rearranging his whole face. Skeeter had been shot outside the Carlton Club, as well, saved only by his Kevlar vest, and had almost been killed at the bell foundry . . .

She and Noah had nearly reached the floor when the inevitable shout came.

"*It's Jenna Caddrick!*"

The roar hurt Jenna's chest. She flinched back from the solid wall of noise, having forgotten during the weeks in London just how terrible it was to face a sea of screaming reporters.

"Steady," Noah muttered at her elbow. "I don't see a sniper anywhere."

Not yet . . .

She glanced back and found Skeeter Jackson right on their heels, his face still a mirror of Noah's. He gave her a brief, tense smile. "You've got that Kevlar vest of mine on, right?" She nodded and Skeeter muttered under his breath, "Good. I *know* it works." Then they were down the last of the steel-grid steps and pushing foward between a cordon of security guards.

Questions battered her from every side. Reporters screamed her name, demanding to know where she had been, how she'd escaped the *Ansar Majlis* death squads, a thousand, million questions that raked up old wounds and inflicted new ones. Then her father was there in front of her, open-mouthed and staring. Shock had dilated Senator John Paul Caddrick's grey eyes. A white pallor washed across his face as he met her gaze. She wondered how she had ever looked him in the eye without a reptilian loathing.

Then he recovered his composure. Her father presented the cameras with a smile worthy of an Oscar and cried, "*Jenna!* Oh, thank God, baby, you're safe . . ." He rushed forward, arms outflung. Jenna had no idea what she intended to do or say. She'd been thinking about this moment for weeks, drenched in sour-smelling terror sweat each time she imagined it. But when he rushed at her like a demon from her worst nightmares, Jenna reacted without a moment's hesitation.

She slugged him, point-blank. Slammed her fist so hard into his nose, the shock jarred her shoulder and left her hand numb. He staggered back, blood welling from both nostrils. For just an instant, a sewing needle dropped to the concrete floor would have sent echos bouncing through the vast station. Even the reporters had turned to stone, stunned motionless.

Jenna drew a sobbing breath. "*Don't touch me, you murdering son-of-a-bitch! You* paid those bastards to kill Aunt Cassie! *You* paid them to pose as *Ansar Majlis,* so the hit couldn't be traced back to you. Damn you to hell, you *murdered* her, and you murdered my fiancé, then you put out a contract on *me,* you sorry sack of shit! I've got enough proof to bring you down, you and your mafia pals with you. Gideon Guthrie's been singing for his supper and believe me, they're gonna throw away the key! If they don't pull the switch on the electric chair. And frankly, after what you did to Carl and Aunt Cassie, I'd pull it in a heartbeat. I hope you fry!"

Her father stood swaying, waxy-pale, mouth working soundlessly. As the crowd roared its shock, his face twisted in a blurred grimace. Then he snatched open his coat and jerked out a small-caliber handgun. Noah Armstrong flung himself forward. The detective slammed Jenna down, away from the discharge of flame erupting from the muzzle. Another shot exploded as her father snarled, "Goddamn you to *hell,* Armstrong!"

Then Skeeter Jackson was on the floor beside her, swearing in some language she didn't recognize, with a hole torn through his coat where her father's shot had barely missed him. Jackson's reflexes were *good*—he twisted aside even as her father fired again, mistaking him for Noah. The real Armstrong lay full length on top of Jenna, face down to protect her. Then a swarm of security officers buried her father, shoving him down under an avalanche of live bodies. The mob went mad, shrieking and hurling abuse that left Jenna numb. Skeeter Jackson grunted once, lying prone practically on top of Noah, and muttered. "I gotta get my own face back . . ."

Jenna just shut her eyes, quaking under Noah's weight, too exhausted to move.

"C'mon, kid," Noah's voice finally broke through, "you've got to testify, make it official."

"Yeah . . ."

Security officials were pulling them to their feet, surrounding them in a ring five bodies deep, hustling them out of the danger zone to a waiting security cart. Skeeter dragged himself up and followed. Through the numbing roar of the mob, another shocked cry went up.

"*Ianira Cassondra!*"

Then Jenna and Noah were thrust into the cart. Skeeter slid in after them and scooted over as Ianira and her family crowded in. The children sat on the floor, dark eyes wide and scared. The driver cranked the siren up full blast and the cart shot down Commons, taking them away from the whole screaming mess. Ianira leaned down to wrap both arms around her frightened children and Marcus held Ianira. Jenna's vision blurred as she met the *cassondra*'s gaze. Ianira, at least, had come home. The *cassondra* and her family would be welcomed by people who loved them. Jenna had no one left in the world who cared about her. No one at all. Except her unborn child.

And Noah Armstrong.

Jenna leaned her elbows against her knees and buried her face in her hands and cried. *Welcome home, Jenna . . . welcome the hell home.*

A quarter of an hour later, Jenna told her story to a roomful of station officials, Interpol officers, and a whole, terrifying retinue of I.T.C.H. agents. Jenna would've frozen up, tongue-tied and shaking, if Noah hadn't been there, backing her up and presenting their evidence. Her father was in jail, sedated and under heavy guard. Skeeter Jackson was with Jenna, testifying under oath. Margo Smith and her grandfather, Kit Carson, had already given their sworn affadavits. When everyone had finished their preliminary testimonies, Skeeter handed over the tape from his scout log, recording Gideon Guthrie's confession to posing as Sid Kaederman in order to murder her and Noah.

A long silence fell, finally broken by Agent Inga Kirkegard, the senior ranking I.T.C.H. officer. "I'll start by acknowledging the courage it took for all of you to do what you've done. You've saved countless lives, shut down a major international terrorist organization, exposed a ruthless conspiracy between mob interests and government officials, and kept this station operational. Not to mention ridding the world of Jack the Ripper. And you did so with surprisingly little loss of life, when the Ripper cults are taken into account." One corner of her mouth quirked slightly as she inclined her head toward Kit, acknowledging his pivotal role in on-station events Jenna had learned about on the way to the station manager's office.

Then Kirkegard's eyes frosted over and she stared coldly at Jenna. "However, your methods are something else entirely. We won't even list the number of laws and temporal-travel regulations broken in this unfortunate situation. I suspect most charges will be dropped, since it is quite clear you and Mr. Armstrong acted in self defense, killing the contract murderers sent after you. There is also a matter of jurisdiction, since the killing was done down time.

"In light of the large number of mitigating circumstances, I will recommend a judicial review and waiver of fines, rather than formal charges. That goes for all station residents who participated in the efforts to extract you and Mr. Armstrong alive. Now, Senator Caddrick brought a number of charges against the management of this station," Kirkegard said, turning her gaze to Bull Morgan and Ronisha Azzan. "After a thorough investigation of those charges, as well as countercharges filed by Mr. Carson, this team has officially dismissed all criminal counts initially brought by the Senator. Those charges were clearly part of the overall fraud he perpetrated upon the public, including those made personally against you, Mr. Morgan."

A weight visibly lifted from the station manager's broad, squat shoulders. Bull Morgan settled back in his massive chair and switched his cigar to one corner of his mouth. "Much obliged."

Kirkegard nodded. "Ms. Azzan will be receiving a commendation from the Inter-Temporal Court for her superb handling of the multiple crises which struck this station in rapid succession, while Mr. Morgan was incarcerated. So will Mr. Carson," she glanced gravely at the world-famous former time scout, "for safeguarding hundreds of lives and restoring the station's normal economic operations through his ingenious solution to the Ripper difficulty. We've taken into custody those members of the Ripper cults your searchers apprehended. They will be prosecuted to the full extent of up-time law. As will Senator Caddrick and Mr. Kaederman, or rather, Mr. Guthrie."

She then turned her attention to Skeeter Jackson, who sat up straighter in his chair and swallowed hard. "It has come to our notice that you have led a rather, ah, checkered career, Mr. Jackson. We uncovered several old warrants and complaints filed, regarding your activities during the past several years." Sweat popped out along his brow. Kit Carson sat sharply forward, the brooding look turning his eyes abruptly dangerous. Jenna gulped, abruptly thankful she wouldn't be the one on the receiving end of Kit Carson's temper. Agent Kirkegard flicked a glance up at Kit, then smiled slightly. "Given the pivotal role Mr. Jackson played in this case, plus the character testimonials filed by this entire group, I believe the Inter-Temporal Court will vote to grant a general pardon and amnesty, in lieu of a commendation for services rendered."

Skeeter relaxed so abruptly, Jenna thought he'd fainted.

"I would suggest, Miss Caddrick, that you and Mr. Armstrong consider remaining on TT-86 for some time. Until the members of Mr. Guthrie's organization are rounded up and jailed, this station is without doubt the safest place for both of you. I.T.C.H. and Interpol can provide additional security to screen persons entering the station from New York. You will need to testify at the trial, of course, but I suspect you would prefer staying here to being placed in a witness protection program."

Jenna shuddered. "No contest."

Noah gave the I.T.C.H. officer a wan smile. "After my experience in London, I may just switch careers and offer my services as a temporal guide."

Kit chuckled, startling everyone. "I'd say you've stumbled onto a lucrative career opportunity, there. Granville Baxter is always happy to find guides who know how to disappear in a down-time crowd."

Armstrong grinned. "I hadn't thought about guiding in quite that way."

"Consider it. I'll tell Bax to give you a call. You'll stay at the Neo Edo, of course, until permanent quarters can be found in Residential. Penthouse suite. And don't even try to argue. My pleasure."

"Thank you," Jenna said quietly. "There isn't much I can do or say to show how deeply grateful I am to all of you. You helped save all our lives. My father may be a sorry bastard, but I won't forget that kind of debt. Ever."

"Neither will I," Noah agreed. "And I suspect Mr. Jackson wants his own face back, after nearly taking a bullet meant for me. Twice, in fact."

Skeeter grinned. "Now you mention it . . ."

The meeting broke up with Bull Morgan handing around congratulatory drinks, then they crowded into the elevator. Noah slipped an arm around Jenna's shoulder where they stood jammed together in one corner. She leaned her head against the detective's shoulder, grateful for the warm gesture and so weary she could have fallen asleep on her feet. Kit Carson was saying, "Malcolm is still in surgery, but the orderlies left word. He's doing just fine."

"Thank God," Margo breathed out.

"By the way, if you're interested," Kit chuckled, "I've got another little job lined up for you, in a few weeks. A real field test of your scouting skills."

"The Ripper Watch *wasn't*?" she shot back, causing even Jenna to smile.

"Well," Kit shrugged, "we had a major new gate open up while you were chasing Jack the Ripper."

"We did?" she asked breathlessly. "Are you really going to let me scout it?"

He shook his head. "Sorry, imp, but Ripley Sneed already did." His apology visibly deflated her hopes. "But it's a real dilly. Ought to give you a good workout for your final field test."

Margo caught her breath sharply in the crowded elevator. "*Final* field test?" It came out tiny with breathless hope. "As in, final exam before I really start scouting?"

He chuckled. "If you pass. And no solo work for a good long while, yet, even if you do pass the field test. Malcolm goes with you or you don't go at all. I'll conduct the field test and put you through your paces, myself. And this is one gate you won't have to worry about shepherding tourists through. Bax has already agreed. Scholars and scouts only, for the next couple of months."

"Just where does this thing lead?" Margo asked warily.

"Chicago. 1871."

Intrigued despite herself, Jenna sifted back through her skimpy knowledge of American history, randomly absorbed during her academic career. What was so special about Chicago in 1871?

Margo's eyes had narrowed, however. "What *month* in 1871?"

Kit grinned. "October."

Margo's eyes shot wide. "*Really?* Omigosh! How soon do we leave?"

"Four weeks. You'd better hit the books hard, imp."

"You're on!"

Jenna couldn't stand the suspense. "Where are you going? What's so special about Chicago in October of 1871?"

Kit chuckled. "Well, Miss Caddrick, my granddaughter and I intend to discover whether Mrs. O'Leary's cow did or did not start the Great Chicago Fire."

Jenna's eyes widened. Skeeter grinned. Noah started to laugh.

"I have a feeling," Jenna muttered, even as her lips twitched, "that living on Time Terminal Eighty-Six is going to prove very interesting . . ."

She fully intended to enjoy every minute.

(((Epilogue)))

At four o'clock in the morning on November 9, 1888, the Ripper Watch Team's video cameras captured James Maybrick committing the brutal slaughter of Mary Kelly in the cramped little room at number thirteen, Miller's Court. At eight o'clock that morning, those same cameras captured the arrival of a midwife who was known to perform illegal abortions for girls in trouble. The woman let herself in with a key Kelly had taken from Joseph Barnett after he and Kelly had quarreled and separated.

The horrified midwife, who slipped in the blood and gore, badly staining her clothing, changed into one of Mary Kelly's dresses and shawls and burned her own in the hearth before fleeing the room, too deeply shocked and terrified to go to the police or even scream for help. Doing so would have required explanations for her arrival in the first place, which would have led to a stiff prison sentence. Mrs. Caroline Maxwell, a neighbor in Miller's Court, glimpsed the midwife leaving Kelly's room and mistook her for Mary Kelly, herself, thus confusing police with sober testimony that Mary Kelly had been seen alive at 8:00 A.M.

London police never solved the Ripper mystery and never made a major arrest, although many suspects were named. The case destroyed Sir Charles Warren's career as police commissioner and sparked a massive social reform movement to alleviate the appalling conditions of poverty in which the Ripper's victims—and more than a million other souls—lived. The following spring, James Maybrick died of acute arsenic poisoning. His complicity in the Ripper case did not come to light for another century. His innocent American widow, her unfortunate affair with Mr. Brierly having come to public notice, was convicted of murder—largely because of her adultery—in a trial that shocked all of England and sparked a decade and a half of protests from the American State Department. Florie Maybrick served fifteen years in prison, then returned to the United States and lived in quiet anonymity under an assumed name, never realizing she had lived in the house that Jack built.